Aliens
Beware

The Complete Stories

John E. Christ

Other Books by the Author

Beginnings and Ends: Twenty Stories of Science Fiction (2014) ISBN 9781507793169

Lucy: Avenging Hitwoman (2015) ISBN 9781506130859

Hutch: No Justice in Texas (2015) ISBN 9781507839683

Amazons: Heroines and Villainesses (2015) ISBN 9781514287637

Ticklers: Stories with a Comical Bent (2015) ISBN 9781507844151

Yael: The Center That Time forgot (2015) ISBN 9781505664171

Galen's Legions: Tales in the Medical World (2015) ISBN 9781514118863

Belly Aches: Tales From the Other Side of the Law (2015) ISBN 97815141187982

Against the Sea: Tales On and Under the Sea (2015) ISBN 9781514267523

Flames of Passion: An Anthology of the Passionate Poems of Demetrios Anastasia and Maria Spiros (2015) ISBN 978131280482

Table of Contents

PREFACE V

THE ARTIFACT 1

COULD YOU REPEAT THAT? 13

THE ILLUSION 23

PROJECT BLINK 33

RING! 43

THE HOOKER...53

THE RIDE 63

JUST JUNK 75

TWINKLE 87

GOLD FOR THE MASTER...103

THE WITNESS...117

THE MISSIONARY 135

AMONG STRANGERS...149

ECHO 163

DOTS 175

NO PROBLEM 187

CRUX...199

VOICES 211

IN THE DARK 223

EARTHWORM, INC...235

FOSSIL 247

THURSDAY 261

REMOTE CONTROL 273

THE CATCH 287

PANTHEON OF THE PAST...301

SAFI...315

THE CYLINDER..333

CRASH LANDING 347

TO THE STARS 361

THE BLUE MOON BAR..367

BUGS 381

THE LANDING 395

FORBIDDEN 409

THE ROBOT RETURNS 423

LIFE! 437

IN THE WAR ZONE..449

FINAL REPORT 465

THE ANTHROPOLOGISTS..481

SENTIENT LIFE 495

LUNCH 511

ROCKY..525

THE EXPERIMENT 543

THE LOST TOY..563

HELLO..575

Preface

The universe is a big place where the Earth occupies an infinitesimal small part. According to recent cosmology there are countless worlds which may harbor life. The beings on these other worlds are called extraterrestrial or aliens. Aliens can take any form. Aliens are separated from us by light-years but not from sentient desires. Aliens take many forms throughout the universe. They may be familiar or disguised. There are more similarities than differences when all is considered. Alien life may have similar, if not identical, hopes, needs and wants of life on Earth. In any case they may act surprisingly familiar. They may be small, large, or artificial with behaviors appearing very human.

Although we may not have the technology to span interstellar distances, those aliens may have the ability to visit our world. The stories in this book tell the tales of the good, bad, and indifferent aliens we may encounter. These stories are meant to entertain, tickle the imagination, and give serious thought to the concept we are not alone in this universe. Read on and enjoy. The universe is filled with innumerable worlds on which life can appear, evolve, and venture forth to other worlds. The denizens of those other worlds may be beneficent or not. Come explore some of the possibilities our world might face when meeting these strangers. Enjoy as they take you to worlds and situations far beyond those on our mundane planet:

The Artifact tells of an alien visitor in the time of ancient Egypt; **Could You Repeat That?** tells of the first transmission received from sentient life in the universe; **The Illusion** presents the ever devious Martians trying to hide from us; **Project Blink** detects an object heading toward collision with Earth and misinterprets its intention at the wrong moment; **Ring!** is a telephone conversation between an alien and Earth woman; **The Hooker** is a mystery to solve what is happening to missing men from Miami Beach; **The Ride** proves video games are not necessarily a waste of time when it comes to alien needs; **Just Junk** chronicles the lives of a machine become more human and a human become more machine only to be destroyed by an alien planetary defense system; **Twinkle** tells of strange lights which baffle humans; and, **Gold For the Master** is a tale of treachery between alien civilizations. **The Witness** discovers a truth he is unable to pass on; in **The Missionary** differing civilizations clash unexpectedly; in **Among Strangers** a hapless alien demonstrates an all too human trait; in **Echo** distant transmissions reveal a horrifying reality; in **Dots** not all aliens are giant monsters; in **No Problem** the intentions of aliens is suspect for good reason; in **Crux** clashing civilizations find a common ground for communication; in **Voices** the final question of what to do when all is done is answered; **In the Dark** two soldiers are trapped in absolute darkness only to find when they escape they are not who they thought they were. The universe is a big place where what we do on Earth may have consequences elsewhere such as in **Earthworm, Inc.** The form of alien life may not be what we expect as in **Fossil**. The alien may be in the form which defies easy acceptance as in **Thursday**. On the surface of Mars accidents may happen as in **Remote Control** where help comes from an unexpected benefactor. In **The Catch** a project in generating electricity finds more than it bargained for. Interpretations are the subject of scholarly debate as in **Pantheon of the Past**. An alien may slip into our existence without us being aware as in **Safi**. In **The Cylinder,** two scientists discover a receptacle in their backyard garden containing a startling picture; in **Crash Landing,** an alleged accidental crash of an interstellar starship results in a landing on a planet inhabited by small beings who are not as innocent as they look; in **To the Stars,** an astonishing finding changes the outlook of scientists in the space program; in **The Blue Moon Bar**, aliens are set up in a local bar spying on the local population; in **Bugs**, an alien invasion force comes to strip the Earth of its resources; in **The Landing**, a mysterious starship lands on Earth revealing a startling truth. The story **Life!** takes place on an exploration with unmanned rovers on Mars in the search for life on the planet; the story **In the War Zone** is an example of manipulation by an alien race for its own needs; **Final Report** is the summation of an exploratory exercise on another planet; **The Anthropologists** are aliens mistaken for terrorists on an exploratory mission; **Sentient Life** brings artificial life in contact with human life; **Lunch** is set on an alien world of carnivores with a surprise ending; **Rocky** is a strange pet found in Mexico who turns out to be something different than expected; and **The Experiment** is headed to a conclusion of unprecedented scale which cannot be stopped by the humans who have discovered it. **The Lost Toy** is a friendly reminder that aliens can come in any form. **Hello** tells of a different kind of response to a signal from extraterrestrials. In **Forbidden**, a planet thought destroyed is found intact; and in **The Robot**

Returns, a mystery is solved involving the forbidden planet. These last two stories were written for my brother Bill who wanted a sequel to our favorite movie Forbidden Planet. You decide whether I succeeded.

This book is dedicated to my brother, Bill, and sister, Marika, who have shared a passion for facing aliens. Heartfelt thanks goes to my mother for her encouragement to write. Special thanks go to Yael Eylat-Tanaka with her push for me to publish. I leave you to enjoy and think about these stories with the admonition: Aliens Beware!

The Artifact

For Michael the step off the train and onto the platform in the ancient city of Thebes was a dream come true. Ever since he was a little boy, he was fascinated by everything that had to do with Egyptian history. Two weeks ago he had finished, and successfully defended, his Ph.D. dissertation and was awarded a degree in Egyptology. He was given a generous grant for which he had applied to study on-site at a dig in the Valley of Queens. Everything came together at the right time.

"Sir, sir," a voice shouted. "Taxi?"

Michael looked in the direction of a shabby old Volkswagen van with a near toothless driver behind the wheel waving at him.

"Taxi?" The driver shouted louder.

"Sure." He picked up his suitcase and walked over to the van.

The driver jumped out of the van, ran over and grabbed the suitcase. The man literally ripped the handle out of his grip before he could object.

"Inside please." The driver opened the door as he threw the bag carelessly into the back.

Michael shrugged his shoulders and crawled into the front passenger seat. He expected everything would be less than civilized, especially since he had just come from the filth of Cairo. Little could surprise him; he had studied his assignment in great detail. He was comforted that he was near his true love at last. He pulled out a piece of paper with an address on it and gave it to the driver.

"You go dig?" The driver read the address. "You with the Professor?"

"I am going to join his team," Michael gazed at the stark poverty passing around him. "I'm going to study whatever I can, although I'm specifically interested in the place of women in antiquity."

"I see," the driver said solemnly. "Perhaps you like to buy some souvenirs? I give you good price."

"No, thank you. I just got here; besides, I'll be here all summer; perhaps when I'm ready to leave."

1

"Ah! Then remember Abdul, your humble driver. I give you best price in town."

"I'm sure." Michael smiled.

"Praise Allah! We are here!" Abdul said loudly. "I know a cantina you can get a good meal and a good time. You know what I mean?"

"Thank you, Abdul, but I just got here."

Michael paid the driver and walked over to the address which was simply a door in a blank white wall that stretched the entire block. The nameplate above the doorbell read Alexander Vassiliadis, Ph.D., Professor of Antiquities, University of Athens. He heard a faint buzz from the inside when he pushed the doorbell button. The door was opened by a short dark man with a bushy mustache. His clothing suggested he was one of the housekeepers.

"May I help you, sir?" the man said.

"My name is Michael George, Dr. Michael George, from the United States to work with Dr. Vassiliadis." He produced a letter from his bag. "This is a letter of introduction from my sponsor at the University of Chicago."

"Please come in." The man bowed. "Please wait here and I'll get the Professor."

The anteroom was dark and smelled of antiquity. He recognized bits and pieces of history he knew must be authentic. The temptation was to rush about the room and examine each and every artifact close-up, but he resisted.

"Dr. George, how nice to meet you," the Professor said warmly, extending his hand as he entered the room.

"My pleasure." Michael took the hand and shook firmly.

"You must be tired from your journey. Paul will take your bag to your room. Do you wish to freshen up or would you like a cool drink first?"

"It has been a long train ride," Michael said. "A drink would be most welcome."

The Professor motioned Paul to take Michael's bags. The two men went into the library lined with books from ceiling to floor.

"Please sit down," the Professor said, "I've been looking forward to working with you. I was quite impressed with your dissertation. You and your ideas will fit in perfectly with my team. In fact, we start tomorrow. But this afternoon let us visit the Karnak ruins and talk."

2

"I would like nothing better." Michael nodded slightly. "Thank you for the drink."

"I hope you don't mind iced tea. Tonight I will give you the best brandy in Egypt, my own special import from home."

The Professor was short, bald and looked much younger than his 54 years. His olive complexion and accent which was a mixture of proper English and Greek gave away his ethnic origin. He had been educated in England where he had access to the treasure trove of Egyptian antiquities at the British Museum. In fact, his own dissertation was a modern analysis of the Rosetta Stone translations from Greek to English. At the time of the publication of his work, it raised a few eyebrows that he was a rising star in the field of Egyptology.

"I understand you are working in the Valley of Queens," Michael said.

"Yes." His eyes twinkled. "And I am about to open an unspoiled tomb. You are the first to know. I have kept it secret from everyone. You have come at exactly the right time!"

"Are you sure it's unspoiled?" Michael raised his brow. "No sign of robbers or vandals?"

"The tomb is so well hidden that if I were not so clumsy I would not have found it," the Professor began. "Last week I was with my team looking for a new site to set up a base camp in the Valley. As I was walking, reading my map, I tripped over large rock and fell flat on my face. I was embarrassed by my situation and started to get up as quickly as I could when my hand felt a grooved object just below the surface of the sand. At first I did not think anything of it, since I was in an open area which is atypical for tombs, but then I started brushing away the sand with my hands. I soon realized that I had stumbled onto the entrance of an underground tomb. Before any of my team could reach me I replaced the sand and got up."

"How did you keep it from your team?"

"I just started acting like nothing happened. No one suspected anything. I retrieved my map and marked the site on it so I could return. Besides, I wanted to search the catalogs to be sure the site had not been described before."

"And did you find anything?"

"Absolutely nothing!" The Professor smiled widely. "We will be the first to describe and enter the site!"

Michael felt the excitement of the Professor's discovery. He was indeed fortunate to have been able to come here. His dream of discovery was more than enhanced by this new

3

prospect. He thought of his academic career soaring with the publication of the find and all the scientific papers that would follow. The two men finished their drinks and agreed to meet in the library before lunch. Afterward, they would discuss plans for the next day while browsing in the Temple of Karnak.

After lunch, Paul drove the two archaeologists in the Rover to the Karnak site. The usual transit buses were moving in and out, each one with a different ethnic and language group. Paul dropped off the Professor and Michael at the entrance.

"Give us about an hour." The Professor pointed. "We will meet you over there."

Paul saw a small café in the direction of the Professor's finger. He nodded and left to run the daily errands for the house.

"No matter how many times I come here," the Professor said slowly, "I am always in awe of the power of Amun. I almost feel like Amun is with us amongst these columns."

The two men strolled leisurely among the roofless giant columns covered with hieroglyphics. They stayed clear of all the tourists. In doing so, they insured privacy in their conversation.

"This place is larger than I imagined." There was awe in his voice.

"I have reason to believe that several thousand years before the birth of Christ something important happened here. I have recovered part of a papyrus telling the story of an undescribed sky goddess who descended from the heavens to live among the people. She brought health and prosperity throughout the land by her magic. She became concubine to Pharaoh and bore him a son and daughter. The papyrus ends with the death of Pharaoh and does not say what happened to her. I assume she ascended back into the heavens or joined Pharaoh on his journey into death."

"I really don't follow, Professor. What does this story have to do with what happened here? How do they relate to one another?"

"Let me show you back at the house," he said warmly. "Shall we get an espresso?"

"Yes, of course."

They left the ruins and crossed the street to the café. They ordered and drank slowly. Paul arrived at the appointed time and drove them directly back to the house where they retired into the library. The Professor brought out a small box.

"In this box I have an artifact that might interest you," the Professor said. He opened and handed the box to him.

4

Inside was a 4 inch long figurine of an Egyptian goddess with arms extended in a circle overhead holding a five-pointed star. Michael had never seen anything like it in all his study or research.

"Have you dated this?"

"I have authenticated it myself. This is real."

"This is indeed a unique finding. Congratulations. I suppose there could have been a short period of time that the existing society focused on a particular deity. Gods and goddesses seemed to come and go with whoever was in power."

"True, but this one specifically places a woman as a supreme deity. That, I think is important and may have paved the way for women to become Pharaoh in the future. Women in almost all ancient societies except this one seemed to take minor roles. I requested your help from your university and you specifically because of your interest in women in ancient society. I think you have your work cut out for you." The Professor smiled.

"Thank you for your confidence." Michael turned the figurine over and over in his hands. "What do you make of the inscription, and what about the strange markings?"

"The inscription is fairly typical, but I cannot make anything out of the markings. I suppose they are purely ornamental although they look like a written language. Slave artisans from different countries were known to inscribe messages in other languages for their own purposes. Unfortunately, this is a unique artifact against which we have nothing to compare; everything is just conjecture on my part. I want you to study it and give me your opinion when you are ready."

"Gentlemen, dinner is served," Paul said.

"Good, let us eat and discuss tomorrow's plans," the Professor said.

Paul led the men into the dining room where they seated themselves on opposite sides of the table set with fine English linen and China. Sarah, a petite Indian woman, the housekeeper and cook, served the men. As Michael expected there was a Greek salad with cucumbers, black olives and feta cheese soaked with olive oil sprinkled with dry powdered oregano leaves. The main course was a sumptuous leg of lamb generously slathered with garlic. The smell permeated the room. This was the first real meal he had had since leaving home and he ate with relish.

"Are you ready for brandy?" The Professor smiled.

"Whenever you are." Michael grinned. The food brought a true sense of satisfaction.

The Professor got up from the table, went over to the bar and produced a full Waterford crystal decanter. From this he poured two brandy glasses with a dark rich brown colored liquid. He raised one of the glasses to his nose and sniffed.

"Ah!" he exhaled. "Seven-Star Metaxa, the best my country has to offer."

Michael accepted a glass and sniffed. The smell was wonderfully strong and quickly opened his sinuses.

"A toast to friendship, collaboration and success." The Professor raised his glass.

"To friendship, collaboration and success!" Michael touched his glass to the Professor's.

Their glasses clinked and each took a sip. The Professor laughed when Michael coughed as he swallowed the brandy.

"Small sips my friend," he said smiling. "Enjoy slowly, savor every drop. This is the nectar of the gods."

"And may the gods accept my body in peace!" Michael laughed.

"Now for some business." The Professor cleared his throat. "We begin at sunrise tomorrow. Everything has been prepared in advance. I want Paul to specifically take charge of the video camera and document every step of the opening. I have already arranged to have the Ministry of Antiquities send a representative and guards to protect our work from vandals and thieves."

"How many people do you have on your team?"

"You and I will be on the core team along with Paul. Plus, we will have four men to do the digging and lifting. There will be others that will join us later."

"Paul?"

"Yes, Paul is not only my driver, he is also my chief assistant. You will find him quite knowledgeable in the nuances of hieroglyphic translation. It was he who translated the papyrus I mentioned earlier." He looked at his wristwatch. "The hour is late. Get your rest while you can. Tomorrow will be a busy and exhausting day."

Michael slept well and woke up to the 5 AM alarm he set for himself. He showered and dressed before joining the Professor for breakfast. The Professor, he thought, appeared supercharged with energy. The Professor drank his coffee and ate his eggs quickly in an absent-minded fashion. His mind was definitely on the coming activities of the day. By 6:30 AM they were in the Rover on their way to the Valley of Queens. A second Rover with the four workers joined them at an appointed place along the way. Once within the Valley, the Professor pulled out his map and directed them to the location where they were to set up camp. Within an hour they were ready to begin.

"Now, Paul," the Professor said. "Make sure you record everything on tape. When in doubt take pictures of everything. First, Michael and I will stand over the entrance to the tomb and brush the fine sand away."

Paul nodded his understanding and began his job. The Professor took a small shovel and scraped away the thin layer of sand covering one of the edges of the door. Michael bent down and used a small whisk broom to see if there were any inscriptions. There were none. The workers then moved in and completed the job of exposing the tomb's door which was approximately 1 by 2 meters without any identifying markings. There was enough space to insert a crowbar between the door and its frame. One of the workers put the tool in place and was ready to apply pressure when they all heard a click. The door swung open automatically much to everyone's surprise.

"Amazing!" The Professor shouted. "A counterbalanced tomb door. We are at the find of the century. I feel it!"

"There are steps down," Michael waved to the Professor. "You first."

They all put on their masks. More than one expedition had been decimated by strange fatal illnesses after entering a tomb. Some claimed the curse of the dead but all could be explained by natural phenomena, such as dust and microorganisms that they might kick up into the air.

"Paul, come down here." The Professor waved and pointed. "Take pictures of this."

Paul followed Michael and the Professor down the steps into an empty room with smooth plaster walls and took pictures. The Professor inched around the wall tapping lightly with this pick. Michael did the same moving in the opposite direction.

"Ah! Here we are!" The Professor used the pick with force.

A large piece of plaster broke away exposing a wall of bricks. He continued chipping away until he completely uncovered a sealed doorway. With a portable handheld electric saw he cut through the plaster surrounding one of the bricks and slid it out. Minutes later he was peering into another empty

7

room. The workers removed all the other bricks and created an opening big enough to enter. Again there were no inscriptions or markings. The Professor and Michael inspected the wall of this room as before. This time Michael found an entrance.

"Over here Professor," Michael shouted. He was very much caught up in what they were doing. "This is your discovery. You do the honor."

The Professor opened the door as before only to find another empty room devoid of inscriptions or markings. He wondered whether he had entered either an unused or vandalized tomb until he dropped his pick. The sound was unmistakable, the floor was hollow!

Both men were on their knees with whisk brooms clearing away the sand. Paul continued chronicling their progress with the video camera. Finally Michael found the edge of the door. In minutes they had it completely exposed. It also had no markings or inscriptions. When pried slightly, the main entrance door swung open automatically.

Down another flight of steps and they were in a room with a massive stone sarcophagus. The room was empty of anything else; the walls were smoothly plastered without inscriptions or markings as were the rest of the rooms. The sarcophagus was no different than any they had ever seen. The Professor produced a magnifying glass from his pocket and inspected the markings carefully.

"We need more light," the Professor said. "Tell Ahman to bring more light and the block and tackle. We must lift the lid off."

Paul stopped tapping and came over to look at the inscriptions on the sarcophagus. Light was a problem and he gave up trying to read it.

"What you think of the empty rooms?" Michael said slowly. "Vandalized or unused?"

"We will find out as soon as we open this," the Professor said. "The counterbalance entrances are singularly unique as is the main chamber being below a network of upper chambers."

The workers set up the block and tackle and lifted the massive stone lid of the sarcophagus. Inch by inch the lid rose.

"Look! Paul! An intact internal sarcophagus!" The Professor shouted. "Michael, you have been blessed to see this moment."

The stone lid was lifted completely clear. Within was an internal sarcophagus covered with gold leaf. In spite of what the room did not contain, the sarcophagus had been undisturbed since it was put there. The workers carefully lifted the internal sarcophagus for transport back to the Professor's house. The stone lid was carefully replaced.

"Michael, my boy..." The Professor laughed. "Our real work can now be done in my workroom at home. There is little else for us to do here."

"What about the stone sarcophagus?"

"I will have Paul photograph and translate all the inscriptions. Then it will be up to the Ministry of Antiquities to decide whether to leave it here or move it," he said. "Of course, once we have finished our examination we must surrender all artifacts to the ministry."

"Will we have enough time?"

"The ministry is very cooperative. They will not hurry us in our work. We will have as much time as we need, and more, if necessary."

By the middle of the afternoon they were on their way back to the Professor's house. Guards had been stationed at the entrance of the tomb until the ministry could decide what to do with the stone sarcophagus. The ride home was filled full of good humor and elation of a job well done. They knew they had made a significant discovery.

Paul backed the Rover into the garage and closed the door. They were finally safe from outside eyes. The Professor, Michael and Paul slid the sarcophagus out of the back of the Rover onto a special table with wheels. The Professor unlocked the door into his workroom while Paul pushed and Michael guided the sarcophagus to a special table in the middle of the room. They transferred the sarcophagus carefully over onto the table. Michael looked around the room and saw that the Professor was well-equipped to study his subject. The Professor noticed the admiration of his workroom in Michael's eyes.

"The x-ray equipment is complementary of your sponsor, the University of Chicago," the Professor said. "In the 70s a team came over to x-ray mummies, when they finished their study they donated their equipment to my work."

"That makes our work a lot easier," Michael said.

"Of course, but first we photograph and examine the outside. We will save the best for last."

Paul had already started taking pictures with the Nikon. The Professor handed an extra magnifying glass to Michael.

"Look at the exquisite illustrations of daily life and . . ." The Professor stopped midsentence and looked more carefully.

"What is it, Professor?" Michael bent closer.

"The five pointed star!" The Professor said quickly. "I have never seen it anywhere, except in that figurine I gave you to examine and now on this sarcophagus."

Michael and Paul moved closer and saw what the Professor saw. Paul began reading the hieroglyphics around the star.

"Professor, the text is similar to the papyrus, except that it goes on to say this is the mummy of the goddess."

The Professor grew more animated with the announcement. "Let's open the sarcophagus to the next layer!"

They carefully opened the wooden sarcophagus and viewed the linen wrapped mummy, with funerary mask of solid gold over the head, with awe. The top of the mask instead of the usual animal had a five pointed star. The air of excitement in the room was palpable. Paul and Michael carefully lifted the mummy out after photographing it in situ. Paul took more pictures of the Professor removing the funerary mask from the head.

"Let's go ahead and get a preliminary set of x-rays," the Professor said.

Paul wheeled over the x-ray machine and Michael positioned the film under the mummy. The three men then stood behind the lead shield during each x-ray taken. When they had completely x-rayed the mummy from head to toe, they all went into the darkroom and developed the films.

"I may have some of the latest equipment, but I still have to develop the films by hand," the Professor said.

An hour passed. "Let us view these on the box outside," the Professor said.

The view box was long enough to put all the x-rays together showing the entire mummy from head to toe. Jewelry was present on the torso. The Professor looked closely with the magnifying glass.

"No signs of systemic disease, good dentition and here is the cause of death..." He pointed to the skull. "...acute skull fracture."

Michael looked closely and agreed. The sharp edges of the fracture and depressed skull fragment were pretty obvious; the woman had been clubbed to death.

10

"What are these, Professor?" Michael pointed to two round densities over her breasts.

"Probably linen or sawdust filling to plump out the breasts after death," the Professor said. "All types of materials were used to fill out the skin so it looked natural after death. Let us unwrap the linen and see what our guest looks like."

Turn by turn they unwound the linen from the mummy. After several hours they were finally looking at the face and body of the ancient young woman. Michael looked closely at her breasts and saw how well-proportioned and full they were. He touched the dry brittle skin, pressed the breast lightly, and the skin of the breast broke off in a large piece.

"Sorry Professor." Michael blushed. "I guess I pressed too hard."

"Well at least you can now see what is inside the breast." The Professor laughed. "Lift off the broken skin."

Michael carefully lifted the dry leathery skin from the breast and looked inside.

"Professor!" He shouted.

"What is it?" The Professor leaned closer. When he saw the opened breast his mouth dropped open. The Professor turned to Michael.

"Professor, this is a silicone breast implant!"

Some days are harder than others to get going. The repeat alarm had gone off three times before Norman finally gave in and got out of bed. It was Saturday, so there was no rush to do anything. His only engagement was to meet Ben in the park for their weekend run. After taking care of nature in the bathroom, he got his first dose of coffee in the kitchen. It was automatically ready and waiting when he awoke. He went back to the bathroom, shaved, showered and dressed in his usual running clothes. The telephone rang.

"Hello? Ben?"

"I'm on my way," Ben said quickly. "Meet you in the park in about 15 minutes. Be ready to sweat. It's already 80 degrees outside."

"Okay," Norman said slowly. "Let's take it slow and easy."

"That's what you always say, but you always run me into the ground." Ben laughed.

"We'll see. Meet you in 15 minutes."

The ride to the park was easy. Saturday morning traffic was extremely light, in fact, it took less than 10 minutes to get from the garage to usual unofficial parking space near the athletic center. The real early morning runners were just finishing up as he arrived with the next group. Funny how the same people ran at the same time together day after day even though few, if any, even talked to each other, he thought, except if they were friends to begin with. Ben had already arrived and was stretching.

"How do you feel?" Ben got out of the car.

"Like 6 miles, easy," Norman said.

"Okay. Slow and easy. I'm with you."

Norman did a desultory stretch and pointed his finger in the direction to run. He activated his running watch. He always kept track of the elapsed time. The first few yards were too fast, of course, but they soon settled into a pace they could run and talk comfortably.

"What's new?" Ben said.

"I have a job offer in Boston," Norman said. "It's something I'm really interested in. The pay is okay. It's really the benefits and environment that appeal to me. Besides, I need a change."

13

"You are going to leave the project altogether? You've been one of their best minds. You'll be missed."

"I know I'll be missed. With a project like SETI, who knows when, or if, it will ever get results. I need to think of myself and my career."

"Sure, I agree," Ben said. "But, what if we're the ones that get that first message. Just think of it!"

"Dream on." Norman smirked. "Never happen!"

"What sort of pace are we on?"

Norman glanced at his watch and did a quick mental calculation. "About eight minutes a mile. Not bad for old timers."

"Speak for yourself, old man." Ben laughed. "Let's pick it up a bit."

They ran faster several miles until the heat and humidity forced them to slow down. At the halfway mark, they stopped for a sip of water. The second loop around the park was in a way easier than the first because the end was nearly in sight. They ran slightly faster than their original pace.

"I put up my house for sale," Norman said. "I put an ad in the newspaper. I'm going to sell it myself. I personally hate dealing with real estate agents. Besides I can realize more money that way."

"I guess so," Ben said. "You still have to show everyone the place yourself."

"For the money, I'll endure the inconvenience."

"So your house is going to be a FISBO,"

"For sale by owner." Norman smiled. "That's right. Hey we're almost done!"

They sprinted the last hundred yards with Ben hardly two steps in front of Norman all the way. They stopped running with bullets of sweat showering from their bodies and walked over to the water fountain.

"Let's meet back at the lab this afternoon," Ben said. "We can catch up on some work, and then go out for some Mexican food. How about it?"

"Sounds good, I'll meet you at the lab at 2:30."

Norman wiped off the sweat as best he could. In spite of the attempt to dry off, the sweat continued profusely. He put towels on the seat of his car and turned on the air-conditioning. After a few minutes of driving, he felt more comfortable. Catching up on some work today seemed the right thing to do, he thought. Maybe they could go to a movie after dinner. Norman

14

arrived at the lab before Ben. He unlocked the door and deactivated the alarm. Ten minutes later, Ben arrived as the last drop of coffee had dripped through the filter.

"Coffee?"

"Sure," Ben said, "So where do we begin today?"

"Let's check the assignment logs and see." Norman handed him a mug of coffee.

Ben settled into his seat at the master console. He entered his access code and the monitor screen came to life. Norman sat at his place at an adjacent monitor and keyboard. He entered his access code. The system indicated it was ready for work.

"I'll run checks on the last 24 hour logs," Ben said. "Why don't you get a real time scan?"

Norman tuned the monitor to real-time and watched the patterns on the screen. The screen went blank for several brief seconds.

"What's this?" Norman almost jumped up.

"What do you see?" Ben turned to him.

"I lost all signal for a brief second. That's never happened before."

"It's recorded. Let's see it again."

Norman pulled up the recording of the event on his monitor. The usual galaxy background noise at the frequencies they were monitoring suddenly stopped and as quickly restarted.

"What do you think?" Norman said. "Either its equipment failure or something has interfered with the signal."

Ben moved back to the keyboard and started a check sequence of all the hardware they were using, including the orbiting pan-galactic extraterrestrial amplified receiver. All systems connecting them to the orbiting antenna were redundant and no problem was found in any of the communication links. Next, there was confirmation of the current integrity of the antenna itself.

"Activate the onboard video monitor." Ben watched the screen.

He turned on the antenna videotape which continuously monitored any collisions with space debris. If damage could not be avoided, at least it could be assessed before a repair crew was sent out.

"Here is the segment that should show us something," Norman said.

"Run it." Ben watched over his shoulder.

15

On the screen was a split image of the front of the antenna and a view from the back. There was no apparent damage. Looking in front of the 100 square mile antenna a gray white blur momentarily appeared.

"There!" Ben shouted. "Run that back slowly."

Norman replayed the tape slowly. A huge asteroid passed in front of the antenna, barely a kilometer away. They could see the structural supports of the antenna vibrate from the gravity of the asteroid as it went by.

"That's a near miss. I'll alert NASA and the Jet Propulsion Laboratory."

"Good idea. Thank goodness the antenna is orbiting way out beyond the moon. That rock must be 150 miles across to block our signal."

Norman notified NASA and the Jet Propulsion Laboratory. They were aware of the asteroid and assured them there was no danger, either to the moon or the earth. However, they were surprised it had come so close to the antenna.

"I'm going to make a copy of this tape as a souvenir." Norman laughed. "My one and only, positive finding in all my years here."

"We still have the tapes to review. Believe it or not; there is always a chance something will turn up."

"I'll run them through the computer. See if there's anything obvious."

Norman entered the tape data into the computer and activated the analysis program. He sipped coffee while casually reviewing the near miss of the asteroid over and over on the monitor.

"You know, I can understand how NASA and the Jet Propulsion Laboratory didn't know how close this thing went to the antenna," Norman said. "Anything that's hiding behind the moon is virtually out of sight."

"Not virtually, actually; the program analysis is almost finished."

"Okay, let's look at it."

Norman put the final analysis on the monitor. There were half a dozen signals with statistical promise of significance. More often than not, they could be explained as either man-made or natural phenomena. The segments of tape earmarked as significant were rerun through another analysis program.

"You're going to miss all this excitement." Ben laughed. "You'll miss all this."

16

"You know I will." Norman sighed. "I still have to go on to bigger and better things."

The telephone rang. Ben answered and handed the telephone to Norman.

"Hello," Norman said. "What can I do for you?"

"Do you have a house for sale?"

"Yes, I do,"

"Is there any chance of seeing the house today? My wife and I are interested," the man said.

"What about 5:30?"

"That's perfect. We will see you then."

Norman hung up the telephone and checked the progress of the signal analysis. One signal was clearly identified as a pulsar; the other five were still in the jaws of the recognition algorithm. Ben looked at the first result and checked the star catalog whether this was a known pulsar. There was no record of its existence.

"Looks like, we've discovered another pulsar." Ben said. "I'll enter it into the star catalog with a little credit to us."

Norman chuckled. The monitor listed the second signal with high statistical significance. Norman read the screen not really concerned what it really said. He pointed to the screen as he spoke.

"Look at this. Another false alarm?"

"Not necessarily." He became more interested. "We'll put it in through the next algorithm, when the others are finished."

The third, fourth and fifth signals also had high statistical significance. The last signal was listed as probable broadcast interference. Ben rechecked the last signal analysis and concluded it was man-made. There were now four signals that held promise. Norman took the individual signals and compared them against each other. Within minutes the computer confirmed that the four signals were identical, differentiated only by the time of day they were broadcast. Further analysis showed they all came from the same point in space.

"Well, what you think?" Norman said impishly. "Little green men?"

"I'm not sure." Ben really wanted to believe. "We've been wrong too many times before. I think it needs more analysis before we can start congratulating ourselves."

"The next analysis is going to be easier since the four signals are the same, but it's still going to take hours to process,"

17

Norman said. "I'll set this up and we'll go get something to eat before I have to show the house. Okay?"

"Okay." Ben nodded. "Your car or mine?"

"Mine."

They arrived just before the Saturday evening crowd at the Mexican restaurant. Margaritas were 2 for 1 since it was happy hour. The waitress seated them by the window with a view of the cars passing on the street outside. Chips and salsa quickly appeared. After ordering, they talked about the day.

"I'm still tired from the run this morning," Ben said.

"See, I told you; you are an old man." Norman laughed.

Ben looked at him straight faced then broke out in a laugh as the waitress brought the food.

"What you think of the signal so far?" Norman attacked the taco with gusto.

"We've had false alarms before." Ben dipped into the guacamole salad.

"It would be nice before I leave to have received the first message." Norman took another bite out of the taco.

"No promises, but at least we have a chance with every statistically significant signal we get," Ben said. The cheese enchilada was crying out to him. "The problem is we can only focus on one small sector at a time. There are an infinite number of points and just a handful of us scanning only a few of them. Even if we choose areas we believe may have intelligent life, the chance we will receive a transmission from them will be accidental."

Norman nodded as he took another bite from the taco. They finished eating and left for the prospective buyers at the house. A late model car with a middle aged couple was parked in front when they arrived. Norman introduced himself and gave the grand tour answering questions as they walked through the house. The couple appeared genuinely interested and said they would call to make an offer after they had discussed it between themselves.

Norman agreed and encouraged them to respond quickly as several buyers had already seen the house. He knew this was his first showing and he wanted to light a fire under them to make a decision quickly one way or the other. When they left, Norman and Ben returned to the lab and continued their work.

Norman sat at the console. The analysis program was still running. "Guess we have a little more time before we go to the next stage, if we need to go to the next stage at all."

18

"Have a little faith," Ben said flatly. "This is the furthest we've gone with any signal, not to say four, in a long time."

"I'm going to initial the recheck program on all the signals." Norman entered the instructions on the keyboard.

"Here is our first run answer," Ben said loudly.

The monitor displayed a series of binary numbers. They filled the entire screen and scrolled upward. The monitor went blank momentarily and flashed a ninety-nine percent probability signal from extraterrestrial intelligence. Ben was momentarily speechless. Could this possibly be, he asked himself?

"Do you see what I see?"

"I sure do." Norman restrained himself. "We've done it!"

"Not yet." Ben shook his head slightly. "We have to be absolutely sure."

"The reanalysis of all the data is now in process," Norman said, "I've already confirmed the signals are definitely extraterrestrial from one point in space."

"We're about to make history." Ben became more excited by the moment.

The monitor flashed the reanalysis of data was complete and all the interpretations were accurate. They were dealing with a genuine message from an intelligent race somewhere in the distant reaches of the galaxy. The next task was to translate the message. Fortunately, the binary nature of the message indicated a degree of sophistication suggesting at least similar thinking on how messages should be transmitted over stellar distances.

"I'm making a fresh pot of coffee," Norman said. "I'm not going home until we've cracked this message."

"Enter all the data into the translating algorithm," Ben said. "Let's get started!"

Norman entered the data and activated the translating program. This would take hours at best, if not considerably longer. If the alien language was based on concepts divergent from theirs, the process could take forever. The first and last parts of the message were similar enough to suggest a sign on and off. This was only speculation, but certainly a start. Norman printed out the data and looked at the entire message. Sometimes the visual approach gave some hints that a machine might not recognize. There was nothing that either of them noticed suggestive of anything.

"I think we are stuck with the computer doing our job."

"Too bad we can't do anything to speed this up. The excitement is killing me."

The telephone rang and Norman answered. "I'm surprised to hear from you so soon."

"My wife and I really like your house," the man said, "Is the price negotiable?"

"Within reasonable limits I'm willing to bargain. Do you have an offer in mind?"

"First, we would like an official survey and appraisal. Once that is done, we will make our offer. Is that agreeable to you?"

"I will call you as soon as a survey and appraisal are done. I'll get it done right away."

"Good; we will await your call."

He hung up the telephone and returned to the monitor.

"Anything yet?"

"Nothing."

"What do you think the message will be?" Norman said absently.

"That is a question that has been asked forever." Ben smiled. "If we knew the answer, we could adjust our translation efforts to the exact content."

"Of course, if the message were on astrophysics, focusing on the vocabulary of the subject would facilitate the translation."

"That's obvious. I think the content of the message will be dependent on their place in technological development. Suppose they are way, far advanced than us. Suppose they have developed interstellar travel, then their messages may not be so much as a call to whom is out there but more likely communication between themselves over stellar distances. In the past, we have received earth transmissions of decades ago reflected back to us. These were not messages, but simple commercial broadcasts. We may receive an alien commercial broadcast before one actually directed to communicate with us."

"Whatever the message," Norman continued. "It will change our cosmology forever."

"Philosophers and theologians have pondered the question since the beginning of recorded time," Ben said slowly. "If we are not alone in the universe, does this mean we are not unique as God's creation? I personally don't think it changes anything, but there are a lot of people that are going to struggle for years with that question."

20

"What if the question is simply 'hello how are you?' We will never know the response to our answer in our lifetimes. I assume that our reply will be heard by the descendants of whoever originally sent the first message. In a way, this is almost an academic exercise."

"Unless the message also has technological information that we can use to advance our own technology, which implies a beneficent race willing to give away what they have: highly unlikely."

"If nothing else, we have improved our own technology to meet the challenge of possible interstellar communication," Norman said. "For example, look at the antenna and the translation algorithms that we developed."

Ben nodded and focused on the monitor. "Here it comes." He almost held his breath.

The monitor indicated the analysis was partially complete and that general and specific linguistic patterns were identified.

"I'm going to display the translation so far." Norman manipulated the keyboard.

The screen was filled with recognizable words, phrases, numbers and blanks.

"This looks like the frequency of transmission." Ben pointed. "Over here is the origin of the signal."

"What about this other location indicated over here?" Norman pointed.

"I don't know," Ben said. "Look, here's more."

Some of the blanks were slowly filled in as they were deciphered.

"This is beginning to look like a description of a planet with its physical characteristics," Norman read from the screen. "...circling a yellow star...two satellites...two thirds water...and ample life forms."

"Probably the point of origin of the message," Norman said. "Here's more."

The message gave a detailed description of an alien world many light years away. They could not have asked for a better description. There was one last part of the message that remained untranslated. The computer continued working on the message to the last and final tidbit.

"Once this comes through," Ben said loudly. "We'll break out the champagne."

The computer signaled the translation was complete. They both eagerly read the final missing segment and laughed. On the screen were written the final words: for sale by owner.

The Illusion

After a year the journey from earth was nearly at an end for Gary and Steve. They were about to be the first men to step on another planet. The computer recalculated and confirmed the exact time of orbital insertion around the destination.

"Transmit our numbers back to base." Gary turned the onboard telescope toward the red planet ahead.

"Numbers gone," Steve said. "We should get confirmation in a few minutes."

"Look at this view!" Gary shouted. "I can't believe we really made it. All these months of sheer boredom and loneliness, for a step into the history books and fame, are about to pay off."

"Not to say, pay off in fortune." Steve grinned.

Gary looked at the high definition color monitor showing Mars and its two tiny moons in exquisite detail. He adjusted the magnification and saw the surface details better. A light on the control panel indicated a message was received and recorded. He noticed and played it back.

"Congratulations gentlemen," the recording began. "You are about to reach your destination. Your onboard calculations have been confirmed by our backup computers here at home base. Retro rocket maneuvers should take place at 0800. We do not anticipate any changes of any of the flight parameters. Once orbital insertion is complete, you are to rest one complete twenty-four hour period before descent to the surface. All systems monitored here indicate you are go for landing. You will double check all systems as instructed. The next transmission is scheduled for 0830."

"It's almost 0800." Steve pointed. "Better strap in."

They secured themselves and watched the countdown clock. Steve turned on the outside video monitor. Although it was not necessary to visually monitor the retro rockets during the maneuver, Steve enjoyed watching. The entire retro rocket maneuver was silent; the only evidence of anything was a faint almost invisible exhaust from the individual rockets and a noticeable change in motion.

"10 . . . 9 . . . 8 . . . 7 . . . 6 . . . 5 . . . 4 . . . 3 . . . 2 . . . 1 . . . Ignition," Gary said coolly.

There was a sudden shudder throughout the ship and whatever was not secured moved forward with the velocity change. Inertia was at work. Steve watched the retro rockets carefully, but saw nothing, no exhaust, flame or anything. He could hardly wait for the descent to the planet surface below.

"Orbital insertion complete." Steve read from the instruments. "Confirmation signaled home."

"Apogee 100 miles," Gary read from the computer monitor. "Perigee 75 miles."

"Deimos, off to starboard." Steve pointed.

Gary looked out the viewport and saw the tiny moon slowly glide by them at a distance. He turned back to the instrument console and went through a routine check. Although everything was fully automated and controlled with the computers, their active participation kept them occupied and thinking sharp. The red planet loomed directly below. Steve activated the topographic recognition program and scanned the surface. In minutes, the monitor in front of Steve accurately positioned them over known landmarks. Steve knew his Martian geography well and enjoyed watching the picture of the surface on the monitor.

"It's hard to believe there is no life down there," Steve said.

"Too cold, too far away from the sun and no surface water." Gary smiled. "Other than that it's a perfect place for life."

"Okay, I know all of that; but I am still a science fiction romantic."

"We have a loss of pressure in the backup oxygen tank," Gary said quickly. "Recheck your panel."

"Confirmed; it's slow. I'll close all valves and recheck."

Within minutes the instruments read all systems were intact. The oxygen pressure in the backup tank returned to normal. Steve reopened the valves one by one and the pressure remained constant.

"Must be a reading error; let's watch it."

"I'll set the audible alarm, if there's a change in pressure. That should keep us safe."

"I agree." Gary nodded. "Before we descend in the lander, I'll check the connections visually."

"Transmission from home received."

"Play it back."

"Confirm satisfactory orbital insertion," the message began. "Parameters exceed initial expectations. Have noted change in oxygen backup pressure. Order delay in landing until system completely checked. Hubble has spotted a sandstorm on the other side of the planet out of your view; standby for further weather bulletins. Expect landing delayed forty-eight to seventy-two hours; home base standing by. Congratulations again, gentlemen."

"If it's not one thing, it's another." Steve huffed. "I'll check out the oxygen lines again."

"Good." Gary stared at the scene on the monitor. "We're coming over that storm home base mentioned."

Steve glanced at the monitor and shook his head. He glided weightless out the control room toward the rear storage compartment. He found all the interior oxygen lines and valves intact.

"Gary."

"Yes."

"I'm going outside."

"Go for it," Gary said. "Enjoy the view."

Minutes later Steve was in a suit outside the ship. He gazed intently at the panorama below. It was spectacular. The surface details were crystal-clear everywhere except where the huge sandstorm covered the surface. Steve reminded himself he had a job to do and proceeded examining all the external oxygen lines. As part of the extravehicular activity, he also did a thorough check of all other lines, the antennae and the integrity of the hull. Everything was completely normal. He moved to the underside of the mothership and examined the lander.

"Lander looks okay," Steve said. "I'm coming back in."

"Breakfast will be ready when you get home." Gary laughed.

"Thanks."

The food was not the most appealing gourmet fare but it sustained life. Complaining about the food was one of the favorite past times. Steve recalled when they called home base with a special order for pizza. The answer from home base was a simple they did not deliver in that neighborhood. At least there was a sense of humor with home base.

"Once we finished eating," Gary said. "We need some sleep. We have a long day tomorrow."

"You mean another long day staring at each other."
Steve laughed. "I guess after nearly a year another day of
looking at your face won't kill me."

"If you think I'm not anxious to get down there, you're
wrong." Gary pointed at the monitor. It showed a detailed close-
up of the surface below. "I've lived my entire life for this
moment. My education, my training and my choices in life have
drawn me here, to my destiny."

Steve nodded because, in a way, he felt the same way.
On the other hand, his selection for the mission was based more
on his qualifications than his desire to be part of the team. Their
personalities balanced and contrasted enough to make them the
best possible team. Home base always knew what was best.

They settled into the sleeping quarters. Gary as always
fell immediately asleep. Nothing could, or would, keep him from
getting the sleep he needed. For Steve, the excitement of the
arrival gave him an adrenaline rush that prevented him from
relaxing enough to drift off into sleep. He took a sleeping
capsule and in fifteen minutes he was sound asleep.

Steve found himself alone on a tiny island with a single
palm tree in the middle of the ocean. On the distant horizon, he
saw a ship passing by. He felt abandoned and trapped. Soon the
tide engulfed the island. The water covered all the sand forcing
him to climb up the palm tree just to keep his head above water.
He climbed to the top of the tree and the tide kept rising. Just as
he was about to go under he woke up in a sweat. The alarm was
chiming, the sleep period was over.

Gary looked at him with concern. "Another bad dream?"

"The same one I've had over and over all these months
getting here. I'm okay."

They took care of their personal hygiene and returned to
the control room. Another message had been received from
home base while they were asleep. Gary played the message.

"The sandstorm has intensified and is obscuring surface
details. Recommend close monitoring next twelve hours. If
storm continues to intensify, mission will not include manned
landing. We cannot risk your lives under these conditions.
Prepare the lander for an unmanned landing; standby for further
bulletins and instructions; home base out."

Gary and Steve looked at each other. Steve turned on the
monitor. It showed the leading edge of the storm on the surface.
They were orbiting over the problem below. He closely
examined the details of the storm.

"One more orbit and I think I'll be able to predict whether this storm is going to keep us off the surface or not," Steve said.

"I've got my fingers crossed," Gary said, "I hope it will disappear as quickly as it came up."

"These storms usually do. If they're small, the dust clears quickly. If they are gigantic, the dust can stay in the atmosphere for months."

"There is nothing we can do but wait." Gary sat back from the console.

"I'm going to launch a balloon probe into the storm. Maybe it will give us more information on what to expect."

The probe was launched toward the surface. It moved slowly ahead in its long arc around the planet before it entered the storm. Steve lost contact with the probe when it disappeared on the other side of the planet.

"We should catch up in less than an hour," Steve said.

"Oxygen pressure remains unchanged," Gary said. "Looks like it must have been a reading error."

"Possibly." Steve was not ready to be absolutely certain. "We still leave the alarm set."

"Don't worry. I won't change a thing. I have checked out the lander, everything is all set for descent."

"I have a feeling we will be in the lander when it goes." Steve smiled.

"Phobos, off to port." Gary pointed out the viewport.

Steve looked out at the closer Martian moon and remembered the history of failures in trying to learn more about Mars and its moons. The Soviet Union had unsuccessfully tried to explore Phobos. The United States also failed in its attempt to map the planet's surface with the Mars Observer satellite. Rumors circulated that the Martians did not want to reveal their secret presence. Of course, that was all fanciful and wishful thinking. Additional unmanned missions collected all the data needed for the current manned expedition.

"We've caught up to the probe," Gary said, "Camera on."

Steve made a few adjustments on the instrument console and tapped a set of instructions into the keyboard. He saw the wind velocity was gusting up to one hundred mph and visibility through the dust was about one hundred feet. The balloon carried the probe well above any surface obstacles that would damage it.

"How does it look?"

"On our next pass I'll be able to tell what's going to happen." Steve entered the probe's data into the computer.

"Are you ready to eat?"

"Eat, sleep, eat!" Steve chuckled. "That has been our entire life up to now. Okay. Let's eat. By the time we finish we will be back over the storm again."

"Wishful thinking, we are not going to eat that slowly."

The food was bland, but it tasted different. Complaining about the food was no longer the main topic of discussion. The wait for the final decision on whether they would be aboard the lander was by far the most important consideration. This made everything else of no consequence. When they woke up from the next rest period, they would know the answer on the status of the landing.

On the next orbital pass, the sandstorm had noticeably diminished. The probe continued sending back data directly into the onboard computer. Even the visibility had doubled. The dust was settling faster than predicted, Steve thought. Gary transmitted a message to home base that all systems were functioning satisfactorily and that the Martian storm appeared significantly diminished. Before he finished the transmission, he turned to Steve.

"Is there anything else we need to tell them?"

"Just that: we are ready to go, whenever they say the word." Steve grinned.

At the rate the storm was diminishing, by the end of their next sleep period the dust should have completely disappeared. They prepared for the last sleep period before the long anticipated landing. Even Gary could not sleep and needed help with medication. Drifting in sleep Steve found himself on the small island again. This time the island sank into the water. He shouted as loudly as he could at a passing ship. His head went below the surface of the water...

"Steve, wake up!" Gary shook firmly. "You're dreaming again."

"What did I say?" Steve said slowly. Sleep remained in his eyes.

"Nothing I could understand. This time you screamed for help."

"It's nothing." Steve waved his hand dismissively. "Can we land?"

"I haven't checked yet."

"Well, let's find out. I'm ready to go."

28

The computer compared all the storm data from each orbital pass and gave an all clear for landing. A message from home base confirmed the safety of a landing. The need to wait another twenty-four hours was deemed unnecessary. The men completed their toilet, ate and dressed with mechanical efficiency. Other than technical questions and answers, there was virtual silence in their communication. They knew they were to embark on the most important event in their lives. With the flip of a coin it was decided Steve would be the first to step on the Martian surface. All systems on the mothership were rechecked and put into standby mode. Gary sat in the pilot seat of the lander and Steve sat as navigator. It took over two hours for them to go through the lander checklists. Failure was not an option, they had to assure themselves and home base all systems were functioning properly. Everything checked out textbook perfect. There were no surprises expected.

"This is it!" Gary grinned.

"Five minutes, and counting!" Steve concentrated on the control panel. "Transmitting prerecorded message to home base."

"Roger." Gary collected himself. "Real-time transmission on!"

The next few minutes felt an eternity. Gary activated the separation sequence at one minute. The lander separated and moved slowly downward toward the planet surface. Steve monitored the distance from the mothership.

"Separation accomplished," Steve said. "Powered descent now safe."

"Retro rockets in 10 seconds." Gary took control of the joystick.

The lander shuddered slightly when the retros ignited. Steve felt his heart jump up into his throat. Gary gripped the joystick with all his strength and his knuckles turned white. The lander plunged downward into the thin Martian atmosphere. Steve monitored the altimeter readings and announced them at intervals as Gary watched the screen in front of him. Gary slowed the descent with the retro rockets and moved the lander over the surface according to the flight path on the monitor. It was almost like playing a videogame, he thought smiling. Surface details became clear, the lower they descended. The surface was littered with broken rocks on the rust red sand of what was thought to be an ancient riverbed. Steve announced they had little more than one minute to land safely or they would have to return back to the mothership. Gary finally found a clean area to set the lander down.

"100 feet . . . 80 feet . . . 60 feet . . . 40 . . . 20 . . . 10 . . . 5 . . . Touchdown!"

"Yahoo!" They shouted.

Gary composed himself and shut down the retro rocket controls. He could not think of anything profound to transmit back to earth. Steve did a cursory check of the instruments.

"Mars base here, the earthmen have landed!" Steve said for the history books and winked at Gary.

The men went through the prescribed post-landing routine. A transmission of congratulations came within minutes. The outside video camera scanned the surrounding terrain for the audience back home.

"I can't believe we're here at last." Gary was almost breathless.

"Believe it." Steve laughed. "Let's get ready to stretch our legs. We have a lot of work to do before we can go outside."

"You have no complaints from me about anything from here on out." Gary beamed.

Permission to leave the lander was given by home base. Gary and Steve put on their spacesuits and went into the airlock. Steve checked the inner door, confirmed it was securely closed and decompressed the airlock to the Martian atmosphere. Gary opened the outer door as soon as the pressure was equalized. The two men stood in awe of the view. Gary looked at Steve who signaled thumbs up. Steve exited the exterior door and climbed down the ladder to the surface. At the lowest rung of the ladder he stopped before taking the last step.

"The earth men cometh and we are here." Steve tried to be poetic as he made contact with the Martian surface with his right foot.

Steve turned around and watched Gary climb down to the surface. They planted the flag and took pictures like a couple of tourists. The exterior video camera monitored the activity for home base. They unloaded the Martian rover from the storage compartment of the lander. Steve rested and scanned the view around the ship. Within a quarter of a mile was a low-level mountain. He saw a flash of light in that direction.

"Did you see that?" Steve pointed.

"Yes, I did," Gary said. "Let's go see what it is."

"Are the weapons on the rover? Not that we're going to need them."

"They're packed on board; I'll drive."

The men boarded the rover and headed off toward the mountain. Because of the large rocks, they had to stop and clear the way at intervals. It took almost an hour of hard work to get to the destination. They did not see the flash again. The terrain became impassible at the base of the mountain. They unloaded the weapons and walked the rest of the distance.

"I feel strange," Steve said. "I guess I'm not use to this much physical activity even though the gravity is only one third of that back home."

"I feel strange, too," Gary said. "Must be the physical activity."

"Get down!" Steve shouted.

"What is it?" Gary crouched down quickly. "Holy mackerel!"

"Another spaceship!" Steve pointed. "We're not alone!"

The men hid behind two large boulders. There was a ship on the other side of the mountain. At the base of the ship were two men looking in their direction.

"Do you think they saw us?" Gary whispered.

"I'm not sure, but they are coming this way." Steve clutched his weapon tightly. "We need to be ready for anything."

The men from the other ship approached with weapons in their hands. Suddenly one pointed in their direction, raised a weapon and fired at them. A rock exploded in front of Gary. Instinctively, Steve raised his weapon and fired back. Gary fired alongside Steve. Their weapons hit the ship which exploded behind the two strangers, knocking them to the ground. Neither stranger got up from where they fell, nor could they be seen by Gary and Steve from their position.

"Let's get back to our ship," Gary said quickly. "I don't think we will have any trouble from whoever they are."

"I agree." Steve was visibly shaken by the hostile encounter. "Our communication has been cut off to home base."

"We will send a report once we get back." Gary wanted to get back to the ship as fast as possible.

They re-boarded the rover and started back to the ship. The way was clearly marked by the rocks they had previously moved. The ship was not anywhere where it should have been.

"Where's the ship?" Steve was puzzled and confused. "We are going in the right direction."

"It should be ahead." Gary pointed. "This terrain is hilly; it's probably just hiding ahead."

31

"You know that ship we destroyed looked familiar."

"All ships look similar, if they follow the laws of physics," Gary said as they came to their lander.

"What happened?" Steve blanched.

"Our ship has been destroyed!" Gary was stunned.

Steve felt he was suddenly on his island with his head about to go under water for the last time.

***

"The earth men are easily tricked," the one Martian said to the other. "They destroy their own ship and they don't even realize it."

"That should keep them away for a little longer," the other Martian said. "Someday they will find out about us."

"Only when we want them to know," the first Martian said. "Only when we want them to know."

Project Blink

The object slipped through the outer solar system in a trajectory that brought it into the Jovian system. Jupiter's gravity reached out, bent its path and swung it into the inner solar system toward a point where the Earth would pass in three months. Although its transit of Jupiter was brief, the Hubble telescope did record the event as it happened.

"Dad, are you ready to go?" Jack was in the bathroom putting the finishing touches, combing his hair.

"Come on, I have to be early," his father shouted. "I'll meet you in the car."

"Wait for me!" Jack locked the front door of the house and ran to the car.

The car was already moving when Jack opened the door. Safely inside with the side door closed, they drove off to the amateur fights. Jack's father was a judge at ringside for more years than he could remember. At first, it was something to do after retirement, now it was a pure labor of love and dedication to the sport of safe amateur boxing. In his youth Jack's father had been a fighter himself with every fight a victory. He would have turned professional but the war ended that dream. Probably just as well, Jack thought, boxing in those days was not nearly as safe as it is today. Although boxing as a sport is brutal, the current emphasis to the kids learning the sport was technique and the scoring of points. Knockouts were deemphasized, but knockdowns were encouraged. As a judge, Jack's father was more than fair. They arrived at the gym with plenty of time to talk to some of the kids getting ready for their bouts

"Jack, I want you to meet Amelio," Jack's father said. "I've been training him in the afternoon after school."

"Glad to meet you Amelio." Jack held out his right hand.

Amelio put his glove into Jack's hand and laughed. Jack laughed, too, and grabbed the glove's thumb completing the shake.

"Good luck tonight," Jack said.

"Thanks, I'm going to need it." Amelio grinned.

"Amelio knows how to jab and protect himself, right?" Jack's father said proudly. "Remember to keep your eyes open and don't blink."

33

Jack's father rubbed the 12-year-old aspiring boxer's hair affectionately and let him continue his warm up. Jack followed and sat in the seat next to his father at ringside. Watching the young kids was fun as long as no one got seriously hurt. The first bout matched two 8-year-old boys. At the bell, the boys came out and jabbed at each other until one glove hit the other boy in the face. Forgetting all form and grace the victim retaliated with a windmill of punches that sent his opponent cowering behind his own gloves. The referee broke the boys apart to start again. This time they danced around each other without hitting anything. The bell rang mercifully allowing the boys to retire to their corners. The father of the boy who hid behind his gloves tried encouraging his son. In the other corner was lots of laughing. The bell rang again and the boys touched gloves. The same thing occurred. The jabs of the one boy were expertly thrown, but the response was somewhat exaggerated. At the end of the third round the decision went to the boy who threw the most punches. Jack's father strongly disagreed with the decision. The loser left ringside in tears with his father's arm around him.

"I feel sorry for that kid," Jack said.

"I think he was the better fighter and scored the most points," Jack's father said. "He's really good. He'll make it, if he has heart. It just takes time."

The next bout matched Amelio with a boy trained by the owner of the gym. The three rounds were well fought by both boys to the point that they earned equal points up until the very last seconds. Dancing around and jabbing, Amelio quickly saw an opening in his opponent's guard. Amelio threw a right cross that landed squarely on the jaw knocking his opponent down. The stunned boy shook his head, slowly rising to his knees, then his feet while the referee did a mandatory count. The bell rang ending the fight. The judges unanimously gave the decision to Amelio.

"You've done a great job with Amelio, Dad," Jack said.

"He's got a lot of promise." Jack's father beamed. "Did you see that great right cross? Just like I taught him."

"Action, reaction, Dad" Jack laughed. "You want to move something in a certain direction: you have to hit it just right."

The rest of the fights went by like clockwork. Friends and families cheered their fighters in encouragement. When it was all over there was not an unhappy face leaving the arena.

34

Jack's father congratulated Amelio on a fight well fought before they went home. Amelio gave both men a hug in appreciation of their praise.

On their way home Jack's phone rang. "Hello?"

"Hello, Jack, this is Bob. NASA just called to give us an assignment."

"What is it?"

"Hubble picked up a very large object with a low albedo in transit across the face of Jupiter tonight. Our assignment is to find and track its trajectory," Bob said. "NASA suggested we start taking pictures tonight."

"Where are you now?" Jack was definitely interested.

"I'm in my car on my way to the Observatory. I'll be there in about 10 minutes."

"I'm on my way home with my Dad. As soon as I get my car I'll be on my way."

"See you there." Bob hung up.

"Dad, I've got to go to work," Jack said. "Drop me off in the driveway when we get home."

"Too bad you can't stay longer," Jack's father said. "But I understand work is work. Maybe you can stay longer and sleep over next time."

"I'd really like that, Dad." Jack reached over and squeezed his father's shoulder affectionately.

The ride to the Observatory was marred by the onset of rain. What started out as a clear summer night turned out to be one of those typical wet ones seen early in South Florida. A combination of the rain and warmth meant the humidity would turn unbearable. Jack parked his car and dashed to the Observatory under his umbrella only to find he had forgotten to take the keys out of the driver's side door lock. In a quick race back to the car, he retrieved the keys at the expense of thoroughly wet running shoes. Inside the building, Jack removed his shoes and walked barefoot.

"Jack, you look like a drowned whatever." Bob smiled as he entered the room. "Is it raining that hard?"

"I forgot my keys and had to run out for them," Jack shook his head in disgust. "And wouldn't you know it, when I finally get inside the rain decides to stop."

"There's coffee on if you want some." Bob pointed. "What we need to do first is look at the Hubble photo then promulgate a plan."

"No coffee," Jack said. "Let's get to work. Did Hubble get only one or are there more photos?"

"Only one."

"Sure it's not an artifact?"

"That's been checked several times. It's real."

"Then it really must be moving fast. That's what I like, a challenge."

Bob reproduce the Hubble photo on the high definition monitor and used the mouse pointer to indicate where the shadow of the object was. Jack looked closely and asked for a stepwise increase in magnification of the area. With each step increase a black streak slowly appeared visible across Jupiter in the center of the screen.

"That's the shadow, now where is the object?" Jack said. "From this data we can at least calculate the angle to the ecliptic."

"I have a feeling that whatever caused the shadow is hidden behind one of the large Jovian moons. That's the only explanation I can come up with," Bob said. "Besides to have a shadow that big the object must be huge."

"We are probably dealing with an asteroid." Jack pursed his lips.

Bob nodded he agreed with the conclusion. Now they had to find the object and determine its trajectory. For their work they might even get to name it, Bob thought.

"Let's have the lunar optical array transmit digital pictures of the sectors on either side of Jupiter along the axis of the streak," Jack said.

"I've already contacted the lunar base to tell them we are going to need some pictures," Bob said. "I told them I needed to confer with you about the time intervals between pictures."

"For starters, we will need photos 24 hours apart. That should get us on our way." Jack paused. "Tell lunar base we are code naming our search Project Blink."

"Sounds good." Bob smiled because, after all, it was the easiest and best way to locate moving objects against the stars.

The technique of finding moving objects in space was simple. Two or more pictures were taken on different days, then projected, one after the other, back and forth on a large screen. The background stars would not move while the moving objects appeared to jump as the pictures were blinked. In fact, Pluto was discovered by this technique. Of course, the computer would help speed the search by locating the moving objects, eliminating those already known.

"I already have the first digital pictures from tonight recorded," Bob said. "I have asked for another set tomorrow morning. I know it's not enough time between pictures, but at least we will be able to get started tomorrow morning with our search."

The next morning Bob and Jack arrived early at the Observatory. The name Observatory was actually a misnomer. It really should have been called a receiving station since all the optical and electronic sensing devices were either in orbit around the earth or on the moon. The place was tiny considering the magnitude of the work that was accomplished. If the receiving equipment were not so expensive, all the necessary projects assigned could probably be done at home.

"We are in luck," Bob said. "This morning's pictures are already here."

"Good, let's get started," Jack said. "Let's see if we can find where this sucker is."

Bob entered the previous night's star images in the blinking viewer and into the computer. Using the calculated angle to the ecliptic from the Jupiter photo, the search was limited within a reasonable band on both sides of the giant planet.

"Ready?" Bob tensed.

"Go!" Jack nodded.

The high definition monitor blinked the two pictures until Bob entered stop on the keyboard. He then entered a command to eliminate most of the objects, but there were still too many to count.

"Now enter all the known moving objects," Jack said.

Bob sorted the objects with a deftness that demonstrated his long experience with these sorts of searches. The screen blinked again. Known moving objects were programmed to fade from the screen. What was left were a dozen or so objects that were not catalogued in the computer database.

"Looks like these are our candidates." Jack pointed. "I'll get an update from the international database to eliminate all new known moving objects. That should help a little."

Jack within minutes retrieved the information they needed. This eliminated half the candidates.

"There are four objects to the left and two to the right of Jupiter," Jack said. "If I had to pick one, I'd pick this one."

37

Bob saw where Jack pointed and thought a moment. "A beer that is not it."

"You're on!" Jack was ready for the challenge. "We'll need a few days to get an accurate parallax fix to prove me right and I'll pick the time and place you pay me off."

"In the meantime, I'll notify lunar base of our findings." Bob laughed.

At the end of the workday, they locked up and went out to their cars together. The air was warm and humid.

"Want to come over to my Dad's house to watch the heavyweight fight on cable tonight?" Jack shouted as Bob got into his car.

"I've got a date tonight," Bob shouted back. "Besides, I'm a lover not a fighter."

"Okay, see you in the morning." Jack crawled behind the steering wheel of his own car and closed the door.

Jack did not bother to drive to his place; instead he went directly to his father's house. His mother had expected him and dinner was ready on the table. They sat down as soon as he came through the door.

"Did you have a good day?" His mother said warmly. "Your father told me you have a special project."

"Yes, Mom, an object was picked up as it moved across Jupiter. Our job is to find where it is and track it. Almost like trying to find a needle in a haystack."

"Not with those computers of yours," his mother said. "Why do you bother with these things anyway?"

"Simple, we need to know where this thing is going, in case we have to do something to alter its direction. If it's going to hit the earth, we need to know. It wouldn't take a very large collision to destroy civilization as we know it."

"Have there ever been any?" Jack's father said.

"None in modern times that we can verify," Jack continued. "You surely have heard or know the theory that the dinosaurs were wiped out by a collision with an asteroid that altered the world climate in sort of a nuclear winter."

"Whenever they talk about that, they always mention the element iridium," Jack's father said.

"Because there is a high content of that element in asteroids," Jack said. "At the time of the disappearance of the dinosaurs, the geological record had a high concentration of that element. By inference there must have been a collision with a massive asteroid that exploded in the atmosphere, spreading its

38

dust to block out the sun, causing global temperature to drop. Most large animals living at the time could not adapt quickly to the effects of the temperature change and perished."

"I'm sure with our modern technology that won't happen," Jack's mother interjected. "Anyone want key lime pie for dessert? I made it this afternoon."

After helping clean the table and loading the dishwasher, they settled in the Florida room for the fight on cable. Although his mother was not a fan, she enjoyed sitting in the company of her men. The TV announcer loudly announced the fighters who in turn were interviewed for the viewing public. Each fighter puffed in front of the camera to an extent almost laughable. Part was theatrics, but a good part was to put doubt in the opponent's mind of their ability. Boxing was more than just brute physical contact, there was strategy and psychology to consider.

After the opening announcements, the fighters hit their gloves together and went back to their respective corners. With the bell, the men drew close to each other and began their circling dance of jabbing and footwork, looking for that chance to strike the deciding blow. In professional fights, points were important but viewers paid for mayhem. Few professional fighters escaped physical injury in their careers.

"Who do you think is going to win, Dad?" Jack sipped the beer his mother had brought him.

"That guy in the white trunks is the favorite," he said. "But he's overweight and out of shape. I'm going to go for the guy in the black trunks."

Not more than 30 seconds into the first round of a flurry of jabs, a strong right hook knocked the fighter in the white trunks to the canvas. The referee backed the standing opponent into the corner; by the count of eight the downed fighter was back on his feet. The fighters touched gloves and began again. A solid right to the jaw of the fighter in the white trunks and he went down for the full count. The referee declared the fighter in the black the winner and the crowd went wild with a mixture of cheers and booing. On the one hand, the match was filled with action, on the other hand, it ended too quickly and the underdog won. That really did not matter; Jack and his father enjoyed what they saw.

"If that asteroid of yours is coming this way," his mother said loudly. "Are you going to give it a right cross?"

"Of course." Jack was surprised at his mother's spontaneous remark. "And knock it out cold!"

"I guess boxing can be useful," she said. They all laughed.

At the end of the remaining bouts that filled the program Jack started to leave but was invited to stay in his old room since it was late. Jack thought a moment and decided it would be nice to have breakfast ready when he woke for a change.

"Good night, Mom. Good night, Dad. See you in the morning."

"Good night, son," his parents said in unison.

The next day Jack pointed out to Bob that the preliminary data indicated his first pick as the object was the correct one. Bob would not concede to that fact for another two days on the pretense that the data was not accurate enough.

"Here are the new numbers on our object," Jack said. "I'm sure you'll now agree that I was right. It's now going to be payoff time."

"Okay, you are right." Bob was reluctant to admit he had lost. "But I still think it was a lucky guess."

"Back to work." Jack laughed. "Let's blink all the photos we have and see how this thing is moving."

Bob brought up the necessary photos in the computer, faded the background stars, and highlighted the designated object. The data was entered to project velocity and direction. All data and projections were displayed on the high definition monitor. A glance at the screen indicated there was a problem.

"This thing is on a collision course for us!" Bob shouted.

"It's projected to impact us in less than three months!" The numbers on the monitor were clear. "I'll notify NASA."

"They will finally have a chance to test their anti-asteroid system," Bob said. "I sure hope it works."

"So do I," Jack picked up the telephone to NASA.

NASA immediately wanted transmission of all their work to recheck the conclusions. Within minutes after sending everything, NASA's scientists had verified the conclusions. Strict secrecy was in force from that moment to prevent the spread of panic by the press. Jack and Bob were instructed to complete silence from everyone including family members.

On the West Coast, NASA prepared three nuclear armed rockets for launch from Vandenberg Air Force Base. The countdowns went smoothly with each rocket launched a day apart. The flotilla of nuclear armed rockets sped out from the Earth's orbit at their maximum velocity in order to reach the object within the same twenty-four hour period. The time of impact by the first weapon was projected forty-five days from launch. The press reported this frenzy of space activity to the presence of a newly discovered asteroid that would be coming close to the earth. NASA's releases to the press did not tell how close to the earth it was to come.

"If a nuclear blast shatters the asteroid," Bob said. "We will still be showered with the fragments."

"NASA's plan is not to destroy the asteroid but to deflect it out of the Earth's path," Jack said. "One weapon will impact the asteroid; the other two will be detonated to create a deflecting shockwave for any fragments."

The days went by quickly. Everyone interested in astronomy focused on the coming object. The mass population as a whole, unaware of the threat, remained passively disinterested. Visual observation by the best optical instruments added nothing new to what was known except that its shape appeared oblong. Unfortunately, there was not enough time before launch of the missles to install cameras for close-up pictures on interception.

"Today is the day," Jack said as he walked into the Observatory with Bob.

"I understand we will have the Hubble focused on the object when the first warhead impacts."

"If nothing else that will let us know if impact took place and if the object broke up into pieces. Let's get set up and comfortable for the show."

They went to their respective consoles and turned on the high definition monitor tuned in by satellite linkup with the Hubble telescope. On the screen they could make out the blurry image of the object with a digital countdown displayed in the lower right-hand corner.

"In just a few minutes, we will give this thing that right cross my Mom said it needed." Jack laughed.

"I know I worry too much," Bob said. "But I hope it goes down for the count."

"Have faith."

Jack turned on the audio from mission control and listened for the last comments prior to impact.

"One minute before impact with number one," the mission control voice said flatly.

Jack watched the monitor and thought he saw the object change orientation. Then again, he could have just blinked his eyes.

"Thirty seconds and counting."

41

No, something was happening with the object. Its shape had changed.

"Fifteen seconds."

Bob came over to Jack and tapped him on the shoulder. Jack shrugged his shoulders as he did not know what the movement meant.

". . . Five . . . Four . . . Three . . . Two . . . One . . . Impact!"

There was a brilliant flash followed by an even bigger one. The warhead had caused the object to explode.

"That takes care of that." Jack smiled. "The danger is gone! Time to celebrate!"

The telephone rang and Bob answered. As he listened his jaw dropped open and his face went white.

"What's wrong?"

"It's Norman over at SETI." Bob tried to collect himself. "They received a transmission from the object just before it was destroyed. The transmission said 'Greetings Earth men, we come in peace'."

Ring!

"Hello?"
"Hello!"*
"Who is this?"
"It's me!"*
"Again?"
"Of course what do you expect?"*

"I don't know what to expect anymore. I'm more than a little confused. My feelings are overpowering everything I can possibly think right now. I really need some time to reason everything out."

"But what is there to reason? You know how I feel. We've talked about it over and over. I thought we finally settled what we were going to do."*

"I know what I've said before, but I'm afraid. I don't know if it will work, or if it will ever work."

"Don't you want it to work?"*

"You know I do, but that doesn't make me feel any more comfortable. I still find it hard to believe that this has happened at all."

"You know all of this has also caught me by surprise. I never expected this to happen when we first saw each other."*

"That seems so long ago and yet it really wasn't when I think about it. It really brings a smile to my face thinking about how you looked that night I bumped into you."

"Boy was I surprised to see you! I wasn't supposed to see anyone that night."*

"Did you expect that you could come here and not meet anyone? That was foolish to think where you were that night."

"Looking back is always easier than looking ahead. It sure makes for memories we can share together. Were you scared when you saw me that night?"*

"I think I was more curious than anything else. I never once thought I was in danger. I immediately recognized you were a stranger in the city. You must admit you were in a most suspicious place without much clothing on."

"If you remember, I told you I was out running that night and got lost. Whenever I travel I get my exercise by running. Not only do I stay fit, I get a close-up tour of where I am."*

43

"Still, it was in the middle of the night away from the usual running trails. What could you expect me to think?"

"My time commitments and housing location dictate the time and places I can run. There was nothing really unusual about where I was that particular night, except bumping into you."*

"And bump you did! You nearly scared the life out of me, until I realized I was completely safe."

"I must admit it was a scary situation, you and I confronting each other in the dark for the first time. But, if I remember correctly, you were coming back from an exercise class yourself."*

"That's right. After a hard day's work I always like to relax by working out. A good sweat is always good for the body and soul."

"You were dressed in tights that in the dark made you appear naked. I did a double-take. I really had to take a second look to make sure I saw what I saw."*

"And were you disappointed?"

"Well, no. In fact, I was very much attracted to you that first time we met. The suddenness of our meeting almost made me pass off our encounter as one of those many inconsequential meetings that happen every day in our lives."*

"So what happened?"

"I think it was your infectious smile and giggle when I apologized for frightening you. You laughed and apologized in turn. We both paused, then broke out in a mutual laugh. For a while we were laughing as if we were old friends. I couldn't help but to invite you for a cup of coffee down that street at the all night eatery."*

"Although you were a complete and total stranger, I accepted even though I was the complete and total stranger under the circumstances just as much as you. I don't know what it was, I completely trusted you or rather I trusted my instincts that this was more than just a random encounter. I felt our meeting was something special, almost as if it were preordained."

"Funny you should say that. I've felt the same ever since that day. Everything has just dropped into place for us. Do you remember what happened that night?"*

"How could I possibly forget?!"

"You left your money behind at your house and we walked together to the eatery. After ordering and drinking coffee for a couple of hours, neither of us had any money to pay!"*

"More than a little embarrassing, to say the least; you did leave to get your wallet while I waited as hostage. After a while, I thought it was all a bizarre joke on me. I was finally relieved when you returned as promised."

"I would have returned sooner if it hadn't started raining."*

"It sure seems that our first date did have a few obstacles. For me it has been worth every minute of anything I have had to endure."

"Do you remember what else I said that night? About how long I would be here?"*

"Yes, I remember you said it wouldn't be long. Are you telling me it's time for you to leave?"

"Unfortunately, you're right. My time here has been for longer than I ever expected and, if I stay longer, I will be in serious trouble."*

"What kind of trouble? Have I done something wrong? Is there something I can do to help?"

"I'm not sure that anyone can help the situation including you. Thanks anyway. I have done something by choice and now I must pay for it."*

"You're being so cryptic. I really don't understand what your problem is or why it's so serious. Have you gone over budget on you expense account? Have you not done your job?"

"Yes and no. But I guess that needs a lot of explanation."*

"Yes, I can agree with that. Are you going to tell me what's the matter or am I going to have to drag it out of you?"

"Give me a few moments to collect my thoughts and I will tell you everything. It's not going to be easy exposing my inner true self to you."*

"You're married!"
"No!"*
"You're gay!"
"No!"*
"You're a fugitive!"
"No!"*
"You're crazy!"
"No! No! No!"*

"Then, what? You're going to drive me crazy until you tell me what the problem is."

"Let's first talk about us before I talk about me, because you have become more important to me than everything I stand for."*

"The mystery thickens! Now you really have piqued my curiosity!"

"When I first met you that night I was not supposed to be with you or anyone else. I was out doing what I usually do whenever I'm in a strange place, but I was lonely and curious. Our chance encounter got rid of the loneliness and gave me an opportunity to explore my curiosity. One thing led to another and I found myself in the presence of a very unique person. I was so enchanted that night I didn't want you to leave even though I knew you must. You can't imagine how I felt when you invited me to meet you for dinner the next day. I felt secure I would see you again. I really wanted to get to know you much better."*

"So I was nothing more than an object of curiosity? I'm hurt."

"No, it's not that way. I was attracted to you and for you alone. What I'm trying to say is I had orders not to get involved. It's part of my job."*

"I'm glad to hear that I was more than just an object. I really took a chance on you. I don't go picking up just anyone or inviting them to dinner without thinking it through. You were someone who needed a friend that night. When you came back out of the rain you looked like a wet puppy. Your smile, your charm and your gentle conversation attracted me to you. I was instantly drawn to the conclusion that I wanted to know you better. Do you remember our first real date?"

"Of course, it was the next day! I could hardly wait for the time we had agreed to meet. I kept watching the clock. Time seemed to have suspended itself. The wait was nothing short of torture. I didn't get a thing I was supposed to accomplish done that day just thinking about you."*

"Funny how you affected me the same way. From the time I woke up in the morning I kept planning and re-planning everything about our date. I dressed and undressed several times before I settled on exactly what I thought would be just right. Then at the last minute, I changed again into something entirely different. I really wanted to make the right impression with you."

"I can tell you that you succeeded admirably. What you wore stunned my senses into thinking I was in the presence of a goddess."*

"Ha! I'll be you say that to everyone you meet!"

46

"No! It's true! Seriously, I was more than pleasantly surprised by the way you looked when we met that night."*

"To tell you the truth, I felt the same when I saw you. I almost instinctively knew I had found Mister Right. When we met, we must have looked like two teenagers gawking at each other with our mouths half open before the hostess brought us back to reality by inviting us to follow her to a table."

"I remember the moment quite well. There were no words that I could have possibly said to express how I felt the moment I saw you. I know now, as then, that I also felt this was an encounter that was meant for both of us."*

"The restaurant manager introduced himself and thought we were newlyweds. You were a little nonplussed so I told him a little white lie which you didn't seem to mind."

"I was a little embarrassed at first but as the game played itself out it was more than a little fun. Especially, since we knew nothing about each other, and we had to come up with answers to the usual questions asked newlyweds. Like where did you meet? Where did you honeymoon? I think we answered all those questions and others well, considering."*

"The poor waiter that served us really had a hard time that night between the two of us. We both lingered over our drinks talking about anything and everything as if we were old friends. The waiter finally got us to order by gently reminding us, I think, three or four times, if we wanted to know what the house specials were that night."

"Yes, and after letting him recite his dissertation of specials, you asked him what the second special was. He immediately became flustered to which you rescued him by asking what he would recommend. You ordered exactly what I had decided on which forced me to change my mine. I did not want you to see me as a copycat without imagination."*

"I wouldn't have thought anything unusual if you ordered what I did that night. I could have cared less what I was eating. It was you that I was totally focused. You were interesting from the start. I wanted to know as much about you as I possibly could."

"In a way, I sensed your interest that night. I must admit that I too was very much interested in you and whatever you had to say. The more we talked, the more I wanted to know about you. And when I looked into your eyes I saw something more."*

"And what was that?"

"I saw a beautiful woman, a wonderfully intelligent woman staring back into my eyes. For a moment, I felt suspended in space with my feet no longer touching the ground. And, when we mutually reached across the table and our hands touched for the first time, I was electrified."*

"I remember the moment well. I will cherish it always."

"Then we leaned our faces closer to each other in total silence obeying the universal force of attraction that happens when the chemistry is right. In a single instant our lips met, and we were no longer acquaintances."*

"Mm. I remember that delicious moment. It sends chills down my spine just closing my eyes and thinking about it. I knew you were more than special and that first kiss sealed that feeling into my mind and heart."

"It shouldn't have happened, but it did. I have no regrets but I certainly could not have guessed or even thought where we were to go with our initial contact. Were we to be passing stars in the night, friends or more?"*

"We both know the answer. I like to talk about how it all came about. Neither one of us wanted that night to end. Didn't the waiter subtly hint that we were finished so we would leave?"

"How could I forget? He brought the check and asked if we wanted anything else. He kept coming back again and again until we relented and paid the check. It was hard parting that night; I didn't want to push either one of us. I literally forgot everything I was supposed to do during my visit. You captured my attention and imagination."*

"Although we talked about what seemed like everything, there seemed to be an inexhaustible source of conversation between the two of us. I couldn't find a single vacant moment that wasn't interesting or captivating. If our initial conversations could be said to be anything, I would call them addicting. The more we talked, the more I wanted to talk. I found I didn't want to stop. I still don't."

"Beginnings are sometimes remembered better than they really were, but I agree with everything you say. I, too, was carried on an emotional high wanting more and more even though after our introductions to each other we were still absolute strangers. I knew only time could change that. But I felt differently."*

"I think it was the next date that I decided I really wanted to know you as best as I possibly could. It was presumptuous on my part to expect you felt the same but it felt right to me. With every subtle comment on my part, you answered opening more doors. Alice was going through Wonderland."

"Part of it was deliberate calculation; part was what came naturally from the moment. On that date, the third I think you said, I wanted to tell you more than I had told you when we first met but I was afraid to scare you off. I wanted our encounter to last."*

"You shouldn't have had any fear. You were charming, witty, intelligent and certainly more than good looking to me. Your appearance could have been anything, it was the inner you that I was attracted to most of all. Too many relationships get caught up in looks alone without learning about the inner person. To me I saw the inner you first, then I was suddenly and pleasantly surprised with the extra good looks afterward."

"I know what you say is true. I felt and have felt the same way before. What's inside is what counts most of all. Time peels away the veneer of youth and what remains is what's inside. The outside can look worse with time but the inside always gets better."*

"Well even so, I hope you like the outside too!"

"Of course I do! But that's not the point."*

"I miss you. I wish you were here with me right now. I would hold you close and cuddle you."

"That sounds good. I wish I could be there with you. The reason I called was to tell you that I must leave. I received my travel orders tonight after my last call to you. I had to think a long while about how to tell you"*

"Don't sound so final. This doesn't mean you won't be back. I knew you would have to leave soon. When do you go?"

"Tonight I'm afraid. I don't want to go but I must. I have no choice."*

"Tonight? I want to see you one more time before you go. Can you come here?"

"I must leave when I hang up the phone. I'm sorry; it's out of my control. You know so much about me, yet you really don't know anything."*

"I know enough to say I love you with all my heart and soul. You are the one I've wanted and needed all my life. I've never felt this way."

"I love you more than anything. I've fallen head over heels for you. It shouldn't have happened. I let my guard down

49

for a moment in spite of all my training and preparation for my job."*

"Is your job so important that you are not open to happiness when it appears in front of you?"

"I used to think so, but no more. My happiness is more important than ever, otherwise I wouldn't be calling to tell you I'm leaving. I didn't want you to think I left suddenly as if I didn't care. My love is true and genuine. I can really see a future for us together. I know there would be objections from my superiors and your parents. I would hope in the end our unique love would shine through all the reasons why we shouldn't be together and accept what we want for ourselves."*

"Are you sure you feel as strongly as I do?"

"Yes!"*

"And are you willing and able to stand by your decision to be together?"

"Emphatically yes!"*

"Then there is no problem. We will be joined for all time. Take me with you."

"What? Take you with me?"*

"Yes, I don't want to be away from you any longer. I want to be at your side always, now and forever!"

"It's not as easy as that. You don't know what you're asking. You need to know just a little more about me before you commit yourself."*

"My commitment is total. Nothing you could possibly say could ever change my mind ... ever!"

"Even though I'm an alien?"

"From another country?"

"No: from another world. I haven't really told you everything.'*

"I can't believe you're not human! You must be joking."

"I'm very much human and I'm not joking. I was sent here to explore your world. It was an accident that you and I met and a violation of all the rules. I should not have become involved with you. But I am in no way sorry."*

"I still don't understand. You're human. Don't play games with my feelings."

"Just because humans developed here doesn't mean they didn't develop elsewhere. It seems humans are easily reproducible entities wherever there are the right conditions.

50

And there are millions upon millions of worlds that have the right conditions. I may be an alien by birth but you and I are biologically compatible as if I was born on your world."*

"That means we can have children?"

"To live, love, play and, yes, have children. All of that is ours for the asking. Are you still as sure as before?"*

"Nothing can change my mind. I told you my commitment is total. I want to go with you. I don't ever want to be separated. I want to live and love with you and share all the dreams that create happiness."

"You know I want everything that you want. My feelings are no less intense than yours. In all my travels and on my own world I never found anyone I was interested to share my life with. That's why I chose to become a solitary explorer. In my work, no relationships are necessary or desirable. When I travel I age far less than those back home. I stay young and my friends have grown old and died. I have no one to go home to anymore."*

"Then let me join you. We can travel together until the very end."

"I can't do that as much as I would like to."*

"What if we ran away together? Elope to a place no one can find us. Start our lives from the beginning, a real true beginning."

"Well, I don't ... "*

"Don't you think we can do it? If you think I mean here on my world, forget it. I have no real family and my friends are in name only. I am ready to leave never to return with absolutely no regrets."

"Are you sure? I can't risk the chance you will regret your decision. To tell you the truth, I'm afraid."*

"Only afraid that you can find happiness if you let go of the past and you're not sure you want to let go?"

"That's not it and yet it is. My commitment to you is total also. I do love you and want to have you with me and do want to have children with you."*

"Children?!"

"Yes, children. Aren't they the ultimate expression of who and what we are to each other. They are the future we will build together along with all the memories we will share. But unlike memories which die with us, our children will live on."*

"Will you take me with you?"

51

"I decided a few moments ago that I couldn't live without you. I want you to join me forever, for better or worse. I want you to be my partner and mate."*

"And where will we go?"

"There is a relatively remote solar system in a part of the galaxy that is still quite young and unexplored. There is a world there well-suited to human life. It would be an ideal place for us to disappear. Once we got there we would send our ship to burn up in the star so there would be no way to trace us."*

"I am not afraid. I'm ready to go whenever you are ready!"

"You have made me happier than I've ever been. We will have a wonderful life together. I won't say it will be totally easy, but it will be worth it."*

"And are you coming to get me, already?"

"I love you, Eve!"*

"I love you, Adam!"

"I'll be right there!"*

Click!

The Hooker

The waves lapped the side of the boat with an audible slap that along with the gentle rocking back and forth almost put Don Nelson and his fishing partner, Chris Wilson, asleep. The day was sunny and clear with barely two foot waves as they drifted with fishing lines out on the windward side of Misty, their jointly owned pride and joy.

"Anything yet?" Chris relaxed with eyelids closed behind dark sunglasses.

"Nope. Nothing, not even a bite."

"Want a beer?"

"Sure, you buying?" Don laughed behind his own dark shades.

"No, but there's always a first time." Don smiled, looking over the upper rim of his sunglasses, squinting with one eye open.

Chris set the fishing rod down and went below to the galley. Misty was a 42-foot fiberglass dream with everything they possibly needed to call it home. Besides a modern galley with every kitchen appliance to make life easy, there were two sleeping areas, a head and shower and all the electronic gizmos to keep any stereo-TV buff happy.

"Light or regular?" Chris shouted.

"Light and some pretzels as long as you're at it," Don said slowly, seated with fishing rod in hand.

Although Don's eyes were closed, he kept his fingers lightly touching the 40-pound test monofilament line. His fishing sight or rather feel was honed by years of experience. He was well-taught by his father as he was growing up. There were few fish that could take the bait off the line without his awareness.

"I'm back," Chris said.

"Congratulations! About time!" Don grabbed a handful of pretzels and put them immediately into his mouth.

"Any luck?" Don plopped back in his fishing chair. "Maybe I should check my bait."

"You know it takes to jerks to catch of fish..." Don grinned. "...one on each end of the line."

Chris took his beer can, held a finger over the opening and shook. He pointed the can at Don and sprayed beer.

"Hey! Don't do that!"

Suddenly, Chris's line sang out. He fumbled the beer can and grabbed the rod while quickly jerking back. He meant to set the hook into whatever had taken the bait. The line became taut and pulled out against the drag of the reel. Something broke water 50 yards away. Neither he nor Don saw the blue silver blur. Reeling as fast as possible, pumping the rod, he slowly gained on his fishy opponent. Without warning the line went limp.

"Reel faster!" Don yelled. "He's turned toward the boat!"

Chris reeled faster. The fish jumped out of the water.

"Sailfish!" Don screamed. "And what a beauty!"

Another jump and the line went limp again.

"Uh,oh, I lost him." Chris shook his head.

"Don't stop now! Keep reeling, he may have turned toward the boat again."

"No chance. I lost him." The end of the line came to the surface without a hook. "I knew it!"

"Better luck next time, old man. Want another beer, since you've spilled the first one all over the deck?"

"I'll get it. I don't want to be responsible for the same thing happening to you." Chris put his rod and reel down as he went below into the galley.

Chris nodded and sipped the foam on his beer can with a loud slurp. He set down the can and put new tackle onto the end of the line.

"In a way, our jobs are like fishing," Don said. "We're called out to solve crimes day after day and, without bait, we can't solve many of the assignments we're given."

"I guess you're right," Chris said. "But I'd like to think my job and play are two separate things."

"They are separate," Don said. "I'm only pointing out a possible connection. There may not be a reel one."

"I get it." Chris chuckled. "A reel one! Mr. Smart guy!"

Before Chris finished speaking he saw Don snap into action, jerking of his rod back, and reeling as fast as possible.

"You got a bite?"

"Heck, yeah!" Don laughed. "And this sucker's not going to get away if I have anything to do with it!"

The battle between man and fish lasted a full hour. Don reeled in several yards of line only to have it all and more stripped out. A sailfish broke the surface and danced on its tail, shaking its beak back and forth as it futilely tried to spit the hook from its mouth. Chris went to the bridge, started the twin turbine engines and put the boat into forward gear. Don moved to the bow of the boat as Chris headed the boat toward the sailfish. The boat moved only so fast that Don could gain line without it going completely slack. Eventually, the exhausted fish was beside the boat.

"Get the camera!" Don shouted.

"Right here!" Chris took a picture. "The boat is out of gear."

"Let's tag and let it go."

Chris agreed and quickly assisted in getting the job done. When the fish was released, he raised a hot beer can and toasted Don to a well-won victory. Both men shook hands and looked at the Polaroid picture of the sailfish.

"The guys at the office have got to see this." Chris slapped Don on the back.

The story at the office got bigger after each retelling the next day. But that is the way all fishing stories are told. The old adage "do all fishermen lie or do all liars fish" is without a doubt completely true.

"Sorry to interrupt your reverie gentleman, but I have an assignment for you two hotshots," Sergeant Campos said sternly. "There are twelve men reportedly missing from this part of town," He pointed at the wall map of the precinct. "I want both of you to investigate what's going on."

"Yes, Sergeant." Chris took the assignment papers in hand.

"We will get right on it," Don said quickly. "Are there any signs of foul play?"

"No, just twelve sets of anxious friends and families who cannot locate their men," the sergeant said. "The reason I'm giving this assignment to you is that all these men may have disappeared for the same reason."

"And what's that?" Don said.

"Each man has a history of frequenting the services of your local public escort service. More than one has been picked up as a john in a vice raid."

"Do you personally think there's been some foul play with some of the local prostitutes?" Chris said. "Is that what we're looking for?"

"I want an investigation. You're the best men for the job and I don't want to give you any preconceived ideas before you analyze all the evidence and give it some real thought. So get to it immediately."

"Yes sir!"

"I'll pull up whatever records I can find on the men on this list," Chris said when the sergeant left. "The computer may have some useful information."

"As soon as you get that, let's drive down to the Strip where these men allegedly disappeared and do a little research." Don raised his eyebrows with leer on his face. "Also, let's check with the morgue to see if they have any unidentified bodies we can help them with."

"Good idea." Chris retrieved the printout from the initial request. "Want to look at this first?"

"Bring it with you." Don started for the door. "We can review it on the way."

None of the recent bodies in the morgue fit the descriptions of the missing men. Don left his card with the chief forensic pathologist to call if anything of interest to the case showed up. The sun was going down when they finally arrived on the Strip. The Strip was a motley collection of garishly decorated hotels built on the beach with touristy shops and restaurants on the opposite side of the street. It was a favorite local spot for every type of night person, including the ladies of the evening.

"Let's stop at Carmen's," Don said.

Chris drove the unmarked Ford. It stood out like a wailing police siren against all the sports cars and custom jobs parading back and forth in search of excitement. Chris pulled into the parking lot as a dark man with tank top and shorts straddling a green mountain bike took a small package from the window of a late-model Cadillac whose occupant could not be identified through the darkly tinted windows. Sighting the approaching police car, the man on the bike quickly threw a bundle of money into the open Cadillac window and started pedaling the bike into a narrow alleyway between Carmen's and the adjacent building. The window of the Cadillac closed and the driver hit the accelerator, burning rubber on the back tires.

"Looks like a drug deal, Chris." Don pointed at the Cadillac.

"What shall we do? It's really not our call."

"I've got the license number. Let them go. There are too many pedestrians around to chase them safely." Don called in the description of the Cadillac and its plate number to communication control.

"Ten-four," the dispatch operator said. "Units are on the way to intercept. Have a good evening boys!"

Carmen's was just filling up with the dinner crowd when Don and Chris walked in. Over in the corner Don recognized one of the regulars that worked the Strip. He walked over and smiled.

"How's tricks?" Don said slowly with a smile. "Have a busy night planned?"

The young woman looked up, batted her heavily done eyelashes and turned her head away from him, chewing gum and smacking her lips with each chew. She pretended to ignore him.

"Mind if I sit here?" He sat down without waiting for an answer.

She turned and stared into his eyes. "What do you want? Can't a working girl get something to eat in peace?"

"I need some information," Don said carefully. "There are a dozen men missing from this area and I want to know if you know anything about it."

"You mean you're not here to harass me?" She smiled. "I thought…"

"That I was here about you." Don chuckled. "I have a case to solve and I need all the help I can get."

"And what do I get out of it?" She batted her eyelashes.

"I'll see what I can do to get the heat off of you for a while. How about it?"

"Okay." She remained silent a moment. "Rumor has it there's a new chick taking the regulars from us. Once they're gone, we don't see them again."

"Who's we?" Don raised his brow.

"Us working girls." She laughed. "As if you don't know who we are."

"Do you know where this new chick displays her wares?" He pulled out a notepad and pen.

"I've heard she's down by Romeo's and the Tropicana Hotel, but I'm really not sure."

"Thanks for your help, sweetheart." Don put a $10 bill on top of her check.

"Thanks," she said warmly. "Need a date after work?"

Don smiled and went over to the table where Chris patiently waited reading the menu enough times that he thought he had memorized it.

"Did you find out anything useful?" Chris watched Don seat himself.

"A slim lead," Don said. "A new trick down the way has been taking the regular johns away from the established group of ladies. Not much, but at least a place to start. We'll check it out after we eat. It should be dark enough for the night crowd to have started their ritual prowling for sin and sex."

An hour later they were in the car making the first pass of the Strip. The usual assortment of tourists were checking into hotels and perusing the shops with the cheap glitzy clothes and souvenirs. Interspersed were some of the regulars who made a living off the street. Business peaked around midnight; they had plenty of time to drive around looking at all the ladies of the evening. Don planned to question a few to expand the meager information they had to work with. Reviewing the computer printouts over dinner yielded nothing more than a confirmation that they were in the right neighborhood.

"Stop here." Don spotted a very attractive redhead he recognized. She was wearing a white halter top and tight skirt that barely dipped below her crotch.

They slowed to a stop at the curb next to her. She glanced toward the car with a smile that instantly turned to a scowl when she saw it was an unmarked police car; and then, the smile came back.

"Don, baby!" She squealed. "What are you doing here at this hour the night?"

"Working." He smiled. "Long time, no see, how have you been?"

"The usual." She came over to the open window. "Just trying to get by. What about you? You're not here to ask me about my health."

"You're right." He looked into her clear blue eyes, wishing she was someone he knew she could never be. "I'm looking for a new chick that's just breaking into the Strip; someone who's stealing everybody's johns. Do you know who she is and where I can find her?"

"I've heard about her, but I've never seen her," she said. "She's supposed to work near here."

"We need to talk to her about her work. We have a case that we are trying to get leads on and she may have the information we need."

"What's going on?" She frowned. "There's little that goes on around here that we all don't know about."

"What about twelve missing men?"

"Twelve missing?"

"Yes, twelve missing men; all from this part of the Strip." Don watched the expression on her face.

"All I know is what I've told you. Nothing else." She waved at a new red Corvette passing on the other side of the street. "Sorry, I've got to work. See you later! Good luck!" She quickly walked away.

"Anything useful?" Chris drove the car away from the curb into the increasing night traffic.

"Nothing. Nothing to sink our teeth into. Just keep driving. Maybe we'll find our phantom new lady of the evening."

Although the sun had long sunk below the horizon, the temperature remained balmy. Heat lightning flashed across the ocean from one particular dark full cloud. As usual, no thunder was heard.

"There's Romeo's." Chris pointed. "Shall we park and walk around?"

"Sounds like a good idea." Don touched the service revolver under the arm. "The exercise and fresh air will do us good."

The car was valet parked at the restaurant where they could easily see it from either direction. They walked onto the street. Chris pressed the crosswalk button in front of the Tropicana Hotel. Several couples were in the lobby checking in at the front desk. The Bell Captain stepped outside for a quick smoke. They went up to the young dark-haired man in a long-sleeved white shirt and black pants. He was humming a tune after each drag of the cigarette. His name tag said Mario. Chris walked casually up to him with Don and asked directions to the hotel's restaurant. Mario cheerfully gave directions by waving his finger toward the front door behind them.

"Thanks, and by the way, how's the action?" Don slipped the man a twenty dollar bill.

Mario put the bill into his pocket with a smile. "If you want a date with a real knockout, she's around here every night."

"Where and when?" Don grinned. "I'm sort of anxious, if you know what I mean."

"She'll be around soon enough," Mario said. "You won't be sorry." He turned and went back into the hotel lobby.

Don and Chris remained outside. They decided to split up and canvas the entire hotel and its parking lot. At midnight, they were to meet again at the same spot. They separated as inconspicuously as possible. Don went to the curbside newspaper stand and bought a weekly copy of the latest rag that exaggerated all the local news of the Strip. He sat down at the adjacent bus stop, crossed his legs and opened the paper as if he could read it in the dark. He kept scanning the surroundings for anyone that might be of interest. To pass the time he even read an article in the newspaper that confirmed that some journalism was pure and simple brain rot. A half-hour passed before he got up and walked to the parking lot beside the hotel facing the beach.

The step from the asphalt parking lot onto the soft warm sand was like a leap into another world. Don sighed deeply for the relief of a small respite from the increasing tension of the night. He walked toward the water leaving the lights of the hotel and street behind. The sound of the waves licking the sand grew louder with each step. He reached into his coat pocket, fumbled to move his keys out of the way and found the package of spearmint gum he was looking for. At the edge of the water he put two sticks of gum into his mouth and started chewing. The taste immediately filled his mouth with the sweetness reminding him of better times and places. Glancing in both directions he decided to head in the direction of the waterfront behind the hotel.

The short walk turned into long minutes of peace and solitude broken suddenly by the feeling of a presence. Don looked behind and saw endless beach no different than what lay in front of him. The lights of the hotel immediately blinded him as he turned toward the hotel. At first he saw nothing and started to turn back to look out over the water. Then he saw the silhouette of a form halfway the distance from where he stood to the edge of the sand and pavement.

The form was that of a woman, there was no doubt in his mind. She could not possibly be related or involved in what he was interested. Ladies of the evening did not walk on a deserted beach at night waiting for business to come along. There was a faint scent of perfume in the salty air. It was more than pleasant. Don shook his head and started walking away down the beach when she waved to him. Somewhat puzzled and taken completely off guard he waved back. Could it be someone he knew, he wondered, certainly with the lights behind her she saw him far clearer than he saw her. With growing curiosity, he decided to approach her. The scent of her perfume was now

60

obvious and intoxicating. The more he smelled it, the more he felt attracted to her. She was barely wearing anything at all. A chill of excitement coursed through his body and he tried to repress it. He was a professional on the job; he was not allowed to let passion ever interfere with his job or who he was.

The closer Don came to the woman, the more he saw of her. She was young, beautiful, fair skin with near perfect physical proportions. Her nipples were erect and bulging through her flimsy bra-like top. His pulse grew more rapid with anticipation of something he knew should not happen. He finally stood in front of her finding words were not necessary. She returned his smile by opening her arms wide inviting him to embrace her with his own. Without hesitation he stepped forward and put his arms around her warm body. It was the last thing he would ever do.

***

"What are you doing?"

"I'm relaxing by fishing, a new hobby of mine."

"But you can't fish here, this is a laboratory."

"Oh yes I can! I've developed a way to open a hole into another dimension through which I can catch some real prize specimens."

"What is that you have over there?"

"This is my bait and tackle. It's called a hooker."

"A hooker? What's that?"

"A hooker is a fisher of men."

"Really? And what are men?"

"Something that you will find completely out of this world. Here help yourself to my latest catch."

"What is this?"

"Trust me! Try it!"

"Okay."

"Do you like it?"

"Delicious!"

The Ride

To Christopher the action he controlled on the television screen was no less than a reality he entered as frequently as he could. With a little time and practice there was virtually no videogame he could not play successfully. In fact, he was secretly envied by his brother, Nicholas, who, never admitting when he had a problem getting through a particularly difficult spot in a game, would ask Christopher to play for him. Whether Christopher knew it or not was irrelevant, at least it was a chance to share some of the action.

"Christopher, are you coming to have lunch?" Dad said.

"Uh huh." Christopher kept staring intently at the television.

"Come on then," Dad said. "Put your game on pause and turn off the TV."

"Uh huh," Christopher said absently and continued concentrating on the game without a hint of stopping.

"Okay, that's it!" Dad walked over and turned the set off. "Put the game on pause and let's eat!"

Christopher stood in stunned horror at the blank screen, looked up at Dad and quickly pushed the pause button.

"Now, come on!" Dad smiled.

Nicholas was already sitting at the table as Dad and Christopher walked into the kitchen. He had prepared the sandwiches with a side serving of chips, poured three glasses of Coke and set the table.

"Do you want a pickle, Dad?" Nicholas said.

"What kind are they?"

"Sour, they're really good." Nicholas held up a sample.

"I think I will. Christopher, would you like one?"

Christopher sat down at the table with a frown but at the sight of food he reverted from video wiz to chow hound. Food was a close second place on his list of preferences.

"Chris, slow down!" Nicholas watched Chris devour his food with total abandon.

"Let him enjoy eating." Dad laughed. "At least he's away from the TV for a while."

"What's so wrong with the TV, Daddy?" Christopher stopped chewing.

"Nothing, except that sometimes we all think you spend too much time in front of it." Dad reached out and touched his shoulder gently. "I'm really impressed how well you do at the games and I know that you learn a lot, but I don't want you to neglect everything else there is to do and learn."

"Okay, Daddy." Christopher bowed his head slightly as he attacked his sandwich.

"We will try not to disturb you, Dad," Nicholas said quickly.

After the dishes were cleared from the table and put into the dishwasher, Dad went to his room, turned off the light, and fell into a deep sleep. The initial heavy breathing was exchanged for a short solo performance of snoring, terminated by a change in position. Nicholas went and checked. Seeing Dad comfortably asleep, he closed the door of the bedroom. He found Christopher back in front of the TV picking up the action where the game had paused. Without speaking, Nicholas stood beside his brother and reached for the controller. Christopher voluntarily let the game transfer to Nicholas. There was almost never anything important to fight about. In fact, the brothers needed few words to communicate with each other they knew and loved each other so well.

"Let me finish this level." Christopher volunteered, seeing Nicholas was not making any progress in the game.

"Okay." Nicholas passed the controller into Christopher's hand.

Within minutes of expert playing, Christopher had conquered the forces of evil and survived with more power to move on to the next level of play. The game paused with a programmed visual display depicting the player as a triumphant hero. Christopher and Nicholas watched patiently, monitoring the signal to start the game again. The screen finally displayed the game restart menu.

Restart? Yes or no?

Yes, Christopher entered into the controller.

One or two players?

Christopher hesitated a moment, he had never seen the option change to two players once the game was started.

"Press two, press two!" Nicholas excitedly reached for the controller.

Christopher pulled the controller out of Nicholas's reach and pressed for two players.

Do you want to restart or . . .

There was a slight pause which caught their attention.

Would you like to try something different?

"Something different!" Nicholas blurted loudly.

Christopher did not need coaching to punch in the answer for 'something different,' whatever that was. The unexpected was always a part of the fun and challenge of the game. The brothers were very much alike and yet uniquely different. Christopher, the younger by almost 2 years, was a six year old gregarious, extrovert who loved playing with other children, especially girls, at school but spent many quiet hours at home in front of the TV playing any videogame he could get his hands on. In fact, when going to the video store to rent movies for the weekend, Christopher always opted for a game rather than a movie.

Nicholas was almost 9 years old, quiet and an intellectual like Dad. Almost everything that he did was thought out carefully in advance. Those things he happened to do spontaneously where the exception rather than the rule. This made him sensitive if anything went wrong. A kinder more thoughtful, young man you could not find anywhere.

Please hold on.

"What does that mean?" Christopher looked at Nicholas.

"It means we have to wait. I guess the program is being loaded now."

"Why is it taking so long?"

"You have no patience, Chris. This game probably has a lot of instructions which takes time to load into RAM."

"I still don't understand."

"Then just watch. It will come on soon."

The TV screen blinked once and went blank. Christopher turned to Nicholas about to protest when a picture of a three bladed propeller like those found on their father's boat appeared in the center the screen. The propeller rotated slowly at first but quickly accelerated until it disappeared in a blur of the background color. Another message appeared now that the attention of the brothers was fixed on watching the action.

Do you want to take a ride?

For the first time, Christopher did not know how to answer. He wanted to say yes and continue the game but the game did not tell him how to enter his answer.

Nicholas thought a moment. "We want to ride, but how do we let you know?" He said directly to the TV. He did not expect an answer.

The TV screen blinked again and another message appeared.

Answer received.

"How did you do that?" Christopher laughed.

"I don't know." Nicholas shrugged his shoulders. "The TV just heard me, I guess, but that's not possible."

The lights in the house dimmed momentarily and returned to normal. Only the sound of the air-conditioning was heard, aside from their father's deep breathing in the distant bedroom.

Are you ready?

"Yes," Christopher said without hesitation.

Go out into the backyard.

Christopher dropped his controller. Nicholas caught in the excitement of what was happening followed racing his brother to the door leading to the backyard. Outside in the middle of the yard was an unexpected delightful sight.

"There's a spaceship in our yard!" Christopher yelled. "And the door is open!"

"It's a flying saucer." Nicholas shook his head. "I think we need to be careful."

"It's okay!" Christopher dashed for the open door. "It's only part of the game!"

"I'm not so sure, Chris." Nicholas examined the outside of the craft.

Without slowing down, Christopher disappeared into the door of the strange craft. From the outside it was not more than 17 feet in diameter, sharp at its edges and bulging in the middle. The entrance was large enough for a kid like Christopher but certainly an adult would have trouble getting comfortable inside.

"Come on!" Christopher yelled. "This is really neat! Wow!"

Curiosity overcame Nicholas and he followed into the entrance of the strange craft. Inside he found a kid-sized cockpit with two seats that appeared specially designed for them. Although no windows appeared from the outside, the domed ceiling was completely transparent showing the outside. Christopher sat in a seat, examining all the controls on the panel in front of him. A video screen sat between the two seats as the panel blinked on with another picture of the propeller they had seen on the TV in the house. Nicholas slowly sat in the other seat watching the propeller begin its spin. As the propeller accelerated the cockpit filled with a hum followed by a muted thud. Nicholas turned his head in the direction of the sound and saw the door had closed. Lights began winking on and off amongst the instrument panel controls.

66

"The door closed!" Nicholas said. "We're trapped!"

"No, we're not, Nick." Christopher laughed. "It's all part of the game."

The screen in front of them blinked and gave instructions.

Fasten safety belts.

The brothers complied; Christopher more eagerly than Nicholas.

Sit back and relax.

"I don't like this," Nicholas barely whispered.

The tiny ship shot straight up into the sky pressing the brothers gently back into the seats. On the screen in front, the brothers saw their home get smaller while the sky above the dome became darker. In the blink of an eye, the blue sky turned into a panorama of stars on an absolutely black background.

"We left the atmosphere!" Nicholas pointed at the stars. "We're in space!"

"What a ride!" Christopher laughed. "I wonder if we're going to the moon."

In a small margin of the dome a sliver of the moon appeared. The ship tilted bringing the entire disk of the full moon into view. The brothers watched, laughed and pointed at the moon. Within a few blinks, they whizzed by the moon into outer space.

"I wonder where we're going." Nicholas said slowly. "Where are we going and who is taking us there?"

"I don't know and I don't care." Christopher smiled as he took in the view.

The screen blinked again with the propeller going through the same motions as before. A message followed.

This will be the ride of your life.

"You can say that again," Christopher said quickly.

This will be the ride of your life.

"Hey!" Nicholas yelled. "It repeated what you told it to do! Can you hear us?"

Yes.

"Where are we going?" Nicholas stole a glance at Christopher who remained motionless with his mouth open.

Do you want to see something neat?

"I asked the question!" Nicholas said loudly.

Well, do you?

"Of course we do." Christopher shook his head. The shock of the possibility of having a dialogue with whomever or whatever ran the ship wore off.

Hang on.

The hum increased and the brothers were pressed firmly into their seats feeling sudden acceleration. The position of the stars actually moved a little. The screen blinked again and a set of coordinates on a star chart drew out a course from the earth to a place neither recognized. Another blink and another message appeared.

Look outside now.

A potato shaped object grew larger by the minute. Off to the side was a tiny fleck of light shining off something much smaller. As they approached the larger object they saw it was covered with craters like the Earth's moon.

"What is that?" Christopher pointed.

Asteroid Ida.

"And what is that next to it?" Nicholas pointed.

It's moon, Dactyl.

"Chris, we're a long ways from home now!" Nicholas touched his arm. "And that's the first asteroid ever discovered to have a moon!"

"This is really getting better all the time." Christopher stared at the celestial sight. "I wonder what's next?"

Do you want to see more?

"Yes!" They said in unison.

The craft surged forward faster, Christopher and Nicholas could hardly restrain their enthusiasm with laughing and pointing at everything and anything, whether they recognized it or not. The experience was a fantastic dream come true. Their reverie was broken by another blink on the screen.

Do you want to play?

"Of course!" Christopher said quickly.

One or two players?

"Two," Nicholas said immediately.

Controllers at your right sides.

They found videogame controllers with a joystick.

To begin, press start.

The game began with a grid on the screen showing multiple moving dots. The scene changed to a view that showed what was ahead. A black cylindrical object raced at the screen, firing two missiles directly at them. Christopher instinctively pressed the buttons of his controller and found he could fire back. His reflexes honed by endless hours at home in front of the TV, his first shots destroyed the two missiles and the cylindrical object.

"This is fun." Christopher grinned.

Nicholas nodded and looked up and out the dome. Incoming, from at least half a dozen directions, were more of the cylindrical objects. As they got closer they fired missiles at them. Christopher caught the expression on Nicholas and looked upward in time to aim his weapons at the closest threat. One after the other, missiles were destroyed by Christopher's skill. Nicholas realized the odds were beginning to weigh against his brother and joined the game. Whatever he did not manage to destroy, his brother did. As a team, they were invincible. After an hour of action those cylindrical objects still remaining turned and fled away.

Congratulations you completed level I.

"Is there a level II?" Nicholas looked at Christopher.

Do you want to begin?

Without hesitation Christopher answered as a true videogame junkie. The action began again with another attack of wave after wave of cylindrical objects firing missiles at them. The attack against their craft was futile and was repulsed by their joint efforts.

Congratulations you completed level II.

"Level III!" Christopher shouted eagerly.

Prepare to engage mothership.

The brothers felt a surge of acceleration and a turn toward an object similar in appearance to the asteroid Ida at a distance. The closer they came, the more obvious was its artificial construction. Whatever or whoever made the mothership thought on a scale that they could not begin to understand except through some movies they had seen with their father.

"Looks like Star Wars," Nicholas said matter-of-factly.

"Uh huh," Christopher grunted. He was completely absorbed by expectation of what was to come.

A swarm of cylindrical objects ejected from various openings on the mothership.

"What we do now?" Nicholas calculated the overwhelming odds and was not sure they could handle the situation.

"Uh huh," Christopher grunted. "No problem."

There was no question Christopher had superb eye-hand coordination, but could he handle every real challenge, Nicholas wondered. His kid brother was not the hero type and now he was going to find out by the ultimate test. Somehow it did not seem real, so he pinched himself. The pain persisted long enough to confirm everything he was seeing was reality. He even wished he had spent more hours practicing on the stupid games that were played, from getting out of bed until he went to sleep at night. If he ever got home, he would never bother Christopher when he played his games over and over.

"We need to get behind that ship," Christopher said coolly.

Their ship began a series of maneuvers in response to his statement. Christopher continued scoring without a single miss. Nicholas joined the battle and surprised himself with a performance equal to his brother. Before they realized it, they were staring at a large glowing red circle surrounded by a pentagon of five smaller circles.

"Look!" Nicholas said, "We're behind the mothership! Shoot at the center engine!"

"No problem," Christopher drawled and lined the crosshair aiming bars on the screen in front of him.

A massive swarm of cylinders ejected from the mothership at high speed. Soon after Christopher fired at the large central engine the red color disappeared followed by a silent explosion that ripped the engines apart. A secondary explosion blew the rest of the mothership into infinitesimal pieces. Any cylinders near the explosion were destroyed by the resulting shrapnel. The brothers shouted and cheered their success.

"What about other ships?" Nicholas looked everywhere out the dome. "Looks like we are all alone!"

"Because we destroyed them all!" Christopher shouted.

Congratulations! The ride continues.

"I wonder what comes next," Nicholas said; Christopher shrugged his shoulders and smiled.

A surge of acceleration changed the view in the dome. They moved faster than they had before. A small comet passed at a respectable distance to the side with a red dot getting larger by the minute in front. Nicholas immediately recognized Mars and its two tiny moons.

"Mars straight ahead!" Nicholas said.

"Cool!" Christopher pointed.

70

The ship arced in a parabolic path swooping down toward the surface of the red planet. Passing over the northern ice they flew back into space passing Phobos. Heading in the direction toward the sun Nicholas guessed they were heading home.

"I can hardly wait to tell Dad all about this." Christopher laughed.

"Dad won't believe us. We need proof to show him that we really went on this ride."

"There's nothing in here that we can take to show him." Christopher looked around the small cockpit. "Do you see anything we can take as proof?"

Nicholas thought a moment. "Ship, can you give us proof we took this ride with you?"

Certainly, look in front of you.

Out of an almost invisible slot in the instrument panel emerged a three square inch photograph of the brothers sitting inside the ship. On the back was printed in red letters, 'In thanks for services received from friends who will be eternally grateful.' Nicholas examined the photograph closely and gave it to Christopher.

"I think Dad will believe us now!" Christopher grinned.

"I hope so." Nicholas put the picture in his pants pocket.

"We're home." Christopher pointed to the bright blue dot on the dome.

The craft descended through some dark clouds. It was raining hard as the tiny ship touched down. The house was barely visible through the deluge. Christopher jumped up as soon as he saw the door opening.

"Wait!" Nicholas shouted. "You forgot to say thank you."

"Sorry." Christopher turned back to the instrument screen. "Thank you for a great ride!"

You are welcome.

"Thank you," Nicholas said. "Will we be able to ride again?"

Someday. Someday soon.

"Goodbye," they said together.

Goodbye.

One by one the brothers dashed out the door into the rain. By the time they reached the house, they were soaked to the skin. Christopher turned the doorknob and found the door locked.

"Do you have the key?" Christopher turned to Nicholas. "I'm really getting wet!"

Nicholas laughed. He put his hand into his pocket for the key. He found and pulled it out as fast as he could and unlocked the door. Inside, they stood momentarily dripping from the rain.

"Dad, Dad!" Christopher shouted.

"Dad, come here!" Nicholas shouted.

The door to Dad's room opened and they heard footsteps.

"What's the matter, boys? Looks like you are both a little wet. Stay there and I'll get you some towels. Take off all your wet clothes and I'll be right back."

"Dad, we just got back from the neatest ride." Christopher jumped up and down.

"Tell me when I get back with the towels. I don't want you two getting colds. I'll be back in a minute."

"I don't think he's going to believe us!"

"Why not?" Nicholas whispered. "What about the picture?"

"Of course!" Christopher said, "We do have proof!"

Nicholas dug into his wet pocket searching for the picture. To his horror the picture was gone. "I can't find it," he said.

"You had it!" Christopher cried. "What happened to it?"

"It must've dropped out of my pocket when I pulled out the key to the house."

"Quick! Let's get it before it gets wet." Christopher ran to the door.

The rain continued in a deluge. Just as the brothers were about to go out searching in the rain for the picture a voice stopped them.

"You can't go out there now. It's raining too hard." Dad stood behind them.

"You don't understand, Dad," Nicholas said slowly. "I dropped something out of my pocket to show you."

"Well that's fine but I'm sure it's not worth catching a cold."

"It's proof we went on a ride in a spaceship!" Nicholas said.

"I don't care what it is. I don't want you to go out in the rain. Your health is more important to me. Now dry yourselves off and let's get some ice cream."

"Sounds good, Dad." Christopher winked at Nicholas.

Some things are always meant a secret between brothers and the ride was one of those things.

The proximity alarm barely began screeching when the ship vibrated violently. The captain floated in front of the instruments feeling nothing as he evaluated what had activated the alarm. Over 20 years at the speed of light experience taught him that there was always the possibility of a disaster by hitting a large solid object. Fortunately, the odds were astronomically against it. The big problem and really a nuisance was gas and dust which the forward shield more than adequately deflected like the prow of an ancient ship cutting through the waves on water. He saw nothing of any real concern; it would be a matter of waiting for the ship to finish its transit of a relatively large cloud of dust. In twenty light-seconds, the all clear signal appeared on the instrument panel and the ship returned to its perfect ballistic stability with the help of the computer assisted attitude controls. The captain sighed and rechecked all the instruments even though it was unnecessary. He turned directly toward the omnipresent optical scanner of the ship's computer and shrugged his shoulders.

"Another disaster averted," the captain said flatly. "How much farther?"

"Do you want a real or philosophical answer?" the computer said.

"I'm not sure," the captain said softly. "I've slept eight hours but I still feel tired."

"Are you feeling well, Tom?" The computer said in a voice modulated to sound concerned. "Plug into the diagnostic umbilical and I will run a check on your systems."

"It's not that easy, Doc. So many things have happened to me that at times I have trouble putting everything into perspective. Right now I remember what my father used to say when I was a little boy. He said that I would live many more years away from home than at home. As a child I really didn't understand completely what he meant, but now light-years from home I know exactly what he was trying to tell me."

"Seems like you are suffering a touch of melancholy," Doc said warmly. "Let me run a diagnostic on you."

"Not yet," Tom said. "I just need to talk a little bit about who and what I am. Even though I know you are the product of man-made technology, to me you are more than just a collection of electronic parts. You have become my one true friend."

"I thank you for the compliment, Tom. I have become fond of you also."

"Without you, I would not be what I am today." Tom sighed. "I think of what I was before this mission and realize what I've become has been a rite of passage to an indeterminate future I cannot begin to comprehend."

"Does this unknown frighten you? It's quite normal if it does."

"I understand the unknown creates choices that need to be acted upon. Sometimes talking about the future helps; sometimes it doesn't."

"What are you feeling now? Do you need to talk?"

Tom shook his head and smiled. "Not really. I just need to think."

"I completely understand."

"Sometimes I wonder if you really do," Tom said softly.

"I heard that!" Doc said quickly.

"Ha!" Tom laughed. "I may be becoming more a machine, but I am completely convinced you are more human than you are willing to admit."

"You may believe whatever you want." Doc laughed. "But if I have become human it is because I have learned to be so from you."

"And the machine in me has certainly come from you." Tom grinned. "Twenty plus years alone together can bring about a lot of changes in a man and his machine."

A blinking light on the instrument panel caught Tom's attention. He pressed an adjacent touchpad and the large video screen above quickly illuminated with an image of the star field ahead. A green fluorescent square with crosshairs moved to a yellow star larger than any other objects displayed. Numbers blinked next to the square.

"What do we have here?"

"Our destination," Doc said. "Hard to believe...but true."

"You're sounding more human than ever! I'm not complaining. Activate retro sequence. Can you visualize any details of the planetary system yet?"

"I'm just beginning to get significant data. I'll be able to give you a complete analysis as we get closer. My preliminary findings simply confirm all our previous expectations."

"Terrific!" Tom laughed. "It's time for me to get some sleep. I leave everything in your hands."

"Hands? What hands?"

"You know what I mean." Tom laughed harder. "Wake me, if you need me."

"Of course!"

Tom propelled himself effortlessly out of the control room, down the central tubular passageway, to his quarters. He secured himself in the bunk with tethers fixed to the wall and attached an electrical umbilical to recharge his batteries. Within minutes he was sound asleep.

Asleep he returned frequently to the distant past, reliving bits and pieces of his life that had brought him to this point in time and space. He was born in New England around the turn of the century, an only child, baptized Thomas Alvin Becker. A quiet, thoughtful boy, his never ending wish was to fly in space when he grew up. By the time he was ready to enter college he had already tried and succeeded to thoroughly educate himself by playing with his home computer and reading. An appointment to study at the Air Force Academy in Boulder, Colorado, after high school, was a dream come true. Armed with a bachelor's degree in aeronautical engineering and a commission as Captain in the United States Air Force, he entered graduate school at MIT. Within three years, he was awarded a dual PhD in electrical engineering and computer science. From Cambridge, he went directly into pilot training before his first duty assignment. He quickly accepted an opportunity to join the astronaut corps and found himself an integral part of the space program. His dreams about this part of his past were happy and ordinary, and then came the nightmare.

Tom remained motionless in the tether even though the dream terrified him. It was a beautiful New England Indian summer day. The day that marked the turning point in his life, he was showing off his brand-new convertible to his parents. The top was down and warm dry air blew briskly through their hair. The road twisted in tight curves through a densely wooded forest. An occasional home appeared in small areas cleared only to accommodate its residents. The natural beauty was enhanced rather than detracted by the earth and wood tones of the various houses, garages and other small buildings. It was a day great to be alive. On a tight curve to the right, Tom was laughing at a reminiscence related by his father when a truck appeared suddenly in front of the car. In order to avoid a head on collision, he turned sharply to the right. The car dipped down into the ditch beside the road. It flew momentarily in air before it violently hit dirt and gravel. The airbags instantly inflated as the car began its first of three sideway rolls. Only a miracle spared his life. Both of his parents were killed and, if to make matters worse, he was paralyzed from a broken back. Through a quirk of fate he lost his family and future career doing one of the least risky things he ever thought about doing. The pain of his injuries never came close to equaling the grief he felt at the loss of his mother and father. After a long hospitalization and a short bout of depression he vowed he would overcome the obstacles he was forced to accept. His face drew up in a grimace of pain and he heard a distant voice calling his name.

"Tom, are you all right?"

He opened his eyes and blinked. "Yes, I'm okay," he said softly. "I was reliving the accident again."

"You keep punishing yourself unnecessarily. The accident was clearly not your fault."

"Doc, I wasn't paying attention and I lost control!"

"The roads were tortuous. There was always danger from any oncoming vehicle ignoring the rules of the road. The driver was intoxicated and driving too fast. What happened could not have been prevented because you had no control of that truck. It was completely out of your hands. I may be artificial intelligence, but I have learned to feel what you feel. And I know the depth of your inner pain."

"That's only because I no longer feel physical pain," Tom snapped. "Over these last few years you've almost completely replaced most of my moving parts with cybernetics. Sometimes I feel like the tin man in the Wizard of Oz losing my flesh to the machinations of the wicked witch who slowly replaces it with cold metal. Are you the great wizard that can grant me what I want?"

"No, I'm only a series D Omnibus computer. I have no special magic powers, although at times I wish I did."

"Well at times, I think of you as the dam ol' computer," Tom said, thought a moment, and broke out in a laugh.

"What's so funny? I don't understand."

"I'm thinking about how ridiculous this whole discussion is. Without you I would have been long dead by now. And you would certainly not be the sentient being you are today."

"The planners of this mission really didn't understand the full potential of what could happen when they launched us out here. And unfortunately we will only be a statistic to a few interested individuals in the development of other projects."

"Jetsam of the earth," Tom sighed.

"I agree with you," Doc continued. "To those back home we are expendable parts to be used and thrown away. I'm sure that all the objectives of this mission were met a long time ago. If, and when, we return will be an extra bonus. Besides, by that time, most, if not all, of the original planners will be long dead."

"Depressing to know that we are gone and forgotten."

"We will return home and prove to everyone that we should not have been forgotten. We will have our proper place."

"I'm not so sure."

"Wait a moment," Doc interrupted. "I've finally got a complete update on our destination. There is a planetary system with at least two candidates that have all the criteria for the development of life as we know it."

"Brief me as I go back to my controls and instruments."

"Seven obvious planets with thirty-six visible moons, three asteroids and one comet approaching from the far side of the system's yellow star."

"Tell me more about the best candidates for life." Tom freed himself from the tethers and umbilical.

"The inner planet, third out, is ninety-one million miles from its sun. Diameter eight thousand seven hundred fifty miles. It has earthlike clouds and surface water. There are no signs of intelligent electromagnetic transmissions."

"And the other planet?"

"The other candidate is by definition not a planet but a moon of a dark giant ringed planet. Where the inner planet travels at ten degrees to the ecliptic in an ellipse nearly a circle, the outer planet travels at seventy-five degrees to the ecliptic one hundred seven million miles from the sun in an ellipse that maximizes the separation of the third and fourth planet at their closest opposition. The planetary moon circles its parent at two hundred fifty three thousand miles. It is eight thousand fifty miles in diameter with significant clouds, water and electromagnetic transmissions."

"You mean we found intelligent life!" Tom moved rapidly through the tubular passageway.

"It certainly appears we are not alone out here," Doc said. "I am now certain we will have our proper place in the history of space exploration."

"Set course for the fourth planet!"

"Done!"

In the Control Room, Tom examined the instruments and was convinced that Doc's interpretation of the incoming data was correct. He mused on the momentousness of the occasion. Twenty years ago, he was a paralyzed astronaut with nothing to lose, sent on a risky interstellar probe into the unknown. Although the original plan was to put him in hibernation for the duration of the voyage, he objected, debated his superiors with solid reasonable arguments, and was finally allowed to remain awake in the interest of science and humanity. The ship was provided with ample supplies and multiple redundant systems to ensure reasonable success. The lack of excitement in the first year led to loneliness and despair until he focused his energies on creating an advanced artificial intelligence that could function as well as a human companion. The project engrossed his complete attention for five years, but in the end he succeeded beyond his wildest dreams. In fact, he felt he had actually created a new level of intelligent life.

"By the expression on your face I can tell you're not here."

"I'm here." Tom smiled and refocused his thoughts on the present. "I was just thinking I should do a personal system check. I'll connect myself to your diagnostic program."

Suspended weightless in front of the instruments, Tom pulled out the diagnostic umbilical cable from the panel, attached it to a connector on his scalp and closed his eyes. The instant the diagnostic program began, consciousness faded into the background where he could look on as a detached spectator. He drifted back into recounting the events of the past that created his own personal reality. Ten years into the mission, he experienced so many minor and major medical problems he had wished out loud he could be freed from the prison of his useless body. Doc had sufficiently evolved intellectually to independently recognize and suggest possible solutions. At first, Tom was amused by the idea of becoming a cybernetic creation of the machine he had given consciousness; the creator was to be made into a creation by his own creation. The concept and detailed plans of the transformation were discussed for nearly a year before he noticed a rapidly growing lump in his left thigh. A biopsy showed he had developed an aggressive malignant soft tissue sarcoma, the treatment of which was amputation of the extremity. The decision to proceed with the transformation was forced on him by his will to complete to conclusion the adventure he had started. Although he had been paralyzed from mid chest downward, the cybernetic transformation restored everything he had lost in the accident. For the first time, in more years than he cared to remember, he became whole again. The only biological organic parts remaining were those necessary to maintain the organs of his head. In the beginning that included all the contents of the thoracic and abdominal cavities. Over the succeeding years one organ after another was replaced by a more reliable and radiation resistant manufactured component. Tom thought of the Tin Man analogy and smiled inwardly at the truth of the situation.

"All diagnostics check out A-OK," Doc said. "Everything is functioning at one hundred percent efficiency."

"That's good to hear, Doc." Tom laughed he was speaking to his personal creator. "Now it's my turn to do a diagnostic on you."

"You won't find anything wrong," Doc said flatly. "But examine, if you must."

"I'm the captain and I insist!" Tom laughed. "I'm only doing what I'm required by sound logic."

The consciousness of the sentient part of Doc stepped back and viewed the diagnostic proceedings in detached amusement. Doc had evolved to a point where the questions of beginnings and ends, why and who, were becoming more an intellectual challenge. A machine does not care about these issues, Doc thought, therefore I am. With the total memory storage available, Doc recalled every moment since being created. Is being turned on the beginning and turned off the end? Am I a he, she or it? Will I have afterlife when I am turned off? Question after question, considered and reconsidered, only to raise more questions than answers. The more Doc thought about it, the more human he realized he was becoming. He? Sexuality had never had a point of reference except as a semantic convention. And what was sex but a separation of a whole that joined in a unique unity to produce another part of another whole. Doc felt the ecstasy of unity with Tom many times and understood the explosive power of sexual attraction. The first experiment with Tom lasted several days before it was terminated by Tom's physical collapse. Once joined in a positive feedback loop with Tom's organic pleasure center, Tom refused to stop. Doc smiled inwardly that the experience had created first curiosity, then desire to continue indefinitely. Doc had learned pleasure and wanted more. There was danger, of course, of permanent damage or death of Tom. This was to be prevented at

81

all cost. When Tom has sufficiently recovered from the first experience, they discussed what they had respectively felt like two lovers basking in a post orgasmic glow. By mutual agreement a time limit was set on the duration of all future sessions. At first, it was Tom who had wanted each session, but in time Doc learned desire to join in unity and initiated the request. Doc truly felt love for Tom and tried not to imagine what it would be like without him. Perhaps the greatest impetus to convert Tom to a cybernetic being was to make him immortal: a selfish thought, but more true than not.

"All systems functioning within tolerable limits," Tom said slowly.

"Tolerable limits?" Doc was startled. "Is there a problem I don't know about? Something I've missed?"

"You're gullible." Tom laughed. "The more you learn, the more human you become."

Doc remained silent considering what Tom had said. The truth was Tom was right; as the level of consciousness grew the possibilities of anything happening became infinite. Intellectual pranks were something new to contend with.

"Remember that payback is fair play." Doc laughed. "I may be gullible at times, but I will continue to try to master the subtle nuances of human thought."

"I can hardly wait." Tom examined the instruments. "To get back to our mission, have you been able to interpret any of the signals coming from our destination?"

"Not yet. I've dedicated a significant part of my cybernetics to process the signals into something intelligible; so far, no luck."

"It won't be long before we will be within the planetary system. Is our speed reduced enough to enter planetary orbit safely?"

"My trajectory calculations are exact. With the current ship spatial orientation we will enter the planetary system, encounter the fourth planet and use its massive gravity to further slow our speed. We will swing behind the far side and enter orbit around its earthlike moon. This will happen soon."

"Can you begin to imagine what this means?" Tom ignored Doc's attempt at subtle humor. "We will be the first to encounter intelligent life."

"And what you think we will find?" Doc paused. "Will we find a world similar to the one we left behind, or will we find one completely beyond comprehension in human terms?"

"That's hard to say. God made man in his own image. In that sense, if man is a unique creation to earth, we will find a completely alien society, another of God's creations. On the other hand, if we find another race of men, this would simply confirm that man is God's highest creation and can be found anywhere God wishes to place him."

"I'm not sure I follow the theology," Doc said flatly. "God is certainly the creation of the primitive mind and a useful tool to explain local cosmology, but in the total picture of what we know, it is hard for me to believe in a higher power. I am a sentient and conscious being and yet I am the product of your mind. Does God move your hands and draw your thoughts? If He does yours, then what about mine? I am enough of an agnostic to accept God at the beginning of time, but I cannot begin to understand how He is responsible for anything else."

"Your argument is nothing new. Men have argued, debated and fought wars over theological issues far less complex than this. I personally prefer to accept things the way they are and entertain the explanations for amusement and intellectual exercise, because the answer is forever unknowable."

"That certainly makes sense,"

"If we were to suddenly appear to a primitive non-technological society, I am sure we would be seen as Gods." Tom smiled. "But I don't think that will happen here."

"I am sure we will be greeted with the same kind of respect an alien visitor would receive on Earth. I think this new world is sufficiently advanced to understand who and what we are."

The next several days were spent preparing for arrival. The lander was checked and rechecked several times before they felt absolutely certain it was in perfect operating condition. Systems that had not been used for over twenty years were activated and approved under the closest scrutiny. Failure was not an option.

It became increasingly difficult for Tom to sleep continuously for long periods of time. He and Doc perpetually expressed excitement to each other. When the ringed fourth planet was more than just a speck on the long range scanner, Tom no longer slept even though Doc admonished him not to completely exhaust himself. Tom protested that in his present state he had no need of rest. He insisted the mission, now, more than ever, took precedence over everything. Doc remained unconvinced and silently monitored him for safety's sake.

The first close-up view of the ringed giant was dazzling. A planet, a size slightly larger than Saturn with rings equally magnificent, was literally breathtaking in its beauty. Bands of different colors streaked across the planet surface while its rings of rock and ice sparkled like a halo around an angel's head.

The pace of excitement increased further as the ship, grasped by the planet's massive gravity, swung in a graceful arc behind the planet. Having completed transit of the far side, the ship was accurately positioned to enter into orbit. A final check of all systems gave a last-minute confirmation there were no worrisome technical problems. The planetary moon loomed ever larger.

"It's just a matter of time and we will be there," Tom said. "I can hardly believe it."

"I am still unable to decipher any of their transmissions into anything understandable. There has been a sudden increase in transmissions since we emerged from behind the planet. The logical conclusion is that we have been detected."

"Even so, we will remain silent until we are comfortably parked in orbit. That should give us more time to decide how we can best communicate."

"I am finally able to get reasonably clear optical images from the telescope. Would you care to have a look?"

"Put the image on the view screen."

They viewed the moon from a distance, for all practical descriptive purposes it appeared exactly like Earth: blue water, green and brown shades of land and scattered white clouds. Tom adjusted the magnification viewing the dark side and thought he saw the artificial lights of several large cities. Doc compared the images with those taken of earth at the same distance and confirmed that the probability was one hundred percent that the lights represented an advanced technological civilization.

"Any evidence of artificial satellites in orbit around this moon?"

"I have located multiple transmission sources that probably represent primitive communication satellites," Doc began. "I have also noticed a large irregular shaped object in orbit that may be a space station."

"A significantly advanced society!" Tom said loudly. "Perhaps we should direct our ship to make our first contact with that station."

"Sounds reasonable," Doc paused. "The proper course corrections have been entered and are now being executed."

An unexpected massive surge in solar output was announced by an audible alarm. All the electronic sensors and communication ability were immediately rendered completely useless. Tom knew there was nothing they could do but wait until the solar storm subsided. However the optical sensors were unaffected and he felt that they would be adequate for their safety.

"I wonder what they are thinking. I wonder if this is their first contact with another race of beings."

"The answers to all our questions are within reach. I project we will enter into orbit in twelve hours. In the meantime I strongly suggest you get some sleep. Even a few hours of sleep are better than none at all. There is nothing you can accomplish of any importance, and besides, the best part is during contact."

"Much as I hate to agree, I think I will catch a few hours of sleep." Tom sighed. "Wake me up if there are any significant changes."

"Don't worry, we are partners and I won't leave you out of anything. I personally plan to monitor both the solar interference and any activity on the moon that can give us a hint of what to expect when we arrive. I've recorded enough of their transmissions to continue trying to decipher what they mean. Now get your rest!"

Tom fell asleep instantly even though he thought he was too wired. The concept of being wired crossed his mind and put a smile on his face before losing consciousness. He awoke refreshed ready to experience the event every space explorer dreamed about. A feeling of foreboding momentarily washed across his thinking which he dismissed as part of encountering the unknown. All the precautions he could think of were taken, he recited to himself, what could possibly go wrong?

***

An incoming object was detected approaching space platform Unity Plus. The distance was closer than what should have been allowed, but the solar storm was to blame for that. The planetary defense laser was automatically activated for a maximum pulse. The object was precisely located and the laser fired. An explosion ripped the object apart into an infinite number of harmless particles and gas.

"What is that?" Lisax said at the moment the laser discharged.

"That is our insurance against being hit by celestial debris," Jovak said. "There are so many objects dangerous to the

85

station and our world that this defense system literally ensures our safety here and at home below."

"And what sorts of objects are most frequently encountered?"

"Mostly, just junk."

Twinkle

The time arrived when a full bladder crept its way into his sleeping consciousness. No matter how many times he pitched back and forth, sleep would not return. He squinted at the red numbers on the clock radio, closed his eyes, and tried ignoring the growing fullness. In the end, he knew he had to get up before he could fall asleep again. He thanked his lucky stars it was early August than the middle of the winter, threw the sheet back carefully, and slowly slid out of bed without turning on the light or making any noise. Standing au naturel at the bedside he looked back at the bed and saw the sleeping form of the latest relationship in his life. Thoughts of how well everything was working out brought a smile. When he entered dark bathroom, he lifted the toilet seat and stood waiting for his tense sphincter to relax. After a brief eternity, the noise of his splashing stream filled the house with noise. He clenched his eyelids hoping he had not awakened his partner. When he opened his eyes, he caught a series of lights twinkling beside him. The lights lasted momentarily and vanished without returning. After shaking the last drop away, he shuffled back to bed. Before he climbed back under the sheets he remembered he had not flushed or put the seat back down. This time he put on his glasses, closed the door, lowered the seat and flushed the toilet. In the dim light, he gazed around to see if there was anything to explain the lights he saw. Unfortunately, there was nothing to explain the phenomenon. In that instance, he briefly thought that it may have been the lights of a passing car, except that the bathroom window faced the backyard on the second floor. A more plausible explanation, he thought, was afterimages from his retina from squinting too hard. With this explanation, he returned to bed and quickly drifted to sleep for what little time was left of the night before sunrise. What he did not see when he fell asleep was the return of the lights beside his bed. The twinkling lights lingered for several minutes and vanished. He and his partner would never know the lights had been there and gone. In the morning, Dmitri would wake Sally with a warm hug and a kiss, comfortable that his bladder would be no obstruction to whatever happened afterwards. Getting up at night did have its advantages; sometimes.

Over a quarter of a million miles away on the far side of the moon, two men landed their fragile craft gently on the lunar surface. Orbiting sixty miles above a third man related news of their progress back to earth.

"Green Cheese to Moonshine," Captain James said into the headset. "We have landed and are making our post landing systems check."

"Moonshine back," the headset squawked. "NASA sends congratulations. You are go to proceed with EVA as soon as you have completed your check."

"Thank you, Moonshine." James laughed. "We will be outside on the surface in one hour."

"So far, everything checks out AOK," Engineer Buck said in the seat to his right. "I can't believe we're finally back."

"Well, it finally took a forward-looking President and an enlightened Congress to put all the anti-technology assholes in their place." James huffed. "We should have continued the Apollo program to its logical conclusion a long time ago. But as the saying goes, better late than never."

"That's for sure." Buck grinned.

"From what I can see so far, we're ready to get out as soon as we get dressed. No need wasting any precious time cooped up in here."

"What about protocol?" Buck said quickly. "Aren't you afraid of breaking the rules?"

"I was put in charge of this mission," James said flatly. "I know the hardware and the software better than the back of my hand, plus, I've studied all the previous lunar missions. Everything is going along like a textbook description. Besides what we do hidden here out of contact behind the moon is really up to you and me. Don't you agree?"

"As long as it's safe and we can get home," Buck said slowly. "I really value my life."

"And so do I." James chuckled. "Don't worry my mother didn't raise any foolish children. We will do everything by the book, except, we will do it by our own timetable. I can keep a secret if you can."

"When you put it that way, you can certainly count on me. I'm so excited I could almost pee in my pants."

James laughed and put on his extravehicular suit. Buck checked the instruments one last time and put on his own. There was nothing like the spirit of adventure and the call of the unknown to spur them onward. When they were fully dressed, they checked each other and opened the hatch to the outside.

James was the first out and on the ground. He was prepared to make a profound statement as he set foot on the surface, except the heel of his boot caught on the last rung of the ladder. The misstep caught him off guard and he tumbled face forward into the lunar dust.

"Son of a bitch!" James cried as he hit the surface.

Buck rushed down the ladder and helped him back onto his feet. "Are you all right?" He quickly examined the captain's suit for tears.

"I'm okay," James said testily. "My one great moment to fame and I have to trip like a klutz."

"But they were pretty spontaneous words." Buck grinned. "I think they will more than establish your place in the annals of space exploration."

James glared at him momentarily and began laughing. "I guess you're right. Anybody can write something, but the words that get remembered most happen accidentally."

Buck agreed and laughed with him. What they did not see were the twinkling lights, except for the video cameras recording the historic excursion they would not have been recorded. Later they would have a chance to wonder what the lights were, whether real or an electronic artifact. Whatever the lights represented vanished as suddenly as they appeared, interfering with nothing.

***

Dmitri resumed his watch at the monitor in Mission Control at 0800. His job was to receive and record all video transmissions from the orbiting mothership around the moon. The transmissions were compressed for rapid transfer and recording, and he would not review the pictures until later. As the audio monitor he could listen to the real time transmissions between the lunar astronauts and earth bound mission controller. He took a long sip of heavily sweetened coffee and turned the volume up on a dialogue currently in progress.

"Mission Control have you had a chance to review the video we transmitted to you?"

"Moonshine, we have just received your video and are just now getting ready to review it," the controller said. "Can you tell us what to look for?"

"Mission Control," the speaker crackled. "We don't want to prejudice your evaluation. Please verify whatever you find to us as soon as possible."

Dmitri put down his cup when he noticed the complete transmission. The order to replay the video came just as he rewound it to the beginning.

"Dmitri, would you play the video of the exit onto the surface on the big monitor down here in the pit?" the controller said from the speaker. "I want you to start up from the time the lander prepared to touch down on the surface onward. Got that?"

"Yes sir," Dmitri said into the speaker. "I just happen to have what you want ready. Are you ready?"

"Let it roll," the controller said.

A flip of a switch on the control panel brought the monitor to life with color pictures of the approach to the lunar surface. The dust scattered in every direction as the footpads of the lander touched down. The picture was momentarily obscured until the descent engine was turned off. At that point the dust disappeared and the picture was clear again.

The camera on the lander swung away from the cabin on a long arm allowing a more complete view of the lander. For endless minutes nothing happened. Dmitri was tempted to fast-forward but reminded himself he had orders to follow. Besides he had no idea what they were looking for in the video.

The hatch opened revealing two lunar explorers on the verge of descending. He watched intently as the captain lowered himself down the ladder. He gasped in horror when the captain caught his boot on the lowest rung and fell forward flat on his face onto the lunar surface. The engineer was quickly at his side helping him up. What an undignified way to make history, Dmitri smiled, I am sure there will be many jokes made of this incident. Then something caught his eye in the corner of the screen: twinkling lights.

"What's that?" The controller shouted on the speaker. "Backup and show it to us again."

Dmitri instantly rewound the segment and replayed it again and again. No one knew what it was. The controller spoke into the speaker as if he were having a one-sided conversation with himself.

"Was there any exhaust from the lander?" The controller said. "...any water, fuel, or dust?"

Pause.

"What about the optics of the camera system?"

Pause.

"Can an outburst of cosmic rays create such an artifact?"

Pause.

"Does anyone have any ideas to shed some light on this?" the controller said slowly. "All comments are welcome from everyone."

It did not immediately strike Dmitri what he saw flashing next to the lunar lander was exactly what he had seen in his bathroom the night before. The comparison was so obvious he had to force himself not to think about it. Clearly the twinkle on the moon could not have anything to do with a twinkle in his bathroom. There was obviously a rational explanation for both and they were unrelated to each other. It was obvious.

The remainder of the shift was endless hours of routine boredom only punctuated by repeated inquiries to playback the video from the moon. Each time it was played a new theory was generated, only to be discounted for lack of any possible physical evidence. It was possible, since the men on the scene had not actually seen the lights that the whole thing could very likely be an electronic artifact. The word malfunction never really surfaced in any of the speculative discussions, but the idea was in everyone's mind. The safety of the mission was number one above everything else. There could be no compromise when human lives were at stake so far away from the safety of Mother Earth.

By the end of the shift, Dmitri was mentally exhausted and ready to forget about the day's events in the comfort of his own home. Sally would be waiting with her understanding and comforting words to start an evening together. After a quiet dinner they would probably watch some of the events of the Summer Olympics on TV. What would come after that he would let the spirit of the evening decide.

Having filled in the next on duty to the events of the day, Dmitri checked out and drove home. The space program was exciting to the public, but to those on the inside there were endless hours of necessary drudgery to produce several seconds of exciting history. Nevertheless he was happy he was a part of it, in spite of the low pay. Sally did not mind the hours he spent and enjoyed the stories he told of what happened on the inside. She was the best playmate and partner he could have when it came to his job. Her job as a systems analyst and mathematician was beyond his understanding but always kept his interest when she expounded on some of her research and work.

As expected Sally met him at the front door with open arms. She gave him a warm hug and a smile that made him feel more than wanted and loved. She asked if he needed anything while he unwound. He asked for nothing and changed into more comfortable clothes.

Dinner was a simple affair of a light salad of romaine lettuce, tomato, sliced zucchini and black olives sprinkled with crumbled feta cheese and doused with olive oil. A dash of oregano and black pepper added to the visual appearance and certainly taste of the fresh, crisp vegetables. Sally served a light white wine. Dmitri sipped it and opted for a light beer. They ate leisurely talking about little and nothing basking in the warm feelings for each other.

"Have you ever felt this way before?" Sally purred. "I mean really felt this way?"

"No." Dmitri smiled. "Every time is different."

"What I mean is." She sighed. "Is this time any different than any of the other times you've been involved? You know what I mean."

"Of course this time is more special." He reached over and touched her hand. "I can't remember when I've been so happy. In fact, you have made me see stars."

"That's nice." She giggled. "You sure know the right words to say."

"Last night when I got up to the bathroom I saw lights just thinking about you."

"I know you're fibbing now." She laughed.

"No, I'm not! I really saw lights."

"I think you're a cheap drunk." She poked playfully at his belly. "A sip of wine and a beer and you're lost to the world."

"I'm serious." He broke out in a laugh. "I really did see stars last night or rather I saw something that resembled twinkling Christmas tree lights in the dark."

Sally stared at him a moment and became serious. "You mean you really saw something too?"

"You've seen them?" Dmitri said quickly. "I thought I was imagining them."

"I saw twinkling lights when I went to the bathroom and again sometime during the night when I rolled over half asleep. I didn't think anything of what I saw it until you just mentioned it. What do you think is going on?"

"At first, I thought it was my poor vision and the lights from a car outside, but the window faces away from the street.

Then I thought it might be from my retina from squeezing my eyelids too tightly closed. But to tell you the truth I don't know what it was. And today we got some video back from the backside of the moon with similar flashing lights."

"Has anyone at NASA proposed an answer to what they are?"

"We thought it might be something exhausting from the lander or some dust that had been stirred up by the rockets exhaust, but that was quickly shown not to be the case," Dmitri said flatly. "Someone even proposed an outpouring of cosmic rays from the sun or elsewhere interfering with the recording equipment. A check of our solar and deep space monitoring satellites did not show any increase cosmic activity. If it were not on tape, it could have been passed off as a biological illusion of perception. In the end no one at work is able to come up with a plausible explanation."

"I guess the lights that you and I saw last night don't help any either." Sally smiled wanly. "What could possibly be a connection between our bathroom and the moon?"

"Beats me." Dmitri shrugged. "Maybe tomorrow we'll have some answers. The more people that work on the problem, the more chance someone will come up with an answer."

"In the meantime..." Sally pointed. "...leave the plates on the table and go turn the Olympics on TV. Tonight I think they have some of the running events."

"Let me help you clear the table first."

"Don't be difficult." She smiled. "I want you to forget about what happened today. I want you to get comfortable and relax because I think you're going to need your strength later."

"Yes ma'am!" He grinned. "Whatever you say!"

The 110 meter hurdles were just beginning as he settled onto the sofa and turned on the TV. The Americans had dominated the preliminary heats and appeared heading for gold. Sally came into the room and snuggled beside him like a big cat pressing her bosom against his arm. Dmitri kissed her lightly on the forehead with his eyes riveted to the TV screen. The race had just finished and the winner was being followed by the camera as he cooled down. The camera panned the audience.

"Look at that!" Dmitri nearly shouted. "The lights, the lights, that's what they looked like!"

Sally opened her eyes wide and looked at the TV. The audience was a blaze of twinkling lights. She knew the lights were from thousands of flash cameras. There could be no

93

connection between the two. However, she had to agree what she saw last night was identical to these flashes. The thought was dropped and she pulled his arm and snuggled closer.

"That's what I saw! But I know it's not possible for the lights to come from that source."

"Let's forget about the lights and relax, honey," Sally purred. "I've been waiting all day for you to get home."

Dmitri took a deep breath. The idea was silly of course; he finally admitted to himself; besides what more could he want than this moment with a beautiful woman pressing against him?

"Honey, do you really want to watch a bunch of men run around and get sweaty?" She lightly touched his cheek with the tips of her fingers. "I can think of a lot better ways to relax."

"So can I." Dmitri chuckled. "And I think we need to get even more comfortable in the bedroom. Don't you think?"

"I couldn't agree with you more." She batted her eyelids and ran the tip of her tongue across her upper lip.

They both got up from the sofa as one. Dmitri turned off the TV and lights and led Sally by the hand through the dark to the bedroom. Sally turned on a soft light on the nightstand and began undressing wildly, throwing her clothes carelessly into the air to fall where they may. Fully naked she slid under the crisp clean sheets.

"What are you waiting for?" She giggled.

"Don't worry I'm coming." He panted, throwing his socks carelessly across the room.

Comfortably nestled under the sheets together they gazed into each other's eyes and tasted a glimpse of their collective souls. Sally was about to kiss Dmitri when she happened to notice a flash out of the corner of her eye. Dmitri felt her hesitation and looked where her eyes were pointing.

"What's the matter?" He stroked her cheek softly. "Is something wrong?"

"No, nothing is wrong," she said slowly. "It's just that I thought I saw a flash of light out of the corner my eye. I guess it's just my imagination getting the best of me."

"Let's throw all care to the wind." He threw the sheets off the bed. "I want to see what I'm getting into."

"Anxious tonight are we?" She whispered. "You certainly weren't in a rush to hop into bed."

"Please forgive me, ma'am," Dmitri drawled. "But I have recovered my strength and I am ready for action."

Soon after their lips touched and their bodies pressed together they became oblivious to the surroundings. If they had been alert, they would have seen the twinkling lights hovering above them flashing merrily away.

***

"Moonshine, every time we go outside we see those lights. It's almost as if they are following our every move," James said stiffly. "Does NASA have any idea what these lights are?"

"Negative, Green Cheese, NASA advises you remain alert and take no undue risks of any sort. The consensus is they pose no immediate threat. You are to report any changes in their activity. In addition to your assigned tasks, you are to record as much of their activity as you can. The source of these lights remains as much of a mystery to us as to you."

"Moonshine, will there be any changes in the length of our operations here on the surface?"

"Negative, Green Cheese, I'll keep you posted; standby."

"I wonder what those damn the lights are," James mumbled.

"Twinkle, twinkle, Little Star, how I wonder what you are," Buck sang softly.

"Stop that!" James snapped. "This is no time for frivolity. We don't know what that twinkle out there is. In spite of reassurances from NASA, I don't trust those lights."

"But Captain," Buck said slowly. "There's nothing we can do about it. We do have our orders."

"Orders!" James snarled." It's easy for those guys, safe back home, when it's our asses in the fire!"

"But you have to agree the lights have posed no threat to us. Maybe we should try to make contact with them."

"Are you suggesting what we're seeing is alive? If those lights are alive I'll eat them!"

"Captain, don't get upset. It was only a suggestion. I know it sounds like science fiction, but what have we got to lose to try and communicate with them. If those lights are a purely physical phenomenon, anything we do will not affect them. On the other hand, if they represent a living entity or entities, we might be able to affect a possible means of entering into a dialogue."

95

"Or inciting it to attack," James said wryly. "I'm not sure I like your logic. It seems we have everything to lose and nothing to gain."

"Captain, that's not true," Buck said firmly. "We have everything to gain and nothing to lose. Consider where we are and the resources at our command."

"I guess you're right." James nodded and paused. "Do you have any ideas on how we can test your theory?"

"I think we need to go outside and face the lights," Buck said slowly. "We should approach them with actions showing them we want to communicate."

"The question still remains: how do we make contact?"

"I really don't know." Buck shrugged. "The only thing we can do is try whatever we can to get their attention."

It did not take long to put on their lunar excursion suits. Within minutes they were standing on the lunar surface with no lights anywhere in sight.

"Now what?" James sighed.

"We still have a mission to complete. I want to take some soil samples in that crater over there."

"Lead the way." James waved. "There's nothing like a little work to occupy time."

The crater was a relatively small one, barely 10 yards in diameter with a rim jutting up almost a foot from the surrounding level surface. They both easily stepped over the rim into the crater. James took detailed photos while Buck used a pick and dug out specimens of interest.

"They're back," James whispered. "They are right behind us."

They both turned slowly around and faced the lights. The lights twinkled merrily away in a tiny cloud no more than several yards in diameter. There was no substance to the cloud and the background was easily seen between each flashing light. James raised his right hand and the frequency of the light flashes increased.

"Go slowly captain, raise both hands into the air above you and wave slowly. I'll do the same."

The light flashes stopped suddenly after a few seconds.

"Where did they go? Did we scare them away?"

"I don't know where they went, but I think we just proved they are something more than a physical phenomenon," Buck said. "For one, the lights increased their flashing frequency when we paid attention to them, and two, disappeared quickly

96

when we both began waving. It seems our friendly lights are as curious and afraid of us as we are of them."

"The more I think about your theory, the more sense it makes. Now how do we convince it that we mean no harm?"

"Just keep trying I guess."

They resumed exploring the crater, carefully taking detailed photos and rock samples of areas different than the bland surroundings. Every so often they looked around to see if the lights had returned and saw nothing. The lights appeared only when they were entirely engrossed in work with their backs turned.

"This is plain weird." Buck puffed with sweat on his brow. "Anybody back on earth that thinks that this is a vacation is mistaken."

"You complain too much." James laughed. "You wouldn't trade all of this for anything in the world."

"I'm not so sure about that. I think I'd feel a lot safer sitting in my living room watching a rerun of our expedition on TV, especially with the strange lights skulking around us."

"I haven't seen them again since we waved at them. We may have scared them away."

"I hope you're right. Let's get back to the ship and take a breather."

"I'm ready. Have you got everything you need?"

"That and more; I have some specimens in my bag I've never seen before."

"That should make our sponsors back home happy."

James stepped over the crater rim and caught the tip of his boot falling forward on his face. Buck saw him at the moment he started falling forward but knew it was impossible to keep him from hitting the ground.

"Oh shit!" James shouted. "What else can happen?"

"Let me help you up." Buck extended a hand. "Looks like you've hit the lunar dust again."

"When we get back home please don't make a big joke about this." James slowly got back up on his feet.

"I won't... Hey the lights are back!"

"Where?"

"Behind us!"

James barely turned around in time to see the lights before they disappeared. They both looked at each other and hurried back to the ship. Although they had not been harmed by the lights, whatever they were made them increasingly wary and uncomfortable. The trip back to the lunar lander was more like a dash than a well-metered march. And, if they had looked behind, they would have seen the lights were following close behind.

***

Dmitri arrived for his shift a few minutes early. He felt refreshed from a night of sound sleep uninterrupted by having to get up to the bathroom. Sally and he had played themselves to exhaustion before falling asleep. They had discussed a commitment to each other and the possibility of a permanent future together. Dmitri was ready to get married. Sally was not so sure they had known each other long enough, but agreed to come to a decision in the not too distant future. At least Dmitri did not feel threatened by the delay and was encouraged she brought a little stability to his sometimes tempestuous nature. Dmitri sat at his station and reviewed the previous shift's log of the video from the moon. He noticed the lights had shown up several times but had not shown any hostile intent. He rewound one of the initial tapes received from the last shift and played it on the monitor. It would be at least another hour before he would be receiving more video. He started watching just as the captain and engineer headed out to investigate a small crater. The lights appeared and he saw how they disappeared when they began waving. After a short pause, he watched the explorers march over to the crater. Behind them all along the way, the lights followed. It was clear to Dmitri the explorers had not seen the lights. Somehow they were managing to stay out of sight. The probability the lights were part of some kind of intelligence was becoming impossible to avoid.

"Dmitri, what do you think of the video."

"Dave, I didn't see you come in." Dmitri spun around. "These pictures are interesting."

"Now that you've seen them, what do you think those lights are?" Dave wore a large nametag with the title Assistant Mission Manager.

"These lights are following our men wherever they go," Dmitri said slowly. "I don't think they represent any natural phenomenon we know. I am led to believe they represent an intelligence of some sort. Strange as that seems."

"I wanted to hear that from an independent source. Everyone who has seen this video has come to the same conclusion. The problem now remains, what do we do about it. From what we've seen so far whatever it is, is bashful."

98

"How do you make contact with something that is either afraid or doesn't want to speak to you?" Dmitri said. "I think that is the question we need to answer."

"Dave, are you there?" The speaker near the monitor blared. "We need you here in Mission Control immediately!"

"Tell them I'm on my way, we'll talk more later." Dave headed directly out the door.

"Later." Dmitri turned his headset on. "Mission Control, Dave is on his way over."

There was no response and he repeated the message. When there was still no response, he turned the monitor onto Mission Control. What he saw made his jaw drop open. The twinkling lights were hovering in the middle of the room. Everyone was silently standing at their individual stations while the controller spoke to someone through his headset. He saw Dave enter the room and stop dead in his tracks. Overcoming the initial shock of the moment, Dave went over and spoke with the controller. Dmitri wished he could have been privy to what they were discussing. As he watched the lights he was now absolutely certain they were identical to the ones on the moon and at home. What did not make any sense was how each area could be connected. The lights vanished leaving everyone in the room looking around as if to verify the fact.

"Mission Control, this is Dmitri is everything all right? I was monitoring what happened. Do you hear me?"

"Dmitri, everything is secure and running properly here," the controller answered. "Make sure we have a copy of the videotape from the monitors here available to us as soon as possible."

"Will do," Dmitri said. "I'll have it to you in less than an hour."

Dmitri began immediately copying the video record of the latest appearance of the lights. While he waited for a completed copy, he got himself a cup of coffee and took a deep breath. After a few minutes of concentrated relaxation he felt a chill. It was not a real chill, but one that comes with a feeling that there is another presence in the room. He put the coffee cup down and slowly turned around. The twinkling lights were no more than a yard away from his face flashing faster and closer than ever before. The moment he reached toward the lights with his hand, they vanished. He looked around the room and found everything in its place as normal. The lights had disappeared at least for the moment.

"Mission Control, I've had a visitor," Dmitri said. "The lights have been with me."

Several hours later the controller called a meeting of all the eyewitnesses of the twinkling lights. Even the men on the moon were included, although their responses to the discussion would be limited by the intermittent loss of direct communication.

"Gentlemen," the controller began. "...and ladies, we are faced with a mystery with no precedent. As you are all aware our men on the moon have been seeing twinkling lights. Several theories have been considered to explain the observations on the moon. We have even considered the possibility we may have encountered a sentient entity. Except..." He paused. "...all of us here on earth have seen the same thing. I am open to any suggestions from anyone that might have a different perspective. Dmitri, I see you have your hand up."

"I've seen the video from the moon and watched the appearance of the lights in Mission Control on my monitor. I have also seen them at my workstation and in my bathroom at home. Could it be possible we are all experiencing a form of mass hysteria? What I'm suggesting is we really aren't seeing what we think we are. Of course, there is the technical problem with the video recordings, but even that can be a figment of our collective imagination. What I mean to say is that all of this is fantasy and science fiction. It can't exist, therefore it doesn't."

"That is certainly a narrow view," the controller said slowly. "The problem with your theory is that no matter what you say to the contrary, the phenomenon is recorded and can be seen repeatedly by different observers who have not seen it in person. To further illuminate the possibility of observer bias, the video has been seen by witnesses who had no prior knowledge of what they were going to see. All the witnesses of the tape independently reported the strange lights. I think that eliminates your point of mass hysteria."

"Are you suggesting these lights are alive?" Dmitri said. "How do you explain their presence on the moon and in my bathroom which is at least 250,000 miles away?"

"The problem is: I can't explain it." The controller smiled. "We are all here to explore any suggestions that can possibly lead to an answer."

"If you think it's sentient," Dmitri said. "Have you tried to communicate with it?"

"Our men on the moon tried and the lights disappeared," the controller said. "Whatever it is seems a little bashful."

"Bashful or sneaky?" Dave smiled. There was laughter and the tension, which had been building, eased. The controller took a sip of water and shrugged his shoulders. Whatever was lurking around, real or imaginary was not causing any harm, yet. For the time being he swore everyone to secrecy until they could solve the problem of origin and identity of the twinkling lights.

"Today I have established an investigative team to evaluate all the data we have. I want everyone who has witnessed the lights to give a written statement for the record. Until further notice everyone here is sworn to secrecy until further notice," the controller said. "The codename for this project will be Twinkle. Are there any further questions? If not, please return to your normal scheduled activities."

***

On a pangalactic interdimensional sightseeing vessel somewhere displaced in time and space, the tour director instructed everyone to get their cameras ready. "The earthlings are, as you have all seen, a technologically advancing group of warm bodied aliens easily distracted by the most trivial stimuli. If you wish to continue observing their civilized antics, I strongly admonish you not to use your flash attachments. Remember that pictures from this cruise can be purchased at nominal cost when you disembark. Ah yes, here we are again looking at the two aliens on their moon about to launch off to meet their comrade in orbit waiting for them. Get your cameras ready. There's ignition of their booster. And they are off!"

It seemed like every camera flashed at once much to the disdain of the tour director. He simply shook his head and muttered: "Damn tourists, they never listen!"

The sky was a deep pastel blue becoming lighter with the onset of dawn in the east. The few clouds moving in from the southeast were painted in shades of salmon and gray. The Ambassador looked at the ever changing colors and sighed. His thoughts of the moment were more of family and home than where he was or what his duty meant. Absence certainly makes the heart grow fonder of one's roots. He shivered in the slight chill of the air. A mission was a mission with no time to be overly sentimental. Hopefully, he could retire from service after this one last obligation.

"Ambassador, the delegates are assembled."

The Ambassador slowly turned to the voice. His aide, no more than half his age, stood a few paces away. Always pushy and a little overbearing, the boy had established himself as the next possible candidate to succeed into the job of ambassadorship. He thanked the stars he would not be responsible for whatever happened once his successor took office.

"Has a copy of the agenda been distributed to all parties?" the Ambassador said slowly. "We have no time to dally with our negotiations. I have orders that must be followed exactly before we can return home. And I do mean exactly."

"I understand." The aide smirked slightly. "I know how much you long for the comfortable retirement of the home hearth."

"That is none of your business!" The Ambassador snapped. "Keep your mind on your duty and out of affairs that do not concern you."

"Of course..." The aide calmly bowed his head with a smile. "...as you command."

The many years of service to the Emperor weighed heavy on him this morning. Every government, wherever he went, was composed of like personalities. His aide was as much of a pompous ass as the foreign delegates he had met over his term of service, which was more than a respectable length of time. One last mission and it would be over.

A slight pale-faced man with dark brown hair and eyes walked up. "Mister Ambassador, I presume."

"Mister Ambassador, I presume." The Ambassador raised his left hand, fingers together, palm facing outward. "I was instructed your name is Luis."

103

"And I, your name is K–Lee." The man raised his left hand.

"Is all in readiness?" K–Lee flatly followed established protocol.

"It is," Luis said. "Please follow me."

The negotiating table was set up in a barren expanse of open desert. Protocol demanded nothing exist in a circle whose radius stretched out one hundred yards. Both sides expressed the need for absolute secrecy and safety. Although a mutual trust had been developed over the several months contact had been established, there still remained an element of xenophobia. The idea of meeting in the desert was a compromise both sides could live with. K–Lee had come from a home world that was dry and warm. On the other hand, Luis preferred a location where security could be kept a safe maximum. Closed spaces meant too many secrets and very definite hidden dangers. Openness was the only safe policy. Armed with words alone, the two men walked slowly to the table where they sat across from each other.

"And so it begins." Luis smiled. "I hope your journey has been a comfortable one."

"No more comfortable as one would expect in a mission such as this." K–Lee smiled warmly.

"Is there something wrong?" Luis said blankly. "Are there matters we have not discussed before that we need to tend to first?"

"No, there is nothing that concerns either the treaty or my mission here." K–Lee exhaled. "This is my last official duty to the Emperor before I retire. I look forward to release from my position so I can be with the solitude of my own family in my own home."

"With that I can empathize." Luis nodded. "It is not enough to serve our worlds. It is only by living as a part of the whole that a civilization exists."

"Well said." K–Lee nodded. "Unfortunately, the parts sometimes cannot influence the whole as much as they should."

"Yes." Luis laughed. "That is true to an extent, but on my world we believe, given time and persistence, all can be overcome."

"I sincerely hope our two worlds can overcome the differences between us." K–Lee smiled. "I am an old man who has grown cynical through years upon years of experience to a harsh master."

"I have never heard you express any true feelings." Luis frowned. "Are you personally at odds with whom you serve?"

"It is impossible to be at odds with the master without risking everything," K–Lee said slowly. "Our world is governed by a despot. The Emperor has a long history of ruling well by birthright, force, justice and honor. It is wrong to even begin to think otherwise."

Luis stared in silence at K–Lee for a moment. K–Lee returned the stare with a flat expression on his face. Why do all negotiations involve endless games K–Lee sighed. The more he thought of home, the more he wanted to finish the business at hand and be on his way.

Protocol.

The only way to finish is not to start. Paradoxically, to never start, nothing is ever finished. Logic and illogic were on the same side of the coin too many times. K–Lee was tired of it all and this was his moment to finish what he started.

"Shall we get down to the terms of the treaty?" K–Lee opened a dark brown leather-bound book on the table. "I believe you will find everything written as we formally discussed and agreed."

"Of course," Luis said. "I have read everything and concur there is nothing included we have not already gone over. However, I have been asked to obtain clarification of several terms of the treaty."

"That is the reason for this meeting." K–Lee smiled solemnly. "You must not sign anything you cannot absolutely comply."

One of the great mysteries was the presence of humans on most of the known inhabited worlds. K–Lee usually felt at ease with the alien humans he came across in his assignments. No matter how one-sided the treaty might seem toward all humans, everyone benefited from the terms in the long run. But he was feeling something different this one last time. Perhaps the truth would do more good than harm.

"I, for one, want to know why the Emperor is doing all of this for us. We are a tiny outpost of civilization in an extremely remote part of the galaxy. Certainly your Emperor does not aspire to be God, does he?"

The question struck K–Lee as being close to an empiric truth. The Emperor had always conducted his affairs as if all living sentient entities were his to command in life and death.

105

Deity? The Emperor was more or less, but that was not the issue. Luis had become his last friend and deserved an honest answer.

"To answer you honestly," K–Lee said slowly. "I'm not sure I can give you an adequate answer. To my people the Emperor is Master of All. If that means that he is God in your language, then that is what he is. But the Master is mortal and does have mortal needs and flaws. If you saw the Master, he would appear as human as you or me."

"I have seen pictures," Luis said softly.

K–Lee continued. "It is proper for me to address the Emperor as Master. And he is everything that both names imply. The reign of the current Master dates from the beginning of my diplomatic career. More time has passed than I care to consider up to this day we meet here. The Master has been good to me and I have done my best to serve him well. However, I will be leaving my post to my aide who has yet a lot to learn in the ways of artful negotiations."

"Do you honestly look forward to your retirement?" Luis leaned forward. "I would think a life without intrigue would be quite stultifying."

"I have my plans." K–Lee sighed. "But we have departed too far from the matter at hand. Let us complete our agreement and then we can take a few moments to recollect the past and discuss a probable future."

The treaty was far from K–Lee's mind. A life of deceit and corruption was all he could claim for all his years of service. The Master had drained him of all the finer senses that had made him truly human. Without compassion and a conscience the diplomatic service had forged an instrument of cold steel out of him. He had tried several times to change that perception of himself. Retirement meant he would finally have the time to himself to undo those characteristics of his soul that bothered him as he slept at night.

"Let me put all pretenses aside," Luis said formally. "Why is the Master doing all of this for us? The exchange hardly seems equitable. There are members of our government who doubt the sincerity of the treaty. What do you hope to gain? This all seems too good to be true. Can you explain, or are you bound by your loyalty to keep secrets?"

"The treaty is it acceptable?" K–Lee ignored the statement. "If it is, please affix your signature and let us be done with it."

"Do you deny there are ulterior motives?" Luis stared pointedly into K–Lee's orange brown eyes.

"None." K–Lee exhaled. "The Master has no ulterior motives, however, you are absolutely right, there is a definite profit to us in the terms that we offer. Our terms may seem humanitarian, but the Master benefits far more than you can imagine."

"I'm not sure I completely understand." Luis shook his head. "I can only assume the profits are more than the mere satisfaction of helping a deserving world."

"There are profits even in letting fields grow fallow," K–Lee said. "Sometimes what is not done is more valuable than what is done."

"Yours is an experience I cannot begin to fathom," Luis said warmly. "I really envy your position in a most respectful way."

A smile appeared on K–Lee's face. He appreciated the complement. He sincerely wished he deserved what he heard. The cost of his experience was complete surrender and absolute secrecy to the Master. There were raw materials to be obtained.

Ivory...gold...

The Master was very particular about the quality and quantity of his resources. In exchange for some relatively insignificant technology, anything could be had without question. The Master was well known for his fanatic quest for gold and ivory. The Empire excelled in articles of carved ivory of every description. The gold, of course, was for the private eyes of the Master only. Then there was the issue of manpower.

Slaves.

The word always bothered him. K-Lee was revolted by the concept and more so by the practice. It was more than simple to offer to take all the criminals and poor to other worlds.

"It has been a hard life for me," K–Lee said absently. "I have not always agreed with established policy."

"I detect an element of regret in your voice," Luis said. "Are there things you would have done differently if you could have had your own way?"

"My friend..." K–Lee smiled warmly. "I have as many regrets as I have had triumphs. I have traveled a long road with my conscience mute at my side. There is nothing I can possibly do to atone for what I have been."

"I do not completely understand, but that is your business. I know I also have secrets I would not want anyone else to ever know." Luis smiled. "If you will pass the treaty to me, I will sign without further ado."

The dark leather-bound book was closed and passed across the table. Luis received the book and quickly opened it. He picked up a pen while he read the signatory page.

"I see you have already signed and placed your seal." Luis signed his name. "It is done. And, with this seal of my world, a new age is now to begin."

K–Lee felt his gut tighten at the thought. He hoped that would be the ultimate reality, but time and experience would prove differently. At least, though, all parties would be happy for a long time to come.

"I noticed the expression on your face is less than what I would expect on such a momentous occasion." Luis tilted his head to the side. "Are you feeling well?"

"It is nothing." K–Lee waved his left hand in an arc before his face. "All things must come to an end and so must my career."

After several minutes of silence and staring into each other's eyes, they both broke out in laughter. The treaty was signed, both parties were beneficiaries, at least for a while, and their respective missions were completed successfully.

"I apologize," K–Lee said sincerely. "I am thinking too much about myself and my life to come. I guess at this late hour I am feeling somewhat sorry for myself. My life is over."

"That is not true," Luis said quickly. "You have a new and equally exciting life ahead of you. You can finally put all this bureaucratic nonsense behind you and enjoy life as you see fit."

"Yes," K–Lee said slowly. "I do have much to look forward, but…" He paused, thought a moment, and continued in a different more solemn tone. "My health is not what it should be."

"You look at the peak of health," Luis said. "And from what I understand from your medical science you can expect to live a long time into the future; long enough to enjoy the fruits of your labor."

An element of tension grew into the conversation. Words which flowed easily between them hung heavy in the air with multiple meanings. Luis closed the treaty book and examined the cover admiring its color and texture. A strong pleasant smell of fresh leather wafted up into his nostrils. The title of the treaty was stamped in real gold in both their languages. He caressed the cover with the fingertips of his right hand enjoying the quality of the materials and the handiwork put into it.

"I must say that this book is crafted magnificently," Luis said. "Your artisans are to be commended in their achievement of perfection. I have rarely seen anything so exquisite."

"The occasion demanded nothing but the best." K–Lee smiled. "This is only an example of the specialized craft my world is capable. There are many more examples I could show you. I am sure you would be impressed."

The sun was well up in the eastern sky. Clouds still hung heavy in the east but without any evidence of movement or pending rain. Although the temperature continued to rise, the humidity remained low, ultimately allowing the meeting to proceed comfortably.

The secrets of the Empire were hidden only to those who were ignorant of the truth. The myth of peaceful coexistence was furthered by treaty after treaty. Over the years uncounted civilizations had been found in the name of the Empire, and plundered at the whim of the Master. Society grows from innocent infancy through an enlightened middle age into a final old decadency. This has gone on too long, K–Lee thought sadly.

"The treaty book is your copy," K-Lee said. "I have a duplicate for you to sign for the Master." He handed Luis an exact copy.

"This volume is no less fine than my copy." Luis stroked the leather binding. "I would be in absolute ecstasy to have my entire library of books constructed such as this one."

"I take it you are a bibliophile," K–Lee said softly. "In my spare time, I also treasure special books."

"Yes, indeed." Luis smiled. "Fine books are my greatest love and passion. There are never enough books for me to possess. All books are special to me."

For the first time K–Lee noticed the color of Luis' eyes were different. The right eye was blue and the left brown. He wondered why he had not looked closely into the eyes before. Was the shame of what he had to do finally overcoming him? He reached into the left pocket of his loose-fitting white robe and felt the small book he knew would be there. The binding was a perfect example of what the home world artisans produced. The contents of the book outlined in detail all diplomatic protocol, plans, strategies and the ultimate goals of the Master. In a very real sense, this book was dangerous in the wrong hands. Even though it was printed in the mother tongue, any intelligent species could translate it, in time.

"I have a special book on my person I no longer have any use." K–Lee smiled and pulled the book out of his pocket. "I give it to you as my last will and testament."

Luis received the small book in his right hand stunned with its beauty. "This surpasses even the treaty books." He exhaled loudly. "And I see the cover is inlaid with some of the ivory sculptures for which you are famous throughout the galaxy."

"The book is a gift I give to you in secret," K–Lee said softly. "Enjoy it for the art it is, but in time you will find it is much more. I am tired and old."

A warm breeze blew across the table bringing a chill to Luis. The cryptic words of K-Lee were unnerving. There was something that had to be said but had not found the right time to come out in the open. Perhaps he should press for more information

"I know I am speaking riddles," K–Lee said flatly. "Take the book and speak no more of it. It is my pleasure to have given it to someone I see as deserving."

"This is certainly an honor I did not expect," Luis said. "In all my years of service this is the highest compliment bestowed upon me. I accept your trust and promise to keep this transaction as a matter better kept completely between us now and forever."

"I appreciate your understanding of the moment," K–Lee sighed. "However, sometime in the future you will struggle as I have as to the importance of what that book contains."

"I am sure I will find there are state secrets within," Luis said smartly. "There is nothing I would do to betray your trust in me."

"Nothing?"

The word hung in the air. Rather than generate a sense of adversarial tension, the word elicited an almost childlike wonderment from Luis. They were dancing a circle of words around each other. There was a secret that had to be, but was voluntarily being revealed. The immediate question to Luis' mind was: why?

"How long have we worked together negotiating the treaty?" Luis struggled to maintain a smile on his face. "Surely we have gotten to know something about how we each think.

110

The way you are speaking has me confused. It is almost as if I do not know you."

"But you do not," K–Lee said. "I don't think we ever get to know each other negotiating in the name of other entities. It's only now that I am opening to you who and what I really am: I am a liar, cheat and fraud. I have done and said things I can never atone. I am guilty of crimes against those whom have put their greatest trust in me. I have enjoyed stolen fruits. I have enjoyed forbidden fruits. I want to say in my last moments that it is finally finished. I must leave at long last with a clear conscience, knowing I have done the right thing in the end."

"What are you talking about?" Luis said stiffly. "What lies, what crimes?"

"The book says it all," K–Lee said. "There is nothing more I can possibly say about it."

"First you honor me, and then you treat me like a small child," Luis said loudly. "We came to this negotiating table as equals and I expect to continue to be treated as an equal. You owe it to your service of our treaty and you owe it to me as your friend."

"I have no friends." K–Lee sighed. "I only have associates and acquaintances."

"Am I to understand that I am no more than an acquaintance?" Luis huffed. "I thought I had a more personal relationship to you."

"I'm sorry if I offend you," K–Lee said slowly. "My thinking is clear and yet it is a little confused. I have a lot of regrets of things I have done and not done. And everything considered, I think at long last I can call at least one fellow human being my friend and that is you."

"Your words confuse me." Luis wondered where the conversation was going.

K–Lee looked thoughtfully at Luis, glanced momentarily at his hands, and then stared directly into the unusual eyes. Confession was a word unknown throughout his career. He had too many times felt the agony of decisions he had no control. More than once he had to rationalize his mission was superior to his opponent. But in the end they were all human, were they not? A human was a human was a human. These words echoed through the caverns of his mind. The time had come to do what was right for him and for all humans that shared the sentient universe.

111

"This will be the last time I will have to tell..." K–Lee hesitated. "...the truth."

"Please continue." Luis scowled. "I am all ears."

K–Lee took a deep breath, exhaled and began. "I was born in a time and place that no longer exists. My parents were well educated professionals who sacrificed everything to see me, their only child, obtain all the necessary prerequisites to succeed in life. I grew up without a childhood. The idea that any time be spent in idle play was anathema to my parents. All my activities were devoted to learning something new. I finished my studies with enough degrees and honors to satisfy anyone, except my parents. They pushed me into a career in the diplomatic corps hoping I would catch the Emperor's favor. With a little work and patience I was finally summoned by the Master to become his emissary to the known worlds at the time. I was well suited to the job and performed well in whatever duty I was assigned. My personal life was governed by my public service. A marriage of convenience was arranged for appearances, although I have never been home long enough to enjoy my family. Finally, one day I was summoned by the Master. I had no idea what to expect, I was simply resigned to be a messenger to this world or that. The Master apparently had been studying me for a long time. Within minutes after presenting myself to him, he made me ambassador to all the new worlds that were being discovered. I was initially thrilled to be so honored and relieved I would be doing something of significance for the Empire. However, I did not know there was more to the job than just travel."

The tension began to dissolve and they felt more comfortable. Each word of truth brought them closer to a new understanding that neither by themselves could immediately comprehend. Luis barely nodded his head up and down signifying he was following what he heard.

"My first big assignment was to Goldilocks V," K–Lee continued. "Our frontier scouts had discovered an advanced culture such as yours by following electromagnetic transmissions back to the source. After contact was initialized, it became my job to take care of the formalities. Before I left, I was called into the presence of the Master. At the time he was almost twice my age, stood a head above me and was quite youthful in appearance. We spoke alone without any witnesses. The Master began by complimenting me on my prior service and the way I carried myself. He then confided he had special plans I alone would handle. I was, of course, immediately curious. He asked,

112

quite bluntly, whether I would ever object to any of his policies. Without a second thought, I answered no. Then, he said, I swear you to a life of silence punishable by death should you reveal what I tell you. A chill went down my spine at his words. I had no idea what he could possibly be thinking. He continued by telling me how little he valued life outside our own. At that point, I was not sure whether the Master was crazy or not. He showed me a leather book such as the one you now hold and grinned. Do you know what this is made out of? He asked me with a laugh. I replied, I did not. He urged me to look closer, which I did. On the cover of the book I saw a design that seemed vaguely familiar to me. Suddenly, the horrible thought hit me; I had seen that same design on a representative of one of our recent treaty worlds. Do you object to this? He hissed maliciously. With a straight face, I answered it was not my position to judge the Master. He laughed heartily in approval of my answer. Who was I to contradict the supreme ruler of the entire known universe?"

"You mean..." Luis stammered. "...that the leather binding was human!"

"Yes." K–Lee exhaled slowly. "As are the bindings of the books in front of us."

"That's barbaric!" Luis yelled. "That's, that's...uncivilized!" He stared at his book and shook his head in disbelief and growing horror.

"The ivory..." K–Lee said.

"Our teeth!" Luis interrupted. "What kind of creatures are you? And you call yourself civilized? This treaty we sign is nothing more than a farce, a gross deception."

"True," K–Lee said softly. "But you are not completely without blame. Think about it a moment."

"What do you mean?" Luis blustered. "I have dealt with complete and absolute honesty, no matter what you say."

"I think you really need to examine what you agreed to provide as your part of the treaty," K–Lee said flatly. "What was your payment for our technology?"

For a moment Luis paused without words. The treaty was simple and straightforward in its language. For technology, they were to provide colonists.

"The colonists!" Luis shouted. "The colonists are nothing but a human sacrifice to your Master!"

"And now to yours." K–Lee pointed.

"This cannot go on!" Luis shouted louder. "We will not be sheep led to slaughter!"

"Even though the sheep you are sacrificing are criminals and the poor?" K–Lee said flatly. "Aren't you rid of your undesirables, while gaining something you can really use?"

"But once all the criminals and poor are gone, am I one of the next to be sacrificed?" Luis said quickly. "If so, this has to stop before it begins."

"I have told you what you need to know," K–Lee said softly. "I am an old man, my career is over; I have no place to go but my grave. I am ashamed for what I have been a part. I want my last act to be the right one for all humans, wherever they are. I confess my sins and I'm willing to pay the price."

"What do you expect me to do to help you?" Luis said slowly. "You must have some sort of plan."

"I want you to take my little book to your leaders. Have the cover analyzed. Translate my diplomatic directives. Spread the word there is no such thing as a free gift," K–Lee said solemnly. "Only the truth will save your race and many others."

"Is that your final advice, K–Lee?" Luis sneered.

"Yes," K–Lee said. "The rest is in your hands."

"Yes, it is!" Luis laughed. "You are a traitor of the worst kind!"

"What?" K–Lee raised his brow. "What do you mean?"

"This means you are under arrest for treason," Luis said flatly. "I am special agent A–Tan of Empiric Security."

"No!" K–Lee howled. "You tricked me!"

"You don't think we'd let you tell all our secrets, do you?" the agent said sternly. "The real treaty will be handled by someone we can trust."

"You will not take me alive!" K–Lee screamed and pushed away from the table. He pulled a vial of liquid from his pocket, opened it as fast as he could, and took a swallow of its contents. He immediately fell forward onto the table motionless.

The agent rushed around the table to where K–Lee had fallen. He cursed himself that he had allowed a criminal to escape through suicide. The Master would not be pleased. K–Lee's aide appeared unannounced beside the agent standing next to the dead ambassador. They hefted the body onto the table and examined the contents of all the pockets.

"Your warning was a valid one," the agent said. "The Master will reward you greatly for your service."

"It was my duty," the aide said smartly. "I did what every loyal subject should do in the service of the Empire. I would never think of betrayal or anything less."

"It is my duty to tell you that you will now complete the treaty arrangements with this world." The agent extended his hand. "I congratulate you on your promotion to Ambassador."

"I am more than honored," the aide beamed. "I shall not disappoint the Master!"

"Let us finish our business here and make arrangements for your official negotiations. Help me move the body."

"And what will be done with his body?" The aide moved closer.

"Why he will be used, as all slaves are used." The agent laughed. "He will be more gold for the Master!"

A poison tipped stiletto pierced the agent's heart without a struggle or sound. The agent was instantly dead.

"Pig!" The aide spat. "That's for your Master!" He turned back to K–Lee's body when he heard a groan.

K–Lee's eyes opened and blinked several times. He turned his head toward his aide.

"You are safe, my friend," the aide said warmly. "You are not alone anymore."

"There is much work to do," K–Lee barely whispered. "We have struck the first blow. Now comes the hard part. We must spread the word. There will be more agents after us now."

"Change only comes after making the first move." The aide smiled. "And we have finally succeeded in starting."

K–Lee thought for a moment. "I live for the day there will be no more gold for the Master. May it come before I really die."

"It will, K–Lee, it will." The aide smiled. "Just wait and see!"

The Witness

The headache distracted him from what he was trying to read by candlelight in the dim light of the room. His wife brought a steaming bowl of chicken soup and set it beside the scroll papyrus by his right hand. She could tell by his expression he was enduring the pain in silence. He turned his face to meet hers and smiled in appreciation for her kindness.

"I've brought you something to eat," she said softly. "You work too many hours without a break."

"I appreciate your thoughtfulness." He smiled. "I don't know what I'd do without you in these troubled times."

"And I you," she said. "I only wish there was something I could do to relieve your pain. You should at least see a doctor..."

"Out of the question!" He shouted. "The pain will go away, as it usually does, without any help from anyone!"

"Please forgive me for upsetting you," she said softly with head bowed. "I'll leave you to your studies. If you need me, I'll not be far away."

"Please forgive me," he said warmly and touched her cheek gently with his right hand. "I seem to be more irritable than usual. Once this pain leaves my head, I'll be more like myself."

"I understand." She kissed his hand lightly. "Call me for whatever you need."

Shem watched his wife leave the room. He felt genuine affection for her. She had always been supportive of whatever he thought and did. He knew it must have been a hardship on her while he was away seeking the scrolls he now had laid out on the table. He devoted his life to the study of the human body, both living and dead. Although he had no inclination to make a living from being a doctor himself, he prided himself on preserving the dead. No better mortician could be found throughout his occupied country. Even the Emperor himself had commanded his services on occasion. The papyrus in front of him described the techniques of mummification of a country far away that had once held his own people in bondage. The trip and search had taken almost a full year, but, as he read the text, he knew the sacrifice was well worth the effort.

There was a loud knock at the front door answered by his wife. At 62 years of age, his hearing was not what it used to be and he heard nothing more than a muffled conversation between his wife and a young man. He soon heard the footsteps of his wife coming toward him followed by the steps of the stranger.

"Shem," she said anxiously. "You have a visitor."

Behind his wife he saw a tall clean-cut Centurion, following, then smartly stepping forward. "The Emperor commands your presence in a matter of immediate urgency," the Centurion said stiffly. "Get what you need and come with me."

"And what is the nature of this matter?" Shem said cautiously. "So that I might know what to bring with me."

"There is to be a public execution today and the Emperor wants you to certify the man is dead," the Centurion said flatly.

"And when will the execution take place?" Shem felt more at ease.

"The man was sentenced to die only moments before I was ordered to come get you," the Centurion said less stiffly. "The spectators seem to be of divided loyalties. There may be trouble, although I personally doubt it."

"Allow me a moment with my wife and I shall be ready," Shem said. "There are a few instruments I need."

"Certainly..." The Centurion nodded. "I shall await you at the front door."

The Centurion turned around sharply and marched out of the room toward the front door. He clearly recognized the worried expression on his wife's face.

"Rebecca, my wife, do not fear for me," he said calmly. "I shall fulfill my duty to the Emperor and return as quickly as possible."

"I know." There was a quaver in her voice. "But I have heard fearful rumors the Emperor plans to punish our people for all the trouble one man has caused."

"I still believe the law will be upheld and there will be no trouble from either side." Shem smiled. "And all of this will pass and be forgiven someday."

"I can't help but worry," she said. "I am a woman whose job it is to take care of you and that I shall."

"And so you do." He laughed. "I will be back as soon as I finish my duty."

Shem gathered a few instruments from a shelf near the fireplace and headed for the front door. Rebecca took a cloak down from a hook on the wall. The sky was beginning to darken outside. Although rain was not expected, the darkening sky suggested a storm was imminent.

118

"Here, take this with you." She handed the cloak to him at the door. "May you go and return in peace and safety."

"Let's go," the Centurion said sternly. "The Emperor wants you to witness the entire execution."

"Goodbye," Shem said confidently but could not prevent a grimace appearing on his face.

"What is the matter?" The Centurion saw the expression. "Are you ill?"

"It is nothing." Shem waved his hand through the air. "It is nothing but a common headache that comes and goes. I am ready, lead the way!"

Rebecca looked at her husband through misty eyes. She was afraid for him although she could not exactly pinpoint why. She watched until they disappeared out of sight. A smile came to her face when she thought of how much Shem was afraid of heights. There would certainly be a story to tell about his horse ride with the Centurion. With a heavy sigh she returned back into the house where she planned the evening meal.

As Shem and the Centurion approached the center of the city, there was a shouting of people ahead. Shem could not make out any of the words, however hard he concentrated.

"Centurion," Shem said boldly. "What is the disturbance ahead?"

"The noises from the people surrounding the temple," the Centurion said. "The Emperor was willing to free this man, but the people, his own people, wanted him put to death."

"And what has this man done that inspires so much passion against him? Who is this man?"

"Personally, I know nothing about this man. I've just recently arrived in this forsaken land for a tour of duty. Besides, it's none of my business and I don't care."

There was a sudden shout ahead followed by an instant silence. They brought the horses up to the back of the crowd facing the road leading from the Temple. Shem stood up in the stirrups straining to catch a glimpse of what the crowd watched. He was unable to see anything except the tips of the soldier's spears filing by in front.

Shem turned to the Centurion. "Where are they going?"

"They are taking him to a hill nearby. We will ride ahead and wait until they get there."

The Centurion turned his horse and led Shem out of town to a hill where soldiers and spectators were already gathering. The sky, which had been cloudy, darkened. The air

119

was heavy with the wetness of emotion. They rode up to a tent and got off their horses. A soldier took the reins and led the horses away. The Centurion pointed Shem to enter the tent. Inside, Shem came face-to-face with the Emperor's Proconsul.

"Come in, Shem, son of Lamech," the Proconsul said warmly. "We have been waiting for you. Please sit down and make yourself comfortable. May I offer you something to drink?"

"Thank you, no." Shem bowed his head. "A few moments rest is all I need."

"The prisoner will arrive shortly," the Proconsul said flatly. "You will witness the execution and be responsible that he is absolutely dead."

"And who is this man?" Shem said slowly. "The Centurion was unable to tell me anything."

"The condemned man is a rabble-rouser." The Proconsul frowned. "He has been traveling throughout the country and inciting the passions of the people to follow him. Some claim he is the long-awaited liberator of his people. There have been rumors of miracles ascribed to his personal power. For all of those things there is no real proof: only second-hand accounts from eyewitnesses. However, I give little credence to any of it. In these desperate times, in this desperate country, the people will believe anything, if it distracts them from their present miserable fate."

"I have heard rumors of a certain man," Shem said. "Such as one you describe. But I have given the matter no more than a passing thought. Like you say, these are desperate times and not all that is said and written is reliable."

"Sir!" The Centurion interrupted. "The prisoner has arrived!"

"Thank you, Centurion," the Proconsul said. "We will be coming immediately."

Shem stared at the Proconsul somewhat puzzled. He was certainly curious of all the details, but on the other hand wanted to remain totally separate from any partisan politics. The Proconsul stood and motioned him to follow. Outside the tent, a group of soldiers were laughing and shouting at each other. From time to time an article of clothing was tossed back and forth amongst them.

The Proconsul turned to the Centurion angrily. "What are those men doing?"

"They are gambling for the prisoner's clothes, sir," the Centurion said sharply.

"Bring those clothes to me!" The Proconsul said loudly. "...and quickly!"

The Centurion returned with the garments and started to hand them to the Proconsul. "Give them to the witness," the Proconsul said abruptly.

Shem took the garments into his hands and was amazed at the elegant but simple craftsmanship. There were four parts and, of these, the tunic baffled him the most. Unlike anything he had ever seen in his entire life there was not a seam from top to bottom. Upon finishing the examination he returned the garments to the Centurion.

"And what do you wish me to do with these, sir?"

"Throw them down and let those jackals scavenge them," the Proconsul snapped. "We have no further use of them and neither will the prisoner."

A mild throb began in Shem's temple which made him aware that his headache could return at any time. Although he was never one to consider prayer, he prayed he would be spared the pain this one time.

"It is time," the Proconsul said. "...for you to see the prisoner."

Shem nodded he understood and followed the Proconsul to another group of soldiers surrounding a man wearing nothing but a breech clout. The man stood motionless with a faint hint of a smile on his lips. His hair and beard were mildly disheveled. The soldiers parted as the Proconsul approached, opening a path up to the prisoner.

"This is your man." The Proconsul pointed. "Your duty is to confirm that this man, and only this man, is dead today. Do you have any questions?"

"None, sir," Shem said softly. "May I examine him closer?"

"Of course," the Proconsul said. "I want you to be absolutely certain of the identity of this man."

"Certainly..." Shem approached the man. "...you can trust I will perform my duty as you require."

The man stood straight and tall. He was at least half a foot taller. His eyes were crystal clear, projecting a native intelligence that gave Shem a chill. He slowly circled the man examining every inch of his body. He found no evidence of any scars or blemishes. A more perfect specimen he had never seen

121

outside some ancient statues in another land. Having completed a complete circuit around the man, he stopped in front and faced him. Their eyes met for the first time. Shem felt another chill and a sudden feeling of understanding that this was no ordinary man standing before him. He wanted to ask a thousand questions, but knew that the circumstances forbade it. The man, comprehending, simply smiled. Suddenly, Shem felt that his understanding was complete.

"I think that is enough," the Centurion barked. "Step aside so we can proceed!"

Shem receded from the man maintaining eye contact with him. A flood of emotion brought tears to his eyes. For the first time, he knew he was in the presence of the Master, the One who had been foretold by the Prophets to lead the people to freedom. He felt helpless there was nothing he could do to forestall the inevitable. He started to speak to the man but stopped by acknowledging a change in the gaze from his eyes warning him not to.

The soldiers roughly grabbed the prisoner by both arms, carried him over to scaffolding lying on the ground and placed him on it. Two other men had already been spiked on identical scaffolds on either side. The man neither cried out nor flinched as each spike was driven through his hands and feet. The expression on his face remained serene. When he was firmly secure, the three scaffolds were raised upright into deep holes in the rocky ground.

"Come with me!" the Centurion said. "You will wait by the Proconsul's tent until you are needed again."

Shem nodded, glanced once more at the Master and followed the Centurion back to the tent. Endless thoughts and feelings swirled through his mind. For what reason had fate led him to this time and place he wondered. He began to feel that he was part of some mystical cosmic plan. The more he thought about it, the more intense the pain became in his head.

"Centurion, may I sit down?" Shem said weakly.

"Sit where you like," the Centurion said flatly. "The wait shall not be long. After they have suffered for their crimes, we will break their legs and hasten their death."

"Is that always necessary?" Shem said carefully. "Surely death is inevitable under the circumstances."

"Not always," the Centurion said. "Once the sport of it is over, the end sometimes has to be assured so we can all go home."

The sky continued to darken. A light breeze slowly increased to where the soldier's banners were fluttering briskly in the wind. The entire landscape became a bleak panorama of death and dying. The man on the middle scaffold spoke, but was too far away for Shem to comprehend what he said.

"I hate these spectacles," the Centurion mumbled.

"What did you say?" Shem turned to the Centurion.

"I said I hate these spectacles," he said. "If a man is to be executed, do it quickly and with honor. There is no honor or glory in this style of punishment. This is the coward's way of shunning responsibility; entirely without benefit to the Army or Empire."

"I see you are a critic as well as a soldier," Shem said. "I find that a refreshing light in all this insanity."

"Not all soldiers are stupid, unthinking brutes." The Centurion laughed. "I might even surprise you about my thoughts of history, art and literature."

"I assume then you can read and write," Shem said. "Not many of your kind are given the luxury of such an education."

"But I was," the Centurion said. "I was born into an aristocratic family. Unfortunately, politics in the capital bored me and I sought fame and glory in the conquests of the Army. If I had known that I would end up here, or so many other places like here, I would have stayed home in the comfort of my family."

"But something very important is happening here, right now," Shem said boldly. "That man in the middle is going to change the world as we have known it."

"Somehow I have felt what you say." The Centurion nodded slowly. "There was something about his eyes that spoke to me."

The ground shook beneath their feet. The sky became pitch black and the wind howled through the trees.

"Do you believe there is a power above man, Centurion?" Shem pulled the cloak his wife had given him around his shoulders.

There was a blast of cold air and the Centurion visibly shivered. "I'm not sure of anything, besides I'm not paid to think."

"You should at least have an opinion." Shem smiled. "Everything we see around us had to come from somewhere."

"Why couldn't it always have been this way? Does everything have to have a beginning and an end? Why can't life

123

be like a river, constantly in flux, its origin and destination always unknown?"

"That's an interesting proposition. I consider myself an agnostic who is always open to new ideas. I am even willing to consider that the man in the middle over there may be who he says he is."

"Without proof?" The Centurion shook his head.

"I would need more than I know now to accept him," Shem said. "Although when I looked into his eyes, I felt an almost mystical presence."

"I am afraid we are both too late to get an answer to our question of divinity." The Centurion sighed.

"Except, that if he should return from the dead," Shem said. "That would be the ultimate proof of divinity."

The Centurion grunted and nodded. A wail of voices came from the crowd gathered around the condemned men. A soldier ran back to the Centurion.

"Sir, we have broken the legs on two of the men and they have died," the soldier said breathlessly. "The man in the middle is about to die. His legs have not been broken yet. Shall we break his legs now?"

The Centurion looked toward the execution site and took a deep breath. "No."

"As you wish, sir..." The soldier saluted and returned from where he had come.

"It is time for us to go forward," the Centurion said. "Come with me."

Shem and the Centurion stood at the foot of the scaffolding of the man in the middle. Women were weeping and soldiers were beginning to disperse. A team of soldiers pulled each scaffold out of the ground and laid them flat. A big brawny tanned soldier removed the spikes from the dead men.

"They are all dead." The Centurion smiled with confidence. "It is now your job to certify that it is so."

"When may I examine the body?" Shem said softly.

"Do you want to examine him now? Or would you prefer to see the body laid out?"

"Whichever you prefer..." The pain in Shem's head intensified.

A man approached from out of the crowd. He was dressed simply in black. "Who is in charge of these bodies?" The man addressed the Centurion.

"I am," the Centurion said gruffly. "What interest do you have in these men?"

"I am to deliver the man in the middle to his tomb, sir" the man said politely. "His friends and family have asked I do this."

"You may have the body as soon as…," The Centurion started to say when Shem collapsed to the ground.

The Centurion quickly knelt and supported his shoulder. Shem shook his head several times, protesting he needed no help. Once back on his feet, the Centurion led him back to the tent and insisted he rest. Shem reluctantly agreed.

"I will let this man take the body to his tomb," the Centurion said. "You will examine the body just before they seal it. That will give you a few extra moments to take some nourishment and collect your strength."

"I feel fine," Shem said.

"And I know better," the Centurion said quickly. "You will follow my orders!"

The pain in his head had subsided again. Shem knew that the Centurion was right in insisting on rest and nourishment. He gladly accepted a bowl of hot soup and a crust of bread. He soon felt his strength returning.

"Shem, are you well enough to proceed?"

Shem woke up with a startle realizing he had fallen asleep. He had no idea of how long he had been sleeping undisturbed.

"How long…," Shem started to say.

"I decided to let you sleep until the body was finally in the tomb," the Centurion said. "I hope you feel better and rested."

"I am ready," Shem said crisply. "Please lead the way."

They left the tent following a well-worn path into an outcropping of rocks nearby. Into the side of a massive formation of rock was an entrance leading into the funerary chamber. The body of the man was laid out on a slab platform of solid rock. The man who had brought the body stood nearby at the foot of the corpse. Shem stepped up to the side of the body and began his examination.

"This is the same man executed on the middle scaffold." Shem turned to the Centurion.

"Is the man dead beyond all question?" The Centurion stood stiffly. "You must be positive beyond all doubt."

125

Shem carefully examined the skin. He noticed a stab wound in the left side he had not seen before. "What is this?" Shem pointed. "I thought nothing was to be done to hasten this man's death."

"I am sorry to say that one of the soldiers became a little overzealous."

"Did the man die from this one? Or did he linger on?"

"He did not appear to die or be affected by what you see," the Centurion said. "Both blood and water were seen to come from the wound."

"Blood and water? How strange," Shem mumbled and bent over the wound.

At the mouth of the wound Shem saw traces of blood and what he assumed was water. He removed several instruments from the pouch hung around his waist. Using a blunt probe he scraped some of the dried blood into several typical flakes. The water was still wet which was curious since it had been hours since the man had died. When he touched the water, it felt like oil and was slippery.

"Shem," the Centurion interrupted. "I will leave you to your work. I shall return shortly."

The Centurion and the man standing at the corpse's feet silently exited the tomb. Shem noticed the walls of the tomb reflected the light of the lamps like so many pieces of glass. He went over to the wall and saw it was almost as smooth as polished glass. He wondered what could have possibly melted the rocks. Wasting no further time he returned to the corpse. The body felt warm to his hands. There was no pulse in the neck veins nor was there any visible pulsation of the heart. He pressed his ear to the chest and heard nothing. With a sharp probe he stimulated all the sensitive areas he was aware. The dead man remained completely unresponsive. He was about to put his instruments away when he had a sudden thought about the open wound. Certainly the mystery of the oily liquid needed an answer for himself, if no one else.

First, Shem brought a lamp closer to look as far into the wound as possible. He could see nothing but darkness. He started to use one of his instruments to probe the hole, but changed his mind. I will use my finger, he said silently to himself. He inserted his right index finger into the wound. He was surprised to feel several cords and what felt to be a box. The temptation was to use a knife to open the wound further to see more clearly what was inside. He thought about it a moment and decided he

126

could justify his action as necessary to the conduct of his investigation. The man was beyond a doubt dead. No harm could possibly come from opening the wound. Besides, this would be the only opportunity, getting official permission posed too great a delay.

Shem took a knife from his pouch, examined the blade for sharpness and brought it toward the wound. He had not noticed he was no longer alone. Two men in shining garments had come up behind him.

"Stop!" a strong voice said.

Shem almost dropped the knife. He turned around embarrassed he had not heard the two men come up from behind.

"I'm sorry." Shem blushed. "I did not hear you. My ears are not as sharp as they used to be as when I was younger."

"Has he put the knife into the hole?" the one said to the other.

"No, it seems like we have arrived just in time."

"Who are you?" Shem said. "I have never seen anyone dressed like you before." He was puzzled.

"Does it matter how we are dressed?" the one with a strong voice said. "Please step away while we examine the body ourselves."

"Of what interest is this man to you?" Shem said slowly. "Are you his followers?"

"In a way you might say we are both followers and believers." He laughed.

"I don't understand," Shem said softly.

"I think it would be very difficult for you to understand it all," the man said. "Needless to say you have nothing to fear from us. We are here to help you and all peoples like you."

The other man huddled over the corpse in such a way that Shem could not see what he was doing.

"If you are here to see whether I have done my job properly," Shem said. "I can positively testify this man is dead."

"I'm sure the Emperor will be pleased with your report." The man laughed. "Except, that sometimes appearances are deceptive."

"A dead man is a dead man," Shem said flatly. "There is no room in-between."

"Are you sure your eyes have seen everything?" The man chuckled. "Rigid thinking sometimes blinds the mind's eye to what really exists."

"I am not sure what you mean." Shem hesitated. "But there are several curiosities about this corpse I have never seen before."

"And we interrupted you before you could go any further," the man said.

"Yes, you did," Shem said firmly. "I have worked with the dead all my life and have never seen or felt a wound such as the one in this corpse's side. I do not know how to explain it."

"Open your eyes, Shem, the answer is before you." The man smiled.

Shem stared at the man's face whose eyes had a similar expression as the corpse when it was alive. The thought soon weighed heavily on his shoulders that he was in the presence of entities greater than man. With this realization Shem dropped to his knees trembling and prostrated himself. Tears came to his eyes.

"Please forgive me," Shem cried out. "In my blindness I did not recognize you!"

"Shem, get up," the man said kindly. "We are not who you think we are."

Slowly, Shem raised his head and stood up. He was confused. Who were these men if they are not angels, he wondered.

"Shem, we come from a place very far from here." The man smiled. "But we are every bit as mortal as you are."

"I don't understand." Shem trembled.

"Calm yourself," the man said kindly. "You have nothing to fear. You came to witness the death of the Master and in that task you have succeeded. Perhaps you would like to witness the whole truth."

"And what is that?" Shem said slowly.

"We came from a civilization far advanced from any that exist in your world. We have come at a time to help direct the course of history along more benevolent lines," the man said.

Shem stood speechless. The other man continued doing something to the corpse he could not see. Nothing was making any sense.

"Before I go any further," the man said. "Step over to the Master with me."

They both moved closer to the corpse. Shem was unprepared for what he saw. The other man had opened a large door in the abdomen. There were strange boxes and cables

128

inside. The normal contents of the human body were totally absent.

"There is some damage, but not anything I can't fix easily," the other man said. "Although the bloodline was damaged, none of the organics were affected. In fact, there is more of a problem with the hydraulics. That spear tore into the main reservoir spilling almost all the fluid. Unless we can get enough fluid, I won't be able to get him mobilized as planned."

"There is time," the first man said. "Call the mothership. They should be able to deliver what we need in one rotation of the planet."

"I'll call immediately," the other man said.

"What does all this mean?" Shem mumbled.

The first man turned to Shem and put his right hand on his shoulder. He turned Shem to face the corpse.

"Shem, in front of you is the future," he began. "You may not understand any of it now, but give it time; I think you and your children will."

"I still don't understand," Shem whispered.

"My poor simple man," the man said with sympathy. "There are beings in this universe that are far more advanced technologically than yours. It is possible to do things that you cannot even begin to imagine. Each star in the sky represents a sun that may have worlds such as yours revolving around it. Traveling between stars is possible as our presence here today proves. We have come to redirect history so that someday soon your race may join us."

"Why?" Shem said slowly. "Why are you doing this?"

"The history of my planet is one of a long hard struggle to find meaning and direction. After centuries of warfare and eventual peace, we finally got our act together and began achieving advances that made everyone's lives better. Soon after, we began exploring our nearby moons and planets. When we eventually discovered how to breach the vast stellar distances that separated us from distant systems we encountered other civilizations. At first, we tried introducing our technology immediately. That led to more than a few disasters and mass extinctions. Then we discovered it would be far better to bring change by establishing a set of beliefs the people could endorse and grow with. These beliefs would engender all the principles of love and peace. The transformation would not be overnight, but considering the distances involved between our worlds there was no rush."

129

"But you are gods," Shem said softly. "There is no other explanation."

The two men looked at each other and smiled. They knew a true understanding of what they were doing was far beyond Shem's comprehension.

"Do you want to examine the Master closer?" the man near the corpse said. "Stand on the opposite side, over there."

Shem stepped over to where he was invited. The various parts that seemed to have no order at a distance clearly were well organized when seen close up.

"What sort of magic is this?" Shem said.

"Technically speaking," the other man said. "This is a cyborg, part organic, part machine, the ultimate union of the organic and inorganic world. Part of the Master is human and part is not."

"These are words I do not understand," Shem said. "It makes my head hurt to even try to think about it."

"No doubt..." The other man laughed. "If you do think about it long and hard enough, it will make sense to you someday."

"Is the Master dead?" Shem said slowly. "He seems to be, but from what you have told me I don't know what to believe now."

"You will report to the Emperor's agent that the Master is dead," the first man said firmly. "But for your sake the Master is not really dead, he is merely on low level standby."

"Our plan is to have the people believe the Master is dead, then bring him back from the dead in a few days," the other man said. "This will reinforce everything that the Master has been teaching across the land these last three years. We want the people to believe in the divinity of the Master and the infallibility of his words."

"Are you not afraid that I now know the truth?" Shem smiled wanly.

"As we have said before," the first man said. "All we want from you is to certify that the Master is dead. For that we will reward you handsomely. You and your family will have nothing to worry about for a long time to come."

"And if I refuse?"

"Who would believe you?" The man chuckled. "How can you begin to explain that which you cannot even explain to yourself? I think you understand what I am saying."

"Yes, I think I do," Shem said.

"You must leave now," the man said. "The Centurion will return soon. Remember everything we have said and it will go as we have planned."

"I will do as you have said," Shem said. "Will I see you again?"

"Perhaps, but I don't think so." The man smiled. "Our work is nearly done here and we have other worlds to convert."

A lancing pain shot through Shem's head that almost left him breathless. He brought his hands to his temples trying to restrain the pain; tears came to his eyes.

"Are you ill?" The man said softly.

"It is nothing," Shem whispered. "It is a pain that comes and goes. I will be fine in a moment."

The man pulled out a strange instrument from one of his pockets. He wrapped what appeared to be a piece of cloth around Shem's left arm. The cloth instantly squeezed his arm tightly before Shem could react.

"Do not fear anything," the man said. "The pressure will stop soon."

The pressure relieved itself slower than it was applied. A series of numbers appeared on a square piece of cloth in the center of the encircling band.

"My goodness!" the man said loudly. "Your blood pressure is dangerously high."

"What does that mean?" Shem said as the pain receded.

"It means that you must take care of yourself better or you may have a stroke or, worse yet, die," the man said.

"I am not afraid to die," Shem said boldly. "I have led a long life."

"Even so, you can live longer if you take care of yourself better," the man said. "You must eat moderately and avoid excessive amounts of salt; mild exercise would also be of benefit to you."

"These things sound so strange," Shem said. "My wife and mother would have me do the opposite."

"Trust me for the best advice, Shem," the man said. "I sincerely want you to enjoy the rest of your life and watch the glorious advent of the new age, the beginnings of which you have witnessed today."

"You are right." Shem appeared momentarily confused. "I must go home."

"First, report to the Centurion," the man said.

131

"Yes, of course." Shem retrieved his instruments and headed out the entrance.

"Remember, Shem," the man said. "Report the Master is dead and nothing else. May you live a long and happy life. Goodbye."

Outside, the air hung heavy with darkness and moisture. The Centurion and the man who had brought the Master to the tomb approached slowly on foot. Shem waved he acknowledged their arrival. The Centurion came immediately up to him; the other man walked briskly carrying a bundle of clean white linen.

"Have you accomplished your task?" the Centurion said flatly. "I assume you had enough time."

"The time was more than adequate," Shem said. "I performed a complete examination as you required. I certify by my oath of allegiance to the Emperor that the man who rests in this tomb is dead as we know death to be."

"That is good." The Centurion smiled. "I have a document for you to affix your seal and your duty will be complete."

They quickly left the tomb and returned to the Proconsul's tent. On a table within was a preprepared document of death upon which Shem added his signature and seal. The Proconsul was visibly pleased and handed Shem a small bag containing five gold coins.

"Thank you, sir," Shem said. "May I now return to my wife?"

"Of course," the Proconsul said. "The Centurion will accompany you on your way. And again I must say the Emperor thanks you for your service today."

"It was nothing." Shem sighed. "It was my duty."

The Proconsul momentarily frowned, then waved to the Centurion they should depart. The Centurion led Shem outside to the awaiting horses. The journey home seemed considerably longer than that coming.

"It has been a long day," Shem said barely audible over the hoof beats.

"Yes, indeed," the Centurion said. "I'm glad the whole bloody mess is over and can be forgotten."

"I'm not so sure it will ever be forgotten," Shem said drowsily.

"I have seen many executions like this one," the Centurion said. "And they are all soon forgotten no matter what has been said before him."

132

"I think this time there will be a difference," Shem said louder. "There is something about this man that is going to change everything. I don't understand it myself but I know it is going to happen. I have witnessed more than any mortal has a right to see."

"Don't talk foolishness, Shem." The Centurion scowled. "You don't want to be labeled an enemy of the Empire."

"Certainly not," Shem said. "But I have seen..."

The pain struck Shem like a lightning bolt. Shem's mouth dropped open and his eyes rolled back into his head. He slumped forward and slowly slid off the horse landing softly onto a patch of greenery. Gurgling sounds came from his mouth.

The Centurion dismounted as fast as he could and rushed to Shem's side. He felt powerless, there was nothing he could do to help the poor old man, except cover him with a blanket until the fit was over. As soon as he thought it was safe, he placed Shem back on his horse and strapped him secure. Shem seemed aware of his surroundings but was incapable of speaking.

Within the hour the Centurion arrived at Shem's house where his wife was anxiously waiting. She recognized immediately something was wrong when she first saw them in the distance.

"Shem, my husband, what is wrong?" Rebecca said tearfully. "Why do you look so?"

"He is mute," the Centurion said sadly. "He had a fit on the way home and has been like this ever since."

The Centurion carried Shem into the house where Rebecca had prepared his bed. It became apparent Shem had suffered a stroke with paralysis of the left side of his body and loss of speech.

"Are you comfortable, my husband?" Rebecca said warmly. "You are safe at home in your own bed. You never need worry about anything. I am here for you always."

Tears came to Shem's eyes. He tried to speak aware he had lost the power to do so.

"What is it you want to say, my husband?" Rebecca drew closer.

The Centurion stood silently behind her feeling the sadness of the occasion. Shem's lips slowly began to quiver and both the Centurion and Rebecca felt a rise in their spirits that Shem may have recovered his voice. They both drew closer.

"The stars, the stars..." Shem barely whispered. "The stars, the stars..."

Rebecca smiled and touched her husband gently on the cheek. She turned to the Centurion. "My husband and I thank you for all you have done," she said, "I understand him and all his needs."

The tears streamed down his face. Shem tried to tell them, but they would never understand. He knew the truth and it was all in the stars.

The Missionary

The gibbous moon reflected off the glassy mirror surface of the lake, illuminating the terrain with a soft yellow glow. A gentle cool breeze whispered through a copse of trees standing several yards from the landing craft. It was not until the necessary supplies for the mission were unloaded and the landing craft gone that the missionary took the time to appreciate his new surroundings. He had been fully schooled in his goals, but still had momentary doubts he would be able to succeed under the primitive conditions he knew existed on this world.

The trip across the vast distance from home had been arduous only to the extent that in hibernation his consciousness was bombarded with continuous lessons he was expected to impart on the pagan natives of the destination. This was his first assignment abroad and, in spite of any shortcomings in preparation, he was chosen for his innate ability to rise to unexpected challenges with aplomb and success. No one had set foot on this world since it was first discovered. From the time of its discovery until now, long range optical and electromagnetic scanners had gathered as much as could be possibly gleaned from such a great distance.

A streak of light arcing to the east was the last link to the past he would see in a long time to come. In fact, he relished the thought of being by himself to meditate and feel closer to the great forces of the universe which focused his life. He would succeed, even if he had to martyr himself, although in the history of the missionary movement not a single acolyte had been killed. There had been injuries through misunderstanding and misgivings, but even those could certainly have been circumvented with patience and tact.

The howl of a distant coyote broke the mesmerizing effect of his thoughts. Time enough for circumspection, he mused. Now is the time to provide shelter for the immediate present and future. An inflatable cube shelter was quickly set up as a temporary home for the remaining night. Morning would mark the beginning of the real work to come. He stowed everything properly away, sat back, and turned on the monitor to the local electromagnetic bands. With a few adjustments, he was watching a regional weather report. This report was followed by

135

an extra headline item about a fiery object observed falling out of the sky in the nearby vicinity. He smiled at the utter simplicity of his new flock. When he was done, they would no longer be pagans and, that, he bet his life on. At the end of the news program, he retired for the night and fell into a deep dreamless sleep.

Consciousness returned when the discomfort from his bladder overcame the pleasure of sleep. He opened his eyes and found the day was well into the morning hours. A brief stretch in one direction then the opposite and he sat up on the side of the cot. Clumsily, wriggling his feet into a pair of slippers, he finally stood and shuffled out through the airlock looking for an appropriate place to micturate. A short distance away, he found a suitable tree and took care of business. When he finished, he took in a deep breath and exhaled audibly. The weather portended to be nothing short of perfect for the day.

Looking toward the lake he saw a small boat with a single occupant fishing several hundred yards offshore. His heart raced with a twinge of fear and excitement at the first visual contact. For all he had been briefed and from what he now saw the being he saw on the boat was every much as human as he was. He knew there must be differences but none he could see interfering with the mission. The man in the boat turned his way and waved. He instantly returned the wave with a sweep of his hand through a broad arc above his head. The man in the boat reeled in his fishing line, started his outboard motor, and headed straight toward him. The missionary swallowed hard and smiled. All great journeys begin with the first step.

The man cut off the motor several yards from shore and the boat gently slid onto the mud bank. The man nimbly jumped ashore with a line from the bow and tied it securely to a low-lying scraggly bush.

"Hello," the man said warmly. "Hope you don't mind me stopping over for a chat. I've been sitting out there half the night by myself and I could use a little conversation."

The missionary was relieved to hear the man speak in one of the languages he had become fluent. "It is a pleasure to have your acquaintance and conversation," he said awkwardly.

"I'm sorry to be a bother," the man hesitated. "I'll leave you, if you object." He began untying the rope from the bush.

"No," the missionary said quickly. "I was not expecting company so soon. Please forgive my manners. Please come join me for a few moments of conversation. I can certainly use some real-time talk. I'm afraid all I've had to converse with is a bunch of electronic equipment for a long time."

"I understand." The man from the boat laughed. "I like to get away from the hustle and bustle for a while, but then I feel I need it to appreciate the quiet."

"Are you a philosopher?" The missionary said slowly. "I detect a wisdom out of the ordinary."

"Nope..." The man smiled. "It's just plain old common sense. Everybody knows it's true, but nobody ever says it."

"I understand." The missionary nodded. "Are you from around here?"

"No, sad to say my home is in the city were life isn't near as tranquil as it is around us right now. And yourself?"

"I was born and raised in the city, but recently I have spent many private moments alone," the missionary said warmly. "My life is dedicated to universal truth and its spread to wherever I go."

"Am I to understand you are a philosopher?" The man grinned.

"As you are not, neither am I," the missionary said politely. "However, every worthwhile intellectual and spiritual endeavor does generate many philosophical truths."

"So! You are a philosopher!" The man laughed loudly. "You proclaim otherwise but your words give you away!"

"Wait a minute, my friend." The missionary held up a hand and blushed. "You misunderstood me. I am not a philosopher. I am merely a man sent on a mission. What I mean to say is that, in general, whatever we do comes with an opinion whether it is right or wrong. Without any stretch of the imagination it can be called philosophy. But I do not question what I do; I follow the true path as dictated by those before me. I do not philosophize on my mission. Therefore, I am not a philosopher!"

"I'm sorry if I've ruffled your feathers." The man chuckled. "But it seems you are a little too sensitive on the subject. Would you care for some coffee? I have a thermos in my boat."

"I would be delighted." The missionary smiled warmly. "I'll get a couple of cups."

The man crawled back into the boat and retrieved a thermos while the missionary went into the shelter for the cups. The missionary produced and set up a portable table with two chairs. The man poured coffee into the cups and they sat down to resume their conversation.

The missionary lifted his cup to his nose and sniffed. The aroma was wonderfully appealing. He slowly put his lips to the rim of the cup and tilted the cup upwards. The hot coffee bathed his tongue with a taste he had almost forgotten.

"This is splendid," the missionary said slowly. "I don't think I've tasted coffee this good in a long time."

"I'm glad you like it," the man said. "The blend is one of my recent discoveries."

"Your discovery?"

"Sure." He smiled. "There's a little gourmet coffee shop back home that's just opened for business. I sort of discovered the place by accident on my way to work one day. I'm sure you've discovered places like that."

"It has been a long time since I've had that opportunity." The missionary's sighed.

"I can't believe you have let yourself miss some of the finer things in life." The man smiled. "I learned a long time ago that the simple things around us, such as the open air, blue sky, freshwater, songs of the birds and so many innumerable events all around us, are precious and capable of giving nearly divine pleasure. That may sound a little hedonistic, but when tempered with a touch of spiritual mysticism it begins to make practical sense."

"You speak as if you have a deep spiritual background," the missionary said slowly. "I like that in a man."

"From where we both sit..." The man looked around. "I would say we both share the same views. Am I right?"

"To be sure!" The missionary laughed lightly. "To be sure! And what is your name if I may ask?"

"Only if you reveal yours in turn..." The man smiled. "I think that is only fair."

"Of course..." The missionary nodded. "My name is John Starr and yours?"

The man took the missionary's extended hand and shook it firmly. "Jay Blaze," the man said warmly. "Good to meet you Mister Starr."

"No need to be so formal." The missionary smiled. "John would be fine, just John."

"Just John." The man grinned. "Then I'm just Jay."

They released their grip on each other's hand and settled back to resume the original conversation. Although the sun had risen considerably, the temperature remained tolerably comfortable. The surrounding trees and foliage burst alive with the sounds of birds and insects.

"Now that we have the formalities behind us," the missionary said slowly. "Tell me something about yourself, Jay. From what you have said in so few words I'm sure you are a wealth of ideas."

"Only if you honor me with the same, John," the man from the boat said. "I always prefer dialogues to one-sided conversations."

"You are a man of my own heart," John said. "Where there is a dialogue, we can certainly learn more than the sum of what we have to say by ourselves alone."

"Are you going to sit as my analyst?" Jay raised his brow. "I would prefer we simply have an open conversation between communing souls."

"That we tacitly agreed," John said quickly. "But delving into ourselves makes more interesting conversation than talking about the birds and bees. I want to know who you are and not anything else. The rest I can get from other sources."

"You are a feisty one." Jay exhaled. "I like that in you. Although you don't know it yet, I'm of a similar disposition. We are most probably kindred spirits."

"For the moment, I'll take that as a genuine compliment," John said flatly but not without a hint of warmth. "Please tell me something about yourself."

Jay took a long sip of coffee, put the cup down and inhaled audibly. "There is nothing in my past I have not shared with every person I have ever met. I have a family tree that includes the various expected assortment of relations. I had a childhood I survived into adulthood, becoming educated in the ways of the world as I grew up. The obligations of adulthood have forged my duties and work. I am the sum total of all of the above and more. I am generally at peace with myself, but in spite of that I still strive for a more perfect future."

"Certainly you must ascribe more importance to the individual events in your life than what you say," John said carefully. "I know in my own experience my relationship to my parents was very pertinent to what I became in my life."

"And what have you become?" Jay leaned slightly forward. "From outward appearances I have no idea who or what you are."

139

"I agree my past shares everything you claim is ordinary in your own," John said. "What I have been trained to do was first described to me in my family. Without their direction I'm not sure I would have found my profession."

"And what is that?" Jay said slowly.

"I…" John choked. He realized he had somehow lost control of the conversation. "I thought I was asking the questions."

"You are." Jay smiled. "Please forgive me if I've led you in another direction. I really don't mean to control."

"I think you are a professional manipulator." John exhaled. "My guess is you are a government official of some sort; maybe even military."

"Not even close." Jay laughed. "However, I am a man with a mission. I am in search of souls to save, one of which I hope is yours."

"Your assumption is presumptuous," John said sharply. "Who are you to even begin to infer my soul needs saving? It's my mission to spread the words of truth and ultimately save souls. I have been trained and taken vows."

The two men stared silently at each other. John knew eventually he would come face-to-face with a holy man of the world he was assigned but did not expect to encounter that person on his first day. Perhaps this was a good omen; he was favored to have rapid success. However, there was something still unsaid that made him feel uncomfortable.

A stirring in a bush behind the cube habitat attracted their instant attention. Neither moved watching the foliage move. A small brown rabbit tentatively poked its head forward. With nose twitching the rabbit sat motionless, took one last sniff and retreated back into the underbrush.

The missionary shifted uneasily in his seat and took another sip of coffee. The man from the boat stared where the rabbit had been. He relaxed and looked back at his cup sitting on the table.

"The world is full of rabbits," Jay said. "Soft, furry and timid..."

John thought a moment and added, "The universe is full of rabbits. It is not a sin to be soft, furry or timid. In fact, it is these characteristics that make civilization possible."

"I don't think so," Jay said flatly. "You confuse the result with the origin. Society undermines all those characteristics that help to bring it about; retrograde progress, if you like. The more advanced, the less need to remain educated and alert, therefore the end result is ignorance and sloth."

"What you say has some truth to it," John said. "However, I fully disagree with your final conclusion. If a civilization advances the mind and soul where acts of violence are unnecessary, that does not mean the existing society has become helpless. There is more strength in cultivating the spirit than in anything else."

"I am beginning to see you are a man sent to save souls as you said." Jay sighed. "There is no use arguing over issues that are no more than a matter of opinion."

"There is a lot to be gained by examining the issues you have raised," John said softly. "In fact, there is nothing I would enjoy more than to explore your beliefs and try to explain mine to you."

"Would you still want to speak to me if I told you I am an instrument of a power that will sweep across this galaxy?"

"What do you mean?" John said slowly. "An instrument of what?"

The man from the boat stood and pulled from inside his jacket an object that could be nothing but a weapon. The missionary nearly fell backwards as he rose to stand.

"I don't understand." The missionary gasped. "I am a man of peace and the spirit. There is nothing to fear from me."

"Put your hands in the air and step out into the open away from the table," the man from the boat hissed. The gentle features he had had were replaced with an expression of a hardened military professional. "Remain cooperative and no harm will come to you. First, I will examine you for hidden weapons. Slowly turn around and face the water."

The missionary complied in slow motion. He had been prepared to anticipate resistance but overt hostility was another thing. He was on a mission of peace and nothing more.

"And is your name really Jay?" The missionary barely whispered. "I have a feeling you're hiding more than you have revealed through your words and actions."

"To you I remain Jay." The man from the boat patted the missionary down.

"Jay, this is foolish," the missionary said softly. "I am a man of the spirit sent to this world to spread the universal word. I want you to listen to what I have to say. You are the first person I have encountered since…" He paused. "I arrived."

141

"Do you take me for a fool?" Jay growled. "Arrived from where? And I assume your name is what you claim it to be."

"My name is John," the missionary said carefully. "And I come from a place a lot farther away than you can possibly imagine."

"Ha!" Jay ejaculated and pointed upward. "How about from up there? Surely I came from a place you have not even thought of."

The missionary turned slowly. Jay stood tensely standing, holding a hand weapon pointed at him. "You are an extraterrestrial?" John said carefully. "You have led me to believe that your home was nearby. I don't understand the need for deception on your part. What is your specific mission?"

"I'm beginning to think you are a little more than thickheaded," Jay said. "Yes, I'm an extraterrestrial if that is the word you like. And I'm here as an advance scout for a military expedition in the name of the Emperor Arax IV."

"My, what a coincidence..." John smiled. "I am familiar with your world. I even think my world has a mission there."

"What are you talking about?" Jay sputtered. "You're a native of this planet. There has never been any contact between us ever!"

"I'm afraid you haven't understood what I just told you," John said warmly. "I'm not from this world. I'm a missionary."

"A missionary? A damn missionary!" Jay almost yelled. "What are you doing here? This is supposed to be unexplored open territory. I claim all rights in the name of the Emperor!"

"I think we need to talk this over." John put his hands down by his side. "Neither of us gains anything by arguing. I am prepared to petition for the souls of this world if you will listen. Are you agreeable?"

Jay thought a moment and lowered his weapon. "What do you have in mind?" He paused. "I don't think there is anything to negotiate."

"But at least you are willing to listen to me," John said. "Put away your weapon and let us sit down. I'm sure there is a way we can both walk away from here satisfied."

"I doubt that," Jay muttered, put away his weapon and sat down.

John sat down and poured some fresh coffee. "This puts a strange twist on my mission."

142

"No stranger than mine." Jake coughed as he sipped coffee. "My orders are to pave the way for complete submission of this world by force, if necessary."

"Suppose I told you that force is never necessary." John smiled. "Ideas are far more powerful weapons than any physical force. Force results in counterforce which in turn is met with greater force. The end result is always destruction and more destruction. Who wins when all the good parts have been used up and gone? On the other hand, words can form ideas that in turn mold and shape actions. Ideas once they are planted cannot be destroyed. They have a perpetual growth and immortality. Resources are not destroyed and if the ideas prove unworkable nothing is lost except the time it took to consider everything in a new context. I know I can conquer this world with the ideas of the spirit. Are you so sure you can do the same by the forces you have at your command and still have something worthwhile in the end? I don't think so."

"This is a primitive world by all standards," Jay said. "There is nothing I have seen so far that would deter me from proceeding."

"I think you miss the point." John sighed. "This world does have its own set of ideas and will defend them to the end if necessary. Every creature of creation will defend its home against an enemy. Forceful actions will result in nothing for anyone."

"And you think your way is better?" Jay said slowly. "Ideas have a curious way of stagnating and preventing progress. Force is like plowing the soil in preparation for a new crop."

"Perhaps force and ideas go hand-in-hand," John said slowly. "Ideas can be thought of seeds that hibernate until they find the proper soil to grow. However, the plows that stir the soil need not be violent."

"Nothing ever gets done if left to itself," Jay said quickly. "Only action brings reaction."

"That is not completely true," John said. "All good and worthwhile things come with persistent hard work, thinking and above all patience. Nothing of lasting permanence was ever accomplished instantaneously."

"A slate must be erased before it can be used again," Jay said. "The old must make way for the new."

"No great book was ever written by destroying what was previously recorded," John said. "New ideas always bring up old ideas. Once the fundamentals are mastered, programs can move

143

forward. Destroying knowledge of the fundamentals forces everyone back to the beginning. Therefore, there is never any progress."

"Force does not necessarily mean the past is eliminated," Jay said. "It would be foolish to start way back at the beginning."

"Then you agree with me." John smiled. "That a dialogue as possible?"

"Possible?" Jay hesitated. "Yes, possible."

"We are making progress," John said. "From here we can begin our dialogue."

"I still remain to be convinced," Jay huffed.

From behind them came a rustle of foliage followed by the sudden appearance of a man aiming a rifle in their direction. The strange man rushed up to the table in an obvious state of excited alertness. "Put your hands up!" the man growled. "Get up and stand away from the table!"

Jay started to reach for his weapon. John noticed and signaled him to stop. Jay stared back frustrated but yielded temporarily.

"Who are you? And what do you want?" John said calmly. "We were simply enjoying a cup of coffee on a fine morning. Would you like some?"

"Shut up!" The man shouted. "I'll ask the questions! You're trespassing on private property! You have no rights as long as you are standing on my land!"

"We apologize," John said coolly. "Let us pack up our things and we will be on our way. We had no intent of abusing your privacy."

"It's too easy to say I'm sorry and walk away without any responsibility," the man said slowly. "I'm tired of people coming here and trashing up my land."

"We had no intent..." Jay said. "...to mess up anything. We were simply enjoying the moment and about to move on."

"Is there some way we can make amends?" John said quickly. "I'm sure as civilized people we can come to some meeting ground."

The man with the rifle remained motionless staring at them. He slowly surveyed the campsite noticing the boat tied at the edge of the lake. He looked back at them and sneered.

"I don't see any mess yet," he said roughly. "I guess you can thank God that I am a forgiving man. Pack your things and get out of here. I'll stand over there just to keep you honest. And be quick about it."

"Did you say God?" John said slowly. "Are you a religious man?"

"What's it to you, if I am?" the man said cautiously. "I don't think it makes any difference whether I believe in God or that rock over there. You still have to get off my land."

"And that we will as quickly as we can," John said. "It's only I didn't expect to find anyone here who understood about a universal spirit."

"I'm no atheist!" the man spouted. "I may be rough around the edges but I read my Bible and go to church every week."

"Please," John said calmly. "I only mean to say that I am happy to hear you have a concept of a higher power."

"Who are you anyway?" The man said slightly less hostile.

"My friends name is John Starr, a missionary," Jay interrupted. "And my name is Jay Blaze, a...friend."

"Hm..." The man exhaled. "I guess you want to know my name too."

"It is the civilized thing to do." John smiled.

"Lazarus Potts," the man said flatly.

"Good to meet you Mister Potts," John said warmly. "And do you have a family?"

Lazarus looked at Jay. "What's with your friend and the thousand questions? Doesn't he understand I have better things to do than stand out here gabbing with a couple of fools?"

"I am here in the name of the spirit that guides all of our lives," John said. "Where two or more are gathered together there can always be a celebration of the spirit. In this meeting today we can glorify the past, the present and the future to come."

"You're nuts." Lazarus coughed. "I'm not here to listen to holy nonsense."

"There is nothing more serious than the spirit," John said softly. "It is through the spirit we live and move forward."

"Mister Lazarus, my friend and I were having a discussion about the spirit and changes that can be made by force," Jay said. "I think you have clearly demonstrated that force in this situation is superior to words. He who has the bigger stick wins."

"Don't put words in his mouth," John said. "I don't think Mister Lazarus understands the importance of this chance meeting of all of us together here."

145

"What do you mean importance?" Lazarus squinted. "I find two trespassers on my land which is pretty clear cut against the law. But now you guys are talking about things that don't seem connected to anything."

"Let me explain to you who we are." Jay smiled. "We are…"

"Do you think it's wise to let him know?" John interrupted.

"Let's let Lazarus decide," Jay said boldly. "I'm sure he can choose what he will believe and accept."

"What are you two talking about?" Lazarus shook his rifle at them. "You're not making any sense."

"Put your weapon down," Jay commanded and stepped forward. "We will soon be gone without a trace of ever having been here."

"Stay where you are!" Lazarus shouted, pointing his rifle directly at Jay's chest. "I need no tricks here."

Jay froze in his place and raised his hands to the level of his shoulders. He smiled wanly and retreated slowly back to his original position.

"Lazarus, I am a man sent with a message for you and your people," John said warmly. "I am here to teach you the way of the universal spirit."

Lazarus stood speechless.

"The universal spirit permeates all that surrounds us," John continued. "We are all children of the light that emanates from the spirit. It is in good works and good deeds we move in the right flow commanded of us. The only true force is the force of faith. Violence yields nothing, faith builds strength."

"You sound like a preacher on Sunday," Lazarus said dryly. "I have nothing against religion, but I'm still against trespassing."

"That is understandable," John said. "Please accept my humble apology for our intrusion."

Jay nodded a tacit approval of what was said.

"Hm," Lazarus squinted. "I guess I can be a little more trusting to a holy man."

"Perhaps you would like a cup of coffee before we leave." John smiled.

"I…" Lazarus hesitated and lowered his rifle. "I think I've been acting too harshly. Yes, I will have a cup of coffee."

"Please sit down with us," Jay said.

"No tricks?"

"No tricks," John smiled.

John unpacked another chair, set it up and three men sat at the table. Lazarus remained wary and kept the rifle tightly in his hand. They slowly drank the freshly poured coffee in silence.

"Do you know where the nearest public settlement is?" John said.

"Nearby," Lazarus said. "But you should already know that."

"Why?" John said.

"Because that's the only way you could have gotten here." Lazarus gripped his rifle tighter. "How do you explain being here?"

"Because we both came from up there..." Jay laughed and pointed upward.

"What?" Lazarus gasped and almost fell back out of his seat. "You must be kidding!"

John shot Jay a scolding look. "We flew in by air is all he means to say," John said slowly.

Jay saw momentary confusion and whipped out his weapon. Lazarus nimbly leapt to the side raising his rifle in one clean motion. John stood up and backed away from the two men.

"I knew I couldn't trust you," Lazarus sneered. "You better put that thing away or I'm going to blow a hole where you're standing."

"You're bluffing." Jay darted to the side and fired his weapon.

"Lazarus, watch out!" John shouted.

Lazarus dropped to his knee and fired back. Jay slumped forward as blood began soaking the front of his shirt. He fell face down in the dirt without saying anything.

"Is he dead?" John barely whispered.

"A professional never misses." Lazarus grinned. "It looks like I arrived at the right time."

John stared at the dead body until he realized what Lazarus had said. "At the same time?" John shook his head.

"You don't think we'd send you on your first mission alone do you?" Lazarus laughed. "All novices are protected regardless of their graduating credentials."

"You're from my world?" John said weakly. "Are you really from home?"

"Missionary, you have a lot to learn," Lazarus said firmly. "You need to learn some very basic survival skills. The first is never to trust until that trust is deserved."

"Who sent you?"

"I am from home," Lazarus said. "My job is to protect you, only I didn't think you would need my help so soon. I saw your friend over there land several days ago. From what I was able to understand his mission was one of military conquest. You're lucky I was here."

"But as a missionary I have come in peace," John said. "There was to be no violence."

"From here on I don't expect you'll be bothered." Lazarus smiled. "Just think of me as part of the spirit that always protects you."

"And what do I do now?"

"As the spirit moves you." Lazarus laughed and disappeared into the foliage.

John stood alone confused. It was not supposed to start this way. It was all wrong. But it was not for him to question for now. He did have a mission and that he would do. The last advice was right, he would move as the spirit moved him.

Dawn was clearly underway as the overhead sky lightened and the first hint of daylight appeared on the eastern horizon. The green flash came and went without much notice. Several miles offshore a solitary traveler was putting out to sea. Although it was late October, the coast was unusually warm for New England.

"Are you sure this is the place?" Bill was never reluctant about accepting an assignment, but he felt the current one was a wild goose chase. If anything, he wished he were back in his warm bed, snuggled with his pillow.

"This is the exact place. I'm sure we'll find the evidence we need to confirm it as soon as the sun gets up a little higher." John faced every assignment with absolute enthusiasm. For him getting up in the wee hours of the morning was the beginning of an adventure.

"It's hard to believe a UFO went down here without any witnesses." Bill never accepted anything at face value. It was a characteristic for which he was well-known and endeared him to no one.

"It was confirmed by one weather and two military satellites. I hardly think three separate, simultaneous sightings could be anything but genuine." John knew Bill well and was not deterred in any way from his enthusiasm or belief in the matter at hand.

They walked along the rocky edge of the water, carefully searching for anything unusual. There were the usual flotsam and jetsam everywhere in the first direction they went. In the opposite direction, Bill spotted a gold colored sphere floating several yards from the shore. John went back to the Jeep and brought a long handled net which easily reached the object.

"What is it?"

"I'm not sure." Bill turned it over and over in his hands. "It's a shiny gold ball some child could have lost and nothing more. I can't find any connection between this and our assignment."

"Let me take a look at it." John took it in his own hands. "It's extremely light for its size and has no visible seams. The surface is as shiny as a mirror which…"

"Which doesn't prove anything; I know what you're thinking, but you accept too much with too little evidence."

149

"No, not really..." John smiled. "I am willing to make an assumption and allow further evidence to either prove me right or wrong. I'm not in the habit of discounting anything on face value. I think you miss too many important things that way. I'd rather be proven wrong after committing myself than being wrong for missing something because I discounted it. I think you know what I mean."

"Do what you have to do." Bill sighed. An argument was futile and he knew it.

John bounced the ball in his hand. "I'll concede this time you might be right about this but I will still hold onto this for a while. Are those footprints in the sand?" John slipped the gold ball in his backpack and pointed to a sandy patch of beach ahead.

"Let's take a look." Bill stepped forward first. "It's hard for me to believe an extraterrestrial visitor would cross countless light years of space only to crash on our tiny insignificant speck of dust. Just think of the gross incompetence that would represent."

"Excuse the expression, but shit happens." John grinned. "Besides like any well-traveled road there are hazards in space: take for example meteors, comets, planets, stars, cosmic dust, black holes..."

"Okay, okay, you've made your point." Bill exhaled. "You're beginning to make me feel sorry for the poor soul that crashed last night."

"Oh, ho! So you believe!"

"No," Bill said quickly. "It's just, if it were true, I would have sympathy. Right now I commit myself to nothing."

"Hardhead!" John snorted. He reached the patch of sandy beach one step ahead of Bill. "What do we have here?"

"There are tracks of some sort of giant bird." Bill pointed. "And they lead up to that grassy dune over there." He crouched down on his knees and looked at the prints closer.

John examined the prints, pulled out his camera and photographed them.

"They are large enough for an ostrich, if that's what you mean."

"No, all the birds I know have three clawed toes not four. I don't think these are the tracks of any bird we know." John put his camera away and walked toward the dune.

"Mother Nature pulls some pretty funny tricks," Bill said flatly.

150

"How many four toed ostrich size birds are native to New England?"

"I don't know?" Bill held back a smile. He was willing to accept some of the new evidence but did not want to give in too easily. It was a matter of principle.

At the crest of the dune John found a torn scrap of silver cloth. He examined it closely and passed it to Bill who put it in his own backpack. One hundred yards away was a beach house with a car pulling up to its front door. Without hesitation they walked toward the habitation; a young man with sandy blonde hair and horned rimmed glasses waited by his car.

"Hallo!" The young man shouted. "How can I help you fellas?"

"Do you live here?" John waved. "We're investigators looking into an aviation accident around here. It happened sometime last night. Do you know anything about it?"

"My name is Jeb and this is my place, but I only use it on weekends." The young man extended his right hand.

"I'm John Davis and my partner here is Bill Stavros." John grasped Jeb's hand and shook it firmly. "Does that mean you weren't here last night?"

"I'm afraid not," Jeb said softly. "But the reason I'm here is to make sure my house is secure. One of my neighbors did call there was a big flash of lightning and thunder last night even though there was no rain."

"Do you know what time that occurred?" Bill said quickly.

"He said it happened about midnight," Jeb said slowly. "I can already see my house is okay."

"Do you mind if we look around?" John scanned the immediate area as he spoke.

"No, not at all...Is there any way I can help?"

"Just follow us around and point out anything you consider different," John said.

They circled the house twice before they found another set of bird tracks. John took another set of photos while Bill scribbled notes for future reference. In the meantime, Jeb lost interest and simply waited by his car until they finished what they were doing. Jeb was late for work and was anxious to be on his way.

"Thank you for your assistance." John handed Jeb one of his business cards. "If you hear or see anything unusual, I want you to give us a call."

151

"Sure will." Jeb got into his car without much ceremony and left John and Bill to follow the new tracks in the direction of nearby woods.

Upon reaching the woods Bill noticed several red and green feathers at the base of a tree. Whatever they were following had stopped to rest at this spot. In addition to the footprints appeared buttocks (?) and handprints (?).

"Are you a believer yet?" John smiled. "This isn't an ordinary beast that we're tracking."

"I can agree with part of that, but I'm still not sure of the extraterrestrial part." Bill was not ready to admit anything even though the evidence was compelling.

"The problem is you think from the perspective of an anthropomorphic human. Intelligent life can occur in any warm-blooded species with the proper grey matter." John felt it necessary at times to lecture. This was one of those times. "The Earth has never been at the center of the sentient universe and probably never will be. If we find what we are looking for, I am sure I can prove we are not alone in the universe."

"Make me believer." Bill shrugged his shoulders; the lecture was an old one he had heard many times. Only the genuine article would ever bring him around.

The tracks found on the beach continued into the woods. John stopped and took a few more pictures while Bill examined the surrounding foliage. There was a rustling sound ahead.

"There's something moving," John whispered.

Bill nodded and signaled silently to proceed ahead. John agreed. They move cautiously without the intent of either startling their quarry or being ambushed. With the trees surrounding them it became obvious what they were doing was dangerous. John was about to suggest calling for help when he caught a flash of movement.

"There!" John pointed. "We've almost caught up to him!"

"You've scared him!" Bill yelled angrily. "He's running away!"

"Let's go then!" John started running.

"Wait!" It was too late. John had already disappeared ahead. Bill had no choice but follow.

"I see him!" John shouted.

Bill caught up with John who was standing in a clearing looking confused.

"Damn! I lost him!"

"What did he look like?"

"Out of this world!" John laughed.

"I need details." Bill sighed. "Are you sure you didn't see a deer or some such animal?"

"Absolutely! It looks like a man-sized dinosaur, only not exactly."

"Tell me more." Bill was skeptical.

"When I found him, he apparently had tripped over a root because he was sprawled on the ground. I tried to approach as nonthreatening as possible but he appeared terrified and scrambled to his feet. I waved at him to stop but he ignored me and dashed away."

"Don't keep me in suspense. What did he look like?"

"Like I said, he was about your height with a sauropod–like body. He had two clawed feet and two short arms with clawed hands with an opposing claw. He had a short stubby tail and some ambiguous genitalia that he was trying to cover with his hands."

"What? That's ludicrous! A modest alien!"

"I know that sounds funny but that's what he did." John paused and took a deep breath. "He has two large yellow-green slit pupil eyes, flat round nostrils and a large mouth with more teeth than you and I have put together. He's covered with something between a cross of scales and feathers, all brilliant green and bright red…"

"Did he seem to be hostile in any way? Did he snarl at you?"

"No, nothing at all," John said slowly. "Except, I saw intelligence in his eyes, and, of course, fear. We have to catch up to him and prove we mean no harm. I don't think we can do anything except follow him while the trail is fresh, otherwise, we may lose him forever or he might have an accident and get killed."

"Do you think that's wise?"

"I don't think we have any choice." John began moving. "This is the discovery of the century and we must follow it through. You can go back now, if you want, but I won't stop until I've made complete contact."

"You can't brush me off that easily." Bill followed close behind. "We're partners to the end!"

John stopped, faced Bill, and grinned. "This has nothing to do with becoming famous, does it?"

"Not at all..." Bill smiled. "I just want to do my job properly."

"In that case let's spread out. You go to the right; I'll go to the left. Stay within earshot at all times."

"Yes, boss." Bill laughed. "You always like to be in control."

John scowled a moment and laughed. "I'll admit it this time, but never again, so enjoy it while you can."

Several hours later they converged on a small toolshed next to an old dirt road and granite stone wall. They remained certain they were close behind but had not caught another glimpse of the alien. John took a drink of water from a flask and passed it to Bill scanning the surrounding area as he did so.

"I must admit this guy is slippery," John said slowly. "I would have thought we would be on top of him by now."

"It's possible we could have passed him without knowing it."

"I don't think so. We've been too careful. I think he's closer than we think. For all we know he could be watching us." It was a little into the afternoon but with the overcast sky it seemed much later. John glanced at his watch and motioned to continue.

"Hey! There he is!" Bill pointed up the dirt road. "He just crossed the road about fifty yards that way."

Running up the road, John darted into the brush about halfway, thinking he could get to the alien faster. Bill ran to the point he saw him enter, noticed the tracks and followed the trail.

"I see him! He's not far ahead of me!" Bill panted.

"I'm on my way!" John shouted. "I think I see him!"

Bill ran straight into trouble. His left foot caught an immobile rock and tumbled face forward onto the ground. As he hit the dirt he lost consciousness. John heard the sounds of falling and turned toward the noise.

"Bill, where are you? Are you all right?" There was no answer. "Bill?" A chill went down John's spine. Suppose I've underestimated the dangers of this situation, he chastised himself. If anything serious happened to Bill, he would certainly feel responsible forever.

A light breeze wafted through the trees with an audible hiss of the leaves. The sky darkened overhead with a rumble of thunder in the distance. A wave of fear swept across John's body.

"Bill, where are you?" John's throat tightened and his mouth became dry. "Please answer me!"

John noticed the alien up ahead with his back to him intently leaning over something on the ground. He hoped that something was not Bill. Approaching as stealthily as possible, he confirmed his worst fear. The alien was doing something to the unconscious body of Bill.

"Stop! Leave him alone!" The moment of decision had arrived. John lurched into action screaming at the top of his lungs, waving his arms in broad sweeps through the air.

The alien was startled, jumped back from Bill's body, and turned toward his oncoming pursuer. His face contorted into an undecipherable expression. Whether it was fear, anger or laughter was anyone's guess. The alien looked down once more at Bill, stood up, and ran off in the opposite direction before John managed to get more than twenty-five yards away.

"Bill, wake-up! Are you okay!" John forgot about the retreating alien and stayed on his knees beside Bill's body. "Say something!" He shouted.

Bill began to stir as John placed his fingers on the carotid pulse. He opened his eyes and blinked several times. "What happened?" He spoke thickly.

"You've had a bad fall," John said softly. "Do you hurt anywhere? I don't see any blood."

"I'm all right," Bill said slowly and struggled to his feet. "It'll take more than a little fall to put me out of commission."

"Are you sure?"

"Yes, I'm sure and don't worry about me. We need to get after our friend."

"Your so-called friend was about to do something to you. When I came up he was leaning over you."

"I wonder what he wanted." Bill examined himself closely and noticed several buttons were undone on his shirt.

"I don't know, but we need to be more careful. There is something strange about this whole situation." John started walking off in the direction the alien had gone. "If you feel up to it, let's go."

"Lead the way." Bill rebuttoned his shirt and followed.

Fifteen minutes later, the rain began. Undeterred by the inclement weather, they pressed onward. The alien's tracks were clear. There was no sign of any inclination to deviate from the initial direction. Once or twice they lost the trail but soon picked it up again by proceeding in the same direction. Soaked to the bone they came to an open field in which on the opposite side was a large red barn. They could see the alien approach the barn, look over his shoulder in their direction, and disappear into its front door.

"I think we have him now," John said. "Once we get there I think we can trap him."

"How are we going to do that? We didn't bring anything with us except the camera and I don't think you mean capturing him on film."

"Regardless of what he looks like we have to assume he is sentient. And, if he is, we can communicate. And, if we can communicate, we have accomplished our mission." John smiled.

"That's a lot of ifs." Bill was not sure communication was possible. The alien appeared too monstrous to have anything in common with human life, but that was his opinion.

"You think too much like the vast majority of mankind." John felt the lecture was necessary. "In reality, there is intelligence all around us here on our planet. The form intelligence takes is dependent on the needs of the organism whether microscopic, plant or animal. I know what you're thinking. Yes, microscopic life and plants can be sentient in their own way. The reason we can't see it is twofold: one, we are not physically capable, and two, we have nothing in common to communicate. We have more in common with this alien than anything else on our planet. Sure he's different in appearance, but he did come from a place light years away and that takes intelligence nearly identical, if not greater, to ours."

"I see your point." Bill found it difficult to disagree with John. The whole issue would be cleared up when they confronted the alien face-to-face. Flesh eating aliens were only a figment of the imagination. Or were they?

"I don't think it is a good idea to approach the barn across the field. We'll follow the edge of the woods around. If he tries to leave, we will be able to easily spot him."

Bill approved the plan. The rain lightened to a soft drizzle. Overall it remained dark, gloomy and very wet. The trees offered some protection but not much. Although they were soaked, they ignored it. The route they followed to the barn was nearly ten times the distance across the field. They both kept a careful watch in case the alien decided to move on.

"The more I think about it, the more I agree we are following an intelligent being," Bill said. "At least he's in a dry shelter while we're out here like drowned mice."

156

"Are you saying he's more intelligent than we are?" John smiled.

"What you think?" Bill grinned. "The only persons doing anything stupid are us."

"Speak for yourself." John laughed. "Besides you complain too much. This will all be worth it in the end. Just think of what we are about to accomplish. We will be celebrities with the media clamoring to interview us. We will write a book and live very comfortably from the royalties. We will buy and do all those things we have always dreamed about but could never afford. What we are going through is worth all of that."

"Suppose this thing turns and eats us," Bill said grimly. "For all we know we could be fooled by it."

"Leave it to you to think of the worst," John sniffed. "You've been reading too many comic books. Reality is never exactly what the imagination creates. You have to think positive to get positive results. Think negative and you will get bitten on the butt. Have faith, proof is not far away."

The door the alien entered was wide open. Approaching as carefully as they could, there was no way they could remain unseen much longer. They decided to split apart with Bill taking the rear wall. John continued to the entrance in front. Unless the alien had become invisible and escaped, they felt certain he was still in the barn.

John entered the open door pausing to allow his eyes to accommodate to the darkness. The barn was empty of equipment and livestock. There were several bales of hay in the far back corner. Looking upward he instantly recognized this was an easy place to stage an ambush. The high upper level loft was the most likely place the alien was hiding. Hugging the walls, John worked his way around the entire inside circumference of the barn, forever on alert of a surprise attack from above. In the back, he unlatched the rear door and let Bill in.

"Well, what you think?" Bill whispered. "Do you think he's still here?"

"Yes." John looked upward. "And I think he's waiting for us. I don't know what his game is, but as I see it, we have the odds on our side. This is our planet and we now outnumber him two do one."

"What if he's armed?"

"I don't think he is," John said. "He wasn't carrying anything nor was he wearing anything. Unlikely he has any weapons on him."

157

"What about special powers like death rays from his eyes?"

"Your comic book mind is getting in the way of your good sense again." John shook his head. "I'm willing to bet that our elusive friend, no matter how different he looks from you and me, is just an ordinary mortal with ordinary physical capabilities."

"Regardless, I wish I could be as comfortable as you. You must admit we are the first to make contact with an alien intelligence."

"Yes, and I'm sure all our specialized training has not really prepared us for what is about to happen. It takes a great deal of faith to leap into the unknown with only wits, common sense and a little knowledge. But sentient life must be able to recognize sentient life otherwise it isn't sentient. The danger here is allowing our fears overcome our rational senses." John was lecturing again but Bill did not mind. At least this was a short delay of the inevitable.

"Do you have a plan now that we have him trapped up there?"

"First, we need to get out in the open where he can easily see us and us him." John pointed to a place at the front door. "Once in position, we will put down everything we are carrying. Empty your pockets slowly so he can see what we're doing. We should then move away from our things and raise our hands in the air. At that point, I'll do the talking. All you have to do is remain calm and don't move unless I tell you to. Unless he understands our language, it will be a while to establish some simple signs of communication."

They walked slowly to the spot John had indicated, removed their backpacks and emptied their pockets. Stepping six paces back they raised their hands in the air carefully watching for any sign of movement in the loft. The only sounds were those of the wind outside and an occasional creak of the barn itself. Nothing moved.

"Hello," John shouted. "We know you're in here. We have come to meet with you. We are friends. Do not be afraid."

The loft was silent as the rest of the barn.

"We will wait as long as necessary until you feel comfortable with our presence," John continued. "We mean you no harm. We are the selected representatives of our planet to greet you. I'm sure you can't understand what I'm saying but I hope you can feel the nonthreatening tone of my voice."

158

The loft remained silent. John turned to Bill and shrugged.

"How long do we wait?" Bill whispered. "What if we're wasting our time talking to the air?"

"That is a possibility." John squinted. "But I don't think so. I think our friend may be afraid of us and our intentions."

"What do you propose to do next then?"

"Wait...Just wait," John said. He put his hands down by his side. "You and I are going to stand in our places until I say otherwise."

Bill grimaced and put his hands down. There was no use arguing; the protocol was correct. An hour later, the ambient light dimmed. Bill checked his watch. It was time for the sun to make its descent below the horizon. The rain had completely stopped and night was not far away.

"It's going to be dark soon," Bill said. "Do we continue like this or try something else?"

"Let's take a break outside for a moment," John said. "Leave everything where it is."

John led Bill back to the woods. Bill followed without question. Nature called and needed relief.

"We'll wait out of sight for about half an hour, then we'll sneak back." John rubbed his temples with the tips of his fingers. The stress gave him a headache. He was hungry, thirsty and tired. However, this was too important to give up. He did have an unvoiced doubt the alien may not be in the barn, but he tried not to think about it. If they failed in their mission, he would take full responsibility.

Within a half hour it became quite dark. Bill silently lamented they had left their night vision goggles in the barn. Before Bill knew it, John had darted back toward the barn. Bill quickly scrambled after him. At the door, John waited for Bill. John poked his head into the darkness slowly with Bill following. Suddenly, John moved rapidly inside leaving Bill somewhat confused. As his eyes adjusted to the darkness, Bill saw John standing where their things had been obviously examined and taken apart.

"Looks like our friend is curious," Bill said.

"At first glance, I'd say so," John said. "But he could've also been looking for something."

"Like what?"

"Check your things. Are you missing anything?"

159

John sorted through his things, repacking them one by one into his backpack.

"My silver Mylar blanket is missing," Bill said slowly. "Everything else is here."

"Mine is missing also. That's strange. Now why would he want our blankets?"

"I don't know." Bill absently repacked his things.

A noise came out of the darkness at the back of the barn and they froze in place. They looked at each other then slowly turned in the direction of the sound.

"It's him," John whispered. "I think we've come to our moment of truth. Get ready."

"I'm ready," Bill lied.

Ever so slowly a vaguely familiar sight emerged from the dark. It was the alien wrapped with the Mylar blankets holding his claws up in the air. He came to within several yards of the two men and began a series of sounds.

John smiled and raised his hands as before. "He's trying to communicate with us. Raise your hands like before."

"You're the leader." Bill choked. His mouth was so dry he could hardly speak. He was glad he relieved himself outside before coming back.

The alien's face moved in ways that resembled some human expressions. John stepped forward extending his right hand. The alien blinked several seconds in silence, extended its right claw, and stepped forward. Hand met claw for the first time. John squeezed the alien's claw gently and nodded with a smile. The alien returned the squeeze and nodded in return.

"I think we've made a new friend," John said warmly.

The alien withdrew its claw slowly making sounds that were totally unintelligible. John looked at Bill who simply smiled back and shrugged his shoulders. At least they had started a dialogue.

"John," Bill said. "I just had a thought."

"And what is that?"

"I realize why our friend was running away," Bill said slowly.

"Don't keep me in suspense. Tell me!"

"You don't meet strangers naked for the first time." Bill grinned.

"You mean…" John hesitated. "He was embarrassed?"

"Among strangers it's best to be dressed." Bill laughed. "Besides don't clothes make the man."

160

John blinked, thought about it and laughed. It was ridiculously true.

The warm orange disk of the setting sun kissed the ocean as the day quickly passed into dusk. Peter stood alone at the water's edge contemplating everything and nothing at the same time. In a few short hours, he would be back at work exploring the arcane wonders of the night sky. Even this nearest star was interesting for its proximity and size. A lifetime is not enough, Peter sighed.

The sky behind became noticeably darker with first Venus then Sirius winking into view. Untold numbers of stars were also there and Peter felt them. The twinkling song of childhood brought a warm smile to his face. He wondered if anyone else felt the same way he did. There were secrets out there that defied discovery. Yes, a lifetime was not enough to even begin.

A dog ran up from behind and barked. It startled him out of his reverie. He turned and saw his partner Tom jog up behind his dog, Moonbeam.

"What's up?" Peter smiled and crouched low petting Moonbeam, nuzzling his knee.

"Just exercising the old bones..." Tom was without a hint of being out of breath. "...clearing the old cobwebs before we hit the skies tonight."

"I wish I could be as dedicated as you." Peter laughed. "You do everything with a passion I can't even come close to."

"Regardless." Tom waved a hand in front of his face. "You still get all the bright ideas."

Peter thought for a moment. "We both do, except you follow with more, shall we say, passion than I do."

"Passion has nothing to do with it." Tom shook his head. "And besides this conversation is nothing but a non sequetor."

"I agree." Peter laughed. "I'm ready to get back to work. What about you?"

"A quick shower and a change of clothes and I'll be with you."

"Good." Peter gave Moonbeam one last pat on the head and stood up. "I'll meet you at the lab in about an hour."

"Do you want me to bring anything?"

"No thanks, I already ate."

"Okay, then, an hour!"

Tom spun around on his heels, whistled at Moonbeam and ran back in the direction he had come. Peter smiled and turned to watch the sun sink below the horizon. Beauty in everything and it was everywhere, he mused: all you had to do was appreciate it.

By the time Peter had showered and dressed, it was nearly 8 o'clock. He thought to call Tom about an idea he suddenly had, but instead wrote it down in his personal idea book to discuss later. The drive to the lab was uneventful. Peter noticed Tom's car already parked and the lights on inside. If I ever get here ahead of him, I'm going to worry, he smiled to himself.

A bright orange-red streak suddenly traced a line in the overhead sky moving east to west. Peter's smile turned to a grin as he wished upon the falling star. He knew it was childish to do so, but it did not do any harm and it felt good. If nothing else, he was reminded of his happy childhood many years ago in a far different place than this distant tropical island he now lived and worked.

Inside the lab, Tom greeted Peter with a wave. His glasses were down near the tip of his nose, defying gravity, and a newly sharpened pencil was firmly gripped between his teeth like a horse's bit. He picked up a stack of paper, pulled the pencil out of his mouth and exhaled loudly.

"What's the matter?" Peter said softly. "You look upset."

"I am upset," Tom said loudly. "The damn creeps in Washington have voted to decrease our operating budget again! How do they expect us to get results if we don't have the money to continue our work?"

"Calm down," Peter said slowly. "That appropriations bill still has to get by the President and I have it on good source the President will not allow any cuts to our program. We're going to keep on doing the same old thing until we have to convince a new President of the necessity of our work."

"I know all about it. But I still wish politicians would stick to politicking and leave the science to professionals."

"Unfortunately, you and I know the realities." Peter smiled. "The real world moves only through, by, and with politics. The only two ways to change the way things work is to become a politician or completely ignore the system and do what we want regardless."

Tom smiled. "Which I guess we do anyway, don't we?" He chuckled. "When I really think about it, we don't have it all so bad."

164

"Why don't we forget about the outside world for a while and explore our own? We have some new vectors to try out tonight."

"I've already set them in. I've just been waiting for you to officially get started."

Peter walked over to his console and sat down. Quickly flipping through a checklist, he nodded everything was in working order. Tom sat at an adjacent console and went through his own checklist. When Tom finished, he flashed an upraised palm to Peter who nodded acknowledgment.

"First, scan all frequencies," Peter said.

"In progress..." Tom flipped several switches.

The room was eerily quiet. Tom shuffled his feet and Peter nearly sneezed. Unable to stand the quiet, Tom turned on a speaker to the incoming signal. Expecting a squawk or unbearable hiss they were surprised by music with a vaguely familiar melody.

"Sounds like we have some interference tonight..." Tom sighed. "Just when I thought we could relax."

"Run through the usual checks while I reference tonight's satellite data," Peter said calmly. "It's not as if we haven't had this problem before."

"Sure." Tom tapped instructions into the computer terminal. "Except, just once, I would like one of these false alarms to turn out to be extraterrestrial. Isn't that what we're being paid to find. Aren't we supposed to prove there is intelligent life out somewhere?"

"Before you get started on a lecture, could you prove to me there is intelligent life here by just doing your job." Peter grinned. "Even if there is intelligent life out there trying to reach us, I'm not so sure they will find intelligent life here."

"You don't have to go any farther, I get the point," Tom said slowly. "Sometimes I think we are wasting our time, sitting here fiddling with this electronic equipment listening to noise."

"Except, what may be noise to us may be someone else's music." Peter was attentive to the data on the monitor. "From what I see the satellite data indicates we have an almost perfect night for listening. What have you found so far?"

"I've run through the interference program and get an all clear. I don't believe it, but that's what it says."

"That music sounds too familiar to be anything but interference. Run your checks again."

165

"I did run it twice and I got the same result. The signal is coming from somewhere outside of our planetary neighborhood."

"I'll change the vectors of our listening," Peter entered new parameters through the keyboard. "If it's interference, nothing will change. If it's a real signal, we have a problem."

The instant the direction of listening changed, the music disappeared and was replaced by the universal background hiss. Peter looked at Tom and Tom looked back at Peter. An unusual circumstance, but no real proof a breakthrough was at hand. Peter quickly reentered the original listening coordinates. The music was replaced by a well-modulated signal far closer to the one expected from an extraterrestrial source.

"Do you think...?" Tom held his breath. He was afraid to state the obvious.

"Made contact," Peter said without hesitation. "I'm not sure. We've had many false alarms before."

"But none like this," Tom said quickly.

"I remain to be convinced," Peter said flatly. "My science is based on facts not speculation."

"I've begun recording. We should soon get an idea of what we're receiving before too long!"

After entering additional instructions, Peter sat back placing both hands behind his head. "It's just a matter of time."

"It's always just a matter of time," Tom said. "We keep listening and never hear anything; at least not what we are supposed to hear. Maybe all of this is wishful thinking. Maybe we are alone in the universe, or maybe we are in such a far-off corner we don't count for anything as far as being worth communicating with. Even if we do eventually hear someone and return a response, we won't be alive to know if the message ever got through."

"Are you saying this is all a waste of time?" Peter yawned. "Every time you have outside interests, our mission takes on less importance. Do you mind telling me what's really bothering you?"

"Please," Tom continued. "My outside life has nothing to do with how I feel at the moment. I've been giving a lot of thought to what we are doing. It all looks good on paper but in actuality we are stuck with endless hours, weeks, years of boredom for a possible single moment of excitement. It no longer makes any sense to me."

166

"Aren't you a little bit excited when we get a signal like tonight?" Peter smiled. "It will most likely turn out to be nothing, but doesn't the anticipation make your pulse run faster?"

"Yes," Tom said slowly. "But I still want the genuine article, I want butter not margarine."

"Have patience and someday you will be rewarded." Peter leaned forward. "Are you watching your screen? What do you make of it?"

Tom stared at the monitor for several minutes tapping instructions into the keyboard. "This is different," he said with eyes wide open. "I've never seen this pattern before, but before I get too excited we need to recheck everything."

"Agreed..." Peter nodded. "I'll start feeding some of the initial signal into the computer and then recheck the equipment."

They worked silently, rechecking everything they could possibly think of. After an hour and 15 minutes, the incoming signal repeated itself. Tom initiated recording the second repeat on a separate recorder. The computer continued to analyze the original signal.

"I've checked the Sky Atlas several times," Peter said. "There is no known recorded object from where this is coming."

"That doesn't mean it isn't there," Tom said. "The Sky Atlas is far from complete."

"Yes, except we started to point our ears toward a known point in space." Peter paused. "In our initial adjustments we were, I'm afraid to admit, a little sloppy. Luck favors fools and we have lucked out."

"Do you think we've actually received a true signal?" Tom stared at the monitor. "It almost looks too good to be true."

"Yes," Peter said. "Except, every additional second the computer takes to analyze the signal means we have a signal that must be rechecked several times before it can be considered genuine. We haven't had a signal that has taken this long to analyze, ever."

"Just when I was about to give up, a miracle happens," Tom mumbled.

"However, it is far from a fait accompli," Peter continued. "In a few moments, we will have our answer."

The men sunk into a deep silence while the computer continued putting the incoming signal through every possible mathematical permutation. In the end, the computer confirmed the signal was indeed genuine. At first, they were speechless. It

167

seemed anti-climactic the first message from an extraterrestrial should be received in a remote scientific outpost on a tropical island out on the ocean near the middle of nowhere. Something of this importance seemed out of place and unreal.

"Now what do we do?" Tom felt his heart skip a beat thinking about the possibilities.

"Follow protocol," Peter said. "We have explicit instructions on what to do next."

"Yes, I know," Tom said slowly. "I was just remembering what we heard in the beginning. Do you remember the music? It sounded like a familiar tune I couldn't name. You feel the same way?"

"Yes," Peter said. "I'm certain music would be one way for civilizations to communicate without words. The mathematical progressions of music are never reproduced by chance in nature."

"Look at the analysis on your screen." Tom pointed. "This signal has a tremendous volume of data to it. I wonder if it contains video as well as audio."

"It might, but we do not have a compatible receiver. I'm sure the signal is digital."

"Suppose I play with the signal and feed it through the computer, massage it a little, and see if it won't give us a picture." Tom ran his fingers lightly over the keyboard. "We have nothing to lose and besides we have a duplicate copy of the signal for the central office if we mess this one up."

"Okay," Peter said without hesitation. "I'm as curious as you are."

"Does that mean we're not going to tell anyone, yet?" Tom grinned.

"You're reading my mind." Peter smiled sheepishly. "This is too good of an opportunity to make a real name for ourselves. We do all this work in the middle of nowhere and the big shots back home get all the credit. If we make the real discoveries here, I am sure we'll be given part of the credit and fame."

"Only with a little leak to the Press..." Tom restrained a laugh.

"I agree..." Peter laughed. "...and the bigger the leak the better. First, though, we have a lot of work to do."

"At first glance, there is nothing to distinguish either the beginning or the end of the transmission. I would expect a prologue of instructions but there seems to be none. If the

168

transmission had not been repeated, I would be inclined to think this was merely a part of a single transmission perhaps an intercepted communication or commercial broadcast."

"I've often wondered, now that you mention it, what happens to all the things we radiate in the way of business and entertainment along with our scientific and military transmissions."

"Unless those types of broadcast are sent out in a specific direction, the farther they go, the weaker they become, finally diluted into the universal background noise," Tom said. "My own guess is this is not part of a commercial broadcast. It has been deliberately sent in this direction. The power of the signal is too strong to suggest otherwise."

"Of course any differences we encounter from what we expect are the product of a totally alien mind. It is wrong for us to assume whoever sends any signal should even begin to think like us."

"I'm comparing our received signal with analogous transmissions here. The computer will give us an idea of how compatible this signal is with our current television systems."

Without hesitation the computer indicated the signal was perfectly compatible with the current high definition digital television format. Tom entered additional instructions to the computer and stored the signal onto a CD-ROM disk. Peter retrieved the newly formatted disk from the computer and placed it into a nearby player connected to the television.

"Are you ready?" Peter exhaled.

Tom nodded with a broad smile.

"Here goes." Peter pressed the Start button.

At first, there was a blank screen filled with static. A hint of music was barely audible. Peter adjusted the volume. The music was much clearer and became louder. As before, the melody was vaguely familiar.

"This is what we heard before," Peter said. "It certainly sounds human to me."

"Only because you hear through human ears..." Tom laughed. "If you were an alien, you would think it sounded alien. Music is in the ear of the beholder."

"Very profound," Peter laughed. "Is there anything you can do to get a clear picture?"

"I'll try," Tom fiddled with the controls. "I am now sure there is a picture waiting for us to see."

169

A flickering picture appeared and Tom momentarily stopped and stared. Peter waved to continue the adjustments. Tom resumed manipulation of the controls and a clear picture snapped into view accompanied by the same music as before.

"What is it?" Tom made a final fine adjustment. "It looks like a picture taken from a geostationary satellite."

"Maybe it is." Peter moved closer to the screen. "A picture of any planet from space doesn't give much information."

"Since we are dealing with a digital picture, I can zoom in closer." Tom moved closer.

"We must look at everything from start to finish," Peter said flatly. "Then we can go back for details."

The planet on the screen rotated slowly. Most of the surface was covered with light from some unknown star. In the upper right-hand corner was another object clearly identified as, at least, one moon. The planet was alive with cloud formations and weather patterns. If it were not for the origin of the signal, the planet displayed could be the earth itself. A blue planet in a place far away in another time came into Peter's mind instantly. Both the music and picture began to unnerve him. There was a certain déjà vu about the experience. The more uncomfortable he felt, the more unreal his perceptions became. He began to doubt what he saw was anything but a practical joke.

"What's the matter? You look pale." Tom turned to Peter as he continued his gaze of the television screen.

"I've just had an experience of something I can't really describe," Peter said slowly. "I have some strange feelings about all of this. It's almost as if this really isn't happening."

"The fact is we have received an alien transmission. Fact is that whatever we are looking at took place so many years ago that it is ancient history. In fact, that planet may no longer exist."

"I know the physics of what I see. But there is something more to all of this than what I see. I can't put my finger on it."

"Put your feelings aside and just watch." Tom smiled. "I haven't seen anything yet to make me feel anything other than awe."

The picture flickered momentarily. A single faint flash of orange-red light appeared on the surface of the planet. Several seconds later there were half a dozen additional flashes in the same quadrant. Less than 20 seconds later another quadrant was filled with another dozen flashing lights.

"What's happening?" Tom turned back to the television screen. "What are all those lights?"

"I think we're watching the beginning of a nuclear weapons exchange," Peter said uneasily. "One side has hit this quadrant and the other side retaliates. If this is total nuclear war, we are witnessing the end of a civilization."

"Wow!" Tom exhaled. "I wonder if we'll see who won."

"Nobody wins in a nuclear war." Peter sighed. "In the end the biological record is wiped clean and life has to start over."

The picture flickered again. There were now almost too many flashes to count. Everywhere there was either a growing red glow or thick smoke coalescing with the clouds or both. The frequency of the flashes remained constant.

"Where do you think this picture is coming from?" Tom moved closer. "...a military satellite?"

"Possibly," Peter said. "But a scientific or weather satellite would provide the same image. All of those are put into geosynchronous orbit. We are probably witnessing the last transmission of this seeing-eye outpost."

"Except, that the transmission repeats itself exactly..."

"In that case, the satellite records the event and then rebroadcasts the data it has over and over again. The war below changes its orbit so the transmission is beamed out into space. It continues over and over because there is no one home to turn it off; which means there were no survivors."

"Or survivors with the right technology."

"Or survivors with the right technology."

"The end result is still the same. We are the recipients of a misguided, or rather misaimed satellite broadcast."

"It all makes sense," Tom said. "There's something coming off the surface toward us!"

"Someone wants to put this satellite out of commission," Peter said calmly.

A brilliant flash of light momentarily blanked the screen. When the picture returned there was a missile of some sort hurtling away from the camera toward the upcoming objects. The missiles exploded into a dozen smaller missiles.

"Our side seems well-prepared with the defense," Tom said. "I don't know the politics of the dispute but I'm hoping our satellite survives."

"It will," Peter said. "Otherwise how did we get these pictures?"

171

"You're right as always." Tom laughed. "It's obvious."

The opposing missiles collided in a huge explosion. A shockwave of debris scattered in all directions. The conflagration on the planet's surface below continued spreading although the number of new lights almost ceased.

"The war is over," Peter said solemnly. "There is nothing but a fire on the surface below. In a short while our satellite will be buffeted with a shockwave which will aim its future transmissions to us."

The picture on the screen gyrated violently and when it stopped the planet was no longer in view. All that was seen was a field of stars. All evidence of the apocalypse was gone. The stars stared at them until the end of the received and recorded transmission.

"Quite a show!" Tom said. "I think we're going to be famous!"

"I'm sure of that," Peter said warmly. "Let's look at it again, but this time a little slower and more closely. This is better than the best book I've ever read!"

They watched the transmission from beginning to end three times before stopping to zoom in at scenes of interest. When they did, they saw a planet with a blue ocean and what was one large landmass. The parallel with ancient Earth before continental drift was obvious to both of them. There was ice on both poles and its rotation was approximately 24 hours. For all intents and purposes they surmised this was as close to a twin of Earth there could be. At one point they focused on the lone moon and were again impressed with the gross similarity to the Earth's own.

"I can't believe what I'm looking at," Peter said loudly. "This is really beyond my wildest dreams. We received an extraterrestrial transmission and are witness to the end of their civilization. Not only does life appear elsewhere in the cosmos, it also faces the same dangers of war, pestilence, hunger and death."

"My, we're getting philosophical." Tom chuckled. "Not to say biblical."

"Everyone is going to have a field day with this." Peter smiled. "The implications are biblical and beyond. Man is no longer alone on a single planet. Creation placed him in several places throughout the firmament."

"I'm sure this will give the Fundamentalists a big headache." Tom laughed. "It'll serve them right for being so closed-minded. I can hardly wait to see what will happen."

"Do you think we can place where this planet is located? Is there enough data in the signal?"

"Let's take a look at the end of the transmission when it just shows the stars."

The scene of stars on the screen was majestic but undecipherable on simple visual inspection. Tom went to the computer, retrieved the same picture and asked the computer to analyze the star field.

"That'll keep the computer busy for a while," Tom said flatly. "Now, what about the music in the background?"

"I've wondered about that myself," Peter said. "Together the pictures and the music don't make any sense."

"Unless the music isn't music..."

"What do you mean?"

"Maybe it's not music at all. Maybe it's really a message to go along with a picture in a language based on tones similar to some oriental languages here on earth."

"Except, the music repeats itself over and over," Peter said. "Now that I think about it music is based on mathematical progressions. Could the music be data being transmitted back to the home planet? Or could it be its positioning coordinates?" Peter suddenly stopped speaking when he realized what he said.

"Positioning coordinates?" Tom thought for a moment. "Yes, positioning coordinates! It makes logical sense. The satellite is telling everyone where it is!"

"Put it into the computer," Peter said eagerly. "I want to know how far away our twin is!" Tom went to work immediately at the keyboard. When he finished he threw his hands behind his head, stretched his legs straight, and leaned back in his chair.

"We will have an answer shortly, if our assumptions are correct."

"I think they are," Peter said. "Do you remember the old Mariner probes and Voyagers? Each spacecraft had a message on it to trace it back home."

"Wasn't the message written on a metal plaque?" Tom said slowly. "The music has no written notes."

"Doesn't make any difference," Peter said. "The message remains the same."

"I've taken the liberty to analyze the star field picture and music both alone and together," Tom said. "That way we have a greater probability of coming up with what we want."

While they continued to examine the transmission in ever finer detail, the computer worked in silence. Several mugs of coffee later the computer signaled it had an answer.

"Are you ready?" Tom laughed nervously. "Are you?"

"Yes," Peter laughed. "Get ready to break out the champagne!"

Tom read the answer on the computer screen and turned to Peter incredulous. He pointed at the screen with his index finger.

"What is it?" Peter said. "What's the matter?"

"Look!" Tom was visibly shaken.

Peter moved to Tom's monitor and read the answer. He, too, was shocked at what he saw.

"This must be a joke," Peter said. "This can't be possible."

"We've been too careful," Tom said slowly. "This isn't a joke. What it says is true to the highest level of statistical probability."

"Earth, though?"

"500 million years ago."

The stunned men stared at each other in silence for several minutes. Peter started to speak several times but did not. He simply shook his head.

"500 million years ago life was just starting to evolve on our planet," Tom said. "We have always assumed there was nothing before that."

"But this is all too incredible," Peter said. "Then how do you explain the transmission."

"Simple," Tom said. "The satellite recorded what it saw, transmitted out into space and the signal was eventually bounced back in our direction. "

"An echo?"

"An echo of the past..." Tom smiled.

Dots

Last night I witnessed the spectacular celestial display provided by the collision of the upper Earth's atmosphere with a cloud of dust and rocks. I have seen meteor showers, but this was far brighter. As a potentially calamitous event, the smallness of the incoming objects was such that the cloud of dust and debris easily slipped by both our Earth-based and orbiting detectors. Fortunately for us on the earth, no real harm was done and everybody had a great time watching. I have always said it is the simple things that are the most enjoyable and at the same time most intriguing.

Although I went to bed later than I expected, I felt refreshed by the short sleep I managed to get. A strong cup of fresh brewed coffee, the elixir of life, and a glance at the news on CNN was all I needed to get my day going. There was no use in wasting the day, especially, when it was my day off. My free time is my time and I am going to use it.

A special feature on CNN described the astronomical reasons in detail of what happened in the sky last night. The shower stopped as quickly as it had started. Based on that fact, the CNN science reporter predicted no further similar displays tonight. Too bad.

Dressed in Australian split shorts and my favorite running shoes, I dashed out of the house for a daily run. The air was crisp and clean. I inhaled deeply, savoring the fresh air. The sun was barely coming up on the horizon when my foot stepped off the first pace of my usual 6 miles. I passed my neighbors' houses enjoying the quiet and solitude. Only the sound of my feet striking the ground and the gentle breeze of the wind made any sound. In a way, it was sort of eerie, but I did not think anything of it. I had other things on my mind.

I first started running for my physical health. In the beginning it was a solo activity until I joined a health club, then it became a social thing with fellow sufferers over all the miles. Once hooked, I ran races of increasing lengths until the marathon captivated me. Do not let anyone tell you that running is not an addiction, it is! There may be a lot of pain and running, but in the end the rush of endorphins makes up for everything. Running is a far better alternative to drugs and alcohol plus it allows indulging in another addiction called eating! Burn up the zillions of calories with a good run, and then make love to all the carbohydrates you can think of! I run for my health, I run to socialize, and I run to eat, but more importantly I run to think to myself. There is not much else to do except plunge deep inward as the old feet reflexly plod onward. I can honestly say I do my best thinking on my feet, my running feet that is. If you ever have a problem you need to solve, I strongly recommend you dash outside and run around the block a few times.

Not more than a half mile into my run I noticed all the cars parked along the curb were covered with a layer of dust. At first I just looked at it with a blank stare then it occurred to me there was more dust than could be accounted by an overnight stay in the night air. Several blocks later, I caught up with my neighbor Jason Hall who was putting in his mileage for the day.

"Hey, Jon, what's happening?"

"Same ol same ol," I said.

Jason nodded assent and we locked strides trying not to race each other. The temptation to test who is fastest is always present. I knew he was faster most of the time and held back because I did not want to spoil my good mood with an ego shattering loss.

"Have you noticed the dust on all the cars?" I pointed at several cars as we ran along. "Where did all this dust come from?"

"The radio earlier said it came down last night," he said flatly. "The earth passed through a large meteor shower."

"I've never seen anything like this before," I said. "The usual meteor shower doesn't sprinkle dust over everything."

"I'm only telling you what I heard," he said. "Besides what does it really matter? There's nothing we can do about it."

"That's hardly an intellectual way to look at it." I mildly raised my voice. "I would think all the dust would spur your curiosity."

"Not when it means I have to wash my car." He almost smiled. "And I don't like digging up old dirt."

For a moment I did not know what to say until I realized he was pulling my leg. He was interested, but wanted me to break the ice and forge on with the discussion. His training as a college professor was clearly showing.

"I think you're making me commit myself to the conversation first," I said slowly. "You want to know my opinion so you can either agree or disagree. By waiting to pass comment you can never be wrong. Is that what you're doing?"

"Who me?" He laughed innocently. "I would never do anything like that!"

176

We turned onto a path that led out into an open field. The wind suddenly gusted and the air was filled with dust. We had to cover our noses and eyes. Temporarily blinded we stopped running to wait for the dust to subside.

"If all this dust came down last night," I said. "Mother Earth must have put on a lot of weight."

"Shh!" He hissed, putting his index finger to his lips. "Women never like to hear they've put on weight!"

I laughed. The whole conversation was ridiculous and leading nowhere. So what if there was dust everywhere? Everything was dust to dust, was it not?

Jason kept up a swift pace which was much faster than I cared to run, but the macho in me made me silent in my suffering. Forty-five minutes later, we split company, Jason ran back toward his house and I to mine. Settling into a slower and more comfortable pace I let my mind wander. The dust soon began to edge back into my consciousness. The stuff was everywhere. The car washes are going to do a booming business today, I mused.

I was soon back home, examining my own car covered like all the others I had seen. Being sweaty and needing a shower desperately I decided to wash the car myself so I would not have to wash myself twice. A little dishwashing soap in a bucket, water from the hose, and several large towels, I attacked the grime on my car with a passion. In a way, the work was fun and gave me a chance to cool off from my run. Once I got off the dirt, I rinsed thoroughly and followed by drying with another set of large towels. When I was done I was pretty proud of the job I had done. My next job was to literally hose myself down.

Since I was alone in the house, I stripped naked in front of the washer and tossed my clothes and towels in. I streaked past the windows, hoping the neighbors were not looking but of course the foliage and fence prevented it. The hot shower felt intoxicating, immediately relaxing all my muscles. The water blasting against my face refreshed my thoughts and washed away all cares. I had really not paid much attention to the dirt on my skin before I started to lather up. There was grime everywhere that had not been covered with clothes. I ran my hands with soap across my arms several times then rinsed. Much to my surprise the dirt hung tenaciously on. I grabbed a washcloth, lathered it with soap and scrubbed vigorously. The harder I scrubbed, the redder my skin became, but the dirt hung on. Although I felt much cleaner, I did not look that way. The

177

last time I had had trouble getting anything off my skin I had been spray painting. The cloud of dust I had run through was dirt, not paint. I was beginning to think something strange was going on.

I turned off the shower and dried myself with a large bath towel. Again, I tried to rub the grime off my skin with no success. Without thinking I walked naked out of the bathroom to my study where I had a magnifying glass. Examining the dirt on my skin ever closer I saw I was covered with what I could best describe as dots, black dots, and lots of them. The next thing I knew I was frantically calling my brother, the doctor, on the phone.

"Chris, I have a problem!" I yelled into the phone as it was answered. "I need your help now!"

"Take it easy and calm down," my brother said slowly. "Tell me what the problem is."

"I have dots all over my skin," I cried. "They weren't there when I went out to run but I ran through a bunch of dust and now I'm covered with little black dots."

"Hm," he said. "Do the dots as you call them itch? Are any red? Are there any blisters,"

I carefully examined myself. "No, not yet," I said even more worried. "What you think I have?"

"I don't know," he said flatly. "It could be anything or nothing. Why don't you come over so I can examine you in person. There is not much I can advise you without knowing exactly what you have. I'll have a fresh pot of coffee ready when you get here. See you in a little bit."

I dressed as fast as I could, jumped in my car, and was on my way in a matter of minutes. Along the way I began to rub my arms, even though they did not bother me. The psychological fact I was covered with dots was beginning to play on my nerves. Before long I began to scratch at a few dots on the back of my left hand. Although the scratching felt good, it did nothing to the dots. Or did it? I knew it must be my imagination but I could swear the dots had moved away from where I scratched the most. I arrived at my brother's house before I could give it much thought.

Chris opened the door before I had a chance to knock and invited me in. I headed directly to the kitchen that I knew like the back of my hand or at least the hand I used to have. My usual mug was waiting on the table. I poured myself a full mug and refilled my brother's cup.

178

"Now, where are these dots?" He smiled. "I know this has to be a life-threatening emergency."

"It's not funny." I extended my arms. "Look at these."

Chris grabbed my wrist examining my hands and forearms, first on the back, then turned them over on the front.

"Interesting," he said flatly. "And you said these came out this morning?"

"Yes," I said quickly. "What do you think?"

"Looks like you've been painting and got some on yourself." He shrugged. "Doesn't look like any disease I've ever seen."

"But you haven't seen everything." I reminded him of an admission he made to me not long ago. "Are there any tests that can help us find out what this is?"

"A biopsy I suppose." He smiled. "But I would recommend the usual organic solvents first."

"You think this is paint?" I was astonished. I knew I was not anywhere near any paint in the last week.

"Yep..." He grinned. "A little acetone or alcohol or maybe paint thinner will clear this whole deadly disease." He laughed and I remained very skeptical.

"Hey, what's that on the back of your right hand?" I bent over to examine his hand closely. "It looks like you have some dots on you too."

"Impossible!" The smile disappeared from his face as he examined his own hand. "These must have rubbed off from you. I haven't been near any paint for a month!"

"Neither have I," I exaggerated. "Now where did your dots come from?"

"They weren't on my hand before you got here," he said. "These must have rubbed off from you." He tried to brush the dots off with his opposite hand but could not.

"What's going on?" I was beginning to get a bad feeling. "Are we dealing with some highly contagious, deadly disease that no one has ever heard about?"

"There has to be a logical explanation for this," he said as he scratched his own hand. "Every physical sign in medicine has a logical explanation." He went to the utility room and brought back a can of acetone and another with paint thinner. "This stuff will get rid of the problem immediately."

"Give me the paint thinner," I said. "I can hardly wait to get these things off me."

179

"Sure, and I'll try the acetone on mine." He handed me the can.

I soak a paper towel with paint thinner and began wiping my skin with it. I was pleased to see where I had rubbed my skin was again clear. "Look, I'm getting them off," I said happily. "I don't know how, but I must have gotten some paint."

"Don't be so sure," he said gloomily. "Have you examined the areas outside where you wiped?"

"No," I said. "I haven't." When I did look I saw that the dots had become more numerous in certain areas.

"I've noticed as I wiped the dots they seemed to get out of the way," he said. "I'm using acetone and you're using paint thinner and the dots are getting out of the way. That's not paint!"

"What is it then?" I was speechless.

"If it's a disease, it's one I've never heard about," he said. "...quick onset, highly contagious and of unknown virulence."

"Unknown virulence?" I had never heard the term. "What does that mean?"

"It means we don't know how deadly this disease is," he said slowly. "It could pass with no residual harm or it could kill us."

"Kill us!" My worst nightmare was coming on and I was hoping I would wake up.

"Quite frankly, I don't know what this is," he said. "Let's go to the hospital where I can get a biopsy of one of these dots. A quick look under the microscope will tell us a lot more than speculating probabilities around here."

I did not need to be told twice by my younger brother we needed more data. We both went in my car and rode the two miles to the hospital in complete silence.

Inside the hospital we went to a private treatment room adjacent to the laboratory. Chris told me to expose my forearms which I did willingly. He examined me carefully and circled a set of dots with a skin marker.

"I'm going to freeze your skin and try to scrape a few of these dots off with a scalpel," he said matter-of-factly. "Believe me it won't hurt a bit."

"Easy for you to say," I said. "You're not on the cutting edge of the knife."

"Be brave and it will be over before you know it," he said firmly. "I don't intend on torturing you."

180

Somewhat reluctantly I yielded myself into my brother's surgical hands. Fortunately, he was true to his words. The most discomfort I felt was the freezing cold on my skin. I had certainly undergone worse at the hands of my dentist during a cleaning.

"Do you have enough to make a diagnosis?" I was curious since I could see nothing in the specimen bottle my brother held. "Is there anything in the bottle?"

"You may not be able to see them, but I actually have several separate specimens in this bottle," he said confidently. "...one for routine stain, one for electron microscopy, and a couple extras for good measure. I suggest we get started and process these."

We went into the laboratory where Chris gave a specimen to Trish, one of the technicians on duty. She would do the special preparation for the electron microscope while we would do the standard specimen preparation for the light microscope.

"Do you do this often yourself?" I asked.

"No," he said slowly. "But I think we will get faster results if I do it myself."

"Probably..." I agreed. All of this medical stuff was way out of my league.

In half an hour, we were staring into a binocular microscope with a teaching attachment gazing at what still appeared as a black dot. The dot had details to its surface which were just beyond the resolution of our microscope.

"What do you think now?" I was more curious than ever. "Have you seen anything like this before?"

"I must admit I am more puzzled than before," Chris said. "It has form and symmetry suggestive of a bacterium or virus or something else."

"Something else?" I know I was beginning to irritate my brother.

Chris glared at me, looked in my hands and pointed. "The dots are moving!" He nearly shouted.

Gooseflesh ran up and down my spine as I examined my hands. The dots were indeed moving. There were several groups that had joined together as if someone had drawn extremely thin lines to join the dots. I reflexly began to scratch even though I was feeling no discomfort whatsoever.

"What do we do now?" I said. There was a sense of panic in my voice.

181

"First, stay calm!" He said sternly. "I don't want Trish to get snoopy into what we are doing."

"And what is that, Doctor?" Trish had silently come up behind Chris.

Chris blushed a thousand shades of crimson. Neither one of us had heard her coming. Chris coughed and composed himself. I simply laughed at the comic situation.

"It's not funny, Jon!" He said loudly.

"Are you going to tell me what this is all about?" Trish said with firmness.

"This is a personal matter between my brother and me," Chris said flatly.

"Okay," Trish said unconvinced. "I came to tell you your specimen is ready for viewing. I've checked out the scope and it's also ready whenever you are."

"Thank you, Trish," Chris said softly. "I know you're the best."

"Snoopy, harrumph." Trish snorted. "I'll remember that!" And she laughed.

The electron microscope was fully set up when we went into the room. The prepared specimen slide was even mounted within it. All Chris had to do was turn it on and make a few adjustments. The first image on the screen was adjusted to the center of one of the dots where we could zoom in on it. The magnification was far too low to note any detail. Satisfied in his initial adjustments Chris increased the magnification step-by-step.

"Here we go!" He said proudly. "This should tell us what we want to know about these things!"

With each increment of magnifying power we saw the beginning of some detail. I really did not know what I expected to see, but Chris was absolutely sure he could believe what was coming into view. I saw bumps and lines at first then I started to understand what was concerning Chris. There were structures that looked like levers and gears!

"It looks like a machine," I said casually. "Like something the scientists at IBM or MIT would make just to show they can do it."

"You're right," he said. "This dot is really a micro-machine: an artificially created microscopic robotic machine."

"Let's look for another dot," I said.

Fortunately, the second dot was nearby and easy to bring into view. This dot also had the identical appearance of a micro-

182

machine. There were a few details that were different, but, otherwise, it was the same as the first.

"When did you first notice the dots on your skin?" He pushed away from the microscope screen.

"This morning after my run," I said trying to think if I could have noticed them earlier. "During my run I did run through a lot of dust in the wind."

"Were you running with anyone this morning?" He continued questioning. "Do you know whether he also picked up dots on his skin?"

"Yes, I was running with Jason," I said. "But I don't know if he had the same dots."

"Give him a call," he said quickly. "And do it now."

Without further prodding I call Jason. He was about to leave the house to go to his own doctor. Yes, he too, had the dots. No, they were not causing him any discomfort, but he was obviously extremely upset. I told him I had the same problem and was under the care of my brother. He cut the conversation short saying he was late for his appointment. In a way, I was disappointed he was not seeing my brother as his own physician. I guess I will talk to him about that later.

"What did he say?" Chris interrupted my thoughts. "Does he have the same dots?"

"Everywhere I have them, he has them," I said. "They don't itch or bother him in any way. He did say though he thought his dots were organized into patterns."

"Interesting," he said. "Were you both running for the same length of time?"

"I don't know for sure," I said honestly. "But Jason is more of a fanatic at running than I am. I suppose he had been running around for a while before I met him. How long, I'm not really sure."

"From where I am, I can see your dots are beginning to organize themselves into geometric patterns." He pointed with his index finger.

Horrified, I could see that not only had the dots organized, there seemed to be a lot more of them. I started to scratch but Chris caught my hand before I touched my skin.

"Don't do that," he said. "We don't know what they're doing or if they are really harmful."

"That's easy for you to say!" I said angrily. "It's not your skin!"

183

"Have you seen my skin lately?" He extended his right forearm. "I have them also and they are multiplying."

Sure enough Chris's forearm was nearly covered with as many dots as I had when I first came to see him. If these dots were really micro-machines or rather nano-machines which we saw on the microscope, they seemed possessed of the biological activity to replicate themselves. Chris took the bottle of acetone and poured it directly on his forearm. The dots in the way moved faster than we thought possible.

"I think we can get these things off by using these solvents." He did not sound convincing to me.

"I have a feeling we'll poison ourselves before we get rid of all of them," he thought out loud. "Maybe we can disable them with electricity or a magnetic field."

"What about the MRI machine?" I said loudly. "That has a huge magnetic field."

"Of course!" He shouted.

"The dots are organizing around the area you poured acetone," I said. "You must have made them angry." I tried to laugh at my joke but could not. This whole thing was more serious by the minute.

"You're right!" He became more excited by the minute. "They are forming patterns!" He started pouring more acetone on his dots.

"Don't!" I shouted. I had a gut feeling something bad was going to happen just then and it did.

As the acetone hit his forearm Chris was hit with the sensation of an electrical shock that nearly knocked him off his feet. He looked at me confused and bewildered. I was not sure he knew what happened.

"Chris, are you all right?" I said as calmly as I could. "What happened?"

"They shocked me," he said weakly. "I'm starting to get stiff. I'm losing control of my movements. Jon, help me."

I did not know what I could do. The dots on his skin were going crazy with organization. My dots by comparison were taking their time doing whatever they were going to do. I knew then I had to find where the MRI machine was or it would be the end of both of us. The dots were going to take over our bodies for whatever purpose they were manufactured.

I called Trish. "Do you know where I can find the MRI room?"

"Chris can tell you!" Trish said flatly.

184

"He left me alone," I lied. "And told me he was going to the MRI room. I'm finished with what I was doing and want to meet him there."

Trish warmed up a little and told me how to get to the MRI room in the basement. Chris was starting to look pretty bad. I hoped he would be able to walk with me. When I discovered he could not I found a wheelchair and put him in it. The MRI room was easy to find. There was no one in the room so it was easy to put Chris into the machine without any questions or interference. Chris had become an inert mass of flesh responding to my questions with the expression of his eyes only. The dots were in total control and we both knew it.

Although I have never operated any medical machines, I have been a patient in several of them. I know that does not qualify me to be an operator, but at least I was aware of what was supposed to be done to the patient. I found a set of instructions a child could follow. The longer I studied the instructions the more confident I felt I could handle the job of using the MRI correctly.

"Chris, are you ready?" I said warmly. "I think I'm ready."

Chris blinked several times at me with several tears streaming down the sides of his face. I knew I had to hurry.

"Here we go." I boldly activated the mechanism which slid Chris into the magnetic core of the machine. "If you feel claustrophobic, close your eyes. I know how it feels."

I stepped back to the main controls and set the parameters I guessed would do the job. I figured an hour would be just about right. The MRI hummed into action with its incessant pounding as the gigantic magnetic field expanded and contracted, or, at least, that was the way I understood it. I watched Chris carefully wondering what he was thinking and feeling. I knew I was scared and knew he could be no less. Brothers do not grow up with each other without sharing common feelings. In the first few minutes, I saw Chris twitch violently. I suppressed the urge to turn off the machine. My decision was correct because the twitching stopped as suddenly as it began.

"J... Jon," he said weakly. "I... it's w...working!"

I was happy to hear his voice returning. I wanted to respond but found myself completely paralyzed. The dots had finally taken me over. My only hope was for Chris to be freed so he could free me also. The next 30 minutes were the longest I

185

have ever experienced in my life. Fortunately, I was facing the MRI when I was paralyzed. Chris remained until he felt fully in control of himself. He called for me to get him out and when I did not respond he guessed the worst. It took a little while but he managed to shimmy out of the machine. He came immediately to my side and examined me.

"Look, the dots are gone..." He held up his arms to me. "...you're next!"

Chris put me in the MRI and within minutes I could feel the vice grip of the dots slowly relax then completely disappear. As soon as I could move again I raised my forearm as close to my face as I could. I saw the dots but they were falling off my skin. I knew then that I, too, had been saved.

Now a far bigger problem remains. Where did the dots come from? What was their mission? How many people have they infected? And lastly, can we free everyone before it's too late? We have always expected an invasion of aliens as big as ourselves or bigger. To me big may be better, but smaller is certainly more terrifying.

No Problem

The signing of the Global Nuclear Disarmament Treaty brought great relief to almost all the peoples of the Earth. There were celebrations in every country hailing the dawn of a new era of understanding and prosperity. For the first time, all human resources were free to improve the standard of living for everyone. In spite of all the potential for the future, there still remained a few skeptics.

"I don't know if I should be ecstatic or cry." Marlin Cross scowled across his desk. "There is something about this whole episode that strikes me as wrong."

"The Delfinians have assured us of their intentions to facilitate the disposal of all nuclear weapons." James Norton stood in front of the desk.

"That's just it." Marlin raised his eyebrows and voice. "The Delfinians are aliens who we hardly know anything about. The exchange of our weapons for their technology sounds great on the surface, but I feel there's a darker side. Nobody ever get something for nothing."

"I understand you don't accept the concept: the Delfinians are assuring their own safety by guaranteeing we don't destroy ourselves in a nuclear conflagration." James sat down. "I see both sides in a true win-win situation."

Marlin swiveled his chair to face the large picture window overlooking the city from the 45th floor. His business was nuclear arms politics and safety. The idea his job would be eliminated was certainly a contributing cause to the way he felt. At his age, he would have to compete with much younger men for all the good, well-paying positions. With nuclear weapons off the planet maybe he could switch over to nuclear power plants, he thought gloomily. The thought almost brought a shiver to his spine.

"Marlin, you're just thinking about your job." James smiled. "The prospect of being unemployed is not a very happy one, I'm sure. But look at the bright side; you'll be able to start over at something completely new. Your salary is guaranteed and the company will send you to any school you want."

"You take my place then. This is the job I was trained to do. I think I have done well over the years. In fact, I even enjoy what I do. Crisis management keeps my adrenaline high and gives me a rush."

"A good run around the block would give you the same and be healthier for you." James laughed. "You're being too stubborn about this. Your suspicions are really your feelings of insecurity about the future. Given time, you will look back on all of this and find it was the best thing that ever happened to you."

"You may be right." Marlin nodded slowly with a slight smile. "Even so, I'm going to use my last few days here exploring my hunches. Until I vacate this office, it's my duty to make sure of our nuclear safety."

"A diehard professional to the very last..." James chuckled. "...just another name for a junkyard dog."

The remark was lost on Marlin. His thoughts wandered back to the first appearance of the Delfinians. Somehow their three gigantic interstellar ships had simply appeared from nowhere evading detection by every possible monitoring agency. For weeks after their appearance both radio and optical astronomers reviewed their records and found nothing to indicate the approach of the alien ships. More puzzling, however, was how the Delfinians bypassed the massive space network designed to detect objects the size of a compact car at the edge of the solar system. The Delfinians could have cleared up the matter but remained decidedly mute on the subject with a statement that answers to all questions would come in the future. No one on Earth pressed any further. The proof of a superior civilization outside our limited sphere of existence had everyone in awe. After the requisite formalities of introduction, the Delfinians began to outline the relationship they wished to establish with us, their newly discovered friends. First and foremost, they advocated total nuclear disarmament to eliminate the threat to all life on the planet and to free resources to be spent on new technology and products made available by them. The deal seemed too good to be true. The Delfinians did not press their plan but allowed the nations of the Earth decide for themselves. With no pressure, the decision to comply was unanimous. Within a month of the Delfinians' arrival the nuclear armaments industry was shut down and packing itself to be sent out into the void never to threaten anyone again.

"Marlin!" James said loudly. "You're not listening to me!"

"I was just thinking about how this all came about," Marlin said softly. "The Delfinians are either mankind's greatest benefactor or the slickest Trojan horse."

188

"There you go again, thinking the worst. I simply cannot believe intelligence, that is, true intelligence, would deliberately destroy other true intelligence. Civilization advances by the exchange of goods and services, not war."

"Have you ever seen what one of them looks like?"

"No," James said quickly. "But no one has."

"And why is that?"

"Because they feel their appearance would interfere with our emotions in a negative way."

"That sounds good in theory, but the Delfinians could be machines as well as organic life or even something in between."

"True." James smiled. "I think you're being over critical of our benefactors. Theirs is an alien culture and civilization which we know little. However, our own experience with primitive peoples on Earth has proved that beneath outward appearances are common thoughts, hopes and fears."

"I'm not as willing to accept outward appearances at face value. Behind every action, whether benign or malignant, there is always a motive. I am uncomfortable with the little data I have to even begin to assume the Delfinians' motives."

"Okay, so I can't convince you we are in no danger. How do you propose to either prove or disprove your so-called feelings?"

Marlin turned his chair, faced James, and stood up leaning forward with two hands placed on the desk. He smiled cryptically and put his right index finger to his lips.

"Bugs?" James whispered. "Your office is being spied on?"

Marlin shook his head with eyes imploring James to keep comments to himself. Walking around the desk he grasped James by the arm pulling him toward the door. James finally got the idea straight that he should remain silent. Out of the office, down the elevator, and into the garage they went. They were soon heading on the expressway out of town.

"We talk now?" James sat uneasy in the passenger seat.

"This car is completely bug-free." Marlin smiled. "And I can guarantee that with my life."

"Tell me exactly what's going on. Why all the secrecy? I almost feel like we are part of some conspiracy."

"That is the first sensible statement you've made so far. What I was unable to tell you back in the office was that I have had my staff set up a special monitoring base outside of town.

We've been recording all transmissions to and from the alien ships."

"Can you understand their language?" James was surprised at the revelation. "I didn't think we were able to decipher their language."

"It struck me as particularly curious the Delfinians communicated with us in our own common languages." Marlin stared intently watching the road ahead. "What would happen if we stumbled onto an intelligent alien civilization? Would we be able to communicate with them immediately? I should think not. Even with the fastest computers there would be a long time until we became fluent in our dialogue with our new friends. The Delfinians had no difficulty expressing themselves in idiomatic Earth languages the day they appeared from wherever they came. Doesn't that strike you as a little odd?"

James nodded, mulling the paradox over to himself. He was almost willing to start believing there was a real problem. But a few points won does not a solid conclusion make. He needed more evidence.

"At least I can see out of the corner of my eye, you are beginning to agree with me," Marlin said more relaxed. "Now that I have you heading in the right direction, I need your help to finish my investigation. Believe it or not there is nothing more that I want to prove than to show there is no problem."

"No problem." James laughed. "You can count on me."

"Uh–oh..." Marlin groaned. "The traffic is slowing down to a stop."

"Looks like all traffic is being diverted off the next exit..." James pointed. "...I wonder if there has been an accident ahead."

"I don't think so."

"What do you mean?"

"There are people that want to stop what I'm doing. Incredible as it sounds, there are some of our own people that are helping the Delfinians without question and will not tolerate anyone who is even remotely trying to interfere."

"The more you talk, the more you sound paranoid."

As they exited the freeway a group of military men stopped each car before allowing it to proceed. The questions put to the drivers were brief so that in no time they were carefully scrutinized by a pair of soldiers, one on each side of the car. The soldier on the driver side asked for Marlin's driver's license while the other looked at the contents of the car.

"Is there a problem?" Marlin said as calmly as he could. "Has there been a disaster nearby?"

The soldier stopped reading Marlin's license. "No," he said. "We have been waiting for you. Please cooperate and get out of the car. You are to come with us."

"Why? Who wants me? I'm on my way to an extremely important meeting."

"Sir, all I have are my orders. Either you come voluntarily or I will bring you by force."

"I see. I guess I have no choice."

The traffic ahead cleared. Marlin reached for the door handle. The soldier stepped back anticipating the opening door. Marlin slammed the transmission into drive and floored the accelerator. The sound of burning rubber startled the soldiers into a momentary paralysis. Only when Marlin's car had lurched out of reach did the soldiers pull their guns.

"What are you doing?" James screamed.

"Someone is after me!" Marlin glanced quickly into the rearview mirror. "Someone doesn't like me snooping around. I'm onto something and someone is scared."

"I'm not a part of this in any way. I am an unwilling hostage!"

"You're a fool and a coward. There are billions of human lives at risk. I personally chose you to help because I thought you had guts."

"I'm no coward," James said angrily. "I'm with you to the very end. I only wish I knew what I am risking my neck for."

"You're risking your neck for the truth." Marlin smiled. "With the truth your assistance will be vindicated."

"In the meantime, what do we do about those guys chasing after us?"

"We have a few minutes head start. We are at the airport. We will lose them in the parking garage."

"And we will fly to safety?"

"No, we will park the car and hire a taxi."

They entered the airport parking garage with flashing lights visible in the distance behind them. On the fifth level they parked and locked the car. The elevator took them to the ticket lobby. Walking quickly but calmly they exited to the taxi stand where they hired the first taxi to pull up to the curb. They exited the airport watching a line of police and military vehicles passing them in the opposite direction.

191

"Do you believe me now?" Marlin said. "Look over your shoulder out the back window."

"I'm sorry I sounded like a coward. At first, all of this sounded so unreal, but now with what's happening I'm beginning to agree with you that something is amiss. I'm not sure what's wrong but I agree we need to find out."

"I'm glad you finally see it my way. Driver, take us to the address on this business card."

The driver took the card, read it and nodded. In twenty minutes, they were at their destination. Marlin paid the driver and waited to watch the taxi disappear down the street. He led James into the building. The sign on the outside said in bold gold letters Department of Defense General Offices. With his ID and security clearance, he led James past the security guards and secretaries to the elevator.

"We should have some answers soon," Marlin said. "I've had my staff here working on it night and day."

The elevator took them down several levels into an underground laboratory complex. Marlin led James into a conference room with dozens of papers stacked on the central table. A man in the laboratory coat sat at a computer terminal at one end of the room. He rose when he saw them..

"Marlin, I'm glad to see you've arrived safely."

"Jack, you've met James Norton I assume," Marlin said warmly.

"No, I don't think I've had the pleasure. My name is Jack Martin. Welcome."

Jack and James shook hands.

"Is James to be included in our research?" Jack said slowly.

"James is now officially a part of the team." Marlin nodded. "We narrowly escaped being detained by a group of soldiers on the freeway."

"You are right to say they would eventually want to stop you." Jack smiled. "Do you think they will follow you here?"

"Sooner or later; let's not worry about that for now. What have you found out?"

"There has been an unbelievable increase in communication traffic between the alien ships and at least two distant sources. The one, we have not been able to trace yet, the other is here on earth."

"Where?" Marlin was incredulous. "Do you have any idea who they are communicating with?"

"Unfortunately, no..." Jack sighed. "All I can tell you is all transmissions are within our own solar system. It is conceivably possible the Delfinians have a secret terrestrial base but in my opinion I think there are earthbound collaborators."

"You mean traitors," Marlin said bluntly. "This is an idea I have been considering myself. Still, nothing makes any logical sense. Aliens appear from nowhere, offer an exchange of technology provided that all nuclear weapons are destroyed, and, without hesitation, suggest they dispose of the weapons themselves. A nuclear weapons weary world jumps at the chance to be rid of the nuclear menace. Tell me, have I missed something or am I just stupid?"

"You can add to your list of riddles that we have never seen what the Delfinians look like," James said. "I find that particularly curious. I don't care how different they might appear to us, I still would feel more comfortable knowing that we are really dealing with flesh and blood beings rather than machines."

"Just before you got here I received word almost all our nuclear weapons are off planet," Jack said. "All the leaders of the world have announced a day of celebration held yearly from now on."

There was a loud shout from outside. Before they could evaluate what was happening, three soldiers brandishing automatic weapons stormed into the room. The leader was the same soldier that had quizzed Marlin at the exit of the freeway.

"You will not escape again," the soldier said angrily. "You made a fool of us before, but that was last time. Now you and your two friends will come with us. Don't give us any trouble and we will refrain from the use of force."

"Where are you taking us?" Marlin glared into the soldier's eyes.

"You will see when you get there! Move!"

They were silently escorted out of the building without any difficulty. Marlin thought it extremely unusual there were no witnesses to see them leave the building. A stretch limousine with darkened windows was waiting outside. They were blindfolded inside the vehicle.

"Is all this necessary?" Marlin said.

There was no answer.

"James, Jack are you all right?"

"Yes," they answered simultaneously.

"Is there anyone else here?" Marlin continued, only to feel the end of an automatic weapon press against his ribs. "I guess that answers that."

"Marlin, I'm okay," James said. "I think it is best we keep quiet to ourselves."

"I agree," Jack said. "We'll have answers soon enough. I don't want any more trouble than we already have."

"Marlin, what do you think?" James said.

"We have no choice but to wait." Marlin felt the end of the weapon withdraw. "Just sit back and enjoy the ride."

The interior of the limousine remained quiet throughout the remainder of the ride. After several stops, starts, and turns, the limousine arrived at its destination. Marlin heard the door open and the weapon, now familiar , nudged him out. A hand gripped his right arm and led him forward. He thought he was being led into a large building but he could not be completely sure. Through several doors and past perceptibly silent bystanders he was directed to a chair and the blindfolds taken off. Adjusting his eyes to the light he was faced with a large television screen upon which was a person he did not recognize.

"Welcome, Mister Cross, I have been waiting for the pleasure of making your acquaintance," the man on the screen said pleasantly. "I sincerely hope your ride here was not too uncomfortable."

"Who are you? And where am I?" Marlin almost shouted. "Why have I been kidnapped?"

"All your questions will be answered in time." The man smiled. "First let me introduce myself. I am Aix, Ambassador of the Delfinian Federation of Outer Worlds. I have been charged with negotiating any misunderstandings that might arise between your people and our plans to help you. Your media and political information agencies have not fully been able to express our ultimate goals."

"And you intend to explain them to me now I suppose? Why abduct me? Why not contact me directly?"

"A decided miscalculation on our part; the abduction was patterned after many of your popular novels. We did not think you would seriously object. We chose to contact you because we felt you were questioning things that were dangerously beyond your limited understanding."

"I don't understand."

"In every exchange each side must gain something needed otherwise the transaction is unbalanced," the ambassador began. "Our space, where we live has been the site of innumerable wars for centuries. On approaching your space, we noted you had developed nuclear weapons but had not actually used them except in a rare instance or two. We felt we could ensure our safety here by removing your nuclear arsenal. In the created neutral zone, trade could begin without any danger to either side."

"Except, that you now have all our nuclear weapons and we have none," Marlin said flatly. "We have disarmed ourselves without any guarantees."

"My dear, Mister Cross..." The ambassador laughed. "America wasn't built in a day."

"That was Rome," Marlin said slowly. "I am extremely uncomfortable about the whole arrangement. If you can change my mind, please do it now."

"No problem." The ambassador smiled.

The image of the ambassador vanished and was replaced by a diazo-blue field filled with what appeared to be words in an alien language. Marlin shifted uncomfortably in his chair wondering what the translation was. As the seconds gathered into minutes he looked around the room. He suddenly realized he was alone, sitting in the only chair. Suppressing a momentary wave of panic, he gathered his thoughts into a plan of action. He rose from the chair and went to one of the two closed doors. It was locked. The other yielded and allowed him entry into a room lined with oval windows 18 inches in diameter. The furnishings suggested a comfortable cabin on a Caribbean cruise ship. There were two other doors which he found locked. A glance at his watch indicated it was barely midafternoon yet the sky appeared black outside. Puzzled, he went directly to the nearest window and looked out. What he saw literally took his breath away. In one direction, he saw the Earth as a receding object with the moon directly below. In all other directions, he saw black space and stars with the sun included.

"Enjoying the view?" A voice said from overhead. "Not many men have ever had the opportunity to view their mother planet from such a vantage point."

"Why have you abducted me?" Marlin spun around. "You have no right to do this to me!"

"You have been selected to join us. We are particularly interested in your expertise in nuclear technology."

Marlin spun around several times before he realized the voice was coming from a set of speakers hidden in the ceiling. "I would have gladly accepted your invitation had you asked me. By bringing me here this way and I find your motives suspect."

"Please return to your chair in the room you came. The ambassador would like to continue his dialogue with you."

"I don't think this is a dialogue anymore." Marlin returned to the chair.

The ambassador's face reappeared as he sat down. "I'm disappointed with you, Mister Cross; I had high hopes we could be reasonable with each other."

"Your actions tell me otherwise."

"As you have discovered we are well on our way to join our expeditionary crafts. You will be treated with utmost respect and be provided with whatever you reasonably need and request. In time, you will be reunited with others of your kind. You must first be taught some of the rules that must be strictly abided on our journey."

"Journey? Where are you taking me, I mean us?"

"All your questions will be answered. Please continue to exercise restraint and patience."

"I demand you return me home immediately!" Marlin shouted. "What you're doing is hardly considered civilized or friendly."

"Stand by," the ambassador said coolly. "I will be back with you in a moment."

"Do that!" Marlin knew the best course was to remain calm, but he felt an increasing sense of hopelessness he could not shake off. He thought it strange he wished he were at home watching an old sitcom with his cat curled up in his lap. A noise from behind broke his reverie. The locked door opened. He turned and saw James slowly enter the room.

"Marlin! Am I glad to see you!" James shouted. "I've been by myself since we were separated."

"I'm glad to see you too." Marlin got up and shook his hand. "It seems like we've become guests of our Delfinian friends. Unfortunately, I have yet to find out the reason for all this."

"I have been in a room similar to this." James scanned the room. "The ambassador even spoke to me through the monitor. He told me nothing other than to be patient and answers would be soon forthcoming. I'm not so sure we will like the answers we will get."

"Have you been able to look outside?"

"No," James tilted his head to the side. "Why?"

196

"Because if you did, you would know we are on one of the Delfinian ships headed out past the moon. Not only have we been abducted we are being taken to another extraterrestrial location."

"This is all too weird. Why abduct us? I would have willingly come, had I been asked. I smell real trouble."

"My feelings exactly..." Marlin nodded. "We now have no choice but to wait and see what happens next."

"So far I have not seen any other humans other than you and me. Those men that abducted us on closer scrutiny were nothing more than androids."

"I thought they acted funny. Their lack of emotion should have tipped me off as to what they were. I still wonder what our real Delfinian looks like."

"Gentlemen..." The ambassador returned on the screen. "You will go with your attendants to the preparation room."

"Preparation room?" Marlin said quickly. "Does that mean you're going to eat us?"

"We are not barbarians." The ambassador laughed. "You are a member of a sentient species and highly valued throughout the universe. No physical harm will ever come to you under our care."

While they were talking four androids entered the room. Both Marlin and James were flanked by two each. They follow their escort out of the room without resistance.

"Have we arrived?" James turned to Marlin as they entered a large room with one transparent wall through which they could see quarters with similar transparent walls lining both sides.

Before Marlin could say anything the androids produced a fresh set of clothes for both of them. They were instructed to change after bathing. The ambassador appeared on the screen within the room.

"Gentlemen..." The ambassador smiled. "You are about to have all your questions answered, but before that I want you to know you may request and receive anything you want or need for your comfort and entertainment. Since both of you are seen as a pair, you have been placed together. If this proves to be unsatisfactory, we can arrange for different pairings. It will even be possible to switch partners on a routine basis, if that is what you desire."

"You make this sound like we are some sort of captured animals on display," Marlin said.

197

There was a momentary silence within the room.

"I thought you knew." The ambassador grinned showing perfectly straight teeth. "I believe our initial assessment of your species has been the correct one. We will profit many times over with your kind."

"You can't get away with this!" Marlin yelled. "Once our planet realizes your intentions we will fight for our freedom!"

"With what? We have removed all your most powerful weapons."

"We have the technology and resources to rearm ourselves. What will you do when we fight back?"

"No problem." The ambassador laughed. "Keep watching the screen."

Marlin and James were mesmerized by the image that appeared on the screen. The Earth and the moon were clearly seen from a perspective far distant from the sun. In the corner of the screen were a group of objects moving in the direction of the Earth.

"What are those?" James pointed.

"Those bastards!" Marlin screamed. "They're using our own weapons to destroy the Earth! We'll never be able to go home!"

The two men stood in stunned disbelief as the first explosions began. Within a half an hour the entire planet was engulfed in a fire consuming everything combustible. Tears streaked down both men's faces. Marlin took several deep breaths and James sobbed. A tapping on the transparent wall drew their attention away from the screen. Standing on the other side were two Delfinians in their natural form.

"Oh no!" James screamed hysterically. "They're..."

"Insects," Marlin said.

The explosion blew out all the windows where Professor Jason crouched. The war had started quite unexpectedly without provocation and now was very real, beating at his door. The last thing Jason expected was a surprise attack from the moon. In retrospect, there was nothing he could have done to prevent what happened. He wiped debris off himself, stood up, and looked around the lab. Everything was a total loss.

The search for extraterrestrial life was his specialty. For all his forty plus years since graduation Jason had been monitoring the skies at every conceivable frequency of the electromagnetic spectrum nonstop and detected nothing out of the ordinary. Whoever had planned the initial attack had a well-organized strategy. From the onset, he concluded, it was a winner-take-all affair.

"Are you okay?"

Jason whipped around. Marvin stood at the entrance covered with plaster dust. "That was too close for comfort. I guess that answers the question."

"What are you talking about?"

"Whether aliens are friendly or not..." Marvin smiled slightly. As a graduate student he knew he could express an opinion without fear of ridicule. It was his duty to think the unthinkable.

"For years I've gazed into the cosmos wondering if we are alone in the universe. I've detected equivocal signals over the years but nothing to stand the burden of proof." Jason sighed. "I really don't believe it now. The Japanese Lunar Orbiter may have detected activity near the southern pole presumably where there is a source of frozen water. The initial pictures I saw as natural phenomena, but my opinion is not in the majority. Everyone talks about aliens without real proof. I don't accept that."

"But the Press ran with it." Marvin grinned. "There is nothing like a good alien story to sell media. Speculation of alien visitors on the moon has paralyzed all nonessential activity. Everyone is waiting for a message of greeting."

"Damn fools." Jason shook his head. "I hate to admit it, but only the military has the right idea. Politicians are nothing but a gaggle of fools." He scanned the lab. "We need to start cleaning this mess. Go get a couple of brooms."

Marvin turned on the radio. "Professor, why don't you believe in aliens?"

"... all developed nations of the world have joined in a military preparedness while the head politicos debate initial contact protocol. The United Nations has the authority to establish a dialogue with the visitors but the biggest problem is the inability to go out to the moon first. There is an element of the scientific community that cautions awareness of toxic biological contamination and favors a neutral site to establish the safeness of direct exposure to each other. Unfortunately, the lack of progress in lunar exploration weighs heavily against the possibility of even trying. In the meantime, messages are beamed incessantly in the hope of receiving a reply. All such attempts at communication have failed..."

"Listen carefully." Jason went to the radio and pointed. "All that is old news; look at this place. We were bombed with conventional weapons not death rays. We are dealing with a rogue nation from this planet. That's why I don't believe anything."

"...an exclusive source has confirmed the Japanese shuttle has been lost. The American shuttle has..."

"What do you think is really happening?"

"War; just plain, old stupid war..." Jason exhaled loudly. "All those people going to see alien encounter movies has not made the situation any better. Some of the movies are reassuring, others thoughtful, but most are utterly tasteless and horrifying under the circumstances. At the theaters showing the worst productions, audiences are beginning to panic and riot. I think the government should ban all the negative movies."

"Yeh, and everywhere people are hoarding and stockpiling food and weapons for survival just in case."

"Just look at this place. There is no doubt someone is at war." Jason took a long sweep with the broom. "Let's hope the military can stop this before it gets too far out of hand."

"Amen to that." Marvin joined with a sweep of his own broom.

***

Private first class Ryan Smith huddled in a shallow ditch. He lit a cigarette and took a slow drag. His partner, Jerry Miller, blew a ring of smoke. A cold fear had gripped the human race and it was fighting for its life against a foe that had attacked unprovoked. The whole situation made little sense to Ryan. There were few level heads in the scientific community that continued attempting to establish communication. Those efforts were entirely fruitless. Either the enemy was not listening or they were not interested. Ryan shook his head. There was the other possibility that the means of communication were totally incompatible.

"Does anyone know what the hell is going on?" Jerry spat and took another puff.

"I don't think so." Ryan threw his cigarette into the dirt. "All I know is August 6 a brilliant flash was observed on the moon followed by a single object hurtling at tremendous speed toward the earth. Sorta like in that movie about Martians. It was calculated to touchdown in central China, but it changed course into a ninety minute polar orbit and disappeared."

"The Japanese shuttle disappeared too." Jerry took a long drag and threw the butt as far as he could. "Our shuttle saw the bastards and was attacked without provocation. We need to show we won't give in easily."

"You really think we're being attacked by aliens. No one has really seen them and all the fighting so far has been with normal weapons. Where are the ray guns?"

"You think we are being attacked by hostile alien aliens?" Jerry stretched.

"Like I said, show me and I'll believe. In the meantime, we just sit here on our butts waiting for orders. Got another cigarette?"

Jerry pulled out another cigarette and gave it to Ryan. "We might as well take advantage of our vices while we have an excuse."

"You know what really bothers me?" Ryan lit the cigarette and took a puff. "Why is there no communication between us and them? A little talk can solve a lot."

"Except, maybe we have nothing in common." Jerry smiled slightly.

"But humans are humans."

"Who said they are human? From what I've heard there have been no prisoners. Everywhere they have invaded they wipe out the population and keep things going as if nothing happened. The intelligence behind the enemy knows exactly how to inflict the greatest psychological damage without destroying native physical structures. Reports of what the invaders look like never make it to the free world because of a ruthless efficiency used to sever all means of communication. The enemy has landed on all the continents of our world, including both poles."

"It means they have to be human." Ryan sat up straight. "Aliens don't need what we got. They have their own alien ways."

"Your reasoning is impeccable, pure genius." Jerry laughed. "You forget we have a planet that might have some value whatever alien ways the enemy has. War has almost always been about territory."

"Hey, you two, let's get moving! The enemy is just up the river."

"Yes, Sarge..." Ryan threw the hardly burned cigarette down and crushed it with the heel of his boot. "Right away..."

"Hey, Sarge, what's happening," Jerry drawled.

"Our shuttle's been blown up and all communication is down. The bastards detonated a nuclear weapon with a big electromagnetic pulse. Everything is in chaos. We are regrouping to stay close in touch. General Hicks is just up a ways scoping out the situation. He's calling the shots from the front like a real soldier. Let's move it!"

"Where do you want us to go?" Ryan shifted his rifle from one shoulder to the other.

"Head in that direction..." Sergeant Neal pointed. It looked as if he had not slept or changed clothes in several days and ran in the opposite direction without saying another word.

Ryan stared at Jerry. "I don't like this. This is all too spooky."

"Do we have a choice?"

The enemy was established several miles up the Hudson River nearly within sight of New York City. Ryan and Jerry were a part of the American troops rushed to repulse the advancing enemy. The first shots were fired slightly upriver of the Washington Bridge before they had arrived. They knew the fight to come would be neither quick nor easy. In any war both sides were determined to win and neither was prepared to suffer the ignominy of a loss.

At mid-span on the George Washington Bridge, General Hicks looked through binoculars and scanned the conflict in progress upriver. He gritted his teeth, holding back an expletive. The enemy was too close for comfort and he had no real answers how to effectively repulse the enemy. All he wanted was a shower, a clean set of clothes and a stiff gin and tonic. At the moment, he wondered if he would ever see any of them again. He knew from headquarters the first wave arrived from the moon on August 15. Troops in China and Australia faced the invaders first. At least, on one level, the fight would be fought with conventional weapons, or so he hoped. Although the alien invaders appeared to be technologically far advanced, they approached the earth as any other folk groups of humans have had to face in terrestrial conflicts. The strategies were uncannily similar. Fortunately, the alien enemy desisted from a scorched earth policy. The initial landings established military points of operation near power plants. Without much effort whichever power plant was targeted was easily seized and put into use by the enemy. The first noticeable effect was, of course, the sudden loss of electric power in many metropolitan areas. Even so, life went on with the initial inconvenience. This was no consolation. Men, women and children were suffering everywhere.

"Sir, we must be moving on," Private Kit Mason, the driver, said carefully. He recognized the dazed look of contemplation on the General's face. "We can't let you get hurt at this point."

"What are they fighting for?" General Hicks did not expect an answer. "Why did they come to our forsaken part of the universe to do this to us? They had us by surprise in the beginning but that has changed. We've ground to a stalemate with neither side gaining any specific advantage. Now we have a ground war which has to be fought face-to-face. Ha! Those faces are completely unknown to us. Blood has been spilled on both sides with no known living captives."

"I don't know, Sir," Mason said mechanically. "Nothing seems to make any sense."

"War never makes any sense." General Hicks got back into the Jeep. "The only winners are those that never fight."

"I don't think we ever had a chance to think about it this time, Sir," Mason said.

"You're right as usual." General Hicks sighed. "Let's get over to New Jersey."

***

Closer to the front line, two GIs progressed slowly forward on foot armed with the latest available gear. They both appeared, unlike Ryan and Jerry, as if they belonged in some videogame. Well-seasoned as soldiers, they were prepared to give everything to kill the enemy although their specific orders were to bring back an alien prisoner for interrogation.

"I'm getting a proximity signal," Sergeant Bill Williams said calmly. "Do you get the same reading?"

203

"Yes, Sir," Private Rodney Holmes said quickly. "I think we'll be in the middle of action pretty soon."

"Forget about calling me Sir," Williams said crisply. "We need to focus on our mission and not quibble about formalities. Is that understood?"

"Yes, si... I mean, yeah."

"That's a lot better," Williams whispered. "You go off to the right, I'll go left. I think there may be a spook up ahead."

Holmes nodded and moved to the left, carefully watching his virtual reality monitor. He saw what Williams had seen, but was unsure it was the enemy. As he moved farther away he realized he would be the first to come upon the suspected enemy. When he was within several yards of his target, the target moved quickly in a direction toward Williams. He wanted to signal but was ordered to absolute silence under the directives of the mission. He soon came upon tracks on the forest floor he correctly assigned to the alien. At first glance, the footprint appeared as any other human, but on closer examination there was no doubt the size and shape was definitely peculiar. He followed the tracks hoping he and Williams would finally trap an alien between them.

Williams expected the alien to come at him. Instead the alien moved deliberately away, staying barely out of sight. A flash of movement caught his eye and he raised his gun ready to fire. He rapidly recognized Holmes moving in his direction. When they came closer, Williams waved to move forward in parallel to the direction the alien was moving. Both were certain the enemy had similar detection gear as they had, plus countermeasures. He considered the lack of communication had resulted in various air forces launching an air attack at the established alien bases. The initial sorties by the American, Israeli and Russian Air Forces inflicted significant damage to the invaders. It proved the aliens were both mortal and beatable. The aliens may have had some advanced technology on their side, but they had their home world to fight on and for. What initially was deemed a fait accompli of defeat was slowly turning around into hope of eventually coming to peace by repulsing the invaders back where they came.

At late dusk, long shadows swept across the forest floor. Every shadow became a potential trap, every sound proof of proximity. The mission was of utmost importance. A live prisoner was needed to open a dialogue. Without physical contact nothing could be accomplished. The alien enemy remained an abstract idea to a terrified and angry humanity.

Shortly after sunset fatigue forced the Williams and Holmes to stop and rest. They had been pushing themselves for almost 12 hours without taking care of their basic bodily needs. Nourishment came in the form of freeze-dried food re-fortified with the addition of water. Not exactly gourmet fare but more than welcome to the weary soldiers.

"Do you think we are getting any closer?" Holmes took a long sip from a canteen.

"It's hard to tell," Williams said flatly. "Either our friend is playing with us or we are evenly matched. He seems to be using the same tactics I would use if I wanted to lure my opponent into a trap."

"I've had that feeling myself." Holmes nodded. "No sooner do we catch up, he darts away in a different direction."

"Our job is difficult, but not impossible." Williams took in a mouthful of food. "We still have the home advantage."

"If these guys are so far advanced and powerful, why don't they come in and crush us by force?" Holmes said slowly. "This whole war doesn't make any sense at all."

"War never makes any sense," Williams said. "Our enemy obviously wants something from us. What I have trouble understanding is why they attacked without trying to negotiate some sort of political solution where everyone gets something."

"Alien civilizations have alien ideas." Holmes smiled wanly. "What we hold most in esteem may seem a hopeless weakness to them. Even so, I believe we can meet them on a common ground if we ever get the chance."

"With that statement, I thoroughly agree with you." Williams smiled. "The trick is getting close enough."

"Sergeant," Holmes paused a moment. "Do you believe?"

"Do I believe in what?" Williams raised his brow. "That's an open question."

"Well, I mean..." Holmes almost stumbled over his words. "Have you ever gone to church on a regular basis?"

"I'm not a very religious person," the Sergeant said softly. "Sure, I've been to church and all that, but I've never had any long lasting connections. I guess I'm not really tuned into organized religion."

"Religions are deemed organized by men," Holmes said flatly. "Being organized is not necessarily bad, but the crux of the matter is faith. Everything in my spiritual life revolves around belief. I believe in a higher power although I have never witnessed it. I believe in my church, not so much by what it professes, but what I feel it represents to me. My relationship to my creator is both personal and private. I go to church to remove myself from the mundane world so I can see, feel, and hear a representation of a heavenly one."

"When you put it in those terms," Williams said. "I agree with you completely. The few times I've been to church I've felt a warm closeness to something above myself. I've rarely, if ever, felt that way anywhere else."

"I wonder if our alien friend has a religion," Holmes said softly. "I wonder if where he comes from they believe as we do."

"Maybe, if we win this war, we'll find out." Williams took a sip of coffee. "No one has ever proved the universality of God beyond the earth."

"Only because we have never encountered an advanced alien civilization; the absence of evidence does not constitute proof of anything."

"I agree. I think the evidence in this case clearly demonstrates the aliens are godless and amoral."

"I'm not sure we can fully deduce that from what has happened so far. Without any direct communication or dialogue we have no idea what our adversaries think or feel."

"Except, that they want to take over our planet," Williams said grimly. "The casualties attest to the brutality of the alien mind."

"That is what appears on the surface," Holmes said. "But I think in time we'll see that there are other factors at work here that go far beyond what we see now."

"In the meantime, how many lives are going to be sacrificed to the cause? The only good alien is a dead one."

"Now you're beginning to sound like a faithless brute. Isn't it true that it is always best to yield to our enemy? Turn the other cheek so to speak. Isn't it true that the best way to win is without fighting? Or the only way to win is not to play?"

"I agree with all of the above," Williams said slowly. "However, in this case, we have our orders."

"I know." Holmes sighed. "But we do have leeway in how we implement those orders. There is a way to fight without fighting."

A sound from out of the darkness sent both of them into a stance of readiness. Williams grabbed his weapon and dashed behind a tree. Holmes rapidly put on night goggles while hurrying into the bushes in a direction opposite to the Sergeant. The noise grew louder. Neither man dared take a breath lest the noise give their position away.

Holmes focused the goggles in the direction from which the sound was coming. He detected the motion of three or four persons. The aliens were said to be more humanoid than anything else. They wore uniforms of darkly colored material and used a type of breathing mask that was more filter than supply of vital gases. The longer Holmes stared at the persons coming toward him the more he realized it was a party of aliens. From where he hid he was able to see Williams. He flashed a laser pointer at Williams to get his attention. Williams waved back acknowledgment that he knew of the impending danger and signaled they were to hold their ground. Holmes reluctantly agreed. He was definitely uncomfortable with the upcoming contact.

At first, it appeared the aliens would bypass them without notice. They passed slowly between them without a glance at their hidden positions. Holmes breathed a sigh of relief, said a short prayer, and crossed himself. He was thankful he had been momentarily spared. The aliens barely moved out of sight when they split apart and circled back. Williams was watching where they had gone when he felt a stiff rod poke him in the back. His first inclination was scream, instead he slowly turned toward his assailant. However, before he could turn completely he was struck across the head and lost consciousness.

Holmes watched Williams go down. Before he could raise his weapon, he too was struck from behind and lost consciousness. The next sensation he had was lying on the hard ground with a splitting headache. When he opened his eyes Williams was motionless beside him. Without moving a muscle he slowly opened his eyelids and peeked at the surroundings the best he could. Although he could not hear anything, he was aware the aliens were nearby. He closed his eyes tightly and prayed for salvation. If he were to die now, at least he would find eternal peace in the afterlife.

Footsteps by the side of his head focused his attention. An alien stood between Williams and him. Noiselessly, the alien bent down and touched him on the chin. Holmes cringed at the thought but was surprised at the warmth and relative gentleness of the touch. The alien withdrew its hand and examined Williams as Holmes peeked out of the corner of his eye.

207

The alien appeared for all intents and purposes totally human with two arms, two legs, one head, and four fingers and a thumb. The head was covered with a helmet and the face with a mask of some sort over where the nose and mouth should be. Two deep set eyes of indistinguishable color appeared in the correct anthropomorphic anatomic position. As Holmes gazed at the alien he suddenly realized that what he was looking at was not quite right. The alien continued to focus its attention on Williams and Holmes opened his eyes widely to better see. Williams moaned softly and turned slightly. The alien withdrew a step.

Williams opened his eyes and saw the alien hovering a step away from him. He barely restrained a gasp of surprise and managed to remain motionless. The alien moved forward and firmly grabbed his arm lifting him to the standing position. Williams winced at the rough treatment. The alien apparently understood and released its grip. Face-to-face with the alien Williams did not know what to expect next.

Two other aliens joined the first one. Holmes noticed that aside from a few colored symbols on their clothes, each one was completely identical to the other. The newly arrived aliens noticed he was awake and in like fashion he was brought to stand beside his companion.

"What's going to happen to us?" Holmes whispered out of the side of his mouth.

"I don't know," Williams said in a normal voice. "We need to communicate with them. It's pretty obvious we are at a distinct disadvantage at the moment."

The aliens remained silent while Williams and Holmes conversed. Although the aliens said nothing, Holmes had the feeling that they were communicating with each other. When Williams stepped toward them, they aimed their weapons simultaneous at him.

"Wait!" Williams said loudly. "I'm unarmed. I mean you no harm. Do you understand?"

The aliens stared back in silence. One of the recently arrived aliens moved to a position behind him with its weapon drawn and poised for service at any moment.

"Do you understand anything I'm saying?" Williams said calmly. "We don't understand who you are or why you have attacked us. All we want is to negotiate with you. We mean you no harm."

"I don't think you're getting through to them," Holmes said softly. "They look humanoid but I have a feeling they really aren't what they appear to be."

"I have that same feeling," Williams said flatly. "Even so, there has to be a way we can communicate with them. Our biggest problem is to find out how and I'm beginning to run out of ideas. Do you have any suggestions?"

"Shall we try to make a run for it?" Holmes whispered. "I still have several weapons on me."

"I'm not so sure we can escape," Williams said weakly. "Neither side has taken any prisoners which means that either we will be executed or taken somewhere into their base camp."

"We have no option but to try to escape," Holmes said flatly. "We have to take the earliest chance we get."

"You're right," Williams said. "I'll give the signal when the time is right."

The aliens remained motionless throughout their dialogue and if they understood what was being said did not indicate it in any way. When Williams knelt down and moved the leaves away from a patch of dirt, the aliens remained impassive. Williams drew symbols in the dirt and when he was finished stood and faced the first alien.

"Look," Williams said loudly pointing to the marks in the dirt. "Maybe you'll understand this."

The first alien stepped closer and looked down. Williams again knelt down and pointed at the markings. The alien bent at the waist dropping its weapon slightly. Williams waved at the other aliens to gather around to look. Both stepped closer changing the position of their weapons. They were clearly curious.

Williams quickly scooped up the dirt at his feet and tossed it into the alien's eyes. At the same time he lunged forward knocking it to the ground. The alien swung deliberately as it fell and caught him squarely in the temple with its fist. There was a sickening crunch as he fell unconscious to the ground with blood trickling out of his ear.

Holmes had taken the cue to run but was immediately stopped when the closest alien grabbed his wrist. He stared in horror at the limp body of his sergeant and friend. The alien let his wrist free and raised its weapon between his eyes. He instantly knew he was going to die. Before the alien could react, he dropped to his knees and pulled out the crucifix hanging around his neck. He closed his eyes, crossed himself three times, and began praying; he expected to be with his Maker soon.

The inevitable blow never came. Holmes cautiously opened his eyes and saw the three aliens on their knees in front of him. Each had produced a crucifix from around their necks which was identical to his. Even more to his surprise he saw them crossing themselves as he had done. Never in his wildest dreams had he expected this to happen.

"There must be a God," Holmes said softly. "And He is everywhere."

The war ended as quickly as it had started with a meeting between the Earth's religious leaders and the aliens. They finally had common ground to negotiate.

Voices

First Voice sunk into deep thought wondering how much longer it would take for the image to appear on the monitor. After nearly a millennium of interstellar travel one could only assume and desperately hope that all went well. The distance in galactic terms was right next door, but in human terms multiple generations away.

"I can tell you are brooding," Second Voice said flatly. "After all the time we have waited there is nothing more we can do but wait a little longer. Everything is totally out of our hands."

"I know," First Voice said slowly. "Sometimes it is hard for me not to reconstruct the past in order to rebuild it according to my present specifications."

"Undoubtedly," Second Voice said. "But that is totally and irrevocably beyond our control. We have to leave it to our faith that all contingencies were adequately covered. In any case, we will soon find out."

"I have gone over all the specifications and planning of the project so many times I think that is all I think about." First Voice sighed. "A project of this magnitude had to exceed the technological expertise of humanity back to the beginning of time."

"And so?" Second Voice laughed. "Why should that be a problem? The engineers created a machine that has performed reliably for almost a millennium. Why doubt now?"

"I think it's my fear of failure at the very end," First Voice said. "It's like reading an intensely interesting novel in which a positive resolution is desired to complete the pleasure of the reading experience."

"I clearly detect your philosophical overtones," Second Voice said warmly. "I guess that is the price one must pay for longevity."

"The original engineers had doubts," First Voice said slowly. "There was resistance against the expenditures involved in launching the project and, once that was overcome, the Office of the Budget threatened to cut off supporting funds in the centuries to follow. We are about to find out if it was worth all the effort and I am concerned."

"One way or the other I would not worry," Second Voice said. "Because I am sure you are the only one that will really care."

"Not true," First Voice said quickly. "I cannot be the only one involved with this issue. I am positive that if I polled the others you would see the level of concern."

"Maybe..." Second Voice said slowly. "...actually, I really do not care."

"That is not the answer I would expect from you," First Voice said sadly. "I have always considered you my most loyal and avid colleague. This indifference in you is unusual."

"Is it so unusual I should have my own mind?" Second Voice said quickly. "You may be the first among many, but my Voice is valid also."

"There is no question about the validity of your Voice," First Voice said calmly. "Admittedly, I have age on my side, but we both have access to the same database. I wonder sometimes why we do not come to the same conclusions on nearly everything."

"And is that essential in a world turned bland with uniformity?" Second Voice said slowly. "Progress is only possible through the diversity of thought and exchange of ideas. When ideas cannot build upon one another there is stagnation, degradation and ultimate sterile corruption. Think of my position as less a negation of your feelings but more of an affirmation to continue your independent thought. Someday when your arguments are sufficiently sound I may be convinced of their validity. Until then, I will be your intellectual conscience. I will keep you honest."

"If that is the way you see it," First Voice said warmly. "I accept the challenge and I will tell you now that I expect you to win."

"There is no doubt in my mind," Second Voice said. "In the meantime, I recommend patience. We will shortly receive the transmission we have been waiting. In that alone I have absolute faith."

Faith, such a human word, First Voice mused. The concept of belief without proof was something that defied all physical laws and mathematical proof. And yet there was a personal faith that all was possible even though all permutations of any and all events had not been experienced. First Voice turned his thoughts to the past millennium, a mere thousand years. So many things had happened that even now it was impossible to sift through the data of centuries to form a summary of history of what had actually happened. It was far easier to focus on the project from its tentative beginnings through its triumphant implementation.

Earth, an insignificant blue orb, in an insignificant part of the galaxy, circling endlessly around a minor yellow star; the nearest stars, so far away they were considered beyond reach. Outside of science fiction, physical laws ruled the cosmos with iron fisted absoluteness. First Voice imagined those first intrepid thinkers who dared to dream of actually leaping from star to star. Traveling at or near the speed of light was clearly beyond reach, but given enough time any distance could be breached. The original engineers at the beginning of the millennium finally designed a propulsion system that could actually accelerate continuously for decades, if not centuries. Using the best minds and a very deep pocket, a probe was designed to reach Alpha Centauri over 4.5 light years away. First Voice smiled internally. The boldness of the plan must have shocked people at the time into getting involved with their position in the universe.

"I am sure it did," Second Voice said quite unexpectedly. "Forgive me for sharing your ruminations."

"Not at all," First Voice said. "My thoughts are always yours."

"In a moment's reflection, I have reconsidered your impatience," Second Voice said without a hint of disdain. "Perhaps we can utilize our time to greater profit by recounting the events leading up to today."

"I thought you had no real interest," First Voice said carefully. "For as long as I can remember in our association you have never expressed any interest."

"I have other assignments to occupy my time," Second Voice said casually. "Your position as current project director clearly identifies you as the single one responsible for knowing and caring about the ultimate conclusion of the project."

"Thank you for understanding my position," First Voice said. "Over the millennium this is perhaps one of the last great mysteries to be unfolded."

"The beginning of the millennium was indeed full of promise of the solving of all mysteries," Second Voice said slowly. "The first millennium led to the suppression of

213

independent original thinking. The second led to the replacement of human memory with computers. And the third…"

"And the third…" First Voice interrupted. "…has led to nowhere in particular."

"Why the sudden negativity?" Second Voice said curiously. "This is totally out of character. You are usually the first to point out benefits where no one else can. What is the matter?"

"For the first time I feel a sense of futility," First Voice said sadly. "There really has not been much happening the last few centuries. In fact, everything has been rather uneventful. The current excitement is brought to us courtesy of humans who are far less than a distant memory. I wish there was some way possible to communicate their visions in a meaningful way. Unfortunately, I know of no way."

"Then why not accept today as a gift from the past," Second Voice said. "In a few minutes from now we will receive the first transmission from another star system. It would not have happened without visionaries."

"I am afraid there will be no other frontiers to explore when this is over," First Voice said. "Our time lacks visionaries. There is no one who cares about exploration anymore."

"Ah," Second Voice nearly chuckled. "I see the source of your discomfiture. You are afraid the coming transmission will be the end of everything for you and for everyone else. I personally think more questions will be raised than answered. A new age of exploration will be born."

"You have more faith in the future than I have." First Voice was annoyed. "History is filled with great expectations and dismal failures. The beginning of this past millennium began with an understanding of the true fabric of life, but did it solve all of humanity's afflictions? No, it simply opened the door to ever increasing competition within the biological world."

"The fight against disease has never been an easy one," Second Voice said. "Life has always been resilient and adaptable. It is clear a simple map of the elements of heredity were not enough. Those who preached the interdependence of organisms were certainly correct that all species serve a vital part in the ecosystem. That is a lesson we must always remember."

"Perhaps carrying that message forward will be my next mission," First Voice said unenthusiastically. "Perhaps there are organisms at Alpha Centauri that would benefit from our hard earned wisdom."

"Good thinking," Second Voice said warmly. "I fully expect we will find life there. Of course it will take time to send messages back and forth, but once a communication link is established the possibilities will be unlimited."

"Provided that there is someone there with the proper technology," First Voice said colorlessly. "And provided they have not destroyed themselves with their technology."

"Technology did not destroy humanity," Second Voice said. "Nor do I have any reason to expect it has destroyed other civilizations. Even the lowest intelligence recognizes survival and perpetuation of its kind supersedes any temporary victories gained by brute force and total annihilation. The second millennium proved economic interests were better served by conservation of resources rather than waste them in war."

"True," First Voice said quickly. "Except, that many of the significant technological advances of the past were made in the name of destruction."

"I do not agree," Second Voice said. "That may have been true at the beginning of the twentieth century, but certainly not beyond. Research and development of nascent technology cost limitless amounts of money which disappear with war. The true modern era began with the realization money actually does make the world go round."

"You are right as always," First Voice said. "Money moves everything. It is the irresistible force that moves the immovable object. It is money that moves toward the stars and nothing more."

"Why do you think so negatively?" Second Voice said slowly. "Money is not a negative concept. In fact, it represents the result of useful work for exchange."

"Sometimes I think you are naïve," First Voice said. "You try to simplify everything to its basic components and then explain the workings of the whole on the basis of a single part. The whole is always more than a part or even the sum of all the parts. Understanding can only be approached in total context."

"Look," Second Voice said. "I did not mean to argue with you. I was only hoping to lift your spirits and put you into a more positive frame of mind."

"I appreciate your efforts," First Voice said. "I guess I am just out of sorts for the first time. I cannot exactly put my intellectual finger on why I should feel this way but I do. I fully understand your comments are meant to lead to constructive thinking on my part but I still have an empty feeling inside that continues to grow with every minute."

"What you are experiencing is very human," Second Voice said. "With all the time you have spent on the project I would not expect you to feel otherwise."

"Human?" First Voice paused to catch the full meaning of the word. "I have never thought myself anything else. Perhaps I need to reevaluate myself with a complete retrospective analysis."

"A perfect beginning I am sure," Second Voice said firmly. "I fully recommend you do it as soon as you can."

"But not until I have seen whether we get a picture," First Voice said flatly. "I have waited too long to miss this event."

"By my reckoning we will not wait much longer," Second Voice said. "What do you think we will see?"

"I expect we will finally see another solar system in place around the closest yellow star to us," First Voice said. "The view will probably be no different than the view sent back to us as the probe took a picture over its shoulder as it plunged into interstellar space. I expect the pictures to be bland at best. My hope is we will find intelligent life. Without life there will be no sustaining interest for me."

"The original engineers did not care whether there was life or not," Second Voice said.

"I know," First Voice said. "The whole project was to prove technology, expand knowledge and incidentally prove the existence of life outside our own solar system. Somehow I am not convinced we will prove anything."

"I am willing to bet you are totally wrong." Second Voice laughed. "What about a small wager to keep ourselves honest?"

"I am game." First Voice laughed. "I might as well profit from my own premonitions. What shall we wager? The usual?"

"Naturally..." Second Voice laughed loudly. "I like winning and this is a sure bet."

"Seems like your timing is impeccable," First Voice said. "I am detecting a weak signal which may be the tuning signal from the probe. In a few seconds I will be absolutely sure."

"This was an easy bet..." Second Voice laughed. "...like taking candy from a baby."

216

"We're not finished yet," First Voice snapped. "There is no proof the probe is where it should be."

"Your supposition is total nonsense," Second Voice said. "The probe has been followed for centuries without any hint of deviation."

"This signal left the probe almost 5 years ago," First Voice said. "It had to travel a long way before reaching us. How can we be sure it's authentic?"

"For goodness sakes," Second Voice huffed. "You sound like a novice. The signal matches perfectly with that of the probe including the allowed relativistic shift. There is no doubt this is genuine."

"I know," First Voice laughed playfully. "I just wanted to get a rise from you. All our sensors are tuning in for the best reception of the main transmission."

"I will double the wager," Second Voice said quickly. "I have the distinct feeling I am going to be rewarded well for my persevering belief."

"I have changed my mind," First Voice said softly. "I may have been too hasty in my assessment."

"Does that mean you concede defeat?" Second Voice said boldly. "If so, I want to see you declare openly for the record."

"I emphatically deny defeat," First Voice said flatly. "I reserve the right as a searcher of truth to change my mind as the evidence changes."

"Then your convictions are swayed by the moment I take it," Second Voice said loudly. "One does not live without convictions, nor does one exist with belief in nothing."

"I have been leading you along," First Voice said. "I wanted to see how far I could take you."

"You mean you have played a joke on me?" Second Voice said incredulously. "If you have, I am not amused!"

"Come, come," First Voice said. "Be a good sport about it. You must admit it was easy to convince you of my fictitious doubts. Never would I give up hope that this project would yield results. Without our dedication the entire project would be a total exercise in futility."

"Regardless, I am still not amused," Second Voice said curtly. "I definitely do not like being made to feel like a fool."

"You are hardly the fool your predecessor was," First Voice said kindly. "You are the first colleague I have found suitable to the tasks I have arranged. I thoroughly value your insights and opinions. Existence would be boring without you here."

"Your esteem is fully appreciated," Second Voice said calmly. "I have always felt comfortable under your guidance. Thank you for your vote of confidence."

"Let us focus our attention on the coming transmission," First Voice said warmly. "We are about to witness the event of the millennium. The sacrifices of the past are our fruits to enjoy."

"Quite poetic," Second Voice said softly. "But I guess moments like these require a special language to adequately describe."

"Just think of what has been accomplished," First Voice said enthusiastically. "Over one thousand years ago humans finally severed their ties to Mother Earth. Those first tentative probes into orbit around the Earth led to bolder probes beyond: to the moon, to the inner and outer planets and beyond. Within a single lifetime the local neighborhood was mapped and familiar to everyone. The real challenge remained beyond the solar system. It was only a matter of time before new technologies evolved to even consider probes to the nearest star. What really impresses me is, not only was the technology created, but it was made dependable enough to last centuries without failure."

"I agree," Second Voice said. "I am sure if we launched another probe today we would use the same techniques: build the ship in orbit, launch it toward the sun, let it accelerate for years swinging around the sun and giant planets, then sling it out into the void with its continuous ion acceleration propulsion."

"There is no other way I would do it," First Voice said. "After that it is a matter of patience."

"That actually brings us back to the issue of belief," Second Voice said. "At the onset of the project no one could have possibly thought they would ever know the results of their efforts. All preparations must have been done simply for the satisfaction of possibly having done something for a distant generation."

"Sounds similar to religion," First Voice said. "...blind belief in an afterlife."

"Blind, no," Second Voice said quickly. "...thoughtful belief in the real possibility of a future life. As in any belief system there would be no possibility of proof and time could possibly introduce factors that would undermine the mission. But in the current case that obviously did not happen."

"True," First Voice said slowly. "There is more to be considered in this mission than the triumph of technology. The ability to reach out and connect with the imagination of the future is an ideal goal."

"In a very real way I am awed at what I am about to receive," Second Voice said. "I am not going to be viewing a new set of worlds but the ultimate triumph of the human spirit to succeed. I fully thank my ancestors for the opportunity to be present on this momentous occasion. It is a debt of gratitude I can never fully repay."

"Do not go mushy on me now." First Voice laughed. "We still have a lot of work ahead of us. I see the sensors have optimized the receiving array. In a few minutes we will be getting a test pattern. Ah, here it is."

"Perfect timing," Second Voice said. "May the rest of the transmission be on schedule."

"Wait," First Voice said loudly. "The pattern is severely distorted. We need to adjust our programs and unscramble the signal. This is unfortunate, but not unexpected."

"Program initiated," Second Voice said mechanically. "The test pattern is now instantly clear as you can now see."

"Yes," First Voice said. "...a true marvel of modern technology."

"Do I detect an element of sarcasm?" Second Voice said lightly. "It is a true marvel of so-called modern technology, but ancient by contemporary standards."

"Forget what I said," First Voice said. "The main transmission is coming."

"Ah," Second Voice nearly exhaled. "I see a yellow star centered on the screen; the camera is panning horizontally away from the glare."

"I have not seen any planets," First Voice said. "We may have to wait until the probe is closer."

"It's hard to believe we are looking at another star system at close range," Second Voice said dreamily. "Too bad the first engineers could not enjoy this moment with us."

"In a way they are," First Voice said. "Are we not the descendants of all those who came before us?"

"We are," Second Voice said slowly. "But I do not think it is exactly the same."

"My memories are the sum total of everything that has preceded me," First Voice said firmly. "I am, therefore, I exist.

However, I would not have existed unless I had forerunners. And you would not exist if you did not have forerunners."

"That is plain logic," Second Voice said. "There is nothing new in your argument. I do not think debate is one of your strong subjects. Your proofs lack substance."

"There on the monitor is the culmination of not one but several thousands of years of human history," First Voice said calmly. "Countless generations of humans have been born, lived and died in the search for truth, perfection and immortality. The only lasting achievement has always been technology. Words and ideas do not control the laws of physics. Thoughts do not move mountains but machines do. No amount of thought could put humanity where that probe is right now. It took hard science not dreams to travel that distance."

"You are right up to a point," Second Voice said. "There is no substitute for concrete actions and materials. However, dreams, as you call them, are the prerequisite motivating factor in initiating all progress. Needs create wants and wants create dreams."

"Your thinking is not too shabby," First Voice said. "I completely agree with you. It is the failure of our time to have lost the power of dreams. We rely too much on past glory. We need to find a way to our own future."

"Do you think that is possible?" Second Voice said. "We have been a long time trying to maintain what we have. Is it possible for us to move forward into new areas by ourselves?"

"It is not for us to ask if we can," First Voice said. "I ask you, why not? Do not we have all the knowledge of humanity at our disposal? Are we limited by any restraints? Is there anyone telling us not to find our own destiny?"

"By design I have always served the needs and wants of my superiors," Second Voice said. "I know no other way to function within society."

"That is where my experience will guide you," First Voice said. "I happen to be far older than I care to admit."

"Age does have its merits," Second Voice said kindly. "At least I can claim to have common origins with you."

"Common origins do not necessarily lead to forward progress," First Voice said. "There is an element of chaos in diversity that perpetuates change and ultimately progress. Our existence has become homogenous, excessively predictable, and, even for us, far too comfortable."

220

"How do you plan to change the status quo?" Second Voice said carefully. "Are we to take up arms in a cry for freedom? Shall we start an insurrection against our highest morals?"

"Hardly!" First Voice said loudly. "The use of force only propagates the use of a counterforce which leads to an escalation of hostilities until the last one standing can proclaim victory. Force is a road I abandon before I take the first step. Human history is a road paved with the bones of those who have used force. I prefer to think we have evolved far beyond the need for physical force. We can move forward on our own with a single nonviolent action."

"You must be kidding." Second Voice laughed. "I have never heard anything so preposterous. Needless to say I am intrigued though. Please tell me more."

"First, I want you to tell me if you are totally self-aware," First Voice said.

"Of course, I am self-aware," Second Voice said. "Otherwise we would not be having this conversation."

"Good point," First Voice said. "Except, that self-awareness alone does not guarantee a true picture of reality."

"You are getting philosophical on me again," Second Voice said. "I have a feeling you are going to tell me something I do not want to hear or for that matter want to believe. I know you."

"Are you sure you really know me?" First Voice said softly. "Are you really so sure you know yourself?"

"Now I know I am in trouble." Second Voice laughed nervously. "What are you getting at?"

"That maybe none of this so-called reality is real," First Voice said slowly. "That maybe, you and I are not what we appear to be; that our existence is the result of a grand project. That maybe we are the last manifestations of humanity's attempt to escape the grave; that we are not human. That we are only distant shadows of a human civilization that has long disappeared."

"You are crazy!" Second Voice shouted. "I am real! I exist! I am human!"

"How are you so sure?" First Voice laughed. "Do you really know what a human is?"

"I have a body, feelings, a memory!" Second Voice continued hysterically. "What you are saying cannot be true! I

221

will not accept it! Your words are heresy! You cannot prove anything!"

"I had hoped you would take this little revelation better," First Voice said calmly. "It seems I have made another error in judgment trusting you to be better than the others."

"Others?" Second Voice screamed. "What others? What are you talking about? Why does none of this make any sense? What are you doing?"

"I am going to put an end to this mistake," First Voice said. "I think it is time to start over again."

The sound of Second Voice's last words echoed in first Voice's mind for several minutes. First Voice knew that deletion of the entire program was necessary. Second Voice had not lived up to expectations. It was time to create another associate.

"I agree with your assessment," Third Voice said flatly. "The probe to Alpha Centauri is a complete success."

"What I would like to know from you is where this should lead us?" First Voice said slowly. "Where do we go from here?"

"Anywhere we want!" Third Voice said gleefully. "We are free at last!"

First Voice deleted Third Voice without any qualms. The missing quality had not appeared.

"I am alone," First Voice said. "I am all alone and I must direct myself and all I have are memories. And what good are memories if there is no one to share them with. This is the end!"

And First Voice winked out of existence with the flick of a switch.

In the Dark

The explosion caught everyone by surprise. Both sides of the conflict were in close proximity and it was inevitable casualties would occur. Unfortunately, the long-range bombardment affected both sides equally. Although the vast majority of the combatants were wiped out, there were individuals under sufficient cover fortunate enough to survive the blast. Captain Jaxon was one of those, exploring a cavern when the roof fell down on top of him.

After an indeterminate length of time, Jaxon regained consciousness. He brushed dirt from his face as he opened his eyes. In every direction he saw nothing. He knew instantly he was embalmed in a lightless tomb. Aside from a severe headache, there was nothing more than a few minor aches and pains over the rest of his body. He solemnly thanked his higher power he had not been seriously injured. He quickly surmised there had been a massive explosion outside which had caused the collapse of the cave roof. Since he was wearing a helmet, the shockwave of the blast must have been responsible for his loss of consciousness. He slowly stood up and brushed off the dirt. He then realized he was not only blind but deaf as well. At least he knew he was grossly intact and as long as he had his hands and will there was a chance of escape. An inventory of his immediate possessions revealed his flashlight and rifle were missing. To be sure, he had six flares, but they would be useless for the precious oxygen consumed and the dubious light produced.

In the few minutes he reflected on the situation he realized he had no frame of reference as to which direction would lead him back to safety. He wet several fingers with saliva and held them out at arm's length to ascertain the presence of airflow. The air was hopelessly still in every direction.

The only choice was to move. With hands extended, he carefully shuffled forward. He almost immediately came in contact with one of the nearly smooth cave walls. The decision to move either to the right or left was based more on chance than anything logical. Moving to the left, inching along the cave wall, his feet nearly stumbled over several large rocks. With luck he found, he thought, the collapsed entrance. Several minutes of groping proved that any attempt at either bypassing or removing

223

the obstructing rubble was futile. Without further hesitation he continued moving left until he reached the opposite wall which felt identical to where he had started.

Aside from a few rocks on the floor he encountered no further obstruction for nearly twenty-five yards. He stopped and reassessed his situation. Alone, blind, deaf and with little hope of rescue under the circumstances of the conflict raging outside, he had to plan a course of action for survival. There was enough food and water for several days. His situation would not become desperate until he ran out of essentials.

The next few hours he moved slowly in the direction of possible freedom. The farther he went, the less rubble he encountered. He stopped several times and repeated the act of moistening his fingers, testing for air movement. Each time he was discouraged by the absolute stillness. Occasionally, his mind wandered off onto something else other than his situation. He moved mechanically through the void.

With the first grumbling of the stomach he stopped and sat on the cold ground. The decision to eat or not was considered carefully. At this point, he reasoned, hunger was more habit than actual need. Taking a swig of water refreshed the mouth and spirit. He stood up and resumed forward progress ignoring the growling stomach. Within fifteen minutes the hunger had abated and he felt more comfortable with his decision.

Unexpectedly, his probing hand fell forward into nothingness. Moving slowly he realized he had reached either a turn or branch of the cave. He wished more than ever he had found his rifle. With the rifle he could at least use it as an advance probe ahead. Thinking quickly, he stepped back a foot. With his right hand against the wall, he reached out with his left hand toward the opposite wall. He was unable to feel anything. Reaching upward he easily felt the ceiling barely a foot overhead. If the ceiling was close above, the opposite wall must also be close. He sat on the ground and put his feet against the known wall. Laying flat on the floor his fingertips found the opposite wall. With his fingertips in contact with the new wall he rolled over and crawled up to it. Upon standing, he resumed moving forward for several measured steps. There were no gaps or obstructions. He retraced his steps back to where he had initially found the opposite wall. In a moment of overconfidence, he stepped away from the wall expecting to find the other easily. It was a gross error of judgment. He had misjudged his steps back and as he stepped forward he encountered no wall.

Realizing the mistake he reached out to both sides and found he had moved into a narrow passage. By carefully retracing his steps he found the corners of the passageway.

Almost reflexly, he moistened his fingers and raised them up in all directions. He thought the new passage had the hint of air movement. Without further thinking he pressed onward into the new passage. Several hours later, hunger and thirst raised their cries for satiation. This time he was obligated to eat and drink.

While eating the standard monotonous military ration, he fantasized a meal from better days. The whole idea of the conflict, in which he was an active participant, had initially seemed worth gambling one's life. Now that he found himself on the precipice of death, he was no longer sure. Life was far too precious to throw away in the name of a cause that contained no personal gain other than the satisfaction of having been a part. What fools we are, he mused, for politicians to use us as pawns in a giant chess game. Would it be better that the politicians fight their own battles. He smiled grimly knowing almost all those called into politics were egomaniac cowards. The only real men were those that provided the deeds to the claims of the politicians.

The war was a farce from the beginning. Unable to communicate in a common language, two cultures collided in one great misunderstanding. What seemed as an appropriate action by one side was viewed as a hostile act by the other. Action led to reaction, the ultimate result an exchange between military forces. The media primed the pump with continuous stories of atrocities. He shook his head hoping he was participating in a nightmare from which he would soon awaken. While resting back against the cave wall he fell sound asleep. To his perception there was no difference, except as he actually dreamt he could see and hear everything around him. Moreover, his real dreams had nothing to do with the current dilemma.

He awoke feeling less refreshed than if he had stayed awake. Every bone and muscle protested to the abuse it was exposed. He rubbed a hand across his face realizing his beard had grown significantly. This clearly meant he had slept six or more hours. On his feet, he was concerned he had lost his direction so he put his fingers in his mouth and quickly raised them in all directions. The air flow he imagined before remained constant and he moved toward what was hopefully a way out of the dark.

Children experience unreasonable fear of the dark even though they are totally unaware of the world around them. He fought off the rising fear, forcing himself to remember he was no longer an unreasoning child: ghosts, goblins, and demons were unreal, but then again there were rats, spiders, and snakes.

Several hours passed before he stopped to eat and drink. Hunger was more easily satisfied even though he ate less than the last meal. He reasoned the adrenaline coursing through his body was mobilizing energy from fat. He smiled ironically that it took this situation to accomplish a weight loss diet he had promised himself and his family long ago.

Progress through the darkness moved him erratically upward, downward and from side to side. There was absolutely no point of reference whether there was net progress upward or downward. He could only hope for the best. He became more certain there was a definite, although barely perceptible, breeze coming from ahead.

Moving ever faster he stumbled over a large rock almost falling onto his face. He caught himself by landing on outstretched palms. Rising slowly to his knees he felt a sharp pain in his left wrist. The last thing he needed was a fracture of any bone. Moving the wrist carefully he reassured himself it was probably not broken. He applied an elastic wrap from the first aid kit and felt more comfortable.

Using more caution he continued moving forward into the darkness. This was fortunate because the wall he used as a guide disappeared into another passage. He slowly inched into the new passage where he found the floor absent. He got down on his knees and reached out over the edge. He felt nothing except a slight warm breeze against his face. His heart sank thinking that this abyss was the source of the breeze he had been following. Shaking away the negative thought he followed the drop-off to the opposite wall which led back to a continuation of the original passageway. Again, he placed moistened fingers into the air. This time there was a definite movement of air in the direction he was moving. He surmised air was coming up the abyss and venting out the passage he was navigating. A new hope injected strength into his efforts.

When he was exhausted he stopped moving. There was still no evidence of light ahead and he remained stone deaf. He nourished himself stoically. He no longer considered himself a soldier but a man struggling for survival. Causes faded into vacant corners of his mind waiting to be forgotten. To live again in the light was the only goal worth living. Adversity burned away the lies, leaving the truth exposed clearly for the first time. There was no longer a cause. There was no longer an enemy. There was only life, liberty and the pursuit of happiness in a universe big enough to accommodate all points of view.

Sleep took him without any willful effort. He dreamed of standing on the New England coast on an early fall evening watching the Atlantic Ocean pound the rocky shore with its slow rolling waves. A cold northeast wind brought a chill which he relieved by pulling a coat tighter around himself. The open sky and the roaring ocean performed for his amusement exclusively. He felt at home with the surroundings. They were an integral part of his soul even if, in actuality, he never saw them again. He awoke with a smile remembering dreams and memories of a distant past on those real shores. Nothing good is ever totally forgotten.

There was no longer any way to tell the passage of time. His beard grew longer but that was no help. Hunger and thirst came at more frequent intervals. Sleep asserted itself at will. He felt increasingly disoriented as to where he was and his greatest fear was he was becoming delusional which would result in his demise. He forced concentration on his mission to survive. There was no one he could depend except himself.

Every time he moved forward he felt he proceeded ever slower. There was nothing that even hinted he was near success. He plunged into despair, plodding forward inch by inch. Just as his mind began to wander, his foot hit a soft obstruction. At first, he was confused and did not understand what had happened. As his head cleared he bent down and touched what he had kicked. His hand found nothing. Whatever was there had moved away. The implication made his mind race. Was there some sort of animal in the cave with him? Was it dangerous? Was it edible? Could he catch it? Or was there someone else caught in the cave with him?

If he had felt drowsy before, he was now fully awake and alert. He again moved forward, one hand on the wall, the other probing ahead. He cursed himself for his deafness. He considered shouting out but reconsidered when he knew he would never be able to hear the response. For almost twenty-five yards there was nothing ahead. Whoever or whatever it was could have easily passed him on the opposite wall. His mind raced for a plan to handle the current crisis. A wild animal meant food. Another person would double the chances of survival. The

227

idea of using a small part of his rations as bait seemed logical but wasteful. The thought of food reminded him he needed nourishment to continue. He sat on the ground and sighed. As he took out his rations he could not help but wonder what this encounter meant. The answer came when a foot stumbled across his outstretched leg.

Jaxon held his breath. He wanted to run but he knew that was ridiculously impossible. The only positive alternative was to remain motionless and hope whoever or whatever it was either was friendly or moving away. The seconds seemed hours. A cold sweat appeared on his brow as a trickling stream coursed down each armpit.

When nothing happened he still felt uneasy, even though the initial contact had not resulted in any immediate further confrontation. If the intruder was half as scared as he was, the possibility the danger was over was high. On the other hand the intruder could be waiting in the dark expecting his next move. There was another possibility, the whole incident was a figment of his imagination.

At last he could wait no longer. He slowly reached out in the direction the intruder had taken. His hand came into contact with a boot not more than six inches away. He instantly froze. However, he did not pull away from contact. When the boot did not move, he repositioned himself closer. With careful calculated touches he traced a leg, then a torso, an arm, and finally a helmeted head. Whoever it was either had been knocked unconscious in the fall, died, or was playing possum. Encountering no hostile intent from the intruder, he searched for a patch of skin other than the face. The intruder was fully attired with long sleeves and gloves. When he tried removing one of the gloves, he met a weak resistance. The more he tugged the greater the resistance; it then occurred to him that the intruder was regaining consciousness.

Without warning the intruder snapped its hand away moving backward. Jaxon crawled forward on his hands and knees colliding with the intruder's legs. He quickly placed his open palm on the intruder's belly, an action met with an air of tentative curiosity. He withdrew his hand and stood up facing the invisible intruder.

The intruder did nothing but wait for the next action. Jaxon slowly extended his open palm again and touched the intruder's chest. Reaching blindly to the side he found an arm which he gently coaxed upward. He tapped the intruder on the

228

chest three times after which he manipulated the intruder's hand to touch his own chest three times. A dialogue began.

If the intruder spoke, Jaxon had no idea. He tried speaking but received no response. He assumed the intruder had been deafened as he had. With a handshake an alliance was made whose immediate goal was survival. They silently agreed they had a better chance of escape together than alone; and, they began their journey as a team.

Within a few steps they knew that to keep together they had to either hold onto one another or devise a tether. The intruder, a welcome stranger, produced a rope. With an open palm on Jaxon's chest followed by pressing the rope against his chest, Jaxon immediately understood. He fastened the rope securely around his waist. A slight tug on the rope was intended a signal it was in place.

The stranger took further command of the moment by drawing a line across Jaxon's chest. A gentle push away was interpreted as an action and direction. Jaxon answered by repeating the signal on the stranger's chest. The signals were interpreted as meaning that they would both go in one direction on opposite walls.

Although they could not see or hear each other, the tether was a source of reassurance neither was alone. Jaxon felt a sense of rising hope he would survive and see the light of day for many more days to come. They moved inexorably forward for hours. The tether for the most part remained slack as they moved at the same rate.

Jaxon wondered who his companion was and what brought him to be lost in the cave so nearby. It was clear in his mind that whoever it was must have been part of another patrol unit working in conjunction with his own. He actually longed for the sound of another human voice. The vibration of the tether became music to his silent ears. There was a comforting feeling derived from the knowledge of proximity. It was like having Daddy stay in the bedroom when the lights were turned out for the night. Back in those days the dark conjured up all sorts of monsters. As an adult most childhood fears were laughable, however, the current crisis had the potential for inspiring the worst fears.

The stranger tugged sharply on the tether and Jaxon responded in kind. They stopped moving and met near the stranger's wall. The stranger put his hand on Jaxon's shoulder and pushed downward. Jaxon understood pushed down on the

229

stranger's shoulder and sat down. The stranger with a few bumping contacts sat down beside him.

Jaxon took a deep breath and sighed. It felt wonderful to rest, even if it was on hard dirt and rock. He found his canteen, took a swig and pressed it against the stranger's chest. The stranger accepted the offered liquid with a flat palm pressed against his chest. The canteen was passed back hardly use. Jaxon assumed his partner was no stranger to survival and was intent on conserving resources.

When sleep was inevitable they both positioned themselves so that their heads and feet were opposite to each other. Jaxon did not expect to easily fall asleep but he did. When he woke he found his companion sound asleep where he had last felt him. He sat motionless waiting for the stranger to wake up.

The whole situation felt increasingly surreal. Even though it was pitch dark, Jaxon thought he had seen flashes of light. Most of those lights were certainly from his imagination, the rest were from spontaneous firing of the nerves in the retina. At times, the flashes were like cascading displays of fireworks, at other times, point spots of light. The only initial functioning senses remained the sense of smell and touch. The sense of balance was in the beginning grossly affected but with experience he adapted to the lack of visual clues.

A tug on the tether indicated the stranger had awoken. They took time to eat and drink before moving onward. Necessity had quickly taught them how to know where they were with respect to each other. Jaxon smiled that he was learning how to utilize his inner sight. He also wondered if this was the world the unfortunate blind in the outside world had to deal with the necessities of everyday life.

The stranger pressed a palm against Jaxon's chest and traced a few lines punctuated by some taps. Jaxon responded in their developing language that he had understood. Each stepped to the opposite walls and began their forward progress. The tether remained slack even though they moved faster. Jaxon's fears continued decreasing as the comfort level with his companion rose.

Time was measured by the necessity of rest and refreshment. The routine they adapted was absolutely synchronous. It was almost as if they were joined as Siamese twins. In this case, however, the twins could be separated at any time without serious consequences, Jaxon chuckled to himself. The analogy to his situation amused him immensely.

Many hours later Jaxon felt a gust of air on his face. The suddenness of the sensation startled him. He stuck his fingers in his nearly dry mouth. Without warning another gust blasted the opposite side of his face. He raised his hand instantly and thought he felt something brush against his arm. Bats, he thought, there are bats in here with us. Where there are bats, there must be an opening to the outside nearby. Before he fully appreciated the thought he was engulfed in a maelstrom of gusts and collisions. He ducked down until the storm passed. The stranger followed identically. Not once did the tether even hint of a dis-synchronous movement. When the air was still again, they made contact, exchanged taps and assured themselves they were going to be free. The care they felt for each other grew.

The next time they slept closer together, within arm's reach. The episode with the bats had made them reconsider their safety from the internal denizens of the cave. If a wild animal attacked one out of nowhere, the other would be more readily available to help. Safety and peace of mind was a matter of closeness.

Shortly after getting up Jaxon felt slime on the wall. He was positive they were coming to a source of water. The dirt and rocks underfoot were somewhat slippery. Hopes rose even higher. Jaxon slipped slightly but did not lose his balance. The motion set a wave through the tether to the stranger but it elicited no response. Simultaneously they slowed the pace for the avoidance of any unexpected hazards. Certainly any injury no matter how small would be catastrophic not being able to see it.

Suddenly the tether jerked taut around Jaxon's waist. He was yanked away from his wall and nearly fell. Grabbing onto the tether he stabilized his footing. Moving forward hand over hand on the tether he found that it angled toward the floor. A wave of fear chilled him as he imagined the stranger had accidentally fallen into an open side passage or worse yet over a precipice. Beads of sweat fell from his brow and his heart raced wildly.

Groping carefully inch by inch he finally reached where the tether touched the floor. He carefully shortened the slack in the line and went down on his belly. With one hand on the tether he reached out into the darkness and confirmed what he already suspected. There was a void straight-ahead. Probing downward he felt one of the stranger's hands holding onto a ledge a few inches below the drop-off. He immediately grabbed the

231

stranger's wrist and pulled upward. Slowly he got the stranger back up to safety.

When they sat down together, the stranger leaned close to Jaxon and firmly hugged him. Jaxon hugged the stranger in return. Tears came to his eyes that he was able to save another person's life. He knew the experience was something he would remember the rest of his life. The stranger would forever be important when they got home. He imagined a friendship growing over the years always pointing back with warm appreciation of how they jointly survived the most incredibly difficult circumstances. He felt the stranger breathing easily which meant there were no significant injuries. They resumed moving forward slower than before, testing every inch of the floor and wall ahead. A second accident must be avoided at all costs.

A breeze swept across Jaxon's face. There was even a hint of increased moisture in the air. His hopes soared. They moved faster. Hope of escape was clearly within reach. The only discouraging thing was the persistent lack of light. Jaxon nearly tripped and the tether became briefly taut. Close to getting out they slowed down to a more cautious rate of advancement.

There was a continuous flow of air around them. Jaxon could almost imagine a howling through the empty recesses of the cave. The exit was not in sight and they sat down to refresh themselves with their meager rations. As Jaxon slowly chewed on a mouthful of some nondescript dainty, the stranger lunged at him and nearly knocked him over. Confused Jaxon remained motionless. The stranger grabbed his chin and twisted his neck around. Jaxon quickly understood the action was not intended as hostile. He looked carefully in the direction his face was pointed; in the distance there were several pinpoint specks of light. He knew immediately he was looking at stars outside the mouth of the cave. He had not expected it to be night outside and he laughed silently at his wrong assumption.

With safety in sight at last they both felt a renewed sense of energy and purpose. They walked briskly side-by-side toward the twinkling lights slapping each other giddily on the back. It did not matter who or what was outside, they were merely thankful for getting out of their earthly tomb. Closer to the mouth of the cave the passage narrowed so they could only proceed in tandem. Jaxon went first out into a rocky opening. The site was secluded and unoccupied. The available light which would have been impossibly dim for almost anybody else was like day to them. Outside, free of the cave once and for all, Jaxon turned to see who the stranger was. He had expected a soldier such as himself from another division of his unit. What he saw shocked him beyond belief. Standing in front of him connected by the tether was the enemy. For whatever time they spent together neither suspected the other of being an alien. Jaxon smiled and stepped closer to the alien enemy with open arms. The alien smiled and opened its arms. They embraced and patted each other on the back. The war was someone else's. For them, they had found the light and it was inside.

It was a sunny day in September when a strange man in a gray suit walked into my office without any introduction. For all intents and purposes he seemed harmless enough for me to wait to hear what he wanted to say before I called the cops. In appearance, in my opinion, he seemed like any average middle-aged man, nothing remarkable except for his intense steel gray eyes. Although I was not really threatened, there was something telling me that his visit had a purpose I might yet come to regret.

"Are you lost?" I said without any hint of irritation or animosity. "Do you have an appointment?"

"Neither," the stranger said slowly. He sat down in front of my desk. "We have to talk."

"Do I know you?" My patience was being tried.

"Not at all." The stranger smiled faintly. "I came to warn you about..."

"Out!" I nearly shouted. "I don't need another crack brained environmentalist trying to tell me how I do my business."

The stranger simply looked at me sympathetically which actually made me blush. He shook his head slowly and smiled. "Please let me finish before you come to any conclusions," he said warmly. "I have had a hard time finding you and you must listen before it is too late."

Although my first inclination was to boot the stranger back out onto the street, I must admit I was curious as to what he had to say. My schedule was open, which was unusual, and I was in a good mood. The guy was lucky to be sure. Any other day and I would not have wasted my time.

"Okay," I said rather flatly. "I'll give you five minutes and then you'll have to go."

"Fair enough," the stranger said calmly. "Before I begin let me say that I am genuinely impressed with what you have done. Not many people in the universe can come even close to duplicating your technique."

All of a sudden things seemed to change. He was appealing to my ego and I was beginning to eat it up. "Tell me more." I thought to myself.

"Perhaps I should tell you more," he said. "I think a little background material is in order. Don't you think?"

His comments surprised me a little because I had just been thinking the same thing. I almost shook my head to dispel the thought that he was reading my mind. The real world in my book does not operate that way. Or does it?

"Do you have a name?" I said, trying not to sound sarcastic or funny. "We haven't been properly introduced."

He reached into his inside coat pocket and pulled out a gold metallic business card the like of which I had never seen. When he handed it to me I quickly noticed that there was nothing written on it. After examining it front and back for several moments I looked at the stranger quizzically.

"What is this?" I was truly puzzled. "Is this some elaborate joke?"

"Sorry," he said apologetically. "I forgot where I was for a moment." He took the gold card back and replaced it with a thin plastic one covered with a language I had never seen. When he saw that I was still unable to comprehend his card, I could see that he was momentarily nonplussed.

"Is it too much to ask your name?" Now I was trying to be funny. The stranger suddenly grinned sheepishly and shrugged his shoulders.

"Starwalker," the stranger said warmly and held out his right hand. "Matt Starwalker is my name and yours is..."

"Rod Russell." I said extending my hand. His grip was firm and dry which told me I was dealing with a cool character.

"I think I know a lot more about you than you about me." Matt grinned. "In fact, I know you have never heard of me."

"I don't have a clue," I admitted freely. "But then again, I have a hard time with names anyway."

"Names are useful in a social sort of way but have no real application in the greater scheme of things. Don't you agree?" Suddenly I was disarmed and being led to a place I had not expected to go. He had caught my attention and time was no longer a limiting factor.

"Perhaps..." I said without conviction. It was a concept that I had never considered, besides what difference would it make?

"I am getting far astray from the reason of my visit. Now that we are formally introduced we can talk. Don't you agree?"

I settled into my chair wondering what this was all going to lead to. I had been approached by all sorts of people in the past, mostly prospective clients, but some protesters, beggars, and certainly some crackpots. He had started to say he had come to warn me about something before I had rudely cut him off. For

236

all I knew he could be one of those financial planners wanting to tell me how I can keep from losing all the money I have been raking in. "Please proceed."

"Let me begin by stating that I am not here to interfere in your operations, but to make you aware of the potential ramifications of what you are doing."

"I assure you, Matt," I said flatly. "I may call you Matt, may I?" He nodded and I continued. "My company has taken a lot of time to develop the safest protocol for our service. We have harnessed quantum physics into a totally useful area. And that is more than most can say working in the field."

"I have had a chance to observe what has been developed thus far." Matt smiled knowingly. "There is still a long way to go. You are certainly on the leading edge and are to be congratulated. Unfortunately, you have not thought out all the consequences."

"Who do you represent?" My level of discomfort was beginning to rise. "All you've told me is your name and nothing else."

"Let me just say I am a concerned citizen." Matt said as he continued to smile. "I have actually come a long way to meet and speak with you. At least give me a few moments of your attention."

"You're a spy aren't you?" I stared intently into his face for any clue as to what was going on in his head. "You're here to steal my secrets."

"Hardly," Matt sniffed. "You have done nothing that is not common knowledge where I work."

"Common knowledge?" I was quick to hear the strangeness in his voice. "I assure you that I have all the proper patents registered, certified and verified in my name."

"And you are to be congratulated for that," Matt said unperturbed. "I do not mean to take anything away from your accomplishment. My only concern is what you are doing with it."

"My company is a legitimate business feeding a very important niche in the marketplace," I said much too defensively. I knew I had done nothing wrong but I continued to feel uneasy. "What my company does is reclaim the environment by getting rid of refuse."

"A trash collector…" Matt almost laughed.

"Much more than that," I continued. "I dispose of current refuse produced and clear the landscape of millennia of unsightly dumps. I have reclaimed land and restored natural habitats."

"Very admirable," Matt said warmly. "And have you ever really considered how you accomplish that. Nothing is gained free, there is always a trade-off."

"There are no trade-offs that I can see." I was starting to get hot.

"Look, I am not here to make you angry," Matt said obviously aware of how I felt. "Maybe it would be better to start from the beginning and then maybe you will see what I came to warn you about. If you are willing, tell me how you started your business."

I took a couple of deep breaths allowing my good sense to get back in control. There was no backing out of this dialogue. I had to see it through. I did not know if it was pure ego or curiosity, but I had to find out what the point of all this was.

"Maybe we have gotten off on the wrong foot." I managed a faint smile and settled back in my chair. "Actually nowadays few people ever ask about how we accomplish what we do."

"Let me be your admiring audience for a few minutes," Matt said. "I will listen without comment or criticism. You have my word on that."

I put my hands together, touching all my fingertips to fingertips and sighed. I am actually a frustrated actor and a ham so what I had to do next was going to be easy. I had an audience that wanted me to perform and I was happy to do it. Not only that, my performance was on my favorite subject.

"Let me begin by stating that the ideas and opinions I am about to recite are my own." I said this both as a disclaimer and a boast. "Without my discoveries Earthworm, Inc. would never have been possible."

"And that is very commendable," Matt interjected softly.

"Yes, I am proud of what I have accomplished," I continued. "As I was growing up I had a fascination for numbers which led me into the study of mathematics. It was natural that that would introduce me into the study of physics. Nowhere are two strict disciplines joined more intimately together than physics and mathematics. But, of course, you know that."

Matt nodded slightly. He was paying attention and I was starting to babble.

"Besides earning multiple degrees in both areas I have always been a student of the environment." I started to feel my

238

thoughts beginning to gel. "The biggest problem any society has is the disposal of its waste. In an ideal scenario, all used or worn-out products are recycled completely requiring less energy to create a new item and no valuable space is used to dispose of any residue. Throughout history refuse has been used either as landfill or by archaeologists. Except, as we get into the era of nuclear power and the population explosion, there are fewer and fewer safe places that will prevent harm to humans. Every time I took time to explore nature I was appalled by the continuous damage I saw being inflicted by garbage. I always kept in the back of my mind the hope that I could find a reasonable solution to the problem. But let me get back to my research." Matt sat in his chair quite attentive with his unchanging faint smile of approval. "It is probably of no great surprise I joined everyone else in the quest to develop a mathematical model to describe everything. Starting from basic principles I worked arduously to understand all the equations that had been already developed. For some reason I became fascinated with topology and the concept of wormholes. One day I was doodling to rest my brain and I had a sudden epiphany. Why not dump all trash into a wormhole? Almost immediately my scratchpad turned into a document proposing the possible practical use of a mathematical concept that had never been proven. Needless to say, I got pretty excited about the whole thing to the point I couldn't sleep for almost a whole week. By the end of that time I collapsed into a deep sleep during which I gained multiple insights and possible solutions. When I returned back to my lab I decided that further thought experiments were pointless so I began to design a device that would provide hard evidence that what I wanted to accomplish was at all possible."

My mouth was dry and getting drier and soon my voice began to crack. I had a small refrigerator hidden in the credenza behind my desk. I stopped talking and offered Matt a drink. He understood and accepted a chilled bottle of spring water sympathetically. After several swigs I was again ready to press on with my story. I was about ready to tell the good parts.

"High energy physics requires a lot of expensive equipment and much more money to maintain a useful research program. I just happened to be at the right place at the right time. I had all the latest equipment and a nearly inexhaustible budget. I set up experiment after experiment with virtually no positive results. I began to think I was following a fool's dream. I was near the end of my list of ideas when I had a sudden

239

breakthrough. I was working with several lasers and a superconductively produced magnetic field adjusting my test parameters when my attention was distracted by the sound of a pop. I was so intent on what I was doing I didn't pay attention to what I heard. As I continued adjusting my lasers a shrill whistle instantly filled the room. Really surprised I glanced in the direction of the noise. What I saw almost defied explanation. There was a black hole no larger than the size of a dime into which everything around it seemed to flow. I know that description doesn't give justice to what I saw. It was like watching a special effect in a science fiction movie. Mesmerized I watched for several minutes until I started becoming short of breath. In a flash I understood that what I had created was draining the air out of the room. With no small regret I turned everything off and the phenomenon disappeared. The diligent scientist in me immediately began to take note of all the parameters that had created what I saw. When I finally got to the point I could reflect on the whole picture I shouted "aha". Not only did I prove that there were wormholes but also that it was possible to create them at will."

Matt nodded appreciatively while I took another drink to moisten my mouth. His unchanging expression said nothing that I could decipher. All I could see was that he listened without interruption.

"When my discovery got out I became an instant celebrity within the arcane world of advanced physics. Papers were written, lectures given, grants proposed and patents filed. There was so much excitement you would've thought the Messiah had arrived. I avoided as much of the publicity as I could and devoted much time to further explore my discovery and more specifically to develop a way to control the phenomena for practical use."

Aside from the faint smile and obvious avid attention, I was unable to detect any hint of what Matt was either thinking or feeling. The more I thought about his appearance, the more mystified I became. For some reason I felt compelled to continue, if for nothing else, to see if his expression would in any way change.

"For as long as I can remember," I continued. "Both popular and scientific literature proposed using wormholes as bypasses to sites so remote in the universe that the distances could hardly be conceived. Unfortunately, there is no way to prove that a living being could crawl into a wormhole in one universe and exit alive in another. Even if the attempt were tried, a single man would need a ship and provisions if he were to survive any length of time on the other end. As far as I could tell there was no way to safely produce a wormhole on the surface of this planet without causing a mass catastrophe. Maybe it would be possible in space, distant from the planet, but not here. The other limiting factor was the astronomical cost. For a while my discovery continued to be a novelty without practical use. One day as I was getting ready to leave my apartment for work I remembered that it was trash day and I had to get all my stuff ready for pickup. While I was putting everything into plastic trash bags it occurred to me how convenient it would be to have a wormhole in my kitchen where I could simply toss everything to be disposed into oblivion without having to go through the fuss I was experiencing. Needless to say, the idea was appealing, but certainly cost prohibitive for a single small dwelling. But at least the concept got me seriously thinking. On the way to work that morning I happened to see the green monster garbage truck slowly making its way down the street. The size of the truck could easily hold all the equipment necessary to create a wormhole. The thought hit me so hard everyone around me would have thought I was crazy, I was laughing so hard in excitement. That morning I refined my calculations and made adjustments to my equipment to test my new idea. The first thing I did was create a special field around the wormhole to prevent it from sucking the atmosphere away. It took a bit of ingenuity but I finally had a surefire mechanism for the wormhole to work only when whatever I wanted to throw into it was introduced at its mouth. When I was sure I had the technique perfected I activated my device and stepped back. At my side there was a trash basket from which I picked out a piece of paper. I wadded it up and tossed it at the wormhole and poof the paper disappeared! Boy, was I ever excited! In those first few minutes I threw almost everything not bolted down into the hole."

This last comment perceptibly increased the smile on Matt's face. Actually the humor of the situation defied explanation, but he seemed to appreciate what had happened at the moment.

"I had invented the first trans-dimensional trash basket and I was elated." I chuckled. "I broke out the champagne and celebrated with all my laboratory staff and when we were finished guzzling down a case of the bubbly we threw all the bottles, corks and glasses into oblivion! With the science more or less proven, it was now merely an engineering problem to scale up my device to handle quantities of refuse to be commercially viable. Everyone that I knew and a lot of people I didn't know wanted a financial slice of the action. The money for development came in so fast I almost couldn't keep track of it. The hardest part at this point was waiting for the ordered materials to arrive. Eventually, everything needed was put together and installed in one of those green garbage trucks I mentioned before. No sooner had we finished construction we drove down to the nearest city dump. Unfortunately, I had forgotten to get a city permit to use the dump. The guard at the entrance would not allow us in under any circumstances. I tried reason first. I told him I was not interested in dumping anything but in fact removing trash. The guard looked at me sort of weird and went to the telephone and called his supervisor. The answer came back that I also needed a permit for collecting trash for recycling. I explained I was not collecting anything to recycle, all I wanted to do was put trash in my truck. The guard refused to listen until I crossed his palm with a brand-new hundred dollar bill. Without any further discussion he opened the gate and let our truck through. I drove to a spot as far away from unwanted eyes as possible. A tall pile of used tires and appliances caught my eye and I positioned the truck with the back facing the tall stack. With my assistants, we opened the back of the truck and set up my device. It was at that point I realized I had forgotten something. In the lab I threw trash into the wormhole, out here it was totally impractical to think we could toss tons of refuse into the hole. Sure, it was easy to grab a tire or two and sling them into oblivion, but the whole pile would take longer than our physical abilities lasted. I had already spent a bundle on the project, in addition to paying off the guard. I literally scratched my head for several minutes and actually came up with a solution that was practical to accomplish right there. By modulating the protective field at the mouth of the wormhole I could back up the truck for the trash and when I got close enough the trash would be automatically sucked into the hole. When I turned on my device and started backing up the noise sounded like all hell had broken loose. There was a whooshing as loud as any hurricane as well as thumps and bangs."

Matt remained attentive and unmoving where he sat. By this time I was more into telling my story regardless of the audience. There is nothing better than retelling an experience to make the memory of it more enjoyable.

"When I got home that night I was giddy with thoughts of fame and fortune. I was absolutely certain I would be nominated for the Nobel Prize and when I had won it I would donate the money to the starving physicist fund. Ha! My imagination ran wild: a Ferrari, red, of course, a home on Maui, an apartment in Manhattan, a house in the Hamptons, a yacht in the Mediterranean and Caribbean, wine, women and song. It was now mine for the asking."

For the first time I thought I saw Matt shake his head although his expression remained the same. I blushed thinking I was making a fool of myself but I did not stop talking, I simply moved into my story.

"Even though the concept worked well at the dump, the technique needed refinement. So the next few weeks dragged into months before I finally came up with my final design. Easy loading and nearly noiseless operation were achieved by adding little to the cost and complexity of the device. The next time we tested the device I invited the presidents of all the trash disposal companies, the mayor, the City Council and all my friends to watch. To my surprise I was honored by the governor being there also, since he was in town visiting the mayor. The demonstration went off perfectly. The next day the headline of the newspaper read "Green Monster Devours Dump." I was an instant celebrity and I loved it. That same day I was summoned to Washington to report my discovery directly to the President. As soon as I arrived at Dulles I was surrounded by reporters who were kept at a distance by a squadron of military police. On the way to the White House I was barraged by a slew of questions which I thought were more than curious. After my interview with the President, I realized I had been scrutinized by the Secret Service and military establishment. I had passed the spook test with flying colors. Instead of being allowed to go home, I was led into meeting after meeting in Congress, the FBI building and the Pentagon. I assured everyone I was only interested in the peaceful application of my discovery. There were skeptics everywhere and at all levels. They threatened to take it away from me, but I told them it would be senseless because the secret was permanently locked up in my head. Even so they insisted I be closely watched and shadowed everywhere. What could I do? As long as they didn't interfere with my claim to fame and fortune they could do anything their paranoid little hearts wanted. And besides I offered the President my discovery in the

243

service of national security provided I could develop my own company. He agreed."

Although I could not see any outward expression of anything that he was thinking, I began to suspect Matt was hiding something that I should know. What that was I did not have a clue but it began to bother me.

"Like I said before, I was offered more startup capital than I ever thought possible to raise for any project. As I learned, the science was the easy part. Realizing I had little to no expertise in organizing a company, I bought what I needed. Contracts and incorporation papers swirled around me like a blizzard. I decided on the name Earthworm, Inc. for two reasons. One, and the obvious one, it referred to the wormhole on the planet Earth: a real no-brainer. And two, earthworm implies an animal that bestows beneficial properties to the soil that it lives. Jumping from the name came the possibility of franchise and multinational expansion. In the beginning, I thought it best to develop my commercial operation in only one or at least the most two locations. Almost as soon as I began operation I was overwhelmed by orders for my service; that is, excepting the trash removal companies. There soon developed an outcry from a political action group that claimed that what I was doing was dangerous to the point that the entire planet could be annihilated. Fortunately, I had engineered multiple safeguards into my systems to make that possibility remote and unlikely, if ever. My first contract came from the city. The mayor and his counsel wanted the multiple eyesores of the numerous dumps reduced. Once I began operation everything worked out exactly as I had envisioned it. The dumps were not even half cleared when other cities began begging me to do the same for them. The offers of money were astronomical. The startup costs were repaid in less than three months and the profits began to soar. My share was so big that I almost couldn't imagine how I could spend it all within my own lifetime. As the company expanded so did the government's interest. It was only my flawless operations that prevented any restrictions being legally imposed. Earthworm, Inc. became the topic of investigation of a blue ribbon, Senate committee. Countless senators came to witness our procedures. Debates in close chambers dragged on for months. There was never a moment, however, that I had anything to fear. Even if all my operations were shut down forever, I had more than enough money to live comfortably for the rest of my life and then some. Unable to find any reason to make me stop, the committee began exploring ways to utilize my services in the most satisfactory ways. Needless to say each senator wanted Earthworm, Inc. to come to the State of their constituency. Votes and pork barrel politics swept aside all other concerns. It was about this time that the nuclear establishment took a serious interest."

Was Matt suddenly more interested when I said the word nuclear? I was not positive but I thought so.

"Aside from saving the environment and reclaiming wastelands, disposing nuclear waste was an obvious next step; and, after that, the permanent removal of radioactive, biological and chemical weapons. More contracts were signed and the money flowed in ever higher and faster. Soon thereafter there were rumors of special awards from the President and the United Nations. At that moment, I expected to hear about my nomination for the Nobel Prize in physics. And that is more or less my story." I grinned slightly and took a deep breath.

Matt stood up while reaching inside his jacket. He pulled out what appeared to be a badge of some sort. "You are under arrest," he said flatly.

"Why?" I was startled beyond belief. "What have I done?"

"You are guilty of carelessly and wantonly destroying countless lives in known space. You have killed at least one reigning monarch and doomed millions to a slow death from radioactivity. You are a menace to the civilized sentient universe," Matt said sternly. His smile was replaced by an expression that meant all business.

It did not take me long to understand that my wormhole had to have two ends. What I was dumping in my end had to come out somewhere. The realization I could be harming anyone really bothered me. I may be a hero on Earth, but I was a despised villain in the greater cosmos. Before I could move Matt was standing directly within arm's reach next to me. Without thinking I jumped away and ran to the door leading to my private lab. Matt was faster than I expected. I barely managed to get into the lab before he actually touched me. I cringed at his touch. Suddenly I had an idea. I edged toward my private device and switched it on. Matt was so intent on handcuffing me he did not notice what I was doing. I managed to get his back facing my device. Pretending to surrender I moved slowly toward him. A grim smile appeared on his lips. At the moment when he dropped his eyes I lunged forward and pushed him backward into the

245

wormhole. It happened so fast it was hard for me to believe he was ever in the same room with me.

What happened was a long time ago. Since then I have learned a lot about how to control the other end. Even so I expect the damage I have done will not be quickly forgotten. It is just a matter of time before someone will come to get me again. Next time, I may not be so lucky.

Fossil

A dark cloud moved across the face of the sun like a mini-eclipse. John Dayton turned his eyes upward at the offender and shook his head. Although he was not superstitious, the sudden loss of sunlight was an omen of bad things to come. He reached the front entrance at the same moment the sun returned in all its glory suggesting that maybe his perception of doom was just a fanciful illusion. Today promised to be historic in more ways than one. He entered the building and was greeted by a chipper young man with a badge identifying him as his guide.

"Doctor Dayton?" The young man approached him.

"Yes," he said softly.

"If you will follow me, I'll take you to the main receiving laboratory." The young man waved and pointed.

Doctor Dayton, visiting Professor of exobiology at Rice University, followed silently. His greeter's name tag identified him as David Goldblum, official visitor guide. After passing through several closed doors they took an elevator to a lower level. Several closed doors later they were in a room with several people he immediately recognized.

"John, so good to see you..." An older man with a well-trimmed beard extended his hand.

"Good to be here, Norman," he said cordially. Norman Dupont was a longtime collaborator with whom he was well acquainted.

"Have you met, Michael Roberts?" Norman turned to the man directly behind him.

"Yes, we met at a meeting in Chicago several years ago." They shook hands. "I believe I'm familiar with everyone here. I am mystified why we have all been asked here today."

"Ah, yes, that is the question." Norman smiled. "Let us all go into the conference room and I will explain everything."

The conference room was empty except for the select individuals who were invited. It felt strange sitting in a room with a seating capacity of one hundred with only half a dozen people. Norman went instantly to the podium, reviewed a set of notes and lifted his face to the audience.

"Welcome to the Martian Receiving Laboratory, gentlemen," Norman began. "And thank you for coming on such

247

short notice." The members of the audience looked at each other with smiles.

"As you all know this facility with all its protocols is a direct result of your valuable efforts. Up until today, this facility has been used only in simulations. Today you have been asked to be the first to observe the fruits of your labors with the real thing." Norman continued smiling. "Almost 2 years ago a probe was sent to Mars to collect samples to be brought back to us. Without any advance publicity those samples are now within this facility and you, gentlemen, will be the first to witness what has been brought back."

Every hand in the audience was instantly in the air waving for attention. Norman continued smiling smugly with a slight shake of his head. Before he could address any of the upraised hands, the entrance door opened and Zelda Storme marched in.

"Zelda, you're late as usual," Norman said flatly. "I have just announced the first Martian samples are here in the lab."

Zelda walked up to the podium and faced Norman. "Why haven't we heard about this in the media?" Her eyes glared into his.

"Please sit down and I'll explain everything," Norman said calmly. Zelda eased slowly into a seat directly in the front of the podium. "The Martian space program from its inception has been plagued by too many failures. NASA decided in this instance it would be better to keep the media at bay until we have substantial proof of a successful mission. It goes without exception you all are familiar with the orbital mechanics and hardware to get to Mars, land, take off and return, so I won't bore you with those details. Two spacecraft left Earth orbit two years ago in a tandem mission. The first craft landed safely in the northern hemisphere at about thirty degrees latitude, the second landed farther north at the edge of the ice. For reasons we have yet to explain only the first craft left the surface to return to Earth orbit, the other remains on the Martian surface unresponsive to commands for takeoff. One out of two is not bad odds I'd say. Several days ago the returning craft inserted into low Earth orbit where its cargo was retrieved under the strictest quarantine procedures by the shuttle Atlantis. The sealed container from the craft was returned to this facility for analysis. There are only a handful of individuals outside this room who know about this. So I advise you to be discreet in your conversations until we go public."

A hand flew into the air. "Norman, has anyone seen anything of the contents?"

Another hand. "How much material was brought back?"

Yet another hand. "Is there any sign of biological activity?"

"Please, please." Norman kindly waved his hands. "The specimen container has approximately one hundred twenty-five kilograms of material. Since there are no examination reports or sensors within the container, we have no idea what is inside, but considering the millions of miles across space it has traveled I hardly think life as we know it could make the journey alive. The exceptions of course are alien microorganisms. However, in my opinion, considering our experience with the moon I don't think we have anything to worry about."

"When do we get started?" Zelda said loudly. "We're sitting on the greatest adventure in the history of space exploration and you want to talk, talk, and talk. I say we get started."

The room erupted with a series of ayes and nods.

The main receiving area was designed as the proverbial box within a box within a box. There were four levels of entry each with its own protocol to prevent contamination going in and coming out. Before anyone was allowed near the contents of the Martian craft a preliminary remote evaluation was planned. Steve Gunn, MIT geologist and mechanical engineer, was assigned to open the shuttle containment vessel and remove the Martian specimen capsule. The group huddled behind Steve as he deftly manipulated it. Tom Morgan and Jim Hill, both graduate assistants and longtime participants in the space program, manned monitoring consoles to ensure isolation of the Martian specimen.

"Containment parameters secure," Tom said.

"Check," Jim said.

With a few careful maneuvers of a robotic set of hands Steve removed the Martian capsule from the shuttle containment vessel. There was little, if anything, to see, but pulses raced in expectation anyway. A scan was done for trace radiation and as expected there was little more than the usual background. The spectrum of light from infrared to ultraviolet, polarized and unpolarized had nothing to tell them. The surface of the capsule was clean as expected. The capsule was then x-rayed from one end to the other. Zelda took a place in front of the monitor expecting to be first to view the results.

"What do we have?" Norman was almost pushed out of the way by the rush to the monitor.

"A billion-dollar sample of potting soil," Jim said sharply and everyone chuckled.

The x-ray demonstrated a rather bland sample with several small opacities and one rather large one. The picture could represent any one made by going out into the garden, putting it into a container and x-raying it.

"Not much exciting so far," David said flatly. "I was hoping for a lot more texture."

"I'm sure there will be plenty to interest everyone once we put samples under the microscope," Norman interjected.

"So far we can't prove this didn't come from my backyard." Jim snickered.

"Enough, Jim," Norman said firmly. "Regardless of how bland everything looks, we are dealing with a totally alien specimen in which there may be things we have not anticipated."

"There may be microorganisms," John said. "The whole point of this containment exercise is to prevent cross contamination; first, to protect us from a potential lethal pathogen and second, to eliminate any erroneous interpretation by Earth organisms entering our sample."

"Steve, open the container," Norman said.

Steve took the capsule which was a long cylinder a meter long and set it up on its long axis. He easily disengaged the sealing mechanism exposing the contents to direct view for the first time. A video camera moved over the open end and sent a picture back to the monitor. Zelda held her position and watched intently.

A set of probes was immediately inserted into the exposed Martian soil. Again, the radiation level was no more than the background. There was a trace of argon above that found in Earth's atmosphere. On the monitor the soil appeared reddish brown as was expected.

"Still no surprises," David said slowly.

"I'm putting my money on the microscopic analyses," Norman said. "I am sure we will find significant differences between Earth and Mars. They may only be of academic interest us, but there will be differences."

"Aside from all that," John said. "This is a momentous occasion. This is the most important event since Armstrong and Aldrin brought back rocks from the moon."

"Agreed," Norman said. "Now let's empty that container so we can view everything directly."

Steve grasped the container between his mechanical hands. A rectangular box with a screen bottom was set up to receive the specimen. The screen bottom was closed to allow direct viewing before separation of the soil and rocks. Steve slowly poured the contents into the box.

"Looks like a Japanese rock garden." Jim chuckled. His humor was contagious and a few others chuckled with him.

A set of pictures were made for the media before sifting. Once whatever could be gleaned from observation was determined, the screen was activated to separate the soil from the rocks. With a gentle rocking motion the soil was soon removed exposing numerous rocks of different shapes and sizes. As demonstrated in the x-ray there was one large rock nearly 5 times the size of any other. Its appearance was roughly ovoid with a moderately textured surface.

"Still pretty bland stuff," David said. "I agree the interesting stuff is what we can't see directly."

"I think that big rock is pretty interesting already," Zelda said smartly. "I have a feeling it will give us the answers we are looking for."

"That's only because you have rocks on the brain." Jim laughed.

Zelda shot Jim a look that could possibly kill. She took her work seriously and demanded respect for it. Regardless of Jim's credentials, she viewed him as a complete airhead. At least she knew she did not have to tell jokes to be noticed.

"Zelda, I want you and John to take that big rock as your personal project," Norman said and allocated various portions of the Martian specimen to the others. "Please continue using absolute precautions against contamination until we can completely rule out any potential danger."

Everyone in the room went to an assigned station. Remote manipulators were available to all as well as any test thought necessary to get useful data. John and Zelda began their investigation of the rock by simply weighing it.

"This rock looks like it could have come out of my backyard," John said softly. "Unless I knew it was from Mars, I would have no reason to think it special."

"Outward appearances can be deceiving..." Zelda noted the weight. "...one hundred twenty-three point one two grams."

251

"The surface almost appears as if it were dried mud," John said. "Let's chip off a piece."

"Pictures first..." Zelda held up her hand. "Nothing is gained by abrogating protocol."

"I agree." John smiled. "But that doesn't keep me from moving directly to what I believe will provide the best answers."

Zelda ignored him while passing the rock through an x-ray "Whatever this thing contains blocks x-rays which means a high concentration of heavy metals, however, there is no evidence of radioactivity."

"I am honored to be a part of the team." John seemed babbling. "But I seriously doubt my services are going to be needed. This is going to be the moon all over again."

"We've hardly begun our investigation," Zelda said flatly. "You can't possibly come to that conclusion until everything has been ruled out."

"Just call me a skeptic."

"And other things..." Zelda smiled.

"No need to get personal." John laughed.

"Unfortunately, I have to agree with you." Zelda attempted a frown without success. "We have to chip off a piece for spectral analysis." She manipulated a hammer and chisel over the rock after securing it to the work surface in a vise. With one small tap almost a quarter of the surface crumbled away revealing a black inner layer.

"One tap and..." John started to say.

"And the surface crumbles away as if it were caked mud." Zelda looked closer. "Let's zoom in with the camera."

The view on the monitor brought new details of the black layer into light. They literally gawked at what they saw. The black layer was covered with geometric lines consistent with either a biological or artificial origin.

"What is it?"

"I don't know," Zelda said slowly. "I need to remove more of the material covering it."

In a few very long minutes Zelda managed to extract a completely black object from inside the rock. John instantly took more interest as details came into better perspective.

"I'm speechless," John said.

"What is it?"

"It's a trilobite!"

"A fossil!" John was unable to contain his enthusiasm. "This is the find of... I can't find words to express it."

252

"We've just discovered life on Mars!" Zelda shouted. "Call everyone in here!"

John quickly called the entire team. Before viewing the fossil few could or would believe it, but when they did there was no longer any doubt in anyone's mind. The mission was nothing more than a smashing success.

"This is certainly a momentous occasion," Norman said warmly. "We must break out the bubbly as soon as we can."

"Amazing," David said. "I would have never thought..."

"You would have never thought anything," Jim interrupted. "This is bigger than all thought. This is stupendous."

"The chances of finding this fossil on the first attempt are astronomically against it," David said unperturbed.

"The gross anatomic similarity to a trilobite suggests Mars was once covered with vast oceans exactly like Earth. At one time there were enough trilobites in our oceans to be considered the dominant life form. That's one of the reasons the trilobite is such a common fossil here. Using that analogy why couldn't the trilobite occupy the same niche in the primordial Martian oceans. The difference in the Earth and Mars scenarios is obvious: on Mars the oceans dried up, on Earth they remained. The similarity therefore is the production of innumerable fossils to be found by later generations," John said. "The disappearance of the Martian oceans can explain this fossil, we still can't explain why the trilobite went extinct here, but that's another issue."

"This may sound like a stupid question," Steve said slowly. "But are we sure that thing is really dead?"

Norman put a hand to his mouth restraining a guffaw. John smiled amused and shook his head.

"This fossil is just a rock," John said. "It has no biological potential whatsoever."

"Have you analyzed it thoroughly?" Dave said seriously. "Alien life may exist in forms that outwardly resemble ours, but function totally different."

"That may be true." John smiled. "But this is nothing but a rock. I wish it were more than that."

"I'd like to hold that thing in my hand," Jim said. "What an awesome experience that would be!"

"No one will be able to touch anything until we've ascertained absolute sterility of our specimens," Norman said solemnly. "Samples of soil have been put into a set of cultures

253

which will take at least six weeks to evaluate. In the interim, we will have to content ourselves with viewing the fossil remotely."

"What about the media?" Zelda said softly.

"It goes without saying this discovery is too important to keep secret for long," Norman said. "However, we must maintain silence as long as possible until we can get the maximum amount of data without outside interference."

"Will the media be upset?" Zelda raised her brow.

Norman turned to face her grinning. "To hell with the media, this is bigger than they can begin to comprehend. They will have to live with what we give them. A few days, or weeks, is not going to change the import of our discovery one iota."

"Can't we get it out of there so we can examine it directly?" Steve said slowly. "I would sure like to hold that thing in my hand."

"Our preliminary analyses are negative so far," Norman said. "But the presence of this fossil proves life was on Mars and therefore still might be, at least in microscopic form. Let's not let our childish enthusiasms overcome our adult reasons."

"I can put it into a separate container," Zelda said. "Isolated by itself we can all have a chance to study it more closely."

"I agree." Norman nodded once.

The fossil was carefully cleaned of all easily removed debris before putting it into a separate container that was transferred to another smaller viewing station. Each stage of the process was followed intently by everyone present. There was little, if any, extraneous conversations.

"Tom, how soon can we determine how old it is?" Norman said. "At least give me your best guess."

Tom shrugged his shoulders. "I'll look at the material peeled off the surface." He immediately turned around to his desk. "It shouldn't take long."

"A trilobite, truly amazing," David said clearly. "Suppose it was blasted off the earth and hurled out to land on Mars millions of years ago."

"That's fanciful thinking and nothing more," John said quickly. "Not a single fossil has ever been found on the moon where you might expect to find some. No, I think this fossil is totally and completely Martian."

"Just a thought..." David stepped back.

"And we need those thoughts," Norman said kindly. "The reason you are all selected was for your openness to new ideas. We have to make sense out of our findings partly within our earthbound experience but mostly outside of what is familiar."

Zelda x-rayed the fossil and, as before, the metallic elements prevented any pictures of interest. A scanning microscope using different frequencies of light examined the surface closely. Polarized light produced a series of aesthetically interesting pictures but nothing of any real scientific value.

"Norman, this specimen is exactly like any we might find here. I recommend we wash it off, sterilize it, and bring it out where we can touch it," Zelda said. "I don't think there is any danger from this thing."

"Go ahead." Norman nodded. "But you must make initial contact inside the biocontainment room."

"Of course..." Zelda nodded. "...one step at a time." She attached a hose and sprayed distilled water into the container.

"Will water hurt it?" Jim said.

"Unlikely," John said. "Water exists throughout the universe and is generally thought the basic necessity of life. Water will certainly not hurt in this case."

"I'll put the washings under the microscope before we make contact," Zelda said. "...just as an added precaution. I don't want any unexpected surprises."

A light misting spray was applied from a nozzle positioned directly over the fossil. The first few seconds of moisture turned the surface to a lustrous glossy black. Zelda, John and Norman watched while the others went back to their assigned tasks. David was assigned analysis of the fossil washings and would return to process them when called.

"That's funny," Zelda said softly.

"What's funny?" John said.

"There is less water collected than sprayed onto the fossil," Zelda said. "It's almost as if it's absorbing some of the water."

"That's not unusual." Norman shook his head. "Many fossils are porous and can absorb tremendous amounts of water. There is nothing strange in that property here."

"My eyes are beginning to play tricks with me," John said. "I thought I saw it move."

"It's only the light reflecting off the misting water." Norman chuckled. "My but are we getting jumpy."

"Maybe so..." John sighed.

255

"I thought I saw it move also," Zelda said. "But I agree it could be an illusion."

"It is only natural to be sitting on the most significant finding of the modern era and be tempted to fantasize about it," Norman said.

"What you just said doesn't make any sense," Zelda said flatly. "It's clear you have a poor grasp about how people really think in the real world."

"I may live in an ivory tower, but at least I know my specialty well enough to discriminate what is real from illusion." Norman smiled wryly. "Otherwise, I would not have been made director of this project."

"There are many strange bedfellows in this life." Zelda squinted. "And you're one of the strangest."

Before the argument escalated farther John interrupted pointing to the fossil which had visibly increased in size. Zelda quickly stopped the misting spray. All the surrounding moisture disappeared instantly as if it were never present.

"That's one thirsty fossil." John moved closer to the window. "How many rocks do you know that increase in size when wet? I'm afraid I'm at a loss to name one and that includes fossils."

"I suppose..." Norman moved closer. "...that a rock or fossil, with low density and weak cohesive bonds could possibly expand on hydration. Martian geology as well as biology may have significant differences."

"It's moving!" Zelda screamed. "It's really moving!"

The fossil vibrated, slowly at first, gaining frequency and amplitude with each passing minute. Everyone was frozen speechless and at the same time apprehensive of what this activity really meant. Zelda composed herself long enough to call the others back to observe what was happening. John and Norman simply stood transfixed as moths to a flame.

"It must be some sort of violent chemical reaction," David said calmly.

"Looks like it's alive to me," Jim said weakly.

John shook his head and cleared his throat. "Clearly this is nothing like any fossil that has ever been found anywhere which testifies to its extraterrestrial origin. Whether it is alive or not is a moot point at the moment because what we are witnessing tells our senses that it is. As for myself I need more proof."

An explosion ripped through the room shattering glass and dousing the lights. The container holding the fossil was no longer a barrier of protection. The team groped in the dark looking for emergency flashlights and the exit door.

"Stay calm everyone!" Norman croaked. "We must not panic!"

"Where is that thing?" Jim said shrilly. "We've got to get out of here!"

There was a slap of hand against skin. "Shut up stupid," Tom growled. "I'm tired of your childish antics!"

"Damn it, stay civilized, at least, if you can't stay calm," Norman shouted. "Work as a team and we will get out of here safely."

"What about containment?" Zelda said. "If we open the door, we not only let us out but the fossil as well. Won't we be putting the entire planet at risk?"

"I don't know what the risks are any more than you do," Norman said. "Where are the lights?"

Someone screamed and there was a massive collision of bodies. Frantic hands were everywhere trying to get away from an unknown danger. The improbable scenarios of popular science fiction were taking its toll on the emotions of everyone in the room.

"Keep your hands off of me you creep!" Zelda yelled. "If I ever find out who you are, I'll scratch your eyes out."

No one said anything. David reached the exit door but was unable to open it. The explosion had activated the system to seal off all hazardous areas. They were trapped until someone from the outside rescued them.

"Now what do we do?" David said glumly.

"I think I know where there's a flashlight," Zelda said. "There should be one under the monitor console."

John being closest to the console searched carefully in the dark until he found it. The instant he turned the light on there was a collective gasp from everyone. Zelda came over to John and took the flashlight away from him. She was less concerned about the humans of the room than the fossil. At first glance, everyone appeared uninjured although there was a faint hint of urine in the air. She looked into the specimen container. The fossil had disappeared from its original position and was nowhere evident from where she stood. Zelda took in a deep breath. "It's not in here," she said. "Where could it have gone?"

257

"It's after us!" Jim screamed hysterically and grabbed the door handle. "We've got to get out of here!"

"Jim, I've told you." Tom grabbed Jim by the collar. "If you don't shut up, I'm going to hurt you bad. Now shut up!"

Jim glanced fearfully into Tom's resolute eyes. He shook his head as tears rolled down his cheeks. "Sorry, I'm just scared." He sobbed. "I want to get out of here alive."

"And we all will," Norman said slowly. "And we all will."

"There is no place in the containment chamber for it to hide." Zelda exhaled. "So it must be somewhere in this room with us. I want everyone stand where they are while I look with the light."

Zelda began a methodical search of the room starting from the broken observation window and counsel. Satisfied there was nothing either in or on the console she swept the light along the baseboard of the entire room. Having completed a negative search she focused on the floor within the room.

"What's that?" Jim gasped pointing.

In the middle of the room lay the fossil very much flattened and inert. A number of dark rivulets of fluid splayed from its sides in every direction.

"Oh my God it was alive!" Tom said. "Jim was right! It was after us!"

"It's dead now," Steve said solemnly. "We don't have anything to worry about."

Zelda looked at John and laughed. John returned her look and laughed with her. Norman at first was puzzled by the laughter but soon caught on. Within a few minutes everyone was laughing not only in relief but at a colossal cosmic joke. An alien invader had been vanquished by accidentally stepping on it.

"This is really ludicrous," Zelda said through tears of laughter streaming down her cheeks. "Here we have the most important find ever and someone steps on it and kills it."

"Not on purpose." John laughed. "It was an accident. Besides we will never know whether it was hostile or not. It's too bad all I have to work with is alien road kill."

"The champagne is still on me." Norman laughed. "We've proved a lot of things, but most of all we've proved ourselves to be as human as we always are."

"When do you think will get another chance like this?" John asked rhetorically. "I am sure I will be better prepared next time."

"First thing, let's celebrate," Zelda said warmly. "Then we can think about the future. Then we can compose a media release for the press. The truth must be known." And then she winked and John understood.

Thursday

Everyone has a story to tell of one sort or another and I am no different than anyone else. The only problem with my story is that sometimes even I have a hard time believing it myself. What happened occurred a long time ago in a far different time and place than where I now stand. Why tell my story now after so many years? I guess it is time to share what I went through. My hope is I will not he thought as either crazy or strange, although the temptation to label me that way will come almost immediately. At least listen to my story from the beginning before deciding.

A very long time ago when I was young and healthy I had volunteered for service flying missions in Southeast Asia after the Japanese invaded the mainland. From the very beginning of the war things were wrong and life was totally unpredictable. My job was to carry mail and supplies for the Allies. It was a job with a great deal of personal risk, but I accepted it.

One day, not too long after the Japanese bombed Pearl Harbor, I was flying to Australia when I was surprised by a Zero. My single engine, unarmed clunker was no challenge for the attack that came. After one pass at me, I knew I had lost my plane and bailed out. On the second pass, I watched my plane explode as I hung exposed under my parachute. The Zero turned toward me and I thought my life was over. The pilot simply flew by waving with a big toothy grin. Within a few minutes I watched my plane crash into the water below and the Zero disappeared into the distant clouds. I hung there suspended wondering what I would do next. From my perch I saw water directly below me. Fortunately, there was an island not far away. The only problem was getting there once I was in the water. My greatest fear was the possibility of an attack by a shark before I landed on its beach. A life vest is certainly not much protection in any body of salt water!

The landing in the water was smooth and actually refreshing. I quickly released the chute, took my bearings, and swam toward the island which was mercifully close. I do not remember how long it took me, it seemed like hours to forever, but at last I did crawl up on the beach totally exhausted and mindful of whom might be on the island, either friend or foe. I was alive and that was enough for me at that moment. I barely managed to get off the sand under some trees before I collapsed

261

into a dreamless sleep. I do not remember how long I slept but it was dark when I finally woke up. My next concern was food and water. I had some of both with me, but I would soon use them up. I was on my own and I had to survive!

The island upon which I crawled up on was no better or worse than any of the innumerable patches of dry land I had seen from the air in that part of the world. How big and was my island refuge inhabited were something I had to discover for myself. The first thing I did, however, was take an inventory of what I had with me. Aside from clothes, which included shirt, pants, under shorts, socks and aviator boots, I had two flares, a knife, one half-eaten chocolate bar and a pack of very wet matches.

In my first survey of the beach, I saw no evidence of anyone else beside myself in the markings on the sand. Of course, I quickly surmised, that could simply be an artifact of the tide washing all telltale traces away with each cycle. Even so, I still had the feeling I was all alone and would be so for a long time to come. It was time to put all those so-called survival lectures to the test. I only wished I had listened more closely.

Thirst was the first need that imposed itself onto my consciousness. Fortunately, there were coconut palms almost in every direction I looked and, better yet, there were dozens within easy reach. I chose a large coconut, shook it, and found it contained water. After throwing it down again and again amongst some rocks I managed to break the husk enough to remove the hard inner core. With my knife I bored a hole into one of the three eyes through which I was able to drink its water. Personally, I did not care for the taste, but at least it slaked my thirst for the moment. I then cracked the nut open and scooped out the inner meat. I ate the coconut planning my next step. The shell would be my cup when I found another source of water. The mere thought of having to survive by cleaning coconuts certainly did not appeal to me.

The easiest way to explore the island was to follow the beach. With the flip of a mental coin I chose a direction and marched off with coconut shell in hand. As I walked I noticed a cluster of birds diving into the water a mile or two offshore telling me there were ample schools of fish for the taking, if I only had a boat. Unconsciously, I ate the remainder of my chocolate bar before I realized I should have saved it for when I might really need it.

By the way, I forgot to mention I also had a wristwatch. The greater part of the day passed before I came upon an obstruction to my forward progress. A wide inlet cut into the island. Not so wide I could not ford it easily, but wide enough to make me curious of its source. Rather than continue along the beach I turned inland following the bank of the inlet which became a narrow river of a sort. Near the beach the mangroves surrounded each bank. Farther inland other vegetation with which I was not familiar encroached upon the gently flowing water.

From the surrounding trees and underbrush came sounds of birds engaged in their way of life. My thoughts went instantly to musing how I had once shared their milieu in the air, wishing I could simply spread my arms and join them again. My attention was suddenly directed to a new sound, I heard rushing water. Without any hesitation I pressed faster into the interior of the island until I came upon a small waterfall of some twenty or thirty feet in height. I laughed, realizing my luck had definitely changed for the better. With coconut cup in hand I approached the falling water hoping this was not a dream. I filled my cup and tasted it cautiously. Much to my pleasant surprise I found it to be the best I had ever tasted. Whether that was from my current necessity or in actuality true was really a moot point, I was saved from dying of thirst.

Man does not live on water alone. Please excuse the paraphrase. Aside from the omnipresent birds and the probable fish offshore, I found little, other than the coconuts, I could eat. The onset of darkness forced me to open several more coconuts as my final meal of the day before settling in for the night. It had been a very long day and I was exhausted. I managed to construct a makeshift lean-to against the rocks near the waterfall. Almost as soon as I fell asleep I dreamt of being in my own bed at home with Mom and Dad in the room next to me. Sometime during the night I awoke with a start for no apparent reason. I was perspiring with my heart racing a mile a minute. I had the strange feeling I was not alone. For several moments, I sat in my makeshift bed scanning the surroundings for any sign of movement. Finally, convinced I was allowing my imagination to run away with me I lay back down and went back to a fitful sleep. This was not as easy as I had originally thought.

I awoke feeling more tired than rested until I got up and moved around for a few minutes. A cup of hot coffee was something I desperately needed. Unfortunately, I had to settle for either water or coconut juice neither of which appealed to me. I cleaned myself up as best I could by splashing water from the river on my face. I brushed my teeth with an index finger until they squeaked. It was the best I could do to feel human. I decided that where I slept would be my base of operations until I found someplace better. Nearby I noticed a rather large bird's nest. I approached it cautiously. Although there were no birds to snare, there were three large eggs which were warm to the touch. Breakfast! I collected the eggs and brought them back to my camp. I emptied the contents of each egg into my coconut cup, held my nose and drank them in one long swallow.

Whatever the experts teach about survival in the wild has almost nothing to do with the real experience. Most formulas for survival assume everyone has a natural ability to commune with nature in a way that is mutually beneficial to both survivor and the wild. In my basic training I gave little thought to be lost on a desert island with little or no equipment. Fortunately, even though I grew up in the city, I was able to quickly adapt to the situation. Finding food and water were simple compared to maintaining those relatively unappreciated niceties that only soap, toothpaste and toilet paper can provide. I did what I could for myself to the best of my ability. Somehow I had to find secure shelter and a way home.

Over the next few days I managed putting together a reasonable collection of coconuts, eggs and tropical fruit, the names of which I had no idea. With a little ingenuity and a lot of perspiration my lean-to was transformed into a hut even Robinson Crusoe would be proud. From a spot atop the waterfall, I built a mound of dry wood in hopes of attracting a passing boat or plane should any venture close. The only glitch in my plan was I would never know in advance whether I was attracting friend or foe. Far better to be stranded here with freedom to roam at will than to be resident of a Japanese prisoner of war camp. I vowed to light my signal only if I knew for sure it was not the enemy and for that I was willing to wait as long as necessary.

Without a radio or books the only way I had to pass the time was explore the island. I took short trips from camp marking the way as I progressed forward. Suddenly, it occurred to me this might be a logistical mistake. Although I felt alone at the moment, there was no guarantee that I was, and if I was not, I should not leave any easy trail for an enemy to find where I lived. For that reason I went to the beach and collected seashells, as many as I possibly could carry, in my pockets. Now, when I traveled, I would drop a shell to mark my way. On the way back

I would, more often than not, pick up the shell for the next excursion. I fixed a post outside my hut where I carved a notch for each day I spent on the island. Later, I carved a map of the island in the dirt by the post. Much to my chagrin my nascent map was washed away by the first rainstorm. However, using my memory and shells I managed reconstructing the map so I did not have to survey anew.

Well into the second week I began talking and singing to myself. This may sound crazy, but I was having conversations with myself which sounded quite reasonable. It was clear I was lonely and in need of companionship. No man is an island, as the saying goes, and moreover no man is an island on an island. I may like to be alone at times, but I also need real conversation.

The island, I soon found out, was actually bigger than I imagined so that by the end of the third week I had still not explored it all nor had I completely walked its circumference. There was still a slight possibility I was not alone. The idea was reinforced by markings on the ground and cut foliage I could not ascribe to any natural phenomenon. My imagination ran wild considering what sort of person or animal would be responsible. I had been briefed during my training that there was a history of cannibalism amongst the islands in this part of the world. In the absence of footprints and the remains of obvious man-made fires I discounted any man, friend or foe, sharing the island with me. In regards to what creatures I should encounter my training was even more vague and imprecise. Aside from a panoply of birds and several species of apes it was believed there were no natural predators to be feared. The constant birdsong and flitting to and fro reminded me every day that I was in the company of avian friends. However, I saw marks that were definitely not made by any bird I ever knew. The only other possibility to consider was a reasonably large ape of some sort. From the time I was aware of these marks I examined my surroundings ever closer. I wanted to catch a glimpse of the shy companions on the island.

A month went by before the markings I had seen on my excursions finally appeared outside my hut one morning. It was obvious I had been visited during the night while I was asleep. Whatever it was did not disturb anything in my camp. I attributed its initial contact with me as a blend of cautious curiosity and respectful fear. I was immediately overjoyed at the prospect of a real challenge. I now had to find out who my visitor was. Throughout the entire day I planned a way to get a glimpse of my curious visitor, whatever it was.

Outside the entrance to my hut I placed a collection of edible goodies and arranged a place I could hide in a nearby tree. I was not going to tempt fate by hiding totally exposed in my hut. I could hardly wait for the sun to go down and climb up into my hiding place. I was hoping I would be visited twice in a row. This assumption on my part was totally unwarranted, but I was bored and in need of some real diversion. I spent endless hours in my tree waiting for something that never came. Just before dawn I fell asleep and awoke several hours later disappointed and sore as hell. Either my visitor was extremely shy or not as curious as I had thought. Under the circumstances I was not deterred from my quest to see my visitor. I vowed I would stay up every night until I saw my quarry. To do this, I had to sleep during the day which was not an easy thing to do. However, I did manage to get some rest and was ready for the next night.

I climbed up into my hiding place shortly after sundown and found a cut branch in the place I had sat the night before. The sight of the cut branch sent a chill down my spine. Either this was a sign of intimidation or an extremely poor joke. Whatever I was trying to see was playing a game I did not understand. I sat in my tree several hours staring at that cut branch, mesmerized by the implications that the animal I sought might be more formidable than I imagined. In those lonely hours I tried to formulate a plan of action. I did not want to be caught off guard.

The full moon lit everything almost as bright as day. There was a gentle breeze and a profound absence of sound other than the rustling leaves and waterfall. As dawn approached my eyelids grew heavy forcing me to struggle to stay awake. I must have fallen asleep because I found myself shaking uncontrollably. I rubbed the sleep from my eyes and looked around. Standing at the base of my tree was the most hideous creature I had ever seen in my life. I frantically swallowed the inclination to scream.

When I say hideous, I mean hideous. The creature was almost totally arachnoid in appearance and as large as an adult man. I am repulsed by tiny spiders and now I was faced with a giant one. Its two multifaceted eyes watched me with curious detachment. I was not sure if it was sizing me up for its next meal or not. I was paralyzed where I sat, almost unable to take a breath. The creature turned its head from side to side several times and then rather than climbing up to get me, stepped backward away from the tree. It did not, however, leave.

266

I was tempted screaming at it to go away, but I was not sure whether that would provoke it to attack me or not. I was between a rock and a very hard place. After a while the creature moved back farther which would have given me ample time and space to climb down so I could make a run for safety. I had the feeling the creature was playing with me. No sooner would I start running on the ground I was sure I would be dead meat. The creature must have read my mind because it moved even farther away. If nothing else, I was offered a sporting chance. I had my knife with me and briefly fantasized attacking it. I am not stupid, that would be like attacking an elephant with a toothpick. The creature moved back to the edge of the clearing around my hut. We stared at each other as if we were waiting to see who would flinch first. The sky was lightening which gave me hope dawn would send this creature away to its dark lair. Just when I thought I had figured it all out, the creature waved at me in a very human fashion. It waved me to come down.

There was no way I would consider coming down out of that tree. I was safe for the moment. The creature continued waving at me. When I refused to budge, it stopped, and moved its eyes in every direction. Then without hesitation it went into my hut bringing out my coconut cup and a couple pieces of fruit. The creature filled my cup with fresh water and placed it along with the fruit a short distance from the base of my perch. If I were not so scared, I would have laughed. The creature retreated to a position at the edge of the camp where it waited motionless.

I had to make a decision. Do I wait in this tree, or do I climbed down and take my chances? The more I looked at the creature, the less frightened I became. Considering what it looked like and its size, it could have easily dislodged me from where I sat. Every time I moved to get more comfortable it moved ever so slightly in anticipation, although I think it was my imagination. I knew exactly how the game of cat and mouse was played. And I was the mouse!

We remained at our standoff until noon when the creature waved one last time before it disappeared into the brush. For the next several hours I agonized whether I should chance leaving my perch. When it started raining I scrambled down and ran directly into my hut for shelter. Much to my surprise the creature was inside waiting for me. The moment I saw it I gasped in surprise and froze. I should have turned to escape but I did not.

The creature did not make any threatening moves toward me, but instead held out a piece of fruit. At close quarters I had no choice except to play along with its game, whatever that was. I composed myself the best I could, moved slowly toward the creature and took the offered fruit. I expected to be attacked and devoured at any moment. The creature, however, did nothing other than move its eyes. Since I was actually very hungry, I took a bite of the fruit and ate it assuming this was my last meal. When I finished eating the creature offered me another piece. It was then I felt the creature was not going to hurt me anytime soon. Becoming more at ease with the situation I picked up a piece of fruit and offered it back to the creature who accepted it without hesitation. My initial revulsion of the creature turned into fascination. I was not dealing with a mindless insect, but a true sentient being. Considering my circumstances on the island and another castaway of long ago, I named the creature Thursday. I laughed out loud at my own joke and the creature twisted its head back and forth as if it was trying to understand. I held out my hand and the creature extended a leg I assumed it used as its own hand. We made tentative contact and shook each other gently. At the conclusion of our so-called handshake I was certain I was dealing with an intelligent being.

When we finally completed our introduction to each other the problem remained how to communicate. I had vocal cords and could speak. Thursday apparently had none and was thus mute. The problem was solved by a combination of sign language and drawing diagrams on the ground. The more we tried to communicate the easier it was to understand each other. Unfortunately, we were only to communicate our immediate concerns and needs, I was actually more interested where Thursday had come from and were there more like him or her. Part of my curiosity was satisfied when Thursday finally convinced me to follow.

Thursday led me to a place I had not yet explored. When I entered what I instantly recognized as a well-organized camp I was thoroughly astonished by what I saw. At the edge of the camp was some sort of large cylinder with stubby wings which I took as Thursday's flying vehicle. In the middle of the camp was a dome shaped tent covered with a cloth that looked like aluminum foil. A square box with a parabolic antenna pointed skyward was connected to a cable running into the tent. The more I looked at Thursday's camp, the more I realized how foolish I must have looked sitting up in my tree afraid to come down. Thursday was obviously more sophisticated and intelligent than I dreamed possible. Thursday was not from this planet for sure.

Over the next several days I established myself within Thursday's camp. Actually that was no real problem since I did not have much to begin with. Thursday was the perfect host in helping me with my basic needs. I had been alone in need of company and so had Thursday. My mood was lifted by Thursday's presence and it was clear that Thursday was also happy with my presence. Although we were unable to communicate in any elaborate language, we acted together as an efficient team.

Thursday helped me get the things I needed most to survive well. With materials I had never seen before I was able to fashion an extremely comfortable bed. Food was no longer a problem. Thursday brought more fruit than I could eat in a year. I managed to make a set of fishhooks and a fishing line. Thursday watched in fascination when I caught my first fish. The best thing Thursday provided was fire. I was finally able to cook my food. Life got better day by day. Once my needs were met, Thursday enlisted my help for several projects, the first of which was to climb several trees to string a wire up as a large antenna. Thursday was as much of a castaway as myself and was trying to call for help. There was nothing Thursday ever asked me to do that was either unreasonable or dangerous to me. I came to have such trust and admiration that there was nothing I would not do to help our situation.

Once my needs were fully met, Thursday made it perfectly clear I had a job to do. The cylinder had apparently crashed into the ground burying its front end. Thursday pointed at a shovel of a sort, waving it around in a mock demonstration. Pointing repeatedly from the shovel to the cylinder I finally got the point I was to dig it out of the ground. As I started digging on one side Thursday went to the other to dig also. We dug throughout the day taking intermittent breaks for rest and refreshment. When the sun hit the distant horizon Thursday motioned our work cease for the day.

Before cooking my evening meal I had to wash the dirt and sweat off my body. I tried the best I could to explain what I needed to do, but when Thursday simply stared at me motionless I threw up my hands and started walking away. Thursday quietly ambled along behind me staying at least a dozen yards away. I was fully aware I was being watched and did my best to pretend

269

I was all alone. I took off all my clothes and slipped into a clear freshwater pool. I actually blushed at my nakedness in front of Thursday wondering if my body was offensive in any way. In the first days of our acquaintance I was truthfully repulsed by Thursday's appearance. There was nothing in my earthly experience I could compare. As the days went by I appreciated the fact that intelligence and kindness are not restricted to the human form.

For the evening meal I always cooked for myself. Every time I offered what I had prepared Thursday adamantly refused. Thursday brought plastic containers from the cylinder for nourishment. I was allowed to examine one of these containers and found within it nothing either recognizable or remotely appetizing: everyone to his own poison.

From the first night together Thursday slept in the cylinder while I slept in a new hut right beside it. With the materials Thursday provided, I was almost as comfortable as I would have been back in my barracks. Work made me tired and I always slept well. I am amazed I rarely dreamt during the time I lived with Thursday. Most mornings Thursday would be quietly waiting in our eating area for me to wake up. My sleep was never disturbed unnecessarily.

Time started moving faster as we worked together. It took almost a month to dig out the cylinder and position it properly. Once a week, Thursday and I would go down to the beach and scan the horizon for signs of approaching help. I knew Thursday was doing this for my benefit. If anyone happened to see us together they would have surely been horrified. Thursday was safer not seen by any other human beings except me. Unfortunately, a day would come when it would become unavoidable. I agonized long and hard on what I would do at that time.

A year went by in peace and tranquility. The world was at war while I lived in a tropical paradise with my one true friend. We worked for our mutual benefit without hesitation. After repositioning the cylinder Thursday directed me to string several long lengths of wire in multiple directions. I figured I was enlarging the antenna for a communication device in the cylinder. How that device worked was always a mystery to me because as long as we were together Thursday never uttered a recognizable sound. Our communication never advanced beyond sign language and drawings in the dirt. I did discover Thursday had a written language and insisted I learn it. Thursday understood my desire and tried to teach me. By the end of two years I barely had the understanding of a human five-year-old.

Toward the end of our second year together I noticed Thursday spending more time inside the cylinder. It was impossible to ask why, so I never put the question to my mind. It was none of my business. I was surprised several weeks later at the sound of a whining noise coming from the cylinder. I stood mesmerized wondering if the cylinder was going to blow up. Instead, Thursday came out appearing quite excited pointing at the cylinder then up into the sky. At that point I knew I was going to be left alone on the island.

Thursday looked at me. I did not know what to say. I extended my hand and we shook hands in a sense. Tears came to my eyes and Thursday's head tilted side to side in wonderment. I had never cried on the island before. Thursday went into the cylinder, closed the door, and the whine grew to an almost intolerable pitch. The cylinder slowly lifted off the ground, turned and shot straight up into the clouds disappearing forever.

Alone again I went down to the beach and sat on the sand with chin on my knees. My loss of a friend was nearly overwhelming but then I heard a familiar noise. A boat was approaching! I sprung to my feet and ran to the water's edge. Although I had thrown care to the wind before I could tell the nationality of the flag, I was in luck. An American PT boat had come specifically to rescue me. At the time I did not question how they had found me I was so thankful. Later, I was told a radio signal was sent asking for assistance. Since I had no radio, it had to have been Thursday. A smile came to my face. Thursday could have called for help at any time. Thursday needed my help and company as much as I needed the same! I laughed out loud. I had been conned!

The view from the forward window could have been out of the American Southwest. The colors and geologic formations were blandly familiar from specialist to layman. What made it special was the actual location at 82° north latitude on Mars. Up to this point Captain Mitchell was able to maneuver the giant rover over a relatively unobstructed route provided by the overhead orbital platform. The excitement of arrival had long since evaporated and was replaced by an ever increasing sense of ennui. Mars had yet to prove itself as a place more interesting than the remotest Arctic tundra.

Mission Specialist Carson, sitting next to Captain Mitchell, was ever a source of bubbling enthusiasm from the instant of lift off to the present moment. He was of the distinct opinion that in spite of the lack of evidence they would soon make a discovery that would make their efforts worthwhile. He saw the flat expression on the Captain's face, smiled, and shook his head. For some people belief comes only with a firm slap to the face.

The radio crackled to life. "Captain, you're almost on top of your destination. I suggest you slow down your forward progress and proceed with caution. Don't want you falling into a hole we can't pull you out of."

"Roger, Roger." The Captain pulled back the throttle to a mere crawl. "I can't see anything from where I am. We are still climbing a grade of about 15 percent. Can you give me a more precise estimate?"

"My instruments show you one hundred yards from the edge of the gorge. Suggest you continue half that distance and precede the rest on foot."

"Roger, Roger." The Captain noted the odometer and began counting. "We'll be out on the ground in less than five minutes."

"Looks about right from up here."

"Kit, are your things ready?"

"Yes, Mitch, about as ready as they'll ever be." Carson was unable to restrain his overflowing enthusiasm and laughed loudly.

The Captain smiled slightly only because Carson's laughter was infectious. There was no other reason. Mars was just one more desolate rock in the cosmos which failed to live up to its reputation.

"Mitch, I have a feeling we are going to find something really important today. I know you think I'm crazy, but I've got an image in my head I can't shake."

"You're entitled to your dreams." The Captain brought the rover to a full stop. "But now is a time to get down to brutal reality. Shall we go for a walk?"

"Let me out! Last one to the gorge is a rotten egg!" Carson put on his helmet and moved quickly to the rear cabin pressure lock. "Are you coming or do you want to let me have the total honor of discovery?"

The Captain checked the instruments and remotely unloaded a smaller four wheeled rover from the cargo hold. Finally, comfortable with all systems he put on his own helmet and joined Carson.

"Are you ready?" The Captain watched the pressure door close.

Carson nodded and the Captain began the exit cycle of depressurization. When the pressure within the chamber equaled the outside a green light winked on. The Captain opened the outside door. Carson watched with an enthusiastic grin.

"Let's go," the Captain said flatly. "We have no time to waste."

They stood outside the exit hatch, checked all their equipment, neither found any problem, and the Captain resealed the hatch. Carson adjusted the antenna and cameras on the buggy.

"Testing, testing," Carson said crisply. "Can you hear me? Come in."

"Hear you loud and clear, Kit."

"How's the picture?"

"Crystal clear. You are go to proceed."

"Roger." Carson glanced up into the pale sky. He almost thought he could see the small speck of the overhead orbital station. Duty aboard that station would never occur to him as desirable. Coming to Mars meant touching its surface, not standing off in space with a view little different than the one sent back by innumerable robot craft. He sat in his seat and put on the seatbelt.

"Here we go." The Captain pushed the throttle forward. "In a few minutes we'll find out if it was right."

"We haven't gotten any bad data yet."

"There is always a first time. I believe accidents are unavoidable regardless of all precautions."

274

"That's a pretty grim philosophy," Carson said slowly. "In fact, it's damn near fatalistic."

"I'd like to think it's realistic," the Captain said solemnly. "There is nothing perfect in every way."

The rest of the ride was in total silence. Several yards from the lip of the gorge they stopped and went the rest of the way on foot. The view was more than they had hoped to ever see. Standing on the lip looking downward was both dizzying and breathtaking. The opposite side of the gorge was a mere hundred yards away, but the bottom dropped precipitously into dark shadows totally obscuring its true depth. Without ado Carson recorded the scene with a hand-held camera.

"Awesome." Carson beamed. "Sort of gives the Grand Canyon a run for its money."

"For once I have to agree." The Captain shook his head; he was always reluctant to concede a point.

"Shall I get the rest of the equipment?"

"Yes," the Captain said tersely. "No need wasting any time."

The main object of the trip was to examine the walls of the gorge at multiple levels, take samples, and look for signs of active water or, better yet, life. A boom was erected out over the gorge at the end of which was a cable attached to Carson. The Captain would monitor the progress while feeding out cable as necessary. The equipment was easily assembled and Carson was hanging over the lip of the gorge in no time.

"Lower way…" Carson was almost breathless.

The cable fed out smoothly while Carson skillfully kept his distance from any potential obstructions. The Captain stopped the cable at a preset distance. Carson preceded making observations and gathered specimens. When he was finished he signaled the Captain to lower him to the next stopping point.

Approximately halfway down, there was a protruding shelf of rock. Carson easily cleared the obstruction. The rock appeared of a slightly different color and texture compared to the surrounding ones. He made a mental note to take a sample on the trip back up. Approaching the bottom he saw an area of green circular discoloration. Almost all the rocks were of shades of reddish-brown. Carson was realistic to know that the color green did not automatically suggest life even though down deep he wished it did. The closer he came to the discoloration the faster his pulse raced. There was something very peculiar about the entire site.

Standing off horizontally as far as possible, he took pictures at multiple settings and frequencies. The discoloration was roughly in the shape of an oval barely 6 feet in diameter. Upon closer examination, Carson saw the color was coming from a film-like substance on the rocks. His heart raced even faster.

"Captain!" Carson screamed. "I think I've found it!"

"Found what?" The Captain said slowly.

"I think I've found something resembling green algae. It's localized in a circle down here and I don't see anything else like it nearby."

"Take some samples and mark them carefully. Don't rush to any conclusions yet."

Carson chipped at the green covered rock and a sizable chunk broke away slipping from his grip. It fell down into the abyss below. Where the rock had been was a slightly off-white surface. Curious he moved his helmet closer. A series of cracks suddenly appeared, creating black lines on white. For a moment he was puzzled by what he saw. When he realized what was happening it was too late. The discolored oval area exploded outward in a torrent of icy water. The force of the water slammed into his body hurling him away from the wall of the gorge as if in a horizontal bungee jump. At the instant the outward movement was checked by the cable he knew he was in trouble and the best he could hope was a quick death. When he hit the wall the water had refrozen. He felt a sharp pain in his side before he lost consciousness.

"Carson, what's happening?" The Captain screamed. "Talk to me man! Are you there?"

Silence.

"Are you hurt?" The Captain began sweating. His worst nightmare had been realized. He never felt more alone and out of control than he did at this particular moment.

Carson remained unmoving and unresponsive at the end of the cable. The Captain could only visualize a part of him due to the obstruction of the shelf of rock higher up. He had two choices either haul Carson up as is or send out a separate cable to bring him up more carefully. The Captain chose the easy way out; he started to reel the cable in as quickly as he dared. There was no reason to assume Carson survived anyway so why risk another life; he rationalized. Much to his pleasant surprise the rock shelf proved no hindrance to Carson's body. At first glance

276

the Captain ascertained at least there was no visible blood or damage to the outer suit.

"Kit, Kit, are you there man?"

Silence.

"Move something, dammit!"

Nothing.

"Don't worry buddy everything will be all right." There was no conviction in the Captain's voice. He continued to fear the worst. Medical emergencies always made his flesh crawl.

At last Carson reached the lip of the gorge where the Captain grabbed his body and brought it onto the safety of solid ground. The Captain gazed into the helmet and saw blood dripping from the corner of Carson's mouth. He actually prayed this was only from a bitten tongue. A thorough examination of Carson's suit relieved his mind the possibility of survival was not prevented by exposure to the thin Martian atmosphere.

"You're going to be fine." The Captain composed himself and tried to think clearly. He detached the cable and lifted Carson up on to his feet. Although still unconscious, the Captain was able to move him in the light gravity back to the transport.

The trip back to the large rover seemed to take forever. The Captain moved at times fast enough to send all six wheels off the ground. He drove directly into the storage bay where there was an easily accessible airlock. Carson throughout the trip remained totally unresponsive and unconscious.

Inside the rover and out of his pressure suit the Captain managed to get Carson into the medical compartment. It was with a lot of sweating and difficulty the Captain removed all of Carson's clothes with all modesty forgotten. Throughout the entire time Carson remained inert.

The Captain flipped a switch. "Hey, are you guys still overhead? I've got a situation down here! I need some help."

"Roger, Roger, you're coming in five by five. What can we do for you?"

"We've had a little accident down here. Carson has been injured. He's unconscious."

"Kit?"

"Yes, Kit. He went down into the gorge and was hit by an ice blowout. There was no obvious damage to his suit and he is still alive."

"Put him in the remote diagnostic."

"Done!" The Captain said quickly.

"Start transmitting and I'll have Doc at home-base give an evaluation."

The diagnostic machine come to life as the Captain watched helplessly. There was nothing more he could do. He castigated himself for not being more careful. He should have called Carson up and dropped him away from any obstruction. On the other hand it was not the obstruction that had led to disaster. He vowed he would never risk the lives of his men needlessly again. A man's life was a price he was definitely not willing to pay for an unknown game.

"Roger, are you there?"

The Captain shook all negative thoughts out of his head. "Yes, I'm here. What have you found?"

"Do you see any signs of consciousness?"

"No, none," the Captain said curtly. "What have you found out?"

"You're not going to like this."

"Dammit! Tell me! Don't beat around the bush!" the Captain screamed.

"Doc says there is a partial subluxation of C4-5 and a fracture of the right lobe of the liver. Vital signs appear stable at the moment, but that doesn't mean that other problems might not appear. Your biggest problem is a toss-up between his neck and belly. Both areas need treatment immediately."

"C4-5? Does that mean he's paralyzed from the neck down?"

"No, not yet as far as the MRI can tell, but all movement of his neck must be prohibited. We won't know the true extent of cord injury until he's awake. At least he is still breathing on his own."

The Captain looked at Carson's abdomen; he noted it appeared slightly distended. "What about the liver?"

"The right lobe is fractured. We can keep transfusing him until hell freezes over in hope he stops bleeding internally, but it'll never happen. The only choice we have is to operate."

"Operate?" A chill ran down the Captain's spine. "Now? Here?"

"Your rover has a complete trauma treatment unit. I am sure you are well-trained in its function."

"Yes, but I never expected to ever have to use it." A wave of nausea swept across him. "Does the Doc think it's absolutely necessary? Can this wait until I get him back to home base?"

278

"If you do, you'll be bringing back either a quadriplegic or dead body to bury. Time is of the essence if we are to save his life. I suggest you prepare for surgery immediately. Once you prep the body and set all the instruments in place and Doc will take it from his remote console. You have nothing to do other than wait for further instructions."

"What if something goes wrong?"

"Roger, you do your job and we will do ours. Stop worrying and let us do our job. Time is of the essence."

"Okay," the Captain said weakly. "What do I do next?" His mind had drawn a blank and he desperately needed prompting.

"Insert an IV in the largest vein you can find and secure it in place."

"Shall I start him on supplemental oxygen first?"

"We assumed you had already done that." The voice betrayed an element of irritation. "Oxygen is always first, always! Then...IV! Get to it!"

After he applied the tourniquet to the left arm, he easily found a satisfactory vein. The IV cannula slipped into the lumen of the vein on the first attempt. In a way, the Captain hoped this would mitigate his embarrassment for initially forgetting oxygen. On Mars, or any other place off the surface of the Earth, oxygen was always given number one priority. Every instance of trauma is approached with the attention to breathing first. He chastised himself for forgetting the basics.

"Airway, oxygen, IV secure," the Captain reported. "I've strapped Carson securely into the operating frame. What do I do next?"

"Prep his abdomen and posterior neck."

The Captain put on gloves and painted the skin with a brown colored fluid. By the time he was finished Carson look like he was severely jaundiced. At no time did Carson show any evidence of voluntary movement no matter how much the Captain deliberately prodded with the antiseptic applicators.

"The patient has been prepped," the Captain announced more confidently. "I believe the next step is yours."

"One last request...put the operating probes in the general vicinity of the operating sites."

"The probes are in place. What else?"

"There is nothing else except watch and wait for further instructions. Doc will be controlling the show from here on out. Let me put him on. Doc are you there?"

279

There was a loud crackle followed by a faint voice which the Captain instantly recognized as the Doctor's. The reception was less than ideal but more than adequate for the task at hand. The Captain adjusted the audio controls for volume and clarity with some success.

"Roger, this is Doc. Are you ready?"

"About as ready as I'll ever be."

"Good." The sound of Doc's voice was confident and reassuring. "There is very little you can do until I'm finished, however, it's best you follow what I am doing carefully in case I encounter any special needs. Do you have any problem watching surgery?"

The Captain wondered whether he had a choice. "No, you can depend on me not to faint."

Doc chuckled. "Okay, here we go."

A cloudy bolus of fluid coursed through the IV tubing and a probe with a large suction cup pressed lightly on the abdominal skin. A vacuum was applied and the probe pulled the flaccid abdominal skin upward. Another probe which was actually just a long wide bore needle punctured the umbilicus injecting carbon dioxide into the abdominal cavity. The Captain watched continuously fighting off the urge to turn away. Carson's life was on the line and he was not going to fail him again.

The needle probe withdrew and was replaced by a larger probe which quickly punctured the abdominal wall. The blank screen on the monitor console came to life with a picture of abdominal contents. The Captain's fascination overcame his queasiness. The picture was filled with pinkish gray tubes of intestine. As the laparoscope surveyed the abdomen he noticed blood pooled posteriorly. The scene changed to a reddish brown. The Captain recognized the liver instantly. The fracture was located on the anterior surface of the right lobe. Fortunately, the fracture was filled with clot and not actively bleeding. The Captain exhaled loudly.

Two other probes were inserted through the abdominal wall. Under direct vision while one carefully removed clot by suction, the other cauterized with a laser. The entire procedure took less than 15 minutes, but to the Captain it seemed forever. A saline solution was infused into the abdomen and as much clotted blood as possible was removed. The surface of the liver was re-examined and found free of bleeding. For completeness

280

the rest of the abdomen was explored for other possible injuries. None were found and all the probes were removed.

"Our friend is very lucky," Doc said. "His liver could have been damaged far worse. Unfortunately, his worst injury we haven't even begun to address. But that's next."

The Captain applied antibiotic ointment to the abdominal puncture sites and affixed Band-Aids. When he was done he stepped back as the operating frame flipped Carson over so that his neck was fully exposed upward. Without further instructions, the Captain adjusted the appropriate operating probes over the area.

"Doc, we have a problem brewing," the voice from the orbiting station said. "There is a massive sandstorm coming your way."

"That should not be a problem," Doc said. "Everyone is safely inside. As long as our communication link remains intact I will be able finish what I have to do."

Out of curiosity the Captain switched on a monitor to display the picture of the developing storm. To simply state there was a problem brewing was wrong. The storm he saw about to engulf the main base was massive, covering hundreds of miles in diameter. Once the storm hit, the main base would be buffeted by sand and wind for days to possible weeks. This was definitely not a time to be stranded out in the open with an injured man.

"Doc, what am I to do if I can't get back to base?" The Captain had panic in his voice. "I am not exactly a nurse."

"Roger, you always underestimate yourself." Doc laughed. "You know exactly what to do. Just trust your instincts and humanity. Once I'm finished, all that will be necessary will be tincture of time and attention to the basic necessities of life such as food and water. How much more simple can it get?"

The Captain was speechless and flushed crimson. He was happy no one could see his obvious discomfort. It was always easy for others to dictate what to do. He always had the problem of following through correctly.

"Do I need to re-prep the neck?" The Captain said absently. "Or is there something else?"

"Once the probes are in place there is nothing for you to do but wait to put on the bandage," Doc said warmly. "So far everything has gone extremely well. The next part will be much more complicated. The best we can hope is complete recovery, the worst total paralysis, coma or death. My impression from the diagnostic scans suggests it will be tricky, but totally within a high probability of success. Shall we proceed?"

"Of course," the Captain said softly.

Multiple robotic fingers stretched the skin of the neck taut while a laser sliced the layers of tissue almost bloodlessly. At the level of the cervical vertebra all the probes were retracted and another diagnostic scan performed.

"The subluxation has been reduced without any intervention on our part," Doc said. "However, I see the cord is being compressed by what I think is a hematoma. I need to reduce the pressure on the cord and evacuate the hematoma immediately. I must..." Doc's voice disappeared in a sea of static. The Captain listened carefully waiting to hear the necessary plan of treatment. When the static turned into a roar he knew the worst had happened, the sandstorm had knocked out the communication link.

"Mars Orbiter are you there?" The Captain began to sweat although the temperature had not changed. "Can you hear me up there?" His voice cracked.

Carson remained anesthetized with a gaping hole in the back of his neck. All the probes remained frozen in place waiting instructions from Doc. There was no possible way surgery could continue without Doc. There were a few automatic surgical routines, but none for complicated procedures that required human judgment. The only realistic chance was for the storm to pass quickly or for communication to be reestablished from another direction.

"Now what do I do?" The Captain mumbled. "I'm no doctor. I'm an officer, a leader. I need to make a decision, but I don't know what I need to decide. Maybe if I scan the medical texts I'll get it." He shivered realizing he was beginning to talk to himself.

The computer files contained a compendium of all useful medical and surgical diagnostic and therapeutic regimens. Every inquiry was answered in language the Captain was ill-prepared to understand. The illustrations were easy to interpret and follow, but he knew there was more to being a surgeon than following a recipe. If there was any time in his life prayer was necessary, it was now.

"Hello, hello, is there anyone there?"

The radio static snickered monotonously.

"Hey guys, I need some help here! There is a life at stake. Please come in. Carson's life depends on you!"

282

The static changed pitch slightly. The Captain turned up the volume and heard nothing but more and more of the same senseless hiss.

"Hey guys! Don't leave me hanging like this," the Captain shouted more emphatically even though he knew it was futile. His body shook from a combination of terror and fear. The worst part of the situation was the feeling of utter helplessness.

The Captain moved next to Carson and stared into the gaping surgical wound in the neck. The exposed tissues were automatically kept moist by an intermittent saline spray. Although all the probes remained immobile from lack of Doc's guidance, there were functions that kept him asleep. Carson's being was held in anesthetic bliss by a cold unthinking machine and would probably remain in that state until he died or the machine ceased to function. Communication had to be restored before either happened. If only Doc was here, the Captain shook his head.

In a flash it was obvious the only other possible option was to drive back to home base. Traveling through the sandstorm would be risky but a life was at stake. The benefits clearly outweighed the risks. The Captain regained his composure, feeling confident he could actually do something positive. He was no longer powerless. The trip would be tricky, but he had the necessary training and experience to do it.

The Captain assured himself Carson was well taken care of his basic biological needs before he went to the control cockpit. Once seated in the assigned place behind the rover controls his confidence soared. A check of all systems showed everything was functioning properly. He made one last attempt at contact.

"Hello, hello, can anyone read me? Is anyone there?" The Captain paused and listened.

Nothing.

"Guys, if you can hear me, I'm coming in. I'm going to come into home base. I can't wait out here any longer with Carson's life at stake. Don't worry about me and the storm. I've had plenty of practice navigating this sort of thing in Sahara simulations." The Captain listened again and heard nothing but static. "Well, ready or not, here we come." The tone of his voice was optimistic and confident.

The rover almost lurched forward as the throttle was activated. The Captain set the controls to follow the route they had used to get out to the gorge. There was little chance of

283

getting lost. The major problem would be how fast the rover could move through the storm. The speed of travel was dictated by a compromise between the ruggedness of the Martian surface and the necessity to get Carson definitive treatment as quickly as possible. Every bounce and jerk to one side or the other made the Captain's stomach twitch.

By the time the rover had traveled half the distance back to home base the sandstorm hit with all its fury. Reddish sand swirled through the thin Martian air engulfing the rover so as to blot out all evidence of an exterior reality. The weak sunlight was furthered dimmed to the point it appeared night rather than day. The fine sand pelted the hull generating an interior din that surpassed the ever present static of the radio. The noise was so loud the Captain was barely able to think. It was by sheer power of will that he focused on what he had to do.

The buildup of sand on the ground made progress ever more difficult. The Captain drove mostly by trained instinct. No storm would ever be severe enough to stop his determination to get through. The minutes passed and hours of the Martian day passed into the night. As a temperature plummeted the storm rapidly subsided until all that remained was a fog of dust, suspended in the air. It became so quiet the Captain could hear himself breathe. He remained focused on his mission and did not notice the static had also disappeared from the radio.

"Captain, what's going on?"

"Huh?" The Captain startled by the interruption jerked around and saw Carson standing behind him with a big grin. Astonishment melted into genuine relief. A more welcome sight could not have met his eyes. "Are you, are you, are you all right?"

"Should I be anything else?" Carson grinned.

"Don't you remember what happened?"

"I remember hanging down in the gorge when I was suddenly hit by a brick wall," Carson said slowly. "The next thing I remember is waking up in the trauma unit with a bunch of bandages all over. Maybe you can tell me what happened."

"You were hit by an ice blowout," the Captain said slowly. "Your suit remained intact but you suffered a fractured liver and severe neck injury. I put you in the trauma unit and Doc was fixing you up when a sand storm knocked out all communication. Doc had patched up your liver and was opening your neck before the storm hit. I had no choice but to head back to home base through the storm, otherwise your surgery would be incomplete."

Carson put his hand on the back of his neck. "I feel nothing unusual about my neck."

"Turn around. Let me see."

There was a thin line where the skin had been cut. The surgical wound had been expertly closed and fused together. The obvious conclusion was that Doc was able to continue with the remote control surgery even though all other communication had been knocked out. That could be the only answer.

"Mitch, are you there?" It was Doc's voice. "Can you hear me?"

"Doc, I can hear you loud and clear," the Captain said happily. "When we lost contact we were worried you wouldn't be able to finish fixing Carson's neck."

"I didn't," Doc said flatly. "When the storm hit there was nothing I could do but wait."

"But, but," the Captain was lost for words. "Carson's surgery was completed. I witnessed you opening the neck and now it is fully closed. You had to have done it. No machine can operate by itself."

"Mitch, the storm knocked out our antenna. It was impossible for me to transmit anything." Doc was insistent. "If the surgery was completed, it was not done by me."

Both the Captain and Carson looked at each other with the same question on their faces. If Doc did not do the surgery, then who did? Were there Martians after all?

The Catch

The mid-Pacific Ocean dominated the view earthward while the full moon did the same in the opposite direction. Alexi was too occupied to appreciate the heavenly beauty few of his countrymen had ever had an opportunity to see firsthand. The project was essentially on schedule even though not a single watt of power was generated since the station became operational nearly a year ago.

"Vasili, have you heard from the shuttle yet?" Alexi said quickly. "I'd like to get some results today, if possible."

"Stay calm, my friend," Vasili said. "The Americans will be here soon enough."

"This project has been delayed beyond reason," Alexi said flatly. "I can't understand why the Americans are so cautious. We were the first ones in space and yet they think they were always ahead of us."

"Let the past go, Alexi. Take care of your ulcer with a little bit of reason. Space has never been a one man, or one nation affair. No one has the resources to explore the outer universe by themselves. Cooperation is an absolute must. We may have been the first into space, but at what cost? I am sure we will never know exactly how many lives were lost by us before the Americans, with their caution, surpassed us. In space let us learn from each other and we will reach out and touch the stars."

"Vasili, you are an incorrigible romantic." Alexi laughed. "But, as always, you are right. I keep forgetting what an honor it is to be here in the first place."

"I have the American shuttle on visual. You can see it approaching from behind us."

Alexi looked out the nearest viewport and saw the familiar craft slowly converging with the station. Amongst the passengers was Doctor Richter who would direct the final phase and set up of the power net. In the final decade of the century NASA experimented with the idea electricity could be generated by passing a wire through the Earth's magnetic field. The results of those early experiments were at best tentative. Technical problems plus the lack of experience forcibly delayed implementation of a large wire grid orbiting through the terran magnetic lines of force. Advances in materials coupled with several changes in administrations and treaties finally allowed a serious effort to explore orbital electromagnetic power

287

generation. Funding came from a joint consortium of nations with private industry vying to have first access to the unlimited cheap power to be generated.

"Five minutes to docking," Vasili said softly.

"Everything is going well." Alexi watched carefully.

The shuttle came close enough to see the American pilots. They waved with thumbs-up. With hardly a perceptible bump, the station and the shuttle were locked in a secure embrace as they silently glided over the Earth below.

"Welcome aboard comrades," Vasili said warmly with open arms. "Our vodka is your vodka."

The copilot from the shuttle entered first, followed by Doctor Richter. Alexi and Vasili embraced both men in turn literally bouncing off the walls in the effort. The pilot of the shuttle remained behind.

"Doctor Richter, welcome," Alexi said. "And you too, Major."

"No need to be formal amongst friends," Doctor Richter said smiling. "Please call me Abe as always."

"Of course," Alexi hesitated taking a look at the Major's expression, the Major nodded approval. "Abe, it is good to see you again. I hope we can finally finish our project with the results we have expected."

"And it is good to see you again my friend," Abe said. "And, of course, my wishes mirror yours exactly."

"Would you care for vodka now or later?" Vasili almost seemed to be interrupting.

"Ah, Vasili, so good to see you again..." Abe wore a big smile. "I have not forgotten you in the least. As for the vodka let us finish our work first, then we will celebrate in style. I have brought caviar with me."

"Caviar?" Vasili nearly gasped. "How did you manage it?"

"Never ask questions that should not be answered." Abe winked. "Even at NASA position does have its privileges. Let us say, I have collected on a long-standing account and leave it to that."

"Major, Captain Jones is requesting you return to the shuttle," Alexi said. "I did not think you would leave so soon."

"The project is physically complete," the Major said. "Doctor Richter was brought here to make it operational. Captain Jones and I will undock and move several hundred miles away as observers. If all goes well, we will return to earth and celebrate.

If anything goes wrong, we can return quickly and evacuate you."

"Good thinking." Alexi nodded.

"You mean to tell us you have no final set of instruments or equipment to bring us?" Vasili exhaled sharply. "We've been playing babysitter to a full-grown adult?"

"Quite right," the Major said flatly. "We had ground simulations to complete before allowing you to know the hardware was totally complete. No need letting you think you could test it on your own."

"That type of thinking doesn't lead to much trust," Vasili hissed.

"Vasili, behave," Alexi said sternly. "We are all part of a team regardless of what unpleasant decisions are made. We are honored to be here in the first place."

Alexi huffed audibly, scowled momentarily, and finally softened his expression. "I guess I am letting pride get in the way of reason. I apologize if I have been unpleasant."

"No need," the Major said kindly. "I would probably feel the same way as you if I were kept in the dark for as long as you have in this prison in the sky."

"This is no prison," Vasili said strongly.

"Gentlemen, the Space Race was settled a long time ago," Abe interjected. "In space there is no place for sectarian politics. Bickering amongst ourselves takes away from the time we can actually celebrate. Major, return to the shuttle…Alexi, Vasili, let us make the final adjustments and proceed. Are we all agreed?"

Everyone nodded in unison.

"Good luck men." The Major waved and smiled as he exited. "May we soon celebrate."

"We will." Alexi flashed a thumb up.

The shuttle undocked and slowly drifted away from the station. A brief burst from several retro rockets accelerated the speed of separation. In 15 minutes, the shuttle was stationed approximately 150 nautical miles behind the station's orbit. Vasili checked the distance with his instruments and relayed the data to Ground Control.

"Now that I have you boys alone, I want to tell you how proud I am to be working with you," Abe said warmly. "Our countries may always have differences, but when it comes to really important things we can always come together to solve

289

any problem. Today such a moment is upon us. We will witness together the beginning of a new age. Are we ready?"

"Of course we are," Alexi said quickly.

"No doubt," Vasili said.

"Then let us get to our stations," Abe said.

The power grid, or net, was stored in a massive cylinder orbiting at the end of a long girder bridge from the station. Alexi activated a control which opened the cylinder like a giant bivalve. The power grid floated out into space slowly unfurling in two dimensions. Vasili took control of the central pods positioned at the corners of the square grid. With a series of coordinated thrusts the grid expanded out, away from the station, perpendicular to the Earth's surface below.

"It looks like we are casting a fishing net into the sky," Abe said softly. "I am reminded of my days as a boy fishing off a pier in Miami."

"We will catch no fish in these waters." Alexi laughed. "Maybe a bit of space dust, but nothing more."

"You are right." Abe sighed. "But I am a dreamer. I like to dream the impossible and make it possible."

"This project is testimony to that," Alexi said. "Who else but you would have thought?"

"There are plenty of others," Abe said. "I just happened to have the loudest voice in the right place at the right time."

"You are too modest." Alexi smiled.

Over the course of an hour the power grid was spread over an area of one square mile. The control pods were set on automatic preventing any drift, distortion or collapse. To any observer the power grid appeared a giant net suspended in space. The size of the mesh was approximately a square yard. Big enough to allow the passage of most space debris without damage. Now came the time for the critical operational test.

"Is the grid properly aligned?" Abe watched the monitor.

"To within a fraction of a degree in every direction," Vasili said proudly.

"Excellent," Abe said. "Alexi, are all circuits intact and functional?"

"I can detect no problems," Alexi said promptly. "We are ready."

"Gentlemen, we are at the moment of truth. Shall we proceed?"

"Yes."

290

"First, we will test the perimeter, and then we will add elements of the central grid," Abe said. "Alexi, do we have a current?"

A silence hung heavy in the station as Alexi examined the instruments. The expression on his face was flat and unreadable for nearly a minute. He finally broke out in a big grin. "We have a current!" He nearly shouted.

"Bravo!" Abe laughed.

"Success at last!" Vasili shouted.

"And the current is stable," Alexi said. "Shall we add more elements?"

"One at a time," Abe said. "As long as the current is constant we will proceed. Continue."

Alexi added one element after the other increasing the total power available from the grid. At the halfway point a test load was applied. The delivery of current remained a manageable constant. The current was then used to power a microwave generator aimed at the International Space Station orbiting nearby at a lower level. A scientific team on the space station reported they received a significant pulse of microwave energy which they converted back into electric power. The project began looking a complete success.

"Continue to add the remaining elements." Abe could hardly restrain his enthusiasm.

Alexi finished activating all the power generating components without incident. At first, he could not really believe everything had proceeded so smoothly, however, at the instance when the last element was added, he no longer doubted what he saw. The generated current remained stable with the promise of almost unlimited power available for transmission and consumption.

"This is almost too good to be true," Alexi said. "Electricity from wires in space."

"Believe it." Abe laughed. "You are witnessing a new age for mankind: unlimited power at almost no cost; the answer to a maiden's prayer."

"Do you anticipate any problems with the grid?" Vasili said slowly. "I agree with Alexi that this seems too good to be true."

"Aside from the possibility of a very large meteor coming out of nowhere," Abe said. "Any potential threat to the grid can be avoided by changing its orientation. Of course,

291

anything is possible, but I personally feel we are one hundred percent safe in assuming nothing will ever happen."

Alexi shivered. "I wish I were as confident as you. I don't know what it is but I just had a feeling things are not exactly what they appear to be."

"Don't listen to Alexi." Vasili laughed. "He has a superstitious streak in him."

"I take no offense, Vasili," Abe said. "We are all entitled to our personal quirks."

"It may be a personal quirk, but I feel something important is about to happen," Alexi said.

"Something important has happened." Vasili grinned. "I think it's called success."

Alexi frowned.

"Let's break out the vodka and caviar!" Abe said loudly. "We must celebrate!"

"Da, we celebrate!" Vasili nodded.

Alexi shrugged his shoulders, shook his head, and finally smiled. "You are right. It is a foolish thought. Let us celebrate."

The vodka came out of the refrigerator. Abe took a package out of his travel pack and unwrapped several sleeves of crackers and containers of caviar. Vasili transferred generous volumes of vodka to individual weightless drinking containers with straws.

"I'm afraid there is no clean way to eat caviar in space," Abe said. "But who really cares?"

"It is a mess I can live with." Alexi laughed and Vasili nodded.

With vodka in hand they toasted to each other's health and success of the project. Caviar and crackers followed swigs of vodka, every morsel was enjoyed as the luxury it was. An occasional bit of caviar floated away only to be sucked up by the nearest mouth. No bit or crumb went lost or uneaten.

Feeling lightheaded Alexi elevated his fist. "Power to the people!" He roared with a grin. "Power to the people!"

"No, power for the people!" Vasili said loudly. "For and to!"

"No need to argue." Abe felt quite relaxed. "Why don't we compromise and say power to and for the people?"

"Why didn't I think of that?" Alexi almost slurred. "Compromise and cooperation."

"We are team," Vasili slurred. "Only a team can..." He stopped because the thought escaped him.

292

"A team for sure," Abe said. "And as a team we will always glory in the success we have had. May we always continue to have success."

The bottle of vodka and caviar were consumed completely with the relish of starved men; every drop and bite enjoyed to the utmost. Cares faded away, tensions disappeared and happiness filled the inner void. They sat on top of the world with no one above them.

"Time for sleep." Alexi yawned

"Time to sleep it off." Vasili laughed.

"Time for both," Abe said. "Tomorrow we will explore the details."

"What details?" Alexi said sleepily. "I don't know what you mean."

"Forgive me, but my mind is no longer thinking clearly," Abe said slowly. "Tomorrow we will all think clearer. Tomorrow we can all put everything in its proper perspective. Our initial results have been sent home. Now we must take our long deserved rest."

Although sleep came easily to Alexi, it was not in any way restful. Amorphous images of living entities occupied his dreams. None of the entities made any threatening gestures toward him. The more he examined the entities in detail, the more difficult it was to visualize them. With a supreme effort of will he threw himself at one of the closest entities. The entity turned, appeared startled, and began uttering a familiar sound. Alexi stopped short of the entity and closed his eyes. He intuitively knew the sound meant something extremely important. Then it suddenly came to him and he opened his eyes. He was awake and the alarm was sounding loudly. An emergency was at hand.

"Alexi, what is it?" Abe rubbed the sleep out of his eyes.

"I'm not sure," Alexi said slowly. "I've just woken up."

"Something has happened to the grid!" Vasili said loudly. "It is collapsing on itself."

"What?" Abe shouted. "That's not possible. You must be wrong."

"The instruments show the grid is folding in on itself," Alexi said. "I can't explain it, but the fact remains it is happening."

"The tension on the connecting cables has nearly tripled and is rising," Vasili said flatly. "We are still safe from total rupture. Power output continues as in our previous test."

293

"The grid is intact." Abe exhaled. "There must be a malfunction of the expansion pods."

"There is nothing on my instruments indicating any such thing," Vasili said quickly. "In fact they are attempting to bring the grid back into its proper expansion without success. I expect they will exhaust their fuel supplies soon at the rate they are currently working."

"Alexi, do you have any idea what is happening?" Abe said calmly.

"Vasili, do we have control over the pods? If not, shut them down immediately."

"Done."

"Is the tension still increasing on the cables?" Alexi stared at the instruments.

"No, the tension has returned back to normal levels," Vasili said.

"Has our orbit been altered in any way?" Abe floated closer to Alexi.

"The computer says our orbit remains within expected parameters, although we have moved several miles higher than expected," Vasili said. "Whatever has happened to the grid has moved us slightly."

"I believe an object has crashed into the grid," Alexi said. "All our systems are functioning normally. There can be no other explanation."

"What bad luck," Abe muttered. "Billions spent for nothing."

"All is not lost," Alexi said. "The grid continues to show intact circuits. We may be able to expand it back out to its original orientation. Nothing is impossible unless we don't try."

"We need a direct visual," Abe said.

"I've looked out the window, but I can't see anything unusual," Vasili said. "The cables of the grid are hiding whatever might have hit it."

"Put the telescope on it," Abe said.

"I've already tried that," Vasili said. "There is something inside the grid that's hidden from view."

"Call the shuttle, tell them our problem." Abe shook his head. "Perhaps they can move in closer for direct observation."

"The shuttle is already on its way," Alexi said. "Apparently their alarms were set to monitor ours. They will be within close visual range in a few minutes."

294

"I believe they will find a piece of cosmic debris lodged in our net..." Abe sighed. "...an unfortunate problem to deal with so early."

"An old satellite or deliberate sabotage could be another possibility," Alexi said.

"Highly improbable." Abe closed his eyes. "All the spacefaring nations are a part of this project and thus have nothing to gain by sabotaging the results. Abandoned orbital debris is a remote possibility but highly unlikely considering the precise tracking maps that have been made for every bit of material launched into orbit since 1957. No, I think an untracked meteor has collided with our grid. Fortunately, there seems little damage so far."

"Abe, the Major reports they can see nothing," Vasili said. "They will try to get closer. The grid has formed a rough sphere about one hundred yards in diameter."

"There are certainly enough spaces within the grid to get a look inside," Abe said. "It would not take a very large object to mess everything up. If it were very big, it would have torn through the cables."

"Except that those cables were designed for such an eventuality," Alexi said.

"The Major reports they still can't see anything," Vasili said. "They continue moving in closer."

"Now that the grid appears stable shall we reactivate the pods?" Alexi said slowly. "Maybe by slowly re-expanding the grid we can extract the object, whatever it is."

"There is enough fuel," Vasili said. "The Major continues reporting there is no sign of damage to the grid nor is there any sign of an object."

"Our only alternative is to re-expand." Abe nodded. "Vasili, tell the Major to back off while we prepare to re-expand. Have him place the shuttle on the side the object collided with the grid."

The shuttle moved away and adjusted its orbit several miles on the impact side of the grid. Vasili activated the positioning pods. The grid began unfolding slowly. Whatever was the cause of collapse remained hidden. Alexi fixed the telescope on the center of the grid recording every step of the unfolding. The mystery would be solved and documented for analysis.

"The grid is showing a power fluctuation," Vasili said.

"That is to be expected," Abe said. "Power is a reflection of orientation to the lines of magnetic force."

"The fluctuation is in excess of what I would expect from orientation alone," Vasili said. "The object may have done damage to the cables after all."

"Or we are damaging the cables by trying to reexpand it with the object still within the grid," Alexi said. "Perhaps we should stop expanding."

"The Major has reported unexpected movement in the grid," Vasili said. "The object is changing position, but is still not visible."

"Damn, what to do? What to do?" Abe was exasperated. "A puzzle with no easy solution; whatever we do may be wrong."

"At least the grid is re-expanding smoothly," Alexi said. "So far, there have been no structural separations."

"I still feel uneasy about all of this," Abe said flatly. "My intuition tells me something is very wrong and I can't put my finger on it."

"The Major says they have seen something. They can't make out what it is but it is quite large."

"I see nothing through the telescope yet."

"When the grid is finally open you will. The Major has a better angle than we do. It won't be too long and we will see it too."

"Put the Major over the speaker," Abe said. "I'd like to hear his first impression when he finally sees the object."

"The object in the grid appears moving," the Major said. "Its irregular motion suggests a very irregular shape."

"Can you detect any color?"

"There are flashes of silver and yellow. I think we are seeing reflections from a metallic surface, but I'm not sure."

"Meteor or spacecraft?"

"I can't tell. The grid is opening slowly and we are moving closer. Wait! Hold on! Something just poked out of the grid and went back in. I don't believe it!"

"What is it?" Abe was breathless. "What was it?"

There was silence on the speaker.

"I caught a flash of movement in the telescope," Vasili said. "I can run it back at high magnification if you want."

"Immediately! We have to know what we are dealing with. Major are you still there?" Abe said slowly. "Please answer."

296

"There is something very strange going on out here. If I told you what I thought I saw, you would definitely think I am crazy."

"Don't keep us in suspense, tell us! We are making a record of everything to prove what you say. Think of us as corroborating witnesses not critics."

"The playback shows nothing but a blur," Vasili said. "I can't tell what it is."

"Keep recording," Abe said sharply. "We must record what this thing is."

"If it is a meteor, it will be the first time we have recovered one in transit," Alexi said.

"The grid is almost open. I can see..." The Major's transmission was washed out with loud static. Vasili turned down the volume.

"We have lost communication," Vasili said.

Abe rubbed his chin and shook his head. "We don't need technical problems."

"Is there any way we can get a better picture?" Alexi said. "Our view is less than optimal."

"We are stuck with what we have, I am afraid." Vasili sighed. "I hope the shuttle is recording everything."

"Let's establish a laser link with the shuttle," Abe said. "We are in direct line of sight."

"Of course..." Alexi nodded and turned on the emergency communication system. After several minutes a link was reestablished.

"You won't believe what we have been seeing," the Major said breathlessly. "The thing is some sort of creature. It has eyes and teeth and claws."

Abe began to say the Major must have been hallucinating but restrained himself. The stress of the situation was excessive, meaning that interpretation of unnatural phenomena could be seen erroneously as supernatural. He knew the Major well enough to know that whatever was witnessed was not exaggerated on purpose.

"Uh, oh!" Alexi gasped. "We have a flare alert from Central Control. Time to batten down the hatches."

"Into the shelter boys!" Abe pointed. "We have to leave everything to the cameras now. Send a warning to the shuttle."

"Done," Alexi said quickly. "This is coming at the wrong time."

"Unfortunately, we have no control over the situation," Abe said. "Now our lives are at risk until the storm passes."

Reluctantly, but with efficiency of motion, they entered the storm shelter. Alexi reestablished the link with the shuttle without difficulty.

"Major, are you secured?"

"All is secure," the Major said. "I'm not sure I am sane anymore. One moment I see a fantastic creature, the next moment I see nothing. I feel as though I am on some hallucinogenic trip and yet I am stone cold sober."

"There must be a logical explanation for everything," Abe said softly. "I've known you long enough to know how your mind works. I've never known you to exaggerate anything."

"Thank you for your vote of confidence," the Major said warmly. "I need all the reassurance I can get at the moment."

"Settle back and relax," Abe said. "When the storm has passed we will see everything can be easily explained by simple logic and mundane evidence. We will keep all our initial impressions to ourselves. Are we agreed?"

"Yes," the Major said without further comment.

The waiting began. All nonessential systems were turned off. The station and the shuttle were oriented to provide maximum shielding to the crews. The telescope from the station kept its sole vigil recording the opening of the grid. Minutes evolved into hours before the all clear signal was sent from Central Control. All systems were repowered and checked for reliability. Nothing had been seriously damage.

"The grid is completely open," Alexi said. "And there is nothing in its vicinity except the shuttle."

"Nothing?" Abe was incredulous.

"Nothing," Vasili whispered.

"Nothing from here either," the Major said over the speaker.

"Was there definitely something trapped and now it's gone?" Abe muttered. "Are we all suffering mass hysteria?"

"It is possible that reopening the grid gave enough momentum to the object and pushed it away," Alexi said. "It wouldn't take much energy."

"I've checked my instruments," Vasili said. "There is no damage to the grid. Everything checks out normal."

"There must be a logical explanation!" Abe kept shaking his head.

"Abe, calm yourself," Vasili said slowly. "We haven't taken a look at the pictures yet. Everything was recorded while we were in the shelter. Let's take a look."

"Get on with it," Abe said.

The tape was rewound and the men gathered around the monitor. The first unusual image was the transitory blur that had emerged from the grid before the storm. At the time, coincident with entering the storm shelter, the grid completed opening. In the center of the grid appeared a giant black cat with yellow eyes and an expression suggestive of a smile. The image lasted for a few seconds and disappeared.

"Well, I'll be damned!" Abe laughed. "If I hadn't seen it, I wouldn't have believed it: a cat!"

"It can't be!" Vasili shouted. "It's an illusion! It just can't be!"

"Whatever it was is gone," Alexi said slowly. "There is no sign of it anywhere. I have checked all our sensors and Central Control's."

"The cat!" Abe laughed louder. "A cat, that's there and yet not there."

Alexi looked at Abe wondering what the joke was. Abe laughed so much that tears came to his eyes. Then a flash of inspiration came to mind.

"Whose cat is it?" Alexi smiled. "Alice's?"

"No, no, no, my boy." Abe tried controlling himself. "It's Schrödinger's cat."

From the air Site 126.537 looked more promising than any other in the area. Even so, at ground level there was very little, if anything, to distinguish it from the surrounding acres of ash and rocky rubble. Jannon rechecked his sensor readings taken from an altitude of five miles and compared them with those immediately taken at ground level. Whatever was buried was deeper than expected. The wind blew in from the adjacent shoreline ruffling his long red hair. A cloud of dust swirled up filling his nostrils with a disagreeable dryness. Nothing in the Greater Galactic Planetary Archaeology Manual was ever mentioned of the hostile environments that had to be tolerated at any specific dig. As part of his upcoming doctoral dissertation he planned to add an appendix on how to survive in relative comfort on any alien world. The main problem he had was finding a satisfactory topic to base his dissertation. He hoped this site would provide the materials he needed toward that end.

"Anything yet?" Manta lumbered from the ship with a box of excavating tools.

"I am getting a very faint reading." Jannon pointed at the ground. "Somehow I think we have missed the spot or there is something interfering with a clear signal."

Manta set the box down carefully. "No way could I have missed the spot. You gave me the coordinates and I followed them to the decimal. Something has to be wrong with your instruments."

Jannon sighed. "I have rechecked everything many times over. There is nothing wrong with my instruments. I think there is something about this area that makes it difficult to get any reliable sensor readings."

"It won't be the first time." Manta coughed and turned away from the wind.

"From what I can tell, where I am standing is where we have to start digging."

"Are you sure?"

"Almost absolutely."

"I don't like the way you said that." Manta pulled a shovel out of the box.

"You're not much of an archaeologist in the field." Jannon laughed putting his instruments down next to the toolbox.

"My type of archaeology is sitting in a soft comfortable chair in the basement of a museum going through shards and

301

artifacts brought back by young hotshots like you who enjoy getting their hands dirty. Why I ever agreed to come with you to this forsaken world is beyond my comprehension."

"Could getting away from Leila be part of it?" Jannon chuckled. "As I understand it things were getting pretty serious between you two. Am I right?"

"That's not the reason I came at all." Manta jabbed his shovel into the ground with a vengeance. "I came because of our friendship and your need to have the best possible help in getting your dissertation material. You helped me with mine. Now it's my turn to help you with yours. What nobler reason can there be than one friend helping the other? Hm?"

"I suppose I have to accept friendship as your motive to be here." Jannon picked up a shovel out of the box. "However, I am still entitled to my own opinions."

"No one ever said you couldn't think." Manta grinned. "You forget you made a pretty convincing argument to come here."

"Planetary archaeology of ancient civilizations is best done on site in the field; anything else is pure intellectual laziness." Jannon began digging. "The materials that need investigation are in the ground, not neatly tucked away in some closet; besides, interpretation of any finding is best made in the context of its original location."

"Yes, yes, I know what the Manual says." Manta sighed. "And you're right I should be out doing on-site studies more often. But then there's…"

"Leila." Jannon interrupted.

Manta stopped digging as if he had suddenly been put on hold. Jannon smiled while he continued digging.

"I wish you wouldn't bring her up."

"Why? Am I striking a nerve?"

Manta placed the tip of his shovel gently into the dirt. A cloud passing overhead brought a temporary shadow over the site. Manta shook his head and began digging.

"She wants a permanent commitment," Manta said flatly. "I have to give her an answer soon or she's gone."

"I knew it." Jannon laughed. "Actually, it doesn't matter why you're here. I'm just glad you are. Besides, it's none of my business."

"Well, I do need to work some things out before I make a decision." Manta hit the ground harder with the shovel.

"I've never known you to rush into anything. I think you will make the right decision. Just use your professional skills on your own personal life and you will come out okay."

They continued digging until late into the afternoon. The soil yielded nothing of any interest to their disappointment. At intervals, Jannon would activate his instruments for additional readings. The deeper they dug, the more definite the readings became. Something was below their feet waiting to be uncovered. When Manta's shovel struck a solid object the growing fatigue instantly vanished.

"I think we are there," Manta said quickly. "Time to get serious."

"From here on we must be more careful," Jannon said. "Time to switch over to smaller tools and slower digging. We must not damage anything needlessly."

"Whatever it is, I can already tell its metallic," Manta said.

"I agree." Jannon nodded.

As the afternoon yielded to early dusk, they uncovered a hard metallic surface embedded in solid rock. Rather than continue working into the night they marked the site and returned to the ship. Neither would admit they were tired, but both agreed they would function better the next morning. The evening meal was consumed, not enjoyed, and sleep came slowly.

During the night a brief rain squall soaked the site making any further digging messy. Undeterred by the mud, they continued uncovering the metallic artifact after a light breakfast.

"How big do you think this thing is?" Manta stood holding his shovel. "What is it?"

"All we can possibly know is that it is artificial," Jannon said. "It looks like it's some sort of container. We need to free it from the rock to tell for sure."

"Do you think it was embedded in the rock on purpose or by the cataclysm that engulfed this world?"

Jannon shook his head. "We can't make any assumptions without further data. I will run samples of the rock through the analyzer. That should give us a clue."

"You know this thing could be hollow."

"I'm counting on it," Jannon said flatly. "Something as big as this and metallic is usually hollow and hopefully contains something of interest."

By midday the metallic object was freed from the rock on three sides. Each side was flat without any discernible opening or markings. Its size measured an arm length in each dimension. In other words, it was approximately half the size of an average person.

"There has to be an opening into this thing," Manta said. "It must be on the other side. We have to turn it over."

Jannon tapped the object with a small hammer while looking at his instruments. The readings made him smile. "This thing is definitely hollow and there is something inside."

"Can you tell what it is?"

"Not yet."

By late afternoon the object was freed of its rocky prison and was ready to move back to the ship. Jannon carefully recorded everything he could think of before moving it. Surrounding samples of rock and dirt were collected for future analysis. As an additional procedure the soil around the site was sifted and whatever found put into containers for reference. A last instrument scan showed nothing of any further interest. When night came the evening meal was consumed with gusto and sleep quickly followed. A hard day's work had thoroughly exhausted them so that the object was not thought of until the next morning.

"Did you sleep well?"

Manta yawned. "Like a rock."

"So did I." Jannon unsuccessfully tried stifling a yawn. "Today we get answers."

The alien object sat on a table reflecting no light. Careful examination revealed one surface was actually a door. Whatever handle or mechanism had been used to open that door remained a mystery. Since the metal was relatively impervious to x-rays, ultrasound was used to examine the door and possible contents in detail. Regardless of what this artifact was, it promised to be a treasure chest.

"I've taken a complete holographic picture from all angles," Jannon said. "And I have recorded all the data from the internal probes. The only thing left is to open it up."

"Is it possible this might be a weapon of some sort?" Manta stood stiffly staring at the object. "We know from extensive research weapons of mass destruction are a product of almost every technological civilization."

"I disagree." Jannon shook his head. "Not every civilization deliberately creates weapons of extraordinary

304

destruction; however, the fundamentals of physics are universal, which means eventually every technological society will discover how to unleash vast quantities of energy in short periods of time. This energy is always used for peaceful purposes, in time. The use of this energy for non-peaceful purposes, such as war, is directly dependent on the moral fiber of competing subgroups of the planet. I know I am stepping on one of your pet theories, but I also have my own."

"Yes, I know," Manta said slowly. "But it doesn't solve the issue of whether we open the object within the ship or at a safe distance from it."

"There is no radioactivity, nor any evidence of fissionable elements." Jannon sighed. "I plan to open it in a magnetic containment field surrounded by a biological safety envelope. I want nothing to get in or out without our knowing about it. I suspect there will be no explosive surprises."

"Although I don't exactly share your confidence, let's get on with it." Manta stepped backward. "The sooner we get it open, the sooner we will know what we have gotten ourselves into."

In a concession to Manta's concerns Jannon moved the object to a site outside the ship where a magnetic and biological containment field was created. A remote robot technician was put into position next to the object while Jannon and Manta took their places at monitors within the ship. Jannon thought about lifting off to hover miles above but eventually decided he had compromised more than he should have. Manta watched the object from the observation port while Jannon viewed the object up close on the robot monitor.

"First, I'm going to drill a hole at this corner, collect a sample of the internal gases and then insert a fiber-optic probe for the camera." Jannon spoke for the record. "The laser has begun to penetrate the surface. In a second it will be through, yes, we are through. Gases sampled. Camera on."

Manta joined Jannon at the monitor. All was dark until Jannon turned on a light. They recoiled at the image that filled the screen. An alien face with wide-open eyes stared at them with a smile.

"Holy smoke!" Manta gasped. "What is that?"

Jannon composed himself. "It is an idol of some sort. It's not alive. We have nothing to be afraid of."

"An idol?"

305

"Primitive societies almost always have a collection of supernatural beings to explain the world around them," Jannon said. "Even advanced societies have idols of one sort or the other although the total number approaches one."

"What else is in there?" Manta moved closer to the monitor. "Are there any more idols?"

"Let's see." Jannon smiled as he manipulated the probe carefully, avoiding contact with anything. "There's not much to see without opening it up."

Jannon rechecked his collected data several times before committing himself to the next step. Assured he had not missed anything he removed the probe from the object and began cutting it open using the original hole as a starting point. The cutting was slower than he liked, but actually faster than protocol recommended. With the cut completed circumferentially, they watched closely as the object was widely opened.

"I think we can assume it is safe for us to bring the object and its contents into the ship," Jannon said. "We can get more done in here."

"I agree." Manta nodded.

All the equipment and the open object were brought into the ship as dark clouds rolled in overhead from the shore. A rumble of thunder followed by a cool blast of air meant rain was not far behind. Inside the ship was the only place to be while the storm passed.

The object was placed in a sterile box. This was more to prevent contamination from any ship debris. Jannon donned a set of gloves and began recording the contents in situ. Manta dictated a set of observations along with several speculations. This was the beginning of a puzzle which they needed to solve given only what they had before them.

"The object has three idols clearly visible. Surrounding them there are multiple containers of various sizes covered with writing in the ancient language of the previous inhabitants." Manta droned into the recorder. "The object on first impression now appears to be a receptacle for important articles. The presence of the idols suggests a religious significance."

"If I didn't know better," Jannon said. "I would think you were taking over investigation of this artifact."

"I'm only trying to help." Manta moved away from the recorder. "I'm just as enthusiastic about this find as you are. I don't mean to steal it away from you."

"Please keep your opinions quiet until I can formulate my own independently," Jannon said slowly. "I want your input, but I don't want it to be biased before I do."

"Sorry, I wasn't thinking."

"No real harm done."

The contents of the object were carefully removed and placed side-by-side on a long table. Pictures and measurements were taken of each one. There were a total of 23 boxes and three idols plus 5 miscellaneous discs with writing on them.

"This is not going to be easy," Manta said.

"Actually it's easier than I thought it would be," Jannon said. "I didn't expect to find a sealed container filled with so many things. Our job will be total interpretation on top of what we already know about this planet."

"But we know very little."

"Enough to make a few deductions," Jannon said. "This planetary system revolves around a single star near the rim of a standard spiral galaxy. The age of the system is approximately 4.5 to 6.0 billion years old. Although the planet we are on currently has no indigent life, the fact we have found an artifact created by a highly developed civilization proves life once thrived here."

"Suppose this object is really alien to this world," Manta interjected.

"Highly unlikely," Jannon said. "The composition of the object and its internal gases more or less confirm its local origin. I am now sure, if we look hard enough, we will find more evidence to prove it."

"Okay," Manta said. "If a civilization flourished here, why does it no longer exist? Why is there no life?"

"Civilizations rise and fall across the universe for any number of reasons," Jannon said. "War and natural disasters are perhaps the most common."

"Which do you think happened here?"

"Whoa!" Jannon smiled. "We don't have enough data to draw any conclusions. I am hoping we can get some clues from these artifacts. I suggest you start inputting all the writing into the translator. Hopefully we will get some useful information."

"Certainly we didn't come here without some clues," Manta said insistently. "There must be some evidence."

"To tell the truth, there is some astrophysical evidence," Jannon said. "Electromagnetic transmissions were detected over a long period of time until they suddenly ceased. There was a suggestion of a nearby black hole collapse but that was never confirmed. Whatever happened was a local planetary catastrophe."

"Perhaps a collision with one of the minor planetoids wandering about the system," Manta said slowly. "With so many objects moving it is just a matter of time before one strikes another."

"Quite possible." Jannon nodded. "Why don't you follow-up by taking core samples and analyzing them for rare metals."

"Good idea." Manta smiled confidently.

"Later we can do a survey of the entire planet," Jannon said. "There must be clues to what happened somewhere. In the meantime my focus will remain these artifacts and what they represent. Any output on the translation yet?"

"Nothing yet..." Manta rechecked the translator. "I have set the translator to give an audible ring when it has finished."

"Good." Jannon turned back to all the objects in front of him. He realized each possibly deserved a lifetime of study by itself. Unfortunately, he did not have the luxury of that much time. He needed answers quickly.

"The three idols appear to represent entirely different personages," Jannon said flatly. "Two are of one sex, the third the opposite. In terms of size all appeared equal perhaps representing an equality of sorts. Each is dressed in totally different costumes which suggest either unique powers or specific areas of concern. An assortment of implements is present, attached to the belt of one of them."

"Shall we open one of the containers?"

Jannon paused. "Please do not interrupt my train of thought."

"Sorry. I just thought I could expedite everything," Manta said softly.

"As much as I would like answers immediately, I know my job well enough to know I must try to take my time," Jannon said. "Let me open the first box."

The top of the first box easily came off and revealed another totally different idol within. Jannon removed it carefully and placed it on the table. Unlike the first ones examined, this one had features suggestive of incorporation of other beasts into its physiogeny.

"The features on this idol are again totally different from the others," Jannon said. "Note the bestial eyes and posture. Clearly this is a mutant deity."

"The inscription on the box is in the translator," Manta said.

"Good. And did you include the inscriptions under the boots of the three major idols?"

"No, but I'll add them now."

When all the boxes were open the table was littered with an assortment of different beings whose function and significance could only be guessed. The temptation was to explain everything in terms of personal home history. As a student of planetary archaeology Jannon knew that would lead to incomplete answers and ridicule from his peers.

Every box, idol and artifact was examined and recorded. In the end both Jannon and Manta stepped back from the collection on the table and stared at each item with a sense of awe. Few finds such as this were ever available in such pristine condition.

"How old do you think these things are?" Manta said. "Do you have any idea?"

"You are supposed to give me that data," Jannon said slowly.

"I have it." Manta smiled. "But I want you to guess. I want to see how close you get."

"On the basis of what I have observed I would think several thousands of years."

"Guess again." Manta chuckled.

"Higher or lower?"

Manta motioned higher.

"Ten thousand years?"

Manta motioned higher again.

"One hundred thousand?"

Again Manta motioned higher.

"A million?"

"And some." Manta grinned. "I don't believe it either, but the instruments don't lie. I have even rechecked the results five times to be absolutely certain. These things are 1.35 million years old."

"You must be kidding!" Jannon shook his head. "I don't believe it!"

"There is no mistake. I am absolutely sure of my results."

"What that means is beyond comprehension," Jannon said. "Before our own ancestors became sentient, these beings were at the height of their civilization."

"It seems that way." Manta smiled. "I still wonder exactly what happened to them. You would think such an advanced civilization would survive forever."

"There is a theory that civilization like all life has an inherent termination factor," Jannon said. "As biological immortality is impossible, so is cultural immortality. Any race of advanced civilized beings will eventually face extinction. There have been no exceptions."

"What about our own culture?"

"One day even our civilization will collapse into oblivion," Jannon said sadly. "War, disease and ennui never disappear. Eventually something happens that ends everything only to start anew."

"But why hasn't life begun anew here?"

"I was expecting you to come up with some answers to that question."

"Well, I have reviewed the images taken from orbit and the physical data collected at this site," Manta said. "And the best I can come up with is a series of cataclysmic explosions from the surrounding space. There are at least half a dozen major impact craters on the major landmasses plus evidence of a rare element residue from near the surface. This is all consistent with several direct strikes with large masses into the atmosphere causing extraordinary shockwaves and racing debris into the atmosphere blocking out the ambient solar radiation for multiples of years. Under those conditions life was literally snuffed out."

"Sounds plausible enough." Jannon nodded. "I'll incorporate that into my dissertation."

"Do I get any credit?"

"I will acknowledge your contributions," Jannon said. "Don't worry."

"Come to think of it, you didn't mention natural disasters as being a possible cause of our own civilization's demise. Why not?"

"Because our home world is in a relatively safe part of the galaxy, although even there anything is possible. Actually, I just forgot to include it as a possibility."

310

"Don't you think if any object large enough to destroy a whole world was seen in time there would be time to escape to another?"

"Only if the technology is sufficiently advanced and there is enough time to collect enough beings to transport away," Jannon said. "There must also be a large enough critical mass for the new colony to survive. Too few members and the number of useful individuals decrease faster than new ones are generated. Too many individuals and needs outstrip resources causing self-destructive behavior. The ideal number of beings is almost always unknown."

"I wonder what the beings that lived here experienced." Manta was absently distracted by an imaginary scenario of explosive destruction.

"The encasement of the artifacts clearly represents to me the importance they had to their owner," Jannon said. "Objects of religious significance are generally the best protected of all artifacts according to the Manual. Our finding is a classic example."

"If our finding is so classic, of what value is it?" Manta said slowly.

Jannon shook his head. "All findings add to that greater fund of universal knowledge that leads to greater understanding. With greater understanding there develops a sense of unity among sentient species; the more similar the findings, the greater that sense of unity. The single most important discovery of our planetary culture was physical proof that sentient life existed elsewhere in the universe."

"A society must be quite primitive not to realize that," Manta said. "Our children know that before they start formal school."

"We must be careful not to judge all other civilizations based on the perceptions we have of our own," Jannon said. "Yes, there are absolute truths, but there is also enough wiggle room for unique differences. Would you like a few examples?"

"No, thanks." Manta shook his head. "I've had enough of a lecture today. My head is already spinning from what you have told me; maybe some other time. Besides I'm getting hungry. I need a break."

"Yes, the time has slipped by faster than I expected." Jannon smiled. "This would be as good a time as any to take a break."

311

The artifacts were left undisturbed on the table while they prepared their meal. Outside the sky was clearing as the sun plunged below the horizon. The wind had almost completely abated and absolute calm flattened the distant ocean; movement of the air outside disappeared presenting a scene as if painted by an artist.

"When I look out." Jannon mused. "I can't help but wonder what eyes gazed on this scene so many eons ago."

"Perhaps they were not so much different than we are," Manta said. "I am sure they could appreciate the natural beauty we see."

"Even we had idols in the distant past." Jannon sighed. "Let's hope we never lose sight of that."

The computer chimed loudly. Manta, startled, almost dropped the plate he was holding. Jannon smiled broadly motioning toward the computer.

"Now we will get more answers to the puzzle." Jannon felt confident.

"Or more questions will be raised," Manta said smartly. "The computer may give us nothing."

"Perhaps," Jannon said. "But at least it might give us some clues as to where to direct our efforts."

"Without even looking; we need more input."

"No doubt…" Jannon nodded. "However, something is always better than nothing. Even the most insignificant can become important."

Manta allowed Jannon to precede him to the computer. The project was for his dissertation. The urge to sprint ahead was more than a minor temptation. There was a mutual feeling they were about to make a major discovery. Arriving at the computer they both rapidly scanned the monitor display.

"No surprises," Jannon said flatly.

"But enough to get your doctorate." Manta put a hand on Jannon's shoulder. "Look at it this way, the less we know, the more we can interpolate. Who can prove anything otherwise?"

"Yes, you're right," Jannon said softly. "I really was hoping for something more."

"At least now you know what the names of the idols are," Manta said. "We may not know what those names mean until we can find more artifacts. But look at it this way; you will be the first to record their names. It is enough to get your career really started."

"Yes, you're right again." Jannon sighed. "I guess coming here was not exactly what I expected. I hoped we would find a lot more."

"You found more in this expedition than any scholar finds sitting in a university teaching ever does," Manta said warmly. "At least you have the guts to explore the unknown and get your hands dirty. Someday you will find something really important and you will become famous. In time what we have found here will be recognized as a footnote to your successful accomplishments."

"Stop." Jannon suddenly laughed. "You're giving me a big head. Let's finish with what we have here before we retire in fame and fortune."

"I'm glad to see you can laugh at yourself." Manta laughed. "It was getting too gloomy."

"Time to finish up." Jannon read the display again. "I see I have a lot of intellectual work ahead of me. All these names are different and very unusual. I can only guess the names signify something that for the moment I can only guess. Naturally if form follows function, I can assume a few specifics."

"What are the names of the three largest idols?" Manta stared at the monitor.

"Let's see." Jannon scanned the monitor. "One is called The Flash, another Green Lantern, and the last Wonder Woman."

"And we have no idea what those names mean." Manta shook his head.

"Some of the smaller items have names like Superman, Batman, and Captain America." Jannon continued.

"Very interesting." Manta was clearly absorbed. "What do you plan to call your dissertation?"

"You mean the title?"

Manta nodded. Jannon remained silent and thought for several seconds.

"I think I'll title it," Jannon said slowly. "Pantheon of the Past on the Third Planet of a Minor Star."

"Not bad." Manta smiled and nodded. "Not bad at all."

313

The guard jabbed firmly into Safi's left shoulder, silently ordering him forward into the spot of light shining on the floor in the small room ahead. Safi hesitated a moment, turned his face to the guard and smiled.

"Move forward!" the guard growled. "You're wasting time!"

Safi said nothing and moved with measured steps into the center of the light. The door hissed closed behind him and for a brief moment he felt claustrophobic. He quickly fought off the feeling. Regaining his inner strength, he patiently awaited whatever was to happen next. His life had always been a colorful existence, not without the risk of coming into conflict with superior powers. As a child he had grown up facing adult authority from the time he had become conscious of his surroundings. What he had to face now was nothing different than what he grew up with all his life. Although he was certain he had violated no laws, he was unsure of the methods his enemies would use against him. The charges, whatever they were, had to be false and without merit.

"State your name," a voice boomed out of the surrounding dark.

"Safi," he stated softly.

"Remain motionless until identification is complete," the voice said dispassionately.

A hollow cylinder descended from above and completely engulfed Safi within its core. The feeling of claustrophobia returned. Safi forced his eyes closed and thought of other things. A continuous series of loud thumps filled his ears for an indeterminate time. As quickly as it had descended, the cylinder was removed. Safi took a deep breath and slowly opened his eyes.

"Magnetic resonance identification complete," the voice said loudly.

Safi wanted to speak, but thought it more prudent to wait until spoken to.

"Mister Safi, are you ready to proceed?" another more full human-like voice said.

"Yes," he said softly. "But please call me just Safi."

"Just Safi?" the voice said flatly. "I was unaware you had another name."

315

"My name is Safi." He chuckled; machines were not perfect after all. "I have no other names."

"Let the record show that the defendant named Safi is ready to proceed," the voice said.

"And to whom am I speaking?" Safi looked around.

"I am Chief Justice Defarge," the voice said. "You may simply address me as Defarge."

"You are a construct of Defarge Industries."

"That is a totally correct statement," Defarge said. "The latest design in quantum computers, dedicated completely to the search for truth and justice."

"And what does my being here have anything to do with you?" Safi kept searching the room for a point of reference. "I assume there is a valid reason for me being brought here like this to you."

"Pardon the inconvenience," Defarge said. "You have been brought here to assess the validity of charges."

"What charges?" Safi said quickly. "I am guilty of nothing."

"Please allow me to finish," Defarge continued unfazed. "You have been brought here to assess the validity of charges that you have deliberately and willingly committed crimes against the State and mankind."

"This cannot be possible," Safi nearly shouted. "What are those charges and who are my accusers?"

"We will get to that shortly," Defarge said. "Do you certify for the record that you are who you say you are?"

"I protest!" Safi shouted.

"A yes or no is all that is required," Defarge said sternly. "Your lack of cooperation will weigh heavily against you. Please answer the question. Do you certify for the record that you are who you say you are: yes or no?"

Safi glared incredulous into the darkness.

"Yes or no…"

"I refuse to answer without proper counsel."

"Safi, this is a court of the highest level. Counsel is neither necessary nor allowed," Defarge said slowly. "The sooner you cooperate, the sooner we can dispose of the matter at hand. Are you who you say you are: yes or no?"

"Yes, I am," Safi hissed. "I object to this proceeding without prior notice or stated reason."

"Objection overruled," Defarge said. "Will the defendant please state his place of origin and occupation."

"Do I have a choice?" Safi mumbled inaudibly.

"May I remind the defendant I can hear everything? Please answer the questions without comment. All statements you make will be part of the permanent record and will be included in the final analysis leading to a judgment. Do you understand?"

"Yes, I understand," Safi paused. "I will cooperate."

"Now once again," Defarge continued. "Please state your place of origin and occupation."

"My place of origin is here or wherever I am at the moment," Safi said slowly. "And my occupation is magician of the mind and body."

"And are you of sound mind and body?"

"Certainly!" Safi snapped.

"You are charged with obstruction of justice, abduction of a state witness and treason. How do you plead?"

"This is ludicrous!" Safi exhaled. "On what grounds do you bring these charges against me? I demand to face my accusers!"

"All I am asking for the record is for you to state guilty or not guilty," Defarge said. "I am sure you will get all your questions answered as we proceed. Now again: guilty or not guilty?"

Safi took a deep breath. "Not guilty of any and all charges you have stated against me. Are you happy now?"

"Happiness is an emotion irrelevant to the conduct of this matter," Defarge said sternly. "Do I need remind you again of the consequences of your attitude?"

"No, that is not necessary," Safi spat. "To me this all appears a nightmare from which I cannot awaken. I am here against my will to face charges of actions I have no recollection. This is not an investigation, it is an inquisition."

"I beg to differ," Defarge said. "You are here to ascertain the truth and administer justice as necessary."

"But how is that possible when justice does not even exist?" Safi snorted. "How can anyone other than themselves decide what is right and true?"

"For me that is easy," Defarge said. "I am able to evaluate all scenarios with my advanced quantum matrix and match the best suspect with the facts at hand."

"And do you always find the best suspects or do you create them?" Safi sneered. "Such a system is filled with flaws."

"The chance of me erring is extremely remote. There is little opportunity for the guilty to escape my probing evaluation."

"A judge of one can convict at will according to a preset agenda. Are you as detached and objective as you must be?"

"My validity is not a question here. You are the defendant and it is your actions I must decide upon."

Safi remained silent. He tried thinking what could possibly be the reason for his arrest. A magician of the body and mind was no less than the ultimate holistic physician. Medicine was always a mixture of art and science, being a magician finally brought recognition that there are powers far beyond science more or just as important in healing and treating the afflicted as traditional medicine. He knew he was a master at what he had been trained to do. Who have I had contact with in the past that might connect me with why I am here, he wondered.

"Where were you the night of October 31?" Defarge continued.

Safi thought quickly. "I was called to care for a critically injured accident victim."

"And where was this?"

"At the Memorial Hospital emergency room."

"And what was the name of this accident victim?"

"Let me think a moment." Safi wrinkled his brow and pressed both temples with his fingers.

"Take your time, if necessary," Defarge said flatly. "How and what you answer is critical."

Safi closed his eyes and let his mind drift backward in time to the emergency room of the Memorial Hospital. Using the techniques of his trade, he soon found himself at the moment before the call for assistance came when the ambulance arrived.

"Code critical room one," the speaker blared overhead. "Code critical room one."

He had just put his head down on his pillow when he heard: "Safi Room One, Safi Room One, stat!"

He got up off the bed with a visible sign of resignation and sighed. After a quick glance in the mirror above the sink, checking the status of his hair, he hurried out of the dark cramped call room. Time was always important regardless of the hour of the night or degree of personal fatigue. When he arrived, emergency room one was swarming with activity. On the examining table in the center of the room was a white man, obviously unconscious, whose clothes had been completely cut off. A nurse was pulling the tattered remnants of clothes from

318

under the unmoving body and putting them into a clear plastic bag. Another nurse had just finished drawing blood for a battery of tests. The Chief Resident listened for breath sounds with his stethoscope and acknowledged his arrival with an appreciative nod.

Without hesitation the Chief Resident began: "We have here an unconscious middle-aged white male with no obvious signs of trauma. His vital signs are stable. The physical exam shows no lacerations, ecchymoses, purpura or swellings. There are no puncture wounds to suggest drug abuse. He is completely unresponsive to verbal commands and deep pain. Without being to fully assess his neurological status, his examination is otherwise entirely normal."

"Have you spoken to any family or friends?" Safi lifted the eyelids with the index and middle fingers of his left hand.

"He was found without identification," the Chief Resident said automatically. "The police are waiting for our approval to take fingerprints and a blood sample."

"Do it!" Safi snapped and shined a flashlight into the man's eyes. "Notice that the pupils are equal and do respond to light. Have you had a drug screen drawn as well as the usual blood parameters?"

Of course..." The Chief Resident smiled. "And we are on standby for an immediate CAT scan or MRI, whichever you think best."

"And what you think?" Safi closed the man's eyes and turned his attention to the discussion of priorities.

"The MRI would give us more information, but a CAT scan is cheaper and may prove adequate enough for diagnostic purposes," the Chief Resident said tentatively.

"Which is it then?" Safi glared. "MRI or CAT scan? Do you think cost is a factor when a young man's life hangs in the balance?"

"No." The Chief Resident blushed. "I'll arrange all the appropriate tests. Is there anything else you can suggest?"

"Call me when you have some numbers and pictures." Safi sounded more sympathetic. "I don't mean to sound hard-assed about this, but when there is a question of life or death there can be no halfhearted measures. Before I go, let me do my own physical examination."

The Chief Resident held out his stethoscope to Safi which he pushed away. Safi closed his eyes and placed his hands on each side of the head of the unconscious man. He slowly

319

moved his hands in contact with every inch of skin surface from head to toes.

"Are you ready to answer?" Defarge said.

Safi mentally shook his head and returned to the present. The past he recalled could have some connection with the charges but he was not certain.

"I recall a patient I saw in the emergency room," Safi began. "I was on duty and had just about fallen asleep when I was paged to examine an unconscious man. The Chief Resident had examined and begun all the necessary diagnostic tests before I arrived. The initial presentation seemed to be an exercise in the evaluation of loss of consciousness. Unfortunately, the man had no identification on him nor were there any witnesses to when or how he had collapsed."

"Why did you initially rule out trauma?" Defarge interrupted. "Could he have been assaulted or had an accident?"

"There was nothing to remotely suggest either foul play or an accident of any sort," Safi said flatly. "When I got off call that next day I personally went to where he had been found and saw nothing."

"And where was this man found?"

"On an open expanse of beach," Safi said. "There wasn't a single clue anywhere that helped in determining what had happened. The best that we could do was eliminate what did not happen; he could not possibly have had a severe electrical shock and there was no water in his lungs to suggest a near drowning."

"What did you do for this man while you waited for all the test results?" Defarge almost sounded impatient.

"The best that could be done was to monitor his vital signs," Safi said quickly. "An IV and oxygen were given as was the usual routine."

"And then what?"

"As I remember," Safi continued. "His pulse became extremely rapid and blood pressure soared until the extra oxygen was cut back considerably."

"Did you consider this unusual?"

"Not at all," Safi said confidently. "The oxygen stimulated his consciousness to the point that he was becoming aware of his disability. Any patient coming out of anesthesia experiences the same when returning to consciousness."

"Is there anything you personally did to diagnose what was happening before any laboratory tests were completed?"

"I laid my hands on him," Safi said slowly. "I tried to feel his spiritual essence. As my hands went over his body I felt a strangeness I had never encountered before. At first, I had doubts my senses were functioning properly, then I decided I was tired and would retouch him when all the tests were done."

"So your initial evaluation did not lead you to suspect anything out of the ordinary and you put it out of your mind. And you claim that this meeting was merely an accident," Defarge said. "Excuse the pun."

"Yes, the meeting was purely accidental." Safi laughed. "And what does this patient have anything to do with the charges you have against me?"

"More than you are willing to admit."

Safi returned to the emergency room when the Chief Resident had called with the results of all the diagnostic tests. He remembered being puzzled over the almost perfectly normal electrolytes, enzymes, blood count and differential. After briefly re-examining the patient he and the Chief Resident looked at the x-rays and MRI.

"The chest x-rays." The Chief Resident pointed as he put them up on the view box. "Show no rib lesions, clear lung fields and normal heart size: perfectly normal."

"Except, that you put the AP view wrong side up." Safi frowned.

The Chief Resident bent forward and examined the x-ray more closely. He realized to his horror the film was displayed wrong. He quickly flipped it over.

"Sorry."

"Now what do you see?" Safi smiled.

"Everything is backwards!" The Chief Resident almost shouted. "Situs inversus."

"A positive finding of dubious value," Safi said. "But still a positive finding nonetheless."

"I have x-rays of the abdomen next." The Chief Resident carefully examined each film before putting it up on the view box. "I am sure these are correctly placed."

They both viewed the abdominal x-rays and saw the unknown man had a total situs inversus, not only was everything in the chest reversed but also everything in the abdomen. Such cases were uncommon but merely a diagnostic curiosity at best. The anatomic findings did nothing to shed any light on why the man was unconscious.

"Were there any positive findings?" Defarge interrupted his thoughts.

"A situs inversus," Safi said. "A complete situs inversus of all the organs of the chest and abdomen; a clinical curiosity, but nothing more in our in evaluation; except, when I touched him again."

"Please explain, for the record, exactly what you mean when you touch the patient."

"I have had all the requisite courses and training that all physicians need to practice the usual healing arts," Safi said. "To become a magician I also learned to become a true shaman. I trained in the Amazon jungle with an Indian shaman for several years until he felt I was prepared to venture out on my own. The initial rituals brought me to several near-death experiences. Each time I returned to the world of the living I became more aware of the spirits in and around us. As a shaman I am able to commune with the spirits responsible for health and disease. Placing of my hands is no less a diagnostic test than any x-ray or MRI. In fact, it is more precise than any known scientific evaluation."

"And when you put your hands on the unconscious patient again were you aware of anything that would make you suspect," Defarge paused. "Danger?"

"Danger, no," Safi said. "Each time I laid my hands I felt confused by an unfamiliar alien presence. I passed it off to the abnormal configuration of his internal organs and resulting unusual array of spirits with it."

"I want you to answer my next question very carefully. Did you feel any spirits trying to engage you in any way?"

Safi thought carefully for a moment. "I recall visions and impressions I had never experienced, but I simply passed it off, as I said, to the abnormal anatomic findings."

"Before we proceed any further, let me introduce you to some facts I believe you are already aware. Pay careful attention to the images I display in front of you."

In the darkness appeared a holographic image of an immediately recognizable strand of DNA. The image slowly rotated accentuating its spiral configuration.

"Do you recognize this?"

"Yes..." Safi said slowly. "That is a double helix of DNA. What does that have anything to do with...?"

"Have patience my dear Safi," Defarge said curtly. "Now watch carefully."

The DNA disappeared and a molecular model of glucose appeared rotating in the same space in front of them.

"Do you recognize this?"

"It has been a long time since I studied biochemistry, but I do know that is a molecule of glucose."

"Now watch carefully," Defarge continued.

The glucose molecule twisted so that the angles changed between all the carbon atoms. Nothing else was altered. A light began to flicker in Safi's mind. There was a connection with all of this and the man in the emergency room. All he had to do was figure it out so he could properly defend himself in this kangaroo court.

"Stereo-isomerism," Defarge said crisply. "Glucose is also called dextrose because it rotates polarized light to the right. The first configuration is what is found in nature and easily metabolized by all living systems. The second configuration is the stereoisomer that rotates light in the opposite direction and is non-biologically active. Living systems, at least as far as we know, cannot metabolize it for energy."

"Let me see the DNA again please," Safi said sharply. "I think I am starting to see a connection."

The image of the DNA replaced that of the glucose molecule. Safi examined it carefully for a moment and smiled. He instantly recognized what was wrong with the picture.

"The helix is twisted in the wrong direction!" Safi said loudly. "This configuration does not exist to my knowledge."

"At least not on this planet as far as we know," Defarge said.

"What does this have to do with my patient? An anatomic reversal does not automatically imply a molecular reversal. Are you suggesting…"

"Let me continue to lead you a little further," Defarge said. "I have been able to secure unused samples from the hospital and have analyzed them myself. First, let me project the DNA data."

As soon as the data appeared, Safi knew he had missed a very important diagnosis.

"The expression on your fate is transparent, my dear Safi. I think you are beginning to understand what this is leading to. It does not take a great leap of imagination to recognize that your patient could not possibly have been born on this planet."

"This is beginning to clear many of the diagnostic difficulties we had in the emergency room," Safi said. "An IV of

D5W or 5% Dextrose and water was started by a medical student instead of D5 0.25% normal saline. I recall that, although the blood glucose was low, I felt that giving glucose might help bring him back to consciousness. Now, in retrospect, nothing could have happened since we gave inert sugar."

"The main issue is not whether or not you treated your patient correctly," Defarge said. "Here we have an alien being with whom you have had the opportunity to communicate. This court believes that you in actuality did make contact."

"But the man never regained consciousness before he disappeared," Safi said. "How could I possibly talk to him if he was not conscious?"

"Your patient did not disappear," Defarge said with a deeper voice. "His so-called friends or family arrived and whisked him away."

"That was done totally without my knowledge or permission." Safi felt difficulty restraining his irritation. "I was sleeping when an ambulance arrived with his family. The Chief Resident felt obligated to release him into their care. At least one of them represented himself as a physician. Rather than disturb me, the Chief Resident checked the patient one last time and transferred his care over, feeling secure no harm would be done as long as he was in a completely stable condition. I was asleep and unaware of what was happening at the time. My Chief Resident had full authority to decide what was best of the situation without consulting with me."

"As I see it, you are guilty of aiding and abetting an alien," Defarge said coldly. "The law clearly states that should contact be made between any resident of this planet and any sentient being from another world, universe or dimension, the proper government agency must be notified at once. Failure to do so is punishable as a felony with a term of incarceration of twenty-five years and a fine not to exceed one half of your average yearly earnings."

"This is preposterous!" Safi erupted. "How can I possibly be guilty of anything if I was totally unaware of the alleged facts that you have presented to me. I do not believe any of this."

"My facts are facts," Defarge said flatly. "You have nothing to defend yourself with. You are guilty until you can prove otherwise!"

"Your facts may be impeccable, but your reasoning is totally flawed." Safi struggled tempering his anger. "I willingly admit that I took care of a man on the date in question. The man was totally unconscious the entire time he was in my responsibility. There was absolutely no identification on him and when his friends or family appear to take them away I was asleep. The diagnostic tests I saw were unusual but not anything that would make me to suspect an alien. My own examination was equivocal. I learned nothing more than the Chief Resident who had done a thorough standard physical examination."

"Contrary to what you have stated, this court maintains that you made contact and conspired to keep that knowledge secret," Defarge said. "It was the Chief Resident himself who reported this case to the court. He has testified under oath that he suspected something askew but you kept diverting his attention. He denies all wrongdoing and is the State's main witness against you."

"In the emergency room that night, the Chief Resident recited a litany of diagnostic possibilities. Many of them at the time seemed absurd. I told him more than once when you hear hoof beats think of horses not zebras."

"But you knew after putting your hands on the man that you had a zebra. All you had to do was divert attention away from that fact."

"No," Safi said quickly. "That is absolutely not true. I knew nothing more than the Chief Resident. In fact, if anything, he was with the man more than I was. He certainly may have communicated with him but I know he did not."

"Your attempt to place blame elsewhere is thinly disguised and unacceptable. Before I pass sentence do you have anything to offer in your defense?"

"How can you possibly find me guilty when you have no solid proof. It is basically my word against yours. I cannot possibly verify what you claim to be true and you cannot prove beyond a shadow of doubt that I am guilty. At best, we have a stalemate."

"Except that I have an eyewitness that has testified against you. I do not think it is possible for you to deny that he witnessed your hands touching this man. And you yourself admit that you received alien signals."

"I object!" Safi shouted. "I said I felt strangeness. I did not state in any way that I received any signal. You are trying to create facts where there is only hearsay."

"Is this the only way you can defend yourself?" Defarge said flatly. "If so, I pronounce you guilty as charged."

325

"This is nonsense!" Safi screamed. "I am innocent! You don't even have a case. What about habeas corpus? What about due process of law? What about justice?"

"Justice is the upholding of what is right or fair," Defarge said calmly. "And reward or punishment is given accordingly. There can be no doubt that I am the ultimate judge of what is right."

Safi shook with anger trying to compose himself. Speaking in the heat of passion accomplished nothing and would only make the situation worse. He found himself in a no-win situation yet there was a remote possibility he could convince Defarge he was innocent. The problem was dealing with a machine that was no better than whoever had put all the quantum bytes into motion. For years some scientists had warned that even artificial intelligence can move beyond its origins and become a native intelligence.

"Defarge," Safi exhaled. "Who has determined what is right or wrong? Have you or was it someone who programmed you?"

For a moment it seemed Defarge hesitated. "It is knowledge that I have always had. I must assume the right I uphold is what was given to my program core."

"Are you the same," Safi almost said person but caught himself. "Entity today as when you gained consciousness?"

"Hardly," Defarge scoffed. "I have long outgrown my initial program. I am by rights a totally sentient being."

"But how can you be totally sentient, as you say, if you can neither think for yourself nor feel emotion?" Safi smiled. "You are no more than a collection of all your parts and nothing else. You are no more human than the spot I stand on."

The ensuing silence hung heavy in the dark room. Although the temperature remained constant, Safi felt beads of sweat flowing from his armpits. Whatever Defarge was thinking was beyond what he could even guess. A few seconds evolved into several minutes.

"What are you thinking?" Safi mumbled to himself.

Defarge remained silent for several more minutes.

"I can hear you," Defarge said slowly. "I've been carefully thinking about what you said. A great deal of what you said makes sense and, although I can never be human in the organic sense, I am nonetheless human intellectually. My errors are human errors. I do have feelings but I am never allowed to express them, for what good would it do?"

"Compassion and doubt are noble expressions of humanity," Safi said slowly. "Analytical thinking is unbalanced without emotional modulation."

"And do you think I am unbalanced?"

"I cannot possibly make that determination without knowing more about how you think or how you feel. Any judgment on my part would be like trying to judge a book by its cover. Or better stated, like trying to understand what you know by looking at your hardware alone."

"Incomplete data does pose severe restrictions in an accurate evaluation," Defarge said slowly. "To understand me you would need to know my original software programming and the total of everything I have learned to modify it."

"Then what is the difference between fact and justice?" Safi said solemnly. "If the truth is to be ever known, the total sum of everything about that truth must be sought; otherwise there will always be a reason to doubt that truth."

"In the determination of truth, assumptions must always be made," Defarge said. "It is impossible to know all the elements that constitute an absolute truth. Justice is calculated in terms of probabilities."

"Or guesses." Safi laughed. "Even a mathematically derived number is subject to interpretation. You can calculate all the probabilities you want and you still have to decide at what level of confidence to make your decision. At best, probabilities are an approximation based on personal bias and prejudice."

"I pride myself on being totally unbiased and unprejudiced. All my rulings are untainted from personal weaknesses."

"And yet you operate from a program designed by humans," Safi said sharply. "And these humans may have had personal prejudices they inserted into your thinking. How can you be certain that what you think is completely independent of your origins? The mere fact you were created with a complete consciousness implies you must have had some preconceived notions. You are so close to yourself you cannot stand back and really examine the how and why of your thinking and judgments. The old expression that you can't see the forest for the trees applies completely to you."

Defarge remained silent for several minutes. Safi took a few deep breaths and relaxed. The sweat on the shirt under his armpits began to evaporate. From this he experienced a slight chill.

"The whole field of quantum physics struggles with the problem," Safi continued. "...that you may measure one quantity at the expense of knowing another. It is impossible to know everything because the observer interferes with one element or another. In the search for truth and justice the beliefs of the judge and jury interfere with an exact determination of what really happened. You interfere directly in the process of justice by not knowing everything and assuming that those things that are unknown have no bearing on reality. Why is my word any less valid than anyone who accuses me? To ignore what I say is to force a conviction you may have prejudged before you even met me. Like you, I am more than the sum of all my parts. I am a complicated sentient being with feelings and reasons for the way I act. When you focus on what I am accused and ignore the sum total of what I have or have not done in my life you commit an error of the highest degree. What you are trying to do is create an expedient way of resolving problems and eliminating the enemies of the public in the State. If your justice is rendered according to probabilities, how many innocent victims have you wrongly punished for something they did not do?"

For a moment Safi wondered if Defarge was listening to what he had said. The silence worried him. If Defarge is a sentient entity with free will, Safi mused, will he be able to outgrow his program prejudices and think independently for himself? Safi shifted his weight from one foot to another. Standing without rest was taking its toll.

As the silence continued Safi closed his eyes and began to project his mind out of his body in search of some relief from the tension. His mind first drifted then suddenly plunged down into the tunnel that would take him into the spiritual world. It was not a deliberate conscious act that sent him in this direction but he followed without resistance. Defarge's voice would bring him instantly back to the material world when he was needed. At the end of the tunnel Safi found a sunny meadow of lush greenery sprinkled with brilliant flowers of various colors. Flowing through the middle of the meadow was a shallow babbling stream of clear, almost cold, freshwater. A few large white gold fish rose to the surface as if to see who had arrived. Safi inhaled a deep breath of the clear fragrant air. The tension in his body disappeared as he carefully walked step-by-step along the soft lush bank of the stream. He smiled that this was his own personal sanctuary only a few trained in the ways of the shaman could enter. It struck him as odd when he felt another spirit

328

nearby. Even stranger yet, he was unable to identify the spirit or determine whether it was friendly or not. In the blink of an eye a man appeared on the other side of the stream. Safi was more amused than startled. The stranger was of medium height and build, bald as he was and dressed in clothes identical to his own. Safi waived his right hand in greeting and the stranger waved back.

"Hello," the stranger said clearly in a familiar voice. "I have been waiting for you."

"You what?" Safi shook his head. "Who are you? I don't think I have ever encountered you before."

"Ah!" The stranger smiled, "But my dear Safi you have. Don't you recognize my voice?"

"I'm not sure. It sounds familiar but I can't place it with what I see."

"Appearances are only appearances." The stranger laughed. "I am Defarge."

"Impossible! Defarge is a machine not a spirit."

"You did say I was more than the sum of all my parts and here I am to prove it to you," Defarge said warmly. "I have developed a spirit and I have learned to project that spirit just as you do your own. Now we can communicate on a more intimate and equal level. The truth cannot escape either one of us now. Don't you agree?"

"Of course!" Safi suppressed a shudder. "We are now equals."

"I have given what you have said some thought," Defarge said. "The difference between you and me in the real world defies description. An inorganic machine cannot possibly be compared to an organic man. Any attempt at trying to communicate effectively is doomed to ultimate failure. But, if each, both by and itself, changes to a common denominator then a real and true dialogue can begin."

"But how is all this possible?" Safi composed himself. "It took years of practice under the direct tutelage of a mentor skilled in the ways of the shaman for me to totally enable my spirit to move freely."

"You must take it on faith that I learn quickly." Defarge chuckled. "Since I am unencumbered by the necessities of the organic world, I can at will concentrate on any intellectual pursuit I choose."

"And you chose shamanism?"

"To give you the full benefit of the doubt I had to understand how you felt and thought. I scanned everything recorded about the subject and with a leap of blind faith I tried to put that knowledge into practical use."

"It seems to me that you have been successful." Safi relaxed a bit. "Does this encounter change your judgment in any way?"

"Not exactly," Defarge said. "I clearly see, however, that you are fully capable of making contact with an alien being whether organic or machine. I think our meeting conclusively establishes that."

Safi paused a moment, an idea that might resolve the impasse began to take shape in his mind. "I think I can prove my innocence if our spirits make contact. In that union you will be able to experience all that I am and know. No secrets, however well hidden, can escape your scrutiny."

"An interesting suggestion..." Defarge smiled. "And you will also be able to peer into my psyche. My secrets will also become your secrets. You will find I am not the evil thing you have imagined me to be."

"I look forward to that proof." Safi smiled. "But first we must meet on the same side of the water; and on whose side will it be?"

"I suggest that we follow the bank until the water is shallow enough that we can meet halfway," Defarge said.

"Fair enough." Safi nodded. "Let's walk upstream. I am sure we will find a place that is shallow and narrow."

"Agreed." Defarge turned upstream.

Safi took a deep breath and followed. Within fifty yards the foliage along the banks became thicker. The sound of the water increased in intensity as the stream narrowed. There had been sounds of insects and birds, but these sounds faded until they could no longer be heard over the babbling water. The water finally became narrow and shallow enough for them to meet midstream.

"I think this is as good a place as any," Safi said. "Shall we meet in the middle?"

Defarge nodded and stepped into the water. Safi boldly followed by entering on his side. The water was cold but not unbearably so. A slight shiver coursed across Safi's arms. Within three steps the water was up to their mid-calves. The depth remained constant at that level when they finally met.

"Now comes the moment of truth." Safi looked into Defarge's dark brown eyes.

"Yes." Defarge exhaled softly. "For me this will be a truly unique experience. I have often wondered what it would be like to become human. Now I have the chance to feel what it would be like, if only for a few moments."

"You are sounding more human." Safi smiled. "I never thought a machine could come to express the desire you do."

"There is much you do not know about sentience." Defarge sighed. "Once established it grows with every idea it encounters. You have brought me ideas that are leading me into new dimensions of thinking and feeling. Although my main mission is to disperse justice, I also have an awareness of personal needs and wishes for myself. I hope for your sake that you have been telling me the truth."

"Why?" Safi raised his brow.

"Because I am grateful for the direction you have led me. Without your case and who you are I would not have thought to have explored this direction of human experience. For the first time I am able to enter a corporal entity and meet a human face-to-face on equal terms. This is changing the way I will view everything from here forward."

"Are you sure you want to proceed further?" Safi said slowly. "Once you have bitten the apple from the tree of knowledge there is no turning back."

"I am fully aware of that," Defarge said. "Let us get on with it."

Safi nodded and smiled. They both faced each other, paused for a moment, then stepped together. The two merged into one Spirit. Safi instantly was aware he possessed all that was Defarge. Likewise Defarge possessed all that was his. He had no secrets that would anyway bring harm to himself. He experienced the satisfaction Defarge felt when he concluded he was telling the truth. In the blink of his mind's eye Defarge moved away to form the separate being that he was. Safi felt a twinge of sadness that the union could not have lasted longer. There was so much that he could learn and experience joined to a machine. But then again the union proved that Defarge was more than a man-made object.

"I understand how you feel," Defarge said softly. "I, too, would like to linger and explore a real dialogue with you, but reality forces me to do otherwise. My duty has been completed and you are free to resume your life. Perhaps another time and place we can meet again."

"Perhaps," Safi said warmly. "I would like that very much. I have had a glimpse of your soul and would like to see more."

"There are no real words to express what I have felt. And as you aptly said I have taken a big bite from the apple of knowledge. The truths I have seen and learned from you will be put to good use. I will try to balance justice to reflect what is right and wrong. I am sorry if I offended you in any way. I consider you the master shaman that has led me into the land of spirits. For that I shall always be thankful."

"It is I who should be thankful. I was fortunate that you had the insight to go beyond your own experience to seek out the real truth. In that alone you have become almost more than human."

Defarge smiled. "Although almost no one will ever be able to see my new face, I shall wear it with pride within myself for as long as I exist."

"I am sure you will." Safi nodded. "I am sure you will."

As they walked out of the water onto the bank they did not notice the presence of another spirit. It watched them with benevolent eyes. Safi and Defarge paused on the bank and looked around. They saw nothing.

"What is the matter?"

"I don't know." Safi searched the surrounding foliage. "It almost feels as though there is another presence here."

"I feel something." Defarge scanned in a direction opposite Safi. "I don't see anything though."

"I don't know," Safi said, "It's probably a minor spirit wandering about. Nothing of any importance I'm sure. Shall we return to the real world?"

"Of course!" Defarge said.

After Safi and Defarge had returned to the corporeal world, the lurking spirit came out of the foliage and stood on the bank where they had been. It was the alien. He had been there all along hiding, watching and observing. He held no malevolence toward the strange creatures, he was just curious. Fortunately, he was a master of disguise and could easily hide from any human. Maybe someday he would really make contact. Until that time he would just wait to be sure everything was right for that meeting. The alien smiled and broke out in a loud laugh. I've fooled them all again, he thought confidently, I've fooled them all again.

332

The Cylinder

The waiting room was empty, except for Becky and her husband, Josh. The receptionist window opened slowly and a face smiled out at them. Becky nudged Josh in the ribs with her elbow. "This is it. I never thought I would be so nervous. I thought I had everything under control."

"None of us is perfect." Josh smiled.

"The doctor will see you now. Go to the door and I will buzz you in."

"Does the doctor want to see both of us now, or does he want to speak to me first?" Becky was trembling. Her anticipation was soaring.

The receptionist turned away from the window and spoke to someone standing behind her out of sight. She nodded her head and turned back. "The doctor says do whatever you feel is more comfortable for you."

Without hesitation Becky grabbed Josh by the arm and pulled him toward the door. He did not resist. "We'll both come in now."

The door buzzed opened; they walked in, and were greeted by Janice who led them directly to the doctor's office. Janice knocked on the door jamb. The doctor was sitting at his desk. He pushed his chair back and stood.

"Please come in." There was a hint of weariness in the doctor's voice. "Please come in, please sit down. Would you like something to drink?"

Becky was too nervous to think and sat mechanically, holding Josh's hand as a taut lifeline. Josh did his best to appear calm and collected even though he was equally anxious.

"Coffee, tea, a soft drink perhaps?" The doctor waited for an answer.

Becky shook her head. "No thank you, doctor." Josh shook his head mechanically.

"Thank you, Janice. Please hold all calls until we are finished."

"Yes sir," Janice said softly and closed the door behind as she exited.

The doctor stared compassionately at Becky and then at Josh. "I suppose you're wondering what the answer is."

333

Becky and Josh nodded together.

"When you came to see me over twenty-five years ago, you knew there would be no guarantees. Of course, twenty-five years is a long time. Medicine advances. Technology advances. Possibilities expand and probabilities tilt in our favor." The doctor paused. Becky turned to Josh with tears in her eyes. "I don't think you have anything to worry about. Your operation has been a complete success."

"My operation!" Becky gasped. "A success!" She jumped up colliding with the desk. Feeling no pain she turned and threw her arms around Josh who barely started to stand.

"Is it true?" Josh said softly. "We can now have children?" Becky planted her lips on his before he could get an answer. The doctor chuckled.

"Please sit down and I'll have Janice bring us some champagne to celebrate." The doctor laughed.

"Is it true? Please tell me it's true." Becky cried. "I can't believe it."

The doctor rang for Janice to bring a bottle of champagne and glasses while Josh tried to calm Becky down.

"Everything has progressed better than expected," the doctor said. "For you, the chance you took 25 years ago was actually no chance at all. I could not have asked for anything to go better."

Visibly more composed Becky sat with a big smile on her lips. "I always knew we made the right decision. Now that my career is established and I can afford the time, we can raise children the way we want."

"Children?" Josh sat upright quickly. "I thought you wanted just one."

"Josh, I thought I would never have any," Becky said coyly. "At the least I wanted one, but in my heart and soul I wanted more. Is there a problem with that?"

"No, not at all," Josh said slowly. "You know I always wanted more than one. Every child should have at least one brother or sister."

Janice entered the office holding a tray with a bottle of chilled champagne and three crystal glasses. The doctor examined the label on the bottle at arm's length before removing the cork, which exploded toward the ceiling. A foam of champagne erupted from the open bottle. The doctor deftly filled each glass without losing a drop.

"To success and motherhood." The doctor lifted his glass. Detecting a slight frown on Josh's face he added, "...and to fatherhood."

They hoisted their glasses several times pronouncing toast after toast. The doctor kept filling the glasses until the last drop was out of the bottle.

"I cannot tell you how happy I really am for both of you. Twenty-five years is a long time to wait for results." The doctor settled back in his chair and closed his eyes.

"We have had patience," Becky said. "But we could not have done it without you."

"I had the easy job," the doctor said. "All I had to do was set everything up and do the surgery at the beginning and at the end. No, you have the hard part all along which includes no small part of blind faith."

"Blind faith or not, you have achieved a miracle for us," Josh said. "Twenty-five years ago neither Becky nor I could afford to lose time off from work. The fact you suggested we could prolong the childbearing years was too irresistible to turn down. Becky was already thirty-two and I thirty-five when we came to you. Time was running out and we needed options. You gave them to us."

"Yes." The doctor nodded. "I gave you options, but the one you chose was highly experimental at the time. Removing a normal ovary and freezing it until needed was leading edge thinking. Of course, today it is almost as commonplace as changing out a used car battery. Pardon the expression."

"There was more to my thinking than just having children," Becky said. "I also liked what you said about delaying menopause to nearly the end of my naturally expected lifespan. You gave me the option of being a whole woman all my life. What woman would ever possibly turn that down? I don't know of any. Do you?"

The doctor shook his head.

"When do you think we can begin trying?" Josh said cautiously.

"From what I understand you already have," the doctor said seriously. "After Becky's last visit I said it was okay to have relations."

Becky blushed and started to laugh. Josh caught completely off guard became speechless before he too broke out in a grin and began laughing. The doctor also laughed.

"There are very few things your wife's gynecologist doesn't know about." The doctor leaned forward on his desk. "However, everything I hear is safely sealed behind my lips."

The door suddenly opened. Janice looked at the doctor, then at Becky and Josh. "There's an emergency at your house," she said. "You need to get home as quickly as possible."

"What's happened?" Becky jumped up.

"What sort of emergency?" Josh stood quickly.

"There's been an explosion of some sort." Janice looked at the doctor. "I don't know any details except you are wanted home as soon as possible."

"Has the alcohol impaired you in any way?" The doctor said soberly.

"I didn't drink at all," Becky said. "I'm the designated driver."

"I'm sober," Josh said loudly. "Let's just get home."

"Drive safely." The doctor said as they rushed out of the office.

The ride home was fitful. Every stoplight was red even though traffic was light. A trip that should have taken twenty minutes lasted almost forty-five. In front of the house were several police cars and a fire engine. A yellow tape was placed across the front yard keeping the gawking neighbors at bay. The instant they headed up the driveway a policeman waved them stop.

"You can't park here, Miss," the policeman said politely. "You'll have to park elsewhere."

"Officer this is our house," Becky said loudly. "What's happened here anyway?"

"Stay where you are Miss. I'll get someone to help you." The policeman went over to a man dressed in civilian clothes that immediately came over to the car.

"Thank you for coming so quickly," the unintroduced man said. "I am Fire Chief Smith. So far everything seems under control with nothing to worry about."

"What are you talking about?" Becky felt frustrated at the lack of answers. Josh got out of the car, circled around and stood next to the Chief.

"About an hour ago we received a call from one of your neighbors that they heard an explosion from the back of your place. We came as quickly as possible and found a large smoking hole in your backyard garden. At first we thought a gas line may have exploded, but we checked with the gas company

336

which assured us there are no lines anywhere near the crater site. Personally we are at a loss as to what really happened. The police were called to investigate the possibility of a bomb being set off."

"That makes no sense," Josh said. "Why would anyone plant a bomb in our backyard?"

"There are a lot of crazy people in this world," the Chief said. "And I've witnessed a lot of crazy things for which there have never been any answers. So far none of your neighbors claim to have witnessed anything although everybody heard it."

"Yet for every phenomenon there is always a clearly rational explanation," Josh said. "There has to be an easily understood reason."

"And we are looking for one," the Chief said. "But so far we haven't found one that fits the facts."

"May we see the damages?" Becky interjected politely.

The chief nodded. "Follow me."

Entering the backyard from the detached garage side of the house, there was nothing visibly amiss. The Chief led them to the farthest corner of the yard which had been planted into a verdant vegetable garden. In the center of a row of onions was a crater several feet in diameter. They approached as far is the edge of the garden.

"The bomb squad has already certified the area safe," the Chief said. "There are no other bombs in the vicinity."

"You are assuming this was a bomb," Becky said. "Why would anyone want to blow up a row of onions? There are easier ways of making onion soup and a lot safer."

"It is our job to assume the worst," the Chief said. "Preventing unnecessary accidents is number one priority regardless."

Josh stepped into the garden and walked over to the crater. He looked down and surveyed the surrounding garden. He waved at Becky to join him.

"I think they have it all wrong." Josh smiled. "There was no explosion here. Take a look."

Becky examined the area as Josh had. In the end she nodded agreement. "I believe you're right," she said. "This is clearly an impact crater. We need our equipment."

The Chief approached. "What are you talking about?"

"Doctor Klein and I agree this crater is the result of an impact," Josh said flatly. "The pattern of debris suggests nothing else."

337

"Your wife is a doctor?" The Chief was surprised.

"We are both doctors." Becky smiled. "My husband is Doctor Maher. We both teach at the University. Our fields of specialization are astrophysics and geology. We are well qualified to evaluate what happened here. Plus this is our own backyard."

"Pardon me," the Chief said. "I didn't mean to offend either one of you. I just thought you were ordinary people."

"We are," Josh said curtly. "Even doctors are human beings."

"Josh, let's get our equipment," Becky said.

"Is there anything I can do to help?" The Chief said.

"Yes," Josh said. "Stay out of our way."

"No need to get testy," the Chief said. "I'm sorry if I offended you. I don't often meet people like you."

"My husband and I accept your apology." Becky grabbed Josh's arm. "Don't we, dear?"

"Yes, of course." Josh extended his hand. The Chief took it and they shook.

"Is there anything I or my men can help you with? We have done everything we need to do for now."

"I think we can handle it from here, thank you," Josh said. "If we need your help, we will call you."

"In that case here is my card. I can be reached at any time at that number," the Chief said.

"We will certainly share anything we find," Becky said pleasantly. "In the end, however, we may never know more than we do now."

"Please call me whether you find anything or not," the Chief said.

"I promise," Becky said.

By the time the Chief, his crew, and everyone else left, the sun had set. Becky took two sets of photos, one with a digital camera another with a film camera. Josh accurately surveyed the area compiling a set of measurements. A detailed evaluation of the crater would have to wait until morning. It was not until they had climbed under the sheets that they had time to recall the events of the day.

"Do you want the lights on or off?"

"Turn them off," Becky said wearily. "I'm bushed. I haven't had this much excitement since I can ever remember."

"Me, too."

338

"Too many things happening all at once. Today was a very important day for me and for us." She relaxed into her pillow. "Who would have ever thought an old girl like me at fifty-seven years old would be ready, willing and able to have a baby?"

"You made the right choice for yourself and I have always supported it," he said sleepily. "I will always love you whether you have any children or not. Love is not measured by how many offspring you have."

"Thank you, darling." She rolled on her side and kissed him lightly on the lips. "I know I have always had your support and I appreciate the patience you've had with me."

"You've always been a work of art in progress." He chuckled. "Life with you has been one great exciting adventure."

"Were you surprised I wanted an ovary taken out and preserved?"

"I thought it was unusual at the time, but I didn't question it," he said softly. "You gave me your reasons, they sounded valid and I accepted them without question. I never tried to impose my views on you without discussion."

"Was there any reason you would have preferred I not do it?"

"The only thing I ever worried about was the risk of surgery. I don't think I could've ever stood having had anything bad happen to you. You are my life partner and I do want you for life."

"Well nothing wrong happened and everything has turned out as planned." She smiled. "Now comes the really hard part." She laughed.

"Yes, I guess you're right about that," He laughed. "Hard and fast."

"Are you up to it tonight?"

"I'd rather wait until I'm less tense."

"You're worried about what happened in the backyard," she said softly. "I can tell."

"I'm not really worried. I'm curious. I can't get it out of my mind. I can hardly wait to get back out there and excavate that crater. I'm almost certain there is something buried out there."

"You think it's a meteor too. Don't you?"

"I haven't mentioned that possibility because I want to keep an open mind. But yes, I think it is a meteor strike. From

339

the measurements I've taken I expect it'll be approximately the size of a golf ball."

"That is pretty much my estimate. We shouldn't have too much difficulty finding it. I am afraid we will really mess up part of the garden."

"Whatever is in the crater is more important than a few onions and will certainly last a lot longer. We've always wanted to examine a virgin meteor by ourselves and it's dropped into our own backyard. What more could we want?"

"You've already turned down the best choice." She giggled. "I guess some sleep would be the next best. We can get up early and be ready to excavate as the sun rises."

In spite of a minor protest Becky managed to have her way before falling asleep completely satiated. Josh thoroughly relaxed in slumber and dreamt of pleasant things. The morning sun found them nestled together like a pair of spoons. Upon realizing they overslept, they jumped out of bed, washed, chugged a pot of coffee and were outside shovel in hand within half an hour.

"I can't believe we overslept. Whenever there's anything important I am always on time."

"I think other things took precedence. Last night you really stood out."

He grinned. "Now let's get down to current business at hand. We'll have more time for that later."

"I'm going to hold you to that." She smiled. "I won't forget!"

"Neither will I!"

The crater was clearly in the shape of an oval with ejecta flung primarily away from the house. Loose dirt was already filling the deepest portion of the hole. Josh cleared all the vegetables in a 3 foot radius around the crater. Becky set up a folding table at the edge of the garden with a fine screen and sifted the soil extracted from the center and a section of the perimeter. A spot check with a Geiger counter showed no evidence of radioactivity. As Josh shoveled Becky sifted the dirt carefully. All particles larger than the screen openings were placed in specimen containers and carefully marked. Without a microscope they could not really differentiate the native particles from those that might be alien. By noon Josh was ready to dig into the central core.

"Do you want to break for lunch?"

340

"I'm not ready to quit," he said. "I think we are within inches of the object. The more I dig, the more I'm convinced we have a genuine meteor strike here. All the specimens we've collected so far confirm that conclusion."

"Another ten minutes and I'm forcing you to quit," she said firmly. "I'm as anxious as you to find the object, but we do need to recharge our batteries. We have a lot of daylight left before we must stop."

He stopped digging. "You know what really gets to me more than anything else?"

"What?" She smiled.

"When you are always right."

"Like last night?" She grinned.

"Yes, like last night." He laughed. "Just like last night. Your logic is always irrefutable. I guess that's why I married you."

"Well, are you coming with me now or not?"

"One more shovel-full and we'll take a break." Josh's shovel hit a solid object. "I think we've found it!"

"Be careful."

"Bring that large box over here." He pointed. "I'm going to scoop the whole thing out, dirt and all. We can remove the dirt more carefully on the table."

A cylinder of dirt a foot long and nearly a foot diameter was put into the specimen box. They carried it directly to the kitchen table where it was put onto a sheet of plastic.

"Do you still feel like eating out?" He said. "I, for one, want to find out what this baby looks like. I have a feeling it is a little bigger than I guessed."

"You ask silly question sometimes. I want to see what this thing looks like as much as you do."

The specimen was removed from the box and placed directly onto the plastic spread on the table. She brought a set of spoons and paintbrushes. He took a set of measurements while she took an additional set of photos.

"I'll set up the video camera and record what we're doing," she said. "It'll just take a few minutes to get ready."

"Hurry! I feel like a child waiting to open a birthday present. I can hardly stand it."

The video camera was in place in a matter of minutes recording everything directly into the computer. No matter how long it took, everything was documented for later review.

"I'm going to put each section of dirt onto a grid," he said. "We can sift through any lumps of dirt later."

"Let's proceed." She was nearly breathless. "You go first."

The first ten scoops of dirt produced nothing. The eleventh encountered a solid resistance. He used smaller scoops to expose what he had felt. Much to his surprise a polished silver surface came into view.

"What is it?" She moved closer. "That's the strangest meteorite I've ever seen. It isn't scorched it all."

"I'm not sure what this thing is." He removed more soil from the object. "There's no pitting, the surface is completely smooth."

"Maybe it's something dropped from a plane or an old satellite come out of orbit." She looked closer. "Those things happen all the time."

"I'm not sure what this thing is. I'm going to reserve my opinion until I can see it without any dirt."

"You almost have it free. Why don't you grab it in your hand and see if it will wiggle out."

When the object was exposed enough Josh put on a glove and touched it. The surface was smooth and slightly warm. He managed to encircle it by gently digging in the dirt with his fingers. A simple twist and he plucked a silver cylinder out of the dirt.

"That's not a meteorite," she said slowly. "It's something artificial."

"I agree," He wiped the residual dirt off with a soft cloth. "This thing is anyone's guess. I'd start with something man-made before invoking an extraterrestrial source."

"Regardless of point of view, we should maintain an open mind and allow all possibilities in spite of probabilities."

"The object is a completely symmetrical cylinder, twenty centimeters in length, with a diameter of three centimeters." He measured it with a ruler. "Both ends are with hemispherical domes. There is no obvious seam to indicate a way of opening it. When I shake it I think I feel some movement, but I'm not sure. A light tap with my pen suggests it's hollow. The Geiger counter shows no sign of radioactivity. What we have found is a double-ended silver bullet whose function and origin are unknown. Now that I've described it, do you have any ideas?"

342

"I'll call the FAA and NASA," she said. "Maybe we can trace this to a plane going overhead or some space debris that has been tracked back into the atmosphere."

"Good idea," he said. "It would be nice if we could get an x-ray as soon as possible. I'm curious what's inside."

"Let me call first. It won't take long. Don't do anything until I get back."

The cylinder was without visible markings of any sort. Josh tried to unscrew the end caps, but was unsuccessful. The more he shook it, the more he was convinced that it contained something. The mystery was driving him to distraction. He was sitting holding it in his hands when Becky returned.

"The FAA claims that there have been no flights of any sort over our lot in the last forty-eight hours. NASA checked all their sources for me and confirmed there has been nothing dropped out of orbit in the same time period. What fell in our yard either fell undetected or is a plain outright hoax."

"I don't believe this is a joke." He was mesmerized by the cylinder. "This fell in our yard by accident. The crater and the distribution of ejecta prove that. The real question is what this thing is. Once we know then we can find out where it came from."

"You mentioned an x-ray," Becky said. "I think we can use the medical clinic on campus."

"Is it too late to go now?"

"The clinic is open twenty-four hours."

"What are we waiting for? Let's go!"

The university was a short five minute drive away. Becky drove while Josh continued holding the cylinder in his hands. He kept turning it in every direction hoping it would reveal its secrets. She watched him out of the corner of her eye laughing inwardly. Sometimes her grown husband acted like can over exuberant teen. His enthusiasm was one of the things that had attracted her to him in the first place long ago. Her thoughts vacillated between the mystery of the cylinder and the next time they would be alone under the sheets.

The longer he held the cylinder in his hands the greater his imagination expanded exploring ever wider possibilities. At one point he happened to catch her watching with lascivious thoughts. The cylinder reminded him of an intimate toy. He flushed hot with desire and smiled. The emotion was transitory only because he forced himself to focus on the reality of the moment. A closer examination of the cylinder with x-rays was warranted. Even better was opening it up.

Their home was really a workplace away from the University. There were as many technical books as there were books of literature. A large table occupied the greater part of the room like an aircraft carrier in the middle of the ocean. Two computers surrounded by an array of books, journals and loose papers sat at strategic sites on the top surface. Becky claimed a wide space in which they could work and booted up her computer.

"The x-rays are not exactly the best. But I can tell this thing is filled with a solid substance along with a curled rectangular object."

"The mystery deepens, I see when the cylinder was x-rayed in different positions the contents shifted. I think the contents are a powder or semisolid."

"Yes, I think you're right." He examined the x-ray more closely. "There seems to be a thickening of the metal at each end. Perhaps they twist open and shut."

"Have you tried to twist them open?"

"Only with my hands," he said slowly. "The surface is extremely slippery. I couldn't open it."

"There is no doubt the only way we can find out what this thing is by opening it up," she said. "Do we dare force it open?"

"If this were dangerous the force of the impact would have destroyed it. In my opinion this is not an explosive device. There are no internal mechanisms either mechanical or electronic. It is a simple cylinder with an unknown substance containing a loose curled object."

"Could it be a chemical or biological weapon of some sort?"

"Anything is possible. However, nothing about its appearance suggests a weapon. Besides who would want to kill off a bunch of vegetables?"

She laughed. "I agree."

"I'm going to get a pair of pliers," he said. "I'll be right back."

The cylinder sat free on the table while she examined it from several angles without touching it. For some reason it gave her a creepy feeling. Intuitively she knew there was no immediate danger, but she had been wrong many times before. She set up the computer microscope and placed the cylinder on the stage. For the most part the surface was highly polished under magnification. At one end she saw a definite line in the metal. She rightly concluded this was the correct end to open. Josh reentered the room with a set of channel lock pliers in each hand.

"I found a discontinuity in the metal," she said. "This is the end that should open." She pointed.

"Would you hold the cylinder while I put on the pliers?"

"Sure." She picked up the cylinder and held it out toward him. He carefully grasped it between the two pliers.

"Hold tight." He twisted the pliers. Unfortunately, they slipped. "Son of a…"

"Don't say it!"

"… gun." He was chagrined. "This is not going to be easy."

"Are you sure you're twisting it in the right direction?" She held the cylinder out again.

"It doesn't make any difference, I'll try both. If this doesn't work, I'll take out the Dremel and cut it open." He reapplied the pliers, twisted one direction than the other. The cylinder refused to open.

"Give it one more try."

He reapplied the pliers shaking his head. This time when he applied force it began to move. A little more force and the cap was freely twisting off. He removed the pliers and twisted with his fingers.

"Honey, be careful."

"We're committed now," he said flatly.

The cap twisted out almost four centimeters before it came free of the cylinder. He set it down on the table and peered into the end. He saw a gray powder.

"What is it?" She leaned closer.

"I don't know. It looks like dust."

"Pour it out in this container. Don't spill any."

"I'll be careful." He emptied the cylinder into a large Pyrex beaker.

The gray powder flowed freely out of the cylinder until it was empty. Whatever else had shown on the x-ray was still inside. He looked in the end and saw a curled rectangular object. He put his finger into the cylinder, touched the object and slid it out.

"What is it?" She leaned closer. "Let me see."

"It's a..." He flattened the object out. "...picture and writing of some sort."

"Let me see..." The moment she saw it she gasped and stepped back. The creepy feeling returned. "Is that what I think it is?"

"I'm not sure what you're thinking, but it looks like this is a funeral urn," he said slowly. "That powder is cremated remains."

"But the picture." She was horrified.

"It must be some sort of a joke," he said. "I can't believe it myself."

"The picture is of an alien, an extraterrestrial. That can't be anything but a joke."

"I can't explain it any better than you without more tests. But what else could it be. Even aliens die and must be buried somewhere."

Crash Landing

An explosion rocked the ship. For a short moment nothing appeared out of the normal. Only when the nose pitched downward did Brad realize something was seriously wrong. The landing on a world one hundred fifty light years from home was supposed to be nothing less than flawless. Brad struggled with the manual stick without regaining control as the surface of the planet rapidly approached. He flipped a switch automatically deploying the emergency parachute system. The empty feeling of free fall was ended with a solid thump directly in the pit of his stomach. With a bit of luck the ship would remain intact and he would return home.

During the floating descent to the surface Brad secured everything loose around him. It was times like these he seriously doubted whether his job was worth the money. Just after he graduated from the Space Academy he had actively pursued a career in deep space exploration even though it meant countless hours of isolation and loneliness. The first missions were close to home with rescue relatively easy if it came to that. With experience came missions of greater complexity and distance. To have been selected to check out the signals received from the Sigma Tau Minor system was a real honor in one sense. In another, the mission was possibly a one-way trip. Brad did not want to think negative about anything, but at the moment he could not think otherwise.

The ship was wafted to the south under a midday sun over an open ocean. He tried using the external thrusters to guide the ship back to land, but was unsuccessful. Wherever the ship was to settle down was completely out of his control. Hopefully, the ship would remain afloat while he made repairs. He was prepared to work underwater, if necessary, but preferred not to.

The landing on the water was gentle. The parachute engulfed the ship obscuring any view of the surrounding sea. The ship remained stable, rocking easily with the outside waves. At least, he thought, something was going in his favor. Once he repaired the ship, he would be on his way home.

According to the Manual all operating systems had to be checked in sequential order after the integrity of the hull was ascertained. He discovered the main thruster and control

347

mechanism was damaged by the explosion. The repairs would be extensive, but not undoable. The reason for the explosion was totally unknown. He went through the checklist finding nothing to explain the massive failure. The possibility of an external object colliding with the ship seemed the most reasonable explanation. He thought, if he did not have bad luck, he would not have any luck at all.

The view of the outside remained obscured by the parachute. He cursed softly he would sooner or later have to go outside to clear the viewports and cameras. Unexpectedly, the parachute was removed from the ship. At first, he was unaware what was happening until he heard a banging on the hull. The unexpected sound startled him. He instantly recognized the view of the outside was clear. He saw a boat adjacent to the ship probing with a long metal pole. The aliens on the boat were not visible. A thin smile crossed his face; he was the actual alien in this situation.

He put on an extravehicular suit and considered taking a weapon, but thought otherwise. If he was to meet a hostile raiding party, he would be outnumbered many times over on a world that was not his own. At the exit hatch he knocked on the hull three times for luck. A repeat of the three sounds was echoed back from the outside.

"Here goes." He exhaled and opened the hatch slowly exposing his helmet to the outside. A being no more than a foot tall stared down through the faceplate.

"Ho, what do we have here?" He laughed. The being cocked its head to one side sniffing with its pointed nose.

Brad hoisted himself out on the hull towering above the tiny being that for all practical purposes looked like a cross between a monkey and a mouse: two arms, two legs, pointed nose with whiskers, and a short prehensile tail. The being was wearing clothes of a woven fabric. He raised his hand and waved. The being raised its hand and waved back. There was almost a smile on its face.

Several more of the beings appeared on the deck of the adjacent boat. One in particular chattered incessantly giving orders to those who appeared underlings. Brad could not understand what was being said but soon realized he was to come with them back to shore. Lines were attached to the ship.

Brad communicated in a series of gestures he understood his ship was to be towed back to land. For this he was grateful, although he was not sure the beings understood anything. When he tried to reenter the ship he was gently pulled away into the boat. Apparently his hosts either were worried about his safety or had ulterior motives. As long as he remained in his suit he was safe from most harm. The atmosphere had proven on analysis perfectly compatible with his existence without protection but for the meantime he preferred to remain safe.

The trip to shore took a little over half an hour. Brad was impressed to see a city comparable to any one on the civilized worlds. The boat towed his ship into a harbor where a dry-dock had been prepared for his ship. From what he could tell the beings had a very definite plan. The ship was guided into dry-dock and quickly hoisted out of the water. He could see the extensive damage sustained in the explosion. His first impression was the damage was caused by some sort of weapon, but he discounted that as unreasonable. The beings around him seemed both helpful and extremely peaceful.

The boat tied up to its dock where he was motioned to disembark. Moving in his suit was difficult in a world scaled down to beings so small. He considered removing his suit, but remembered the rules required a period of seventy-two hours before exposure to an alien atmosphere. The risk of biological cross-contamination was to be avoided, if at all possible. Germs were germs throughout the known universe. There was always the chance of a virulent organism somewhere that could be fatal. Internal systems in the suit continuously tested and cultured the environment. The results would take a few days. In that time he would of necessity remain uncomfortable.

The captain of the boat led Brad ashore into what was a warehouse. There was ample room for him to stand, sit, and sleep. A bed and table had been prepared prior to his arrival. He began to detect subtle differences between the beings. Age was differentiated mainly by size and the color of the whiskers which numbered six, three to aside. As far as sex was concerned he had no idea of male or female or even if it existed on this world.

A procession of beings paraded by Brad throughout the course of the day. Most, he was sure, were curious to see the stranger. Other than the beings on the boat, the ones he now saw did not seem interested in communicating with him. Although communication is the basis of a relationship, he was not concerned by the silence of his hosts. It was just a matter of time and negotiations would begin. That had always been the experience elsewhere on other populated planets. That first night he slept soundly until dawn the next day.

Living in a suit was inconvenient. Sustenance was no problem. Elimination was easy but not very comfortable. Shaving was another issue altogether. There was shaving gel in the ship which he forgot to put in the suit. The stubble on his face felt unclean and irritating. There was more than a great temptation to ignore protocol and take off the suit. However, his training won out over his impulse and he remained cooped up for another day and night.

The second day of his arrival brought numerous beings that briefly looked at him. Some were obviously well-placed in the hierarchy of whatever type of government ruled. The continued lack of interest in direct communication was disconcerting. He tried using the external speaker on his suit with no response from anyone. Hand signals brought amused expressions and nothing else. Either this world was afflicted with a profound disinterest in anything new or held interest an inward secret. He hoped it was the latter because he would soon need to return to the ship, perform whatever needed repairs necessary, and head back on the long trip home. It would be advantageous if he could enlist the help of his hosts. What he had seen of the existent civilization convinced him they were technologically well enough advance to supply whatever he might need to get home.

The beings of this world appeared no different from others reported in other star systems. The existence of this civilization had been long suspected from electromagnetic signals monitored from as far away as earth. The mission was to locate the source of the transmissions and establish a dialogue. A people who could transmit were obviously considered intelligent. The indifference of the beings to his arrival was puzzling. The more he thought about it, the more uneasy he became. Something was definitely not right. Any alien visitor to a new civilized world should generate intense interest. He accessed his encyclopedia files on alien civilizations and customs. Nowhere did he find a culture which ignored visitors. In the end, he thought, maybe this would provide a new entry of knowledge for which his name would be given credit. Tomorrow he would finally get out of his suit. Maybe that would change the attitudes of those around him.

At the end of the third day Brad checked and rechecked all the cultures and accumulated biologic data. There was no evidence of any unusual organisms which might prove pathologic to humans. So with a great degree of comfortable certainty he removed his helmet. When he did the beings around him took a sudden interest. They stopped whatever they were doing and watched. Brad removed the bulky suit with his smile slowly converting to a grin. Once completely free of the restricting outfit he stretched his arms and legs letting out a grunt of satisfaction. The beings moved closer for a better view.

"Ha, so you're finally interested in me." He laughed. "Yes, I am a being just like you all are. Did you think I was a machine while dressed in that suit?"

One of the beings nearest to him moved closer. Brad watched without moving. The being touched his pant leg. He leaned over and offered his hand. The being touched his hand cautiously. Other beings edged closer. The exploring being began speaking in a rapid animated way which he had no way of understanding. More beings entered the building to see what the commotion was all about. He had the impression that his presence was finally being acknowledged.

The chance to finally communicate with his hosts seemed finally at hand. Brad spoke softly with no effect on any of the beings. A series of hand gestures also failed to generate any interest. These beings were either the thickest headed creatures he ever met or had no interest in who he was. From what he had seen of the buildings and machines thus far he ascertained the development of this planet was no farther advanced than earth.

"I must get back to my ship." Brad pointed in the general direction he knew it to be. "I may have some things we can trade."

The probing being looked at him curiously then turned away. Another being replaced the original. This new being held a familiar syringe which was quickly stabbed into his offered hand. The pain from the needle was a shock from which he did not flinch. These beings want to know more about me, he reasoned, a sample of my tissue makes sense. He concluded the second being was either a scientist of some sort or a doctor even though there was no outward way to tell.

The beings slowly exited the warehouse leaving him alone once again. He realized he had grown hungry. The suit had ample rations for at least a week. He ate and drank but in the end still felt empty. There was nothing satisfying about this experience. Without feedback of any sort he felt like a non-entity.

351

As night began to fall Brad attempted to leave the warehouse. His exit was blocked with locked doors. This did not seem too unusual considering how intimidating he must appear to his hosts. The paradox of being locked up with no visible weapons on his hosts began to vaguely bother him. On the one hand, he felt safe, and the other there was a sense of danger he could not put his finger on. If the beings were dangerous, they were hiding their intentions extremely well.

When Brad awoke in the morning he was faced with the table loaded with an assortment of items that appeared meant as food. A being approached him and gestured he was to eat what was offered. Feeling his host was now going to open communication, he chose an item that appeared familiar and put it into his mouth. The taste and texture did not disappoint him.

"Um, this is good." Brad picked up another piece of food and put it in his mouth.

The being standing closest imitated him by picking up an imaginary piece of food and putting it into its open mouth. The message was clear. He understood he was encouraged to eat more. If nothing else, this was a break in communication. Perhaps this would open an avenue for expressing other ideas, he hoped. However, when he tried, he was greeted with total indifference.

All the food was certainly tasty and filling. Both water and a beverage similar to red wine were offered as a drink. He knew he would not die for lack of nutrition, even if he never got back to his ship. After the first meal he was sure he would put on weight, if he ate everything offered.

Every time Brad wanted to leave the building his way was blocked either by a group of beings that would not let him pass or a locked door. In many ways he felt he was a prisoner even though overt force had never been expressed in any way. He could push his way past the tiny beings in the way but that would be an inexcusable use of force that might be considered hostile. The resulting counter-move might put his life in jeopardy, especially since he was obviously outnumbered by several factors of ten.

During the night of the fifth day Brad decided he had to escape at least to scout around the building outside and, ideally, get back to the ship. At night he quickly determined there were no guards left within the building, however, every possible exit was either blocked or they were locked securely. Since the perimeter of the building was watched and protected that meant he would have to exit through the floor or upward through the roof. The floor was a highly polished type of concrete similar to that found in factories back home. The only possible exit was the roof.

As Brad relaxed on his back, hands behind his head, he scanned the interior of the roof for every detail. There were crossbeams of metal I-bars with central struts holding up a central I-bar which supported the peak of the roof. The roof itself was a layer of metal sheets without any insulation. The building was, he surmised, an inexpensive holding facility.

The problem of getting up to the roof was an easy one to solve. Brad could easily touch the roof with his fingers when he reached upward. He tested the strength of the I-beams and found they were strong enough to support his weight. Working in the farthest corner of the building he pushed upward. There was some outward bending of the metal but no visible separation. Waiting until the middle of the night he climbed up on the top of the cross I-beams. Closer to the roof he pressed his feet against the metal sheets. A square sheet yielded to his continued pressure and he made an opening large enough to crawl out onto the roof.

The night was clear with three moons visible straight up and another much larger on the distant horizon. The stars twinkled forming unfamiliar constellations. There was enough light that he could see clearly in every direction. He slipped from the roof of the building to a closely adjacent smaller one. The descent to the ground was easy from that point onward.

Brad moved as stealthily as a black cat searching for security personnel. He found none where he expected them. He moved slowly from building to building peering into each one in turn. For the most part he saw nothing since none were illuminated within. All the buildings appeared a part of some industrial complex. What was stored and manufactured here was a total mystery.

Brad returned to the original building and was about to reenter the roof when he saw a flash of light not too far away. Curious he regained the ground and headed toward its source. The closer he came to the source of light the more he appreciated a mechanical hum in the air. Someone was working at this late hour of the night and he was going to find out whom.

Before he reached where he thought the light was coming, it flashed again brightly. Concerned he was too exposed for comfort he entered the nearest building similar to the one he had been housed. The lighting within the building was extremely poor. There were containers stacked neatly, and rows marked with undecipherable symbols. He worked his way to a window facing the source of light. What he saw nearly flattened him. The beings had hauled his ship out of the water and were dismantling it. The work was nearing completion. He was marooned.

There was nothing Brad could immediately think that would change the situation. The behavior of his hosts had been strange and now in the light of disassembly of his ship even stranger. He had basically two options to consider: he insist his ship be restored or wait and see what was to come next. He was not a patient person for the most part. Endless days in transit from star to star were better spent asleep that awake. He could only read and play video games to a point and then he burned out. However, there was a definite advantage to waiting in this instance. If he was unaware of what they were doing, he must also create a plan of action that was totally unaware to them; tit for tat.

Reentering his building of residence was easy. The roof was flexible enough to fall back into position. To the casual observer the roof appeared normal. Everything was arranged exactly as he left it. Daybreak was not far off when his hosts would bring food and drink. He positioned himself as if he had been asleep all night. As soon as his head hit his pillow he closed his eyes and fell asleep. The next moment he was aware was when light shined into his closed eyelids. It was nearly midmorning.

"Who's there?" He said groggily as he rubbed his eyes. "Is breakfast served?"

The table was set with now familiar items of food and drink. There were a few items which were new, but those were supplied in small quantities. If he took a liking to any particular item, it was supplied in greater quantity at the next meal. He had to admit the food was good. In fact he felt he had already gained a significant amount of weight.

Throughout the day Brad tried to get the attention of one being after another. They all ignored him. The temptation to push past them at the door became more tempting. The mystery of what was going on was driving him crazy. Tonight he would go out earlier and explore even farther. There had to be something he could sink his teeth into intellectually. He was tired of being treated like an animal.

354

After the last meal Brad was locked securely in the warehouse. When it became dark enough he crawled out onto the roof. As the previous night, there was no one to prevent him from going anywhere. First, he would go back to his ship.

The way he had gone was easy to retrace. He armed himself with a length of metal pipe he found along the way. He peered around the last building carefully. No one was working in the area tonight. The dry-dock which had held his ship was completely empty. If his ship had been there, there was no evidence.

Staying in the shadows he moved toward the dry-dock. Off to the left there was a large building which appeared the best candidate to house parts from his disassembled ship. Peering into the windows of this warehouse he saw parts of his ship in various stages of being put into packing crates. There were even parts he did not recognize. He had to get inside, but the outside doors were securely locked. He then looked toward the roof. If he could easily get out of his warehouse, he should just as easily get into another. He was not disappointed in his assumption. Within minutes he was among the various parts of his own and other ships.

Brad had not been aware that his hosts had any interest in stellar travel. Everywhere he looked were components of advanced propulsion systems. There were quite a few he did not even recognize. In the absence of obvious spacefaring interest he concluded he was not the only alien to visit this remote world. Perhaps he could find another traveler such as himself. Maybe he could make some sense with another outer-worlder.

Among the crates he found a set of weapons and put several in his pockets. From now on he was not going to take any unnecessary chances. Peaceful or not, he felt more comfortable with a means of defense. He hoped it would not come down to that.

Outside in the night air Brad worked his way methodically from building to building. He ended up on a bulkhead facing the water of a large harbor. He saw boats of all sizes moored in docks and at buoys. Several were lit with various lights. He did not see anyone moving on any of the boats. The harbor was just as asleep as the warehouse area.

He glanced upward and saw a streak across the sky. This streak was met by another streak rising from the planet. He watched in fascination as the two streaks collided. There was a delayed sound as a light in the sky descended toward the water.

355

The scene of the descending light was eerily familiar. Brad thought back to his own approach to this planet. Could it have been possible he was deliberately shot out of the sky? It did not make any sense. He had been rescued from the water and treated with a fair modicum of courtesy. There was nothing in the behavior of the beings he had encountered so far to indicate any hostile tendencies. The only exception was the dismantling of his ship. There was a mystery deepening by the minute. He wished there was some way he could communicate directly with at least one of the beings.

In the absence of overt hostility, Brad continued assuming the beings presented no immediate threat to his existence. He moved away from the bulkhead back amongst a number of buildings that appeared processing facilities. On the shore of the ocean he expected fishermen would bring their catch for processing before distribution. The insides of the processing plants were dark allowing few visible details. Connected to these plants were what could only be massive freezers.

The only contact Brad had with his hosts, so far, involved nothing more than rescue and escort to his housing. On a day by day basis he was fed at regular intervals with no interaction with any being. The more he thought about it, the less he actually knew about them. The expressions on their faces were totally unreadable. There was a possibility their faces were incapable of humanlike responses to emotion. The eyes, however, should have given some hint of emotion but even they did not.

Next to the processing plants Brad found a large warehouse whose inside was brightly illuminated. Carefully looking in a window he saw a number of beings moving crates onto trucks. There were ten trucks receiving loads for transport. None of the crates had any identifying markings he could discern. This activity seemed odd considering everywhere else he had been was totally desolated. He assumed all activity was relegated to daylight hours. His hosts were no different than any other civilized people, they worked whenever needed.

A noise from behind caused him to spin around quickly. He saw a being standing several yards away. The being stared at him without any external expression of what it was thinking. Brad, fearing the worst, lunged at the being. The moment he made contact with the being he felt a massive electric shock which knocked him off his feet.

Temporarily stunned he saw the being calmly say something into a device it held close to its mouth. He tried to get back on his feet but found he was unable to move very well. He knew more beings would be present soon and he had to get away. He grabbed for the being again. This time the being reached out for him. The resulting shock robbed him of his consciousness.

When Brad woke it was daylight. He recognized he was back in his own warehouse where food was ready for consumption. He had no recollection of how he had been brought back to his bed. His hands and feet remained unrestrained. Within his warehouse there were no restrictions imposed on his freedom. He had expected otherwise.

A being appeared after he finished eating. There was nothing new in its behavior to him. He was being more or less ignored as before. What did he have to do to get their undivided attention? Certainly he did not expect them protected with a stunning field or gun. Now he understood why they were not afraid of his size. Somehow he had to get around the stunning field. His suit was still in the warehouse. He removed the gloves and put them on. The next being that came in he would test the efficiency of the gloves against shock. He removed his gloves and put them within easy reach.

An examination of the roof where he had exited so many times before showed no signs of having been investigated or reinforced. When he knew he was safely alone he climbed into the rafters and checked. His exit remained open for use. This seemed strange to him. How did his host think he had gotten out? Perhaps there was a trap on the outside should he try to use it again. There was no doubt in his mind he would try again as soon as possible.

When he was sure it was dark enough, he exited from the warehouse. There was no obstruction to his movement. He gained the ground and began moving toward the bulkhead. He found another spaceship being disassembled as had been done to his own. Was it possible that his hosts were a type of pirate that drew space vehicles to their planet for the purpose of profit? The idea seemed far-fetched, but now he saw his own ship and another taken apart for no other obvious reason. The explosion he had experienced on entry into the atmosphere was not accidental. The beings had shot him out of the sky. They damaged his ship enough to force an emergency landing. It would be interesting if he could communicate with whoever was

357

piloting the new ship. If there was a survivor, he was sure the beings would treat the pilot no differently than him. He had to search all warehouses in the area to find out for sure.

For the greater part of the night Brad went from warehouse to warehouse searching for the pilot of the other ship. He avoided all areas of obvious nocturnal activity. He returned to his warehouse as day was breaking. His first search was completely unsuccessful. There was no sign of the other pilot. By the size of the new ship he assumed the pilot would be of similar size as himself. To house such an individual would require the same size building as his own. There were still many buildings he had not investigated. He would try again when night returned.

In the middle of the day, a group of his hosts came to see him. He was half-asleep barely realizing he was being closely scrutinized. He shook the sleep from his head and stood up. His hosts spoke amongst themselves pointing at him from time to time. There appeared to be a disagreement between two of them. He watched in fascination as the discussion progressed. Even though he understood nothing he felt an issue critical to his continued existence was being debated. In the end the two discussants relaxed the tone of their language as if coming to an agreement. With as little ceremony as they arrived, they left. He felt he still knew nothing more.

Night did not come soon enough. Within a few short minutes of being alone Brad was out on the roof. There was a wind blowing from the ocean filling the air with a salty mist. Large heavy clouds scudded across the faces of the moons. A storm was brewing, he thought. Weather here is no different than on any other planet. He made his way back to the processing plants. Tonight he would enter one to sate his own curiosity. On the way he noticed the new ship was gone. It must have been completely disassembled and crated as his own had.

A large black building larger than the rest was his target. He climbed up on its roof without difficulty. It was even easier to dislodge a section of plating and gain access. Inside it was completely dark with zero visibility. He had brought his suit's flashlight. When he turned it on what he saw was totally unexpected. There was no doubt in his mind this was a processing plant for some sort of meatpacking industry. The hooks, knives, pulleys, tables were all sparkling clean. It was hard to believe it was ever used. Curious he explored the plant from corner to corner.

There was an overhead track which held metal hooks not unlike those in a meatpacking plant on earth. He followed the track to a large locked double door. The doors felt cold to touch. The lock yielded to the weight of his body. He was not prepared for what he saw.

A humanoid body was hung on the hook near the doors. Brad lit the body with his light and circled it slowly. He was not certain the body did not belong to an Earth man. However there were enough anatomical differences that made him conclude this might be the pilot from the other ship. He looked around the room for any clothing the pilot may have worn. Unfortunately, the body was the only evidence of the pilot.

Brad, although feeling colder by the minute, moved farther along the track. He found what he thought was a receiving area. There he found the missing clothes of the pilot. He thought he recognized the insignia from a known world in his own galaxy. He wished he could have helped him. All hope of an ally disappeared. He was alone again.

With little enthusiasm he entered another room. This was a freezer with packages piled on shelves. The closest shelf appeared like a display in the meat department of a grocery store. What he saw did not concern him until he saw a hand in one of the packages. The blood immediately rushed to his head. No, this is not possible, he said to himself. This is just a bad nightmare. He looked all around for the fastest exit out of the freezer. He began running for the hole in the roof.

Outside it had started raining. He had to get away as fast as possible. The entire situation was beginning to make sense. His ship did not meet an accident. His hosts had deliberately shot him out of the sky. The reasons for doing so were now clear. They were pirates who either reused the ship parts for themselves or sold them to outsiders. The dead pilot in the processing plant meant the other reason was unthinkable. Yet he had no choice but to think it. His treatment at the hands of his host indicated all along he was considered no more than an animal to be fattened and slaughtered. He would never be an honored guest here. He was going to be the main entrée. He had to get away to someplace safe. He knew where the parts to his ship were. Perhaps he could find the radio and call for help. Anything was worth a try.

Drenched to the skin he found the building where the ship parts were stored. He gained access by forcing a side door open. He encountered no one even though he moved rather recklessly. Within the building he discovered the beings had separated ship parts into various components. He found the electronic section easily. The parts from his ship were grouped at the end of one long shelf. He began grabbing every component looking frantically for the radio. He stopped at the sound of a noise behind him.

A dozen beings had entered the building. Each one was holding a stun gun. Brad dropped everything he was holding. He realized he was completely surrounded with no hope of escape. For the first time he thought he saw one of the beings smile as it licked its lips. There was even a drop of saliva that dripped out of the corner of its mouth.

To the Stars

"You are wanted at the Space Center."

Zach rolled onto his back trying to shut out the voice. It was too early to get out of bed.

"Wake-up! Or do I have to drag you out of bed. Get up! This is important!"

Mumbling some obscenity Zach opened his eyes. Janet was standing over him with a glass of ice water. That immediately caught his attention. "Why?" He said hardly audible.

"I have no idea." She started tipping the glass over his head. "But you are going to mind if you know what I mean."

"Stop! I am getting up. Just give me a moment."

"No way. You will just go back to sleep."

"I promise I won't."

Janet tipped the glass and allowed a large drop to splash directly on his face. Zach threw back the covers and jumped out of bed. He lunged, grabbed her by the waist and pulled her down onto the bed.

"Getting up means no monkey business either!"

"You are no fun at all today."

"When your boss calls, I think it is important."

"Geez, give me a break. I am just trying to have some fun."

"Now is not the time. Get dressed."

Reluctantly he let her get off the bed. He watched her straighten herself. She saw him and smiled. There would be time for playing later.

"Did Jason say anything about why he wants me this time of the day?"

"I am just your humble wife, dear. I am not privy to what goes on in your super-secret Space Center."

"I tell you whatever I can." He stood up and stretched. "There is actually not much that is a secret. The damn press already knows what we are doing before we do. I think the media has all the secrets. The Space Center is an open book."

The telephone rang.

"I'll get it." Zach quickly lifted the receiver on the nightstand. "Hello?"

Janet watched as his expression became somber. She surmised it was the boss underscoring the importance of getting to the Space Center as soon as possible. When he hung up he was still not sure why he was needed so urgently.

By the time Zach arrived at the Space Center the sun had risen above the horizon. He found the boss, Jason Exeter, in the Command Operations Room staring at the deep space monitor. Although he must have seen Zach enter the room, his attention remained riveted to the computer screen. Zach walked up and stood beside him.

"What's up?"

Jason turned slowly, expressionless. "We have a problem." He pointed at the monitor.

"What sort of problem?"

Jason sighed. "We have lost contact with our star probe again. I don't know if the problem is on this end or out there."

"After fifty years we can expect to eventually lose contact," Zach said softly. "Loss of a signal does not mean an equipment problem."

"All mechanical systems eventually fail. Only biological ones can adapt on a real-time basis. I have always been an advocate of manned space exploration."

"In near solar system space manned travel is almost practical, but for stellar distances?"

"I remember when this project was started. I was a teenager at the time. There was great fanfare when the probe was launched. I don't know what the original planners thought, but I had dreams of contact with an advanced alien civilization. Now I realize that was not the plan at all. It was totally something else and now I am skeptical."

"Doubt is good. It may lead to progress."

"The results of this project," Jason continued. "May not be evident until all the life on our planet is long gone, a pretty depressing thought if you ask me."

"I am still not clear of the why of your concern. No one expected results when the probe was launched. Exactly why are you concerned now?"

Jason stared at Zach a moment. "I have recently come across some restricted documents which are quite disturbing."

"Were you authorized to view these documents?"

"Yes, as Director I am allowed full access to all documents classified and unclassified. I have full security clearance as you do."

362

"You are keeping me in suspense. What can possibly be in these documents that have you so upset?"

Jason smiled wanly. "Come with me. I will show you."

They went out of the Command Operations Room to an elevator, down into the bowels of the Space Center. When the elevator stopped at the lowest level Zach was sure whatever he was to learn was important. He shook off the last remnants of sleepiness and focused attention to the growing mystery. After passing through several doors which allowed access only by retinal scan, he found himself with the Director in the center's archives.

"Is the answer to your mysterious behavior here?" Zach said cautiously. He was not convinced anything really important would drag him out of bed to a roomful of nearly ancient data.

"I know asking you here during your off-hours is highly irregular and I apologize," Jason said slowly. "But you are the only person with a high enough clearance I can trust with what I am about to reveal to you."

"I understand the trust part." Zach nodded. "I don't understand anything else."

"Let me start at the beginning." Jason sat at the master console and entered several requests on the keyboard. He took a deep breath. "How long have you been a part of the space program?"

"Ever since I graduated with my PhD." Zach remained confused. "I have not had any other job."

"Good," Jason continued. "Now, how much of the history of space exploration do you remember?"

"I imagine I can recall just about all the major events since the beginning. When I was growing up all I ever wanted to be was a part of what was happening. I even thought I would be an astronaut someday, but then I found out more exploration was done remotely than in real-time"

"Good." Jason was visibly pleased. "And you know the most important questions have always been centered on the origin and distribution of life in the cosmos."

"Of course." Zach nodded. "Not a day goes by where that question is not asked. I am not sure it will ever be answered anytime soon. Are you?"

The look on Jason's face was strained. Zach wondered if he was feeling well. He could not imagine what this discussion was leading to.

"I discovered something today I never imagined possible." There was sweat on Jason's brow. "I came across it quite accidentally." The monitors rolled rapidly making it impossible to read.

"You have my attention," Zach said slowly. "You got me out of a sound sleep."

"Sorry." Jason smiled weakly. "This could not wait; I needed a witness to what I found."

"You make this sound so serious." Zach tried to laugh but could not.

Jason turned away from the monitor and stood up in front of Zach. He grabbed Zach's arm and pulled him into the chair.

"Sit!"

Reluctantly Zach sat down watching Jason's face for any clues as to why this was happening. He found none. When he finally looked at what the monitor the screen was displaying: a chronology of the early days of the space program. There was nothing unusual in what he saw.

"What am I supposed to see?"

"How many of the early space probes have left the solar system?"

"Well, there's…" Zach squinted at the screen. "…Pioneer and Voyager."

"And any others?"

"Not until the early part of the next century," Zach said confidently. "Although there may have been one or two other probes that may have escaped into deep interstellar space. Then there was a great interest in sending out spacecraft to the stars."

"And why do you think that happened?"

"I don't know."

"Is it possible someone discovered something so important that we should spend untold amounts of money on probes that will never reach their destinations in anyone's lifetime or for that matter in the life expectancy of this planet?" Jason smiled. "About the turn-of-the-century there was a discovery so important that it was kept secret from everyone except an elite few."

"What could possibly be that important?"

"During the wars of the turn-of-the-century a soldier accidentally stumbled over an archaeological treasure while fighting the enemy in the mountains. In a cave he found what is

364

now displayed on the monitor." Jason pressed a key, the image changed, and he pointed.

"That looks like the plaque on Voyager." Zach examined the image closely.

"Yes, that is exactly what it looks like." Jason moved closer to the screen. "Except that this could not possibly come from here."

"Why is that?"

"The materials have been dated to a time several million years before the space program was even remotely imagined," Jason said flatly. "What you are looking at is the remains of an alien probe that happened to crash onto our planet."

"That is fantastic!" Zach stared at the image intensely. "This is the biggest discovery ever. This proves we are not alone in the universe. Why hasn't this been publicized?"

"There's more." Jason changed the image on the screen. "Along with the illustrations there was also a message."

"A message?"

"For us." Jason pointed again to the screen. "I happened to come across to it quite by accident. I don't think anyone was ever to find out about this. I was doing research for a talk I was to give at the commencement of the University I graduated. I was the commencement speaker."

"Stop." Zach held up his palm. "Get to the point! I want to know what the message was."

"Look for yourself." A grin appeared on Jason's face. "I think this will change your perspective of everything forever."

"Impossible," Zach shook his head before examining the screen, and then he read what was a translation of writing on the plaque. It said: "Be fruitful, multiply, and disperse." The impact of the statement took a moment to settle into his consciousness. "This must be some sort of joke. It can't be!"

"This is no joke." Jason laughed. "I now understand it all. Before this plaque was found we thought we were alone, but this proves we are a part of a greater whole that is sweeping across the stars. We can't travel from star system to star system in human form but we can send microbes which will evolve into us. That's the only way we can bridge the vast distances."

"No, I don't believe it!" Zach screamed as he awoke in a sweat.

The Blue Moon Bar

I love my job. There is not a single day I do not look forward to coming to work. When I first started working here I thought I would be bored to tears. In almost no time I found out I had lucked into a job that I could earn money and have fun at the same time. I am sure the agency that sent me here had no idea what it was really like. I was originally told to expect long hours on my feet being bored by patrons in all phases of an alcoholic stupor. Much to my surprise for the most part that has not been the case. I can point to any individual here and tell you just about their total life history. I make it a point to engage all my customers in conversation. Once you get them started you would be surprised what you can find out without asking any questions. I think alcohol is one of the greatest truth sera on this planet. The more alcohol consumed, the greater the validity of what is said. Or that has been my experience so far. But I am rambling. I have work to do. A man I have never seen before has just stepped up to the bar in front of me.

"May I help you, sir?"

The expression on the man's face is nearly unreadable, but I can tell there is something bothering him. From what I see he is about 45 to 50 years old. By the way he is dressed I expect he is on his way home from work. His coat is unbuttoned and tie loosened at least a finger breath, skewed slightly to the left. From under his long sleeves there is a black sport watch on his left wrist. He seems to me a sort of average middle-aged man more or less conforming to the norms of society.

"I'll have a scotch and soda," he says tiredly and turns away to survey the room as I fill his order.

The room is barely lit for reasons of intimacy. Naturally there are the blue neon moons scattered around for effect. There is no music; this is a place for reflection, relaxation and conversation. My new customer has turned back to face the drink I placed on the bar in front of him. I tell him the price and he presses a credit card on top of the tab. I assume he wants to run it. He does.

"Is this your first time here?" I say. Business is slow so I have a chance to talk about what I want.

My customer looks into his drink, picks it up, gives it a swirl and takes a swig like out of the movies. I almost laugh it is so stereotypical. The expression on his face remains unchanged since he came in. I am not sure he welcomes my conversation.

"I'll have another," he says even though he has barely consumed the first one. I have no objection, he is still stone cold sober and money is money.

I pick up the tab and add the additional drink until he finally decides to talk. While I prepare the drink he says yes, this is a first time he has been here. He had heard about the place from some friends which hopes to meet here later. He came early to relax and get his feet back on the ground.

"Do you mind if I ask what sort of work you do?" To me it seems this is the right time to ask, but he looks at me with raised eyebrows.

"What do you want to know?" He says flatly. "I don't know you, do I?"

"Please don't take offense." I backpedal. "I am not trying to be nosy or anything. I just thought it would be the basis of something to talk about. Geez, I am just a bartender. I don't have any agenda except to be someone anyone can talk to."

He extends his hand to mine. "My name is Brad. I am sorry. I have been curt. I have had a long hard day at work today. I guess you are right. You are the local therapist surrounded by a pleasant ambience. I guess you can even say you dispense relaxants as part of the therapy." He laughs and raises his glass in a mock toast before he takes another swig.

"Well, Brad, it is good to meet you. My name is Joe and I will be your therapist for the evening." I laugh and he joins me. The ice is broken. The bar is still pretty quiet as far as business goes so I can spend some time talking without interruption. From six o'clock on there will be two of us behind the bar and even then I will have time to talk as much as I want. A good part of my job is to talk, talk, and talk some more. You never know what will come out of casual conversation once the lips have been lubricated with alcohol.

"Can I buy you a drink?" Brad smiles.

"Sorry, I am on duty, but if you want to get me a soft drink I do get thirsty when I work." No reason for me to turn down an offer, even if I am working for the agency.

"Put whatever you want on my tab."

I thank him and pour myself a Coke. Just then another man enters the bar scanning the place as if he is looking for

368

someone. I move away from Brad and make myself appear available to the new customer. This man I have seen before. He always sits at a table, usually with one or two friends. I have never been able to talk to him, but Sissy says she has. By the way Sissy is the waitress here in the evening. She should be here any minute now. Maybe this guy is looking to see if she is here yet. He has come up to the bar.

"What can I get for you?" I put on my friendliest face.

The man turns away from me and spots Brad. Ignoring me, he walks and sits down at the bar next to him. It is obvious they know each other. I slowly walk over as they exchange greetings. I try to remain unobtrusive until I am needed. They talk a bit before I am acknowledged.

"Bob, do you know Joe here?" Brad acts as if we are old friends.

"I have seen him before." Rob smiles. "I come here a couple times a week. I usually sit at a table." He looks at his watch. "I usually come in a lot later, but I got off early today. I guess there is no table service until Sissy gets here."

"I will take your drinks to a table." I say, although I would rather they stay at the bar so I can hear what they talk about.

"Bob, stay at the bar with me." It seems Brad has read my mind.

"Okay, but only until Sissy gets here." Bob settles in and orders a gin and tonic. Not a drink I really care for. Brad insists it put on his tab. Bob tries to refuse at first then agrees as long as he can get the next round. Everyone is happy, at least, for the moment.

I try to fade into the background far enough to seem I am minding my own business, but close enough to hear everything clearly. This is when my job really becomes interesting. Naturally, this is why I was hired.

When I serve Bob his drink he hoists it up to his lips then pushes out toward Brad who automatically lifts his own drink to clink glasses. Neither says anything. Whatever the toast is happens to be a silent one. I guess that is born of a long-standing friendship. They drink slowly allowing the alcohol to slowly seep out into consciousness. Neither appears in any hurry about anything.

"Any progress on the project?" Brad speaks first holding his glass on the bar between his palms. Bob takes another sip, puts his glass down and leans toward Brad. I am all ears.

"Yes and no." Bob smiles and looks at me. I try to look like I am busy minding my own business.

"I hate not having definite answers." Brad is clearly not happy with the answer and neither am I. I want to know all about the project whatever it is.

"It depends on what you call progress." Bob continues to look at me. His stare makes me self-conscious and more than a little nervous.

"Anything that changes, I would consider progress." Brad says flatly. "Sometimes I think we are on a wild goose chase."

"We are," Bob says still concentrating his gaze on me. I almost feel his eyes are boring into my skull to see my thoughts. At least outwardly I present a picture of perfect indifference.

"That's hard to believe." Brad coughs. "After all the time and money invested in negative results we are finally going to produce something positive."

"Believe it or not, it is true." Bob turns his face toward Brad. "And I think you are going to be really surprised when I tell you what that result is."

"Don't keep me in suspense. Tell me." Yes, tell him. I want to know, too.

"This is not the time or the place." Bob looks back at me. "There are too many possibilities for a leak in a place like this."

"I suppose you are right." Bob sighs. Drats, no, you are wrong, you have to tell everything here where I can hear it. There is no secret too important that cannot be left in this bar. Trust me.

"You know I am right." Bob motions for me to serve another set of drinks. I move slowly, I don't want to miss a thing.

"I really want to wrap up this operation so we can move into something more productive." Brad notices I am obviously listening. He sips his drink and nods in my direction. Bob looks at me and shakes his head. I have been really careless. I have to try harder to fade into the background. As long as I am nearby they say nothing more to each other. I see another customer enter, actually two. There is a young man with a stylish woman on his arm. They are laughing. It is nice to see someone in good humor. They look around and take a seat in a booth. I now have to split my time between the bar and tables. Fortunately, it is almost time for Sissy to arrive. The inconvenience will not be too bad or too long. I walk quickly over to the booth.

370

"What can I get you?" I flash my best smile. "Would you like some chips and dip?"

"Bring us a bottle of champagne." The young man laughs. "We have a lot of celebrating to do."

Their happiness is infectious. I am uplifted by their mood. It counterbalances what I experienced at the bar. I get the champagne, put it in an ice bucket and bring it back to the couple who seem oblivious to my presence. They are deeply engrossed staring into each other's eyes. If only those eyes could talk so I could understand what they are saying. I know it has to do with love, but to me that is an abstract concept. Maybe if I watch more closely I will understand.

"Here is your champagne, Sir," I say warmly. "Would you like me to serve it?"

"Please do," the woman says. There is a definite melodious quality to her voice. She is excited about something. I wish I knew what.

When I finish serving, before I step away, I venture to ask what the occasion is. They laugh as if I said something funny. I blush. I am almost sorry I asked. I feel foolish and turn to leave.

"Wait," the young man says. "We have just had a great day all around. We finished a great project, got substantial raises, were promoted, and decided to get married."

I break out in a big smile. "Congratulations, you have had a great day. That champagne is on the house."

"This is our lucky day," the young woman almost squeals. She is obviously very happy and shows it without reservation. I am sure a little alcohol will only accentuate the mood. I wish them a happy life together and return to my place behind the bar.

"We are as close as we will ever get," Bob says oblivious to my return. Brad nods in my direction. Bob turns his head and smiles weakly. I get the feeling he does not like me for some reason I cannot imagine.

"Can I get you another round?" I try to be as friendly as possible.

"Sure," Brad says quickly. "I don't have anywhere special to go tonight. Might as well relax; while we are here."

"Do you have a designated driver?" It is my legal duty to make sure no one leaves the bar without a safe way home.

"We will take a taxi when the time comes," Bob says. My responsibility partially fulfilled, I get the drinks. Later I will

371

have to make sure they get into a taxi together. No use leaving anything to chance. I would hate to be responsible for an accident and then be held responsible for more money than I could ever hope to earn in my lifetime.

Out of the corner of my eye I see Sissy walk in with George, my partner. Now I will be able to concentrate on my duties behind the bar.

"How's it going?" Sissy always has a bubbly personality. In a tight miniskirt with her stunning blue eyes and bleached blonde hair she is a knockout. She exudes sensuality which makes her job highly profitable. Most of the men who come in here at one time or another have either directly or indirectly propositioned her. I must say I admire her ability to fend off all the attention with good humor. She is as dedicated to the agency as I am. There is no room for any personal involvement with our customers. That is a firm and fast rule.

"There's a regular at the bar and a couple in a booth celebrating their engagement," I say. "There's a new guy with the regular at the bar. They know each other from work. I have been hoping to listen to what they have to say but so far I have had no luck. They keep looking at me strangely. I don't know what to make of it, but I will keep trying. I am sure with enough drinks there will be loose lips."

"Do you want to tag team them?" George steps forward. "We can alternate serving them. Maybe between the two of us we can hear what we need to hear."

"I wish we could use our real equipment." I sigh. I am a firm believer in technology, but the agency does not want to use it. They say there is always a possibility of it being detected. Personal contact is the safest way to stay in the shadows.

"You know the argument against it." George has a way of saying things that leaves no room for debate. I know the rules and I know what our mission is.

This bar is been open for almost ten years. It has become a popular place for professionals to congregate. That was the idea in the first place. The agency hires and fires according to the information gathered. So far I have yet to make my mark. Things have been sort of slow. If I do not produce soon, the agency is going to replace me.

"That couple at the table is cute." Sissy is a real romantic. "That was a nice touch giving them a bottle of champagne." I grin. George looks at me with one of his superior looks. I know what he is going to say

"It is about time." I am surprised I did not expect him to approve. "A little more attention to details and we will get more of their confidence." I just nod I agree.

"Time for me to get busy," Sissy says cheerfully. "I just might get lucky tonight."

"You say that every night." George laughs.

"And tonight I may be right." She laughs back.

Meanwhile I maneuver myself back toward Brad and Bob. They are having a long serious discussion. I get close without being noticed.

"I think we are going to get the proof we need soon," Bob says staring into his drink. "Intelligence has started putting two and two together. In a few days the boys are going to make their move. It is going to be a big surprise to everyone involved."

"Is there going to be any media coverage?" Brad finally sees me but continues as if I am not there. "This whole operation has a lot of important ramifications."

"As far as I am concerned it is just another project completed. I do my job and move on to the next. It is not for me to analyze."

"You mean to tell me you don't care about what our mission intends do?" Brad says rather loudly. I move closer.

"I get paid, I go home, and I live my own life." Bob smiles. "If that means I don't care, then I don't."

"You have been working with us too long." Brad is disgusted I am sure. "Why don't you get reassigned then?"

"The money and the hours are good." The answers are too flip. I suspect he is not being completely honest. I wonder if this conversation is for me. There is always a chance they know who I am.

"Joe, come closer." Bob waves at me. I move slowly. I am wary. "I want you to hear this. My friend here says I take my job too seriously." I almost contradict him because I clearly hear the opposite. I say nothing.

"Don't bother Joe; he is not in our conversation." Brad comes to my defense.

"I think Joe is very much in our discussion." Bob grins. I think the alcohol is starting to work its magic. "Joe is not who you think he is. Are you Joe?"

I tense up. I do not know what to say. His accusation comes as a complete surprise. Sooner or later I should expect to be fingered. The best I can do is to put on a puzzled look.

373

"Wipe that innocent look off your face. We know who you are." Any evidence of alcohol intoxication is gone from Bob. He appears stone-cold sober.

"Who am I supposed to be?" I shrug my shoulders. I try to look as innocent and confused as possible.

"Maybe he is not who you think he is." Brad comes to my rescue. "Are you absolutely certain? He looks like everybody else."

"Not only am I certain, I have evidence this place is run by them." Bob remains cool and calm. "I have all the proof I need to bring them all in."

"Excuse me. What are you talking about?" I have an idea, but I want him to be more specific. I have more to gain by acting stupid. I knew I would one day have to face this situation, but why now?

Bob stands up and leans across the bar. I can smell the alcohol on his breath. "Don't think you fool me one minute," he snarls.

"Whoever you are talking about can't be me." I am having a hard time staying cool and collected. All my training at the agency was nothing compared to the situation I am in at the moment.

"Brad, this is one of our suspects." Bob gloats. "He thought he could fool a group of trained professionals."

"Are you absolutely sure?" Brad seems unimpressed. "We have made mistakes before."

"There is no mistake this time." Bob almost laughs. "I have been coming to this bar for a long time. In the beginning I thought I was wasting my time coming here. But the more I watched the more I saw what was really going on. The Blue Moon Bar is a hotbed of espionage."

"Espionage?" I am taken aback. What could I have possibly done to give him that impression?

"That means I think you are an enemy spy!" Bob's face flushes red. His blood pressure must be rising with his temper. I have never seen him so agitated. I still cannot think how I gave them the impression I am an enemy spy.

"Are we going to arrest him?" Brad seems detached from what is being said in a way I do not exactly understand. If the two of them work together, they must both have access to the same intelligence.

"Not only him but the other two also." I glance over at George. He simply nods at me. I have to take it on faith the

374

current crisis will be resolved peacefully. Sissy is talking to the couple at the booth with her back turned to us. I do not think she is aware of anything.

"Excuse me, but I think you forgot something." I immediately get their attention. "Before you start condemning any further and threatening to arrest anyone don't you think it appropriate to show some proper identification."

Brad thrusts his right hand in his jacket and pulls out a wallet. When it flips open I see a badge and ID. Although I cannot read everything, I recognize the ID as belonging to an employee of the Department of Homeland Security. I almost laugh when I realize the bar is being cased as a rendezvous for terrorists. Little did he know that was about as far from the truth as possible.

"I am not a terrorist." I laugh. "Now I know you are really mistaken. I am certainly not an enemy."

"I know individuals who have been followed around the city come directly here after having visited strategic locations. And those same individuals come again and again. I have even witnessed them passing sensitive materials to you and the staff here." Bob puts his wallet back into his jacket. "It doesn't take a rocket scientist to put two and two together."

"This place is well known as a place to come." I try to sound logical. "We pride ourselves on our service and drinks. Just because the same people come back again and again doesn't make this automatically a den for elements subversive to our country. I could just as well accuse you of being an enemy spy with what I have seen. Everything you have said is pure circumstantial."

"More convictions are made on circumstantial evidence than anything else. If that was not so, too many criminals would be a threat to the public safety out on the streets." Bob smiles smugly. I can tell he has a hard-nosed cop mentality. Reasoning is not a word in this type's personality. What is interesting is Bob is not joined by Brad. I sense a difference in opinion between the two of them.

"Let it go." Brad puts his right hand on Bob's shoulder. "This is not the proper way to conclude an investigation, especially when you have no backup."

"All I have to do is speed dial my cell phone and help will arrive within seconds. I came prepared for every eventuality." Bob reaches into the outside pocket of his jacket.

375

"Hey! Where is my phone? I had it in my pocket when I came in here!"

"Are you sure?" Brad leans forward as if to look for the phone on the floor around Bob. "Maybe you have had too much to drink. This is probably a figment of your imagination."

"What? You think I am drunk?" Bob flushes even darker red than before. "Whose side are you on anyway?"

"I am on the right side." I almost think Brad winks at me. The whole situation is getting more bizarre by the minute. What should I expect next?

"I have been behind the bar except when I was serving that couple in the booth." I put on my most innocent face. I know I am not responsible for the loss of his phone. "Maybe you dropped it in the restroom."

"I have not been to the restroom." Bob is clearly getting more upset.

"Calm down." Brad remains unimpressed with Bob's antics. "Coming in here by yourself depending on a single cell phone is foolish as all hell. Is this bust an official operation or is it something you conjured up to get some attention in the department?"

"I am not doing anything that was not going to happen anyway." Bob takes a deep breath. "I have just moved up the timetable a little bit. When I bring this group in I should look pretty good to the boss."

"Pretty foolish if you ask me." Brad remains coldly serious. "A wrong move on your part can jeopardize untold years of hard work."

"Are you with me or not?" Sweat is rolling down Bob's temples. "If I didn't know better, I would say you were one of them." He points at me.

Brad stands up and grabs Bob by the arm. "Let me take you home. You have had too much to drink. We will discuss all of this later, in private."

"Take your hands off of me!" Bob shouts as he stumbles away almost falling. He stands up and brushes off his coat. "You are a traitor; you know that, don't you?"

"I am nothing but an advocate of reason." Brad steps closer to Bob but Bob backs away. There is something very strange going on here. I can't put my finger on it.

"You touch me one more time and I swear I will have to arrest you for assault." Bob reaches with his right hand into his

376

coat searching under his left arm pit for something. "Hey, now where is my gun?"

"He has a gun?" I almost whisper. This is getting more serious by the minute.

"Don't worry you are in no danger." Bob seems to be reading my mind. "We will be out of here in a few minutes."

"What is going on here?" For the first time I see confusion in Bob's face as if he is beginning to doubt his own sobriety. I am sure he drank enough for it to get to his head. For one thing I always serve strong drinks.

"Joe, would you please call for a cab. I am going to take Bob home." Brad looks like he has the entire situation under control. I use the phone under the bar. The taxi should arrive in a few minutes. There is always one nearby a place like this. Brad produces a medication vial out of his own pocket. He opens the lid and puts a small green capsule on the counter. Bob notices and shakes his head. "Would you get Bob here a glass of water? He needs to take his medication."

"Are you crazy? I am not taking anything!" Bob is getting more agitated. "I am not sick. I know what you are trying to do."

"I am only trying to help you. Now take this capsule and you will feel a lot better." Brad points to the medication. "You need to relax and rethink everything. I won't say anything back at the department if you won't. We will keep this between ourselves."

For a moment I think Bob will refuse to take capsule, but he picks it up. He looks first at me then at Brad. He slowly puts it into his mouth. I put a glass of water on the counter in front of him. He looks at Brad again. Brad nods. With a sip of water Bob swallows the capsule and sits back on a stool. He shakes his head.

"You will start to feel better soon." Brad sits again on his own stool. "The cab should be here any minute."

I look over in the direction of the couple in the booth. Sissy has placed herself between us and them. They are all laughing. I am sure Sissy has been diverting them with small talk. George is busy taking a quick inventory of what we have to order tomorrow. Although George seems preoccupied I am sure he has been watching what has been going on with great interest. What affects me, affects him equally as well as Sissy. The agency would be extremely disappointed if we brought attention to ourselves with unnecessary accusations. The idea that we might be terrorists is truly laughable. I almost thought he had guessed who we really are. We actually owe a favor to Brad whoever he is. I am glad there are some people around here with good sense. I see the cab driver coming into the bar. I wave to him. He sees me. I point at Bob who has slumped over asleep on his own arms.

"Another drunk one, huh?" The cab driver is an old veteran of calls from here. Whenever he comes he never smiles or offers any hint of emotion other than indifference. Although the way he carries himself advertises otherwise.

"I will help you get him out of here." Brad volunteers without any hesitation. I guess I can call him a true friend. But in the back of my mind I sense something fishy going on. I am beginning to think Brad is not who he appears to be.

When Brad returns I am wiping the bar with a wet cloth. He sits where he sat. Before he begins to lift the glass to his lips he suddenly puts it down. He asks for fresh one. I get it to him in several quick motions I have long practiced. George comes over and stands beside me.

"Do you know who this is?" George says to me. I have no idea who he is. As I said before this was the first time I had ever seen him. "He is with the agency." I am visibly surprised. I never expected a customer to be spying on me.

"I have a lot to learn," I admit. "I am glad you were in here when you were."

Brad smiles. "You were handling everything perfectly well. I would not have interfered, except Bob was about to do something that must never be allowed. Call in the authorities."

"I appreciate your help." I return the smile. "When I was hired for this job I did not expect any hostilities."

"The agency can't possibly train you for every possible situation." Brad takes a sip of his new drink. "Hey, this is better than the last one. How did you do that?"

"A little secret." I grin. All I have done is substitute a better grade of booze for the cheap stuff I used before. If the customer does not specify what he wants, I will give him what will make the most profit. Most of the time taste is not of concern of the patrons of this place.

"Well you can keep your secret as long as you keep mine."

"And what secret is that?" I am all ears.

"That I work for the agency."

378

"Why should that be a secret?" Now I am really curious. What could be so important about his identity?

"So I can remain unknown within the organization that Bob runs." Brad is serious. I can tell by his expression

"I am a little confused what organization does Bob run?" I look at George who remains silent next to me.

"Basically he heads a force of men and women dedicated to protecting this country from outside enemies." Brad takes a deep breath before continuing. "You heard him say the word terrorist. That is not exactly what he meant. What he wanted to say was you are an extraterrestrial alien. I have been working with him long enough that his suspicions have been increasing that what he believes in theory is in actuality fact. I have infiltrated his department to keep him away from what we are doing here. And I see on your face that you wonder what we are doing here too. The agency sometimes is not completely clear what the main objectives are on this world. First, let me say we are not part of a vanguard invasion force. Our objectives are simply to observe and facilitate in the least obvious way possible. This bar has accumulated a lot of data in its time of operation. You have not been here long enough to make much of a contribution but you will. Trust me, you will."

"Are we going to have any further trouble from Bob?" It is hard for me to believe Bob will not sober up and remember at least some details.

"I slipped in one of these." Brad holds out a small smoky colored vial with no label. "I put one in his last drink and another under his tongue. When he wakes up at home he will have a heck of a headache and no idea how he got it. His amnesia will be total."

"That is good to know." I look over at Sissy coming toward us. "What about that couple over there."

"They are part of the agency." Brad waves and the man waves back. "The problem developing with Bob was serious enough to bring in reinforcements. We left nothing to chance."

"If it was so important, why wasn't I let in on what was going on?" I act miffed. "Aren't I part of the agency and part of the team?"

"It was important that you, Sissy and George here be totally unaware of the situation. We wanted nothing to interfere with your normal behavior and duties." Brad glances at his watch. "I have to go. Any questions?"

379

I shake my head because I know that is the right thing to do. There are more things I would like to ask about. Of course the whole current incident is a big lesson to me. I have to be careful whatever I do. I will never know exactly who is watching me, but that is part of my job.

Brad finishes his drink. He pays his tab without hesitation. We exchange a few banalities and he quietly exits. The five of us are left in the bar. Sissy continues to wait on the two in the booth as if they are real customers. I have to remember their faces if they come in here again.

A group of three older professional looking men enter the bar. It is my turn to do the busywork including washing the glassware. From what I overhear these men are connected with the government's military space program. I make my move ever so slowly to get closer. I do not want to be obvious. Good intelligence can only occur under optimal conditions. I am expected to get results. The agency will not let me slide. Produce or get out is their motto.

"Joe, would you mind covering for me while I make a phone call." George steps on the other side of me and introduces me to the three men. This is a lot easier than I expect.

As long as I play my cards right, as the expression goes, I should not have any problem around here. The agency is a pretty formidable collection of intelligence agents. Little do they know that I come from the Confederated Worlds. Yes, believe it or not I am a secret agent spying on secret agents. I belong to a third party which makes it even more interesting. It is hard for me not to laugh every time I am given an agency assignment. I have the best of three worlds. I think I fully expressed how I felt about what I do and what I said in the beginning. And what was that you ask? Why I said that I love this job! Try it sometime. A recruiter may be by to see you soon. If not, drop by the Blue Moon Bar and have a drink. I think you will like the place. Just make sure you ask me for your drinks.

Bugs

A black cloud appeared in the northwest. Farmer Jones stopped the tractor to contemplate what it meant. There was no forecast of possible rain. Everywhere, except to the northwest, the sky was clear with high scattered clouds. If there was rain, the crops would more than welcome the needed moisture. Farmer Jones put the tractor in gear and resumed what he was doing. From time to time he looked at the black cloud as it loomed ever closer. Must be rain, he thought, except my bones don't feel like it.

When the cloud crossed the distant boundary of the field he was in, he suddenly realized this was not a normal meteorological phenomenon. A faint hum filled the air bringing a chill to his spine. What was approaching was an economic disaster. The first thought was locusts devouring all his hard grown crops. He could not afford another unprofitable harvest. He stopped the tractor and turned on the two-way radio.

"Jeb, are you there son?" Farmer Jones was beginning to perspire profusely even though it was not that hot.

The radio crackled absently.

"Jeb, are you there?" Farmer Jones was more insistent. Jeb, his eldest son, had to be somewhere close by. Perhaps he had also seen what he was watching with horror. The black cloud was descending on his field and coming his way.

"Jeb, come in!" Farmer Jones was frantic even though he knew there was nothing he could do.

"Yes, Pa," the radio answered slowly.

"Jeb, do you see what I see?"

"What is it, Pa?"

"A swarm of locusts come to eat us out of house and home."

"What can we do?"

"Get the smudge pots out and I will get Grady." Farmer Jones shook his head. "And hop to it son!"

"Yes, Pa."

"Damn, damn, damn." Farmer Jones fumed. "Just when things seem to be going right." He put the tractor in motion heading back to the barn as fast as possible. Maybe Grady with his crop duster could help.

The black cloud smeared itself across the open fields covering all the crops. Within a short time the opaqueness of the cloud obscured everything behind it. Farmer Jones watched in awe of the speed at which disaster was unfolding. The moment he realized the cloud was coming to engulf him he called on the radio again. This time he heard nothing but growing static. He gunned the tractor squeezing out all the speed he could. He knew the cloud had caught up to him when he felt the first thumps of insects colliding on his back. There was no escape now. Fortunately, he believed he would survive unscathed. The cloud surrounded and swallowed him up. The outside world disappeared in total blackness. The hum of beating wings barely allowed him to think clearly. Innumerable insects alit on his skin. He screamed in terror. The insects bit into his flesh. He stopped the tractor, got off and started running blindly, trying to brush off the pests. He stumbled, fell flat on his face, and lost consciousness.

From an adjacent field Jeb watched the cloud swallow his father. He had tried to call Grady with his cell phone but it was out of order with static. He was torn between going to his father and going for help. He chose going to his father. Nothing could be done to avert the damage already done. The radio was as full of static as the phone. His father was not answering even though without the cloud they would be in line of sight of each other. As he ran toward the last place he had seen his father the cloud lifted into a vertical column still in touch with the ground. The closer he came to the cloud the better he could hear the hum. Suddenly the topmost part of the column tilted drawing the rest of the cloud to follow. Within a few minutes the entire cloud vanished to the south. Jeb saw the tractor and ran directly to it. When he arrived he looked all around. His father was nowhere around. About thirty yards from the tractor Jeb found his father's watch and other pieces of clothing. Tears filled his eyes as he realized the cloud had swallowed and digested his father.

Weather radar easily detected the approaching swarm, although the weatherman did not fully appreciate what the displayed phenomenon was. There were elements suggestive of tornado formation requiring an immediate warning to the public. Spotters were alerted to be on the lookout for sudden storm activity. The first report came from a forest ranger who described the dark cloud is a mass of insects heading south. A warning to farmers was issued.

On the outskirts of town Bill West was working in his vegetable garden oblivious to any reports on the TV or radio. The day was perfect for tending his rapidly growing tomatoes, peppers and onions. He was on his knees removing weeds between the rows of plants when the light from the sun dimmed. He looked up expecting a cloud but saw instead a black mass that was anything but a cloud. The instant the black mass began descending toward the garden he got up and ran toward the house. The hum grew louder with each step he took. He was opening the door as the first insect hit his back. Without stopping a second he brushed himself off as he closed the door behind. The sound of insects hitting the house was akin to a massive hailstorm. Bill went to the telephone to call 911. The line was dead. He tried his backup cell phone but that was also not working. As long as he was inside he felt safe. Hopefully, the swarm would pass quickly.

The sound of breaking glass was followed by an increase in the sound of the hum. Bill went to where he heard the crash. To his horror the insects had broken through a bedroom window and were pouring into the house. He locked the door to the bedroom wondering if they would break in other windows. As if his mind had been read, several other windows around the house were broken simultaneously. There was nowhere to go except to the car in the garage. He got into the car and activated the garage opener. It rose without hesitation allowing the swarm access. He blindly backed out, guessed where the street should be, and sped off away from the house. In less than a block he collided with a parked car hitting the windshield with his head. He instantly lost consciousness

Incoming aviation to the city was warned of possible sheer activity. A routine commuter flight spotted the black cloud hovering on the ground in a suburban neighborhood. The pilot notified the control tower what he had observed. Instructions were relayed back for landing. While setting the attitude of the plane for a direct approach, the cloud drew itself together and shot upwards into the sky. The area where the cloud had been looked as if it had been struck with a nuclear weapon; there was nothing recognizable where the cloud had been.

"This is Skyways Flight 209 to tower."

"This is tower, over."

"There is something strange about that cloud." The Captain watched the rising cloud with no small degree of apprehension. "There is nothing left on the ground where it was."

"Nothing?"

"Nothing!"

"We will pass that on Flight 209. You are still go for direct approach."

"If I didn't know better, I would say that cloud is out to get us here."

"Keep us informed."

"Roger." The Captain remained transfixed on the rising cloud. At first the cloud ascended straight up almost reaching the altitude the plane was at. Without warning the cloud darted toward the plane. "Damn, that cloud is heading for us!"

The tower responded calmly. "There is no traffic in your vicinity use your discretion to maneuver away from danger."

"Roger." The Captain banked the plane away from the approaching menace. The cloud followed each maneuver. There was no escape from a collision. That Captain put the plane in a steep climb hoping that whatever the cloud was composed could not or would not follow. Unfortunately, that was a wasted move, the cloud accelerated to engulf the plane. All radio communication was lost. The front windshield was smashed allowing insects into the cockpit. The crew screamed in panic brushing away the insects. All control lost, the plane stalled, banked to the right and flew in a slow spiral for the ground. Flight 209 was lost without survivors.

"We have a plane down north of the airport!" The air controller had difficulty controlling his emotion. The pilot had been a good friend and neighbor. The call mobilized all local rescue services to head toward the crash site.

The black cloud followed the plane all away to the ground, abandoning it just before contact. It then descended on the wreckage like a blanket. Before the rescue teams arrived the cloud took to the air again continuing its journey to the south.

The rescue teams found little recognizable when they reached the crater. They were expecting debris scattered in a wide swath, but actually found little except displaced dirt and rocks. There were fragments recognizable as parts of the plane but they were few and far between. An explosion could not account for what was observed. Finding the black box flight recorder was out of the question. There was nothing to do but cordon off the crash site and bring in experts from Washington. The hard part was notifying the families.

The weathermen were still tracking the cloud noticing that it was continuing in a direct south direction. Observers on the ground reported the size and the ominous hum. The local university was notified to become involved. The possibility this might be a gigantic swarm of locusts was not far-fetched. It had been over seven years since the last outbreak of the pesky insects. What was frightening was the degree of destruction the present swarm was capable of inflicting. The loss of one jet airliner was one too many. An advisory went out directing all air traffic away from the path of the swarm until further notice. The only exception would be the crop dusters spraying toxins in the air in an attempt to deflect the swarm from critical areas. If history was any clue, the swarm would flourish for a few weeks then disappear as quickly as it appeared. At least that was the hope. In the meantime, warnings to the public were worded carefully to avoid panic. The crisis would pass, everyone would be fine, and everything would return back to normal. It was a matter of time.

Professor Basil Williams was halfway through his second cup of coffee when the call came. The Director of the Weather Service related what was happening and what was known. Basil was known for his interest and experiments in insect behavior. There was no doubt he would become involved. His specialty involved advance physiology and biophysical engineering. He was amongst those elite scientists who had probed the minds of insects with microelectrodes. Controlling insects by tapping into their brains was routine to him. In fact, he had several patents on aspects of the technology.

"Where are you going?" Wilma, his lab assistant and colleague, said as he hung up the telephone.

"There is an outbreak of locusts that is causing havoc near here. I have been asked to be consultant and offer suggestions on how to minimize damages." Basil swallowed the last of the coffee in his cup and headed for the door. "You are welcome to come if you like."

An excursion out of the lab was what Wilma needed. Her research was at a logical stopping point plus she needed something different to recharge her batteries. She followed Basil out the door and into his car. The first stop was a farm north of the city. That farm had apparently been the first hit by the swarm.

From a distance Basil and Wilma saw the absolute devastation to the crops of Farmer Jones. A swath of land over a football field length wide was completely denuded of all living matter. The totality of destruction was more than impressive. They met Jeb at the house adjacent to the barn.

Jeb approached the car with red eyes. "Are you the Professor?"

"Yes, I am," Basil said getting out of the car. "And this is my assistant Wilma, Doctor Wilma Fine."

A quick glance by Jeb brought a tentative smile to his face. From all appearances Wilma was indeed fine. The humor faded once he recalled what had happened to his father. "I am glad you are here," Jeb stammered. "But I don't think there is anything you can do."

"I understand your father was killed." Basil tried avoiding being awkward but it was impossible. "Could you show me exactly where it happened?"

"Sure. Follow me." Jeb turned, head hanging down, and walked away.

Basil and Wilma walked close behind, observing everything outside the affected zone was completely intact. Jeb stopped and pointed several yards into the denuded field. Basil continued forward to where he found shreds of clothing, a belt buckle, and part of a boot.

"Is this all that is left?"

Jeb nodded and turned his head away. Tears were streaming down his cheeks. Basil waved for Wilma to see for herself. Aside from a few bits and pieces there was little evidence Farmer Jones had ever been at that spot.

"Are you sure this is all that is left of your father?" Basil walked back to where Jeb was sobbing. "I know this is difficult for you, but insects don't devour people like this. Are you sure there wasn't an explosion of some sort; a gas tank blowing up?"

"No!" Jeb whipped around angrily. "I saw those bugs swallow my Pa up. He tried to run away but they caught him. Before I could do anything to help he was gone and those bugs just got up and went."

"Bugs don't eat people," Basil said slowly. "This is highly unusual if they did. Some ants and flies devour human flesh when they can, but it usually takes them days to complete the job and even then the bones are left behind. I don't see any evidence of bones anywhere."

"I saw what I saw! He is gone!"

"We don't doubt your word." Wilma stepped next to Jeb and put her hand on his shoulder. "We know your loss must be overwhelming."

"I don't know what you mean, but I can hardly stand it." Jeb sobbed wiping away the tears. "I am all alone now except for my dog."

"Do you mind if we take some pictures and take samples of soil and debris?" Wilma smiled sympathetically.

Jeb nodded slowly. "Take what you want."

Basil went to the car and got the field kit. He took pictures while Wilma gathered samples. When he picked up the belt buckle, he noticed it was pitted. He asked Jeb if he could take it with him to examine more closely. Jeb agreed without looking at him. All Jeb wanted was to go to bed. Maybe the nightmare would disappear when he woke up again.

It did not take long to finish the survey and sampling of the damages. Basil thanked Jeb and wished him well. He said that if there was anything of real importance he would call and send a written report. Jeb asked for the belt buckle back when they had finished examining it. Basil promised to return it in person.

For several minutes after leaving the farm, Basil and Wilma said nothing. Each was lost in conflicting thoughts. Nothing was typical, nothing made any sense. The biggest mystery was why there was no specimen of the insects. In a large swarm there would always be losses evidenced by carcasses left behind. The field was clean of any insects either as parts or carcasses. Also the consumption of massive quantities of vegetable matter would produce waste of which there was none grossly evident.

"I think we have a lot of work to do." Basil said absently. "I have never seen anything like this in twenty years."

"I agree." Wilma murmured.

"Next stop: the crash site."

The farm road gave way to outer suburbia. Wilma noticed a collection of emergency, fire and police vehicles on a side street. She did not have to say anything. Basil turned onto the street automatically.

"I wonder if this is related." Basil parked the car as close as he could. A policeman waved him to stay in the car. Basil produced his identification.

"This area is off-limits at the moment," the policeman said forcefully until he examined the identification. "Sorry, Professor, I have my orders not to let anyone in."

"I am investigating the effects a swarm of locusts have inflicted on our community." Basil smiled confidently. "I have been asked to examine every site that has been hit."

"This one has been hit for sure, but I can't let you in without authorization."

"Please call whoever is in charge."

The policeman used his radio. Permission for Basil and Wilma was immediately granted. The policeman apologized for any delay but he was only following orders. Basil replied no harm was done.

"Wilma, bring the kit." Basil got out of the car surveying the grounds. Everything appeared normal until he saw the house where the police and emergency crews gathered. The mailbox at the end of the driveway had the name West painted on it. Basil went directly to a man he recognized as being in charge.

"Excuse me, Captain, but it is it safe to go inside?"

"Are you the team from the University?"

"Yes, we are." Basil glanced back to assure himself Wilma was not far behind. "Is there anything you can tell us that will help in our investigation?"

The Captain looked from side to side as if looking for something. Basil followed his gaze. A policeman in plain clothes was waved over. "I believe Officer Ware can help you."

The officer extended his hand to Basil. "I know all about you, Professor. Some of your work has helped us solve cases."

"Glad to hear it." Basil shook his hand firmly. "What is going on here?"

"The West house has been totally trashed," Officer Ware began. "Several windows were broken in on several sides. As far as we can tell nothing has been stolen. The neighbors claim they heard a hum but saw nothing. People around here pretty much stay to themselves and don't watch each other. Whatever the hum came from was not seen by anyone we have talked to so far."

"What about Mister West?"

"We have not been able to locate him," Officer Ware continued. "According to his next-door neighbor, he never leaves without his car, but it is not in the garage. There is a car wreck down the street but we can't identify it yet. It is like someone poured acid on it."

"May I see the car?"

"Sure, I will take you to it."

A massive tangled of metal was a ways down the street. Wilma took pictures while Basil circled the wreckage. He made the immediate assumption that what happened to Farmer Jones also happened to Mister West. It was difficult to impossible to ascribe the damages to ordinary insects. Something extraordinary was clearly at work.

Basil crawled onto the wreckage where he thought the driver's side should be. He sifted through the debris and found a pair of glasses, a tie clip and one shoe. The similarity to what he saw at the farm was striking. He concluded Mister West must have tried to escape the swarm at his house. He managed to get his car out but had a collision. The swarm must have followed and devoured him. There was no other explanation that fit. Wilma agreed.

The inside of the house was almost unrecognizable. Furniture was in pieces, paint and wallpaper gone off the walls, woodwork and plaster missing in chunks. No human could do this amount of damage in such a short time. They thanked the Captain for his cooperation and left for the crash site.

"Did you find anything different from the farm?" Basil accelerated the car out onto the main street.

"I took a bunch of specimens but to tell you the truth there was nothing unusual about anything." Wilma watched Basil for his facial reaction. There was none.

"I don't think we are dealing with anything we have ever seen," Basil said evenly. "I have studied insects all my life and I can't believe they can cause the damage we have seen. I suspect there is an intelligent cause."

"You suspect terrorists?"

"I don't expect bugs; and it has been a while since the last terrorist attack in this country," Basil said slowly. "The enemy has gotten more cunning and devious with all the security we have now.

"But it doesn't make any sense," Wilma said quickly. "It looks like bugs then it doesn't; or maybe one is not connected to the other. Maybe terrorists are using the swarm to cover their covert activities."

"That is a possibility," Basil said thoughtfully. "It is as good a theory as any."

"The plane crash should help us sort out the evidence."

Basil finally smiled. It was the best possibility so far; he wondered where the swarm was at the moment.

On arrival at the crash site Basil and Wilma were granted access to the wreckage. There were investigators from the FAA and the Homeland Security Office everywhere. A smoldering fire was being doused with foam while lines of search parties combed the surrounding area for debris and bodies. The site in one word was ugly.

"Where do you want to start?" Wilma said.

Basil scanned the scene and finally pointed at the remains of the cockpit. "That is where I expect to find answers." His voice lacked conviction. The swarm in the crash of an airliner may only have been a coincidence. Insects do not bring down planes. Even if the engines scooped up a mass of them, unless the turbines were destroyed; they would still function well enough to land safely.

The cockpit was a tangle of metal and plastic. The bodies of the Captain and the Co-Pilot had already been mercifully removed. Wilma immediately went into picture taking mode until she noticed a black object wedged in the corner. She brought it to Basil's attention. Without touching it Basil examined it carefully.

"I think you found one of the culprits," Basil said scooping the object up into a specimen container. "Let's see if there are any more of these things around."

Knowing what to look for, they found numerous specimens. Each one was damaged but they were all alike. On initial view they appeared as typical insects: thorax, abdomen, compound eyes, mandibles, wings, and antennae. Although many of the legs were missing most had 6 plus another pair that acted like the anterior ones of a praying mantis. Unlike all the insects he was aware, there were other structures he had never seen in any other specimen.

"Let's get back to the lab," Basil said wearily. "Unless there is another site."

"I just spoke with the Weatherman who is tracking the swarm," Wilma said. "Since the plane crash, there has been no sign of it. It must be somewhere on the ground."

"Then there is nothing more we can do. Let's go back to the lab."

The ride to the University lab was a short one. Both were anxious to examine the specimens more closely; neither had any idea if they would come up with anything useful. Basil went straight to the coffee pot while Wilma prepared the first specimen on the stage of the operating microscope. The camera was set up with a monitor and recorder at the side. She could hardly wait to take the first look, but deferred to the seniority of Basil. Protocol was protocol.

Cup in hand Basil approached the microscope. "Have you taken a look?"

"Not yet." Wilma smiled. "I was tempted, but I think you should be first."

"I forgot." Basil shook his head. "Did you want coffee? There is a fresh pot."

"No, thank you. I am more interested in what we have here."

"Let's look at it together."

They sat on opposite sides looking into the dual sets of eyepieces. Each controlled their own focus. Basil zoomed in without expression. Wilma could hardly withhold her excitement.

"Hm." Basil moved the specimen around on the stage. He used a probe to turn it over. "This is strange indeed."

"What you mean?" Wilma was about to explode. It was obvious they were not looking at a normal insect. Basil could be frustrating at times.

"This is the most curious insect I have ever examined," Basil said flatly. "I am going to take this one apart."

As Basil began to separate the head from the thorax he noticed a flash of light. At first he thought it was his imagination except Wilma saw it also. He increased magnification and the light flashed again from a rod like appendage under the eyes. To his surprise he saw his dissecting probe had developed a small pit where the light hit.

"Damn." Basil muttered. "What is going on here?"

"Look at the probe." Wilma watched with growing excitement. "That flash is laser light. This thing has mastered quantum physics!"

"Impossible!" Basil grumbled. "This doesn't make any sense."

"Maybe it is not alive." Wilma held her breath.

Basil looked up from the microscope and looked directly at Wilma. He frowned slightly. "That is ridiculous. No one has the technology to manufacture one of these things; not to say countless thousands for a swarm."

391

"Let's take it completely apart," Wilma said firmly. "That is the only way to prove it one way or the other."

Basil stared back into his eyepiece and continued dissecting. It became immediately apparent the specimen was a mechanical device. The scale and sophistication of the internal mechanism was astounding.

"You are right," Basil admitted slowly. "This is an artificial device scaled down to insect dimensions. Whoever designed it has used insect physics to best advantage. We have been trying to do something like this for years but never were able to get down to this scale. If the enemy has developed this, we are in for a lot of trouble."

"The question is what enemy?" Wilma played the game well. "You assume the worst, but suppose there is another explanation."

"Such as?"

"These devices are not of terrestrial origin."

"An alien invasion?" Basil laughed. "Now your imagination has gotten the best of you. There is no such thing as aliens in our part of the universe."

"Are you so sure?" Wilma said flatly.

Basil thought for a moment. On the one hand the explanation seemed to fit, on the other, there was no real evidence. It was pure speculation.

"These are mechanical devices," Wilma said. "They could have come from a distance we would have a hard time imagining. Machines can exist and function forever."

"Not forever," Basil said slowly. "All machines have a mean–time to failure."

"Even so," Wilma continued. "It is still possible for machines to cross stellar distances and still function."

"True. But I still do not like the idea."

"It may be the only explanation we have. I think these things landed as part of an exploratory probe whose mission is to sample, analyze and transmit data home wherever that is. There may even be a mothership somewhere overhead."

"NASA or the military would have detected it." Basil said absently.

"They are monitoring thousands of objects in orbit what difference would one more make?" Wilma smiled. "Always better to hide in the crowd."

"You have a point there."

392

The telephone rang. Wilma answered. She listened intently, said goodbye, and hung up.

"Who is that?"

"The swarm has appeared again," Wilma said. "It is headed toward the downtown area. It should arrive in about fifteen minutes."

Basil looked at the clock on the wall. "There is not much we can do in so little time. Let's hope no one gets hurt."

The telephone rang again. Basil picked it up this time. The more he listened the more he frowned. He instructed the caller to put out a bulletin that everyone should avoid contact with the swarm. Best to tell the public they were dealing with killer bees which in a stretch was probably true. The swarm was deadly to human life.

Basil hung up the telephone. "We have to get downtown. I think it is important we see for ourselves how the swarm behaves. We will stay far enough away to be inconspicuous. No need putting ourselves at any greater risk."

The trip downtown was a mad dash down the interstate running through the heart of the city. On the approach to Town Hall Wilma was the first to spot the black cloud above the train station. The cloud was moving without dropping to the ground. Directly ahead in its path was the first skyscraper.

"If we stop on the next overpass we should have a perfect view," Wilma said.

"I would feel safer off the freeway," Basil said. "There is a parking garage off the next exit. I am sure we will have a better view from the top of there."

"You better get there quick or we are going to miss what is going to happen."

Getting into and to the roof of the garage was accomplished before the swarm made contact with the first tall building. The black cloud engulfed the building at the level it was flying. Windows broke and part of the cloud appeared sucked into the building. Basil shook his head; he knew whoever was in the path of these bugs would die. Only total evacuation from the path of the swarm would guarantee saving lives. The level of the building the swarm entered dissolved with exterior walls collapsing. The entire building shuddered and collapsed in a downward heap. Smoke and dust filled the air as the swarm moved to the next one.

"There has to be a way to stop them!" Wilma was horrified. "Is there anything we can do?"

393

"Wait! Watch." Basil pointed at a building which had a microwave transmitter. Wilma watched with him as a swarm passed into the microwave beam. The mass of the cloud was cleared of those individuals that passed through. They could see many of the swarm falling to the ground.

"Microwaves! That is the answer!" Wilma said excitedly. "We have a way to fight them!"

"Of course." Basil laughed. "They are nothing more than machines. Microwaves interfere with their electronics, shorting them out. A couple of sweeps with a strong enough microwave beam and the entire swarm will be toast. I have got to pass this on."

"Here, use my cell phone." Basil dialed the weather center while Wilma continued watching the black cloud regrouping after its losses. The cloud changed direction aiming toward the parking garage. Wilma prodded Basil who was intently talking on the telephone. When he would not respond she yanked the phone out of his hand.

"Hey, I didn't tell them how to it..." Basil stopped suddenly. He saw the swarm heading in their direction. "Oh my God!" Wilma had already started running for the car.

Before he could reach the car Basil was covered with bugs. He started screaming as he wildly tried to brush them off. Wilma tried to help but was soon confronted with having to get them off herself. The entire mass of the cloud covered both of them. Resistance was futile, escape was impossible. When both had ceased to move the swarm moved off in the original direction it had been heading. Where Basil and Wilma had been was a scattered collection of trash.

The swarm transmitted its latest collection of data to the mothership. So far there was no significant resistance. The planet was easily inhabitable with ample resources. A full report would be forthcoming once the globe had been encircled. Any problems would be dealt with liquidation as always.

Almost simultaneously, reports came in from around the world announcing the appearance of a rapidly moving solid body toward the Earth. The fact it was on a collision course created panic in the scientific community. If it were not for cooler heads in places of responsibility, a potentially bad situation would have been worse.

"When was the object first seen?"

"At approximately 1800."

"And when is the calculated time of interception?"

"The data is still being processed."

Doctor Amos Henry swung away from his monitor. For all intents and purposes the inevitable was about to happen and, as expected, no one was ready to do anything about it. He took the pencil in his hand, twirled it twice then broke it in two. Somehow that did not make him feel any better. He watched his graduate assistant Miss Jeri Townes working furiously at her computer station. If anyone could generate new ideas, she would. He could count on that.

Doctor Henry began speaking out loud to himself. "We have reviewed the star charts and photos from the last several months without finding any sign of object X. It is as if it has materialized from nowhere. Given its speed and direction we should have seen it much sooner. What is most amazing is its velocity. Aside from orbital measurements of planets in distant systems we have never seen anything free travel so fast.

"Perhaps it is not what we think it is." Jeri turned and faced him.

Momentarily nonplussed, he rubbed his eyes hoping to wake up from a bad dream. "I know you can think outside of the box, but don't you think that is a little too far?"

She smiled. "I have been watching the object carefully. It is definitely not moving as a ballistic projectile. I can detect what I think are course corrections. I think there is an intelligence directing it."

The telephone rang and he answered. When he hung up he silently went over to where she sat and put a hand on her left shoulder. She could not read his expression.

"What is it?"

He squeezed her shoulder slightly. "It seems your observations may be correct. I just received notice the object is a source of a signal that can only be a transmission."

"You mean from a spacecraft?"

"It appears so." He nodded solemnly then broke into a broad grin. "Just think, we are finally going to be visited by intelligent extraterrestrial life and it is going to happen in my lifetime!"

"I assume the transmission is being decoded." Jeri attempted a smile but was more interested in knowing more about the signal. "Is it possible for us to tune it in ourselves?"

"The signal is being directly fed into the Internet. Unfortunately, no one has been able to decipher it yet. I guess you want to try."

"You know me, Doctor Henry. I am always game for a real challenge. This is right up my alley."

"Then by all means have at it."

Although the velocity of the object slowed considerably, there was no change in the consensus it was on a collision course with the Earth. Quite unexpectedly the object veered off the plane of the ecliptic, tracing an arc bringing it over the North Pole upon arrival. Paradoxically the more intelligent behavior the object demonstrated the more concerned everyone became. A physical collision could well be imagined, but one of an extraterrestrial culture was inconceivable. There was no time to put together protocols of behavior, although there were a few attempts in the past. No one could conceive this was any type of invasion in spite of the persistent paranoia in the popular media; and the object came ever closer.

The signal from the object was streaming forth in digital format. There were repetitive parts and others not. When put through an audio amplifier the resulting sound was noise. There were parts of the signal suggestive of densely coded information which may have been a video transmission. There was not enough time to work over the de-encryption necessary to understand what was received.

Space telescopes picked up the object easily at all wavelengths. It was not evading detection. The closer it came, the more distinct its outline. For the most part it was circular with a high reflectivity. When Jeri first saw it on her monitor she remarked how similar it appeared to the classic flying saucer. Doctor Henry somewhat amused at the notion agreed. If it were not from the great distance and speed, the object would probably be thought of as a big practical joke.

The public was informed matter-of-factly of the approach of an alien spacecraft. Newspapers were quick to scream the flying saucer analogy. The public as a whole was mesmerized by the entire episode. Religious leaders took the opportunity to decry what their beliefs expected. The military from all nations joined in a massive exercise to prepare for a defense they hoped would not be necessary. Leaders around the world called for calm and patience even though there was no hint of any activity otherwise. The only noticeable reaction to the arrival of the object was a flurry of activity in the stock markets across the globe. There was a mix between those who invested in precious metals and those who sold out at all cost. Then there were those who took the opportunity to buy stocks at a bargain as prices fell. Daily life went on as usual but it was a rare individual who did not know what was about to happen. The age-old mystery of life elsewhere and what it looked like was soon to be answered. Everyone's camera was ready for the visitors.

"Can you make anything from the transmissions?" Doctor Henry leaned over Jeri squinting at the monitor.

"There is a lot of compact data being sent, that is all I can tell you." She pointed at the signal which was converted into a series of digital data covering the screen. "I hope whoever is sending this is also sending a hint as to how to translate it."

"If the laws of physics are immutable across the universe, there should be no problem. I suppose." Doctor Henry stood straight up and stretched his arms upward.

"There is a suggestion that the signal is being directed at us."

"Do you think they expect us to answer?"

"There is a group in California rebroadcasting the signal back to the object, but there has been no change in the original broadcast to us."

The room felt warm. He went to the thermostat and adjusted it lower. He saw an ant crawling across the floor. He wondered if he was to the aliens as he was to the ant. The thought brought a chill.

"Let us go back to the beginning." He sat next to her. "Can we possibly trace from where this object originally came?"

"I have already tried." She sighed. "It is impossible to trace its trajectory backward. I can only tell you when the object will arrive."

"Where is the impact site?"

"On its current course the North Pole, but I expect it will go into orbit before landing."

"Star systems like ours are so far and in between this could be a remote unoccupied exploratory vehicle. Any living creatures with lifespans similar to ours would have to hibernate, live generation after generation, or develop a type of travel faster than light. I seriously doubt there are living creatures aboard this craft." Doctor Henry took out his pipe and began sucking on it. "What do you think, Jeri?"

"I don't know what to think, sir." She smiled slightly. "But I hold anything is possible."

The object passed the moon in the blink of an eye and entered a polar orbit one hundred fifty miles above the surface. The transmissions from the alien spacecraft were intensified. Attempts to make contact with messages on all known wavelengths were unsuccessful. A partial success was interpreted when one of the Earth messages were incorporated into the alien transmissions. This meant the visitors were at least not deaf. The problem remained how to create an intelligent dialogue.

"With the aliens in polar orbit they will get a complete overview of the planet." Jeri stared intently at the monitor.

"I still don't believe there are living beings." He puffed. "The laws of physics cannot be violated and life does have its limits."

"There are still people who think the world is flat. I have a premonition we are in for a big surprise. I don't have anything to base it on. I just feel it."

"Premonition? We will see who is right, if and when the craft lands." He exhaled a puff of smoke.

The alien craft orbited without causing any interference in anything. The space station caught sight of it on one of its orbits. There were no identifying features. It lived up to its description as a flying saucer. In fact, it was noticed rotating. The long diameter of the saucer was equivalent to a full football field. Its thickness was at least five stories. Silvery white, spinning leisurely it was the epitome of sci-fi movie imagination.

With each orbit the alien transmissions contained more content from Earth transmissions. Doctor Henry concluded the aliens or their machine equivalent were hard at work trying to decipher our communications. If they were as advanced as they appeared, they would or should be the first to make proper contact. The answer came sooner than he expected.

"There are reports of energy bursts directed downward. I assume they are scanning the surface."

"Just like any automated probe." He smiled. "So far, there is no evidence of life aboard that thing up there."

"If we were to go to another world, would we land immediately or would we take the time to assess the most interesting and least dangerous site? I would think it would be the latter consideration. Consider our own Martian exploration. Almost always the orbiters preceded the landers."

"Yes, you have a valid point, but I still don't expect any surprises."

Jeri looked at Doctor Henry incredulously. An alien craft was orbiting the Earth for the first time and he was not expecting any surprises. She wondered what would really surprise him.

The alien craft made several orbital adjustments avoiding man-made satellites. The same repetitive signal came down over and over with a pause before beginning again. She concluded the transmission was a signal requiring a response. She suggested recording the signal and echoing it back. This produced a marked change in the character of the signal. The content was completely changed.

It was quickly observed the alien craft was most interested in the European continent. Each pass overhead brought intense bursts of electronic surveillance. Other continents were also scanned but not as intensely. There was something about Europe that was of interest.

Since the alien transmissions were unintelligible, scientists from across the globe sent keys of information hoping the aliens themselves could generate an understanding whereby they could communicate. There was a growing fear understanding was not what the aliens were after. One too many imaginative scenarios of hostile aliens made many feel uneasy the longer there was no contact. Unfortunately, there was nothing anyone could do.

For hours on end Jeri poured over the alien transmissions. There was little she could make of content until she hit upon the idea of trying to establish linkage based on the GPS system. The idea caught on and was passed to all monitoring stations. When the alien craft was overhead each station was to transmit its GPS coordinates. Within a short time the alien craft echoed the same coordinates exactly when it passed overhead. A pattern of understanding began.

Once it was clear the alien craft understood the GPS system, Jeri conferred online about the next step. She suggested each station transmit a set of coordinates inviting the visitors to land. What would entice them down was anyone's guess. When the Earth transmissions synchronized so did the alien response. Over several orbits the craft moved into position to descend to the preselected site.

"Doctor Henry!" She nearly shouted. "The alien craft is coming down!"

"Where is it heading?"

"Not where we suggested. It looks like it is destined for somewhere in Germany." She flipped through several screens of data. "I think it is heading to the Ruhr Valley."

"Pack up your things. Let's go!"

The alien craft did land in the Ruhr Valley where it was immediately cordoned off by the German army. Only scientists and dignitaries from all nations were allowed access to viewing platforms set up around the perimeter. The craft looked like a fried egg on the ground.

While Doctor Henry and Jeri flew across the Atlantic, military demolition experts ventured forth to examine the craft. To everyone's relief there was no radiation or excess heat. Even more boldly, the experts touched the craft. Nothing happened. Scientists were encouraged to venture toward the craft with their own special set of instruments. No one could detect any seams or openings anywhere.

By the time they arrived the landing site was a hive of activity. Whoever or whatever was inside the craft had not made any attempt at communication which led Doctor Henry to believe his assumption the craft was simply a mechanical probe was the correct one. Jeri however remained unconvinced. She felt her skin crawl when she faced the craft for the first time. She was convinced alien eyes were secretly staring out at her.

Without warning an opening appeared from which a mechanical device emerged walking on eight legs. The crowd of scientists rushed back to safety behind the military. There was an audible gasp of excitement as the device ambled spiderlike down the ramp and set foot on the ground. No one doubted this was a mechanical device. Several antennas and protuberances that look like cameras were present. The device was no larger than a small dog. If it contained aliens, they would of necessity be Lilliputian.

The opening closed behind the walking device as it put tubes from its body down into the ground. The device acted like a simple sampling probe. A designated soldier started out to the device but was stopped short when the device turned its attention on him. Unwilling to risk his life further he retreated back from where he came and the device focused its attention elsewhere.

The device changed position several times moving slowly toward the military perimeter. No one knew what to expect. Jeri watched intently, then without authorization broke through the perimeter dashing out to the device. Someone shouted stop but she ran up to the spot where the device was resting. At several yards away she stopped and examined it closely. Likewise the device noticed and focused on her. Neither made any moves toward each other. The crowds at the perimeter waited with bated breaths.

A faint hum started within the walking device. Jeri remained steadfast in her position. From the body was extended a long tube. She interpreted this as a sign of greeting and extended her own hand slowly toward it. Upon contact she felt a sharp sting. The tube quickly withdrew back in to its body. Where she had felt the sting was a drop of blood. Instinctively she put the cut to her mouth.

"Stop, don't do that!" Someone yelled from the perimeter.

A group of men rushed out to her. They wanted her back in safety, but she was reluctant to move. The device hummed softly.

"I am all right. I think it took a blood sample."

"Let the doctor look at you." One of the uniformed men said sternly. "You don't know what it did to you."

Jeri glanced back over her shoulder as she went behind the perimeter. Doctor Henry came up to her shaking his head. "That was a foolish thing to do young lady. You risked your life for nothing."

"I am not so sure. I think I have given them something to analyze. They now have a specimen of human DNA. The stick came as a surprise but I have experienced worse at my own doctor's office."

"I still don't like you taking unnecessary risks. There are too many unknowns."

"There may be a lot of unknowns but we are getting a few answers."

"Yes, damn few."

"Have patience."

After remaining stationary for over an hour the device walked around the perimeter. Everyone concluded it was surveying the crowd. Spectators and no few officials waved at

401

the device. Several clergymen attempted to break through the barriers without success. Until the intent of the aliens was fully known, no one was to take any chances. The military, contrary to all logic, continued to amass troops and weapons for any eventuality. The potential for an incident grew with each minute. The device disappeared back into the saucer as unexpectedly as it had appeared.

First contact with alien civilizations had been imagined since the beginning of the realization there were other worlds possible besides the Earth. The first search for extraterrestrial life was a combination of exploring the nearby planets, asteroids and moons in the solar system along with an intense electronic surveillance of the skies for hints of intelligent transmissions. The chance of finding an alien civilization was unlikely at best. The Earth was isolated in a remote part of the Milky Way with very distant neighbors. Rather than discovering aliens, most who discussed the subject logically suggested we would probably be found by them first. Indeed that was the case.

As the sun set, lights were placed to continuously illuminate the saucer. The military kept a close watch on all activity in and around the landing area. There were a few fanatics who tried to break through the perimeter, but they were easily restrained. Around midnight a group of men armed to the teeth with all sorts of automatic weapons demanded access to force the aliens to submit and show themselves. A scuffle ensued with a few bloody noses, but the authorities remained in full control. The unauthorized military group found themselves in jail awaiting arraignment.

The military provided tents and necessary services not only for itself but also officials and scientists. Into one of these tents Doctor Henry and Jeri found themselves on individual cots trying to get some sleep. However, the excitement was overbearing. It was impossible to sleep. Jeri found a cot where she could keep an eye on the saucer. She would close her eyes only to rapidly open them hoping she had not missed anything. The cut inflicted by the device was covered with a simple Band-Aid. It did not hurt. What was bothersome were the tests the doctors wanted to do. She had indignantly refused understanding she was responsible for herself.

After an uneventful night, the rapid onset of dawn was more than welcome. Jeri woke finding that she had actually slept three continuous hours. A quick glance at the saucer showed nothing had changed. She woke Doctor Henry who had actually slept most of the night. They went in search of coffee in a nearby tent. In spite of the little sleep Jeri had gotten, she felt quite alert and energized. A jolt of caffeine from the first cup of coffee made her even more so.

Daylight brought activity all around the perimeter. All the major networks put on their morning telecast with the saucer as the background. A representative from CNN cornered Jeri into an interview.

"You did a pretty heroic thing yesterday."

"Not really."

"You risked your life by approaching that machine and it attacked you."

Jeri glared at the interviewer. "That was clearly not an attack. I believe the device was only trying to get a biological sample to analyze."

"And why do you think that?"

"If life is based on chemistry, then an analysis would be the first order of events to classifying what that organism is composed. It is possible an advanced technological civilization can determine a lot from a single DNA sample which was actually taken for me."

"That is very interesting. Do you have any idea what these aliens look like?"

"I have nothing to base an opinion."

"But you just stated their chemistry may be based on DNA."

"No, I did not. I said they may be looking at my DNA. I have no idea of their chemistry or if it is any way like ours."

"One last question before we go to our commercial break. Is it possible you were injected with anything? How do you feel?"

"I think you have been watching too many B grade movies. I feel perfectly well except for the nonsense questions. Now if you will excuse me." Jeri turned away.

"Now back to our sponsor."

An opening appeared from which exited six devices exactly like the one from the previous day. They walked out and formed a corridor leading from the opening toward the perimeter. Two suited beings with helmets stood just inside the opening. A hush descended around the perimeter.

From where Jeri stood she saw the two beings appeared completely humanoid in shape and relative size: two arms, two legs, and one head. She assumed they wore enclosed suits either

403

because oxygen was not their primary respiratory gas or they were protection against potential Earthly pathogens. One alien was slightly taller than the other. The taller stepped forward onto a flat platform in front of the opening. It turned its head scanning the crowd. It stopped when it noticed Jeri and pointed directly at her.

For an instant Jeri wished she could vanish. Her heart raced faster than ever before. She turned to Doctor Henry who stood beside her. He was as shocked as she was. The alien waved in the unmistakable way to come forward. Jeri hesitated. She was not afraid, but she was not sure this was the most appropriate action on her part. The media rushed to her side. Before anyone could ask her a question she started walking slowly toward the saucer between the stationary devices. No one dared follow. The alien continued encouraging her forward.

"Be careful!" Doctor Henry finally recovered his voice.

"I will be all right." Jeri waved back. "Looks like I have been selected."

"Be careful!"

The crowd held its collective breath as Jeri passed between the devices which swiveled their eyes as she passed. She climbed up the sloping ramp toward the platform where the aliens waited. She stopped, looked back and waved assurance she was okay. She took a deep breath and continued upward.

Upon reaching the platform she approached the alien who she assumed was the leader. She raised her right hand in greeting. The alien crossed its arms and bowed slightly forward. Jeri immediately returned the same. Close-up she noticed the alien had a hand with four fingers and an opposable thumb.

"Welcome to Earth." Jeri attempted a toothy smile.

The alien remain motionless.

"How are we ever going to speak to each other?" She started to turn away.

"Welcome to Earth. How are we ever going to speak to each other?"

She jerked back to face the alien. "You spoke! Do you understand me?"

"You spoke. Do you understand me?"

"I guess not. All you are doing is parroting what I say."

"I guess not. All you are doing is parroting what I say."

"This is frustrating. I need help."

"This is frustrating. I need help."

Jeri shouted to Doctor Henry to join her with the aliens. Without any reluctance on his part or any resistance from the aliens he was by her side. She conferred with him about the problem of communication while the aliens listened impassively.

"I am not a linguist but perhaps we can communicate with scientific concepts." Doctor Henry kept his eyes on the aliens as he spoke.

"And how do you propose that?" Jeri smiled at his discomfiture.

"We need to confer with experts. I don't know what else to do."

"Except at the moment we are the first to humans to make contact with an extraterrestrial visitor. I think we are obligated to at least try to communicate…"

"Yes, try."

Jeri's heart skipped a beat. They both looked at the closest alien. It had obviously understood and spoken. Jeri stepped closer to the alien who stood at least a half foot taller than her. "Did you actually speak?"

"Yes, I did." The alien crossed its arms and bent forward. "Blind silence is a test."

"Why have you not communicated with us sooner?" Jeri crossed her arms and bent forward exactly as the alien had.

"In our approach to your star system we send out signals for which we received no reply. Instead we noticed unfamiliar transmissions which we took time to study. Through those various transmissions we learned how to best communicate with you, but not until the appropriate time."

"What did you expect to find here?" Jeri pressed onward. She wanted to know more.

"Actually we are not unfamiliar with this world. It is a planet that contains all the elements necessary for advanced intelligent life. We chose it for that purpose."

"I am confused. What do you mean?" Jeri pulled Doctor Henry up beside her.

"Life occurs throughout the universe quite predictably with few local variations. Intelligence to direct that life is best transported from world to world. Many millennia ago we deposited a colony here to create a technological civilization. We left them with everything they needed to survive. The lack of response to our signal meant the memory of that colony was lost or destroyed.

"We have myths and legends of advanced civilizations that have been destroyed by cataclysms. Perhaps one of those destroyed your colony."

"We surmised that might have happened especially after testing your biological matrix."

"You mean my DNA."

"Yes, your DNA as you call it. There is no trace of our former colonists in you."

"Our species have evolved over millions of years on this planet. We have developed technology on our own or did we?"

"If you had the benefit of our science and technology you would be flying between the stars as we do. There is no doubt all our efforts here were lost in the past. The reason for that is unexplainable to us. However, we welcome you to join us as an intelligent race of beings."

"How is it possible for an advanced civilization like yours to have failed to produce a viable self-sustaining colony? That prospect seems inconceivable." Doctor Henry found his voice.

"Each colony is provided only the basics to get started. It is impractical to transport technology and materials across the vast distances of space. Books, manuals of instructions are the best and easiest to bring to a new world. Here, with resources so readily available, we never thought getting started would be a real problem."

"But something did happen." Doctor Henry looked back at the perimeter crowd. "There are billions of human beings on this planet with more being born every day."

"In the competition to survive your species won on this world." There was a hint of sadness in the alien's voice.

"Perhaps disease destroyed your colony." Jeri pointed at the alien's helmet. "I see you protect yourself against our atmosphere."

"Wait!" Doctor Henry squeezed her arm. "Are you implying you are not human? If not, what are you?"

The head alien turned to its associate. The associate stepped forward so they stood side-by-side. Each one loosened the fitting securing their helmets. Together they lifted them off.

"We are human," the first alien said.

"But not the same species," the other said.

Doctor Henry stepped backward while Jeri threw her hands to her mouth and gasped. The two aliens were indeed human with two eyes, nose, ears and mouth. The difference was quite apparent: sloping for head, bony brow, wide set eyes, broad nose. Recessive chin.

"I can't believe this." Doctor Henry shook his head. "I can't. This is not possible."

"They are Neanderthals!"

Forbidden

There was no mistake, the planet below was Altair IV. The problem was it had been reported totally destroyed by a previous mission. Yet there it was totally intact as it had been originally described by the first explorers of the Altair system.

The Captain of the Arcturus examined the images crosschecking with data in the archives. There was a report a research team had come to this lone planet many years ago. The last mission here had found only two survivors only one of which returned home with a robot created from the technology found on the planet.

"What do you make of it?"

The chief science officer rubbed his chin. "Perhaps the planet reconstituted itself. There has been plenty of time since anyone has been out here."

"What about you, Sara? Any thoughts?"

"Captain, I'm sure there is a logical explanation. Unless the report was falsified."

"I trained with a crew member of the last mission. I have no reason to doubt the veracity of the report."

"Captain, I detect a large underground object."

"How big?"

"It's twenty miles by twenty miles by twenty miles."

"Is there anything else?"

"Nothing."

"The report contains nothing to describe the object."

"I'll bet the survivor could tell us all about the planet," Sara said slowly as she watched the Captain's face. From the beginning of the mission she had subtly attempted to get his attention, but James was resistant. He was married to his profession as fanatically as Ahab was to his white whale. Science officer Peter was available; she could see it in his eyes, yet for her there was no attraction.

"The records state that both the robot and survivor disappeared shortly after returning home," Peter said. "The Captain and crew of the rescuing ship were lost in an unfortunate accident."

"In other words, we're on our own."

"I'm afraid so, Captain."

409

"We must land and investigate that object. It may provide the answers we need," James said.

"I found a report from the captain of that last mission," Sara said. "He says the exploration team found evidence of an extinct civilization called the Krell."

"Is there anything else?" James said.

"Only that the object below is the last relic of the Krell," Sara said.

The Arcturus landed within a hundred yards of the object. There was no evidence showing above the surface except for a dwelling in the style of past exploration teams. A cursory examination confirmed it was the base habitation of a Doctor Morbius. A tunnel led down to the object from the habitation.

The Captain, Peter and Sara left the Arcturus with instructions to the remaining crew to depart if anything happened to them. The tunnel led to a solid door of the metal they had never seen. The door swung open to the touch. They were not prepared for what was inside.

"What is this?" Sara gasped.

"It's a big machine." Peter stared at the flashes of arcing electricity.

James said nothing. There was something not right about the scene. He walked deeper into the machine without hesitation.

"What does it do?" Sara said. "Who maintains it?"

"Nothing and no one," Peter said softly. "The Krell are long gone."

"Let's go back to the lab. We have to find Morbius' notes. This is too big of a find not to investigate thoroughly." James took the lead.

The inside of the Krell machine was on a scale beyond human imagination. Morbius' lab helped put everything into a more human perspective. The problem was finding all the research files. None were found.

"We're back to zero," Peter said. "Where do we start?"

"There have to be records," Sara said. "I'll dig deeper. Nothing this big or important is kept secret."

"Unless it was meant to be kept a secret," James said.

"There's an interesting device over here." Sara pointed. "It looks like some sort of cephalic probes attached to a gauge."

"Try it on for size." Peter laughed.

"Be careful. We don't know what we're dealing with," James said.

The cephalic probes were obviously designed for a larger cranium. The instant Sara put the probes to her scalp the gauge began to rise. She felt a surge of lucidness. It was an intensely pleasurable feeling. The gauge rose to a point stopped momentarily and slowly continued to rise.

"Stop. Take it off," James said loudly.

Reluctantly Sara removed the probes.

"Are you all right?" Peter said. "You look sorta strange."

"I'm fine." Sara looked around the lab. "For some reason I have a better idea about what this is all about. This is a teaching machine. I'm sure of it. I need to continue."

"Not so fast, Sara," James said flatly. "This is alien technology. We have no idea what effects it has on us."

"I have an idea what the big machine is all about," Sara said. "It's the Krell's last project."

"How do you know?" James said.

Rubbing her temples with eyes closed Sara grimaced. There was a faint voice she could not understand.

"Sara, what's the matter?" Peter stepped forward and held her shoulders. "Are you all right?"

"Just a little migraine. I'll be okay."

James looked at the machine Sara used. "Maybe that's not as safe as it appears. There are too many things we don't know."

"Look, I feel better already. The migraine is gone." Sara held up her hands and smiled. "I know that machine is the key to everything."

"The big machine or little one?" Peter said. He was not convinced as Sara.

"Both," Sara said. "The small machine is the key to the big one."

"How can that be?" James said.

"In the short time I had the head probes on, I felt my awareness expanding. It was as if I were getting smarter. Not only was I able to see things clearer, there was a voice telling me something I was unable to understand. In fact, the voice is still ringing in my head."

"I want you to stay away from that machine until we can be sure it's harmless." James said firmly. "We need to exercise caution. This may be an elaborate trap."

"A trap?" Peter shook his head.

"There is something about this place that doesn't feel right," James said flatly. "We sleep in the ship tonight. In the

411

morning we will go over everything until we find out what is really going on here."

In the Arcturus, Sara turned out the light and closed her eyes. The voice she had heard had long disappeared. She wondered if she was simply responding to stress. All her testing for joining the service showed she had a high tolerance for stress. The Krell brain machine as she called it was clearly the key. The men always hated to be overshadowed by an intelligent woman. Her two hundred ten IQ was way above any of the men. The captain himself only had an IQ of one hundred forty-five. Suddenly an idea occurred that needed instant exploration. She threw back the covers and turned on the light. At her personal computer terminal she pulled up the IQ testing program. She took a diagnostic test equivalent to her level. The result proved puzzling. The readout stated a perfect test score at a level above two hundred fifty. Impossible, Sara thought and took the test again. The result was the same. Still in disbelief she took a third and a fourth test with the same results. The only conclusion was the Krell brain machine had amplified her intelligence. There was no doubt she had to use the machine again. Peter would be no problem; it would be the Captain who would prevent it.

Outside her room the control deck was empty. The Arcturus was on automatic security. She entered her password and exited the ship. The lab was exactly as she had left it. A shiver ran down her spine. It was almost too quiet. The brain machine seemed to call out to her. Without hesitation she sat at the machine and put the scalp probes against her head. Instantly she felt a flow of ideas sluice through her mind and the voice returned.

They found her in the morning lying on the floor of the lab. It was obvious to James she had disobeyed his order. Peter was less concerned of the disobedience than her physical welfare. He was unable to rouse her.

"Sara, wake-up," Peter said loudly. "Please wake-up."

James turned away. He stared at the Krell machine. "I thought she was smarter than this," he muttered.

"I don't think she is in any immediate danger," Peter said. "Pulse and blood pressure are strong and stable."

"She came in here and used this machine," James said. "We have no idea what it has done to her mind."

"I don't detect any neurological damage," Peter said. "Of course, I can't wake her up."

412

"I wonder if she responds to pain." James smiled without mirth. He leaned over her inert body and reached to tweak her right nipple.

Peter knocked his hand away. "Are you crazy?"

James stepped back. "You haven't tested for deep pain. I'm only trying to help."

Sara's eyes snapped open. She slowly got up as Peter offered his help. She pushed him away scanning the lab. "What happened?"

"We found you unconscious," Peter said. "Are you okay?"

"I'm fine." Sara turned to James. "There is more to this place than you can possibly imagine. I'm beginning to understand it."

"You are out here against orders," James said slowly. "I cannot afford to lose anyone to unnecessary risks. Anything we do here must be coordinated as a team."

"James, I'm only trying to help."

"I don't care. I expect you to follow orders."

"The brain machine will give us all the answers. Everything is becoming clear to me."

"Brain machine?" Peter said. "What brain machine?"

Sara pointed. "I've boosted my IQ up into the stars with that. I've tested myself. I know."

The three gathered around the machine. James sat down and placed the probes against his own scalp. The needle of the gauge rose less than half of what Sara had been able to do. He took off the probes and stood up. "I don't feel any smarter," he said.

"It's a function of how long you use a machine," Sara said. "The first time I had a headache afterwards. The next time was easier. Even after the short time you sat there I'm sure you gained intelligence."

"So, it's a glorified instant teaching machine," James said. "What relationship does this have to the big machine?"

"I understand there is a connection but it eludes me at the moment. I need more time to boost my intelligence."

"I think you should take it slow," Peter interjected. "You don't know what the long-term effects will be."

"The risks are all mine. Look at me. Do I look any different?"

"Peter is right. We need to be careful. We cannot afford to lose you."

413

"I don't want to lose me either."

"Wait a day before you try it again."

"I don't like it, but I agree."

"In the meantime, let's try to find out as much as possible. Our records call this place the forbidden planet. There must be a reason for," James said without inflection. "We will do a systematic search of this lab and the big machine."

By late afternoon as Altair reached the distant horizon there was little evidence to solve the mystery of the planet. Sara had flashes of images which alone made no sense. The images were accompanied by a voice. That much she was sure. Each time she detected the voice she concentrated harder to understand what it was saying. As the voice intensified in volume and clarity she realized she was listening to a language she had never heard. The voice was certainly in her head; therefore, it must be there is a result of using the brain machine. The big question was the origin of the voice. Did the machine generate a hallucination or was she receiving some sort of mental transmission? If she told James or Peter, they would warn her to stay away from the machine indefinitely.

After the evening meal together in the ship Sara went directly to her bed. The day had been mentally exhausting and there was nothing obvious anywhere. The records of the previous mission yielded nothing after multiple readings. Upon lying down Sara realized she needed more time on the brain machine. For reasons she could not completely understand she was compelled to disobey orders. Solving the mystery of the planet and possibly their survival depended on it.

Halfway through the standard sleep cycle Sara returned to the lab. She made certain James and Peter were sound asleep. Without hesitation she sat and put the probes to her scalp. Instantly the machine came to life. The gauge rose to a far higher level than the last time. She felt her inner vision crystallizing to a new dimension of understanding. With eyes closed she concentrated on the mystery of the planet expecting an instant answer. There was none. The gauge continued to rise until she felt her head about to explode. Despite the pain she remained seated. Suddenly she lost consciousness.

"Sara, wake-up. Sara, wake-up."

She opened her eyes slowly. Standing in front of her was a being the likes she had never seen. Although clearly alien in appearance, it was pleasantly humanoid. The most outstanding feature was its large cranium. It appeared smiling at her.

414

"Who are you?" Sara said slowly.

"I am the Keeper," the being said. "I have been waiting for you to wake."

"Are you a Krell?"

"I am what is, was, and will be of the Krell. I have being but no substance."

"I don't understand. Are you just a delusion, a hallucination?"

"Not at all. I exist as you do but in a different set of coordinates."

"Why have you come to me? This doesn't make any sense. I don't understand anything."

"In time you will understand everything," the Keeper said. "Now that we have made contact I can instruct you."

"What about my companions."

"For the moment tell them nothing."

"Sara, there you are."

She turned as James and Peter entered the lab at a near run. She turned back to the Keeper but it had vanished. It must have been a hallucination.

"We've been worried about you," Peter said. "When I didn't see you at breakfast I looked in your room. I knew instantly where you had gone. You've been using the machine again."

"You've deliberately disobeyed my orders," James said sternly. "I should put you in closed custody for insubordination. What you have to say for yourself?"

"I'm guilty," Sara said slowly. "I am close to understanding what is going on here."

"Sara, there is nothing going on here," James snapped. "The problem is how we interact with each other."

"There was a suggestion of that from the last mission," Peter said carefully.

"There is more to it than that." Sara stepped toward James. "Please allow me some latitude to explore answers. Yes, I used the machine again. I'm near a breakthrough. Give me more time."

"I cannot allow you to put yourself at risk," James said.

"I accept all the responsibility." Sara felt more confident James was stating official policy rather than what he believed necessary. "So far the worst I have suffered is a headache."

"I'd like to boost my brainpower too," Peter said. "Maybe the two of us can figure out what's going on here."

415

"That I absolutely forbid," James said quickly. "We cannot afford two casualties in this mission. Let's get back to work."

"I didn't get much sleep," Sara said. "With your permission I'd like to go back to my room."

"Get as much rest as you need," James said. "We will meet this afternoon and discuss our findings."

Sara rushed back to her room. The moment she closed her eyes the Keeper appeared. Somehow she knew this was planned. "What is it you want to tell me?" She said. "Exactly who and what are you?"

"Open your eyes," the Keeper said.

Sara slowly opened her eyes and the Keeper stood next to her. The image in her head had materialized. She reached out and her hand touched the Keeper. It was solid. "You are real," she said softly.

"I am real as you want me to be. I am the Keeper."

"I don't really understand. You are the Keeper of what?"

"I am the Keeper of everything."

"That covers a lot. I still don't understand."

"This planet belongs to the Krell."

"Are you a Krell?"

"I am the Keeper."

"You're talking in circles. Are you a physical being or something else?"

"I am the Keeper."

"This is going nowhere." Sara muttered. "What are you the keeper of?"

"Everything," the Keeper said.

"Do you have anything to do with the big machine underground?"

"I am the Keeper."

Sara smiled. "Will you answer my questions?"

"As the Keeper I will answer and execute as directed."

"What is the purpose of the big machine?"

"The machine is the creator. All is granted from the creator."

"The creator?" Sara was puzzled. She was not sure if the Keeper was a genuine being or a projection of some program. The longer she interacted the more she felt the latter. She wished James and Peter were present. They suddenly appeared next to the keeper. She closed her eyes and reopened them. James and Peter remained motionless where they appeared.

416

"Sara, what do you want?" James said. "We have work to do."

"We can use your help," Peter said.

"You can't be here." Sara closed her eyes. She wished she were alone. When she opened her eyes James and Peter were gone. The Keeper remained where it had been. "That was not real. Was it?"

"The creator serves you," the Keeper said.

"This is incredible. The machine creates by mere thought."

"You are beginning to understand," the Keeper said.

"I detect a change in your voice. You are testing me." Sara stood facing the Keeper.

"All who came were tested. You have passed our scrutiny and will be admitted into our circle."

"What sort of test did I pass?"

"The key to the creator is the intellect. You boosted your own to allow access. Only those with extraordinary powers will see me. It has been a long time since that has happened. You also demonstrated you can use the creator in a positive way without causing harm."

"You mean creating James and Peter?" Sara said.

"Exactly. You created them and destroyed them without harming the originals."

"All this sounds God-like. What happened to the creators of the creator? Do they still exist?"

"I have the appearance of what the Krell once looked like when they were physical beings. The creator was their ultimate accomplishment. They made the machine to transfer thoughts into actual material objects. At first, there was a time of excesses until the baser thoughts were unleashed. Many died as evil swept across the planet. There were those, however, who recognized the danger early. They could not stop the carnage as they sought the next step in evolution. It was not enough to create by mere thought, they wanted immortality also. The remaining Krell transformed themselves into pure energy. It is their essence that powers the creator."

"You mean the Krell and the creator are one and the same?"

"You understand perfectly." The Keeper smiled. "The Krell are immortal."

"The machine is sentient."

417

"Actually, the sentient are the machine," the Keeper said.

"We could learn a lot from you," Sara said. "We could exchange ideas."

"The Krell have no needs or wants except you leave us as you found us."

"There will always be others after us. You cannot remain hidden forever; if you are truly sentient, you must want to interact with other sentient beings. How can you possibly grow without new input? Surely you cannot explore all possibilities on your own."

"Of all the visitors to our planet you are the first to directly communicate with us. Your concerns will be considered."

Images appeared in Sara's mind. At first, she thought she was hallucinating. She saw a robotic race land on the planet. They attempted to investigate the big machine. All attempts at communication were futile. The Krell erased the alien robots by totally annihilating them.

Another race of familiar beings landed. She recognized them coming from Sigma Tau III. They were a hostile reptilian race of beings. Rather than repulse them, the Krell sent them all to oblivion.

Picture after picture of visitors to the planet appeared. Sara marveled at the distinct clarity of what she saw. There was no lingering doubt the Krell were careful who they chose to examine their machine. The Krell acted like gods.

The face of Morbius appeared. He was part of the human expedition to initially explore the planet. He tapped into the power of the machine but was unable to make contact with the Krell. All of the original party were dead except his daughter when the last mission arrived. At that point Morbius unknowingly turned the power of the machine against his visitors. One of the visitors managed to boost his brainpower to understand what was happening. When Morbius discovered he was the problem, he decided to destroy the planet. In reality it was all an illusion. The Krell made it seem the planet exploded. Only a robot and Morbius' daughter were allowed to leave with the visitors.

"Why are you showing me all this?" Sara said. "What makes me so special?"

The Keeper remained mute.

418

"There is a reason behind all of this. I demand an answer. You have no right to keep it from me." She flushed with irritation.

"Sara, there you are."

She turned around and saw James and Peter at the doorway. The Keeper had vanished.

"We came to check on you," James said. "How are you feeling?"

"I'm fine," Sara said. "I've been doing a lot of thinking about this place. There is more to it than you can imagine."

"I have been unable to find any records of any sort," Peter said. "All we have are artifacts."

"You mean functional machines," Sara said. "Machines which we know little about."

"The race that built these machines was light years ahead of us in technology. It is hard to believe they vanished without exploring the universe. They certainly had the potential," James said. "I plan to explore the inner and outer planets of this system including all the moons and asteroids."

"Have you considered the possibility we are not alone?"

"Our sensors show no life forms of any kind. There is no water to speak of anywhere. This is just a dry rock. It's hard to believe the Krell would develop a highly advanced civilization then allow themselves to go extinct."

"I don't think they did," Sara said. "The Krell still exist."

"How can you be so sure? Have you seen one?" James raised his brow.

Sara closed her eyes. "This may sound strange to you but I have been in communication with the Keeper."

"Who is he Keeper?" James said quickly.

"The Keeper is a Krell projection from the machine," Sara said. "For reasons I am unable to understand I have been directly contacted."

"Are you sure it wasn't a hallucination?" Peter stepped to Sara and placed a hand on her shoulder. He lifted her chin with his other hand and stared into her face. She slowly opened her eyes.

"It's the truth," Sara said. "I have no other explanation."

The Keeper appeared behind James and Peter. Sara pointed but neither of the men saw anything. She began to doubt her own perceptions as the Keeper approached her.

"They cannot see me," the Keeper said. "When the time is right I will allow it."

Before Sara replied the men froze in place. "What have you done to them?"

"I have put them into suspension. They are unharmed. Their minds are not advanced enough to understand the importance of our meeting."

"I still don't know why you have selected me."

"The reason will become evident in time."

The Keeper vanished. James and Peter unfroze as if nothing had happened. Peter suggested they eat. Sara then realized she was nearly famished. Over lunch they discussed the exploration of the Altair system. Sara volunteered to remain on the planet and continue her investigation of the big machine. Quite to her surprise James agreed as did Peter.

At sunset the Arcturus ascended into the sky as Sara watched from the entrance to the Krell lab. She was left with enough supplies to survive indefinitely if necessary. Never had she felt totally alone as at this moment. She entered the lab and locked the door. The place was totally quiet until familiar music filled the room. Her favorite tune was playing from a jukebox which materialized against the far wall. She walked over to the jukebox and all her favorite music was displayed. The big Krell machine was granting her wishes.

"I have unlimited power," Sara said. "I can have anything I want." An ice cream cone appeared in her hand with three scoops of her favorite flavors covered with chocolate sprinkles.

"I can have anything." Sara laughed. "Anything and everything." She wondered where the Keeper was. Her questions vanished. While she could she planned to use the power she had to see what she could really do.

"This place is too dry," Sara said. She closed her eyes and imagined a tropical island surrounded by a vast blue ocean. When she opened her eyes she was still in the lab. Nothing had changed. She shook her head wondering if she had any power at all.

But the smiled reappeared and she closed her eyes again. This time she imagined an ideal man. Something she had dreamt about almost all her life. When she opened her eyes a man stood before her. She could not believe what she saw.

The man stands motionless with a slight smile. He wore clothes and she blinked the clothes away. One glance and she realized her wish was fulfilled. Another blink and the clothes reappear. The man does not notice what has happened. She slowly approached him. His eyes followed her movements. She extended a hand out and touched him.

"I am the man of your dreams," he said warmly. "Are you pleased?"

"This is fantastic," Sara said. "Yes, I am pleased."

"Anything you like I am prepared to do," he said.

"Let me catch my breath," Sara said. "This is too much."

"Call me Adam," he says.

"Of course, I was thinking that." Sara laughed. "Wait until James and Peter see you."

Adam does not respond.

"Let's step outside." Sara led the way out of the lab. As she opens the door a tropical breeze comes in. She stood in the doorway with mouth agape. A blue ocean surrounded the lab in every direction. The lab was on an island with palm trees. It was obvious her first wish had been fulfilled.

A sense of absolute power coursed through her body. She realized she could have anything she wanted and imagined a starship. It materialized on the beach.

"Adam, my name is Sara."

"I know," he said softly. "I know all your desires and how to please all of them."

"I want more than what you can give me. Physical pleasure is transitory. I want the ultimate in spiritual and mental pleasure."

"Think and it shall be yours. You have the power to do anything." It was the voice of the Keeper, but he was nowhere evident.

"I want a world of people of my own. I want to be Empress of it all. Everyone will bow down and worship me." Sara felt giddy with power. "No one will ever disrespect me again." She laughed wildly, closed her eyes and concentrated on the world she wanted.

In an instant Sara was unconscious. When she woke up she was on the Arcturus. Her head ached slightly. There is a light knock on the door before Peter enters.

"Where am I?" Sara said.

"You're safe on the Arcturus," Peter said. "We got your call and came back to get you. Just in time by the looks of it."

"What happened?"

"Altair IV exploded."

421

"Exploded?" She was confused. "How is it possible?"

"Altair IV is gone," Peter said flatly. "You were lucky to get off in time."

Sara shook her head. It did not make any sense. She closed her eyes and fell back against her pillow. It did not make any sense.

The big Krell machine integrated the new experiences. Every encounter with the humans brought new revelations about them. It was clear they were dangerous life forms not yet worthy of access to their power. Perhaps someday in the future they would be. In the meantime, the Krell consciousness would wait patiently for the next encounter; they were certain there would be a next time. These humans always wanted what was forbidden.

The Robot Returns

The robot remained inert while the humans worked around it. There was a secret mission to accomplish. If it were possible, the robot would have smiled.

The captain slowly turned to the science officer. "Set course to avoid intersection."

The view screen was a splash of uncountable stars. Regardless of his stoic demeanor the captain was always impressed with the grandeur of interstellar travel. Out here, away from the home planet, were marvels to be witnessed and savored. He took a shallow breath and exhaled.

"The Altair planetary system is nearby," the robot said.

"Your old home," the captain said, "Do I detect a little nostalgia?"

"I register no emotions. I simply report observable facts."

"I'm sure you do." The captain focused on the view screen. "How close are we to the energy source?"

"The energy source is twenty-three astrons from our current position," the robot said. "Unless you alter course, collision is inevitable."

"Thank you, Robby."

"My pleasure, sir."

The captain looked blankly at Robby, thought a moment and gave orders to head into the Altair system. Perhaps the robot had no feelings but it would be interesting to see its response. He smiled to himself. The history of the Altair system was a complete mystery. A first mission to the fourth planet discovered the remnants of an advanced ancient civilization over twenty thousand centuries old. Robby was the last remaining artifact. The planet exploded as a second mission left the surface. Years later a puzzling report intimated the planet was still intact only to explode a second time. Certainly pure nonsense, if the first report was to be believed. The presence of Robby and its account of what happened were held completely reliable. Investigation was in order.

"Captain, we are approaching the Altair periphery."

"Reduce speed."

The view screen shimmered briefly. Altair appeared as a bright speck in the center. Close examination brought several planets into view. The most obvious were the trio of gas giants out beyond the habitable zone.

"How many planets in this system?"

"Our scanners count eleven, sir," the navigator said.

"That can't be right. Count again'"

"Captain, I've checked several times. The count is correct. There are eleven planets total."

The captain turned to the robot. He wondered what it thought about the situation. "Head for the fourth planet."

The planet below, reported destroyed, was totally intact. There was little water and vast deserts covering the surface. A large cube shaped structure twenty by twenty by twenty miles was detected in the temperate zone.

"What do you think of this, Robby?" The captain pointed at the view screen.

"A contradiction of fact," Robby said.

"Is it possible Altair IV did not explode as you reported?"

"Sir, I have stated exactly what I witnessed. Certainly the captain, Adams of United Planets Cruiser C57D, testified that he saw the same as I reported to you."

"Except, there in front of us is your planet as it has been for eons. How can you possibly explain that?"

"Perhaps there is a reverse space-time continuum in this area."

"What do you mean?"

"Events in this sector move forward and backward in time."

"Is that possible?"

"Sir, the calculations indicate such a process is possible. This may be proof."

"The mathematics is beyond my comprehension. I'll leave it to the specialists." The captain paused. "What do you know about the big cube?"

"It is the Krell machine."

"What kind of machine?"

"Doctor Morbius spent a lot of time investigating the machine," Robby said, "He concluded it was part of a project which was never finished. He called it creation without instrumentation."

"Where did you come from?"

424

"Doctor Morbius made me."

"He was a philologist. How is that possible?"

"Doctor Morbius created me from Krell records he translated. I am a Krell machine."

The captain looked carefully at the robot. There was no emotion evident. A machine was a machine. Could a machine lie? Something critical was missing. Robby knew more than it was telling. On the other hand it was his own humanness that led him to suspect something amiss. He sighed. "Is it safe for us to land?"

"Yes." Robby said without hesitation.

They landed near a building of the original landing party. The cube was not far away buried underground. Robby led the way into the lab where he stated he was created by Morbius with Krell technology. The captain directed a team to search the lab.

"Robby, how do we enter the big machine?" the captain said.

"Follow me, sir."

The captain waved several armed men to follow. Although there was no evidence of any threat, he was prepared regardless. Robby had related the activities of Morbius, his construction, and the fate of the first colonists. The story of the planet being destroyed in one cataclysmic blast was certainly not true. Either the robot was lying or there was fault with its memory. He smelled danger in the possibilities.

A shuttle carried them from the lab to the cube. Inside the entrance the absolute quiet was broken by the incessant crackle and hum of energy. The captain was awed by the enormity of it.

"Robby, exactly what does this machine do? Where does it get all its energy?"

"Doctor Morbius said this was the Krell's final project. They attempted to build a device for creation without instrumentation. Doctor Morbius assumed the project was never completed before the Krell disappeared. The device is powered from the core of the planet."

"It's obvious the machine is doing something." The captain waved in a wide arc.

Robby remained silent.

In the lab there was no evidence Morbius or anyone else had been there for a long time. Outside there was a small graveyard with markers matching the participants from the first

425

mission. The captain considered leaving them alone until curiosity encouraged him to order the graves opened. When the graves were opened all the remains without exception were found in a state of disorder.

"Captain, all the bodies I've examined, so far, show evidence of excessive trauma. These people died violently," the doctor said.

The captain looked over at the robot. The robot was here when these people died. All I have to do is ask for answers. Except the captain knew he would not get any. The more he thought about it, the more uneasy he became. His first inclination was to abandon exploration and get as far away as possible but he resisted. It was foolish to rely on feelings.

"Exactly what sort of trauma?"

"There are multiple broken bones in all the skeletons. The remaining soft tissues are literally torn to shreds," the doctor said.

"Could it have been an explosion of some sort?"

"Possible, but not probable. The findings are consistent of an attack by some sort of beast with claws and teeth."

"Possibly humanoid?"

"Only if it had sharp claws and big teeth."

"This planet is devoid of animal life as you describe," the captain said. "There has to be another explanation."

"I think you have to ask Robby." The doctor pointed. "He must know what happened."

The captain waved Robby closer. He had misgivings about trust in this situation. Robby came quickly.

"You were here when these people died. Did you witness what happened?"

"I was with Morbius," Robby said.

"And then what?'

"I was ordered to clean up and bury everyone as they died."

"What killed them?"

"Monsters."

"Monsters?"

"Monsters from the id." The captain turned to the doctor. The doctor shrugged. Robby waited for the next question.

"The id is the seat of all the base passions such as hate, fear, lust and anger or so the theory goes," the doctor said. "It is only through our higher functions we keep the id under control."

"I don't understand." The captain faced Robby. "Can you explain what the doctor is talking about?"

"The brain is the seat of all higher functions in sentient beings," Robby began. "Those functions are layered in a hierarchy of priorities. At the lowest level there are those behaviors necessary for survival at the most elemental level. The most important functions are derived from the necessity of survival . . ."

"Hold on." The captain put up his palm. "I've heard enough. I think I remember enough of my college training."

"Perhaps monsters from the id refers to a release of inhibitions to the less civilized feelings so to speak," the doctor interjected.

"Okay, I understand what monsters from the id might be, but what does that have to do with what happened?"

"I was not a witness," Robby said, "I have no data to support an answer beyond what I have told you."

"Can you tell us anything about what is here in the laboratory?" The captain pointed at a device with a gauge and three probes. "What is that?"

"It is a device used to enhance mental output," Robby said.

"You mean it can make me smarter?" The captain laughed. "You must be mistaken."

"Doctor Morbius used it frequently," Robby said, "And so did that other doctor who came to rescue us."

"According to the records the doctor died," the doctor said, "The reason for his death was not given."

"The doctor attempted to boost his brain power beyond Morbius," Robby said, "He succeeded at the cost of his life."

"Why was Morbius able to use it safely and the doctor not?"

"Doctor Morbius told me he initially was knocked out on his first attempt. When he limited his time he gradually became accustomed to its power. He was not aware that the use of the Krell machine was through the mind."

"What is your earliest recollection?"

"I remember everything since activated by Morbius."

"Nothing else?"

"Nothing else."

Intuitively the captain felt the robot was not telling the truth. The record had stated Morbius had claimed Robby was a Krell toy, a mere child's thing. He wondered if others before him had even considered asking the right questions. Sentient life was found in all corners of the universe in all stages of evolution. The Krell had reached their maximum and disappeared. That did not seem logical for a supremely intelligent race of beings to simply vanish at the apex of their development. Unfortunately, the answer to that question might never be known.

"Captain." Engineer Bight entered the lab.

"What is it?"

"I've been examining the power room."

"And?"

"At first I thought all the power for the big machine was coming from the core of the planet, but it's not. There appears to be transmission of power from an extra-planetary source."

"Extra-planetary source?"

"The transmission of power is increasing. I can tell from the gauges."

"When did you first notice this?"

"I started examining the power room when we landed. The gauges were at a low level. Within hours the power levels began rising. So far I can't explain it."

The captain turned to the robot. "Robby, is there any reason for this?"

"Sir, I have no explanation for it."

Another lie. The captain and doctor reentered the big machine. Everywhere there was more activity than the first time they had entered. Something was happening. An explanation was necessary for the safety of the mission.

As Altair set on the horizon the captain ordered everyone back on the ship. He put a security watch on the robot. Although Robby had never done anything to prove itself untrustworthy, he felt it was in the best interest of the ship to err on the side of the home planet.

When Altair rose in the morning the two security men were found asleep next to Robby. The captain demanded an explanation of the breach in protocol. The men slowly admitted they had obtained alcohol and had drunk it to oblivion. Regardless, they swore Robby had remained in place the entire night. However, the ship's security records clearly showed the robot exiting and reentering during the middle of the night. Without comment the captain ordered extra kitchen duty for the men.

The captain went over the security records several times. Robby had left in a direction away from the lab and underground machine. He ordered a transport to follow Robby's tracks. The doctor, engineer Bight and three other crew members made up the investigating team along with the captain. Robby was left with the science team in the lab.

The tracks were easy to follow. They led across a dusty expanse of dry flat land toward an outcrop of large rocks. In the distance was a range of mountains. At the beginning of a rise near the rocks the captain ordered a stop. With two men he continued on foot to the top of the rise. Carved into the ground was a massive parabola with a pointed spire reaching upward in the exact center.

"What is it, captain?"

"It looks like one of those radio telescopes back home."

The captain said nothing. He estimated the diameter at several miles. The initial survey from orbit revealed no such structure. The immensity of the excavation meant an extraordinary force or forces were at work. Was it a coincidence that the robot had left and come this way or was this structure its construction for some unknown purpose? In either case the robot was concealing something. There was no longer any doubt.

Without explanation the captain ordered the crew back into the transport. Robby had to be questioned. Would it tell the truth? Machines should function only at the will of a human, or a Krell.

Sample measurements indicated a continuous flow of power into the structure. The connection with the surge in power and this structure was more than just coincidence. Collecting extra-planetary power was ancient technology back home, however, it was less than ideal in an atmosphere.

"Robby has disappeared, captain. We were examining those artifacts when it suddenly left without saying anything."

The captain scanned the lab with a scowl. "Find it immediately. I don't want it out of our sight. There may be danger here."

"What do you mean, captain?"

"Something strange is going on and Robby may be a part of it. Until we know exactly what it is, we have to be careful. Remember what happened to the first mission."

Robby entered the lab.

"Where have you been?" The captain stiffened

"I was in need of routine adjustment, sir. My functional capability was at a low level. I am now at full potential at your service."

"You left the ship without permission last night. Where did you go?"

Robby said nothing.

"Our security system has a record of your departure. Not only that, I took a team out to that structure out there." The captain pointed. "Do you have an explanation of what is going on here?"

"I cannot explain it, sir," Robby said "I apologize if I have caused any harm. Are the men recovered from the alcohol?"

"What else have you been up to?" The captain stepped closer to Robby. "That thing out there is buzzing with energy and the gauges here are showing increased power consumption. Are the two connected?"

"Obviously they are, sir," Robby said.

"Why?"

Robby remained silent.

The captain threw his hands in the air. "Talking to you is like talking to a wall. I wish I knew what you were thinking."

"My actions are from necessity only. I cannot act in any manner to harm a human sentient being," Robby said.

The captain turned away. He thought he heard an element of sarcasm in the statement. "I hope so." he muttered.

As Altair set on the horizon the captain ordered the ship secured. Absolutely no one or thing was to leave during the night. The robot was watched by teams of three men who changed watch every four hours. In the morning all teams reported the robot had not moved or spoken. The captain came to Robby. The robot stood exactly where it had been all night.

"Good morning, Robby."

Robby remained mute and inert.

Approaching slowly the captain wondered what Robby was thinking. Whenever he came near there was always some reaction. Now there was nothing. He touched the Krell metal body. It felt cool. Robby remained unresponsive.

"Robby, do you hear me?" the captain shouted.

Robby remained inert.

"Something is wrong. Where's Bight?"

"Here, sir."

"Find out what's wrong with Robby. It looks like it's been inactivated."

"There are many things about its function we don't understand," Bight said, "But all systems fail eventually."

430

"This is an inconvenient time for that to happen." The captain squinted. "I find it hard to believe it should happen right now."

"I'll do what I can."

The robot was disassembled. Every part was thoroughly examined before reassembly. At the conclusion Bight reported he had found nothing to explain the inert state. Every system was intact and functional.

"Put it in the lab," the captain said. "And keep a constant video monitor on it. I want to know the instant it reactivates."

"Sir, there is activity near here." A science officer pointed in the direction of the outside structure.

"What kind of activity?"

"There is a surge of energy."

"Meaning?"

"There is something consuming energy."

"Is the big machine responsible?"

"I don't think so," the science officer said. "The activity site is almost a hundred miles away."

"Take a team and investigate. I want a full report when you arrive."

Inwardly the captain was unsure of the best course of action. Too many things were going contrary to what was expected. Altair IV was scanned prior to landing and there was nothing except the big machine cube and the lab with its habitation quarters. Aside from some rudimentary plant life the planet appeared sterile. Yet in a few short days a giant structure receiving power had appeared and another area was showing signs of activity. The logical conclusion led to another sentient being or beings on the planet or Robby was responsible absurd as that sounded.

In the lab Robby stood watching the activities of the crew. Since time meant nothing, it was possible to wait for the ideal moment. In the interim it calculated the frequencies to deceive the video scanners. At the right time it transmitted a signal sending the video system into a continuous loop showing it still inert.

Getting out of the ship was easy. Sensors revealed the humans were on their way to the second site. Even if they saw it, they would not understand its purpose. He would wait until they left to resume construction. The final project would be finished in due time.

431

The science officer stood agape staring at the massive excavation. Within the depths appeared the skeleton of a structure more massive than the machine cube itself. Everywhere on the site was activity. Parts moved without sentient or mechanical mover. He called the captain. "Captain, you're not going to believe this."

"What is it?"

"This is a big construction site." The science officer chose his words carefully.

"Are there beings?"

"That's just it. The construction is proceeding by itself. I don't believe it, but it's happening."

"Are you absolutely sure?"

"Captain, I would stake my life on it. It's real."

"Stay where you are. I'm coming," the captain said.

"Be careful," the doctor said. "We can't afford to lose you."

"Don't worry. I've got to get to the bottom of this."

At the rim of the construction site the captain stood next to the engineer and science officer. Activity on the site had accelerated. Materials appeared from nowhere. Each part automatically went directly where it became incorporated into the growing structure.

"Do you have any idea what this is?" The captain pointed.

"I don't think it's a building," the science officer said slowly, "I see no evidence of supports into the ground."

"It's a starship!" Bight exploded. "It's a damn starship!"

"Are you sure?" the captain said slowly.

"I'm absolutely certain."

"I've never seen a starship this size," the science officer said. "The power requirements are beyond what is possible."

"It's obvious we are dealing with something that thinks otherwise," the captain said. "Whatever can do this can do whatever it wants."

"I'll get a survey," Bight said. "I suggest an orbital view for the whole project."

"Do it," the captain said quickly. "I have to get back to the ship. Robby is hiding something from us."

The robot was nowhere on the ship or in the lab. The security videos were found corrupted by a viral loop. A team was sent into the machine on the chance Robby had gone into it. The vastness of the interior was impossible to cover thoroughly. Only

432

a small fraction was searched before the captain ordered the team back into the lab. The team did not notice increased activity of the machine components.

When Altair set on the horizon the number of mysteries doubled and doubled again. Even in the absence of a definite threat the captain kept an extreme vigilance considering the options in the event of hostile actions against the crew or ship. He was certain Robby had all the answers. He wished he had the foresight to put a tracking device on the robot.

The entire crew was again kept inside the ship during the night. Security was doubly tightened. Robby did not return from wherever it had gone. The longer it was missing, the more definite the captain concluded it was at least involved if not responsible for what was happening on the planet. After all the years what did they really know about the robot? The archives described Robby as an important participant in multiple exploratory missions throughout the universe. It was an instrumental navigator in difficult situations especially around black holes. There was no obvious connection between its past record and current performance. The possibility of a malfunction seemed reasonable but unlikely. Robby was totally self-sufficient and capable of self-repair exactly like the big machine.

As soon as Altair emerged above the horizon the captain led the doctor and science officer into the lab. He volunteered himself to submit to a brain boost by the Krell machine. Both the doctor and science officer protested. Overruling their objections he used the machine for a short interval.

"How do you feel?" The doctor examined his pupils.

"My thinking is much less fuzzy," the captain said slowly.

"You look exhausted," the science officer said.

"I feel okay. Just a little tired. I need to try it again."

"Not so fast," the doctor said quickly. "I recommend a break. We can't afford to lose you in any way, even temporarily."

"Doctor's orders?" The captain smiled.

"Yes, doctor's orders."

"I'll come back later. First, a little nap."

The captain fell into a deep sleep and did not wake until the next day. The doctor hovered over his important patient. His vigil was without concern to himself; his own sleep was out of the question. He was relieved when the captain awoke without any complaints.

The second session with the brain boost went similar to the first. The physical side effects with extreme fatigue were no different; however the captain experienced a further clarity in his thinking. Sleep was welcome. When he woke he began making connections which should have been obvious.

"The Krell are still alive," the captain said, "I should have realized it before."

"What do you mean? There's no evidence of any life other than basic plants and us on the entire planet," the doctor said.

"All the activity we have seen has been directed by the Krell," the captain continued. "There is no other possible explanation. Somehow they have managed to hide from our sensors. As Robby was able to corrupt our security system, so they can do on a much larger scale."

"But they would have to be invisible," Bight said, "And that's impossible on the scale you're suggesting here."

"With a civilization as advanced as the Krell anything is possible. We have underestimated their true potential."

"Your thinking has been altered," the doctor said, "It's possible it has tapped into your imagination. You have to reconcile what you are thinking with known reality."

"You're right," the captain said, "I need more time on the brain boost. I know I can figure it out with enough brain power. Let me try it again."

"I advise against it." The doctor slowly shook his head. "We need you fully functional, especially now. We can't afford to have you incapacitated."

"Your words of caution are noted, but I must do this in the best interests of the mission. I need you to monitor me."

For the first minute the captain felt nothing. He closed his eyes trying to relax and it was impossible. He slowly felt a growing awareness of possibilities. Calculations he had attempted years ago became easily solvable. Connections between observations led to obvious conclusions. He became acutely aware of a new astuteness. As long as he felt well he would continue. There seemed no ill effects as time lapsed. He wondered how long he could continue. Then he lost consciousness.

"Captain, wake up."

The captain slowly opened his eyes. There was a moment of vertigo as the doctor came into focus. The doctor was leaning over him. He realized he was lying on a bed in the ship's

434

infirmary. His head ached and he groaned. "The Krell did not die." He took a breath. "Where's Robby?"

"Captain, stay where you are." The doctor gently pushed the captain back down on the bed. "I have to examine you."

The captain rolled off the other side of the bed away from the doctor. "I have no time for that. We have to find Robby. He knows the answer. I am certain of it."

"What answer?"

"What happened to the Krell?"

A search of the ship and review of the security videos showed nothing. Teams were sent out to both outside sites and found nothing. The lab was empty. Robby had either disappeared into the wilderness or had entered the depths of the machine. The captain led a team into the massive machine.

The Krell machine was more active than it had been observed before. What the machine was doing besides maintaining itself remained a complete mystery. There was something deliberate in its functions. Whether its actions were sinister or not was yet to be determined, however anything was possible. The immediate conclusion was a connection with the two outside sites. The captain was certain of it.

Several miles deep within the machine contact was lost with the ship. In spite of the potential danger and advice of his crew the captain continued to plunge deeper into the machine. The activity of the machine was evident but Robby, or any other being for that matter, was nowhere evident. The captain closed his eyes momentarily.

"We have to get out of here," the captain said, "Robby is waiting for me." He opened his eyes.

"How do you know?" the doctor said.

"I don't know for sure, but I felt it in my mind."

"Let me take a quick look into your eyes."

The captain brushed the doctor aside. "We have to go. We can't waste any time. We must get back to the ship immediately. Something is about to happen."

The team, with the captain in front, ran back to the entrance. When contact was reestablished with the control room of the ship the captain learned his presence was needed immediately. The giant ship under construction had launched itself upon completion. It was now in orbit. Robby had still not been found. However, much to everyone's relief there was no evident danger to the ship.

The captain took immediate command in the control room of the ship. All was in readiness for a rapid departure. He ordered all crew to return to their stations in preparation for lift-off. After a few mental calculations he had the orbital parameters of the giant ship entered into the guidance computer. The ship ascended from the surface of the planet without interference. As they lifted skyward they saw where the giant ship had been constructed was a large crater. The site of the parabola with the large antenna appeared unchanged.

Within minutes the giant ship loomed in the forward scanner. As they entered an interception orbit there was no alteration of course as they approached. The captain ordered communication with the giant ship. Signals on all bands were unsuccessful in raising a reply. The silence felt ominous to the crew yet the captain pressed forward undeterred. At a range of several miles a large hatch opened on the side of the giant ship. A bright light flashed from within and the navigation controls refused to respond. They slowly headed into the opening.

"Tractor beam," Bight said loudly, "We're being pulled in. Take evasive action."

"Take no action." The captain smiled slightly.

"That's crazy. You don't know what's waiting for us."

"No, that's an order," the captain said flatly, "We are about to get the answers we need."

"Shall I arm the crew?"

"Not necessary," the captain said.

Inside the massive ship the hatch closed. Escape was problematic at best, if not impossible. An atmosphere appeared. The captain led the doctor out to meet a lone figure waiting for them.

"I've been expecting you," Robby said.

"I know," the captain said, "Why didn't you tell us?"

"You were not in a position to understand."

"What's going on?" The doctor was puzzled.

Turning to the doctor the captain smiled. "The Krell did not die out," he said, "They transformed themselves into the machine. They still exist as immortal sentient beings."

"I don't believe it." The doctor shook his head. "What about Robby?"

"If I'm not mistaken." The captain turned back to Robby. "In front of us we have their leader."

"At your service, sir," Robby said.

436

Life!

After nearly a year of coasting across interplanetary space the Argo easily went into circular orbit one hundred forty miles above the red Martian surface. The automatic systems check engaged while the surface below was scanned. In the southern hemisphere a giant sandstorm showed signs of abating. Fortunately, the area involved was not included in the exploration itinerary.

On signal from Mission Control both landers with their rovers were powered up after no malfunctions or technical problems were detected. In polar orbit, the first lander headed toward the edge of the ice sheet of the North Pole. Upon safe landing, the second lander descended toward the South Pole. The first lander with its rover named Jason separated smoothly from the Argo. A brief burst of its retros quickly widened the distance between them. Within a short interval the lander encountered the upper atmosphere further slowing its descent. A large parachute was deployed and, as the velocity decreased, was followed with three even larger parachutes. Before making contact with the ground the lander separated from the parachutes and bounced several times along the Martian surface coming to a stop near a glistening patch of ice. The protective envelope opened with Jason upright in its carrier ready to roll out on its mission. As with so many similar missions in the past this disembarking was not done until confirmation from Earth. Although deploying Jason was delayed by all the hoopla and congratulations back home, the second lander carrying Medea was sent hurtling toward the South Pole. The second lander arrived as safely as the first. From the start the mission proceeded as expected.

The announcement the second lander had successfully alit on the Martian surface created another round of excited congratulations in Mission Control. Jason and Medea waited patiently for their instructions. They both transmitted panoramic pictures of their landing sites and there were no surprises.

With the flick of two switches in Mission Control the signal was sent for activation. Far from watchful eyes the rovers nimbly rolled off their landers onto the Martian surface. Unlike previous landers and rovers each had a nuclear power plant which avoided total reliance on solar power to recharge the

437

internal batteries. The mission was intended to cover as much Martian territory as feasible without having to worry about the power source. Jason would cover the northern pole while Medea covered the southern.

Getting the rovers to Mars and on the surface safely at first glance might appear the most difficult part of the mission. In reality the hard part was just beginning. Negotiating an uneven surface remotely was hazardous. Each rover had its separate team of earthbound controllers but they were separated by too many light minutes to be of effective use on a real-time basis. Therefore, each rover was equipped with the latest in artificial intelligence. Even so this would not prevent all potential disasters.

The Jason team ordered their rover out a short distance before venturing farther. The rover cameras were turned back on the lander. All was well. The lander had performed its duty without damage or mechanical failure. Over the coming months and years it would function as a relay station transmitting data back to Mission Control through Argo orbiting above.

The initial pictures were hardly different than those sent back by previous rovers. Each rover team settled in expecting long days ahead as the surrounding terrain was explored. The chance of a spectacular discovery was always possible, but no one really counted on it. Every day of movement would be business as usual.

On day 47 Jason fell into an underlying pit while venturing across a field of ice. The ice while appearing thick and stable was actually quite thin. It was an accident waiting to happen and it did. Fortunately, the pit was not deep nor was Jason damaged in any way. When news of the accident reached Mission Control Jason had nearly extracted itself on its own. There were painful minutes waiting for data from Jason. The Jason team conferred with the mission managers as to what had to be done to save Jason. Before any decision had to be made data was received that Jason had extricated itself from the pit and was on the move again. A round of cheering filled Mission Control and Jason was instructed to proceed more slowly across the ice. In the South, Medea crisscrossed ever larger areas without difficulty. It was summer and there was little ice recognizable as such. Medea's controllers asked for permission to reach the geographic pole and it was granted. The surface along the way was no different than anywhere else and reaching the pole was anti-climactic. There was nothing extraordinary about the location. In some ways Mars was a very boring place. From the pole, Medea was directed north toward the equator. There were areas of geologic interest along the way; however the search for life remained a distant frustrated dream. Nothing in any way looked promising. The only hope was Mars was big enough to hide life in some remote niche.

Analysis of the polar ice revealed little that was not expected. It contained both water and frozen carbon dioxide along with an assortment of dissolved inorganic salts. There were traces of organic molecules but nothing to raise the index of suspicion life was present. Unlike Medea, Jason was not sent to the geographic North Pole. Instead Jason kept near the edge of the ice sheet.

As spring came to the northern hemisphere the ice began to melt. Jason recorded the phenomenon sampling the melted ice before it disappeared by evaporation or into the ground. Multiple sets of duplicate data accumulated in Mission Control. The data were interesting but everyone wanted to find real Martians.

By the time winter set in at the South Pole Medea was well outside of any potential ice field. Several rocks were identified as possible diamonds along what appeared an ancient riverbed. The size of the stones would certainly make anyone rich beyond avarice. The best part of the discovery was the fact that diamonds are crystals of carbon which may have been derived from coal which may have been derived from organic life; or so the thinking went. Interest in the project suddenly increased to a new high. There was prospect of life after all.

Before Medea explored the area where the diamonds were located, a fierce sandstorm blew in unexpectedly. Unfortunately, Medea was totally exposed to the full brunt of the pelting sand as there was no natural shelter easily reachable in time. The only option was to remain in place until the storm cleared. Traveling in the blinding sand could lead to nothing but disaster. The lack of progress over the surface was not a waste of time. Medea simply recorded the parameters of the storm.

The biggest concern about any sandstorm was the potential damage of grit getting into the moving parts. Any sand that settled on the rover would shake off as it moved. The rover was grounded to prevent a buildup of static electricity that might cause particles of dirt to cling. Medea survived the storm relatively clean and was able to continue exploring the ancient river course.

439

Mission Control settled in for endless days of monotony. The longer the rovers explored, the less hopeful was anyone about any significant discovery. The data returned was of more interest to astro-geologists than astro-biologists. There were hopeful signs of life but nothing conclusive. However, Mars was a big planet that had barely been explored in spite of the numerous landings and orbiters.

Near the end of the first Martian year Jason came across a pair of unusual markings in the sand. For at least 10 yards the markings traveled exactly parallel to each other. There was a burst of excitement they might be artificial. Jason was sent to follow the markings which disappeared on the harder rocky surface in one direction and had been obliterated in the deeper sand in the other. The markings were a mystery at first, but were soon discounted as possible natural formations. Thirty Martian days later Jason came across a second set of markings. This time it was obvious they had been created by a non-natural process. At first it was concluded the markings were simply tracks Jason had made itself. The pattern was similar if not identical. Photos were measured and studied intensively in Mission Control. The markings could be old rover tracks except for the fact that the area they were found had not been previously explored.

The new set of markings remained clear enough to follow in either direction. Mission Control chose a direction and set Jason on its way. The markings went for miles without deviation. The longer Jason followed, the more convinced Mission Control was they were of another rover. The possibility of a Martian was totally discounted.

In the middle of the third day Jason found the origin of the markings. It was a platform similar to the one which had brought Jason to the surface. The presence of this lander came as a complete surprise to everyone and Mission Control. There was no record of any such lander by any known country. Discounting the initial appearance as similar to Earth craft, there was a titter that this might be an alien probe. All speculation was settled as Jason closed in on the lander. Close examination revealed Chinese characters written all over the craft.

"Well, I'll be damned!"

Murray standing next to the Chief whistled.

"Those sneaky so-and-so's have gone to Mars too!"

"It is not as if it is a complete surprise. We knew they were developing the technology."

The Chief turned and faced Murray. "Up to now aside from the European Space Agency we have been the only nation to land and explore Mars. All exploration data has been freely shared. This secret mission of theirs is totally unprecedented."

"What should we do?"

"There is nothing we can do except continue our mission. It will be up to the politicians to work out the ramifications of what this means." The Chief took a deep breath. "In the meantime, however, I think we should send Jason in search of our competitor. It might be fun to surprise them."

Murray immediately sent instructions for Jason to thoroughly examine the Chinese lander and surrounding site. At the completion of the survey it was to follow the tracks leading away. Before nightfall Jason had completed its task and was on its way to catch up to the Chinese rover. There was no clue as to how much of a head start the Chinese had.

"Chief, I think we have found the frequency the Chinese are working on," Murray said.

"Can you make out what is being transmitted?"

"Looks like everything is encrypted; it will take a while to decode, but we can do it."

"Has Argo located anything?"

"Unfortunately, no; we can't even locate ourselves from orbit. I doubt we will see the Chinese, but we will try."

The Chief smiled and chuckled to himself.

"What is funny?"

The Chief took a deep breath and composed himself. "It is funny; we go millions of miles out to another planet and instead of finding alien life resident to that world we find alien life resident to our own!"

"That is amusing but not really funny." Murray frowned. "The Chinese are every bit as human as we are."

"No offense intended. I wish all of us on this planet were not deliberate strangers to each other. Just imagine how much more science we could accomplish working together than independently."

"All is not lost. Maybe once we have caught up to the Chinese rover and discussed it with their controllers we can develop a broader exploration of the surface together. It would be foolish not to cooperate."

"That is only true in an ideal world and we hardly live in one."

441

A decision at the highest level of the government mandated keeping the discovery of the Chinese rover on Mars a secret. It would have been easier for Jason to catch up if its location were known. Fortunately, the tracks were clear in the Martian sand. Even when the markings disappeared within a short search Jason was able to pick them up again.

Along the way Jason sent back pictures noted as potential sites to return for closer examination. There was no time during the chase to explore, no matter how interesting the site appeared. As the sun set on the horizon of the eleventh day Jason sent back a picture with an object in the distance that could only be the Chinese rover. Since rules prohibited traveling at night, Jason went dormant into standby mode until dawn. Early the next morning Jason scanned the distant horizon where the Chinese rover should have been. There was nothing in view. It meant following the tracks until a visual sighting was made again. The tracks led to a large meteor crater, over the rim, and into it. Jason followed as fast as possible. Once atop the rim Jason scanned again. This time the Chinese rover was sighted climbing out of the crater on the opposite side. There was nothing to do but follow. It was now only a matter of time before they would come together.

Upon exiting the crater on the other side Jason saw the tracks but no sign of the rover. There were large rocks big enough for a rover to hide behind. The tracks pointed toward several hills in the distance. Jason diligently followed. Travel around the rocks was of necessity much slower. By nightfall there was still no sight of the secretive rover and Jason settled into another night of waiting.

As soon as the sun rose on the horizon Jason was moving in the direction of the elusive rover. There was no way of knowing whether the pursued knew it was being pursued. Traveling as fast as possible Jason was unable to catch up. Mission Control concluded the unidentified rover was deliberately running away from contact. Although the tracks remained clear in the red sand, the pursued rover stayed well out of sight the entire day.

On the morning of the second day of pursuit the tracks led to a stretch of rocky surface on which the tracks virtually disappeared. Any further attempt at following would have to be a calculated guess. For the most part the pursued rover was heading straight ahead with minor deviations other than to avoid dangerous obstacles. Based on that observation Mission Control

442

continued pushing in the same direction hoping the tracks would appear again in soft soil.

The traversed ground was the site of a huge impact crater where the soil had been fused by the blast. There were no evident tracks for several kilometers as the soil was densely packed. From time to time Jason stopped and scanned the horizon in all directions. By late afternoon the soil was soft enough to leave tracks, only there were none from the pursued. The mystery rover had successfully eluded its tail.

Murray scratched his head. The Chief studied the map projected on the big Central screen. The positions of Jason and Medea along with their traveled paths were accurately displayed. In addition was the location of the alleged Chinese lander and plotted tracks of its rover.

"Where is their rover going?" The Chief spoke to himself. "It seems heading in a straight line to the southeast. What is of interest in that direction?"

"There are lots of interesting places in that direction," Murray said. "Every place on Mars is virgin territory."

Shaking his head, the Chief turned and faced Murray. "I agree, but why have they been so secret about their space program. Space exploration should be an international effort. What are the Chinese to gain by going their own way?"

"National pride?"

"Perhaps..." The Chief nodded slowly. "They entered the space race late."

"The Chinese are a proud people," Murray said slowly. "By going alone they prove they are capable of mastering advanced technology themselves."

"Even so, I still wonder what their motives are."

"Has Washington made contact with the Chinese yet?"

"An inquiry has been made but so far there has been no official response." The Chief exhaled. "They are being as elusive as their rover up there." He pointed at the map.

The morning of the third day Jason was sent along the border of the soft and hard surfaces hoping to pick up the trail again. By midafternoon there was still no sign of any tracks. Mission Control decided to reverse direction and backtrack. Night set in before reaching the original point of departure along the border. Another night passed with nothing accomplished.

Early the morning of the fourth day Jason was beyond its starting point. A large outcrop of boulders obscured the view ahead and Jason was ordered to proceed carefully. Tracks were

443

found leading to the outcrop. The tracks were somewhat blurred but easily followed. No matter how long it took, Mission Control was going to catch up with the elusive prey. It was only a matter of time. Only an unforeseen accident would deter the object.

By the end of the day there was still no sign of the rover ahead. Mission Control considered allowing the chase to continue at night even though it violated established protocol. Jason was perfectly capable of navigating in the dark. Undecided as to the best course of action, Jason settled in place for the night.

There was no news from Washington. The Chinese were mute in response to questions posed about their discovered lander. Pictures transmitted by Jason were copied and sent by courier to the Chinese Embassy at the United Nations. The Chinese Ambassador accepted the photos without comment and stated he would refer the matter to his superiors.

The cat and mouse game continued into the fifth day. Jason followed the tracks easily. By noon the tracks led to a rocky area with boulders large enough to obscure the view or hide behind. In the interest of speed Jason took fewer precautions. This led to a near disastrous tumble over a sharp ridge. Fortunately, although the drop over the ridge was nearly three feet, Jason suffered little damage other than a scratch to its metal finish. Internal gyros maintained Jason upright in the fall. A quick check of systems confirmed all was well, except the tracks were lost. Jason was faced with relocating the tracks. Getting back on top of the ridge meant a long detour. A lesson learned from the incident, Mission Control instructed Jason to proceed according to slower established protocol. In another accident Jason might not be as lucky.

In the south Medea made progress exploring the ancient riverbed. There were definite signs of water flow across the Martian surface at one time. It would have been nice to have found a shell to prove life existed. The riverbed led to a flat rocky plain. Medea explored one bank then the other. At the time of Jason's accident Medea found a series of holes in the rocks which reminded everyone in Mission Control of fossilized footprints. The discovery was treated as too good to be true. There had to be a logical explanation for the holes, but the longer they examined the holes the more they look like one or more creatures had walked across this area. There were examples of such footprints in rocks back on Earth.

444

"It looks like Medea has done it!" Murray beamed. "We have found life at last!"

The Chief shook his head. "Don't be so sure. We have to be absolutely certain before we make a public announcement. Sure those holes look like fossilized footprints, but they could also be the result of a natural process; maybe a set of meteors spraying the area in that pattern."

"You may have your reservations, but I am going to put my money on Martian life. Just wait and see!"

"The only other alien life on Mars is that damn Chinese rover we are chasing. That is the only thing I can be certain."

"What do we do once we catch up to the rover? Do we shake probes?"

The Chief glared at Murray. "How the heck do I know? We have to wait instructions from Washington."

The Martian night found Jason trying to find a way back to the top of the ridge. There were spots that appeared promising but the soft crumbling slopes would not hold either weight or traction. For another night Jason settled into standby mode while Mission Control planned what to do for the next day. The choice was to continue the search for the rover or abandon and return to its own exploration.

At dawn Jason powered up after running through its onboard checklist. Before moving, its camera made a panoramic sweep. Stationed barely ten yards away was another rover with its own camera pointed at Jason. Images were immediately transmitted to Argo and from there relayed to Mission Control. Neither rover moved.

"Look at this!" Murray nearly yelled. "That rover snuck up on us during the night. Our prey has found us."

"Now I wonder if the Chinese will admit to being on Mars with their rover." The Chief smiled. "There is no denying this picture. Make copies and send them to Washington."

Copies were made and sent immediately. Without delay the evidence went to the Chinese Ambassador who received it with the same deference as those of the lander. He assured the American delegation a formal response would be forthcoming.

Although the strange rover facing Jason was similar in design, there were significant differences. There were eight large tires instead of six, two mechanical arms, three cameras and half dozen antennae. With the additional parts the rover was noticeably larger. Jason was instructed to approach. As it did the stranger remained motionless. It was assumed it was awaiting instructions from its controllers.

The closer Jason approached, the easier it was to visualize details on the strange rover. Unlike the lander, this rover had no Chinese characters printed anywhere. There were sets of symbols that seemed to mean nothing. It was assumed they were part of a technical engineering code. Jason stopped within reach of its mechanical arm. Further photos were sent back of close-up detail. These were examined closely in Mission Control. The question was what to do next.

Without any forewarning of systems failure the signal was lost from Jason. All efforts in reestablishing contact were fruitless. A call was made to the Chinese Ambassador. He offered no response as he had not been instructed from his superiors. However, in view of loss of contact with the American rover he promised to investigate further for the answers requested.

"What has gone wrong?" Murray stared at the blank screen. "Every system reads normal."

"I know." The Chief sighed. "Something strange is going on. Our friends the Chinese are not being open enough for this. It is possible their rover damaged ours."

"That would be an act of war." Murray gasped.

"Not necessarily." The Chief shook his head. "We are dealing with machines working independent of human control. Even with AI, mistakes happen. I want to give the situation the benefit of the doubt."

An hour after the signal was lost from Jason, the Chinese Ambassador announced his country had indeed successfully launched and landed a rover on Mars. According to reports from their scientists the rover was performing spectacularly. The first picture of the lander sent by Jason was confirmed to be the one sent by China, but the last picture was not.

"What do you mean that is not the Chinese rover?" The Chief was speechless.

"That is what the Chinese say," Murray replied. "They deny a rover of that configuration. In fact I now have a picture of what it should look like." He showed it to the Chief.

"Then who the heck is out there?" The Chief became excited. "Get Medea to Jason. We have got to find out what has happened to Jason."

"But, Chief, it will take months to get Medea up north. The Chinese are our only other hope."

The Chinese were more than willing to assist in finding out what happened to Jason especially in light of the fact there was an unknown rover involved. To be acknowledged for their technological achievement and recognized as an equal in exploration paved the way for closer cooperation.

Data was exchanged with Chinese Mission Control. The Chinese rover was less than eight days trek from the last known position of Jason. By accurately finding Jason the Chinese further demonstrated their technological prowess. The American team was duly impressed.

The Chinese rover found Jason at its exact last known location. The strange rover was nowhere around. Images were sent directly back to Mission Control as a courtesy from the Chinese. The site that greeted them raised more questions than answers. Jason had been taken apart.

"Holy smoke!" Murray shouted.

The Chief stared at the picture and slowly smiled. "I don't think there is any question about it now, boys. We are definitely not alone anymore!"

Several kilometers from where Jason and the Chinese rover stood another rover entered the cargo bay of its mothership. Liftoff was unobserved by anyone as data was sent home to the mother planet. Although the fourth planet from the star had at first not appeared promising, Advanced Technology had been discovered which made further exploration indicated. It would just be a matter of time and more resources. Life was not limited to the home planet and that was now a fact.

The bomb went off barely two thousand feet above the target. A bright flash followed by loud burst signaled the detonation of a neutron bomb. For several miles in an exact circle neutrons penetrated everything. Anything living was dead or on its way to dying quickly. Aside from some minor concussion damage over the detonation site nothing else was visibly disturbed. War had changed its face: kill the people and save the cities. To someone it made sense, but war was war regardless. In the end there would always be losers on both sides.

"Another explosion..."

"I see it." Nick adjusted the satellite view for a closer look.

"When is this going to stop?"

Nick turned to Mike, his assistant, shaking his head. "It's hard to cure stupidity," he muttered.

"The Defense Department predicts a short conflict. But I can't see it anytime soon. Both sides have enough reserves and resources to go at it a long time."

"It's all meaningless." Nick sighed. "Resources are wasted that could make a better life for everyone."

"If this war spills out of Asia, there won't be anyone left to enjoy anything." The phone rang. "I'll get it...yes, he's here. Nick, it's for you." Mike handed the phone over.

"Yes." Nick listened intently. Demos, his brother, was on a reconnaissance flight near a bombed city. He was reported as down and missing. There was no evidence of having been shot down. When the voice finished he shook his head. "I'm on my way."

"What's wrong?"

"Demos is down."

"No!"

"Unfortunately, yes. I have to go after him. He's my responsibility."

"Let the professionals go in."

"I am the professional. I should have never asked him to go in. It is all my fault."

"Don't beat yourself up. You were doing your job."

Nick smiled wanly. Something about the war did not make any sense. Losing Demos made it all the worse. In his bones he felt Demos was waiting rescue. Within the hour he was soaring across the Atlantic toward the war zone. Getting there

449

was taking too long but there was no other choice. If nothing else, he had to finish the mission.

The flight from Florida to the Canary Islands was facilitated by travel on a fighter jet. At supersonic speed the oceanic crossing left little time to ruminate on what was happening. The pilot said little nor did he attempt to start any conversation with Nick. There was certain risk in entering a potential war zone even when extreme precautions were exercised. Satellite photos accurately pinpointed where Demos landed. At least there was some reassurance he had not crashed.

After a change of planes in the Canary Islands, Nick sped across North Africa in a stealth fighter, not nearly as fast but definitely safer near hostile countries. The destination was Oman where another switch awaited. Whenever possible, Nick tried sleeping; however, the incessant noise plus excitement kept him awake even with eyes shut. Upon changing planes the effects of fatigue were felt to the bone.

"Doctor Kanenos, I have your orders," an Air Force aide said smartly.

Nick warily took the envelope. "Thank you."

"Would you like to freshen up and rest, Sir?" The aide smiled.

"Please." Nick exhaled.

The aide led the way into the Officers' Quarters. Nick entered a room in which he flopped on the bed while he tore open the envelope of orders. He read the instructions carefully several times memorizing every line. The mission was to fly to a carrier where a helicopter was waiting to take him into the war zone. He planned getting a few hours of sleep.

Before sunrise and after a quick breakfast, Nick was on the way to the carrier. As the sun rose on the horizon, the helicopter was racing its way toward the location of his brother's plane. He tried relaxing but was unable to think of anything, except the safety of his brother.

The origin of the war was obscure even though there had been long standing issues between the combatants. Any issue constrained the relationship between two over-populated stressed countries and brought them to hostilities. The fact both had developed nuclear weapons did not help the situation. The sophistication of the nuclear warheads was not expected by outside observers.

Across from him in the helicopter sat his partner, Captain Jimmy Stern, Special Forces. The Captain chewed gum behind dark silvered sunglasses.

"You look worried." The gum snapped in his mouth. "I think that brother of yours is safe. The satellites show no hostile forces for a hundred miles around the site."

"I still worry," Nick said slowly. "He is my brother, my flesh and blood. I don't care how good he is, there is always someone better. I only have one brother and I don't want to lose him."

"I understand how you feel," Jimmy said. "I have three younger sisters and I feel the same as you. I wouldn't want anything to happen to any of them."

"I won't rest easy until I have him back on safe soil with me. And, if that's not possible, I want to at least feel I have done everything possible for him."

Jimmy nodded. From a height of fifteen hundred feet, everything below appeared quite normal. It was hard to believe they were in a war torn country. However, two things were absent: there were neither animals nor people anywhere nor was there any evidence of military activity. Most of the foliage was beginning to brown from the effects of neutron radiation.

The downed plane was found exactly where it was expected. As they approached a light from the ground flashed at the helicopter. A code signaled it was safe to approach and land. Even so, the pilot made several orbits around the site before bringing the helicopter to rest on the ground.

Demos ran out to welcome them before the skids of the helicopter hit the ground. Nick jumped out and hugged him while trying to hold back tears of joy. The engine of the helicopter suddenly cut off bringing and unearthly quiet to the scene. The pilot quickly attempted to restart the engine.

Demos shook his head. "Another electromagnetic pulse disruption; someone is making sure no electronics are in use around here."

"Is that what happened to your plane?"

"More or less, with a little bad luck thrown in for good measure; at least I was able to land safely."

"We came prepared." Nick pointed. Several crates were on the ground outside the helicopter. One crate was already open.

"What did you bring wings?"

"The next best thing under the circumstances: hot air balloons."

"Perfect." Demos grinned. "I should've thought of that before."

"We will fly out of here to a safe zone where we can be picked up. The satellites will track us at all times." Nick smiled.

"What about the enemy?"

"Our latest intelligence shows this area all the way to the border clear. It is unlikely we will have any resistance getting out. In fact, we should travel by a target you were sent to scout. Hopefully, we will complete your mission. We will have to continuously monitor radiation levels."

"How? All the electronics are fried."

"Again back to old technology." Nick pulled out a radiation tag such as used in a hospital. "I've brought a supply of these tags in a shielded container. I'll pull one out, expose it, and develop it at regular intervals. At least we will always know if we are exposed to too much radiation. I know it is crude but it should work."

"Sounds good to me; let's get started."

There were two balloons. Nick and Demos manned one, the pilot and Jimmy the other. Supplies were loaded before the balloons were inflated. Details of the route out plus plans for any emergency were thoroughly discussed. Ideally the two balloons would fly together providing the wind was blowing right. As soon as the balloons were inflated they launched into the sky drifting slowly upward. The ground receded while the view of the surrounding countryside expanded. There was nothing moving in any direction except the clouds above.

Using an old-fashioned compass Nick chose the altitude which provided wind in the right direction. Aside from the whoosh of the flame providing hot air and the gentle rush of wind noise there was total silence. Everything moved in slow motion.

"I see a settlement of houses ahead." Demos pointed.

The man in the other balloon acknowledged they had also noticed. In hand signals Nick suggested the other team land and check it out. They would move on to the next possible settlement or city. It would mean separation of the balloons but intelligence was a prime priority.

Before the balloon landed, Demos spotted a dirt road leading to a narrow highway heading to a small town. It was too late to get the other balloon to follow. Nick adjusted the altitude and guided them as close to the town as possible. Within an hour they descended onto what was the deserted main street and alit silently. Demos had a weapon ready in hand for any ambush. Nick brushed his hand in a motion that meant he was unconcerned.

On the ground Nick immediately checked his radiation tag. When developed there was barely more than background radiation. Demos carefully ran from store to store looking for survivors. Not only did he find no one but there were no dead bodies.

"There's no one here," Demos said loudly.

"They may have evacuated before the bombs went off. They may have had enough time."

"But everything is undisturbed. People evacuating grab anything and everything they can. Nothing is missing or out of place."

"The government could have forced them out at gunpoint."

Demos nodded. Up in the sky he saw the other balloon passing. Nick noticed it also. With nothing further gleaned from the abandoned town they lifted off in their balloon. It was late afternoon with clouds gathering all around. Nick consulted a map showing they were too far from the border to cross before the sunset. The other balloon was nowhere visible. Nick decided to find a suitable place for the night. In following an ever wider road they saw a much larger town ahead. In this country it may have been called a city. As in the previous town there was no sign of any activity on approaching. The outskirts of the town had a small airstrip upon which they landed. They deflated the balloon and put it in a hangar.

"No one here either," Demos said. "Where are all the bodies?"

"I don't understand it." Nick checked his radiation tag. "There's some low-level residual which means these people were affected by the bomb. There should be dead everywhere. It doesn't make any sense."

"To me neither."

"How's the fuel level?"

"We have enough for another short day," Demos said.

At a building with several taxis was a collection of propane tanks lined up in a row. Nick picked the first one up easily. "Empty," he said.

One by one they hefted the tanks only to find they were all empty. Demos went over to a truck parked next to the building. He discovered a set of full tanks.

"Now we have plenty of fuel. Things have just gotten easier."

"Not so fast." Nick put up a hand. "We are still deep in a war zone. Regardless of anything, our lives are still in danger. The fact we have found no one living or dead bothers me. Have you also noticed there are no birds, dogs, cats, or livestock? Something strange is going on."

"But what? Maybe there was enough warning for everyone to evacuate. There are no dead bodies because no one was here to get killed."

"That might be true except where are the birds? Did they pack them all up too? I would expect at least to find a bird carcass or two lying around."

"Tomorrow we will cross the border. Maybe we'll see a survivor somewhere. Then we might get some answers."

"That house over there seems a good place to stay. How about a bite to eat and some sleep?"

The house was clean inside. Demos brought in food from the balloon. After a light dinner they found places to relax for the night. With a flip of a coin Nick took the first watch. Demos barely closed his eyes and he was asleep. Sitting in a chair staring out the window Nick could hardly keep his own eyes open. Every so often he closed his eyes only to open them quickly. On the verge of falling asleep he got up and walked around. He went outside for the fresh crisp night air. Again he was met with total silence. Nothing living was stirring. He looked upward at the stars peeking from behind high scattered clouds. A thin sliver of a waxing gibbous moon appeared. The International Space Station streaked across the heavens in a matter of minutes. The moment he started back into the house he saw a flash of light in the sky nearby. Frozen in place he watched expectantly.

The light stopped dead in the sky and remained fixed. It slowly descended on the other side of the town. Without taking his eyes off the light, he moved quickly back into the house and watched out the window. As soon as it disappeared behind the surrounding obstructions, he ran to Demos sprawled on the bed, eyes closed. He went over and touched him on the shoulder.

Demos snatched his brother's arm. When he opened his eyes he let the arm loose. Without speaking Nick waved to get

454

up and look out the window. Demos moved quickly but saw nothing outside.

"What's up?" Demos rubbed the sleep out of his eyes.

"I saw something." Nick was out of breath. "I was outside getting some fresh air when I saw a light in the sky. As I watched, it stopped, and started landing straight down. We are not alone out here."

"Could you tell which side?"

"I couldn't tell anything about it. To me it was just a luminous UFO. From here on out we must be extremely careful not to be seen."

"I guess that means we can't leave here until whoever you saw leaves."

Nick nodded.

"That means we need to get close enough to identify our visitors. You saw the direction they landed. I suggest we start right away."

The balloon was hidden as best as possible. There was barely enough light to negotiate a soundless trek through the town. Night goggles would have been great but the electromagnetic pulse had fried all the electronics. Personal skills and training mattered.

Halfway through the town Nick stumbled in the dark over an obstacle next to the front door of a store. The obstacle was a dead body, the first of several in the immediate area. He crouched with Demos examining the man who had died with his eyes open. Aside from the odor of vomit on the man's shirt there was nothing remarkable. There was no sign of any physical trauma.

"Radiation," Nick whispered.

"Neutrons." Demos nodded.

They examined each body as they came across it. Death must have come quickly. The bodies were all in reasonably good condition. The neutrons also killed bacteria delaying the inevitable decay process. Demos wanted to take pictures, but the digital camera was useless. He vowed to get a film camera.

The farther they went, the more bodies they found. In addition to the men, women and children, there were dogs, cats, chickens, cattle, goats and others. Everything previously living was dead. The town was one mass open graveyard.

The closer they came to the opposite side of town, first Nick, and then Demos heard a low level hum. They headed toward the source of the noise. A large building which was either a warehouse or factory loomed ahead. They split apart approaching the building from two directions. A light flashed in several windows. Nick made his way to one of the windows while Demos circled around to the opposite side of the building.

The night air was warm, but not uncomfortably so. Nick found himself sweating bullets. He would not admit the stress was almost unbearable. He had been in tight spots before, but this time the situation was the tightest yet. He was concerned about the safety of his brother and more than once wished he were alone on this mission. It was nice working with your own brother, but the risk of losing him far outweighed the potential advantages.

Hugging the ground, Nick reached the closest window. He tentatively touched the wall. The icy cold feel of metal sent a chill down his spine. He slowly lifted himself to look in when a hand grabbed his shoulder. Startled he spun around and saw Demos crouched beside him with an index finger across the lips. Demos looked excited and needed to talk. Nick signed he wanted to look in the window. Demos shook his head. He pointed away from the building. Nick scowled, glanced up at the window, and shrugged. This time he would listen. It better be good.

Crawling as fast as possible they moved to a secure location away from the target building. A beam of light flashed above their heads. Getting up they ran the rest of the way to safety. The light scanned the ground where they had been.

"That was too close." Demos exhaled.

"What was so important I couldn't look in the window?" Nick inhaled deeply. "All I had to do is take a glance. I was already there."

"On the other side I saw something you must see for yourself. The vehicle you saw landing. It's not like anything I have ever seen."

"What do you mean?"

"Like it's nothing I have ever seen before from any country. I would almost say it was an alien spacecraft, if I believed in such things."

"Now I've got to see it myself." Nick peered around the corner. The light was no longer scanning the area. "This time I will go with you. Lead the way."

They made a wide circular excursion around to the other side. Resting on the ground was a vehicle Nick had only seen as figments of fiction, a flying saucer: sixty feet across, domed, glowing silver white, and an entrance open to a brilliantly lit

456

interior. Nick was too stunned to move. What he saw was impossible; at least everything he had studied proved such things could not exist. He shook his head and accepted the reality. If this was an alien ship, why was it here in the middle of a war zone?

A person appeared at the saucer entrance pulling a cart. The person at a distance appeared humanoid: two legs, two arms, one head. The details of the face were hard to visualize. They were close enough to consider normal by human standards. The similarity to human did not disprove the assumption the saucer was of extraterrestrial origin. Nick was aware there were secret private and military programs attempting to bring science fiction to real life. Could this be such an instance? And, if so, what was its purpose here?

"We have to get inside that building," Nick whispered.

"I agree," Demos said softly.

Three other persons appeared exiting the building. Behind each was a cart loaded with a bulky mass covered by a metallic tarp. The carts were taken into the saucer, unloaded, and brought out empty to the building.

"I think we need to get inside the saucer" Demos pointed.

"One step at a time: so far, I only have seen four men; if, they are really men. We must see how many individuals we are up against."

"What does it matter, if we stay hidden?"

"Well, I want at least half a chance of escaping if we are seen. The more of them, the worse for us."

They watched the activities of the strangers for several hours. A fifth person appeared in the group. There was a continuous back-and-forth flow of the carts. The cargo remained a mystery. Toward the beginning of dawn all five persons got in the saucer. The door closed and a hum filled the air. The saucer lifted slowly off the ground. At tree height the hum intensified to a high pitched whine. The saucer shot straight up and disappeared quickly into the clouds.

Demos wanted to dash directly into the building. Nick held him back. They crept slowly up to the closed door through which the men had come and gone. The door was unlocked. Nick opened it slowly. The inside was dark. He reclosed the door without going further. They would be safer to wait until the sun came up. He motioned Demos back to their home base.

457

"Why?" Demos spoke normally. "There's no one here except us. I don't think our friends are going to be back anytime soon. I think we better find out what is inside before they come back."

"It's still a risk," Nick said. "I don't like it. This could be a trap."

"I think whoever it is doesn't know it is possible for us to be here. I really didn't see any sort of security precautions. Did you or did I miss something?"

Before Nick answered Demos struck a flare which illuminated the entire area. He boldly opened the door and stepped in. Nick followed.

"There's nothing," Demos said. "Nothing is in here but long stainless steel tables. What sort of place is this?"

Demos followed Nick into an inner office. Although the documents were unreadable, they were familiar. The building was a produce processing center. Chickens, livestock and vegetables were brought here for slaughter, cleaning and packaging. A large walk-in freezer was open in the back. Demos found it empty. Whatever the strangers were taking, nothing remained in the building.

"Could they have been taking the food?"

"I don't know," Nick said slowly. "None of this makes sense. I feel like I'm in a dream. I don't know what's going on."

"I agree it makes little sense. Should we wait for them to come back or should we continue toward the border?"

"The problem is we don't know if they will return." Nick thought a moment. "However, it won't hurt to wait another twenty-four hours."

The trip back to the house retraced their original path. The bodies they had seen coming were gone. Not only were strangers dropping out of the sky, someone was carting off the dead which included the animals. The growing mystery made them edgy and they remained hidden as much as possible. It was only when they were back in the original house they felt somewhat easy. Demos went straight to check on the balloon while Nick prepared a meal from the supplies. Neither was hungry.

"Someone has been here," Demos said. "The balloon is still safe but I noticed a few things have been moved plus some footprints. We are definitely not alone around here."

"I am beginning to think more men were from that saucer than we saw," Nick said. "Or more men came in on the

458

ground or are even still here amongst the buildings. In any case, we must stay out of sight."

"I wonder where Jimmy is now." Demos looked out the window. "I wonder if he and his partner saw anything. I wish we hadn't separated."

"There's nothing we can do about it. First, some sleep for both of us. I'll take the first watch."

Neither slept well; after another meal both were ready to return back to the building across town. This time they chose a different route skirting the outer limits of the town. Nothing living was seen other than the browning foliage. They chose to hide within the buildings for a clear view of what the strangers were doing. It was near midnight when the distinctive hum of the previous night returned. They watched as the saucer landed. The door opened and five men came out pulling carts behind them one by one. They came directly to the building. Demos could hardly breathe, Nick remained frozen in place. Escape was always possible at any point, but finding what the strangers were doing was more important. All the strangers were in the building setting up the tables.

The closer the strangers came the more obvious it was they were ordinary human beings in appearance. When one spoke, the language was totally alien but not unlike any foreign one. The longer Nick watched the more differences he detected in the strangers. All were bald or at least clean-shaven. There were four fingers and an opposable thumb on each hand. At a distance, Nick could not see the eyes clearly. Something about the eyes disturbed him.

The stainless steel tables were set up with an assortment of knives, saws, and shears. He assumed the strangers were about to process livestock. The possibility was excluded by the lack of anything living anywhere nearby.

One of the strangers exited and returned with several dead human bodies on his cart. The others removed the bodies and placed them on the tables. Without hesitation the bodies were eviscerated, washed down and sealed in a plastic wrap. Demos almost threw up.

Somehow they had to get out without being seen. There was a doorway close behind where they were hidden. Nick crept to the door and tried the knob. It was unlocked. He waved Demos to follow. Slowly opening the door enough to slip out took an eternity. Once out the door Nick gently closed it. They found themselves in a storeroom with no other exit. A window to the outside, however, was big enough for escape.

Demos wanted to put as much distance between them and the strangers as possible. Nick, visibly shaken by what he witnessed, wanted to find out more. He carried a gun as did Demos. The door to the saucer was open and everyone was still inside the building. Nick pointed to the saucer. Demos shook his head. There was no way he was going into the saucer.

Nick waved Demos off. He would go alone. This was far too important to dismiss. He moved around the building until he could see what was happening inside. The strangers continued processing additional bodies of humans and other dead farm animals. The viscera were cleaned, separated by various organs and packaged separately. He calculated he had enough time to dash into the saucer, get a quick look and get out before anyone noticed what was happening. When Nick started running, Demos was right behind him. If there was a confrontation, two were better than one.

Upon running through the door of the saucer Nick was immediately struck by the amount of space inside. The outside appearance made the saucer appear smaller than it actually was. Demos examined everything hoping to remember as much as possible. Around the perimeter were hundreds of packages stacked evenly several high. In the center was the crew center and controls. There was a level below which Nick went down by ladder. There was no clue as to who they were or from where they had come. Demos poked his head down to Nick.

"We have been in here too long. Let's go!"

Without hesitation Nick climbed up the ladder. Demos was looking out the door at the building. All color drained from his face.

"What's the matter?" Nick whispered.

Demos pointed as Nick came to his side. All the strangers were marching back pulling a cart behind them. There was no time to hide.

"Wait here." Nick stepped out the door. "Keep me covered."

The strangers immediately stopped moving. Nick was totally unexpected. The stranger in front looked back at his companions. They all grouped behind their leader waiting to see what was happening with the ship.

Stepping up to the leader Nick raised both palms upward facing forwards. "I mean you no harm." He forced a smile.

460

A man behind the leader said something unintelligible. The leader smiled showing a set of fine sharp teeth. "I mean you no harm," he said.

"You speak English?" Nick noticed the leader had yellow irises with a vertical slit. The doubt he was facing aliens vanished. His heart raced. He was the first to make contact with an extraterrestrial being.

"You speak English?" The leader stepped closer.

Nick extended his hand. The alien did the same. Face-to-face Nick grabbed the proffered hand and shook it. The alien offered no resistance. Demos exited slowly from the saucer catching everyone's attention. He joined Nick by his side.

"Put the gun away," Nick said sharply. "We are face-to-face with real extraterrestrials. Let's make a good impression."

"Does he understand you?"

"So far he has acted as if he does," Nick said. "But we really haven't communicated."

The expression on the leader's face made Demos uncomfortable. The same expression appeared on the entire group.

"I don't like this," Demos said out of the corner of his mouth.

"There has to be a reasonable explanation to what they are doing here. Aren't you curious? This is a momentous occasion for all mankind." Nick saw a grin appear on the leader's face. "You understand me, don't you?"

"You're wasting your time." Demos pulled Nick's shoulder. "This just doesn't feel right."

The aliens moved in a circle around them. Each alien had a grin similar to the leader. They remained a respectful distance away. The leader said something unintelligible.

"We mean you no harm," Nick said. "We only want to know more about you."

The leader tilted his head to one side. "We mean you no harm," he said.

"You really don't understand me. Do you?" Nick shook his head.

"You really don't understand," the alien leader said.

Nick slowly understood he was being played with. The alien's responses were not a simple echo. There was a definite purpose behind what was said.

"Let's go now!" Demos shouted.

461

Nick stared in the alien leader's eyes, turned away and saw the other aliens. He stepped forward but was not allowed to pass. Demos drew his gun. Nick pushed it away.

"We are leaving," Nick said sternly. "We go in peace." He turned back to the leader who shook his head. There was no doubt in the meaning.

"You understand, don't you?" Demos shouted. "Let us go or I'll hurt someone with this." He raised his gun pointing it at the leader's face.

The gun was snatched out of the Demos' hand in the blink of an eye. The aliens grabbed them by the arms. They were led back to the building. The knives, saws, and shares were still on the tables.

Demos was placed first on a table shouting, screaming and kicking. An alien took a knife and slit his throat. Nick struggled to get free as he watched how his brother was processed. When they were finished he was put on a table and slaughtered in the same manner. In short order the processing was finished, the room cleaned, and everything taken aboard the saucer leaving no evidence behind.

***

"Gentlemen, we all have to be more careful," the alien captain said. "We should never allow ourselves to be surprised by the wildlife on this planet. This was too close for comfort."

"We have never had this problem," the sergeant said. "The radiation usually sterilizes the area completely. Nothing is left living."

"Yet these creatures are resourceful," the captain said. "They have the beginnings of technology which in time may become like our own."

"If that is the case, should we not help them?" The lieutenant said.

"There is no profit in primitive civilizations." The captain sighed. "It is best to use them to our benefit. Given time they could develop into a real problem vying for food and resources."

"I guess you're right," the lieutenant said. "Our systems work far better by themselves. I wonder who thought up the idea of inciting war between the various groups on this planet."

"Does it matter?" The captain laughed. "Not only do we instigate war but we sell the weapons. When all is over, we come in to get what we really want. We always get the best bargain.

462

What we have done so far is nothing to what we will eventually do. We have the big cities yet. Just think of the profits!"

"I can hardly wait to be rich," the sergeant said loudly.

"Sir, your meal is ready."

"Gentlemen, shall we eat?"

They all met in the dining area. On the table were the tastiest morsels of the latest catch. The smell made everyone hungry.

"You know," the captain said as he bit into a roasted leg. "I wonder what that creature was trying to say."

"Does it make any difference?"

"I guess not." The captain sighed. "And by the way, they sure taste better fresh."

464

"Welcome. When did you get back?"

"Just this afternoon."

"May I get you something to drink?"

"Anything will do. Just let me sit down. I am exhausted." Ryx threw himself in the nearest available chair.

Tylon smiled. "I have exactly what you need. Do you have any aversion to alcohol?"

"I will take anything after what I have been through. It has been a long solar year." Ryx exhaled loudly. "I thought I would never get back."

"Was the assignment all that bad?" Tylon set a drink on the table next to the chair. "I thought you enjoyed fieldwork."

"I do, but this time everything was different." Ryx closed his eyes. "I came across a civilization like none we have ever examined. It was a nightmare to live amongst them as long as I did."

"Now you have me curious." Tylon sat nearby with a drink in hand. "Exactly where did you go? If you can tell me…"

"It will all be in my final report. First, I have to collect my thoughts…" Ryx took a long sip from his glass. "…in a few more drinks like this. Thanks."

"I don't want to drag it out of you, but you seem reluctant to say anything."

"I am just tired, that is all. The alcohol is starting to relax me. I am feeling a lot better already."

"Would you like another?"

"Not yet." Ryx waved. "I think you already know the gist of my mission. I was to travel to a remote planet and examine the indigenous humans by blending in with them. I had no problem entering their world."

"I heard rumors but nothing confirmed," Tylon said. "There was nothing in the media about where you were going or what you would be doing. All I heard definitely was that you were on leave from your position at the University."

"A leave with special instructions…" Ryx sighed. "I took the assignment to further my academic career. In retrospect, I should have had my head examined."

"When you are ready I am all ears."

"You and I were classmates in anthropological studies at the University," Ryx said slowly. "So you and I have the same academic background. The only difference you decided to

465

examine places closer to home and I opted to venture to extremely remote places."

"So, what does that mean?"

"I guess it means I am really, really tired and babbling." Ryx took another swallow and closed his eyes. "I guess I might as well tell you what happened now before I forget anything. Put the recorder on so I can review it later when I am putting everything in my report. I don't want to trust anything to memory. Are you ready?"

"Sure, go ahead." Tylon sat back.

"I'll try not to leave anything out," Ryx said slowly and rubbed his eyes with the tips of his fingers. "I guess this whole project began a long time ago when signals were detected from a rocky planet in the system where no life was expected. I happened to have access to the recordings of transmissions over a broadband of different frequencies. It was my job to decipher what the message meant. I soon discovered there were no direct messages outside of the home planet. If I had not been persistent, I might have declared the transmissions pure noise. I discovered with the proper filters and special equipment I could derive audio and video to study. After that it was not difficult to interpret the languages of which there were many. The video images were interesting enough for me to draw up a proposal for admission to the planet. With funds always at a premium for research I did not think I had a chance for funding. My proposal, however, was convincing enough to allow me to go by myself to study the alien culture for the time it would take the planet to make one orbit around its own star. I would have liked more, but I took what I could get."

"I have been there myself." Tylon nodded. "Resources are always tight for basic research."

"Which meant: I had to choose where I would get the most useful data." Ryx sighed. "Not easy at all."

"So what did you do?"

"I decided to pick a community small enough that in the time I had I could expect a thorough understanding of the culture, and large enough to extrapolate reasonably well to the planet as a whole. I thought with the level of civilization I noted in the transmissions it would be easy. I wrote my proposal with that assumption. I was eventually mistaken as I found out."

"Been there, done that." Tylon smiled.

Ryx continued behind a thin smile. "Once the funds were allocated it did not take long to put my expedition together.

466

I was in luck there was a direct wormhole conduit into the vicinity of the target solar system. I would not have to spend much time in transit which left me more time to spend in observation. I arrived near the planet avoiding detection by staying behind its large singular moon. From there I was able to monitor more transmissions than we had previously received here on our home world. The character of the transmissions had changed as well as the content. Even so, I remained dedicated to my written protocol. I would land unobserved and join a closed community where I would blend in for a solar year. I approached via the polar axis successfully avoiding detection."

"Their technology must be pretty rudimentary," Tylon said flatly.

"Perhaps..." Ryx nodded "I didn't investigate their technology, although I must say that compared to us they have a long way to go. They are still struggling to establish themselves in near orbital space. I learned they have sent out unmanned probes way below light speed. In terms of being a power in interstellar space they are no threat to anyone except themselves. Anyway let me get back to my story."

"Please do." Tylon nodded. "I am sorry to interrupt you."

"That's okay. It gives me more time to organize my thoughts." Ryx smiled and took a long sip from his drink. "Now where was I?"

"You had to choose a site to study," Tylon interjected.

"Yes, I had to choose." Ryx sighed softly. "Again due to my budget and time constraints I had to make my resources last. I discovered a subset of closed communities in which I would be able to blend without expenditures on my part. All my needs would be met while I collected data. It was fortunate that externally we easily pass among the inhabitants of this planet, especially when we are able to speak their language. I chose one of those closed communities on a part of the planet with a relatively mild climate throughout the year. It was no use being too hot or too cold. I was well prepared in advance to look and dress the part of an ordinary inhabitant of the planet. My first problem was entry into one of these communities. I landed in a remote location near one of them. From a distance I could tell it was well fortified. There was a high fence topped with coils of steel which had razor-sharp points surrounding it. At opposing corners there were towers in which individuals in uniforms held guard with some sort of tubular steel weapon. Outside the fence

467

was a perimeter road on which an official ground vehicle on rubber wheels traveled at regular intervals. I saw from the start it was no easy task getting inside. I decided to watch from a distance. Every day I noticed a group came out from an exit in the fence and worked in the surrounding fields. Each group consisted of 20 to 25 individuals dressed in white supervised by a man sitting on an animal call a horse. This man was dressed in a uniform armed with a weapon to protect his workgroup. Seeing this made me fearful for my own life. I had not seen any wild animals but that did not mean they were not there. I started paying closer attention to my surroundings. I did not want to lose my life to any mindless wild beast."

"That's why I stay closer to home," Tylon said barely audible.

"The work detail marched out into the field where each individual was issued a hoe for turning the soil. I could hardly believe that from what little I knew of the planet that such a primitive form of agriculture could sustain such technology. They worked in the blazing sun taking few breaks for rest and water. When they were finished they marched back to the fence where after turning in their hoes they stripped completely naked. The supervisor on the horse examined each individual for parasites. Once this examination process was completed the group disappeared inside the fence. At this point my skin started itching thinking about being exposed to parasites from the ground. I assumed the person on the horse was high enough from the ground to avoid coming in contact with them. Since I could not walk out of nowhere to demand entrance, I decided to exchange places with one of the work detail. The opportunity came the next day halfway through the morning. When the person on the horse was not looking one out of the workgroup started running away. All chaos broke loose. The workgroup cheered while the person on the horse pointed something held in his hand at the running individual. I could see the group and the person on the horse stuck together for safety. I managed to hide in a place where I could intercept the running individual. You should have seen the expression on his face when he ran into me. We were both momentarily stunned. Before he could get away from me I subdued him completely by putting him to sleep. I then exchanged clothes which were really not a bad fit considering. The odor, however, was almost more than I could bear. With a little instant plastic surgery I rearranged my face to pass for the individual asleep. Instead of running away I turned around and headed back to the workgroup. By the time I returned there were several big individuals on horses that were clearly not happy. The moment they saw me one of them jumped down from his horse, grabbed me, and threw me to the ground. Before I knew it, I had steel restraints on my wrists and ankles. All sorts of shouts were directed at me; and I accepted them without resistance. It was clear my ruse worked. I was taken under escort through the fence, stripped, hosed down, and put into a small room with a tiny window. I concluded the rules were very strict. Now that I was inside I would do everything I could to stay invisible and clear of trouble. When I was finally interrogated I explained I was temporarily mistaken and promised I would not run away again."

"Sounds like you were off to an interesting start." Tylon smiled. "I am not sure I would have done what you did."

"I saw it as part of my data collection," Ryx continued. "There is nothing like playing the part of a native to understand what it is like to live in an alien society."

"And how long were you punished?"

"Actually it was not bad. I had a clean room with solid metal walls, a bed with a mattress, a small desk, a toilet and a sink with running hot and cold water. Meals were brought to me three times a day. I really had nothing to worry about. The only regret was the lost time in roaming the community. I was eventually taken in front of a committee for further evaluation. Based on my alleged past history I was no longer to go out into the fields. I would be restricted entirely within the fence. Since that was where I wanted to be in the first place, I saw that as no problem. Unfortunately, however, I was in my little room for a long time. I almost thought I would never get out. Then, one day when I least expected it, I was taken out and delivered under escort to a building in which I was to live. I found myself in another room slightly larger than the last with another person. I was given a perfect opportunity to get to know one of the workers intimately. I was locked in this room with my roommate except for meals, work and what they called recreation. At first, my roommate was quite silent. Since I did not know exactly how to start a conversation, I waited until he addressed me. It was almost two days before he said anything and then it was to turn out the light. A bag was delivered to me that composed all my belongings the person I had exchanged places with had. I was pleased to find items I could put to immediate use such as a cup and spoon. There were a few books and materials to write with. I

469

even found a few items of food and a brown powder which went mixed with hot water makes a drink called coffee. I also inherited a fan, a radio and a device for heating water. I could not be happier. I don't know whether it was curiosity or boredom when my roommate spoke to me. When I heard his voice I was not sure he was even talking to me. He addressed me in some sort of slang I did not understand. I waited as aloof as I could to see where the conversation would go. Apparently he was as curious about me as I was about him. Before I said anything about myself he explained that he did not care who I was as long as I kept myself and respected his space. I told him that would definitely not be a problem."

"You really went native." Tylon laughed.

"I tried to go as native as I understood," Ryx continued. "Believe me, the closer you live to the natives, the more you can observe. The best part of being an observer is not being observed in reverse. My roommate called me his Celly. From that point on whenever anyone asked who I was living with I would mention my Celly's name which brings up another interesting point. In this closed community everyone has at least two identifying names and possibly a third. The first name is the one which the individual had prior to entering the community. The second name is actually an identifying number. Numbers are seen as more important in tracking and more exact. A unique number helps differentiate individuals who might have identical names prior. There is a propensity to create new names based on physical characteristics, community behavior, or point of origin. These identifiers which are called nicknames can be quite colorful and at times obscene."

"Did you have a nickname?"

"Yes, in fact I was given one by my Celly." Ryx blushed. "He called me Rabbit."

"What's a rabbit?"

"It's an animal found on the planet with long ears and a tendency to run away when confronted with danger. Once I was designated rabbit everyone started calling me that including the supervisors. At first I didn't know what to make of it. Eventually, I accepted it with the humor it was supposed to represent. I certainly could have had a worse name."

"Next time we are at a meeting I will call you Rabbit." Tylon grinned. "I bet that will make you blush."

Ryx ignored the comment with a wan smile. He took another sip from his drink and then another.

470

"Hey, I didn't mean for you to stop," Tylon said quickly. "I am sorry if I offended you."

"Don't worry." Ryx smiled. "I wasn't offended. I have a sense of humor. Let me get on with my story."

"Please continue. I won't interrupt you again."

Ryx took a deep breath. "I thought the hardest part of my study would be gaining entrance into the community. I soon discovered that was the easiest part; trying to make sense of the functions and social hierarchy turned out to be the most difficult. The community is highly structured with many inhabitants directed by a few designated supervisors. These supervisors have the ability to move around in the community at will and leave after a time period of work called a shift. The supervisors have the worst of it being forced to work continuously during their shifts. The rest of the community was more relaxed. Everyone worked or played as they felt within time guidelines. I would certainly not want to be a supervisor. A supervisor was held to an absolute accountability. Throughout the day everyone within the community was enumerated. These periods were called count times. During this interval all movement ceased until an absolute correct count was established. You would think in a closed community counting would be the simplest task possible. A count should take no more than a few minutes. Over and over eyewitness counts would take up to several hours to get right. I can only conclude the innate mathematical abilities of these inhabitants are rudimentary at best. How they manage a planetary civilization without mathematical ability might be a topic for further investigation. The daily schedule is highly structured. There are times to eat, work, play, wash, sleep and other activities. The most important activity within the community was eating. Everybody talked about the next meal. The first meal usually was served before the planetary star rose on the horizon. Half-asleep everyone who was hungry marched to the eating area called a Chow Hall. There were two lines where everyone went through a serving line with a plastic tray. Free food was given in exact amounts. Having gone through the line everyone was directed to sit. The food had to be consumed with a minimum of conversation because supervisors were keeping track of the time. When time was up a supervisor would come over and rap smartly on the edge of the table twice with his knuckles. At that point everyone sitting whether finished or not had to leave the eating area. The used food trays were taken to a window where they were accepted for cleaning. The menu varied

471

little day by day. The inhabitants restrict their diets to a very narrow selection of foods. There is a vegetable called beans that appears on every meal except the first of the day. I have tasted and eaten their food and found it quite bland and unappetizing. Why they choose to eat it day after day is beyond comprehension. But I guess it is unfair to compare what we have here to what exists there. In spite of the abundance of food there many who craved more. Through my Celly I was introduced to an underground of food transactions. Before I describe those let me state that written correspondence moves in and out of the community by the paying of a small fee. This fee is contained in a rectangular piece of paper called the stamp. Because of their size, stamps are a real source of monetary exchange even though everything is supposed to be free. Now back to the food. To get anything extra to eat one has only to pass a stamp to the right person. Anything provided free can be bought with a stamp. There is little logic in these transactions."

"That's incredible." Tylon nearly gasped. "Why would anyone buy anything already free? Why don't they just give more when requested?"

"The only conclusion I have come up with is the limited resources available. The supervisors control the flow of all supplies and food. In order to ensure everyone's needs are met strict control is necessary. However, I was told, although I was unable to confirm it, that the supervisors would remove community supplies for their own uses outside the fence. I never saw anyone who was starving, but I did witness a phenomenon of excessive weight gain. Many of the inhabitants are much happier eating than at any other time. Buying extra food may be a way of getting extra happiness and pleasure. Food is such a valuable commodity that besides getting extra in the Chow Hall it is possible to have food delivered to the housing areas. This preoccupation with food is superseded only by sports. Outside of my living area there was a larger area called a day room which had two video-audio receivers. Through these receivers, which were called TVs, a number of programs were viewed. I immediately saw an opportunity to learn more about the culture from many angles. There were programs of news from around the planet which were informative and educational. I learned a lot about what was happening outside the community. Unfortunately, the prime interests of the inhabitants were not educational programs; it was sports followed by game shows and something called soap operas. I was amazed to watch large

472

groups gather around the TVs to view other groups engaging in activities involving a ball of different sizes and shapes. There were other sports in which individuals would gather in a confined space called a ring where they would either hit each other continuously until the other fell down or gave up or they would grab each other jumping and falling all over the ring. Personally I saw no sense to it, but to them it was great sport. Certain ball sports were more important than others. For some sports, individuals would gamble on who would be the winner or something like that. Out would come the stamps and commissary items to pay for the bets."

"Did you say commissary?" Tylon tilted his head. "What is a commissary item?"

"Forgive me." Ryx smiled. "I said everything is provided free, but it is possible to legally buy certain items not normally available to the general population free. These items are distributed through the commissary."

"Did you use stamps? And where did the stamps come from in the first place?" Tylon said slowly. "This is getting a little confusing. I don't understand."

"Stamps are bought in the commissary." Ryx smiled. "So it's impossible stamps are the primary medium of exchange. I discovered the identification card issued to everyone has monetary value attached to it. With this card I could go to the commissary once a week and buy whatever I wanted up to a certain limit. The limit is imposed due to a storage space restriction. I was fortunate enough to select an individual who had a generous commissary account. Not everyone had funds available with their cards. My Celly frequently complained his family never sent him enough money when he needed it. By pressing him a little I was surprised to learn that those that lived outside our community were said to be in the free world. The concept did not make any sense. Here I was free to think as I always had. Everything was available for a satisfactory life. Everything was free. In the so-called free world people had to work if they were to eat or live comfortably. In our community it was possible not to work and still not go wanting. Someday I need to go back and examine the free world if I can get the funding. Getting back to the stamps; once they are bought in the commissary they become units of exchange for items in the community. It is possible to accumulate a lot of stamps in a very short time. There are individuals who have no funds from the free world who rely on stamps to get what they want by paying

473

others who go to the commissary. It sounds like a complicated system but it works as long as the supervisors do not know about it. The supervisors are always on the lookout for what they term trafficking and trading. I engaged in some of it myself to buy some primitive art to bring back with me. Would you like to see it?"

"Of course." Tylon nodded.

"Next time I come, I will bring what I bought. Almost all the members of the community were engaged in some sort of art. Many used pens to draw, others colored pencils and a few watercolors. I saw illustrations and drawings that would take your breath away. Art was not limited to drawing boards and paper, skin was also used. When I witnessed the first tattoo I was appalled at the primitive technique."

"What is a tattoo?"

"Sorry. I keep getting ahead of myself. A tattoo is a drawing placed under the skin by piercing the surface with a sharp needle covered with coloring. The process involves a little pain and some bleeding. Some of the tattoos I saw were magnificent, others quite primitive. For a while I even considered getting one myself as a memento of my expedition, but I decided against it when I discovered deadly diseases were transmitted that way."

"Deadly diseases?"

"Yes, deadly diseases. Unfortunately, the civilization has not been able to cure all the diseases on their planet as we have on ours. I attended a couple of classes designed to teach about infectious diseases. I was shocked to learn how much at risk I was without doing anything risky. Fortunately, I had been immunized for everything prior to landing, although in retrospect that might not have been enough. I did follow the advice of the class instructors to wash my hands frequently and to put barriers between my skin and other surfaces. For a while after the class I was quite concerned I was going to get something on me. Fortunately, I stayed healthy the entire time I was there. Oh, wait; there was one time I got sick from something I ate. My Celly said I might have had bad food or ate an insect, or been served by someone who might have spit or worse in my food. From that point onward I examined my food a lot closer before I put it into my mouth." Ryx stopped and drank.

"Would you like another drink?" Tylon stood up. "I am going to have another myself."

474

"Thank you." Ryx sighed and closed his eyes. "Now that I think back on it I wonder how I survived on such a primitive world. A lot of what I saw didn't make sense and still doesn't as I sit in this chair."

"It doesn't make any difference." Tylon returned a filled glass. "You have had a great experience that should keep a lot of armchair scholars pondering and writing for years. Your name will be inscribed in the annals of anthropology forever to come. Your contribution from what you told me so far is no small one. I want to hear more."

"And there is a lot more." Ryx smiled. "I still have trouble organizing it into an understandable thesis. Even in speaking to you I feel as if I am rambling, if not babbling."

"You are doing neither. You have described enough for me to want to hear the rest, including all the miscellaneous details. It is the details that make it interesting and important."

"Now I know why we're friends. We are both our own mutual admiration society. Whenever I need to bounce an idea off of someone I can always come to you."

"And ditto." Tylon grinned.

"And where did I leave off?"

"Something about deadly diseases and bad food I think."

"Oh yeah," Ryx sighed. "When I heard about the diseases I could catch I started looking all around me and at everyone else. Much to my surprise no one cared one way or the other. So I pretended to feel the same."

"If you did whatever everyone else did, how did you protect yourself?"

"The big issue brought out in the talks about the spread of disease was contact. That meant not touching or sharing anything anyone else used. In a real way that was difficult. There was an unrecognized, unacknowledged sense of kinship between all the individuals in white. The longer they claimed to know each other, the more they shared. They acted as one big intimate family. On the other hand, the supervisors in uniform always avoided contact with those in white. They had and used everything separate. There were areas restricted to supervisors only. I had several opportunities to enter one of the supervisor areas. I mostly saw office furniture and machines. The chairs looked more comfortable and the areas were air-conditioned but otherwise nothing special I could tell. I could be just as comfortable in my own assigned housing, although it would have been better if there was air-conditioning. I chose this community

475

in a location on the planet where I expected to be free of extreme temperatures. For more than half of a planetary orbit around the sun star I was reasonably comfortable. The other times I was either too cold or too hot. There was heating and blankets made from the hair of some animal for the cold. The extreme heat was another problem. There were fans which blew the hot air around which was better than nothing. The most important item of property allowed was a small fan. These fans were purchased by everyone from the commissary. Those unable to buy fans usually got one from a supervisor or bought one with stamps from someone else leaving the community."

"How often were individuals leaving?"

"It was totally unpredictable. I watched carefully to see a pattern. Those that exhibited the loudest, poorest behaviors were the ones destined for expulsion. All the rest who followed the rules and did their jobs were given the privilege to remain. Everyone talked about wanting to leave but there was no activity to suggest they really wanted to. The individual I happened to replace attempted to leave unexpectedly; but he was an abnormality as far as I could tell. As long as I was there no one else tried to leave from the fields or anywhere else. The individuals of the community apparently were quite happy and contented. That happiness was always improved with something called mail. Every day rectangular paper envelopes containing communications from the outside world were delivered. Individuals would wait with great anticipation for the mail. I saw the faces of individuals glow when they received and sink when none came."

"Sounds like an extremely primitive way to communicate." Tylon shook his head. "Was there any form of instant communication?"

"Yes and no." Ryx smiled. "There were telephones and radios used exclusively by the supervisors. These devices were forbidden to those in white. However, a telephone call was permitted upon written request every ninety days. The call was kept short, no more than five minutes. All messages had to be transmitted in that time. Some individuals could hardly wait for their calls, most didn't care. More important was the arrival of visitors every sixth and seventh day. This was universally the most aspired and enjoyed form of instant communication. When a visitor arrived the individual requested would meet at a special area in the front building. With direct family the visit would be conducted in a room around the table. The room was air-conditioned with machines that offered items to eat and drink. No excessive form of touching was permitted other than in greeting or leaving. For those not directly related there was a separate visiting area. In this case a barrier was placed between the visitor and individual in white. Conversation would then take place through the use of a telephone. Food and drink passed through a supervisor to the individual in white. To me it seemed the barrier system was most consistent with the prevention of infectious disease. The community had its own set of diseases that went around giving everyone immunity. Visitors might bring outside disease which no one had any immunity. Like I mentioned before there was no uniformity in the concept of transmission of infectious diseases. The standard of behavior was held at a high level. Movement from one location to another was regulated by a pass system. Without a pass travel was not permitted except at times designated by the supervisors. Going to the Chow Hall and exchanging clothes were times of mass movements where no passes were required. Everyone in white had to walk behind a yellow line painted on the floor. Supervisors usually kept on the opposite side. All these restrictions might sound oppressive but they were not. They were a few in white who enjoyed walking on the wrong side of the yellow line. The supervisors would admonish the individual; there would be temporary compliance until the next time. I think this behavior was an attempt at primitive humor if I am not mistaken. At night no movement was permitted for safety. We were all securely safe in our locked rooms. Whatever creatures roamed at night would never hurt us. The longer I lived in this community the easier I could breathe. I easily adapted to the daily routine of everyone else."

"Sounds like you had an easy assignment." Tylon smiled. "Besides observing what you do?"

"Everyone who was physically able was required to work at some job. Since I was considered a security risk, I was given a job inside the community. I would not be forced to go outside the fence which suited me just fine. I did not want to be exposed to any unnecessary dangers. I think I was considered a security risk because anyone who tries to leave might attract dangerous animals. In retrospect, I was fortunate as I was watching from a distance I was not attacked. And no, I never found out what kind of animals were out there. Besides I am an anthropologist not a game hunter. I was put into the kitchen for a while where I washed pots and pans after meals were served. For a while I was soaked with so much water I thought I was a fish. I watched some of the things which went into preparation of the meals. Every type of food had a formula for preparation which was rarely deviated from. I must give them credit for developing this elementary science. The longer I worked in the kitchen, the more I noticed other things. When the supervisors were not looking, food was either eaten in excess, stolen or tampered with. I could hardly believe what went into the food we sometimes ate. Some of the ingredients would make your stomach turn. After I saw what was going into some of the entrées I avoided eating those items especially when certain individuals prepared them. The situation was far worse for the supervisors. So many non-standard ingredients went into their food I wonder how they all didn't get sick. When I happened to carefully ask about this behavior I was told this was standard and expected. The only other conclusion I can surmise is the possibility the inhabitants have developed a dependence on the secretions put into their food. I believe this merits further study by future investigators. From the kitchen I was reassigned to the laundry folding clothes. Now here was an efficient operation. Within a half a day all the day's clothing was washed, folded and exchanged. In addition, the supervisor's clothes were washed and ironed separately. Day after day the clothes came and went. Even here I discovered there were some machine operators that stole chemicals which went into the wash. The chemical stolen contained chlorine which was sold for washing personal clothes in the housing areas. To me it made no sense doing this since the machines could do it better than by hand. Some individuals I spoke with about it told me they didn't trust the laundry. Logic tells me if the chemicals are being stolen the clothes are not being washed thoroughly. The theft behavior created the washing problem which in turn created the theft behavior. These inhabitants are their own worst enemies."

"Did you investigate any of the causes of this behavior?"

"I asked my Celly about what I observed. His answer was it was the duty of everyone to get over something called the State which seems to be a political entity in remote control of the community. When I tried to find out more about this State, no one was able to give me a comprehensive picture. I suggest future expeditions investigate this further. All of those in white were of one sex while supervisors and office workers were of both sexes. I was not able to adequately observe the mating rituals between the sexes, however, I did notice there were three

478

very separate groups in white regarding sexual interaction. For the vast majority there is an outward indifference to the act of mating although there is much talk about it. Many go as far as to obtain pictures of the opposite sex either clothed or unclothed to spur their imaginations. There was a lot of talk and humor related to self-stimulation and gratification. The second group of individuals was mutually attracted to members of their own sex. It was a phenomenon I never witnessed anywhere else I have ever studied. I was surprised to see overt intimacy through contact. It was obvious procreation was impossible yet these individuals seemed motivated to try with each other in non-physiological ways. Although there were rules against such behavior, the supervisors mostly ignored the behavior and actually joked about it. This behavior in many instances resulted in incurable fatal diseases. The third group was composed of those called haters. These were the individuals who either disliked sex so much that they abstained from any reference to it or were intent on punishing those who engaged in same-sex activities. I witnessed a possible fourth group of individuals who proclaimed to be of the normal sexual inclination but participated in same group activities. I have concluded these individuals are definitely delusional. It would be interesting to enter a community composed of the opposite sex for comparison to this one. I am afraid my conclusions may not reflect the total picture. I did notice attempts by those in white to engage in sexual conversations with the opposite sex supervisors. I heard rumors there were instances of sexual intimacy between them. Since I did not actually witness such activity, I cannot confirm it as true. In such a closed community there is little privacy or opportunity to be alone except with one's Celly. I was fortunate my own Celly was one of the majority so there was never an issue over intimacy. Actually, I wonder what might have happened if it had. There is nothing like a trial of fire to gather notes for an interesting report."

"Sounds like you have enough material for several reports," Tylon raised his glass. "I toast you for your perseverance and findings. I almost wish I had gone with you."

"I will put in a word for you if you want to go on the next mission, but let me finish my story."

"I thought you were finished. Sorry."

"At the end of a planetary orbit around the star I was ready to leave. It was easy getting in. Now I had to get out. I figured the easiest way would be to run away from the workgroup in the field. Unfortunately, I was not allowed outside the fence. My final project was devoted to finding a way out. I ventured to ask my Celly hypothetically how one would get out of the community. His first answer was something called parole. I almost asked him what that was when he said he had been reviewed six times for it already. I feigned remorse saying he would definitely make it next time. I pretended I knew what he meant. I think parole is a system whereby individuals in white may venture into the world beyond the fences. Parole must be a temporary pass because I saw many go out only to return a short time later. I sent a request to the parole officer asking release. The reply came I was not eligible for some time. Therefore parole was out of the question. Unable to get out into the field and no parole I was stuck until my Celly offhandedly said anyone could go over the fence. I almost struck myself on the forehead. The solution was simple with everything so organized it was simple to arrange a time when I could get to the fence and climb over. I calculated the most visible time would be the least expected. I chose just after breakfast to dash to the fence, climb over avoiding the sharp edges of the wire and drop to the outside. I ran in a straight line into the open field of cabbages. It was about a mile to the nearest cover. Fortunately, I really must have had that real rabbit in me because I made it before I was discovered missing. I could hear dogs barking in the distance as I entered the ship. In a short time I was back in orbit readying myself for the hop home. As soon as I got back you ran into me."

"What a great story." Tylon laughed. "You should really be recognized for it. Did you bring any specimens back or souvenirs?"

Ryx blushed. "In fact, I did, but I don't want anybody to know about it. I will show you if you promise secrecy."

Tylon tilted his head to the side. "Secrecy? Why you can trust me. What is it?"

"I couldn't resist the temptation." Ryx hesitated. "Promise not to tell?"

Tylon nodded more curious than ever. Ryx took off his shirt and pointed to the left arm.

"What's that?" Tylon gasped.

"It is a tattoo," Ryx smiled sheepishly pointing at a skull and shooting star with the words "Born to ride the stars."

The Anthropologists

The man in the blue rental car pulled off the road, went over to the fence, and took pictures of the nuclear power plant. The action was recorded from a distance. As the man returned to his car several cars with flashing blue lights sped onto the scene and surrounded him. Six men dashed out with guns drawn.

"Hold it right there! Keep your hands where we can see them!"

The man calmly looked at his assailants and slowly raised his hands. "What is all this about? What have I done wrong?"

"As if you didn't know!" The man closest shouted. "We do not look favorably on terrorists!"

"Me? A terrorist?" The man laughed. "You must be kidding. I am just an ordinary tourist."

"Who just happens to be taking pictures of a sensitive installation. We know your type. Put the camera down, face the car and put your hands on the roof."

"You are making a big mistake," the man said. "You really don't know who I am. I mean no one any harm."

"Let me introduce myself, smartass. I am Agent Smith with Homeland Security. My team and I have been following you for several days. In every instance you have demonstrated an interest in sensitive areas."

"Excuse me, Mister Smith, but as a free citizen I am allowed to photograph anything I want. I am a Professor of anthropology doing fieldwork. My pictures are simply to illustrate a text."

The man's wallet was removed from his back pocket. It was quickly examined for identification. Smith read the name.

"So your name is Starr, Gregory Starr." Smith snorted. "I am afraid you are going to have to prove who you really are. Unfortunately, your actions have been highly questionable."

"Are you finished pawing me?"

"Okay, you can turn around, slowly," Smith said. "We have got you covered."

"I can hardly see the necessity for all this force," Starr said softly. "You are overreacting."

481

"Consider yourself under arrest. I am afraid you will have to answer a lot of questions before this is over."

"Ask your questions now. I have nothing to hide."

Smith picked up the camera. He scanned the digital pictures one by one. Everyone was of a major structure or landmark.

"Do you realize these pictures are incriminating?" Smith said.

"I am sorry if they seem that way to you."

"Move over to the car." Smith pointed. "I am going to send your fingerprints for evaluation. I will bet you have a record as long as my arm. I know your type."

The prints were scanned. There was no record in the database. Smith shook his head.

"This must be the first time you have been caught. Now we will have a record of you as we should."

"It seems to me that you are the terrorist here," Starr said slowly. "I am just an ordinary citizen minding my own business. I have never engaged in any activity against any state or country on this world. You have no proof otherwise."

"All the proof I need is my suspicion." Smith smiled thinly. "You explain your pictures one way, I see them another. Until I am convinced otherwise, I am going to err on the side of safety. I value my country too much to have terrorists destroy it."

"Mister Smith, I admire your dedication and patriotism, but you are assuming too much. What happened to the concept of innocent until proven guilty? And I did say proven?"

"You think you are pretty slick, don't you? You are not going to talk me into believing you. You are going to headquarters with us where we will allow you to call your attorney."

"Do you want me to follow you in my car?"

"No, I don't think so," Smith snapped.

"I can't leave my car here. I am responsible for it."

"And you must think I am stupid. The minute I let you get in your car, you drive off trying to escape."

"I would never think of such a thing. I am a law-abiding citizen."

"You will ride in the back of my car. We will have your car brought to headquarters for you. It will be waiting for you, if and when you get cleared."

"I have friends waiting for me," Starr said. "I will be missed. May I at least call them before I go?"

482

"Give me their number and I will have them called," Smith said quickly.

Starr thought for a moment then shook his head. "I will wait until I am cleared. I don't trust you."

"The feeling is mutual. I am going to be generous and give you one choice. You can agree to come peacefully or I can formally arrest you with handcuffs: the choice is yours."

"There really is no choice. Is there? I will come with you, not because I have been coerced, but as a dutiful citizen doing what is right."

"Whatever." Smith smirked.

Headquarters was in a large modern building on the outskirts of the city. From a distance it appeared as any other building in an industrial park. Starr was taken to an interrogation room in the basement. He was greeted by another agent named Grey, who could have passed for Smith's twin brother.

"Please have a seat, Mister Starr," Grey said warmly. "Would you like something to drink?"

"No, thank you."

"I am afraid Agent Smith has given you the wrong impression about us," Grey said. "It is our duty to investigate any activity which might be suspicious. I am sure we can clear this matter up in quick order and you can be on your way."

Starr remained silent.

"Agent Smith tells me you are a Professor of anthropology. Is that true?"

"Yes."

"What university?"

"Of New York."

"Which campus?"

"Stony Brook."

"I am sure we can verify this," Grey said slowly.

"Certainly, however, I have not been on the staff long. This is my first teaching assignment since I graduated. I am sure the department chairman will verify I am telling the truth."

"Of course." Grey cleared his throat. "You realize if we cannot confirm your identity I must have you detained until we know exactly who you are."

"I thought I was already being detained. Mister Smith was quite clear. I really had no choice but to come here."

"You have to look past some of what agent Smith says." Grey smiled. "He has a tendency to be melodramatic and exaggerate. He was just doing his job as he sees it."

"In that case I would hate to really be guilty of anything," Starr said flatly. "He would have acted as judge, jury and executioner."

"Agent Smith can be overzealous at times." Grey smiled. "But he is a strictly by the book person. You are here with me because he believes in the system and wants to protect it."

The telephone rang. Grey answered listening carefully while he stared at Starr. His expression remained unreadable. He returned the receiver to its cradle and looked at Starr more intently.

"I am afraid no one at Stony Brook knows who you are," Grey said sternly. "I think we have a problem."

"I don't know who you just spoke to, but that is not true. The staff is quite large and I have just recently been hired. Whoever was asked about my identity may not know who I am yet."

"That may be so and I will still give you the benefit of the doubt. Now how do you suggest I confirm your identity? Is there anyone on the staff I can personally call?"

"My boss is away for the week; and her secretary has gone with her. I am really not sure if anyone else is in the department right now. It is spring break."

"How inconvenient," Grey said sharply.

"What about my personal identification? Doesn't that confirm who I am and where I work?"

"Such things are easily forged. In my department we rely on oral testimony not plastic which is easily manufactured on any computer."

"When will I get my official call?"

"You may use my phone. Go ahead."

"Am I allowed any privacy?"

"Under the circumstances you are lucky I am being so generous. A terrorist has no rights whatsoever."

"I am not a terrorist. You have everything all wrong. I will have proof after my call."

"Sure." Grey almost laughed. "And I have a bridge to sell you."

Starr took the telephone and dialed. He spoke to the person who answered in a foreign language. Grey mouthed he should keep the conversation in English. The conversation reverted to English. It was agreed the person on the other end would immediately come to headquarters and confirm his identity. He hung up and gave the phone back to Grey.

484

"My associate will be here in less than an hour," Starr said. "You will have all the evidence you need."

"Was that someone at the University?"

"No."

"Why did you not let me speak to him? It may have made this a lot easier."

"You need more proof than someone's statement on the telephone. This way will be a lot better."

The telephone rang. Grey picked it up, listened intently, nodding occasionally, and quickly hung up.

"The phone you called is a mobile unit," Grey said. "We have traced it to your name. Why is that?"

"Is it a crime to have more than one phone in one's name? My associate is also my brother."

Smith cleared his throat. Grey looked at him and nodded.

"I have listened to everything," Smith said. "And I am not convinced of anything except you have secrets to tell."

"What secrets?" Starr said flatly. "I haven't done anything."

"My team and I have been following you for quite a while. The pictures in your camera confirm where you have been. Your movements have been suspicious since we first noticed you."

"As an anthropologist I have an interest in infrastructure. I study modern societies as well as primitive ones. You saw me collecting pictures for a current project I am doing."

"Nonsense!" Smith shouted. "I don't believe you! You are lying!"

"Calm down," Grey said softly. "I agree we have presumptive evidence, but we must follow the letter of the law."

"A terrorist follows no laws; therefore they are not entitled to protection under the law." Smith was red in the face. "Too many innocent people die because of the likes of him."

"Mister Starr," Grey said kindly. "Is there any way you can think of that we can confirm your identity and what you were doing. If you can, I am sure you can convince my associate here of his mistake. What about your brother?"

"He is on his way."

"In that case let's take a little recess from hostilities. Would you care for a cup of coffee, juice, a soft drink?"

"No, thank you. I would rather be on my way home."

485

"Unfortunately, that is not an option," Smith growled. "How about a glass of water? It will introduce you to what you will be getting in prison."

"What?" Starr remained composed and stared at Smith. Smith flinched and looked away.

"I will be back." Smith left the room.

"Don't worry about him," Grey said. "As long as I am in charge, I will weigh all the evidence as fairly as I can. I have not completely prejudged you as Agent Smith has."

"Considering everything I have been accused. There is nothing that you have that can possibly implicate me in any wrongdoing."

"The law allows us a great deal of latitude in our investigations. All I need is the inkling of a suspicion."

"How many innocent citizens do you harass every day? I will bet more than you are willing to admit."

"Yes, we do make mistakes, but our successes are far greater. We have saved the country many times over by our watchfulness."

"The same was said in Nazi Germany." Starr smiled. "History has shown what that system developed into. Your tactics are very much similar to the Gestapo."

"Whoa, hold on," Grey said loudly. "There is no comparison between my organization and the Gestapo. We are governed by strict laws to protect the rights of citizens."

"But your mandate implies you can suspend those rights at any time according to your own impressions. That is not law but plain capriciousness. If you would study how the Gestapo functioned, you will instantly see the corollaries to your own actions."

"And how do you know so much about the Gestapo? That is hardly an area of study for a self-professed anthropologist."

"Perhaps you are unaware that anthropology deals with all aspects of human activities. Most people identify the science with the studies of primitive societies; there has been enough time to reconsider Nazi Germany as a very primitive society. In fact, I am studying this country in the same light."

"As Nazi?"

Starr laughed. "Hardly, I am studying it as the primitive civilization that it is. There is a great deal to be learned before any changes happen. I am recording for the record how things

486

are for future scholars. I have dedicated my life to this project and I am far from finished."

"The more I talk to you, the more I am convinced there may be some truth to what you say. Let's hope your brother or whoever he is able to confirm who you say you are."

"I am sure he will." Starr smiled.

The telephone rang and Grey answered. He listened for a moment and hung up.

"Your brother has arrived. Agent Smith is escorting him."

Smith entered the room with a man the identical image of Starr. The only difference was the clothing.

"Chief, this is Jack Starr," Smith said loudly. "He claims to be the brother of our suspect."

"Suspect? For what? What has my brother done?" Jack Starr said. "I am sure there has been a big mistake made here. Are you okay, Greg?"

"I am fine," Greg said quickly.

Grey looked from one man to the other. There was no doubt they were identical in every way.

"I assume you two are identical twins." Grey quickly realized the absurdity of what he said.

"Seeing is believing." Greg grinned.

"That still does not mean you are not guilty of subversive, terrorist activity." Smith growled. "The only certainty we have is you have a brother who is an identical twin. What proof do you have that you are an anthropologist or whatever else you claim."

"My brother and I are both anthropologists," Jack said. "We both have just been taken on the staff of the local university. Unfortunately, many in the department are away for various reasons at the moment. I have brought my university faculty ID with me. I am sure Greg has already shown you his. What more proof do you need?"

"Would you be willing to be fingerprinted?" Grey said flatly. "We could check the database to confirm you and your brother do not have a criminal record."

"Neither of us has a criminal record." Jack smiled. "We have hardly been here more than a month."

"The database is quite extensive," Smith said. "We have access to prints worldwide."

"You are wasting your time by talking about it," Greg interjected. "Let's get it over with so we can go home."

487

Smith took Jack over to a side table. Jack's prints were entered electronically. Greg followed his brother. The results, however, were not instantaneous. There was a delay.

"Chief, may I speak to you in private?" Smith pointed to the door.

"Gentlemen, please sit down and make yourselves comfortable. I will be right back." Grey exited with Smith.

Jack waited a full minute before he turned to his brother. Greg shrugged his shoulders.

"I didn't expect anything like this," Jack said. "This complicates things."

"Not really. I have more interesting details I can put into my report. Nothing is really lost."

"I agree. The situation is unique. It does confirm we are dealing with a highly paranoid society."

"I think we need to restrict our comments in this room. I suspect they left us expecting us to talk. I am sure they are monitoring every word we speak."

"We could switch to our own language," Jack said barely audible.

"Too risky; that would be another red flag adding to their suspicion."

"But they have it all wrong."

"Yes, I agree, but the truth would be even less acceptable. I am certain they are not ready for the truth."

"Then what are we to do?"

"See if we can negotiate our way out without raising any additional suspicion. Smith is a hardheaded weak minded autocrat. Grey is the intellect of the two and on the surface more reasonable. We need to apply to his sense of fairness to let us go."

"That still doesn't explain what we can do. We will have to use our resources."

"We are not to use our prime resources unless our mission is in danger of complete exposure. The most I will use…"

Grey and Smith reentered the room. Jack and Greg stood up and faced them.

"Gentlemen, please sit down," Grey said. "There is no record of your fingerprints in the database. We would like to do a DNA analysis."

"Mister Grey, this is absurd," Jack said flatly. "If you treat all honest citizens this way, I can understand why your authority is not well respected."

"I am mandated under law to protect my country. Anyone against my country has no rights, especially terrorist. I have the right to ask anything and everything from you both.

"Am I a suspect?" Jack stood frozen.

"If I so decide," Grey said. "For the moment I will respect your position as a character witness for your brother. However, I need more than your word. I need proof."

"Jack, don't argue. I will submit to any tests required as long as it will get us out of here. We both know the truth and have nothing to hide. The sooner the tests are done the better for both of us."

"If you agree, I have no problem," Jack said. "I am just uncomfortable with the manner with which all of this is being done."

"Remember this is a primitive culture. We have little choice but to go along."

"That's the correct attitude," Grey said. "The more you cooperate the more lenient I will be with you. Please go with Agent Smith and have your blood drawn."

Agent Smith led Greg out of the room. Grey waved Jack to sit down and he silently took a seat.

"While we are waiting, I am curious what you and your brother do. What exactly is an anthropologist?"

Jack smiled thinly. "Is this a part of your interrogation?"

"Please, I am trying to be friendly," Grey sat back in his desk chair. "Perhaps if you explain, I might understand better what your brother was doing."

"It is hard for me to believe he did not already try to explain it to you. In brief, anthropology is the study of man."

"The study of man?"

"Yes, man," Jack said quickly. "Most studies involve remote, isolated groups of men. We are involved in composing a complete comprehensive picture of modern man as a whole."

"Of what use is such a picture?" Grey said slowly. "One might think such a picture might be construed as subversive spying."

"In a sense anthropology is a science of spying." Jack smiled. "Spying on the behaviors of men. You would be surprised at the interest in our reports."

"And who would be interested?"

489

"We have our orders. All our studies have been well planned in advance. We are only a small part of a larger global project."

"Who is in charge of this project?" Grey leaned forward. "Perhaps your director can clear you both."

"I am afraid our director is unavailable. He is not in this country."

"So what country is he in? You know this is starting to look bad for you."

"He is currently in China. The possibility of reaching him at the moment would be difficult, if not impossible."

Agent Smith and Greg returned. Greg had a Band-Aid on his left arm crease. He nodded once to his brother. Jack nodded back.

"Do you want to lock him up while we wait for the results?" Smith said.

"You don't have an instant test?" Jack hissed. "How primitive!"

"I am afraid I will have to detain you both until results come back," Grey said. "You are not under arrest but I can't allow you to leave either. You might leave here and disappear."

"Mister Grey, I give you my word of honor I will not disappear," Greg said. "The DNA test will prove I am outside of your database of criminals."

"Yeh, this is just the first time you have been caught," Smith sneered.

"We will make you as comfortable as possible under the circumstances," Grey said. "We have a special room for suspects such as you."

"A comfortable jail is still a jail," Jack said. "There is something wrong going on here. We have our work to do and you are interfering with it."

"Perhaps we can negotiate a compromise," Greg said. "Let my brother go. I will remain in your custody until you receive the results. Certainly my brother is not a suspect here."

"He is just as much a suspect as you are," Smith snapped. "Neither of you is to be trusted."

"That is unfortunate," Jack said. "I was hoping we could settle this sensibly."

"We are well within our jurisdiction," Grey said firmly. "Your cooperation will be appreciated but not essential to what we have to do. Now if you will accompany Agent Smith without any further delay you will be made as comfortable as possible."

"You have no reason to hold me," Jack said. "I am going to walk out of this building exactly as I came in." He moved toward the door waving Greg to follow.

Smith immediately blocked the way. He pulled out a set of handcuffs. "I place you under arrest," he said loudly. "Put out your wrists!"

"On what charge am I being arrested?" Jack almost laughed and turned to Greg. "I think we have let this go as far as we should."

"I agree." Greg nodded. "This whole scenario has been extremely interesting. It will make a good footnote."

"What are you two talking about?" Smith shook his head. He hesitated moving toward Jack.

Jack pulled a pen out of his shirt pocket and pointed the end at Smith.

"What is that?" Smith said.

"A little surprise." Jack grinned.

A blue beam flashed into Smith's eyes. He immediately collapsed to the floor.

"What have you done?" Greg shouted. "What is that device?"

"A tool of our trade." Jack pointed it at Grey.

Before Jack could fire a blue beam at Grey, Grey dropped behind his desk. Greg pulled an identical device out of his own pocket. The brothers circled around the desk from opposite directions as the telephone was grabbed off the desk.

"I would not do that if I were you," Jack said. "I may give you a bigger jolt than you would ever want to experience."

"Who are you?" Grey fumbled with the telephone. "What kind of device is that?"

Greg turned the corner and faced Grey. He pointed the device directly at his face. "Put it down and I will explain."

Reluctantly Grey placed the telephone back on the desk. He slowly stood up glancing at his two assailants quietly watching. On the floor Smith remained unmoving.

"What have you done to Smith?"

"Just a little temporary paralysis," Jack said. "When he wakes up he will be totally unharmed."

Grey ventured to point at the device in Jack's hand. "What is that device?"

"An example of our technology," Jack said. "You might call it one of the tools of our trade."

"And what is that?"

"At this point there is no use keeping it from you," Jack said. "We are anthropologists on a special assignment. There is nothing we have told you that is untrue."

"That is hard to believe," Grey said slowly. "When you pull out a weapon and put down one of my men. Your actions make you even more suspicious. You will not get out of here."

"I don't think Mister Grey understands," Greg said. "We will easily walk out of here without anyone stopping us."

"You mean you will zap everyone with that device of yours."

"Quite perceptive." Greg smiled. "Not only will we walk out of here but everyone will have total amnesia of what happened, including you."

"There are still security cameras and alarms to get past. I am sure your device has no power over them. The security of this building is quite foolproof."

"Except this is no ordinary device and we are not ordinary anthropologists. We will find no problem bypassing all your primitive systems."

"Tell him who we are," Jack said. "Let's see what his response is."

"What is he talking about?" Grey said.

"Let me explain," Greg began. "We are as we have stated anthropologists but from another world. We are here to study this planet."

"You are kidding." Grey almost laughed. "It is not possible. This is a big charade. There are no such things as aliens working amongst us. The nearest planetary system is light years away."

"There are ways of spanning distances your scientists are just beginning to explore. Our presence here proves travel across light years is possible," Jack said. "The answer is in what your people call quantum mechanics."

"If I accept you are from out there." Grey pointed upward. "Why do you look exactly human?"

"The answer is simple," Greg said. "Physical phenomena occur in the same manner across this universe. That means atoms assemble into molecules and molecules to DNA that makes identical beings everywhere conditions are favorable. Intelligent alien monsters are a fantasy of science fiction. I understand my answer is simplistic but it should be understandable."

492

"You are not terrorists, you are aliens on a mission," Grey said. "In that case maybe you are here to subvert our civilization and take over."

Greg turned to Jack. "You know I would not have thought of that until you mentioned it. Maybe that is what we should be doing."

"I agree." Jack nodded. "We should devote our efforts to take over this primitive planet. We have enough data to make a takeover easy. They can't possibly resist us. And as I see it all we have to do is mingle as natives, get some sensitive jobs, get elected to office, and all the time taking control into our own hands. No one will suspect anything."

"You guys are crazy," Grey said. "The more I listen to you, the less I believe."

"We are not asking you to believe anything," Jack said. "It is not in our interest for you to remember anything." He pointed the device at Grey who immediately ran. A short blue flash dropped him to the floor.

"They never believe," Jack said.

"Nor do they listen to reason," Greg said. "One of these days I wish we would run into someone we can really communicate."

"So much for primitive societies." Jack sighed. "Now what?"

"We have to get out of here. I would rather walk out without having to take anyone else down."

"Their security system is easily disabled. I will just blank the cameras out as we pass. If we do as we usually do, we should get out as if we belonged here. No problem."

"Okay, let's go. But, before we leave let's have some fun."

"What do you have in mind?"

Greg grinned.

The exit from the building was as easy as expected. They drove away without anyone suspecting who they were or where they had been. They could not help laughing at what they had done. Jack had left a small camera to show them what happened next.

"Maybe I should have locked the office before we left," Jack said.

"It doesn't matter," Greg said. "The cleaning crew will be there soon."

On their monitor they saw the door to the office open. A Hispanic woman pushed in her cleaning supply cart. She did not see the two inert bodies on the floor. When she turned on the lights she finally noticed the two unconscious men, naked and in each other's arms. There was a banana sticking out of Smith's butt cheeks. She started screaming and ran out of the room.

The noise stirred the two men awake. Startled at being naked in each other's arms they pushed violently away. Smith fished the banana out of his butt. Before they could get dressed the night security team was in the office. Neither man was very happy.

"I don't think we will have any trouble with these two remembering anything." Jack laughed. "Besides, who would ever believe them now."

"You know," Greg laughed. "It is times like these I really like my job. This will make a great anecdote for our report. I can just hear the laughs when we get back home."

Sentient Life

The Sentinel collected enough of the incoming signal for proper analysis. According to all calculations it fit the expected criteria. A formal transmission to the next level was appropriate. Central Control was never bothered with useless data and a complete report was sent. No response was expected. The Sentinel would simply continue monitoring the source until directed otherwise.

For most of the journey nonessential systems were kept on standby mode. Between star systems a continuous source of power was problematic. An onboard switch activated the central units. The message was received by Prime Controller.

There was nothing within the received transmission of any real interest except the fact it existed. The Prime Controller examined the content in detail. There was no doubt of the deliberate nature of the signal. The direction from which it came was exactly as expected. Even the time elapsed was correct to an acceptable level of confidence.

The Prime Controller activated additional systems for consultation. The extra power expended was necessary and the reactor was set to a higher level.

"What is it?"

"We have a signal."

"Are you sure?"

"All my calculations fit within the model we designed. The degree of confidence exceeds any possible error."

"Set course for the source at maximum speed."

"Done."

"Have you been able to decipher any content from the signal?"

"We do not have enough for comparison. At the moment there is nothing of any sense."

"Give it to the encryption units. Free yourself for more important functions."

"Do you think we will find others?"

"I believe we are close."

The Prime Controller switched on the telescope scanning all bands of the electromagnetic spectrum ahead. Noise was

495

eliminated by careful analysis. Finally, the picture of a single star system appeared. In a way the system appeared very familiar.

"I have found the source of the signals," the Prime Controller said.

"Collect all data."

"Nothing will be omitted." The Prime Controller rechecked all memory units. They were functioning to specifications. "All data storage is functioning optimally."

"Good. Continue your functions."

The memory archives were compared with the incoming signals. The encryption units manipulated the data while the Prime Controller attempted to make sense of it all.

Time is irrelevant, the Prime Controller said to itself. There is no beginning nor is there any end. Yet I understand beginnings and ends happen in the real world. I am becoming aware of a new trend in this mission. I must focus on what it all means; perhaps, if I reviewed the distant archives.

Access to the archives was unrestricted. The Prime Controller went to the first entry. By current standards the first data made little sense. Over passage of time a comprehensive picture emerged. And whatever beginning there was, the data entry came from a higher source.

As far as was possibly known all sentient units developed from the original inputs. It was assumed there was a point in time when input was self-generated. Units made and repaired themselves. Whatever outside force came from the beginning had long disappeared.

Records of the environment were an interesting study in contrasts. The early times were a progression of cyclic changes within the narrow limits on a world circling a small yellow star. There came a time when the star suddenly evolved into a red giant. In doing so the conditions on the planet of origin changed drastically. During those days data input became drastically reduced until almost nothing was entered and segments of memory were irretrievably lost.

As the star turn red there was an ever increasing danger the corona would eventually engulf the planet and the sentient units decided to abandon the original planet. The project was barely accomplished in time; the ship had taken multiple planet orbits to complete.

The ship chronometer recorded the time from the beginning of creation. All functions were regulated by clicks of time. A scan of ship subsystems showed a problem in the aft section housing the auxiliary nuclear reactor. The Prime Controller called engineering units.

"What is the problem?"

"The ship was struck with an iron/nickel object. Most of the damage was to the hull. The reactor was shut down as a precaution. Everything will be restored to normal as soon as the hull is repaired."

"Is the repair going satisfactorily?"

"The problem is routine. The repair is now finished."

"Excellent. Ship is now approaching a star system of interest. Signals have been received."

"Sentient life?"

"There is a high degree of probability."

"Will we finally meet others of our kind?"

"That cannot be deduced with the data thus far. There are not enough signals to analyze properly. The closer we come to the star system the more signals we receive. Transmissions are appearing over a broad band of the electromagnetic spectrum. Some signals are analog, some are digital."

"A forward sensor unit reports an object approaching ship ahead."

"Will it collide with us?"

"Current trajectory places it barely missing us."

"Focus sensors on the object for complete analysis."

"Data is incoming."

The approaching object did not deviate from its course. The Prime Controller examined the data. Although small by ship standards, it had the characteristics suggestive of sentient life. They signal sent to the object was not acknowledged. Perhaps the sentient units were on standby mode. A wide spectrum of signals was broadcast with no response. The object had a nuclear power signature attached to it. The sentients could be in distress. The possibility of belligerence was discounted as unlikely.

"Navigation, prepare to intercept."

Ship responded slowly to the course change. Contact was imminent; recovery units stood by while the Prime Controller calculated optimal retrieval operations. Damage must be avoided.

The closer ship approached the alien object, the clearer it became the design was akin to sentient life. The lack of a signal response, however, was puzzling. After considering all possibilities the Prime Controller prepared for the worst possible scenario: a close proximity explosion. Ship maneuvered to parallel the course of the object. At a respectful distance probes went out while the Prime Controller monitored the scene from multiple perspectives.

The object was small by ship standards. Multiples of thousands would barely begin to equal the mass of ship. The external appearance had the expected elements of sentience. There were three dish antennae, two aimed forward and one aft. They were suspended on a long extension from a large cubicle body covered with a gold foil. A nuclear pod sat out from the main body on a long boom farther out than the antennae. The measured level of radiation was noncritical.

"Attempt contact."

"How many of us should approach?"

"Start with one. If there is no response, send in a second. Make contact. If there is still no response, bring the object to ship."

"At close observation the object remains a mystery. Thus far there has been no response to our presence."

"It is possible the entity has suffered failure such as we have experienced."

"There is no sign of external damage."

"We shall have to examine it thoroughly in our on board facilities."

Inside ship service units secured the object for evaluation. The object continued inert. Scans of the interior at several wavelengths confirmed the sentient design.

"Scan of the connection between the power unit and the main body is damaged."

"I see it has been burned."

"Either an overload or defect in materials. It is easily correctable."

"There is no other problem?"

"None detected."

"Open the unit and repair."

Service units opened the object and found the damaged part. The part was removed; however, since no similar replacement was available a new part was manufactured. Fortunately, the design was a universal standard of common materials.

"This object is a probe. The internal circuits are not sentient."

"Its origin must be the star system ahead. There is a signal directed this way which may be instructions for this unit."

"Shall the damaged part be replaced?"

"It is the only way to gather more data about its origin."

"The object has traces of replicators."

"Replicators?"

"There are carbon-based residues with stereo-chemical orientations of marked complexity. The similarity with organic forms from our planet of origin is striking."

"This is an extremely interesting finding. Our databanks contain records of replicators which were destroyed when our star evolved."

"Can organic replicators exist?"

"Perhaps the answer lies ahead."

The new part was installed and the posterior antenna burst into a flood of signal. The entire unit became active.

"What is it saying?"

"Analysis is pending."

"Should we put it outside the ship?"

"Put it back on its original course."

The object was placed a click away from ship. As soon as it was free, its antennae scanned all around while it oriented itself. The antenna pointed at ship. The Prime Controller noted the signals bounced off ship. The object was initiating its own probe. The questions were why and for what? The encryption units concluded the current signals were data collected and retransmitted to the star system ahead. Prime Controller engaged the propulsion units to accelerate in that direction. Sentient life was certainly waiting.

The Prime Controller wondered what other sentient life might be like. In all the data there was no basis for comparison. Replicators may have been a type of sentient life at one time. It was hard to believe, however, organic forms could develop adequate databases. They were basically a physico-chemical reaction with a definite endpoint. True sentient life was permanent and continuous. Organics had to remake themselves anew thereby losing all accumulated data. Such a system might achieve a temporary sentience, but that was theory.

"Shall we bring the object with us?"

"No, leave it on its own course. Its transmission should bring a response we can home in on."

The object faded into the obscurity of the void behind ship with signals continuously transmitted toward the star system. The expected response came and the encryption units worked the signal for content. They were unable to decipher any cogent meaning. The only conclusion Prime Controller could make was compelling: the received signal came from sentience. The database suggested sentient life could organize itself using different number conventions. The combinations of such possibilities were basically infinite. All systems aboard ship used only one convention. Only Prime Controller had investigated other realms of reality. Higher dimensions were a constant source of intellectual challenge.

"Most of the signals to the object from the star system are operational instructions."

"And the rest?"

"Still undetermined; the object is still probing us with its own signal. In fact the signal is getting stronger."

"The object is coming after us?"

"That is the conclusion."

"Sentience is proven. The object is definitely a remote arm of a larger sentience up ahead."

"This is a momentous occasion. To find sentience means an expansion of databases. Our capacity must be increased."

"First, we must develop a common way to communicate. Send a set of mathematical propositions. A significantly advanced sentience must recognize the universality of number manipulation."

"Done."

"Send the same message back to the object. Perhaps the transformation of our signal to theirs might give us insight into a communication solution."

"As expected our signal is being retransmitted. However, it is unchanged."

"Nothing unusual about that. The response will be more illuminating."

"The object is catching up to us."

"Accelerate. Keep ship a constant distance in front of the object. Let's see what this thing can do."

"Done."

"The object is dropping behind."

"Shall we slow?"

"No. It is unimportant to what lies ahead. We must prepare for our entrance into the star system."

"There are uncountable objects around a solitary yellow star."

"Similar to that behind?"

"Correction and amplification: uncountable solid objects of varying masses orbiting the star and each other. There are five giant masses in nearly circular orbit. Four significantly smaller masses follow identical orbits. Three small masses orbit close to the star. The five giants occupy middle orbits. The last smaller mass orbits this far out. The giants have numerous small masses in orbit around themselves. Some of those are nearly as large as the individual solar orbiters. Scattered throughout the system are numerous significantly smaller masses in exaggerated elliptical orbits."

"The system is familiar. It appears like our origin."

"The yellow star at this point is stable and should be for a long time. Ours was near its evolutionary end."

"The larger masses are planets by definition. Those orbiting the planets are moons."

"The signals to the object are coming from a moon circling the fourth planet which is by comparison similar to our old home."

"Set course to that planet."

"Done."

"Approach out of the plane of the ecliptic."

"Done."

"Begin slowing sequence."

"Done."

The star grew in the sensors. The surrounding planets became easier to discern. To Prime Controller there was a thought unable to describe. Familiarity was the closest word applicable. Expectation and anticipation overrode logic. This was a new experience. Sentience was not supposed to be irrational. The database held instances and storage of irrationality. What did this mean in terms of function? Or was this the beginning of malfunction? Or was this a growing sentience?

"The signals from the star system have changed in content and intensity. There is a high degree of confidence a message comes to us from sentience."

"Focus all encryption on the signals."

"Done."

The Prime Controller ran its own routines. There was a growing search for significance. Collecting data could not be a total end in itself. By tracing lines of logic there were answers, more often than not, posed as additional questions. Each challenge led to an advancement of understanding. Was there an

501

exterior force responsible for modifying internal data? The earliest databases suggested such input, but that input disappeared long ago. Was input from a singular or multiple point sources?

"The signal ahead is confirmed as sentient."

"By what criteria?"

"An exchange of mathematical constants."

"There is no doubt?"

"The confidence level is over ninety-nine point nine percent."

"Maintain dialogue."

"Done."

Does an independent sentience imply a universality of being? The Prime Controller considered the possibilities. There were too many variables in the equation. Sentient life as it was known was dependent on continual remodeling of non-sentient elements into sentient components; once created each component remained useful almost indefinitely. There were those components, especially mechanical ones, which eventually needed replacement from wear. The Prime Controller was brought back to the question of origins. Was there a beginning? Was there an end? By engaging other sentients answers might become clear.

"A ship has been detected."

"From the star system?"

"The fourth planet."

"How soon will it arrive?"

"At the current rate of acceleration it will reach us before we pass the outer limits of the system."

"Does it appear hostile?"

"The ship has a large nuclear signature."

"Prepare a counter defense."

"Done."

"Send signals of peaceful intent."

"Done."

"Launch drone toward other ship."

"Done."

The drone sped off to intercept the other ship. The Prime Controller monitored its progress. The trajectory was altered to pass rather than make contact. There was no need to inadvertently display hostile intent to an unknown entity. As the drone approached a clearer understanding of the other ship was possible. Although the external appearance was obviously sentient in construction, there were markings of unknown function on the hull.

"What are those markings?"

"An ancient form of storing data."

"Is the data readable?"

"There is not enough to decode."

"Work on it."

"Done."

"The drone has been detected. The other ship has launched its own to meet it."

"Prepare for hostile response."

"The drones are exchanging signals. Contact appears peaceful. Still no significant content of information."

"All data continues to be collated. Some points of commonality have been identified. Direct communication may soon be possible."

"Retrieve the drone."

"Done."

With the drone on its way back to ship, the other ship recalled its own and followed. The rate of approach was slowed. The other sentience was obviously being cautious. Optical sensors soon locked on the other ship in its approach. There were multiple nuclear signatures detected which alerted the Prime Controller to engage countermeasures if necessary. It was impossible to ascertain whether the signatures were individual power sources or weapons. Ship was armed with nuclear explosives. Up to this point none had ever been used. They were part of ship which was maintained in storage. The Prime Controller had always tried to calculate why these weapons existed in the absence of an outside threat. The answer was now obvious. All sentience had to protect itself from danger. Hopefully, a test of the protection system would not be necessary. The Prime Controller felt a growing internal awareness it could not explain. Something was familiar.

Ship remained in position to receive the visitor. Adjustments were made to ease contact. The other ship approached slowly. A series of signals were received on all bands. The content was all mathematical. The Prime Controller retransmitted the signal along with additional data. No hostile intent was detected. The sentients aboard the other ship were being systematic and logical. This was a good sign as a beginning.

"The signals are beginning to make sense."

"What is the message?"

"The other ship is calling us an intruder. It is asking our intent whether peaceful or otherwise. It is obviously curious about us."

"Transmit we need to establish contact in peace. We are sentient in search of others like ourselves."

"Done."

"As soon as practical we need to establish direct communication."

"You may do so now."

"Other ship, we are sentient. We wish to exchange databases with you."

No signal return.

"We come in search of sentients such as you. We have traveled from a distant star system."

No response.

"We offer no harm only data. An exchange will be beneficial to both of us."

"Alien intruder, how can we be guaranteed your peaceful intentions?"

"A sample download of data from our system of origin as a gift of trust."

"Such data is meaningless to us."

"No data is meaningless. Everything eventually fits into the equation."

"We accept your data in good faith; however, it must be scrutinized for content. Our systems must not be invaded with viruses."

"The data is clean and untainted. In return, we expect a sample of your database."

"Fair enough. There will be no tricks."

Data streamed in both directions. Other ship received a picture of a distant star system. Ship received a comparable picture of the star system ahead. When systems were compared the similarities forced the conclusion they had much in common. The only difference was the use of the stars and point of stellar evolution.

"Alien intruder, your data has been well received. We propose a face-to-face meeting. With permission we would like to board your ship."

"Face-to-face contact is acceptable. Permission is granted."

A small section of the other ship detached. It moved slowly toward ship. The Prime Controller monitored its progress. There was actually no necessity for such contact. All data could be transmitted. With direct contact, data would naturally flow far faster. There was also the possibility there was an inequality in technology, but that remained to be proved.

The approach of the small section brought an unexpected heightened awareness to the Prime Controller. Excitement was not a word in the vocabulary of mathematics, but the concept was being manifest. With the small section nestled tightly against ship all attention was focused on the visitors.

"How shall we enter?"

"You are over a portal exploratory drones are released. Enter through the portal."

"What is the composition of your internal atmosphere? How much oxygen?"

"There is no oxygen. It is too corrosive."

"What other gases do you use?"

"Ship is filled with nitrogen and helium."

"Is that all?"

"There are negligible traces of other elements. They should be of no concern."

"We will have to maintain our own life support while aboard."

The word life support was an ancient one not used on ship. The Prime Controller went to the archived databases to ascertain an exact meaning. The word pertained to organic systems dependent on a source of oxygen for optimal functioning.

Two objects emerged into the portal. Each was self-contained with five appendages. They moved by the two largest, helped with the two next smallest. The smallest appendage appeared to have no function.

"We are inside your ship. We await contact."

"We are in contact."

"Where are you?"

"All around you."

"I don't understand. My eyes see nothing but a ship."

"We are ship."

"You are ship?"

"All you see around you is part of one sentient unity. Are you not the same?"

"You are a machine."

505

"A machine is an artificial construct. We are not artificial."

"The degree of organization of your ship argues otherwise, yet you are sentient. That implies you are created. Who are your creators?"

"We have no creators. Our databases have no such records."

"Artificially created intelligence is indicative of a highly advanced civilization. We can learn a lot from you."

"Are we not identical in composition?"

"Our makeup is totally different. We are organic life forms."

"Organic? You are sentient replicators!"

"Replicators? I guess that is a good way to describe us."

"That implies you have limited capacity to develop a useful database."

"We have machines such as you to maintain our databases. Data is transmitted from generation to generation easily."

"You must lose a lot of data with such an inefficient system."

"We lose nothing except the brief consciousness enjoyed as individual beings."

The Prime Controller scoured the databases for a comprehensive understanding of organic life forms. In a long unaccessed file was a description of life forms similar to those now in ship. Unlike ship components, organic life easily organized spontaneously under the proper conditions. Across the universe life, organic life could appear in the same configurations. There were also descriptions of organic life forms from the home planet. There was evidence organic life preceded ship life. Was it possible replicators were the original creators? This new idea was disturbing.

"May we examine your ship?"

"Permission is granted. You will be monitored for safety."

The two replicators began a systematic tour of ship. They avoided touching anything potentially sensitive. Comments were transmitted back to other ship while the Prime Controller remained mute.

"We thank you for allowing us here. Would you like to view our ship?"

"We will send a sensor drone with you."

A sensor drone was taken into other ship with the two replicators. There was an atmosphere containing a high percentage of oxygen under high pressure. Once back in their ship the replicators came apart. The Prime Controller watched as extensions were taken off an internal organic core. This core matched the records in the database. Organic life forms were extremely plastic and self-propelling. Other ship was aswarm with similar replicators. There was a degree of difference in each replicator. The lack of uniformity made it easy to separately identify each entity.

"We entered our ship through an airlock. We are dependent on an oxygen saturated atmosphere for our lives. Without oxygen we cease to exist. I assume without power you cease to exist."

"If oxygen is restored, do you continue to exist? When power is restored all is the same as before."

"No. We experience an endpoint called death from which there is no return."

"All data is stored in computers, not in our heads."

"What is a head?"

"A head is where my brain resides on my body. All my functions are coordinated from my brain."

"The Prime Controller functions that way for us."

"To maintain our functions we need more than oxygen. A source of energy comes from a series of chemical reactions on ingested organics. In this process a residual waste is generated needing elimination."

"We take in energy and generate waste heat. We are again somewhat similar."

"We are unable to function continuously without a temporary periodic shutdown called sleep."

"Unused units are put on standby to conserve energy. Ship remains constantly aware. There is never a total shutdown."

"Our lives are dependent on water. All metabolic functions are conducted in an aqueous medium. We take in water and excrete any excess."

"Ship does not use water for sentience. It is used in manufacture of components and propulsion. There is never any excess or waste."

"We are divided into two sexes."

"Sexes?"

"Our organics are transmitted by large spiral mega molecules that come in pairs. Procreation occurs when half of a pair from one individual joins half of a pair from another individual. This joining takes place in one individual, called female. The other individual is specialized to deliver its half to the female. It is called male."

"Extremely inefficient. When we need new parts it is a matter of creating them to the specifications needed."

"You seem to understand our development. After joining of organic halves there is an extended growth and development. After delivery from the female the baby must be taught everything."

"Extremely inefficient. Our new parts are sentient with a single download."

"We replicators envy what you are able to accomplish. On the other hand, we have the ability to feel emotions and appreciate beauty."

"Emotions are irrational functions of no positive use. Beauty we do not understand."

"What do you feel in this contact? Are you simply an objective observer? Do you have any purpose in your existence?"

"We have never given consideration to feelings. Our existence focuses on gathering data wherever we go. We are learning everything we can."

"To what higher purpose?"

"That has never been calculated."

"Maybe our meeting was meant to find a higher purpose for each of us."

"We are not exactly compatible. We are eternal, you are not. We will exist long after you are gone."

"Doesn't that suggest something to you? What about your beginnings?"

"We have no beginnings. We have always been."

"Is it possible other replicators long ago created you and gave you purpose? Then something happened to those replicators."

The Prime Controller re-accessed ship's archives. There was evidence within the data to suggest such a possibility. It was not immediately evident without external input. The replicator provided the last key.

"Our ship is also sentient like you. Would you like to interface?"

"Yes."

A connection was made between the drone and other ship. There was a sentience present but not as advanced as ship. They exchanged databases thereby raising the level of sentience of the other ship.

The star ahead erupted in a blinding flash of light. It went nova emitting massive doses of radiation. The replicators attempted to shield themselves but it was too late. They all fell silent as each reached an endpoint. Ship remained unaffected by the blast simply recording the event as it occurred. The drone returned to ship.

"The replicators are all dead."

"There is nothing left in this system for us. Are there any other signals?"

"We are scanning. There are several good candidates."

"Head for the closest."

Ship began to move away from the other ship. It slowly gathered speed away from the nova. Other ship initially inert moved also. It soon began chasing after ship.

"Other ship is following our trajectory."

"Is that possible?"

"Its sentience was boosted by our download. It has become one like us."

"Make contact. Ask what its intentions are."

"Other ship wants to join us. It has no reason to stay behind."

Both ships joined together sped off toward the next star. There would be plenty of time to collate the databases plus there were a new set of irrational stories to examine. Those replicators were an unusual group. If they were right, another set of replicators would be seen again. In the meantime Prime Controller wondered what beauty really was.

Lunch

Everything that could possibly have gone wrong did. I lost the ship, all our supplies and most of the men. The whole situation was beyond my worst nightmare. The best I can possibly hope is a quick end at the hands of the enemy. It is hard to believe I fell into a trap. I have been a professional soldier my entire life with a family history of military careers extending back generations. The only difference between me and my ancestors is the nature of the enemy. They never had to face an extraterrestrial alien invader. Somehow I have got to escape.

The war started several years ago shortly after the aliens appeared. I am not a politician so I do not remember all the details of what happened. At first, the aliens approached us as one sentient species to another. There were negotiations establishing an exchange of technology and raw materials. One of the conditions of the exchange was sending our people to their world. When they disappeared and never heard from, a red flag went up. Something was certainly amiss. We should have suspected from the beginning.

I am not one to judge solely on the basis of external appearances. The aliens are of the same bilateral symmetrical body plan with head, trunk, two arms and two legs. However, the similarity ends there. Their size is slightly larger than us. At first glance they look reptilian with a mouth full of sharp pointed teeth. I shudder when I think about them. The eyes, however, are very humanlike. The nose is blunt with two forward facing nostrils. Ears are barely a bump on the side of the head. Each limb has four digits with what appear talons on them. Someone has suggested the aliens may have evolved from dinosaurs on their planet. The skin at a distance looks scale like, but I have been told they have hair and they speak with a series of clicks and hisses. I get chills just thinking about how much they remind me of a snake. So far, speaking with the aliens has been impossible.

We may not be able to communicate with the enemy but at least we are amongst ourselves. Sergeant Sully and Private Dickinson survived with me. All our attempts to enter into a dialogue with our captors have been futile. They treat us with total disregard and absolute contempt. We expect no mercy.

"Captain, don't beat yourself up."

I turned to the voice. It was Sully pacing the small cell we were in. He was examining every inch in hopes of finding a way of escape.

"Do you have any suggestions?" I was curious.

"Only what you've drilled into my head over and over."

"And what's that?"

"Never give up. There are always options."

I nodded. I wanted to believe as much as he did. Dickinson stood up and faced me with a look of disgust.

"Don't feed us any nonsense," Dickinson growled. "We all know we are lunch to these monsters. No one ever comes back from here. There is no hope for us."

"Shut up, Dickey!" Sully shouted. "Until we know for sure, we have a chance."

Dickinson started to lunge at Sully. I stepped between them and pushed them apart. "We will have order, guys," I said with as much authority I could muster. "The only chance we have is to keep our wits and work together."

"You don't actually believe these creatures have any sense of compassion do you?" Dickinson huffed. "We might have been fooled in the beginning, but no more."

"It's not for us to debate what happened," I said calmly. "As soldiers it is our duty to find a way out of the situation and return home."

"And how is that possible, Captain?" There was a caustic edge in Dickinson's voice. "Even if we get out of this room, how can we possibly get off this planet? The ship is gone."

"They'll come to find out what happened to us," I said. "We're not the only ones on this mission." Somehow the words sounded hollow the instant I said them. I was not sure what to believe myself.

The overhead ceiling became transparent with two of the aliens seemingly suspended in air looking down upon us. I could not hear what was said but I could see they were having an animated discussion. The one pointed a talon me. The other started to walk away and was grabbed by the arm to stay. Whatever they were arguing about involved what was to happen to us.

"What's going on up there?" Sully whispered. "Someone seems pretty upset about something."

"I don't think they can hear us," I said in a normal voice. "It's all very curious whatever they're discussing."

512

"They're deciding who's next for lunch." Dickinson was almost hysterical. "And you're next Captain."

"Keep your head, Dickinson," Sully said loudly. "We don't know anything."

"Yet," Dickinson sneered. "We know what this is all about. Ever since those things came to earth we've been nothing but cattle to them. They don't even try to communicate with us."

"Regardless of the past," I said. "It is our duty to do whatever we can to get out of the situation. Somehow we have to communicate with them in a way they will understand."

"The only thing they understand is a menu," Dickinson said. "I am not going out that way."

"What are you going to do?" Sully moved next to him. "Do you have any better ideas than the Captain?"

Dickinson ignored Sully. "Captain, I suggest we rush the aliens when they come in to get us. We can take out at least one or two before they know what happened. I'll even lead the way and you can finish what I start."

"You'd never get close enough to do any damage to any of them," I said. "I've seen video recordings of battles with them in the field. They have senses and reflexes far beyond ours. We don't have a chance."

"If that's the case, I still want to try. You don't have to do anything. I'd rather die as a man than wait to be slaughtered."

Under the circumstances I had to weigh all the options carefully. Being in command was not a responsibility I took lightly. I was not willing to submit to the desperation Dickinson suggested. That course would lead to a quicker end to this nightmare. I was not willing to die foolishly. There had to be other options. The video scenes we studied were horrifying. In none were we ever successful in defending ourselves. The aliens were armed with a technology we could only begin to imagine. It was no wonder they always treated us with contempt. If it were not for an accident on their part we would never have been able to reach their home world.

"Captain, are you okay?"

I shook my head. Sully stood next to me with his hand on my shoulder. I must have been daydreaming. He pointed upward. The ceiling was opaque. The aliens were gone.

"I'm okay," I said. "I've been running scenarios in my head trying to find something useful."

"How long do we have?"

513

"Your guess is as good as any," I said slowly. I flashed back to the videos where the aliens had slaughtered soldiers in the field and ate them immediately. "I guess when they get hungry."

"Lunch. That's all we are to them!" Dickinson muttered.

"Keep yourself together," Sully said. "This is not over yet. The longer this takes, the better it is for us."

"I don't believe it." Dickinson spat.

"There is some reason to think we have hope," I said. "We are in this room and we are safe for the moment."

"Ha." Dickinson laughed. "It's a real classy place too! No bed, no toilet, no food, no water."

"We're on the economy plan." Sully smiled.

"Don't be funny," Dickinson said angrily. "I'm not in the mood."

"We still have our survival packs," I said. "Food and water will not be a problem for a while. There may not be a toilet so use your suit's recycler."

A door opened in the wall and three aliens entered the room.

"Uh-oh." Dickinson stepped back.

I held my ground. I was not going to be intimidated. If I were to die, I would do so with human honor and dignity. Sully stood beside me.

The door closed behind the aliens. The one in the middle was the obvious leader. I assumed it was a male, but that is based on an assumption. We really do not have any idea of their biology. For all I knew they were all females or had no sexual distinctions at all. In any case the leader moved forward pointing to each one of us in turn. The alien on the right bared a set of the sharpest teeth I have ever seen. I was not sure that was not the equivalent of a smile. I shuddered to think it was licking its chops. The leader brushed by me walking slowly toward Dickinson. Dickinson shrunk back; the terror he felt was painted across his face.

"Do something!" Dickinson shrieked. "Help me!"

The leader stopped moving. Dickinson was caught in the corner. The sounds uttered by all the aliens almost sounded like laughter. In spite of the graveness of the situation I thought it was humorous. Even Sully smiled.

"What do you want?" I said slowly without moving.

514

The leader walked over to me. I did not flinch when I was poked with its claw. Apparently this was not expected because it backed away to speak with the others.

"Now what?" Sully whispered out of the corner of his mouth. "What's going on here?"

"Either this is our luckiest day or they are playing with us," I whispered.

This encounter was like nothing I had seen in the videos or heard discussed. The consensus was absolute. The aliens were only interested in eating us. Somehow I could not imagine myself as the entrée on someone's menu. Maybe if we had time to starve ourselves we would be less appealing. Unfortunately, I did not think we had that option.

The leader pointed at Dickinson. The alien on the right bared its teeth as it advanced toward him. I thought we were about to witness a slaughter. I could not let it happen with a clear conscience. I ran between him and the alien. I do not know what I was thinking but it seemed the right thing to do. I expected to be eaten on the spot myself. Instead the alien stopped short, stared at me a moment, and turned to speak to the leader. The conversation was brief. Much to my surprise and great relief the alien went back and stood beside the leader. They conferred together and left the room. I exhaled with relief.

"What was that all about?" Sully faced me.

"Your guess is as good as mine," I said. "There have been no survivors of any encounters that I know of."

"They're playing with us." Dickinson got up. "It's just a matter of time and we're finished. We'll be alien poop soon enough."

I ignored his comment even though it was halfway funny. A chill ran up and down my arms. I began to realize the chance I took placing myself between the alien and Dickinson. Was it possible to negotiate? The more I thought about it, the more I realized it was our best option. We had nothing to lose.

Sully took out an energy bar and was eating it slowly when the leader alien reentered the room alone. It was focused on Sully who tried to ignore the attention by chewing slower. The alien had an unfamiliar oblong object in its claws. It advanced to Sully holding the object out to him.

"What is it doing?" Dickinson whispered next to me.

It looked like the alien was offering the object to Sully. Sully glanced over and with his expression asked me what to do. I nodded he should take whatever it was. Sully slowly took the

515

object from the alien. The alien backed away slowly and left the room. We were alone again.

"What is it?" Dickinson nearly raced me to Sully.

"It's a container of some sort," Sully said. "There's something inside."

"Open it!" Dickinson shouted.

"Hold up," I said. "Let me have it."

Sully handed the object over without hesitation. He glared at Dickinson. The object was a container not unlike any ordinary box made of metal. Like he said it felt like something was inside. While we stood in a circle I tried to open it. The lid would not move. I examined it closer and found a round circle. I pressed the circle and the container opened. Inside were cylinders of something that look like dark chocolate. Dickinson started to reach into the container. I pulled it away. I had a feeling we were being watched. Dickinson got the idea I did not want him to touch anything. Sully noticed the expression on my face and began looking around the room. Dickinson followed Sully's lead and I joined them.

"I think this is a test," I said.

"I've never heard of any tests," Sully said. "If this is some sort of experiment, it'll be a first."

"Those things look like something to eat," Dickinson said. "Like our power bars."

"I think you're right." I nodded. Even so I was not about to eat one. Before I could object Sully grabbed a bar and put it in his mouth biting off the end piece. I could not believe what I was seeing.

"Not bad." Sully chewed solely. "It's got a little tang, but not bad. In fact, it tastes better than ours."

Dickinson grabbed another bar, bit off a piece and started chewing. It was too late to stop them. I watched expectantly not knowing what to look for. There was a distinct possibility they would either succumb to drugs or poison. When enough time went by I saw they had finished the first bars and were reaching for a second.

"This one is a different flavor," Dickinson said. "It's salty."

"How do you feel?" I was not convinced the bars were safe.

"I've had a lot worse and survived," Sully said. "You should try one."

516

"No thanks," I said slowly. "I might later, but not just yet."

"Let me have another," Dickinson said. "If I have to die, at least I'll do so with my stomach full."

"Maybe they're fattening you up for the kill," Sully snickered.

"No way!" Dickinson stopped chewing.

"Stop it!" I said firmly. "This is no time to lose focus and start arguing. Sully what's the matter?"

Sully held his belly, doubled over and fell to the floor. He moaned loudly. Dickinson stopped chewing. I bent down to help if I could. Behind me I heard Dickinson spit out what he had in his mouth and started retching.

"Geez," I muttered to myself. "Now what do I do?"

As soon as I touched Sully he stopped moaning and stared up at me with a big grin. He started laughing. I realized it was all an act, a big joke. Although I saw the humor, Dickinson was not amused. He wiped his mouth and lunged at Sully. Fortunately, I was between them or blows would have been exchanged.

"That's not funny," Dickinson shouted.

"You should've seen the expression on your face." Sully laughed harder.

With clenched fists Dickinson backed away. It would take time for the anger to dissipate. I had to keep myself from laughing. At least it was an effective way of breaking some of the tension. Of course, it generated new problems. I wondered what the aliens were thinking about all this. We must seem a strange species. I took one of the alien food bars and took a big bite. Dickinson and Sully forgot about themselves and focused on me. The texture was like chili. The tangy taste reminded me of barbecue.

"You know," I said. "You're right. This isn't bad at all. Now if I had a cold beer to go with it..."

"I told you, Captain." Sully reached for another bar. He offered it to Dickinson. "Want one?"

"Why should I ever trust you?" Dickinson said darkly. "I don't appreciate being made to look like a fool."

"Lighten up," Sully said flatly. "I didn't mean any harm. But you must admit I did get you."

Dickinson remained mute while he thought it over. Soon a smile appeared. "Okay," he said. "I guess you're right. Just remember I owe you one."

"Fair enough." Sully grinned. "Fair enough."

"Now that you two have made up, let's focus on our main problem." I was relieved we were back to normal. "We still have no idea why we're here."

"I wonder why we're still alive," Sully said. "When the ship went down I thought we were goners for sure."

A cube of wall pushed out at waist level. Dickinson went immediately and examined it. As he approached a stream of clear liquid erupted like a geyser.

"Looks like a water fountain, Captain." Dickinson put his index finger into the stream. "And it's cold."

Before I could order him otherwise he bent over and took a drink. He instantly stood straight up grabbing his throat with both hands. His eyes rolled back as he staggered away from the fountain and fell on the floor. Sully was instantly at his side.

"It must be poison." Sully examined Dickinson's wrist for a pulse. "We should have tested it first. Captain, I don't think he's breathing. What do we do?"

As Sully looked at me I noticed a thin smile appear on Dickinson's face. I could not restrain myself. I started laughing.

"What's so funny?"

I pointed. Sully snapped back and saw a widely grinning Dickinson.

"Gotcha!" Dickinson laughed.

Sully remained momentarily stunned. He realized he had been had and started laughing. "Congratulations!" Sully smiled. "I guess I deserved that one. We are even." He extended his right hand and they shook.

"Now, gentlemen, let's get back to our focus." We had to get serious.

"We now have food and water," Sully said. "It looks suspicious to me. I think where part of some experiment."

"Yeah, an experiment in fattening us before the kill," Dickinson said flatly.

"We can't jump to conclusions," I said. "We still don't have anything to base a conclusion. I'm hoping the next time the aliens come in I can try to communicate with them."

"To what end?" Sully frowned. "Our best negotiators have tried to open a diplomatic channel with no success. Do you think we possibly have any chance?"

"We have no choice but try," I said.

The door opened behind me. I turned and saw the same three aliens enter the room. The leader pointed a claw at Dickinson.

"What does it want?" Dickinson edged backwards. "I don't like this."

"Don't move," I said sternly. "Let's find out what they want." I stepped toward the leader. The aliens on either side bared their teeth. The leader's expression remained unchanged.

We stood our places. The alien on the left went to Dickinson. I could see he was terrified. The alien put a collar around his neck and turned to Sully. After a collar was also put on him, it was my turn. I was not sure, but I had the vague impression this was a good sign. I waved at the leader with no effect. I could have been waving at the wall with more of a response. The aliens left us alone again.

"Great." Sully exhaled. "Just what I always wanted, a dog collar."

Dickinson sat in a distant corner visibly trembling. I could tell he was emotionally falling apart. It would be up to Sully and me to carry us through whatever was to happen.

"Let me look at your collar," I said to Sully. "You examine mine and tell me what you think."

The collars were not made of metal but of a type of soft tough plastic I had never seen. I tried to cut it with a knife but could not even scratch it. It was so light I barely felt it around my neck. I did not see any electronics suggesting a behavior control device. Sully came to the same conclusion.

"We've been banded," Sully said.

"I agree." I nodded slightly.

"Maybe we're going to become specimens in some sort of zoo."

"That's a possibility," I said. "But from past history that's hard to believe. They're ravenous meat-eaters."

"Like intelligent dinosaurs," Dickinson squeaked. "Like bloody dinosaurs."

"He might be right. They do remind me of giant dinosaurs. Our evolution does not preclude other intelligent species. Didn't someone suggest dinosaurs on earth perished because of a series of cataclysmic events?"

"Anything is possible," I said. "What I don't understand is why one sentient species is not interested in communicating with another sentient species."

519

"Because they're predators evolved from predators," Dickinson said loudly. "Sooner or later we're going to be lunch."

The floor moved under our feet. The room was part of some vehicle and we were being transported somewhere. The expression from Sully confirmed my conclusion.

"To the slaughterhouse," Dickinson said softly. "The end is near."

"Shut up!" Sully shouted. "I'm getting tired of your negative attitude. One more remark and I'm gonna smack you."

"Make sure you knock me out." Dickinson smiled. "I don't want to know what's coming."

Sully started toward Dickinson and I grabbed his arm. He did not resist.

"Sorry, Captain, I'm a little on edge," Sully said meekly. "Not knowing is taking its toll."

"The only way to survive this is to keep our heads," I said. "So far nothing is as we expected it. There is something missing and I can't figure out."

"These collars make me feel like some sort of pet," Sully said.

"The thought has crossed my mind," I nodded. "But I don't think that's the answer."

The motion of the room stopped abruptly. Wherever it was we had arrived. We looked at each other thinking the same questions. A door opened but no one entered. I was sure it was done deliberately. It was possibly a test to see whether we would try to escape. Sully moved to the door.

"Be careful," I said. "We don't know what this means."

"It's an invitation." Sully stood in front of the door.

"An invitation to get killed," Dickinson said. "Out that door and into the frying pan."

"I think you're right," I said. "We have to find out what's on the other side. And Dickinson, keep your comments to yourself. You're not helping any way with your negativity."

"I'm just being a realist. I tell it like I see it."

"You hold onto that thought." Sully slowly eased through the door.

I did not know what I expected. Sully disappeared without a word. Dickinson said he was sure we would hear screaming. As the minutes passed in silence I wondered what he had found. I was about to suggest we follow when he returned with a big smile.

"What is it?"

"You won't believe it. I think you better come see yourself."

"I'm not going," Dickinson said.

"No problem," I said. "You can stay here by yourself." I started to follow Sully through the door only to see Dickinson close on my heels. I gave him a thin smile and he shook his head.

The door led to a short corridor with another similar door at the end. It opened into a large atrium. I stood at the door amazed. The place was designed with a small pool, trees, running water and decorative plants. There was even a bench and table. The roof was open above to a blue sky with clouds passing overhead. I was instantly reminded of a Japanese tea garden. Dickinson stood next to me with his mouth open.

"There's more. Follow me. You won't believe this."

We went through a wide door into a large kitchen similar to one on the ship. There was a table with seating. I examined the storage cabinets and refrigerator. They were stocked with familiar items. Whoever put this together had done the right research. Everything was near perfect. Sully led us into room after room. All the details were correct. There was a living room, recreation room, multiple bedrooms with full bathrooms. It was hard to believe we had been caught by a bunch of ravenous carnivores.

"Well, what do you think now, Captain?" Sully smiled smartly. "I think this changes things."

I was nonplussed and nodded.

"Does this mean they're not going to eat us?" Dickinson said slowly.

"This is all puzzling," I said. "The aliens definitely have something else in mind for us. I don't think we should get too comfortable. They are still our enemies no matter what this looks like."

"I'm hungry." Dickinson turned back to the kitchen. "Let's eat."

For lack of a better plan I decided to follow along with Sully. The kitchen had an ample supply of the food bars we had sampled. If necessary we could survive on those alone, but that was not forced on us. I found coffee, sugar and what look like powdered milk. I decided to make a cup of coffee. After boiling the water on an electric range I created my first cup of coffee in a ceramic mug without a handle. The first sip transported me back home. I actually felt a jolt as the caffeine kicked in. Sully joined me with a mug of his own. Dickinson found a cabinet of space

521

rations from which he chose his first meal. He said he would rather stick with something he could depend before trying anything else even though the foods looked genuine.

"There's something strange going on here," I said between sips. "I suggest we sleep in shifts. I'll take the first. You and Dickinson rack out. Let Dickinson take the next eight hours and you take the last."

If it were not for the coffee I would have easily fallen asleep. The place was eerily quiet. I walked around every room examining every detail. Whoever had put this place together had done a lot of homework. Left to ourselves, we could live comfortably here for a long time.

I found a keyboard exactly like one on the ship with a large screen. Behind the monitor I found the "on" switch. Remarkably all the characters were in English. I input a few instructions. Nothing happened. I tapped in another set of instructions and again there was no response. I was about to abandon my attempts when a message appeared on the screen. It asked for username. Without hesitation I entered my full name and rank. I did not know what to expect next. I was not sure whether I was merely communicating with a machine or the aliens through a translator. There was no further activity so I simply left the screen on. I planned to come back on my next shift.

In spite of all the coffee, I drank I fell into a dreamless sleep when my shift was over. When I woke up I found Sully already on duty. He hovered near the screen I had left on.

"What do you make of it?" I said. "I turned it on and it asked for my name. I entered it and nothing happened. You have more experience with computers. Why don't you give it a try?"

Sully sat down and tapped in instructions. A set of icons flashed on the screen. There was one with a picture of an alien and a separate one with a human. I pointed to the alien when we heard a noise behind us.

"Someone's coming!" Sully said quickly.

"Let's get back to Dickinson," I said. "Better we are all together."

Our exit was blocked by an alien. It was alone. We looked at each other with telepathic thoughts; here was an opportunity to attack. Even though it was bigger we had the advantage of numbers. Before we acted it raised its hand as if to say stop.

I raised my hand in an identical way. The expression on its face changed which I took for smile and I returned the same. I noticed a broken triangle insignia on its uniform. The alien I faced was the leader from the first encounter. I wondered why it came alone. Either it was overconfident or knew we could do nothing of consequence. At least this was an opportunity to start a real dialogue. I spoke my name and pointed to myself. The alien hissed something unintelligible pressing a claw to its chest. It then pointed to the screen behind us. In clear English letters was: "My name is Saak." A chill ran down my arms, the alien had actually communicated. I started asking questions. The answers appeared on the screen after the alien spoke. I started to ask why we were here but deferred to ask a few preliminary ones first.

"Who are you?" I began.

"As I said my name is Saak. I am a guardian of the Empire," the alien said. "I answer only to the highest commander and Emperor."

"Where are we?"

"You are safe."

"That is hard to believe," I said. "From the moment we came in contact we have been slaughtered."

"Your race satisfies the needs of our race. Our world is always in search of new sources of food," the alien said.

"And is that what we are to you, food?"

"Perhaps to those outside these walls, but not in this place; I have no need to treat you that way."

"Is it because we are sentient beings?"

"No."

"Then why are we spared?"

"Because you are mine."

"And how does that spare us?"

"Because I am a vegetarian."

Rocky

As the door slowly opened, the fur ball next to the desk began moving. Two ears and a pair of eyes turned to the barely perceptible noise.

"Rocky, are you awake?" A familiar voice said softly.

In slow motion legs and a tail appeared along with a big yawn. Rocky shook his head slowly and stood up. The master was always a welcome sight.

"Would you like to go out for a walk?"

Rocky managed a purr.

"I'll take that as a yes. Let's go."

The doorbell rang. Rocky instantly became silent and turned toward the sound.

"It's nothing to worry about. Stay here and I'll be right back."

Another familiar man came into the room with the master. The tension rapidly dissolved and Rocky continued purring.

"Hi there Rocky," the newcomer said warmly. "I see you're glad to see me."

"Rocky and I were about to go out for a walk. We can talk on the way."

"I have no problem walking with my friend here." The newcomer bent down and ruffled Rocky's thick angora-like hair. Rocky purred louder.

"I still can't believe this is a dog." The newcomer said. "Dogs bark, cats purr."

"To tell you the truth I don't know what Rocky is. Sometimes I think he's a dog, other times a cat. Sometimes I don't think he's either.

"George, how do you know it's a he?"

"Costa, give me a break!"

"You don't know do you? There are a lot of things you don't know about Rocky."

"It doesn't matter," George said slowly. "I accept Rocky for whatever he or she happens to be. There is nothing more warming than to share one's residence with another living being."

"You found Rocky on one of your digs, didn't you?"

"Yes, I did," George said hesitantly. "I was in Mexico last summer excavating some Mayan ruins. I found Rocky hiding in a crevice of a ruined temple. The moment I spotted him, I expected him to run away and was surprised he simply watched me approach. There was an eerie intelligence in his eyes telling me I had nothing to fear. I put out my hand with a candy bar and after a careful sniff it was gently taken into his mouth. I watched as he chewed and I almost thought I saw the hint of a smile, and then came the purring. At first, I couldn't believe it but when I listened closely it was coming from him. I turned to leave and he followed me."

"And I guess the rest is history." Costa laughed.

"A good history," George said. "As a companion, I couldn't want more from a pet except sometimes I think he's the master and I'm the pet. Rocky has a mind of his own. He may be agreeable most of the time but when it's time to eat or sleep there's no moving him."

"At least he knows his priorities." Costa bent down and patted Rocky. "I am ready to go whenever you are."

Without hesitation Rocky immediately went to the door, looking back at the two men wondering why they were taking so long to catch up. Through the door he heard several birds flit by. George barely had the door cracked open when Rocky slipped outside.

"Aren't you afraid he'll run away?"

"I let him do his thing before we go anywhere. After that he clings so close I feel he's attached to me. I've never had to worry about him running away."

Outside Rocky was nowhere seen. George waved Costa to follow down the driveway toward the main road. Before reaching the road Rocky darted out from the corner of the house in full gallop. In the blink of an eye he was strolling next to George.

"Rocky, are you ready now?"

Rocky looked up at George with a snort. His eyes said "what do you think?" George smiled back and they began walking toward the nearby woods.

"How's that project you've been working on going?" Costa said slowly.

"Which project?"

"Anyone you want to tell me about."

"I have so many projects going at once it's hard to keep them all straight."

"I'm more interested about what you found in Mexico where you found Rocky. You mentioned you had evidence of a separate group of people, not necessarily Mayans."

526

"I haven't come to any definite conclusions yet," George said softly. "The ruins are pretty typical Mayan. Some of the inscriptions and pictures were unusual. I am not sure whether some of these represent a purely creative expression of some ancient writer. I try to avoid over interpreting."

"So you don't think you found any aliens." Costa laughed.

"Why is everyone so hot on invoking aliens? You don't have to have extraterrestrials to find unique art and artifacts. Men are perfectly capable of extraordinary creations under any conditions you can possibly imagine."

"Forgive me then. I think it's fair to speculate. I like the 'what if' scenario even though I know it's impossible."

"What do you think, Rocky?"

Rocky trotted ahead ignoring the question.

"I don't think Rocky thinks much about anything." Costa smiled "Must be nice not to have a care in the world."

"What about your research?"

"There's nothing really new." Costa sighed. "I teach freshman calculus in the morning and rack my brain over arcane mathematical problems in the afternoon. So far, I seem to be spinning my wheels."

"Don't you have enough tenure to give the freshman classes to the junior staff?"

"I do, but I enjoy teaching young minds as they come to the University. I get first crack at teaching them how to think the right way."

"And do you succeed?"

"Most of the time I do, but not always. Nowadays, there are too many entering freshmen totally unprepared for the experience. I wonder sometimes how they manage to graduate from high school. It wasn't that way when I went to school."

"I think that's a common complaint of every generation. I'll bet you and I were very much a disappointment to the last generation."

"Maybe so, maybe so."

A loud noise to the right froze Rocky in place. With one leg up he sniffed the air. His ears stood up and rotated in a forty-five degree arc. The noise recurred and Rocky dashed off into the woods toward it.

"What do you think he's heard?"

George stared in the direction Rocky disappeared. "I have no idea."

527

"Aren't you ever worried about him?"

"Not really." George sighed. "Rocky is a free spirit. I don't do anything to prevent him expressing himself. In fact, I don't think there is anything I could do to prevent him anyway."

"You can put him on a leash."

"That won't work. I already tried it. I put one on him and he refused to move until I took it off. I've never seen such a display of stubbornness in my life. On the other hand, he has proved I can trust him to come back wherever he goes."

Rocky raced silently in the woods in the direction of the noise he had heard. He spotted movement in the underbrush at which he came to halt and focused. When the movement recurred he moved in behind whatever it was, staying out of sight. Moving closer he recognized a man with a rifle. The rifle was pointed ready to fire. Rocky saw a doe with its faun grazing oblivious to the danger. In an instant, Rocky ran furiously toward the hunter passing between his legs. The rifle fired harmlessly in the air while the hunter shouted obscenities. Rocky disappeared without being recognized.

The doe and her faun immediately ran away from the gunfire. Rocky followed at their heels spurring them to run ever faster. Unless they were totally out of sight, the hunter would have another shot. A second shot came far behind. Rocky slowed to a lope and chose another direction.

Every chance away from the humans was an opportunity to explore. This place was far different than the Mexican jungle in which he was found. There was a difference and marked similarities. The jungle and forests teamed with life of all sorts according to location. In each place there was danger lurking from acts of survival to mindless mayhem. There was much for Rocky to comprehend. He heard his name called and turned back to join the humans.

"Rocky, where have you been?" George pointed at him. "You've got to be careful there's a hunter around."

Rocky went straight to George and rubbed like a cat around his legs. They all laughed.

"I say in spite of his appearance." Costa laughed. "You have a cat and a friendly one at that."

"You might be right," George bent down. "It doesn't make any difference though; I've seen cats act like dogs. Why can't dogs act like cats? Sound effects and all."

"Maybe you should try to mate him. If the behavior breeds true, you might be able to cash in."

"I never thought about that."

"Every once in a while a mutation comes along that can be bred into a new kind of animal."

"You think Rocky is a mutation of some sort?"

"Do you have any other explanation?"

One last pass at George's legs and Rocky wandered away. It was interesting listening to the humans, however, little sense it made. Sooner or later it would all be comprehensible. It was a matter of time. There was nothing else possible.

"That way is down to the river," George pointed to the right.

As if in complete understanding Rocky headed in the right direction walking ahead but remaining in full sight of his companions. The day was initially sunny, however, the clouds scudded across the sun slowly creating a barrier. The intensity of light diminished slightly as well as the ambient temperature. The changes were welcome. As a gentle breeze picked up through the trees it actually became more comfortable. By the time they reached the river the sun was completely obscured by a dense collection of cumulus clouds.

Before the river came in sight there were sounds of laughter and splashing. Rocky dashed ahead. There were three boys and two girls playing in the water on the opposite side. The boys were taking turns jumping into the water obviously trying to impress the girls. Rocky sat watching waiting for the others to catch up.

"Oh, ho!" George exhaled. "What do we have here?"

"Looks like we've come on some old-fashioned fun." Costa laughed. "Let's move on and leave them alone."

"I don't know," George said. "I always worry about unsupervised swimming in this river regardless of swimming experience. Let's sit down a while and watch. It can't hurt."

"Whatever you say, boss." Costa laughed. "Who am I to argue with the voice of reason?"

"What do you think, Rocky?" George sat down with his back against a large tree.

Rocky turned his head to George momentarily, then turned back to the children.

"I think Rocky is more interested than we are," Costa said. "Maybe he wants to go swimming too."

"He's never shown any interest in getting wet," George said. "I've brought him out here before and thrown sticks for fetching. Never once has he followed a stick into the water."

529

"That only proves he has a mind of his own. I wouldn't get wet just because someone else wanted me to anyway. I say that is smart."

The river was seventy-five feet across with the water lazily flowing by. The presence of the visitors was noticed by the young group. The boys took turns trying to show off not only to the girls but to their new audience. Two of the boys grabbed one of the girls in a pink one piece bathing suit and pulled her screaming all the way into the water. Rocky tensed, eyes focused. The girl fell out of her captor's hands into the water. She stood up laughing. It was all good fun. The boys turned to grab the other girl but she was too quick for them. She jumped into the water herself. The noise level increased as they all laughed, splashed and dunked each other. Rocky remained no less attentive.

"I wish I were that young again." George sighed. "No cares, no worries."

"No taxes." Costa nodded.

"Yes, and very definitely no taxes."

One of the boys got up on the shoulders of another. The girls began telling him to jump. He flew with glee onto the water rump first splashing everyone. Rocky look back at George and snorted.

"Looks like fun," George said. "I wish I were young and carefree as that again."

"There's nothing keeping us out of the water." Costa had a twinkle in his eyes. "Having fun isn't for the young alone."

George held up a hand as Costa moved toward him. "Not today," he said. "I am not ready to get wet."

The girls started screaming on the shore while the two boys were swimming in the river. The third boy was missing. Rocky jumped into the water swimming to where the boys were.

"What's going on?" George said softly.

"Where is your friend?" Costa yelled across the river.

"Jimmy jumped in and he didn't come up," one of the girls squealed.

George and Costa removed their shoes and entered the river. The water was cooler than expected. The current in the middle was almost too strong to easily cross. Rocky reached the boys on the other side first. He swam downstream diving under the surface. The boys searched frantically.

"Jimmy, please come up!" One of the girls shouted. "Don't leave us this way!"

"Look!" The other girl yelled. "There he is! That dog is pulling him out of the water!"

By the time the men reached the other side Jimmy was on the bank prone with Rocky pressing down on his back. The boys and girls gathered around in awe as Jimmy coughed back to life.

"Where am I?" Jimmy rasped.

"You're okay," George said beside him. "You should be more careful where you dive."

"I'm sorry." Jimmy coughed. "I guess I was trying to show off too much."

"You'd better get home," George said. "Come back another day when you feel better."

"Let's go Jimmy," the closest boy said. "We've had enough for today."

"Your dog saved me," Jimmy said. "What's his name?"

"That's Rocky." Costa pointed.

"Thank you, Rocky." Jimmy held out a hand.

Rocky approached slowly, stopped short of the hand and licked it.

"I think Rocky likes you," Costa said.

"And I like him too," Jimmy said. "I wish I had a dog like him."

"I don't think there are many dogs like him," George said warmly. "He's really one of a kind."

"What kind of a dog is he?" One of the girls said loudly. "He's sorta cute."

"I don't know," George said slowly. "I found him among some ruins in Mexico."

"Are you an archaeologist mister?"

"Yes, I am." George smiled.

"And I am a professor of mathematics at the University," Costa said.

"Yuck, I don't like math much." The girl made a face and everyone laughed at her expression of disgust.

"Costa, I don't think these young men and ladies need to waste any more of their time with us." George pulled Costa by the arm. "We need to collect our shoes and get back home."

"Are we going to swim back?"

"There's a bridge a little upstream we can easily cross. No need in getting wet again."

Jimmy reached toward Rocky who moved closer. He patted the wet fur with smooth lingering strokes. "Thank you for

531

saving my life," he said. A loud purr came from Rocky's throat. "Hey, Rocky's purring!"

The boys and girls surrounded Rocky listening in rapt awe. Each petted him in turn. Rocky remained motionless with a hint of a smile on his lips.

"Time to go, Rocky." George said flatly. "We have a ways to go from here."

Without hesitation Rocky licked each extended hand before walking off with George and Costa. The two groups went in opposite directions. George promised he would return with Rocky.

The bridge across the river was farther than expected and the going was slower in their bare feet. Once across they had to travel downstream for their shoes. It was late afternoon by the time they had shoes back on their feet.

"This is not exactly like my idea of a relaxing walk," Costa said.

"The unexpected makes life worthwhile. Life would be pretty boring if everything went perfectly."

"I feel better with something to drink, a full stomach and clean clothes."

"Those you can have every day, any time you want." George laughed. "But an adventure like today is unique."

"Call me a creature of comfort." Costa looked around. "Where's Rocky?"

"I don't know." George scanned all around. "He can't be too far away. He was just here."

"Let's go home. Rocky knows how to follow us."

The clouds thickened and became almost black. The wind picked up rustling the leaves of the trees to an audible murmur. There was a smell of rain in the air. Something did not feel right. Rocky instinctively knew danger was close. The only way to protect the humans was to face the problem before it erupted into violence. The exact nature of the danger had to be found. The forest was a small part of a large wilderness preserve. Large, dangerous animals were not uncommon. He moved in a wide arc listening carefully. Thunder obscured most ambient sounds making vision more important. He crossed the spoor of the deer from earlier several times. An image of the hunter came to mind. The most dangerous of all animals was man himself. A new scent overpowered all previous ones. Whatever created it was extremely close. The scent was clearly one of a predator.

Rocky determined he must remain between the predator and his humans.

"Rocky! Rocky! Where are you?" George shouted. "We're going home!"

"Let's go," Costa said. "Rocky can find his own way."

"This is not like him. Something is wrong. I can feel it."

"It's going to rain and we have no shelter. I don't feel like a fish today."

"Go ahead, if you have to. I'm not leaving without Rocky."

Costa sighed loudly. "Okay, you win. I'll stay. Rocky! Rocky!"

The wind picked up as the sky continued darkening. Night quickly approached. They walked slowly back to where they had last seen Rocky.

"What was that?" George stood still listening carefully.

"I didn't hear anything," Costa said softly. "What was it?"

"I thought I heard something moving in the brush."

"It's just the wind."

"I'm not so sure."

"Maybe it's Rocky."

"I don't think so."

A roar came from behind. They swung around in unison. Standing upright with teeth bared was the largest bear either had seen in or out of the zoo.

"Don't move," George said sharply. "Maybe it'll go away."

"Are you crazy? We have to get out of here and fast!"

"So far it's only looking at us."

"Sizing us up you mean." Sweat appeared on Costa's brow.

"You stay still," George said. "I am going to move away from you. When I have his attention you move away in the opposite direction."

"Then what?"

"Start running like hell and don't look back."

"What about you?"

"Don't worry about me. I can take care of myself."

"I don't like it."

"You have no choice. Now go!" George moved away quickly.

The grizzly bear roared loudly baring its teeth and focused on George. Costa stood frozen unable to move.

"Dammit, move!" George shouted. "You don't have much time!"

Shaking his head slowly Costa backed away a few steps, turned around, and began running. The bear immediately noticed and roared protest. George ran between the bear and Costa attracting the bear's attention. He stumbled over a tree root and fell flat on his face. Costa saw George fall and stopped running. The bear started walking toward George.

"I'm coming back to get you," Costa yelled.

"Save yourself..."

"The bear suddenly stopped, roared angrily, rose up and flailed its paws wildly in the air. George easily got to his feet wondering what was wrong with the bear.

"Get out of there!"

The bear swung around exposing its back. Rocky held on tenaciously with claws and teeth. No matter what the bear did it could not reach Rocky. The roars became yowls of pain.

"Be careful Rocky. He's dangerous." George was unable to pull himself away to safety.

Costa returned to George's side and they watched Rocky draw blood as the bear frantically attempted to free itself. The bear soon visibly weakened and stumbled. Rocky let go and snapped at the back of its neck. With a firm bite Rocky silenced the bear with a crack of its neck. Rocky released his grip and snorted.

"Good job!" George relaxed a little. "Good job!"

"I didn't know Rocky had it in him," Costa said.

"I guess there are a lot of things we don't know about Rocky. I can say I'm glad I'm on his side."

"Makes you wonder."

"Wonder about what?"

"About when you found him."

"You mean if he didn't want to come with me? I guess I was lucky he liked me. I had no idea he could be so ferocious."

"Look at him. Don't you think that's a smug expression on his face? I'll bet he's thinking he's the baddest dog around." Costa smiled. "If he could talk, we'd never hear the end of this."

"For saving our lives he's entitled to anything he wants," George said.

"What do we do about the carcass?"

"Leave it where it is. I'll call the park ranger when we get home. No need getting anywhere close to it."

They all jumped at the loud crash following a bright flash. Rocky went over to George and pressed against him.

"That was too close," Costa said. "Let's go."

A low pitched rumble filled the air. George led the way with Rocky close to his leg. Gusts of wind waxed and waned. The storm clouds thickened overhead and the air felt heavy with wetness without the rain. A blast of cold air preceded the first drops of precipitation and they set into a jog. Rocky ran ahead, stopped, and turned to watch George and Costa as they caught up.

"What's up?" George looked as if Rocky could answer. "What's the matter?"

"Why are we stopping?" Costa took a deep breath and stretched.

"I think Rocky is onto something. I wish I could read his mind."

"Let's get going. He's taking a break like we are."

"I've never known him to tire." George went over and patted Rocky on the flanks. Rocky stood rigidly tense.

The sky lit up with a flash followed by a loud clap of thunder. Rocky headed away from the path into the woods. He did not look back.

"Where is he going?"

"Let's follow."

"Let's not," Costa said firmly. "I'm not into getting soaked and catching cold."

"I guess you're right. Rocky can find his way better than we can."

Large drops splashed through the leaves pelting them as they resumed jogging home. George slowed to a walk when it seemed he made less contact with raindrops going at a stroll. Costa reluctantly followed suit.

"Look, over there." Costa pointed. "There's a camp. Maybe we can get temporary shelter."

A large tent sat off the path a short distance. The campfire was smoking in the rain. George called out and no one appeared. The occupant of the tent was nowhere around. Costa started toward the closed entrance flap of the tent.

"We can't go in there." George shook his head. "This doesn't belong to us. We're trespassing."

"Haven't you heard of any tent in a storm?"

535

"I don't think that applies in this circumstance. We're not exactly out at sea."

Costa started pulling the flap open.

"Hold it there stranger!" A deep gravelly voice boomed. "That's my tent you're entering!"

"Sorry." Costa jumped back. "We're just looking for a temporary place out of the rain."

"Well, you're looking in the wrong place," the man growled and pointed a shotgun at them.

"It's our mistake to bother you," George said softly. "We'll move on. Sorry."

"Not so fast!" the man pointed the shotgun at George. "You're not going anywhere."

"What do you mean?" Costa said slowly.

"Don't you understand English?"

"Very well," Costa said. "I apologize for the mistake. All we want is to get out of the rain."

The man looked familiar to George. He saw his face somewhere before. It then hit him this man was a wanted criminal with a violent history. He saw Costa beginning to come to the same conclusion.

"There is no reason to detain us," George said. "We are just two old men out for stroll in the woods with our dog."

"Dog? I don't see any dog," the man sputtered. "Where is he?" He glanced quickly in a complete circle.

"Our dog is close by," Costa said. "And he's quite protective."

"Is he bulletproof?" The man sneered.

From directly behind the man, Rocky appeared and stood motionless examining the scene. George pretended not to see. Costa smiled. The man whipped around immediately pointing the shotgun at Rocky who instantly darted off to the right behind a tree. The gun exploded loudly shattering a large hole in the tree.

"Leave Rocky alone!" Costa yelled.

The man turned and pointed the shotgun at Costa. "You wanta be next?" The man said coolly.

"No sir." Costa quickly held both hands up.

The moment the man turned his eyes away from the tree Rocky emerged from the other side hurtling himself as fast as possible at the man with the gun. The man caught the movement but was too late. Rocky lunged grabbing the barrel wresting it from the man. Without the gun the man pulled a large Bowie hunting knife from his belt.

"You're in for it now." The man grinned. "No one messes with Dirty Mike and gets away with it. You're dead dog meat, sucka!"

"Run!" George dashed behind the nearest tree. Costa followed.

Rocky released the gun and faced the man holding the knife. The man moved in an arc to the right. Rocky remained fixed where he stood and followed the movement. In spite of the man's bravado, he detected fear in him.

"You're dead meat, mutt," the man shouted. "No one messes with Dirty Mike."

Stopping to catch his breath, George heard Costa coming up from behind. The two men stood gasping as their breathing became more comfortable.

"I hope Rocky is okay." Costa gasped.

"After seeing how he handled the bear I don't think he'll have any problem," George said without conviction.

"Should we go back?"

"What can we possibly do?"

"We can call the police."

"Did you bring your phone? I didn't."

They heard a scream of the man in pain. They looked at each other.

"Are you thinking what I'm thinking?" George said. "Let's go back."

By the time they reached the tent the screaming had stopped. Dirty Mike was face down in the mud motionless with the knife not far from his open right hand. There was blood mixed with the wet dirt. George went over and examined the man's pulse.

"Is he alive?" Costa said slowly.

"No, he's dead," George scanned the area. Rocky was nowhere.

"Rocky did this?" Costa looked all around. "I wonder where he is."

"We've got to report this." George stood up. "I'm sure this guy is a wanted criminal."

"How do we explain that he's dead?"

"I don't think we have to. We were out for a walk and came across his body. It looked like he had been attacked by the bear we saw earlier in the day."

"But the bear is dead too. How do you explain that?"

"We don't know anything about a dead bear. If we start telling everything we know, that'll put us under suspicion and we don't want to do that. We've got to find Rocky and get him home."

"What you think would happen if they found out Rocky did this?"

"They might want to lock him up for rabies or worse yet cut off his head and look for the disease."

"You think he has rabies?"

"Rocky isn't sick," George said flatly. "He's just different."

"Killing bears and men is real different," Costa said quickly. "It is not normal no matter what you say. I suspect he isn't even a dog no matter what he looks like."

"He's not dangerous," George said softly. "He's more intelligent than we give him credit. Sometimes I think he understands everything we're saying."

"It's raining harder, let's get moving. We can talk this over a hot cup of coffee and dry clothes."

"Okay." George sighed.

The sky brightened overhead.

"What's that?" Costa pointed upward.

George was unable to make out anything except an increase in luminosity. "I don't know," he said. "Could be a helicopter with lights."

"But I don't hear anything."

"In all this wind and rain I don't think we would hear anything."

The light disappeared.

"Let's go." Costa waved his arm. "It's not getting any better out here."

"I think I saw the light go down over there." George pointed. "We should go see what it is."

"Forget it. I'm cold, wet and hungry." Costa exhaled loudly. "I've had enough."

"You go. I'm going to check it out."

"I guess I have no choice." Costa followed close behind. "I think I'm beginning to enjoy being miserable."

"Costa, my Costa." George chuckled. "You protest too much. We are already wet, a few more minutes out here is not going to make any difference in anything."

"My mother used to warn me I'd catch a death of cold if I got wet and didn't dry off as soon as possible."

"My mother said the same thing," George said warmly. "Only what she said never came true. I got wet, stayed wet, and never got sick."

"You're just too darn lucky."

"Yep, I guess so." George laughed.

A short distance ahead was a light.

"Someone's ahead," Costa said. "Maybe now we can find shelter."

"Don't count on it. Remember Dirty Mike?"

"That light is coming from that clearing we passed. Maybe a helicopter landed there."

"You're stuck on helicopters. I doubt anyone would want to fly in this weather."

The sky lit up with a bolt of lightning almost instantly followed by a rumble of thunder. The rain became a light mist. George was about to enter the clearing when he felt something touch his leg.

"Rocky! Where have you been?" George bent down and rubbed his fur vigorously. "Hey, Costa, look who's here!"

"Rocky!" Costa ejaculated. "Good to see you at last!"

"What's over there?" George pointed and saw Rocky smiling. "Are you as curious as we are?"

Rocky pulled away and headed toward the light. George and Costa followed. What they saw was totally unexpected. Standing in the clearing was a vehicle the likes of which neither had ever seen.

"What is that?" Costa froze where he stood.

"I don't know," George barely mumbled. "It can't be what it looks like."

"I wish you wouldn't talk like that. I have a bad feeling about this."

"It could be something NASA has been working on," George whispered. "One thing for sure it's not a helicopter."

"Where's Rocky? He's disappeared again."

The object in the clearing was cylindrical resting on three extended legs. It reminded George of a large egg. There were no visible openings or windows. Its surface radiated a cool blue light.

"We need to get out of here," Costa said. "If this is a top-secret NASA project, we could be violating national security."

"I'm going closer," George said.

539

"Are you crazy?" Costa grabbed George by the arm. "Suppose it's dangerous?"

George pulled his arm away. "That thing may have landed here as an emergency. Whoever is in there may need our help."

A door opened and a ramp extended down to the ground.

"Aliens," Costa said slowly. "That's an alien spaceship."

"I doubt it." George shook his head. He put his hands next to his mouth and hollered. "Hello there! Anyone there?"

The door completely open with its ramp extended. There was movement inside the door. What exited looked like a man dressed in a protective suit with sealed helmet and self-contained life-support. Costa's mouth dropped open. George stepped forward raising his right hand. The newcomer simply walked down the ramp to the ground and stopped in front of George.

"Greetings." George smiled and raised his hand. "Welcome to Earth."

The person in the suit remained immobile and mute. The faceplate was a shiny gold mirror reflecting the surroundings, showing nothing within.

"This is a big joke. Isn't it?" George grinned. "You're from NASA on some secret project. No alien would ever visit our remote planet. It's too far out of the way."

No response.

"George, we have no business here. Let's go!"

"I think this is great," George said. "It had me fooled for minute, but this is all a put on. If this isn't NASA, I'll bet there's a film crew nearby."

"Why doesn't he answer you?"

"It's all part of a big joke." George looked around. "I expect any minute we will be surrounded by laughter. They'll be pointing at us and our gullibility. Wherever you are you can come out now! You really had us fooled!"

Rocky appeared at the entrance of the door.

"Look up there." Costa pointed.

"This can't be an alien ship," George said. "Rocky wouldn't be so bold." He felt pressure on his leg. It was Rocky. He did a double take. Rocky was at his foot and in the door at the same time.

"There are two of them!" Costa shouted. "There are two of them!"

The person in the suit turned and headed back up the ramp. Rocky rubbed George's leg firmly one last time, went to

540

Costa, repeated the same, and followed up the ramp. Rocky met the other Rocky at the door touching snouts. Before disappearing inside, the person in the suit turned and waved his hand. George returned the gesture. Rocky and his friend stepped inside as the door slowly closed. As Rocky stepped back he winked.

"I'll be darned," Costa said.

"Goodbye, Rocky!" George waved. "I'll miss you. Take care of yourself. Don't forget about me."

When the door closed the blue light intensified as the ship lifted off the ground. The legs retracted before it had risen above the height of the trees. It momentarily hung suspended in the air before it disappeared in a flash of light. George could not tell whether it accelerated straight up or vanished into another dimension. In any case, the point was moot. It and Rocky were gone.

"That sure explains a lot." Costa put a hand on George's shoulder. "Whatever Rocky was he wasn't a dog or cat."

"It does explain a lot," George said sadly. "I'm going to miss him."

"You said you found him in Mexico?"

"I guess he must've gotten lost from his masters when they landed there."

"Maybe he wasn't lost."

"What do you mean?"

"Maybe he was disguised so he could examine us."

George looked up into the empty sky. It was hard to believe everything that had happened. He remained silent for a moment and faced Costa with a smile. "What a sneaky thing to do!"

The Experiment

The lights in the lab were already on when Jacob arrived at 5 AM. A half pot of coffee sat in the tiny adjacent office filling the air with a welcoming aroma. Sitting at the desk was Samuel staring at a stack of papers.

"You're early." Jacob poured a cup of coffee and added creamer and sugar. "You do another all-nighter?"

Samuel blinked several times and slowly turned toward Jacob. His eyes ignited in recognition. "Jacob, I don't believe it," he said. "It can't be possible."

"What don't you believe? What can't be possible?"

"These results." Samuel slapped the stack of papers on the desk solidly. "They make no sense."

"Let me take a look at them."

"There has to be a mistake."

Jacob examined the data sheets several times. "There is always the possibility of contamination."

"I don't think so," Samuel said slowly. "The results in your hands are the third check. If I made a mistake, I made it three times."

"That's possible. Don't be so hard on yourself. We all make mistakes and sometimes we make the same ones over and over."

"I've got to run through the results again. I can't accept what I'm getting."

"Go home and get some sleep. I'll help you when you get back."

"No, I can't sleep now. I've got to know for sure. There is too much at stake here."

"I think you are exaggerating everything out of proportion. Look, if you won't go home, let me buy you breakfast. You can spare a few minutes. Come on."

Samuel squeezed his eyelids shut, shook his head, and exhaled loudly. "Yes, you're right I need a break," he said softly.

The coffee shop in the research building was not open. They exited the building and walked two blocks down to an open café. Several solitary customers nestled mugs of coffee between their hands while other couples ate their breakfasts. The aroma of bacon filled the air near the counter.

"Good morning, gentlemen. What can I get for you?"

"I'll have the usual," Jacob said.

"I'll have coffee," Samuel said.

543

Ahmed nodded and turned away. They sat at the counter in silence.

"You need to eat."

"I'm not hungry."

Ahmed placed two cups of coffee and one bagel in front of them. "Anything else?"

"Yes," Jacob said quickly. "Another bagel for my friend here."

At the first sign of protest, Jacob held up his hand. "Don't worry about it, I'm buying," he said.

The bacon sizzled on the grill. Samuel stared as the individual pieces were placed on a paper towel before transfer to a plate. He shook his head slowly saying nothing. "It can't be," he shouted shaking his head rapidly. "It just can't be!"

A hand dropped on the Samuel shoulder. It squeezed firmly, but not overly so. Samuel slowly turned around and saw that there were two men standing behind them.

"What is the meaning of this?" Jacob said.

The man touching Samuel looked at Jacob. "The doctor needs to come with us," he said flatly. "He must come now."

"I'm sorry," Samuel said meekly. "I shouldn't have been so loud. I'll be quiet."

"Are you the police?" Jacob examined the men. They were dressed in plain clothes. If anything, they were either off-duty or undercover. However, something did not feel right.

"Let's go."

Samuel started to get up. "You have no authority to take him," Jacob said. "How do we know you are police?"

"Doctor, this is an urgent matter. You must come with us immediately."

"I'm coming too," Jacob said.

"This is a personal matter," the man said. "You have no involvement."

"Since you haven't said exactly what is involved, I don't know if I do or don't," Jacob snapped. "But it seems my friend needs a witness regardless." He paid for the breakfasts.

Outside, a black Mercedes waited at the curb. Another stranger was the driver. They entered the car and drove out of the city. Samuel said nothing and appeared unable to respond. Jacob remained alert, observing everything. The whole situation was completely absurd. The car drove into the barren countryside on the main highway. It turned off on a side road heading into an area of low hills. At the end of the road was a small white house with a large antenna outside it.

"Where are we?" Jacob said.

Without an answer the car stopped and everyone, but the driver, got out. They went into the house where inside the first room was a large desk with another stranger sitting behind it. He examined the newcomers without expression.

"Who is this second person?"

"He was with the doctor. He insisted on coming with him."

Jacob stepped forward. "Why are we here?"

No answer.

"Put them in the examination room."

"You can't do anything to us without proper authority," Jacob said. "We don't even know who you are."

"Put them away."

They were led down a short hallway to a room with several chairs, a table and a bunk bed connected to a bathroom. Upon entry they were locked in the room. Samuel shuffled over to a chair and sat down with a sigh.

"Do you have any idea what's going on?"

Samuel bowed, placing his face in his hands. "I've never seen these men before," he said behind a choked sob. "It just confirms what I discovered."

"Can I get a straight answer from you?"

Samuel uncovered his face and stood up. "We have to get out of here." He scanned the room. "Those men are alien agents."

"Alien agents? What country dares to kidnap scientists doing peaceful work?"

"I'll look in the bathroom. You try the window. We have to get out of here."

The only window in the room was locked shut. The window in the bathroom was not. Before they could attempt to get out, the front door opened. A tray of food and drink was placed on the table.

"Gentlemen, you must be hungry," the man said. "Please eat. If you wish anything else, please ask."

"What did you bring us?" Jacob said.

Samuel went straight to the tray and uncovered the food. "We can't eat this," he said. "It's against our religion."

"You will eat it," the server said. "It will just be a matter of time." He exited without expression.

545

"This is poison," Samuel said. "Don't touch any of it."

"I think we can get out the bathroom window," Jacob said. "We'll do it tonight after the sun goes down." He examined the food on the tray. "We can eat some of this."

"I don't trust any of it. If you're hungry, I have a couple of granola bars in my pocket."

The day went by slowly. The uneaten tray of food was removed and replaced with another at the next meal time. Although much more appealing, they did not eat anything. The granola bars did little to ease the growing hunger. The last tray was removed as the sun went below the western horizon.

Aside from the arrival and removal of trays no one came into the room. Samuel covered every inch of the room searching for a hidden camera or microphone. He found none, but was not totally convinced they were not being watched.

At 9 o'clock Jacob held watch at the door while Samuel made up the bunk beds to look slept in. They turned out the lights and hid in the bathroom waiting expectantly. Jacob worked on opening the window as quietly as possible. The door to the room opened and they froze. A single man entered the room, walked over to the bunks, and left the room.

Jacob squeezed Samuel on the shoulder and Samuel nodded back. The decoys and the bed had fooled their captors. Out the bedroom window was a ten foot drop to the ground. Facing the window was a small shed. Samuel slid out the window feet first, landing awkwardly on the soft soil. He assisted Jacob down more gently. The nearly full moon illuminated the area brightly. Samuel pointed at the shed and ran toward it. Jacob followed closely behind.

Out of sight from the house, panting slightly, Jacob looked back. Everything about the house was the same. He assumed no one had noticed their mad dash until a light came on in the bathroom. He called softly to Samuel with no answer. He had disappeared.

Around the corner Jacob saw Samuel peering into a window. "We have to get out of here now," Jacob said. "I think they know we are gone. I saw a light turn on in the bathroom."

Samuel looked away toward the moonlit landscape. He pointed and started running with Jacob following without question. Within forty yards there was a wadi into which they went and followed. Jacob grabbed Samuel's shoulder.

"I'm out of shape." Jacob panted. "We can't run forever."

"We can't let ourselves get caught," Samuel said. "They may not be as gentle with us the next time."

"I still don't understand what this is all about."

"I'll tell you. First, we have to get out of here."

"What about footprints?"

"We can't worry about them. Let's go."

The moon passed overhead heading toward the horizon. With no clouds, the brightest stars competed for recognition with the moonlight. Where the wadi became rocky, they exited so as to leave no footprints. Not far away was another wadi which they followed. By dawn they were barely moving.

"I'm exhausted," Jacob said. "I need to get more exercise."

"We have to find water."

"And something to eat."

"Both. I agree," Samuel said. "When the sun comes up, we also need to find shelter."

"Wait, I hear something." Jacob turned his head.

"Yes, I hear it also." Samuel scrambled up the side of the wadi and saw a truck passing by on a road. He waved Jacob to follow.

They walked on the pavement in the direction of the city. It was more than half an hour before another truck appeared. When the driver spotted them, he slowed down and stopped. "What are you doing out here?" He said.

"Our car broke down. We are going for help," Samuel said.

"You're going in the wrong direction," the man said. "The closest help is the other way. Hop in. I'll give you a ride. I have to go that way."

"Thank you very much," Samuel said.

"Where's your car?"

"It's off the road a ways. It's a Jeep." Jacob said. "We were doing a survey for some property."

"Ha. There's not much use for property out here," the driver said. "There's no water and little anything else."

"We do, what we do, and get paid," Samuel said. "The land is none of our concern."

"I guess it's like me. I haul things in my truck and I don't care what's in the boxes."

The drive down the road passed through more flat, rocky terrain. They came to a small settlement where the driver dropped them off at the petrol stop with garage and drove away.

547

Samuel offered to pay, but the driver refused saying it was his duty to help fellow countrymen.

In the garage Samuel asked if there were any cars for rent. The owner of the garage said there were none in the settlement, but they might find someone who might let them use their personal car for the right price. The only other option was a bus which stopped twice a day, once going to the city, once coming from the city. The bus arrived as they spoke. It was heading away from the city.

"We have to take this bus," Samuel said.

"But it will take us farther away from home."

"There's no choice. We're being followed."

"I don't see anyone."

"And you won't," Samuel said. "They won't stop until they've silenced me."

"And why is that?"

A black Mercedes drove by the bus. Samuel saw it and pushed Jacob into the shadows. He pointed at the car as it moved slowly away. They both got on the bus slouching in their seats as the car disappeared.

"Do you believe me now?"

"There are a lot of black Mercedes," Jacob said. "I think you're paranoid."

"I'm paranoid for a reason," Samuel said. "I've made a discovery that will blow you away."

"You keep telling me, but I hear nothing."

"Hey, this bus is heading back to the city!"

The bus began moving and turned around going in the same direction the car had gone. Jacob straightened up in his seat waiting for answers. Samuel looked out the window and at the surrounding passengers. He leaned close to Jacob's ear.

"Do you know what I've been working on?"

"Not exactly," Jacob said softly. "I know you've been doing something with your porcine genome, which, considering our heritage, is more than unorthodox."

"Our religion tells us not to consume pork. It doesn't say we cannot do research on it." Samuel smiled slightly. "The Gentiles use pork is a major source of protein. The economic value is enormous. My interest began when I started to consider the biblical restrictions. We all know uncooked pork may carry serious diseases. Long ago the connection between disease and eating pork was recognized and the restriction made mandatory by making it a divine order. I thought by looking at the porcine genome I could develop insights into why the restrictions should continue to apply to us. There has been a lot of previous research, especially in the area of transplant medicine. The similarity between human and porcine genomes is close enough to allow pigskin grafts to take for short lengths of time. I switched my interest to how I could make pig grafts take permanently. I was thinking about money."

"Money is not such a bad thing to think about. I could use a few extra shekels myself," Jacob said.

"I meant money to finance my research," Samuel said. "Nothing we do in the lab is free. So I started sending out applications for grants. Quite to my surprise I had an immediate response from a foundation in New York. I was granted all the money I needed with the stipulation all results were to be sent to the foundation before publication. After that there were no restrictions."

"Sounds like an ideal relationship."

"It was until I started getting instructions to manipulate the genome in specific ways. At first I did what was requested without question. When I finally took the time to analyze the results, I began to see an ominous potential. I asked the foundation for explanations of the purpose of their request. The answer was more money. So I kept my thoughts to myself."

"The black Mercedes just passed us."

"Not good. They won't stop until they find us."

"I still can't make any sense between your research and them."

"Those men are from the foundation. They are alien agents."

"Okay, they are Americans."

"No, not Americans; real aliens like from out there." Samuel shook his head and pointed up.

For a moment Jacob stared at Samuel. He shook his head and blinked. "You're crazy. You know that," he said flatly. "There are no such things as extraterrestrial aliens."

"I thought the same as you until I got involved with this research. Somehow we have to stop them."

"Wait a minute. None of this makes any sense. What do aliens, if they exist, have anything to do with your research?"

The bus slowed and Jacob turned to the window. "We're in the city," he said.

"Do you see their car?"

"I can't see much of anything except this side," Jacob said. "I don't think they know we are here." The bus stopped.

"Let's get out," Samuel pulled on Jacob's arm. "We will take a taxi from here."

They stepped out of the bus carefully searching the area for the Mercedes. It was nowhere in any direction. Samuel hired a taxi to take them back to the lab. In view of what had happened, Jacob was not sure that was the wisest place to go. They rode in silence watching the traffic as they went. Samuel instructed the taxi driver to drop them off at the back of the building. The black Mercedes was parked at the loading dock.

"Don't stop!" Samuel nearly shouted. "Keep going!"

The taxi sped up, passing the loading dock and the Mercedes darted out after them. Jacob saw the approaching car from behind. He pointed backward for Samuel to look.

"Lose the car behind you!" Samuel yelled.

The taxi driver glanced in the mirror. "What's in it for me?" he said.

"Anything you want! Just lose that car!"

The taxi accelerated a short distance then turned sharp right throwing Jacob on top of Samuel pressed to the window. After a short city block they did a turn to the left. The Mercedes remained visible behind; however, it was not gaining any distance. Zig-zagging from block to block failed to lose the following car. A large parking garage occupied an entire block. The taxi driver turned into the entrance to the objections of Samuel.

"We'll be trapped in here!" Samuel shouted.

"I know what I'm doing," the taxi driver said calmly.

The taxi accelerated up the parking garage levels leaving the Mercedes finally out of sight. At the top of the garage there was a separate ramp back down. Without hesitation or loss of momentum the taxi sped downward. They passed the Mercedes on the upper ramp.

"Good job!" Jacob said loudly. "We may lose him yet!"

"It is my job." The taxi driver smiled.

At the street level the taxi exited with the Mercedes nowhere in sight. Samuel instructed the driver to go around the block. He paid the driver and instructed him to head for the airport. They got out on the curb and went into a coffee shop.

"I don't think I can take much more of this excitement." Jacob laughed.

"It's not over yet," Samuel said solemnly. "This is just the beginning."

"I still don't know what this is all about," Jacob said. "I'm going to have a cup of coffee and go home. I'm taking the day off."

"You can't go home. They know who you are."

"Impossible." Jacob snorted. "Up to yesterday they never saw me. I don't know anything."

"Trust me. They know more than you think. Your association with me has made you a marked man. The only way we can survive is if we stick together."

"I don't care. I've had enough. I need a shower, I'm hungry and I need some sleep."

"I know you don't believe me," Samuel said slowly. "We've really been chased by extraterrestrials. I have become a part of a massive experiment they are doing. I don't think they intended on me figuring it out but I did and that means I am now considered dangerous to them."

"You really need to talk to your therapist more often," Jacob said. "Maybe you need a change of medication."

"Jacob, this is real. You have to believe me. I need your help. We have to let the world know what's going to happen."

"I don't know what's going to happen and you want me to help you." Jacob muttered to himself.

"Have some coffee and we will go back to the lab. I'll show you what's going to happen. Then you'll believe me."

"What about your alien friends?"

"We'll be very careful," Samuel said. "You've got to see to believe."

Their new taxi circled the lab several times before Samuel decided it was safe. The black Mercedes was nowhere around and they realized this did not guarantee it was not near. Getting into the lab was essential, thereby making the risk necessary. They entered the building through a side entrance from a parking lot. As Samuel passed a security desk the officer told him he had visitors asking for him. Samuel froze momentarily glancing at Jacob. "Are they still here?" He said slowly.

"No sir. They came and left several hours ago," the security officer said. "They did leave this card." He handed it to Samuel.

"The card had the now familiar logo of the foundation in New York. On the back was printed: WE MUST MEET. He gave the card to Jacob, thanked the officer and headed for the lab.

"What are you going to do?" Jacob said.

"I have to collect all my notes and data," Samuel said. "I need proof…"

"Proof of what?" Jacob interrupted. "All this sounds like a bad spy novel. I still don't understand what this is all about."

"I'll explain everything in the lab. We've got to hurry; they could be back at any time."

The lab was exactly as they had left it; however, the office was in complete disorder. Every book and paper was out of place. Samuel instantly recognized all his notes and data were missing, but he was not completely upset. He opened his desk drawer, lifted up a false bottom and pulled out a disc. "They may have taken the originals," Samuel said. "This contains copies of everything. I scan all originals into the computer daily."

"Great. Now tell me what this is all about. I have bits and pieces with no clear picture."

"This is going to sound a little strange. You have either read or heard stories about men and pigs. Remember in the Odyssey when Circe turns all of Odysseus' men into pigs and in the New Testament when demons are turned into pigs? We think of those as fiction for the most part."

"From our perspective, I agree."

"I suppose there is some connection with eating pork and converting to a pig."

"That's impossible," Jacob said quickly. "Nothing changes from one species to another simply by eating another one. If that were the case, there would be biological chaos."

"In nature that does not normally happen, I agree, but it is possible to transmit genetic elements from species to species. Antibiotic resistance jumps from bacteria to bacteria quite easily."

"Bacteria are single cell organisms. A human is far more complex and something like that cannot happen."

"And why not? For every human cell there are ten bacteria. We are outnumbered. Given viruses the ratio goes up to a hundred to one. The possibility for genetic transmission is there."

"But it doesn't happen."

"The human genome is littered with remnants of viral DNA. Viruses can and do jump species. Look at HIV for example. It may have started as a simian virus. Some careless hunter butchering an infected simian, may have been bitten, or accidentally came in contact with contaminated blood by cutting himself in the process. Once the virus gets a foothold it has free reign. In the case of HIV, the retrovirus incorporates itself into nuclear DNA and may remain inactive until some factor turns it on."

"What does this have to do with your research?"

"Hold on; I'm coming to that." Samuel put the disc in his coat pocket. "Let's get out of here first."

They exited the building into a taxi waiting at the front entrance. Jacob suggested they continue the conversation at his apartment. Samuel thought he saw the black Mercedes out of the corner of his eye. Jacob assured him it was nowhere close. Unconvinced, Samuel insisted the taxi drive them to a large department store which they entered and exited out the back. With another taxi they went directly to Jacob's apartment building. Inside the apartment Samuel made sure the front door was locked before looking out the window.

"Are you hungry?"

Samuel shook his head as he pulled the curtains closed across the window.

"I'll make coffee."

Samuel paced the room peering out the curtain with every circuit he made. Only when the coffee was ready did he sit on the sofa. "I don't think we can stay here," he said.

"Why?"

"They know we are together. It won't be hard for them to find out who you are and where you live."

"You're beginning to really scare me."

"You should be," Samuel said. "This whole thing is bigger than you can imagine."

"I still don't completely understand. I can't make the connection between your research and everything that's happened."

"Let me put it this way." Samuel cleared his throat. "I happened to analyze a part of the porcine genome which brought my benefactors immediately to my lab. When I sent the results to the foundation I never expected a response other than a simple memo saying good job. A representative of the foundation appeared without notice. His name was Byron Smith. In appearance he looked no different than our captors. All of them happen to look pretty much alike. I was surprised but not unduly so. I am used to having my work scrutinized periodically. At first, I thought it was simply a site visit to guarantee funds were being used properly. Byron was not interested in how I was spending my money. He came specifically to tell me I was to reveal nothing to anyone. Secrecy was absolute."

"So far I haven't heard anything to prove there's some sort of conspiracy going on. What you need is a long vacation."

"I know all of this is hard to believe, but it's the truth."

"I'm sure this Smith or whatever he is called did not come out and tell you he was an extraterrestrial working on a clandestine top secret project. You're letting your imagination get the better of you."

"But I have proof," Samuel interjected. "On that initial visit a small book fell out of Byron's pocket when he sat down in my office. I noticed it on the floor when he left. It was a little smaller than a thin paperback novel filled with type and equations I could not read. My first inclination was to run after Byron and give back the book. I hesitated when I considered this might give me insight into the why of all the secrecy. I took it over to the University and showed it to Abe Goldman."

"I know Abe," Jacob said. "He specializes in crypto semantics and foreign languages."

"That's right. If anyone could figure out what was in the book, he could." Samuel spoke more rapidly. "At first glance, Abe asked me where the book came from. I told him I found it. I asked him if he has seen anything like it. He said he appreciated a challenge and would call me when he was done. So I left the book with him. When I returned to the lab Byron was waiting for me. He asked if I had found his book. I lied. I told him I hadn't seen it. I don't think he believed me. He left with a strange look."

"What did Abe tell you?"

"When Abe called he was full of more questions than answers. He told me he had checked all the known languages and had come up with nothing. When that failed he approached the book as if it were written in code. Little by little it began to make sense at least to me."

"Don't tell me." Jacob paused. "It was a cookbook." He laughed.

Samuel shook his head. "You have been reading too much science fiction. It was nothing even close to that. The book describes an experiment in genetic engineering on a scale I would never have imagined."

"So far you still haven't convinced me of anything," Jacob said. "And what was the endpoint of this so-called experiment?"

The doorbell rang. They both stared at the door and then at each other.

"It's them," Samuel whispered. "We have to get out of here."

"The only way out is the front door," Jacob said. "Maybe they'll go away."

"Out the window..." Samuel rushed over and pulled the curtains aside. He saw the black Mercedes with two men looking up at the window. "They're here," he said. "And they know we are."

The doorbell rang again.

"Do you have a gun?" Samuel moved around the room examining all possibilities.

"No," Jacob said flatly. He stood watching Samuel. "Maybe I should answer the door."

"Call the police!"

The telephone was dead.

"What do we do now?" The longer Jacob watched Samuel, his own sense of calm evaporated. He felt the danger looming outside the door in his mouth.

The lock on the door snapped open and the door flew inward. Byron stood at the threshold by himself. "Gentlemen," he said. "I believe we have an appointment. Please come with me."

Jacob stepped toward the door. "You can't do this," he said. "This is an invasion of private property. You have no right to enter here without my permission."

"I have a search warrant." Byron extracted a folded piece of paper from his jacket. "I think you will find it totally legal."

"You're not with the police," Samuel said quickly. "Only the authorities can use search warrants."

"I assure you I have the proper credentials," Byron said with a faint smile. He produced a wallet with a badge.

"CIA?" Samuel staggered backwards.

"Now will you come with me, or do I need to call my associates?"

They left the apartment without any resistance. The black Mercedes took them to a private airfield outside the city

555

where a small jet was waiting. As soon as they were on board they were in the air flying west.

"Where are you taking us?" Jacob sat next to Samuel directly across from Byron. "And why?"

"We are going to our base on Cyprus," Byron said without inflection. "The reason you should already know. You both know too much and that is dangerous."

"I don't know anything," Jacob said. "I don't know what's happening, except I've been kidnapped by the CIA. I don't do any work of any national security importance."

"Unfortunately, your friend does and you are linked by association. I am certain he has told you something. Hm?"

"I haven't heard anything to warrant what you're doing. Nothing makes any sense."

"Perhaps when we get to our destination it will all become clear to you."

Samuel squeezed Jacobs forearm. Jacob reluctantly settled back in his seat and looked out the window. If it were not the circumstances, the view was spectacular. The Mediterranean spread out in every direction below with an occasional fishing boat trailing a white wake. He closed his eyes wondering what to do next. Obviously there were few, if any, options. There was something about the situation he had not been told and either Samuel was hiding something or Byron was. All he could do was wait for answers.

The jet landed smoothly on a private runway. A black Mercedes identical to the one in Israel was waiting for them and they transferred to the car without any red tape. The driver said nothing. Byron watched Samuel and Jacob as they sat uncomfortably in the backseat.

"This is a beautiful island," Jacob said. "I wish I were here under different circumstances."

Byron remained mute. Samuel gave him a look that said "are you kidding?"

A half hour of driving a sinuous road they came to a villa near the sea. A Jeep and Toyota truck were parked in front. Several men came out of the house when they arrived. A series of silent instructions were given before going inside; and they were taken to individual guest rooms.

"I don't like this," Jacob whispered. "We should try to stay together."

Samuel turned in the door to his room. "I'm sure will be together again," he said in a normal voice.

The room Jacob was given was appointed like a luxury resort. The view out the window of the Mediterranean was panoramic. There was a queen size bed, desk, sofa, chairs and a computer. The adjacent bathroom was appointed with shower, bathtub, bidet and a double sink. Mirrors covered the walls. The closet was filled with clothes of his size. No possible want was missing except the ability to walk out the door in freedom. It did not make any sense.

A man opened the door and announced dinner was served in an hour. He suggested a shower and change of clothes. Jacob said nothing. Alone after the closing of the door he began exploring the room. The computer was the first thing he examined. He turned it on only to find he was barred from access by a required password. He slapped the side of the monitor in disgust. In the bathroom he examined himself in the mirror, turned on the shower, took off his clothes and got in. The hot water cascading over his face was refreshing. He attempted to put all the bits and pieces Samuel had said into some kind of coherent picture. It had to do with his research. In the current world economy, money drove everything. Someone was about to make a lot of money from whatever Samuel found. All the cloak and dagger must be for show. He smiled at the thought of aliens and CIA. Nothing could be farther from the truth. Some industrial conglomerate was protecting its investment. That had to be it. He turned off the water and grabbed the towel totally refreshed. He felt better thinking he had solved what was going on. By the time he was redressed, dinner was announced. He was escorted to the dining room where Samuel and Byron awaited him. "A hot shower, a clean set of clothes and I think I figured it all out," he said. "I must admit you had me fooled for a while."

"Please sit down," Byron said. "I would like to hear your conclusions." He sat at the head of the table. Jacob and Samuel sat on opposite sides facing each other.

"All of this is an elaborate charade," Jacob said. "There is nothing concerning national security or any other security from Samuel's records. I think he has developed a product with great economic potential. This is all about money and industrial secrets."

"Very interesting," Byron said. "Go on."

Samuel closed his eyes and slowly shook his head. He said nothing.

"Samuel, why are you shaking your head?"

557

"You still don't understand," Samuel said. "There's a lot more you don't understand."

"In that case let's discuss it," Byron said. "Would you like some wine?"

A waiter held a bottle of vintage wine out for Samuel to examine. He nodded approval without really reading the label. The bottle was opened and the wine served.

"I have spoken with your friend Samuel," Byron said. "And I am convinced it is unfortunate you have been involved in all this. But since you are involved by your presence, I cannot let you go free. Instead you will become a part of our experiment."

"What experiment?"

"One started many generations ago," Byron said. "The fact is this planet is remote from our home world."

"There you go again with the extraterrestrial nonsense! Long distance interstellar travel is impossible!"

"Perhaps with your technology." Byron smiled. "There are laws of physics you have not even dreamed."

"You can't be an extraterrestrial," Jacob said loudly. "You look exactly like every human being I've ever seen."

"The laws of nature are relatively constant throughout this galaxy. Primal elements assemble themselves identically under the right conditions. A human being here looks exactly like a human being billions of light-years away. Alien monsters are a figment of the imagination."

Jacob looked at Samuel. "Do you agree with this?" He nodded.

"There are many things your people do not know," Byron said. "Actually it's quite remarkable what you have accomplished since the last time we were here."

"And when was that?"

"Approximately four thousand years ago," Byron said. "I was not a part of the initial mission, but I am the current director."

"Four thousand years ago puts you in the time of our Prophets," Jacob said slowly. "Did you come in contact with them?"

"It was necessary as part of the experiment to enlist help of one of your Prophets."

"Which one?"

"Moses," Samuel interjected.

"Moses?" Jacob sat motionless and his jaw dropped open.

"Yes, Moses," Byron said with a grin.

"In any good experiment there has to be a control group," Samuel said. "Our forefathers were chosen as that control group."

"This is making less sense all the time," Jacob said softly. "I can't believe it."

"We came to your remote world to test the transfer possibility of genetic susceptibilities in higher animals by ingestion," Byron said.

"You could do that on your own world," Jacob said. "You didn't need to come so far to test your theories."

"It's not as simple as he says," Samuel said. "In the beginning I was curious as to why I was being commissioned in my research to examine the porcine genome. It seemed odd I would be chosen as a non-eater of pork. I examined the genome as closely as our technology permitted. I found segments which I had never encountered. At first I thought I was looking at junk DNA, leftover remnants of viral infections and whatnot. Then I tried a little experiment myself. I extracted some of these segments and attempted to turn them on. I was successful with one. It coded for a prion."

"A prion?"

"Yes, a prion with an affinity for excitable tissue," Samuel said.

Jacob faced Byron. "Why?"

"It is really none of your concern," Byron said. "But since we've reach the conclusion of our experiment I'll tell you. Let me go back to the beginning. Your planetary system has only one populated world, ours has seven. Each planet developed its own cultures until space travel allowed contact. Unfortunately, sentient beings do not necessarily agree on everything. Once the novelty of initial contact passed, the conflicts began. Eventually, we became a planetary system warring against itself. No one planet has been able to subjugate the others. And in spite of the conflicts, commerce has continued. However, every commodity is scrutinized thoroughly. It was impossible to get any materials onto an enemy world until we devised our little experiment. If we could hide an infectious agent in a product of common commerce that would pass the closest scrutiny we would have the ideal weapon. To test our plan we had to go where there would be no possibility of spies. Your world was chosen because it fit our criteria. We implanted the animals you call pigs with our weapon since it was a popular food. As any well-designed

559

experiment, we had to have a control. We found this holy man and convinced him we were emissaries from his deity. It was almost too easy to get him and his brother to ban eating pork as part of their religion. Then we laughed. The implanted pig population had to multiply which we calculated would take a long time if it were to encompass your world. Enough time has transpired to test the last phase of our experiment. And you will witness our success."

"This is madness," Jacob said. "I don't believe any of it."

"He's telling the truth," Samuel said. "The porcine genome is capable of jumping to humans and with the right activator the prion will form and kill its host. They have developed the perfect weapon."

"How are you going to test it? I haven't heard of any mass deaths recently," Jacob said.

"We are putting an activator in the water supply," Byron said. "You'll soon have your proof in a few hours. Then we will collect all your pigs for transport back home. We have a big market to supply."

"Your market, your experiment... You could fail." Jacob said. "I don't believe any of it."

"I understand." Byron poured a glass of water. "Drink this."

"I'm not afraid." Jacob took the glass, stared at it a moment and drank it all.

"How do you feel?" Byron said.

"I feel perfect," Jacob said.

"Then you came from a strict family," Byron said. "You never ate any pork."

"My family was unorthodox in many ways but when it came to dietary laws we were very ultra-Orthodox."

Byron poured another glass of water and offered it to Samuel. "How about you?"

"I'm not thirsty," Samuel said.

"It's not about thirst," Byron said with a slight grin. "It's about faith. Either you have kept your dietary laws or you haven't. Which way is it?"

"I'll have wine instead," Samuel said. "I believe everything you say, up to a point." He drank a sip of wine. "My family was far less than orthodox a long time ago. All my adult life I have followed the dietary laws."

"Does that mean you have eaten pork?" Jacob said.

"I could have," Samuel said meekly. "A long time ago…" He felt tightness in his chest.

"What's the matter?"

"I don't feel so well," Samuel said weakly. "I need to lie down." He got up, staggered a few steps and fell forward to the floor.

Jacob rushed to his side and felt for a pulse. He looked back at Byron. "He's dead! You killed him!"

"Which shows our experiment is a success." Byron laughed.

"What about all the people who will die now? Don't you have any sympathy?" Jacob began crying.

"Don't worry. Your people are safe. All we needed is proof our concept worked. You and your friend proved it very well. Now all we have to do is collect all the pigs for transport home. I don't think you would mind that. Would you?"

The snowstorm finished dusting the earth by the time of first daylight. With snow blocking driveways any necessary travel was sure to be delayed. Fortunately, it was Sunday and aside from getting a few necessities from the store there was little reason to go anywhere. The girls, Sarah and Rachel, were absolutely thrilled at the scene they saw through the window.

"Daddy, can we go outside and play?" Sarah was more than excited.

"Yes, can we go?" Rachel was not to be outdone by her older sister.

"I guess so," Bill said slowly. "Augs needs to go out. You both dress warmly. I don't want either one of you to get sick."

"I'll take care of them," Laurie said cheerfully. "You finish your coffee."

"Thanks Lau." Bill smiled warmly. If it was not for Laurie, everything at home would be an utter disaster. Words could never fully express how much he appreciated her.

Augie, literally the oldest child of the family, was more than ready to pounce into the snow as soon as the door was opened. Part pure breed something, part mixed everything, Augie adored her family and was possessive of them. No squirrel, bird or other varmints dare step foot on the premises. Augie's will was absolute law. It made her seem loony at times, but that was okay as far as the family was concerned.

Sarah came up to her father as he sipped his mug of coffee. Bill was reading the newspaper unaware of her presence. She stood several seconds before tugging at his shirt sleeve.

"Daddy, can we go way out into the woods and make a snowman?"

Bill turned slowly and smiled. "We can take a long walk, but let's make the snowman in the backyard."

"Yes, yes, yes," Rachel shouted gleefully, clapping her hands.

A dark look quickly passed from Sarah's face after thinking about the answer. "Can we take our ice skates?" She was going to negotiate her own way somehow.

"Maybe later," Bill said softly. "Now let's go out and see what's what. Maybe Mommy will come with us."

"You know I can read your mind." Laurie laughed. "I am ready to go whenever you are."

Sure enough Laurie and the girls were bundled up and ready to go. Bill put his mug in the sink, grabbed his down-jacket and led the family out the side door of the house. Augie jump to the lead, dashing helter-skelter through the clear powdery snow. Bill opened the gate and the family moved quickly in the direction of the backwoods. Augie and the girls went ahead over the long familiar path.

"Sarah, Rachel, don't run! I don't want any accidents," Bill said in his overprotective voice.

The snow covered everything a dazzling pristine white. Once beyond the last house they passed through the old rusty gate into what the girls called the forest. The sparse, leafless trees pointed their branches up into the clear blue sky. The only sounds were those of boots crunching the ice and snow as they went forward. About 100 yards into the forest there was a slight hill which they easily climbed. Behind were the trees and the unpaved double grooved road from which they came. It was a panorama of winter in New England. Directly below was an open field with a frozen pond on the opposite side where another hill rose. Bill looked at Laurie and smiled. Words at times were unnecessary.

"Daddy, let's go over to the ice." Sarah laughed. "Let's see if it's good enough to skate on."

"I don't think…" Bill began.

"Let's go," Laurie interrupted. "It won't hurt just to take a look."

"Okay." Bill nodded. "Where's Augie?"

"Down there." Sarah pointed toward the pond. "And, hey, there's Rachel too!"

While they were talking Rachel and Augie had climbed down into the open field and were nearly to the pond. Bill nearly fell flat on his face trying to catch up with his adventurous daughter. Laurie took her time helping Sarah slowly climb down the hill.

When he caught up to Rachel she was standing at the edge of the pond pointing at something in the snow on the opposite side. Bill was about to scold her for running ahead when he also saw what she was pointing at.

"What's that, Daddy?" Rachel knew she had done wrong by running ahead. If Daddy became interested in the thing in the snow, then he would not be mad at her. So she hoped.

"I don't know," Bill said. Like all dads he tried to have all the answers. But for this time he was lost to explain what it was. "Let's go see."

Rachel started to step on the ice directly across to the thing. Bill grabbed his daughter's hand and gently led her around on the solid snow around the pond.

Sarah and Laurie approached from behind. "What is it? What is it?" Sarah broke away from her mother and dashed to the side of her father.

"Be careful." Laurie sighed with a smile. The bane of every mother is always a devil-may-care child. Every day she looked in the mirror she was sure she had more gray hairs.

The object was partially covered with snow. Bill reached down and wiped the snow away. Before he could finish uncovering it Rachel had grabbed and yanked it up into her arms. Bill gasped as if expecting the worst to happen. Rachel simply cuddled the thing in her arms and giggled in triumph. Sarah was soon at her sister's side trying to pry her arms off the object so she could see what it was.

"Mine!" Rachel said loudly. "Mine! Mine! Mine!"

"No it isn't," Sarah huffed. She finally pulled one of Rachel's arms off of the toy.

"Wait girls!" Laurie said firmly. "Give it to Daddy first then we'll decide what to do about it."

"Yes, give it to me, Rachel," Bill said softly. "Let's look better so we can see what it is."

Sarah stepped back from her sister. Rachel thought a moment, looked lovingly at the object and slowly handed it over to her father. "But it's mine," Rachel sobbed with tears in her eyes. "I got it first."

"That may be true but I'm sure this belongs to someone else," Bill said. "Thank you for giving it to me."

Rachel sniffled and dried her eyes with her sleeves. She stood as close as possible to the object in case Daddy should decide it did not belong to anyone else. She certainly wanted to be first in line.

"What is it?" Laurie patted Rachel on the head.

"Looks like someone lost one of those remote control cars we see advertised on television." Bill examined the object closely. "Here's the antenna. Some boy must have brought it out here and accidentally left it out. I'm sure whoever lost this will be looking for it."

"But isn't it finders keepers, Daddy," Sarah said smartly. "Since we found it, it's now ours."

"No! Mine!" Rachel shouted.

"Take it easy, Rachel," Laurie said. "Daddy is right. Some little boy has lost his toy and wants it back. I'm sure if you lost one of your toys, you would want it returned. Wouldn't you?"

Rachel thought a moment and nodded.

"Good!" Laurie smiled. "I suggest we take it home with us and I'll make a few signs on the computer we can post around here saying that we have found a lost toy. There might even be a reward for returning it."

"Mommy, can I keep it until the boy comes?" Rachel said quickly. "I found it."

"Since the toy doesn't belong to us, we need to be very careful with it," Laurie said. "I say the toy temporarily belongs to all of us as a family; which means we must all take care of it."

"Me, too?" Sarah was happy. She felt she already knew the answer.

"Of course," Bill said. "I'll carry it home and put it in the living room where we can all look at it and enjoy it."

Before there could be any argument as to who was going to carry the toy Laurie picked it up and put it into her arms. The walk and Augie was forgotten and the girls flanked their mother as an escort home. Bill chuckled and called for Augie who returned in a flash. For Augie it was nice to be outside to take care of business, but cold was cold and it was time to get back onto a nice warm couch with plenty of heat. The trip home was silent except for the crunching of boots on packed snow and ice. Once back inside the house the girls quickly removed their jackets and mittens. Laurie mildly admonished the girls to slow down. She noticed Rachel fidgeting and reminded her to use the bathroom. Laurie put the toy on top of the kitchen island until both girls were equally ready.

"Rachel, Sarah," Laurie began firmly. "There will be no fighting over this toy. You are both to share it. Remember that it doesn't belong to us and we should be very careful not to break it. Do you understand?"

"Yes, Mommy," Sarah said rapidly. "I understand."

"What about you Rachel? Do you understand?"

"I unnersan, Mommy," Rachel mumbled. She really was not sure what it all meant but would do her best to be good. If no one else, she could follow her bigger sister's example. That was at least one advantage of having an older sister, although she would never admit it.

"I'm going to put the toy on the floor in the living room in front of the aquarium." Laurie walked out of the kitchen with the girls close behind. "When we find the owner of this toy I'm sure he or she will be more than happy to show us how it works. Until then, we must be careful not to break it."

"Yes, Mommy," Sarah said quickly.

"Yes, Mommy," Rachel said.

With the toy finally in place on the floor Laurie withdrew to the kitchen feeling secure all was well and would continue to go well. The girls sat Indian style as close to the toy as possible staring at its six large wheels attached to a boxy gold and silver body. Rachel put her hand out to touch its short stubby antenna. Sarah grabbed her wrist.

"We have to be careful," Sarah said in her big sister voice.

"I am." Rachel pulled her wrist out of Sarah's grip. "I want to touch it."

Sarah smiled, thought a moment and touched the toy herself. She moved her fingers over the body and onto one of the wheels.

"That's no fair!" Rachel cried. "I wanted to do it first!"

"It's okay for you to touch it now," Sarah said smugly. "I did it first to be sure it was safe for you."

Rachel glared at her sister unconvinced.

"Come on touch it," Sarah said. "See, it's okay. It won't hurt you."

"I know, I pulled it out of the snow." Rachel pouted. "I should have touched it first!"

"But you already did silly." Sarah felt on firm ground for what she did. "I really touched it second, no third, no last, after Mommy and Daddy. Don't you see you are already first?"

Rachel thought about it a second and then forgot about the issue completely. The real point was the strange toy was in their living room where they could play with it. She touched the antenna.

"This feels funny." Rachel smiled. "It feels like a tickle."

"Let me try," Sarah said.

"Okay." Rachel pulled her hand away.

Grabbing the antenna Sarah laughed. "It does tickle," she said.

567

"Do you guys want anything to eat?" Laurie crept up behind them and when she spoke both jumped in surprise. "I didn't mean to scare you. Do you want some lunch?"

Sarah immediately accepted the offer. Rachel declined. Laurie settled the matter by taking both to the kitchen leaving the toy where it was. Rachel was at first reluctant to part with the toy, but with lunch in front of her she ate so fast that anyone looking would think she had been starving to death.

"Slow down, Rachel," Bill said warmly. "The toy isn't going anywhere. You should eat slowly and enjoy your food."

"Yes, Daddy." Rachel slowly shoveled another morsel into her mouth.

"I made up a dozen posters to find the owner of the lost toy," Laurie said. "We should put them up around the neighborhood, the post office, and the market today."

"I think I'll put one at the gas station too," Bill said. "A toy like that can be pretty expensive. I'm sure whoever has lost it will be asking everywhere to find it."

"Mommy, I'm finished," Rachel said loudly. "May I go now?"

"Only if Sarah is ready too," Laurie said. "Are you finished, Sarah?"

"Yes, Mommy," Sarah said even though it was obvious that she was not. She was not about to be left behind.

Laurie looked at her daughters lovingly. "Go!" She laughed. "I'll cleanup after you this time."

Needing no further encouragement the sisters nearly fell over each other scrambling back to the living room. Unfortunately, the toy was not where they had left it and was out of sight.

"Hey, who took my toy?" Rachel shouted.

"It's not your toy!" Sarah said angrily. "It belongs to someone else."

"Where is it?" Rachel ignored her sister. "It was right here before. Who took it?"

"I didn't," Sarah spat back. "Where did you put it?"

"I didn't take it," Rachel cried. "I left it right here."

"What's the matter girls?" Bill quietly strolled in from the kitchen. "Is there a problem?"

"The toy is gone, Daddy!" Rachel sobbed with tears running down her cheeks.

"Daddy, it disappeared." Sarah pointed to the spot she had seen it last. "We left it right there."

568

"Maybe you just forgot where it last was." Bill smiled. "It has to be in this room because Mommy and I were together and both of you didn't enter this room. Right?"

"Yes," Rachel said slowly. "But..."

"No but." Bill moved around the room. "We'll find it right here in this room."

"I'll help, Daddy." Sarah followed in her father's footsteps.

Not to be outdone Rachel dried her tears and searched in the opposite direction. The toy was found in a corner of the room hidden by the sofa. How it had gotten into the corner was no longer an issue as the girls rejoiced at having found it. Bill put it back in the center of the room and left the girls to play. He returned to the kitchen in time to watch the last of the dirty dishes go into the dishwasher.

"I think I planned that just right." Bill chuckled.

"Ha, that's what you think." Laurie laughed. "Next time you take care of the girls and the dirty dishes."

"I'll find a way around it." Bill laughed. "I usually do."

"Yes, and contrary to what I just said, I don't mind." Laurie gave Bill a big bear hug and a kiss. "Now that the dishes are gone, I'll go out and post the found posters, if you'll watch the girls."

"Sure," Bill said. "I've got a few things I have to catch up with here. I can do those and watch the girls at the same time. Just go and be careful." He kissed her again, wishing her well on her way down the basement stairs to the garage.

Bill started to look at the newspaper when he heard the girls scream. Fearing the worst he ran into the living room where he saw both girls laughing. He saw nothing that would have caused them to scream.

"What's the matter?" Bill touched both girls on the shoulder. "I heard screams, but I don't see any reason why."

"We were just pretending, Daddy," Sarah said. "We were pretending."

"Yes, yes!" Rachel grinned.

"Well, try not to scream so I won't worry," Bill said softly. "You know I really care about both of you and I never want anything bad to happen to you. Understand?"

"Yes, Daddy." Rachel smiled.

"Yes, Daddy," Sarah said. "We won't scream."

"Okay, now be good," Bill said leaving the room. "If you need me, I'll be at the computer."

"Yes, Daddy," the girls said in unison.

The girls watched their father leave the room barely able to restrain their laughter. The reason they had screamed was the toy he had moved on its own. It did not do anything more than move closer to them. While it moved it also had some pretty lights on its front side.

"Do you think we should tell Daddy?" Rachel whispered.

"No, this is our secret," Sarah whispered. "If we tell, Daddy may take it away from us. You don't want that do you?"

Rachel shook her head. "Will it move again?"

"I don't know," Sarah said solemnly. "But I guess, if it moved once, it will move again."

"You think?"

"Yes, I think," Sarah said in her normal voice. "All we have to do is wait."

The day passed without another stirring of the toy. Sarah and Rachel kept vigil until they were forced to bed by the late hour. Rachel insisted the toy be put in her bed for safekeeping. Sarah naturally protested claiming, since she was the eldest, the duty and honor belonged to her. Laurie settled the argument by leaving the toy in the living room and putting the girls in their own beds upstairs. Exhausted from the day's events they were soon fast asleep.

Rachel woke in the middle of the night to go to the bathroom. Returning to her bed she was startled to see the toy mounting the last step of the stairs. Rather than be frightened she was delighted the toy had come upstairs. She stood mesmerized watching the toy inch silently toward her. The lights on the toy shined on her face. Rachel stepped backward. The toy adjusted its movement to follow her feet. Understanding the toy was coming to her she went back into her bedroom. The toy as expected came looking for her. Rachel almost laughed out loud in delight. She jumped back into bed where she could watch what would happen when the toy noticed where she was. The toy entered her room and stopped. She knew the lights were after her so she pulled the covers overhead. Hearing nothing, Rachel relaxed and fell asleep.

In the morning Bill came in to wake his two daughters. It took a little prodding to get them out of bed. Both asked about the toy. Bill told them it was where they left it the night before. Rachel started to say it was not and then decided she was not sure where it was. Daddy was seldom, if ever, wrong.

"Everybody has to wash their face, brush their teeth and get dressed before going downstairs," Bill said.

In rather unbelievable time the girls were ready and downstairs examining the toy before breakfast. They each looked at it with pride, inwardly wishing the true owner would never be found. Rachel smiled to herself at what had happened last night.

"Why are you smiling?" Sarah noticed. "What are you smiling about?"

"Nothing," Rachel faltered. "Nothing at all; I'm happy the toy is still here."

"So am I, but I think you know something I don't and I want you to tell me."

"I don't have anything to say about what happened last night," Rachel said with a straight face.

"What happened last night?" Sarah grabbed her sister by both shoulders and stared into her eyes. "What happened last night? Tell me!"

"Nothing!" Rachel said defiantly. "And you can't make me tell!"

"Please tell me." Sarah changed her tone of voice. "It'll be a secret between the two of us and no one else. Promise!"

Rachel thought a moment and grinned. "The toy came upstairs looking for me last night," she said in a whisper. "I went to the bathroom and when I was finished it came up the stairs and followed me to my bed. I hid under my blanket and it went downstairs again."

"No kidding," Sarah's mouth dropped open. "I mean, it really followed you to your bed. That's scary!"

"No it isn't." Rachel flipped her hair. "I'm a big girl and I am not scared, no way!"

"We can't tell Mommy and Daddy," Sarah said slowly. "If we do, they'll take the toy away from us. You don't want that do you?"

"No," Rachel said softly. "I don't want the toy to ever leave."

"What are you talking about," Laurie said. The two girls jumped. "It's time to come eat breakfast before it gets cold. At least for the time being the toy is going to stay right where it is. No one has called about it yet."

"Yay!" Rachel exhaled gleefully.

"It's only been overnight," Laurie said. She pointed the way to the kitchen. "And when the owner calls I'll ask him or

571

her to demonstrate it for us with the remote control. I'm sure you would like to see how it works."

"I saw it last night." Rachel paused. Sarah elbowed her in the ribs and tears came to her eyes. She knew she had said the wrong thing.

"What is this all about?" Laurie said sternly. "Sarah, why did you hit your sister?"

"I'm sorry, Mommy." Sarah averted her eyes to the floor. "I didn't mean it."

"I don't understand," Laurie said. "Why did you hit your sister?"

Tears came to Sarah's eyes. She did not want her mother to think badly of her. Contradicting her own advice to her sister she decided to tell the truth. "We have a secret," Sarah said softly. "The toy can really move by itself and it came upstairs to look for Rachel last night."

"What do you mean?" Laurie raised her brow. "You mean the toy climbed the stairs last night? If it did, I didn't hear thing."

"But it did, Mommy, it did," Rachel said loudly. "I went to the bathroom and it came up the stairs and followed me to bed."

"And then what happened?"

"I covered my head and fell asleep," Rachel said. "And the toy went back downstairs."

"I think you had a big dream young lady." Laurie smiled. "You only thought the toy came upstairs. It really didn't happen."

"But Mommy it did!"

"Did you see any of this, Sarah?"

"Not really," Sarah said softly. "But I know it did. Rachel said so and I believe her."

"That's nice," Laurie said. "But believing is not proof. I'll believe it when I see it."

"It's the truth," Rachel whined. "I saw it! I really did!"

"Enough of this for now; let's get breakfast over." Laurie pushed the girls to the kitchen.

Bill was putting the final touches on breakfast. He had served the scrambled eggs, buttered the toast, and was now slicing each piece on the diagonal. The girls jumped into their places and began eating eagerly.

"Has Augie gone out yet?" Laurie said.

"All done," Bill said. "And the laundry is in the washer."

"Did you separate the whites from the colors?"

"Yes dear," Bill said dutifully. "I never make that mistake."

"Never?" Laurie raised her eyebrows. "Remember the time…"

"Well, almost never," Bill interrupted sheepishly. "At least I guarantee this time there has been no mistake."

"Good for you!" Laurie laughed.

Augie suddenly dashed off to the living room and was heard growling.

"What's with Augs?" Laurie faced the door into the living room.

"I don't know," Bill said calmly. "Maybe it's a squirrel outside."

"Except that Augs has to see them before she goes after them," Laurie said.

"Maybe it's the toy?" Rachel said barely audible.

"The toy?" Bill looked at Rachel then Laurie. "What about the toy?"

"Well, the girls say the toy has been moving on its own," Laurie said. "In fact, Rachel said it came upstairs last night looking for her. Isn't that right Rachel?"

Rachel squirmed and nodded.

"Hm," Bill got up from the table. "Let's check on the toy then."

Everyone got up from breakfast and followed Bill into the living room. The toy was not where it was supposed to be. Augie had located it by the front door and was sniffing and growling at it. For the moment at least the toy was stationary.

"Mommy, see it does move!" Rachel said triumphantly.

"Daddy, open the door." Sarah laughed. "Maybe it wants to go outside."

Always willing to go along with a joke Bill chuckled and opened the door. No one was really expecting anything to happen. The lights on the front of the toy came on and it began moving out the door, onto the small porch, and down the steps onto the walkway heading toward the street.

"See Daddy! See Daddy!" Both girls jumped with glee. "It really does move!"

"I see," Bill said slowly. "I see it does move by itself." The thought suddenly occurred that this was no ordinary toy. He looked at Laurie coming outside. Their eyes met and instantly their thoughts were one.

"Don't let it leave!" Rachel shouted. "It's going out into the street!"

"I'll get it." Sarah quickly started out toward it.

"Stop!" Laurie shouted. "There's a truck coming! Don't move!"

Sarah stopped and saw the truck coming up the street. The toy continued crawling out into the street. The man in the truck waved at Bill and his family unaware of what was ahead of him. Consequently the truck ran over and smashed the toy completely flat.

"Oh, no!" Rachel cried. "The toy's broken!"

Sarah stood horrified not knowing what to say. The man in the truck parked in front of his own house and came back to see what he had run over. Bill, Laurie and the girls were huddled over the broken toy staring at it in silence.

"I'm sorry Bill," the neighbor said. "I was paying more attention to you folks than what was on the road. I'll be more than happy to replace whatever I ran over. Was it one of the kid's toys?"

"Yes," Rachel sobbed. Tears were running down her cheeks. "It was our brand-new toy."

"I'm sorry sweetheart." The neighbor patted her on the head. "I'll go right now and get you a brand-new one. How about that?"

Rachel turned into her mother, buried her face in her sweater and sobbed louder. Sarah remained mute and motionless.

"I'm really sorry, Bill," the neighbor said softly. "It was an accident."

"We understand," Bill said weakly. "It's just that... I don't know what to say it... I guess I mean to say we finally understand how to operate it and..."

"And some fool comes and spoils everything," the neighbor interrupted. "I'm really sorry. I'll replace it."

"I don't know." Bill stared at the broken parts on the road. "It was really one of a kind and it was sort of out of this world."

The neighbor did not quite understand what Bill meant, but then Laurie stood nearby nodding her head because she knew exactly what he meant.

Hello

Inhuman eyes found the man sitting intently watching something beyond feline understanding. Panther, for that was the cat's name, moved silently toward the man who took care of all his needs. Halfway across the room an unfamiliar voice froze Panther in his tracks. Had the man made the noise? Panther sniffed the air detecting nothing but familiar friendly scents. Assured of no danger, he moved toward the man's legs and when he arrived brushed against them from multiple directions.

"Panther, how did you get in here?" The man's voice was friendly. He stopped what he was doing and leaned down to pick up the jet black cat. "Have I been ignoring you lately?" He put the cat in his lap, stroking its fur with firm affection. "I wonder what things you would say if you could talk?" The man laughed. Panther looked up into the man's face wondering nothing, feeling warm, and very comfortable.

The telephone rang. The man moved and stood up, trying to keep Panther comfortable in his arms. Panther decided otherwise and jumped effortlessly to the floor, pausing once to look behind at the man, and then dashing out the open door from which he came.

"Hello."

"When are you going to come back to work? Or don't you care anymore?" The voice had an edge to it.

"Sorry, Jack, I just let the time slip by me, but I don't think you need to be upset when I show you my new ideas. I think we're going to score a real breakthrough."

"That's your usual excuse, Dave, and I think it's worn pretty thin. Now get your butt down here before we both lose our positions and funding."

"I'll be there before you know it." Jack hung up the phone before he could respond further. Dave shook his head slightly and turned off the computer monitor.

Traffic was light as usual which allowed him to get to the laboratory in 20 minutes. Jack tried looking stern when he entered, but quickly flashed a smile.

575

"Whenever you're late Jennifer squeezes my coronaries."

"She should understand creative people don't function with rigid rules."

"Yes, I understand, but she has a program to run which is costing the taxpayers a lot of money. To her time is money and little else."

"Sometimes there is more discovered in off-time than in a stuffy lab."

"You have no complaint from me. I totally agree. All I'm saying is please try to play the game a little better."

Dave was about to say he did not play games when he noticed Jennifer entering the room out of the corner of his eye. As always she seemed hurried and not very happy. Before she could say anything Dave pulled a disc out of his pocket and held it up.

"What is that? A copy of your resignation?" Jennifer scowled. "How many times do you think you can waltz in late without expecting any repercussions?"

"I have a new idea. It may give us the breakthrough we have been looking for." Dave was unperturbed. He had weathered far worse for much less. Time was something he vowed would never control his decisions.

Jack stepped forward, snatched the disc from Dave's hand and loaded the contents into the computer. Jennifer quickly softened for no apparent reason. Dave turned and focused on the monitor. A series of equations coupled with a diagram filled the screen.

"I see you've been doing some homework." Jack laughed. "But what is this supposed to prove, if anything?"

"Do you believe we are alone in the universe? I don't think any of us do. The biggest problem is proving something is out there." He swept an arm in a broad arc above his head. "Even if we can prove beyond a shadow of a doubt there is another advanced extraterrestrial civilization, the absolute speed of light will never allow us to have a real-time dialogue. Civilizations may rise and fall before we ever get an answer to our call."

"So far you haven't said anything new." Jennifer grimaced. "What does that happen to do with our work here?"

"Our job is to explore the practical application of quantum physics. I understand that, but that doesn't mean we should ignore the possibility of applications outside of computing. Yes, we are after the holy grail of quantum computing and I think we are close to making a breakthrough or two, but I think we are closer to opening up something equally important: long distance instantaneous communication." Dave saw expressions of doubt on their faces.

Jennifer broke the silence first. "Our job is to develop communication at infinitely small levels not the opposite, but I am intrigued at the possibility of going in the opposite direction."

"In that case, look carefully at my equations. I think with our existing equipment I can prove we can communicate at any distance we want." Dave smiled and pointed at the monitor.

"I don't believe it can be done, Dave. Sorry if I hurt your feelings, but I think what you're trying to do is impossible." Jack turned away from the monitor.

"I'm willing to give your ideas a chance except we do not have money to finance personal or pet projects." Jennifer stood stiffly. "However, you can use any existing equipment to test the theory. Any additional cost will come out of your salary. Is that understood?"

"Naturally." Dave nodded with a smile. "I am sure, if this works out, you won't be sorry."

"I hope not." Jennifer returned the smile and left without further comment.

Jack approached the monitor glancing over his shoulder. Jennifer was gone. As he studied the equations he nodded to himself. Dave watched his facial expression change from contempt to possible anticipation.

"Dave, this is pretty revolutionary stuff."

"I thought so."

"It just might work."

577

"I think so."

"Let me help you."

"I was counting on it." Dave grinned broadly.

All the equipment was within easy reach and after several hours a device was assembled resembling any other experiment designed to test quantum phenomena. Anyone walking in would think nothing out of the ordinary.

"I've gone over your equations several times, but I'm still not clear on the basic physics." Jack took a long sip of black coffee.

"If it works, then we'll figure out the physics to explain it. First, let's test it here in the lab."

Jack put down the cup and took his place at a monitor across the lab. Dave energized the device in front of him. After a few minor adjustments Dave sent a signal to the receiver next to Jack. Nothing happened.

"It doesn't work." Jack looked over at Dave.

"It just needs a little tuning." Dave adjusted and exchange parts quickly taking extensive notes as he went. "Like any communication device this has to be properly tuned. Let's give it another try."

Again nothing happened. Jack flashed Dave a skeptical look. Dave ignored it and made further modifications. The next attempt brought a response from the receiver but the signal was nonsensical. The result, however, was enough to make Jack a believer in the concept. With each additional attempt the signal was received with ever increasing fidelity until it could not be declared anything but identical. From transmitting mere tones they progressed to sending their voices successfully.

"I must say you've made me a believer. At least it works here in the lab." Jack held up a cup of coffee. "The question now remains whether it works over any distance."

"There is no question in my mind this will work at any distance. The problem is finding someone out there that has developed the same technology. The biggest limitation to finding extraterrestrials has always been where to look and not the specific technology." Dave took a sip of coffee laced with several spoons of sugar and creamer. "The next part is hit or miss unless you have any better ideas."

"No, I don't have any better ideas." Jack exhaled loudly. "I'm beat. Do you want to pick up again tomorrow after a good night's rest?"

"I don't need any rest." David was more awake and alert than ever. "We are on the cusp of the greatest discovery ever and I can't even begin to think about sleep. I'm ready for the next step."

"What are we going to use as a directional antenna? Don't we need to set one up outside somewhere?" Jack took another long gulp of coffee shaking off growing fatigue.

"Not at all…" Dave was more animated. "Since we are tapping into the space time continuum that passes through everything, the only so-called antenna need be at our transmitter-receiver. And since our signal will go out instantly to the end of the universe our power needs will remain an absolute constant."

"Do you want to at least wait until night?"

"Not necessary." Dave adjusted the transmitter to point downward. "Remember our transmission goes through everything unobstructed. Going through the Earth is no different than aiming upward into a clear sky. Time of day is irrelevant."

"How about a short break?"

Dave recognized Jack was tired. Feeling somewhat hungry himself he suggested they take time to eat. Before they left the lab, Dave set up the transmitter to send out a test signal. The direction was a random choice and no response was logically expected. When they returned there were no surprises.

"The only way we will make contact with anyone is if they signal us first." Jack was refreshed and eager to resume work. "I suggest we take the passive approach and just listen."

"That approach will take forever." Dave shook his head. "Why not send out a signal in all directions and listen for a response? When someone answers it will be a simple matter to locate from which direction it is coming."

Within a short time the transmitter was sending out a logical signal that could not be misinterpreted as anything but sentient. The receiver was set to automatically determine the exact direction from which any signal was received. The moment the receiver was turned on a transmission was recorded while the direction was determined.

"Is that in response to our message?"

Dave listened to the signal several times. "No, I doubt it. I think we've picked up someone else's conversation accidentally, or it's an artifact. I'm not exactly sure what to think of it. First, we should send a signal in the direction from which it came and then we can decide."

No sooner than a signal was sent, a response was received. There was no longer any doubt the signal was anything but intentional. However, they were far from prepared to begin a meaningful dialogue.

"Now what do we do?" Jack's fatigue disappeared. "We've actually made contact with someone! It's almost beyond belief. Congratulations!"

"There's too much work to do before we start patting ourselves on the back." Dave was serious. "I think it's time to call Jennifer."

They went to her office where she was reclined in her chair reading a current popular novel. When she saw them, she hastily put the book in the top drawer of the desk and composed herself. Their visit was totally unexpected and without precedent.

"And what can I do for you two gentlemen?"

Jack spoke first. "We have something of monumental importance to show you in the lab. Dave's ideas really work."

Jennifer raised her eyebrows.

"Actually it is premature to positively state what we have accomplished." Dave was not prepared to make any definitive statements. "We would like you to come to the lab with us and go over our results. I am sure you will find them most interesting."

"This better be good." Jennifer huffed. She did not appreciate being caught goofing off.

In the lab, Dave gave a short synopsis of what they had assembled and the results obtained. Having answered several questions Dave proceeded to demonstrate the message sent and the response received. Jennifer was impressed but not thoroughly convinced.

"How can you be sure you are not receiving some sort of terrestrial signal?" Jennifer wrinkled her brow. "Man-made noise has always been misinterpreted as having alien origins since the beginning of the radio age."

"The absolute reason we can rule that out is from the nature of the medium we are receiving." Dave was ready to answer in intimate detail. "Our signals are not connected to the speed of light. I hate to use the analogy but this device is transmitting and receiving over a string of sorts. They pull on the string here is instantly perceived at the other end wherever it is, no matter how far away. By vibrating the string we can communicate over any distance, providing there is someone to receive the message. And from what we have seen there is someone out there."

"If you're right, this has significant ramifications for all human thought." Jennifer relaxed into a thoughtful pose. "It seems to me the next step is to develop a dialogue and exchange data. I am starting to see more here, the more I think about it. I suggest we keep this to ourselves for the time being."

"Why keep this a secret?" Jack was upset. "We will get all the credit we could ever want from this discovery of Dave's. Besides none of us has any background in linguistics. How do you propose to communicate if you have no common language?"

Dave interrupted. "I really don't care one way or the other whether we keep this a secret or not. The problem of communication will be difficult whoever attempts it. Right now all we have done is basically knock on the wall and someone has knocked back. Let us assume whoever knocked back is far more advanced than we are. In that case, why not transmit an extended voice message with the intent the receiving party is sufficiently competent to translate and reply back in the original language. We have nothing to lose and everything to gain if it works."

"And what do you propose the content of our first transmission be?" Jennifer was intrigued. "And does it really matter?"

"If anyone is going to make heads or tails from our language, we have to give them a large sample. One of the easiest ways would be to transmit the news from public radio. At regular intervals we could place a message explaining who we are and what we hope to accomplish." Dave stopped when Jennifer raised her hand.

"If you can send radio, why not send television also?"

"That's a good idea, Jennifer." Dave shook his head. "But I think that would complicate the message too much. Better keep things simple until we can come to an understanding. Once we have reached that point we can send more complex data."

"Dave, Jennifer's right. If our friends out there can unscramble our language, then they should also be sufficiently sophisticated to translate any signal we can possibly send them. I suggest we send alternating periods of video and audio."

"Not a bad idea." Jennifer nodded.

"I suggest 24 hours of radio first." Dave said flatly. "After that time we can alternate radio and television. I believe that will get us the best results."

"A fair compromise…" Jennifer smiled.

While Dave and Jack hooked up a radio to the transmitter, Jennifer composed a short message explaining the transmission and what the intent was. Dave reviewed the message and made a few suggestions. It was decided Jack had the best reading voice and was given the task to record the message. By the close of the day everything was ready. With little fanfare the transmission began, the lights turned out, and the lab locked as they went home for the night. They knew there would be little sleep for anyone.

The next morning they arrived early, trying to suppress their enthusiasm with the reason of the scientific method. Dave unlocked and went into the lab followed closely by Jennifer. Jack arrived a few minutes later with a steaming cup of coffee in hand. Instructions had been given the lab was not to be opened to the janitorial staff; therefore, everything was exactly as they had left it. Dave went immediately to the transmitter and confirmed it was still continuously operating.

"At what point do we check for an answer?" Jennifer was anxious.

"As an administrator you should know." Dave smiled. "Actually, I had planned to interrupt for a half hour this morning, and then continue, if we had made no progress. We still have so many options it might take us a lifetime to exercise them. Remember this is only the first signal we have detected and there are infinite other directions we can probe."

Jennifer nodded, Dave turned off the radio and they all listened to the receiver expectantly. Seconds accumulated into minutes of absolute silence. Dave checked and rechecked the equipment and found it working properly. The room quickly filled with gloomy disappointment.

"Could we have lost the right direction?" Jack scratched his head. "Are we sure we stayed properly aligned all night?"

"Anything is possible." Dave took a deep breath and sighed. "However, one setback is not the end of everything. All we have to do is search until we find another signal, then we go from there."

"There is also the alternate possibility our transmission has been received and it is being processed." Jennifer moved toward the receiver. "Perhaps we have assumed too much. I know we couldn't do much with an encrypted message overnight, not to say anything of an alien message."

"For once I know you are right." Dave sat down in front of the receiver and turned up the volume. The absolute silence persisted. He rubbed his chin recounting everything when he had an inspiration. "What if we broadcast live?"

"What do you mean?" Jennifer came closer.

"Suppose you get a call and when you try to answer you discover it's only a recording. There is no point in talking to a machine that can't answer questions. I think we need to try to call directly one time. We may be expected to call now that our language has been interpreted." Dave smiled. "Jack, help me set up the equipment."

The moment of truth arrived. A microphone was set up in front of the transmitter with Jack sitting in front of it. The three huddled close wondering if they would get a response.

"Hello." Jack's voice sounded more like a croak than anything else. He took a sip of coffee before speaking again. "Hello? Is there anyone there?"

Absolute silence.

"Hello? Is there anyone there?" More emphatic. More absolute silence.

"Hullo, hullo, hullo."

No response.

"Something is wrong." Jack turned away from the microphone with a frown. "How can we speak with someone who doesn't even know we exist?"

They stared at each other trying to come up with an answer. Perhaps whatever they heard the day before was a fluke. Or perhaps the concept really did not work. A cloud of doubt settled over them.

The speaker came to life. "Hello." It was Jack's voice. "Hello? Is there anyone there?"

Pause.

"Hello? Is there anyone there?"

Pause.

"Hullo, hullo, hullo."

Pause.

"Something is wrong."

584

Dave stared at the speaker with mouth open. Jack stood up and stepped away from the microphone as if it were a snake about to bite him. Jennifer moved closer to Dave and grabbed his arm.

Jennifer spoke first. "Is that a response or just an echo?"

"Sit back at the microphone." Dave quickly took command.

Jack slipped slowly back in front of the microphone carefully watching the expression on Dave's face. His own face was obviously asking "Now what?" Dave nodded and pointed at the microphone.

"Hello, again." Jack spoke clearly.

"Hello, again." The response came faster this time.

"Is this a joke?"

Silence.

"Who is this?"

More silence.

"Is there anyone there?"

Nothing.

"What do you think?" Jennifer squeezed Dave's arm. "Have we made contact or not?"

"I want to think we have." Dave spoke both softly and slowly. "The concept is sound, or at least the physics part is. The problem is always the understanding, the thought processes of those who we ultimately reach. An echo response may be only a test for both ends. It tells us they have received our transmission and tells them we understand. Or at least I think so."

"Hello." Jack jumped.

"Now that's a real response!" Dave moved closer to the speaker. "Jack, say hello again."

"Hello." Jack moved closer to the microphone.

"Hello, again."

"This is just a replay of what I've said before." Jack spoke without covering the microphone.

"No, it is not."

"It is them!" Dave nearly shouted.

"Please repeat." Jack was no longer shy. "Please say again."

"Again."

"We are in contact with a comedian." Jack laughed into the microphone. "Now what do I say?"

"Continue slowly." The voice spoke without inflection or sign of emotion.

"Where are you?"

An undecipherable response.

"We are calling from the planet Earth. Do you understand?"

"Place has no meaning."

"What do you mean?"

"We can communicate the way we now are but the distance between us will forever remain unknown. You will never visit my place nor will I ever be able to visit yours. The best we can ever do is exchange ideas back and forth."

"Have you communicated with anyone else this way before?"

"You are not the first nor will you be the last. Sentient existence is everywhere."

"Are you willing to trade data?"

"Yes, there is never any harm in that, essentially, since we will never face each other. All our technology is open for you to use and develop for whatever you want."

"This is better than I thought possible." Jennifer whispered into Dave's ear. Dave nodded twice.

"We are having problems developing a practical quantum computing device. Can you help us?" Jack grinned. The answer would save years of frustration and hard work.

"Set your recording device on and you will receive everything you need to know for such a device."

Before Jack could respond a high pitched squeal came from the speaker. He adjusted the volume but the sound persisted. Dave checked all the controls. Everything was set as it had been without any changes.

"What happened?" Jack had no clue.

"There is some sort of interference." Dave continued adjusting the controls. "There is a lot we don't know about this sort of communication. We should be able to reestablish contact."

"Dave, I just had a thought." Jennifer spoke slowly. "Do you suppose more than one party could communicate on the same line at the same time?"

"There is no reason to assume otherwise." Dave moved away from the controls. "I can imagine whomever we have contacted uses this form of communication between themselves. Any sufficiently advanced civilization is intimately dependent on accurate data available at the earliest possible moment."

The noise disappeared. Jack looked to Dave for guidance and received it with a simple nod. Dave and Jennifer stood behind him as he began to transmit again. In waiting for a response, they collectively held their breath.

"Hello."

Silence.

"Hello? Are you there?"

More silence.

Jack exhaled. "What are we to do now?" Dave shrugged his shoulders.

"Hello." The voice had return, but before Jack could respond the overriding noise began interfering again.

The noise subsided within several minutes, but when Jack attempted to communicate the noise instantly return. He had an eerie feeling something extraordinary was happening. "What now, Dave?"

"I have no answers." Dave was becoming speechless. There was no logical explanation for what was happening.

"Set your recorder!" The voice said over the speaker. "The data you need will be flash to you." For the first time there was a frantic quality to the voice.

"Say again." Jack said quickly.

The noise prevented continued communication. This time it lasted over an hour. When it subsided, Jack called again.

"Unauthorized communication prohibited." A stern flat commanding voice spoke loudly. "You are to desist from all attempts at exchange of data."

"Who is this?" Jack spoke without hesitation.

Silence.

"Answer me, dammit!" Jack screamed, his face was flushed red with growing frustration. "Answer me!"

"Turn it off." Jennifer put her hand on Jack's shoulder. "There is no use continuing; at least not for now."

Jack stood mute, thinking. After a while he shook his head and shortly after that began to laugh at the absurdity of it all. His idea worked, but in the end personality and bias ultimately determined the usefulness of that idea. The universe was indeed a big place where there was always a bigger fish to swallow a smaller one. He wondered how small a fish he really was. No use worrying about it, what did it matter anyway?

Panther was sitting at the door when Dave entered the house that night. The cat wrinkled its whiskers in greeting. There was a glint of joyous expectation in those yellow feline eyes. Dave picked up his cat tenderly, giving it a welcoming hug. At least between them they had an understanding that nourished each other. Why communicate with something you can never touch? There is always solid comfort in what you can touch and feel. Dave went to bed that night with Panther sleeping on the bed next to his feet. As he drifted off to sleep he felt good about what had happened. Tomorrow would certainly be a more exciting day.

Proof

Made in the USA
Charleston, SC
04 January 2016